D1131964

The Short Stories of
HENRY JAMES

SELECTED AND EDITED, WITH AN INTRODUCTION BY CLIFTON FADIMAN

RANDOM HOUSE · NEW YORK

SECOND PRINTING

For permission to include the
copyrighted stories by Henry James,
acknowledgment is here made to Macmillan & Company,
Harper & Brothers, Charles Scribner's Sons

Manufactured in the United States of America
Designed by Stefan Salter

To

MY WIFE

whose unerring judgment
is responsible for much of
whatever value this book
may have

CONTENTS

INTRODUCTION

1. *VITA BREVIS*

In a certain sense nothing happened to Henry James, or rather, the things that happened to him were negative things. The first large event in his life (after his birth in New York City on April 15, 1843) was an accident to his back that prevented him from becoming a soldier in the Civil War (see A Note on "The Jolly Corner," page 641). He never married. He seems to have had no passionate relations with women or with men. He never had to earn his own living. He lived to be seventy-three, suffering only the normal illnesses that come to most mortals.

In his long life there is but a scattered handful of "dates." In 1875 he removed to Europe, and during the next year chose England for his lifelong residence. In 1897 he forsook London for a small house in Rye in Sussex. In 1904-1905 he spent ten months revisiting his native land. With the beginning of the First German War Against Mankind came a sudden outburst of emotion, formally symbolized by his becoming in 1915 a naturalized British subject. On February 28, 1916, he died.

Hardly an active life, one might superficially judge; yet, as one studies its concretion—that is to say, his books—one begins to wonder whether it was not one of the most active lives of the entire century, though it went on almost entirely in his head. The word for James—it is his favorite—is awareness. He must have been aware of more impressions and reflected upon more ideas in the course of a single waking hour than is the lot of you or me in the course of a year or, in more cases, a lifetime. Nothing happened to him except everything, everything that he could observe, relate, weigh, judge. These discriminations produced an incalculable amount of life, an entire population of human beings, a world of connections. And they were continually subjected to control, to a proper and harmonious ordering. Experience assumes meaning when the proper form for its expression is found—and only then. Thus the life of Henry James became identical with the search for and the discovery of the proper form. It became a work of art. This work of art was a growth, like the life of Goethe, minus the pomposity. James began as a mediocre imitator of Hawthorne, as a bright young reviewer, as a purveyor of genteel chit-chat. He ended as a great creative novelist and critic. The progression was not accidental. It was the result of constant self-examination, self-knowledge, self-control—and plain hard work. This is not to deny that the spring of it all—his genius—was in him from birth. It is merely to suggest that, more than any other writer of his time, he converted the potentialities of that genius into the fullest possible actuality.

From the point of view of the typical hero of our time, the success-monger, James hardly lived at all. From another point of view, he lived a life so full, so passionate, so aware, that in comparison the careers of the success-men seem anemic and withered.

The "life" of Henry James need never be written by anyone, for he wrote it himself in fifty remarkable volumes and half a dozen supreme ones.

2. *ARS LONGA*

Daisy Miller (1878) and *The Portrait of a Lady* (1880) stand, amid James's varied and copious works, as the two titles that earned him, during his long lifetime, something like popular acclaim. *The Turn of the Screw* has occasionally been reprinted as a thriller. A few of the short stories and one or two of the longer ones (*The Aspern Papers,* for example) have crept into the anthologies. To the eye of the modern public and the modern publisher, however, he was an unsuccessful novelist. Not only did he not sell; he was not even talked about. Whatever reputation he possessed receded after his death in 1916, though there have been small waves of reawakened interest, the latest during the last few years. With Mark Twain and Melville, he is one of our three greatest novelists, but there is no collected edition of him readily available, and most of his masterpieces are unobtainable.

The case against James is firmly rooted and, to be fair about it, has a certain cogency. Suppose we try to summarize it and then see whether it stands up. It rests on five main points.

1. *He, and hence his work, is rootless.* His alienation from America is exposed in his work and was formally symbolized by his becoming, in 1915, a British subject. He ignored completely the great theme of the late nineteenth and early twentieth centuries—the rise of industrial America. His art is enfeebled by the malnutrition resulting from this split in his allegiance.

2. *His snobbery imposed on him a pathetically limited subject matter.* His mature life was spent among the rich, the well-born, the eminent—or among artists. He had little sympathy for the common man, viewed with apathy the democratic drift of his time, and (except for his literary friendships) attached himself to all that was decadent and artificial in European, British and expatriate-American society. His characters, being drawn from this small and dwindling class, lack warmth, breadth and social gravity. The *beau monde* he knew, but not the big world.

3. *Even within this world his emotional range is narrow.* His early injury may have been the reason for his never marrying. In any case his work shows little realistic expression of passion. It is bare of any representation of violence or of the larger, cruder, more elemental emotions. It is timid, even old-maidish. It lacks masculinity.

4. *He sacrificed content to form.* His elaborate esthetic theories stifled the free flow of his imagination. His interest in "effects," in the mere architecture of narrative, made him draw out his stories to excessive length. He disguised the poverty of his content with the artifice of formal tricks and mannerisms.

5. *His style is esoteric to the point of unreadability.* His dislike of banality swelled, in his later phase, into a mania, the consequence of which was a prose so dense, involved, indirect, and allusive as to amount virtually to a dead language.

Thus, at its most vigorous, the arraignment of Henry James. Those who draw it up do not necessarily deny him genius, but they consider the genius so specialized and rarefied as to be insulated from the general reader. I have tried to be fair in my presentation of their case, all the more because, not many years ago, the shallowness of my own knowledge of Henry James would have placed me more or less in their camp.

I have tried to be fair, also, because the case is not without merit. It is based on what seem to be salient facts. James *was* a man without a country. His characters *are* drawn largely from the rich, the idle, the over-sensitive, often the frivolous. Man as a sexual animal is *not* one of his specialties. He *has* a hypertrophied interest in the problem of literary form. His later style *is* difficult. All this is true. Yet, during the past ten years or so, it has become apparent, at first to a small group of literary critics and scholars, then to an increasingly wider circle of perceptive readers, that it is not the whole truth. Somehow or other, after the charge has been drawn up and its points admitted, Henry James continues to impose himself. There is something in him, large, pervasive and valuable, that eludes the indictment.

James's importance, its quality and extent, may take us some years to assess. We may not even be able to see it clearly, because our attitude toward him is in a sense impure. Perhaps we are getting solace from him, perhaps we are using him as a balm rather than a great writer.

For example, those who care passionately for our English speech find in the precision, the exquisiteness, the close workmanship of James's prose a relief from the careless, uncleanly, and hyperthyroid jargon which currently passes muster for sound writing. James's almost fussy concern for elevated, even noble standards of craftsmanship operates in agreeable contrast to our own fetish of relaxation, our cult of "informality" (a sweet name for mental laziness). Ours is a period in which books are made easy for us to read; in which, if this reading is too hard for us, we are given pictures accompanied by nursery-prose captions; in which, if pictures are too difficult, we are furnished with comic-strips. Years ago James saw all this coming. Indeed he described with stunning accuracy the triumph of our most admired journalism when he spoke of "the bastard vernacular of communities disinherited of the felt difference between the speech of the soil and the speech of the newspaper, and capable thereby, accordingly, of taking slang for simplicity, the composite for the quaint and the vulgar for the natural." To Howells he wrote, "The *faculty of attention* has utterly vanished from the general Anglo-Saxon mind, extinguished at its source by the big, blatant Bayadère of Journalism." Those who find themselves unable to agree that the communication of ideas and feelings must necessarily be on a pre-adolescent level find in the careful complexities of Henry James a welcome challenge.

In our day form and subtlety in the novel are not expected; they are even decried. To those in reaction against the current passion for looseness of pattern and flatness of speech, James offers form and subtlety in heaping measure. Furthermore, at a time when no demands are made for the close, analytic appreciation of literature, James's uncompromising severity of approach, his perfect confidence that literature is a noble thing, worthy of the most unrelaxed attention, has a certain tonic value. It is possibly true, as Spengler declared, that ours is an age of the conqueror and the technician, an age in which the artist (unless he is "successful") will tend increasingly to be contemned. Those unable to accept the conqueror and the technician as paragons of human experience find in James's fervent—even feverish—defense of the creative life a measure of consolation.

Finally, it may be that James's seeming unconcern with social and community problems, his unrelenting preoccupation with the individual (although always with the society-conditioned individual) comes as a welcome counterbalance to our own absorption in the State-man, the Group-man, rather than the individual man.

Yet these are hardly sound reasons for praising James. Are we merely inclining to him because he offers something absent in our own environment, because he soothes some contemporary irritation?

Yes; but I would suggest that the return to Henry James is based also on something deeper, much harder to define. It is based on our sense that here is an author who is subtler than he seems, that there is hardly any end to his complexity, that underneath the surface vein are riches still to be mined. He is a writer with whom one does not easily finish. He exerts the fascination of those devious spirits whose message is neither slight nor immediate. As an artist he is, of course, inferior to such men as Melville or Dante, but he is one with them in that he may be approached on more than a single level of perception. Reread and studied (for, I submit, he must be studied, he asks that we pay *attention* to him) he almost eerily reveals another James lying beneath the James of the familiar indictment.

All at once we perceive that his "rootlessness" furnishes him with an international viewpoint and, indeed, an international style, both far more relevant to our own time than they were to James's period. If Europe was once part of the American fate, America is now part of the European fate. Hence it has come about that those writers who can mediate between the two continents hold for us an enhanced value; and of these James is far and away the most meaningful. Indeed, he is more than a mediator. He is the herald of a time when mediation will no longer be necessary, when mankind will in truth be one. Dimly he perceived the remote future when he spoke of "the multiplied symptoms among educated people, from wherever drawn, of a common intelligence and a social fusion tending to abridge old rigours of separation. . . . There, if one will—in the dauntless fusions to come—is the personal drama of the future."

As for his "snobbery," we note that while on occasion it can be irritating, it more often only half conceals the most thorough, the slyest, the most pitiless of satire on the leisure class. Read *The Princess Casamassima* for proof; or in this volume study the unpretentious story, "Mrs. Medwin." James was occasionally taken in by the leisure class, but not permanently and not deeply. His unfinished novel, *The Ivory Tower,* is a work of social criticism as much as is *An American Tragedy;* indeed, it shows the reverse side of that tragedy.

Seen in the light of what Freud has taught us, James suddenly demonstrates an extraordinary perception of the hidden and even sinister drives of men and women. I think it at least arguable that the distant manner in which he handles sex comes about not through ignorance or timidity but because, like the other Anglo-Saxon novelists of his time, he was forced by the taboos of his culture into reticence or ambiguity. That he does not, except rarely, represent passion directly, is true; but that he understood it and is compelled to express his understanding obliquely is, I believe, demonstrable. Certainly no one will deny (*The Turn of the Screw* is the most forcible instance here) that he had an almost intuitive perception of the unconscious and the part it plays in conditioning behavior.

His absorption in formal problems presents itself as a noble literary conscientiousness, pure, ascetic, but by no means frigid or remote; and the more we study him the more we become convinced that in him, as in any great writer, form and content are one. Even the famous style is seen to be a beautiful machine for the perfect projection of James's complex and curious perceptions. It is a weapon, not a toy.

One makes the general discoveries that James is wonderfully near to us; that he is a *modern* writer, to be ranked with Joyce, Proust, Mann, and not a nineteenth-century writer at all; that his studies of Americans in Europe in 1875 tell us a great deal about Americans in America in 1945; that from the embryonic prefigurings of his own time he foresaw many of the brutal dilemmas American acquisitive society now faces—and is thus extraordinarily valuable, though dead for almost thirty years, as a trenchant critic of the life around us; that (as *The Princess Casamassima* discloses) he knew or rather divined much about the conflict of classes; that his prefaces to his novels, his essays on Flaubert, Emerson, Stevenson, Turgenev, and others entitle him to rank as a master of literary criticism; that, in sum, while a moderate portion of his work *is* trivial tea-table chatter, the larger remainder is devoted to the most profound, ambiguous and touching of the moral experiences of man. I do not see how any unprejudiced reader can study "The Beast in the Jungle" or *The Turn of the Screw* or "The Pupil" or "The Jolly Corner" (not to mention his larger masterpieces) without sensing that James, for all his fussiness, for all the cloistered quality of his experience, had somehow reached out and obtained a firm grasp of that stick whose two ends are labeled Good and Evil. He was, in other words, a philosophical novelist, his concern being generally, though not always, with what is persistent in the heart of man.

He did not, it is true, have the range of Tolstoy or Balzac, but, within his narrower compass, he worked to a great depth. Not satisfied merely to present an understandable, easily graspable report on an individual consciousness, he would not stop, this patient, eager artist, until he had wrung that consciousness dry. When you have finished *What Maisie Knew,* for instance, you do not merely have a clear picture of Maisie. You *know* Maisie; you feel that there is nothing left in Maisie for James to tell you about; she is complete. You may not like James's characters, you may not think them "important," but it is hard to deny that they are exhaustively created. And it is from the exhaustiveness of the creation that one derives the sense that, while he at no time systematizes it, James has a wise and searching view of life. In his preface to *The Portrait of a Lady* he says that there is "no more nutritive or suggestive truth . . . than that of the perfect dependence of the 'moral' sense of a work of art on the amount of felt life concerned in producing it." Where there is enough knowledge, there is virtue.

To James, writing is not an opportunity for self-expression, or at least not merely for self-expression. It is first a problem, not first a solution. He thought about writing as Mozart must have thought about music, as the unsurpassable nameless architects must have thought about the cathedral of Chartres. That writing must express something goes without saying, but everything, for James, lies in the manner, the method of the expression. What is to be expressed must first be grasped in all possible relations (the opposite of impressionism); then a form must be discovered to enclose all these relations in the best conceivable way, which is, of course, the most economical way. James at his finest works on the principle of least action. He may seem elaborate, but that is only because he has seen all there is to express—and the all is multifarious, puzzling, "thick," to use his word. He speaks somewhere of "exquisite economy in composition"; and again of "that odd law which somehow always makes the minimum of valid suggestion serve the man of imagination better than the maximum"; and again—most revealing of phrases—of "the baseness of the arbitrary stroke." Accident James leaves to life, which specializes in it; but art cannot come out of the fortuitous. The artist by accident is a contradiction in terms; the true creator fights all his life against the temptation to take the easy road, to write the "readable," to gain effects by happy strokes. "The effort really to see and really to represent is no idle business," says James, "in face of the *constant* force that makes for muddlement." In James there is difficulty, there is complexity, but there is no muddlement. He is always clear, but only so after we have made a successful, if often an exhausting effort to perceive what it is he is being clear about.

Yeats, in his poem, "The Choice," tells us

> "The intellect of man is forced to choose
> Perfection of the life, or of the work."

When we survey the life and work of Henry James we are filled with a sense that in a manner he resolved the dilemma Yeats poses. As we have seen, not a great deal "happened" to James; but he made everything that did happen pay. Indeed, out of his very sensation of non-experience he constructed two masterpieces—"The Beast in the Jungle," which is about a man whose tragedy is that nothing ever happened to him; and *The Ambassadors,* which is about a man superbly equipped to react to the experiences which came to him too late. James put everything he saw, everything he felt, everything he thought, everything he was, into his books—but only after this everything had been subjected to the most rigorous scrutiny and organization. His work is not, in Yeats's phrase, "perfection"—no life work is—but it comes breathlessly close to it. It is singularly rounded; it increases in importance as James ages. (He is one of the few writers of whom one might say that he would have written better at 170 than he did at 70.) It touches heights in several media—the long novel, the short novel, the short story, the literary essay, the familiar essay, the personal memoir. It is the harmonious record of a life that organized itself consciously, yet without pedantry, almost from its beginnings. And, because its creator rejected the shoddy, the easy, the second-best, because he was always hard on himself, because nothing but the essence, the economized, the beaten gold leaf was good enough for him, what he contrived speaks to us still, and will, in the years to come, still speak.

3. *A WORD ABOUT THIS BOOK*

James wrote about eighty short stories—let's use the term for anything under 20,000 words, and we'll avoid a good many arguments. This is an extraordinary number and would have sufficed to establish James as a prolific writer had he written nothing else. He had a high conception of the function of the short story and, though his output contains many failures, it contains no potboilers. Over-elaboration lies at the root of some of the failures. In other cases the material is too slight, too special, or, let us admit, too strongly marked with the date of its composition.

The seventeen stories I have chosen for this collection do not seem to me slight (except in one or two cases), special, or dated. Particularly do they not seem to me dated. The specific preservative of style works strongly in them, and no less strongly the general preservative which is nothing less than the clear expression of the truth about human nature. The earliest of these stories bears the date of 1877, the latest that of 1909; but the words in them are instant, not remote. Part of that instancy springs from James's refusal to admit background as particularly important in depicting the relations among people. He can do a background as well as any "realistic" novelist, but he recognizes the job for the minor thing it is. Those who do not care for James argue, often quite persuasively, that he depicts manners; and that, because manners change, he will not last. It is true that he often does depict manners, even mannerisms; but they are rarely mere topical documentation; and in his finer stories—such as the ones here included—they occupy a subordinate position.

I hope that this modest collection will lead many readers to the major works; but, even if it does not, those readers, if they are adequately attentive, will have obtained a considerable view of James's mind and method. The stories have been selected in such a way as to profile James's development and bring out in relief the themes that absorbed his creative imagination over a period of more than a quarter of a century. The reader will note a progression from the relatively simple to the supremely complex, from the casual to the concentrated, from the merely serious to the grandly tragic. Yet, though "Four Meetings" is a small thing and "The Beast in the Jungle" a great one, the second is implicit in the first. James is a perfectly ordered, unified personality. He wrote nothing eccentric to himself. Like every human being, and particularly every writer, he occasionally lost confidence in himself; but he never really lost himself, Henry James, the man underlying the confidence or lack of confidence. The perfect recognition of the powers of his own personality is the mark of the master of any art.

As for the editor's notes, if you care to read them at all, please read each one directly *after* you have finished the corresponding story. They are intended to serve two modest purposes: first, to indicate, however crudely, the manner in which James tends to stimulate reflection; second, taken as a unit, to suggest a rough idea of the development of James as a worker in the restricted field of the short story. If, beyond this, they interest you in James generally and send some readers on to his greater and more difficult works, I shall consider my pleasant task amply rewarded.

CLIFTON FADIMAN

May, 1945
New York City

THE SHORT STORIES

OF

HENRY JAMES

FOUR MEETINGS

I SAW her but four times, though I remember them vividly; she made her impression on me. I thought her very pretty and very interesting—a touching specimen of a type with which I had had other and perhaps less charming associations. I'm sorry to hear of her death, and yet when I think of it why *should* I be? The last time I saw her she was certainly not—! But it will be of interest to take our meetings in order.

I

THE first was in the country, at a small tea-party, one snowy night some seventeen years ago. My friend Latouche, going to spend Christmas with his mother, had insisted on my company, and the good lady had given in our honour the entertainment of which I speak. To me it was really full of savour —it had all the right marks: I had never been in the depths of New England at that season. It had been snowing all day and the drifts were knee-high. I wondered how the ladies had made their way to the house; but I inferred that just those general rigours rendered any assembly offering the attraction of two gentlemen from New York worth a desperate effort.

Mrs. Latouche in the course of the evening asked me if I "didn't want to" show the photographs to some of the young ladies. The photographs were in a couple of great portfolios, and had been brought home by her son, who, like myself, was lately returned from Europe. I looked round and was struck with the fact that most of the young ladies were provided with an object of interest more absorbing than the most vivid sun-picture. But there was a person alone near the mantel-shelf who looked round the room with a small vague smile, a discreet, a disguised yearning, which seemed somehow at odds with her isolation. I looked at her a moment and then chose. "I should like to show them to that young lady."

"Oh yes," said Mrs. Latouche, "she's just the person. She doesn't care for flirting—I'll speak to her." I replied that if she didn't care for flirting she wasn't perhaps just the person; but Mrs. Latouche had already, with a few steps, appealed to her participation. "She's delighted," my hostess came back to report; "and she's just the person—so quiet and so bright." And she told me the young lady was by name Miss Caroline Spencer—with which she introduced me.

Miss Caroline Spencer was not quite a beauty, but was none the less, in her small odd way, formed to please. Close upon thirty, by every presumption, she was made almost like a little girl and had the complexion of a child. She had also the prettiest head, on which her hair was arranged as nearly as possible like the hair of a Greek bust, though indeed it was to be doubted if she had ever seen a Greek bust. She was "artistic," I suspected, so far as the polar influences of North Verona could allow for such yearnings or could minister to them. Her eyes were perhaps just too round and too inveterately surprised, but her lips had a certain mild decision and her teeth, when she showed them, were charming. About her neck she wore what ladies call, I believe, a "ruche" fastened with a very small pin of pink coral, and in her hand she carried a fan made of plaited straw and adorned with pink ribbon. She wore a scanty black silk dress. She spoke with slow soft neatness, even without smiles showing the prettiness of her teeth, and she seemed extremely pleased, in fact quite fluttered, at the prospect of my demonstrations. These went forward very smoothly after I had moved the portfolios out of their corner and placed a couple of chairs near a lamp. The photographs were usually things I knew—large views of Switzerland, Italy and Spain, landscapes, reproductions of famous buildings, pictures and statues. I said what I could for them, and my companion, looking at them as I held them up, sat perfectly still, her straw fan raised to her under-lip and gently, yet, as I could feel, almost excitedly, rubbing it. Occasionally, as I laid one of the pictures down, she said without confidence, which would have been too much: "Have you seen that place?" I usually answered that I had seen it several times—I had been a great traveller, though I was somehow particularly admonished not to swagger—and then I felt her look at me askance for a moment with her pretty eyes. I had asked her at the outset whether she had been to Europe; to this she had answered "No, no, no"—almost as much below her breath as if the image of such an event scarce, for solemnity, brooked phrasing. But after that, though she never took her eyes off the pictures, she said so little that I feared she was at last bored. Accordingly when we had finished one portfolio I offered, if she desired it, to desist. I rather guessed the exhibition really held her, but her reticence puzzled me and I wanted to make her speak. I turned round to judge better and then saw a faint flush in each of her cheeks. She kept waving her little fan to and fro. Instead of looking at me she fixed her eyes on the remainder of the collection, which leaned, in its receptacle, against the table.

"Won't you show me that?" she quavered, drawing the long breath of a person launched and afloat but conscious of rocking a little.

"With pleasure," I answered, "if you're really not tired."

"Oh I'm not tired a bit. I'm just fascinated." With which as I took up the other portfolio she laid her hand on it, rubbing it softly. "And have you been here too?"

On my opening the portfolio it appeared I had indeed been there. One of the first photographs was a large view of the Castle of Chillon by the Lake of Geneva. "Here," I said, "I've been many a time. Isn't it beautiful?" And I pointed to the perfect reflexion of the rugged rocks and pointed towers in the clear still water. She didn't say "Oh enchanting!" and push it away to see the next picture. She looked a while and then asked if it weren't where Bonnivard, about whom Byron wrote, had been confined. I assented, trying to quote Byron's verses, but not quite bringing it off.

She fanned herself a moment and then repeated the lines correctly, in a soft flat voice but with charming conviction. By the time she had finished, she was nevertheless blushing. I complimented her and assured her she was perfectly equipped for visiting Switzerland and Italy. She looked at me askance again, to see if I might be serious, and I added that if she wished to recognise Byron's descriptions she must go abroad speedily—Europe was getting sadly dis-Byronised. "How soon must I go?" she thereupon enquired.

"Oh I'll give you ten years."

"Well, I guess I can go in *that* time," she answered as if measuring her words.

"Then you'll enjoy it immensely," I said; "you'll find it of the highest interest." Just then I came upon a photograph of some nook in a foreign city which I had been very fond of and which recalled tender memories. I discoursed (as I suppose) with considerable spirit; my companion sat listening breathless.

"Have you been *very* long over there?" she asked some time after I had ceased.

"Well, it mounts up, put all the times together."

"And have you travelled everywhere?"

"I've travelled a good deal. I'm very fond of it and happily have been able."

Again she turned on me her slow shy scrutiny. "Do you know the foreign languages?"

"After a fashion."

"Is it hard to speak them?"

"I don't imagine you'd find it so," I gallantly answered.

"Oh I shouldn't want to speak—I should only want to listen." Then on a pause she added: "They say the French theatre's so beautiful."

"Ah the best in the world."

"Did you go there very often?"

"When I was first in Paris I went every night."

"Every night!" And she opened her clear eyes very wide.

"That to me is"—and her expression hovered—"as if you tell me a fairy-tale." A few minutes later she put to me: "And which country do you prefer?"

"There's one I love beyond any. I think you'd do the same."

Her gaze rested as on a dim revelation and then she breathed "Italy?"

"Italy," I answered softly too; and for a moment we communed over it. She looked as pretty as if instead of showing her photographs I had been making love to her. To increase the resemblance she turned off blushing. It made a pause which she broke at last by saying: "That's the place which—in particular—I thought of going to."

"Oh that's the place—that's the place!" I laughed.

She looked at two or three more views in silence. "They say it's not very dear."

"As some other countries? Well, one gets back there one's money. That's not the least of the charms."

"But it's *all* very expensive, isn't it?"

"Europe, you mean?"

"Going there and travelling. That has been the trouble. I've very little money. I teach, you know," said Miss Caroline Spencer.

"Oh of course one must have money," I allowed; "but one can manage with a moderate amount judiciously spent."

"I think I should manage. I've saved and saved up, and I'm always adding a little to it. It's all for that." She paused a moment, and then went on with suppressed eagerness, as if telling me the story were a rare, but possibly an impure satisfaction. "You see it hasn't been only the money—it has been everything. Everything has acted against it. I've waited and waited. It has been my castle in the air. I'm almost afraid to talk about it. Two or three times it has come a little nearer, and then I've talked about it and it has melted away. I've talked about it too much," she said hypocritically—for I saw such talk was now a small tremulous ecstasy. "There's a lady who's a great friend of mine—she doesn't want to go, but I'm always at her about it. I think I must tire her dreadfully. She told me just the other day she didn't know what would become of me. She guessed I'd go crazy if I didn't sail, and yet certainly I'd go crazy if I did."

"Well," I laughed, "you haven't sailed up to now—so I suppose you *are* crazy."

She took everything with the same seriousness. "Well, I guess I must be. It seems as if I couldn't think of anything else—and I don't require photographs to work me up! I'm always right *on* it. It kills any interest in things nearer home—things I ought to attend to. That's a kind of craziness."

"Well then the cure for it's just to go," I smiled—"I mean the cure for this kind. Of course you may have the other kind worse," I added—"the kind you get over there."

"Well, I've a faith that I'll go *some* time all right!" she quite elatedly cried. "I've a relative right there on the spot," she went on, "and I guess he'll know how to control me." I expressed the hope that he would, and I forget whether we turned over more photographs; but when I asked her if she had always lived just where I found her, "Oh no sir," she quite eagerly replied; "I've spent twenty-two months and a half in Boston." I met it with the inevitable joke that in this case foreign lands might prove a disappointment to her, but I quite failed to alarm her. "I know more about them than you might think"—her earnestness resisted even that. "I mean by reading—for I've really read considerable. In fact I guess I've prepared my mind about as much as you *can*—in advance. I've not only read Byron—I've read histories and guide-books and articles and lots of things. I know I shall rave about everything."

" 'Everything' is saying much, but I understand your case," I returned. "You've the great American disease, and you've got it 'bad'—the appetite, morbid and monstrous, for colour and form, for the picturesque and the romantic at any price. I don't know whether we come into the world with it—with the germs implanted and antecedent to experience; rather perhaps we catch it early, almost before developed consciousness—we *feel,* as we look about, that we're going (to save our souls, or at least our senses) to be thrown back on it hard. We're like travellers in the desert—deprived of water and subject to the terrible mirage, the torment of illusion, of the thirst-fever. They hear the plash of fountains, they see green gardens and orchards that are hundreds of miles away. So we with *our* thirst—except that with us it's *more* wonderful: we have before us the beautiful old things we've never seen at all, and when we do at last see them—if we're lucky!—we simply recognise them. What experience does is merely to confirm and consecrate our confident dream."

She listened with her rounded eyes. "The way you express it's too lovely, and I'm sure it will be just like that. I've dreamt of everything—I'll know it all!"

"I'm afraid," I pretended for harmless comedy, "that you've wasted a great deal of time."

"Oh yes, that has been my great wickedness!" The people about us had begun to scatter; they were taking their leave. She got up and put out her hand to me, timidly, but as if quite shining and throbbing.

"I'm going back there—one *has* to," I said as I shook hands with her. "I shall look out for you."

Yes, she fairly glittered with her fever of excited faith. "Well, I'll tell you if I'm disappointed." And she left me, fluttering all expressively her little straw fan.

II

A FEW months after this I crossed the sea eastward again and some three years elapsed. I had been living in Paris and, toward the end of October, went from that city to the Havre, to meet a pair of relatives who had written me they were about to arrive there. On reaching the Havre I found the steamer already docked—I was two or three hours late. I repaired directly to the hotel, where my travellers were duly established. My sister had gone to bed, exhausted and disabled by her voyage; she was the unsteadiest of sailors and her sufferings on this occasion had been extreme. She desired for the moment undisturbed rest and was able to see me but five minutes—long enough for us to agree to stop over, restoratively, till the morrow. My brother-in-law, anxious about his wife, was unwilling to leave her room; but she insisted on my taking him a walk for aid to recovery of his spirits and his land-legs.

The early autumn day was warm and charming, and our stroll through the bright-coloured busy streets of the old French seaport beguiling enough. We walked along the sunny noisy quays and then turned into a wide pleasant street which lay half in sun and half in shade—a French provincial street that resembled an old water-colour drawing: tall grey steep-roofed red-gabled many-storied houses; green shutters on windows and old scroll-work above them; flower-pots in balconies and white-capped women in doorways. We walked in the shade; all this stretched away on the sunny side of the vista and made a picture. We looked at it as we passed along; then suddenly my companion stopped—pressing my arm and staring. I followed his gaze and saw that we had paused just before reaching a café where, under an awning, several tables and chairs were disposed upon the pavement. The windows were open behind; half a dozen plants in tubs were ranged beside the door; the pavement was besprinkled with clean bran. It was a dear little quiet old-world café; inside, in the comparative dusk, I saw a stout handsome woman, who had pink ribbons in her cap, perched up with a mirror behind her back and smiling at some one placed out of sight. This, to be exact, I noted afterwards; what I first observed was a lady seated alone, outside, at one of the little marble-topped tables. My brother-in-law had stopped to look at her. Something had been put before her, but she only leaned back, motionless and with her hands folded, looking down the street and away from us. I saw her but in diminished profile; nevertheless I was sure I knew on the spot that we must already have met.

"The little lady of the steamer!" my companion cried.

"Was she on your steamer?" I asked with interest.

"From morning till night. She was never sick. She used to sit perpetually at the side of the vessel with her hands crossed that way, looking at the eastward horizon."

"And are you going to speak to her?"

"I don't know her. I never made acquaintance with her. I wasn't in form to make up to ladies. But I used to watch her and—I don't know why—to be interested in her. She's a dear little Yankee woman. I've an idea she's a school-mistress taking a holiday—for which her scholars have made up a purse."

She had now turned her face a little more into profile, looking at the steep grey house-fronts opposite. On this I decided. "I shall speak to her myself."

"I wouldn't—she's very shy," said my brother-in-law.

"My dear fellow, I know her. I once showed her photographs at a tea-party." With which I went up to her, making her, as she turned to look at me, leave me in no doubt of her identity. Miss Caroline Spencer had achieved her dream. But she was less quick to recognise me and showed a slight bewilderment. I pushed a chair to the table and sat down. "Well," I said, "I hope you're not disappointed!"

She stared, blushing a little—then gave a small jump and placed me. "It was you who showed me the photographs—at North Verona."

"Yes, it was I. This happens very charmingly, for isn't it quite proper for me to give you a formal reception here—the official welcome? I talked to you so much about Europe."

"You didn't say too much. I'm so intensely happy!" she declared.

Very happy indeed she looked. There was no sign of her being older; she was as gravely, decently, demurely pretty as before. If she had struck me then as a thin-stemmed, mild-hued flower of Puritanism it may be imagined whether in her present situation this clear bloom was less appealing. Beside her an old gentleman was drinking absinthe; behind her the *dame de comptoir* in the pink ribbons called "Alcibiade, Alcibiade!" to the long-aproned waiter. I explained to Miss Spencer that the gentleman with me had lately been her shipmate, and my brother-in-law came up and was introduced to her. But she looked at him as if she had never so much as seen him, and I remembered he had told me her eyes were always fixed on the eastward horizon. She had evidently not noticed him, and, still timidly smiling, made no attempt whatever to pretend the contrary. I stayed with her on the little terrace of the café while he went back to the hotel and to his wife. I remarked to my friend that this meeting of ours at the first hour of her landing partook, among all chances, of the miraculous, but that I was delighted to be there and receive her first impressions.

"Oh I can't tell you," she said—"I feel so much in a dream. I've been sitting here an hour and I don't want to move. Everything's so delicious and romantic. I don't know whether the coffee has gone to my head—it's *so* unlike the coffee of my dead past."

"Really," I made answer, "if you're so pleased with this poor prosaic Havre you'll have no admiration left for better things. Don't spend your appreciation all the first day—remember it's your intellectual letter of credit. Remember all the beautiful places and things that are waiting for you. Remember that lovely Italy we talked about."

"I'm not afraid of running short," she said gaily, still looking at the opposite houses. "I could sit here all day—just saying to myself that here I am at last. It's so dark and strange—so old and different."

"By the way then," I asked, "how come you to be encamped in this odd place? Haven't you gone to one of the inns?" For I was half-amused, half-alarmed at the good conscience with which this delicately pretty woman had stationed herself in conspicuous isolation on the edge of the sidewalk.

"My cousin brought me here and—a little while ago—left me," she returned. "You know I told you I had a relation over here. He's still here—a real cousin. Well," she pursued with unclouded candour, "he met me at the steamer this morning."

It was absurd—and the case moreover none of my business; but I felt somehow disconcerted. "It was hardly worth his while to meet you if he was to desert you so soon."

"Oh he has only left me for half an hour," said Caroline Spencer. "He has gone to get my money."

I continued to wonder. "Where *is* your money?"

She appeared seldom to laugh, but she laughed for the joy of this. "It makes me feel very fine to tell you! It's in circular notes."

"And where are your circular notes?"

"In my cousin's pocket."

This statement was uttered with such clearness of candour that—I can hardly say why—it gave me a sensible chill. I couldn't at all at the moment have justified my lapse from ease, for I knew nothing of Miss Spencer's cousin. Since he stood in that relation to her—dear respectable little person—the presumption was in his favour. But I found myself wincing at the thought that half an hour after her landing her scanty funds should have passed into his hands. "Is he to travel with you?" I asked.

"Only as far as Paris. He's an art-student in Paris—I've always thought that so splendid. I wrote to him that I was coming, but I never expected him to come off to the ship. I supposed he'd only just meet me at the train in Paris. It's very kind of him. But he *is,*" said Caroline Spencer, "very kind—and very bright."

I felt at once a strange eagerness to see this bright kind cousin who was an art-student. "He's gone to the banker's?" I enquired.

"Yes, to the banker's. He took me to an hotel—such a queer quaint cunning little place, with a court in the middle and a gallery all round, and a lovely landlady in such a beautifully fluted cap and such a perfectly fitting dress! After a while we came out to walk to the banker's, for I hadn't any French money. But I was very dizzy from the motion of the vessel and I thought I had better sit down. He found this place for me here—then he went off to the banker's himself. I'm to wait here till he comes back."

Her story was wholly lucid and my impression perfectly wanton, but it passed through my mind that the gentleman would never come back. I settled myself in a chair beside my friend and determined to await the event. She was lost in the vision and the imagination of everything near us and about us—she observed, she recognised and admired, with a touching intensity. She noticed everything that was brought before us by the movement of the street—the peculiarities of costume, the shapes of vehicles, the big Norman horses, the fat priests, the shaven poodles. We talked of these things, and there was something charming in her freshness of perception and the way her book-nourished fancy sallied forth for the revel.

"And when your cousin comes back what are you going to do?" I went on.

For this she had, a little oddly, to think. "We don't quite know."

"When do you go to Paris? If you go by the four o'clock train I may have the pleasure of making the journey with you."

"I don't think we shall do that." So far she was prepared. "My cousin thinks I had better stay here a few days."

"Oh!" said I—and for five minutes had nothing to add. I was wondering what our absentee was, in vulgar parlance, "up to." I looked up and down the street, but saw nothing that looked like a bright and kind American art-student. At last I took the liberty of observing that the Havre was hardly a place to choose as one of the æsthetic stations of a European tour. It was a place of convenience, nothing more; a place of transit, through which transit should be rapid. I recommended her to go to Paris by the afternoon train and meanwhile to amuse herself by driving to the ancient fortress at the mouth of the harbour—that remarkable circular structure which bore the name of Francis the First and figured a sort of small Castle of Saint Angelo. (I might really have foreknown that it was to be demolished.)

She listened with much interest—then for a moment looked grave. "My cousin told me that when he returned he should have something particular to say to me, and that we could do nothing or decide nothing till I should have heard it. But I'll make him tell me right off, and then we'll go to the ancient fortress. Francis the First, did you say? Why, that's lovely. There's no hurry to get to Paris; there's plenty of time."

She smiled with her softly severe little lips as she spoke those last words, yet, looking at her with a purpose, I made out in her eyes, I thought, a tiny gleam of apprehension. "Don't tell me," I said, "that this wretched man's going to give you bad news!"

She coloured as if convicted of a hidden perversity, but she was soaring too high to drop. "Well, I guess it's a *little* bad, but I don't believe it's *very* bad. At any rate I must listen to it."

I usurped an unscrupulous authority. "Look here; you didn't come to Europe to listen—you came to *see*!" But now I was sure her cousin would come back; since he had something disagreeable to say to her he'd infallibly turn up. We sat a while longer and I asked her about her plans of travel. She had them on her fingers' ends and told over the names as solemnly as a daughter of another faith might have told over the beads of a rosary: from Paris to Dijon and to Avignon, from Avignon to Marseilles and the Cornice road; thence to Genoa, to Spezia, to Pisa, to Florence, to Rome. It apparently had never occurred to her that there could be the least incommodity in her travelling alone; and since she was unprovided with a companion I of course civilly abstained from disturbing her sense of security.

At last her cousin came back. I saw him turn toward us out

of a side-street, and from the moment my eyes rested on him I knew he could but be the bright, if not the kind, American art-student. He wore a slouch hat and a rusty black velvet jacket, such as I had often encountered in the Rue Bonaparte. His shirt-collar displayed a stretch of throat that at a distance wasn't strikingly statuesque. He was tall and lean, he had red hair and freckles. These items I had time to take in while he approached the café, staring at me with natural surprise from under his romantic brim. When he came up to us I immediately introduced myself as an old acquaintance of Miss Spencer's, a character she serenely permitted me to claim. He looked at me hard with a pair of small sharp eyes, then he gave me a solemn wave, in the "European" fashion, of his rather rusty sombrero.

"You weren't on the ship?" he asked.

"No, I wasn't on the ship. I've been in Europe these several years."

He bowed once more, portentously, and motioned me to be seated again. I sat down, but only for the purpose of observing him an instant—I saw it was time I should return to my sister. Miss Spencer's European protector was, by my measure, a very queer quantity. Nature hadn't shaped him for a Raphaelesque or Byronic attire, and his velvet doublet and exhibited though not columnar throat weren't in harmony with his facial attributes. His hair was cropped close to his head; his ears were large and ill-adjusted to the same. He had a lackadaisical carriage and a sentimental droop which were peculiarly at variance with his keen conscious strange-coloured eyes—of a brown that was almost red. Perhaps I was prejudiced, but I thought his eyes too shifty. He said nothing for some time; he leaned his hands on his stick and looked up and down the street. Then at last, slowly lifting the stick and pointing with it, "That's a very nice bit," he dropped with a certain flatness. He had his head to one side—he narrowed his ugly lids. I followed the direction of his stick; the object it indicated was a red cloth hung out of an old window. "Nice bit of colour," he continued; and without moving his head transferred his half-closed gaze to me. "Composes well. Fine old tone. Make a nice thing." He spoke in a charmless vulgar voice.

"I see you've a great deal of eye," I replied. "Your cousin tells me you're studying art." He looked at me in the same way, without answering, and I went on with deliberate urbanity: "I suppose you're at the studio of one of those great men." Still on this he continued to fix me, and then he named one of the greatest of that day; which led me to ask him if he liked his master.

"Do you understand French?" he returned.

"Some kinds."

He kept his little eyes on me; with which he remarked: "Je suis fou de la peinture!"

"Oh I understand that kind!" I replied. Our companion laid her hand on his arm with a small pleased and fluttered movement; it was delightful to be among people who were on such easy terms with foreign tongues. I got up to take leave and asked her where, in Paris, I might have the honour of waiting on her. To what hotel would she go?

She turned to her cousin enquiringly and he favoured me again with his little languid leer. "Do you know the Hôtel des Princes?"

"I know where it is."

"Well, that's the shop."

"I congratulate you," I said to Miss Spencer. "I believe it's the best inn in the world; but, in case I should still have a moment to call on you here, where are you lodged?"

"Oh it's such a pretty name," she returned gleefully. "À la Belle Normande."

"I guess I know my way round!" her kinsman threw in; and as I left them he gave me with his swaggering head-cover a great flourish that was like the wave of a banner over a conquered field.

III

MY relative, as it proved, was not sufficiently restored to leave the place by the afternoon train; so that as the autumn dusk began to fall I found myself at liberty to call at the establishment named to me by my friends. I must confess that I had spent much of the interval in wondering what the disagreeable thing was that the less attractive of these had been telling the other. The *auberge* of the Belle Normande proved an hostelry in a shady by-street, where it gave me satisfaction to think Miss Spencer must have encountered local colour in abundance. There was a crooked little court, where much of the hospitality of the house was carried on; there was a staircase climbing to bedrooms on the outer side of the wall; there was a small trickling fountain with a stucco statuette set in the midst of it; there was a little boy in a white cap and apron cleaning copper vessels at a conspicuous kitchen door; there was a chattering landlady, neatly laced, arranging apricots and grapes into an artistic pyramid upon a pink plate. I looked about, and on a green bench outside of an open door labelled Salle-à-Manger, I distinguished Caroline Spencer. No sooner had I looked at her than I was sure something had happened since the morning. Supported by the back of her bench, with her hands clasped in her lap, she kept her eyes on the other side of the court, where the landlady manipulated the apricots.

But I saw that, poor dear, she wasn't thinking of apricots or even of landladies. She was staring absently, thoughtfully; on a nearer view I could have certified she had been crying. I had seated myself beside her before she was aware; then, when she had done so, she simply turned round without surprise and showed me her sad face. Something very bad indeed had happened; she was completely changed, and I immediately charged her with it. "Your cousin has been giving you bad news. You've had a horrid time."

For a moment she said nothing, and I supposed her afraid to speak lest her tears should again rise. Then it came to me that even in the few hours since my leaving her she had shed them all—which made her now intensely, stoically composed. "My poor cousin has been having one," she replied at last. "He has had great worries. His news was bad." Then after a dismally conscious wait: "He was in dreadful want of money."

"In want of yours, you mean?"

"Of any he could get—honourably of course. Mine *is* all—well, that's available."

Ah it was as if I had been sure from the first! "And he has taken it from you?"

Again she hung fire, but her face meanwhile was pleading. "I gave him what I had."

I recall the accent of those words as the most angelic human sound I had ever listened to—which is exactly why I jumped up almost with a sense of personal outrage. "Gracious goodness, madam, do you call that his getting it 'honourably'?"

I had gone too far—she coloured to her eyes. "We won't speak of it."

"We *must* speak of it," I declared as I dropped beside her again. "I'm your friend—upon my word I'm your protector; it seems to me you need one. What's the matter with this extraordinary person?"

She was perfectly able to say. "He's just badly in debt."

"No doubt he is! But what's the special propriety of your—in such tearing haste!—paying for that?"

"Well, he has told me all his story. I *feel* for him so much."

"So do I, if you come to that! But I hope," I roundly added, "he'll give you straight back your money."

As to this she was prompt. "Certainly he will—as soon as ever he can."

"And when the deuce will that be?"

Her lucidity maintained itself. "When he has finished his great picture."

It took me full in the face. "My dear young lady, damn his great picture! Where is this voracious man?"

It was as if she must let me feel a moment that I did push her!—though indeed, as appeared, he was just where he'd naturally be. "He's having his dinner."

I turned about and looked through the open door into the salle-à-manger. There, sure enough, alone at the end of a long table, was the object of my friend's compassion—the bright, the kind young art-student. He was dining too attentively to notice me at first, but in the act of setting down a well-emptied wine-glass he caught sight of my air of observation. He paused in his repast and, with his head on one side and his meagre jaws slowly moving, fixedly returned my gaze. Then the landlady came brushing lightly by with her pyramid of apricots.

"And that nice little plate of fruit is for him?" I wailed.

Miss Spencer glanced at it tenderly. "They seem to arrange everything so nicely!" she simply sighed.

I felt helpless and irritated. "Come now, really," I said; "do you think it right, do you think it decent, that that long strong fellow should collar your funds?" She looked away from me —I was evidently giving her pain. The case was hopeless; the long strong fellow had "interested" her.

"Pardon me if I speak of him so unceremoniously," I said. "But you're really too generous, and he hasn't, clearly, the rudiments of delicacy. He made his debts himself—he ought to pay them himself."

"He has been foolish," she obstinately said—"of course I know that. He has told me everything. We had a long talk this morning—the poor fellow threw himself on my charity. He has signed notes to a large amount."

"The more fool he!"

"He's in real distress—and it's not only himself. It's his poor young wife."

"Ah he has a poor young wife?"

"I didn't know—but he made a clean breast of it. He married two years since—secretly."

"Why secretly?"

My informant took precautions as if she feared listeners. Then with low impressiveness: "She was a Countess!"

"Are you very sure of that?"

"She has written me the most beautiful letter."

"Asking you—whom she has never seen—for money?"

"Asking me for confidence and sympathy"—Miss Spencer spoke now with spirit. "She has been cruelly treated by her family—in consequence of what she has done for him. My cousin has told me every particular, and she appeals to me in her own lovely way in the letter, which I've here in my pocket. It's such a wonderful old-world romance," said my prodigious friend. "She was a beautiful young widow—her first husband was a Count, tremendously high-born, but really most wicked, with whom she hadn't been happy and whose death had left her ruined after he had deceived her in all sorts of ways. My poor cousin, meeting her in that situation and perhaps a little too recklessly pitying her and charmed with her, found her, don't you see?"—Caroline's appeal on this head was amazing!—"but too ready to trust a better man after all she had been through. Only when her 'people,' as he says—and I do like the word! —understood she *would* have him, poor gifted young American art-student though he simply was, because she just adored him, her great-aunt, the old Marquise, from whom she had expectations of wealth which she could yet sacrifice for her love, utterly cast her off and wouldn't so much as speak to her, much less to *him,* in their dreadful haughtiness and pride. They *can* be haughty over here, it seems," she ineffably developed—"there's no mistake about that! It's like something in some famous old book. The family, my cousin's wife's," she by this time almost complacently wound up, "are of the oldest Provençal noblesse."

I listened half-bewildered. The poor woman positively found it so interesting to be swindled by a flower of that stock—if stock or flower or solitary grain of truth was really concerned in the matter—as practically to have lost the sense of what the forfeiture of her hoard meant for her. "My dear young lady," I groaned, "you don't want to be stripped of every dollar for such a rigmarole!"

She asserted, at this, her dignity—much as a small pink shorn lamb might have done. "It isn't a rigmarole, and I shan't be stripped. I shan't live any worse than I *have* lived, don't you see? And I'll come back before long to stay with them. The Countess—he still gives her, he says, her title, as they do to noble widows, that is to 'dowagers,' don't you know? in England—insists on a visit from me *some* time. So I guess for *that* I can start afresh—and meanwhile I'll have recovered my money."

It was all too heart-breaking. "You're going home then at once?"

I felt the faint tremor of voice she heroically tried to stifle. "I've nothing left for a tour."

"You gave it *all* up?"

"I've kept enough to take me back."

I uttered, I think, a positive howl, and at this juncture the hero of the situation, the happy proprietor of my little friend's sacred savings and of the infatuated *grande dame* just sketched for me, reappeared with the clear consciousness of a repast bravely earned and consistently enjoyed. He stood on the threshold an instant, extracting the stone from a plump apricot he had fondly retained; then he put the apricot into his mouth and, while he let it gratefully dissolve there, stood looking at us with his long legs apart and his hands thrust into the pockets of his velvet coat. My companion got up, giving him a thin glance that I caught in its passage and which expressed at once resignation and fascination—the last dregs of her sacrifice and with it an anguish of upliftedness. Ugly vulgar pretentious dishonest as I thought him, and destitute of every grace of plausibility, he had yet appealed successfully to her eager and tender imagination. I was deeply disgusted, but I had no warrant to interfere, and at any rate felt that it would be vain. He waved his hand meanwhile with a breadth of appreciation. "Nice old court. Nice mellow old place. Nice crooked old staircase. Several pretty things."

Decidedly I couldn't stand it, and without responding I gave my hand to my friend. She looked at me an instant with her little white face and rounded eyes, and as she showed her pretty teeth I suppose she meant to smile. "Don't be sorry for me," she sublimely pleaded; "I'm very sure I shall see something of this dear old Europe yet."

I refused however to take literal leave of her—I should find a moment to come back next morning. Her awful kinsman, who had put on his sombrero again, flourished it off at me by way of a bow—on which I hurried away.

On the morrow early I did return, and in the court of the inn met the landlady, more loosely laced than in the evening. On my asking for Miss Spencer, "*Partie,* monsieur," the good woman said. "She went away last night at ten o'clock, with her—her—not her husband, eh?—in fine her Monsieur. They went down to the American ship." I turned off—I felt the tears in my eyes. The poor girl had been some thirteen hours in Europe.

IV

I MYSELF, more fortunate, continued to sacrifice to opportunity as I myself met it. During this period—of some five years—I lost my friend Latouche, who died of a malarious fever during a tour in the Levant. One of the first things I did on my return to America was to go up to North Verona on a consolatory visit to his poor mother. I found her in deep affliction and sat with her the whole of the morning that followed my arrival—I had come in late at night—listening to her tearful descant and singing the praises of my friend. We talked of nothing else, and our conversation ended only with the arrival of a quick little woman who drove herself up to the door in a "carry-all" and whom I saw toss the reins to the horse's back with the briskness of a startled sleeper throwing off the bedclothes. She jumped out of the carry-all and she jumped into the room. She proved to be the minister's wife and the great town-gossip, and she had evidently, in the latter capacity, a choice morsel to communicate. I was as sure of this as I was that poor Mrs. Latouche was not absolutely too bereaved to listen to her. It seemed to me discreet to retire, and I described myself as anxious for a walk before dinner.

"And by the way," I added, "if you'll tell me where my old friend Miss Spencer lives, I think I'll call on her."

The minister's wife immediately responded. Miss Spencer lived in the fourth house beyond the Baptist church; the Baptist church was the one on the right, with that queer green thing over the door; they called it a portico, but it looked more like an old-fashioned bedstead swung in the air. "Yes, do look up poor Caroline," Mrs. Latouche further enjoined. "It will refresh her to see a strange face."

"I should think she had had enough of strange faces!" cried the minister's wife.

"To see, I mean, a charming visitor"—Mrs. Latouche amended her phrase.

"I should think she had had enough of charming visitors!" her companion returned. "But *you* don't mean to stay ten years," she added with significant eyes on me.

"Has she a visitor of that sort?" I asked in my ignorance.

"You'll make out the sort!" said the minister's wife. "She's easily seen; she generally sits in the front yard. Only take care what you say to her, and be very sure you're polite."

"Ah she's so sensitive?"

The minister's wife jumped up and dropped me a curtsey—a most sarcastic curtsey. "That's what she is, if you please. 'Madame la Comtesse!' "

And pronouncing these titular words with the most scathing

accent, the little woman seemed fairly to laugh in the face of the lady they designated. I stood staring, wondering, remembering.

"Oh I shall be very polite!" I cried; and, grasping my hat and stick, I went on my way.

I found Miss Spencer's residence without difficulty. The Baptist church was easily identified, and the small dwelling near it, of a rusty white, with a large central chimney-stack and a Virginia creeper, seemed naturally and properly the abode of a withdrawn old maid with a taste for striking effects inexpensively obtained. As I approached I slackened my pace, for I had heard that some one was always sitting in the front yard, and I wished to reconnoitre. I looked cautiously over the low white fence that separated the small garden-space from the unpaved street, but I descried nothing in the shape of a Comtesse. A small straight path led up to the crooked door-step, on either side of which was a little grass-plot fringed with currant-bushes. In the middle of the grass, right and left, was a large quince-tree, full of antiquity and contortions, and beneath one of the quince-trees were placed a small table and a couple of light chairs. On the table lay a piece of unfinished embroidery and two or three books in bright-coloured paper covers. I went in at the gate and paused halfway along the path, scanning the place for some further token of its occupant, before whom—I could hardly have said why—I hesitated abruptly to present myself. Then I saw the poor little house to be of the shabbiest and felt a sudden doubt of my right to penetrate, since curiosity had been my motive and curiosity here failed of confidence. While I demurred a figure appeared in the open doorway and stood there looking at me. I immediately recognised Miss Spencer, but she faced me as if we had never met. Gently, but gravely and timidly, I advanced to the door-step, where I spoke with an attempt at friendly banter.

"I waited for you over there to come back, but you never came."

"Waited where, sir?" she quavered, her innocent eyes rounding themselves as of old. She was much older; she looked tired and wasted.

"Well," I said, "I waited at the old French port."

She stared harder, then recognised me, smiling, flushing, clasping her two hands together. "I remember you now—I remember that day." But she stood there, neither coming out nor asking me to come in. She was embarrassed.

I too felt a little awkward while I poked at the path with my stick. "I kept looking out for you year after year."

"You mean in Europe?" she ruefully breathed.

"In Europe of course! Here apparently you're easy enough to find."

She leaned her hand against the unpainted door-post and her head fell a little to one side. She looked at me thus without speaking, and I caught the expression visible in women's eyes when tears are rising. Suddenly she stepped out on the cracked slab of stone before her threshold and closed the door. Then her strained smile prevailed and I saw her teeth were as pretty as ever. But there had been tears too. "Have you been there ever since?" she lowered her voice to ask.

"Until three weeks ago. And you—you never came back?"

Still shining at me as she could, she put her hand behind her and reopened the door. "I'm not very polite," she said. "Won't you come in?"

"I'm afraid I incommode you."

"Oh no!"—she wouldn't hear of it now. And she pushed back the door with a sign that I should enter.

I followed her in. She led the way to a small room on the left of the narrow hall, which I supposed to be her parlour, though it was at the back of the house, and we passed the closed door of another apartment which apparently enjoyed a view of the quince-trees. This one looked out upon a small wood-shed and two clucking hens. But I thought it pretty until I saw its elegance to be of the most frugal kind; after which, presently, I thought it prettier still, for I had never seen faded chintz and old mezzotint engravings, framed in varnished autumn leaves, disposed with so touching a grace. Miss Spencer sat down on a very small section of the sofa, her hands tightly clasped in her lap. She looked ten years older, and I needn't now have felt called to insist on the facts of her person. But I still thought them interesting, and at any rate I was moved by them. She was peculiarly agitated. I tried to appear not to notice it; but suddenly, in the most inconsequent fashion—it was an irresistible echo of our concentrated passage in the old French port—I said to her: "I do incommode you. Again you're in distress."

She raised her two hands to her face and for a moment kept it buried in them. Then taking them away, "It's because you remind me," she said.

"I remind you, you mean, of that miserable day at the Havre?"

She wonderfully shook her head. "It wasn't miserable. It was delightful."

Ah was it? my manner of receiving this must have commented. "I never was so shocked as when, on going back to your inn the next morning, I found you had wretchedly retreated."

She waited an instant, after which she said: "Please let us not speak of that."

"Did you come straight back here?" I nevertheless went on.

"I was back here just thirty days after my first start."

"And here you've remained ever since?"

"Every minute of the time."

I took it in; I didn't know what to say, and what I presently said had almost the sound of mockery. "When then are you going to make that tour?" It might be practically aggressive; but there was something that irritated me in her depths of resignation, and I wished to extort from her some expression of impatience.

She attached her eyes a moment to a small sun-spot on the

carpet; then she got up and lowered the window-blind a little to obliterate it. I waited, watching her with interest—as if she had still something more to give me. Well, presently, in answer to my last question, she gave it. "Never!"

"I hope at least your cousin repaid you that money," I said.

At this again she looked away from me. "I don't care for it now."

"You don't care for your money?"

"For ever going to Europe."

"Do you mean you wouldn't go if you could?"

"I can't—I can't," said Caroline Spencer. "It's all over. Everything's different. I never think of it."

"The scoundrel never repaid you then!" I cried.

"Please, please—!" she began.

But she had stopped—she was looking toward the door. There had been a rustle and a sound of steps in the hall.

I also looked toward the door, which was open and now admitted another person—a lady who paused just within the threshold. Behind her came a young man. The lady looked at me with a good deal of fixedness—long enough for me to rise to a vivid impression of herself. Then she turned to Caroline Spencer and, with a smile and a strong foreign accent, "*Pardon, ma chère!* I didn't know you had company," she said. "The gentleman came in so quietly." With which she again gave me the benefit of her attention. She was very strange, yet I was at once sure I had seen her before. Afterwards I rather put it that I had only seen ladies remarkably like her. But I had seen them very far away from North Verona, and it was the oddest of all things to meet one of them in that frame. To what quite other scene did the sight of her transport me? To some dusky landing before a shabby Parisian *quatrième*—to an open door revealing a greasy ante-chamber and to Madame leaning over the banisters while she holds a faded wrapper together and bawls down to the portress to bring up her coffee. My friend's guest was a very large lady, of middle age, with a plump dead-white face and hair drawn back *à la chinoise*. She had a small penetrating eye and what is called in French *le sourire agréable*. She wore an old pink cashmere dressing-gown covered with white embroideries, and, like the figure in my momentary vision, she confined it in front with a bare and rounded arm and a plump and deeply-dimpled hand.

"It's only to spick about my café," she said to her hostess with her *sourire agréable*. "I should like it served in the garden under the leetle tree."

The young man behind her had now stepped into the room, where he also stood revealed, though with rather less of a challenge. He was a gentleman of few inches but a vague importance, perhaps the leading man of the world of North Verona. He had a small pointed nose and a small pointed chin; also, as I observed, the most diminutive feet and a manner of no point at all. He looked at me foolishly and with his mouth open.

"You shall have your coffee," said Miss Spencer as if an army of cooks had been engaged in the preparation of it.

"C'est bien!" said her massive inmate. "Find your bouk"—and this personage turned to the gaping youth.

He gaped now at each quarter of the room. "My grammar, d' ye mean?"

The large lady however could but face her friend's visitor while persistently engaged with a certain laxity in the flow of her wrapper. "Find your bouk," she more absently repeated.

"My poetry, d' ye mean?" said the young man, who also couldn't take his eyes off me.

"Never mind your bouk"—his companion reconsidered. "To-day we'll just talk. We'll make some conversation. But we mustn't interrupt Mademoiselle's. Come, come"—and she moved off a step. "Under the leetle tree," she added for the benefit of Mademoiselle. After which she gave me a thin salutation, jerked a measured "Monsieur!" and swept away again with her swain following.

I looked at Miss Spencer, whose eyes never moved from the

carpet, and I spoke, I fear, without grace. "Who in the world's that?"

"The Comtesse—that *was:* my *cousine* as they call it in French."

"And who's the young man?"

"The Countess's pupil, Mr. Mixter." This description of the tie uniting the two persons who had just quitted us must certainly have upset my gravity; for I recall the marked increase of my friend's own as she continued to explain. "She gives lessons in French and music, the simpler sorts—"

"The simpler sorts of French?" I fear I broke in.

But she was still impenetrable, and in fact had now an intonation that put me vulgarly in the wrong. "She has had the worst reverses—with no one to look to. She's prepared for any exertion—and she takes her misfortunes with gaiety."

"Ah well," I returned—no doubt a little ruefully, "that's all I myself am pretending to do. If she's determined to be a burden to nobody, nothing could be more right and proper."

My hostess looked vaguely, though I thought quite wearily enough, about: she met this proposition in no other way. "I must go and get the coffee," she simply said.

"Has the lady many pupils?" I none the less persisted.

"She has only Mr. Mixter. She gives him all her time." It might have set me off again, but something in my whole impression of my friend's sensibility urged me to keep strictly decent. "He pays very well," she at all events inscrutably went on. "He's not very bright—as a pupil; but he's very rich and he's very kind. He has a buggy—with a back, and he takes the Countess to drive."

"For good long spells I hope," I couldn't help interjecting—even at the cost of her so taking it that she had still to avoid my eyes. "Well, the country's beautiful for miles," I went on. And then as she was turning away: "You're going for the Countess's coffee?"

"If you'll excuse me a few moments."

"Is there no one else to do it?"

She seemed to wonder who there should be. "I keep no servants."

"Then can't I help?" After which, as she but looked at me, I bettered it. "Can't she wait on herself?"

Miss Spencer had a slow headshake—as if that too had been a strange idea. "She isn't used to *manual* labour."

The discrimination was a treat, but I cultivated decorum. "I see—and you *are*." But at the same time I couldn't abjure curiosity. "Before you go, at any rate, please tell me this: who *is* this wonderful lady?"

"I told you just who in France—that extraordinary day. She's the wife of my cousin, whom you saw there."

"The lady disowned by her family in consequence of her marriage?"

"Yes; they've never seen her again. They've completely broken with her."

"And where's her husband?"

"My poor cousin's dead."

I pulled up, but only a moment. "And where's your money?"

The poor thing flinched—I kept her on the rack. "I don't know," she woefully said.

I scarce know what it didn't prompt me to—but I went step by step. "On her husband's death this lady at once came to you?"

It was as if she had had too often to describe it. "Yes, she arrived one day."

"How long ago?"

"Two years and four months."

"And has been here ever since?"

"Ever since."

I took it all in. "And how does she like it?"

"Well, not *very* much," said Miss Spencer divinely.

That too I took in. "And how do *you*—?"

She laid her face in her two hands an instant as she had done ten minutes before. Then, quickly, she went to get the Countess's coffee.

Left alone in the little parlour I found myself divided between the perfection of my disgust and a contrary wish to see, to learn more. At the end of a few minutes the young man in attendance on the lady in question reappeared as for a fresh gape at me. He was inordinately grave—to be dressed in such parti-coloured flannels; and he produced with no great confidence on his own side the message with which he had been charged. "She wants to know if you won't come right out."

"Who wants to know?"

"The Countess. That French lady."

"She has asked you to bring me?"

"Yes sir," said the young man feebly—for I may claim to have surpassed him in stature and weight.

I went out with him, and we found his instructress seated under one of the small quince-trees in front of the house; where she was engaged in drawing a fine needle with a very fat hand through a piece of embroidery not remarkable for freshness. She pointed graciously to the chair beside her and I sat down Mr. Mixter glanced about him and then accommodated himself on the grass at her feet; whence he gazed upward more gapingly than ever and as if convinced that between us something wonderful would now occur.

"I'm sure you spick French," said the Countess, whose eyes were singularly protuberant as she played over me her agreeable smile.

"I do, madam—*tant bien que mal*," I replied, I fear, more dryly.

"Ah *voilà*!" she cried as with delight. "I knew it as soon as I looked at you. You've been in my poor dear country."

"A considerable time."

"You love it then, *mon pays de France?*"

"Oh it's an old affection." But I wasn't exuberant.

"And you know Paris well?"

"Yes, *sans me vanter,* madam, I think I really do." And with a certain conscious purpose I let my eyes meet her own.

She presently, hereupon, moved her own and glanced down at Mr. Mixter. "What are we talking about?" she demanded of her attentive pupil.

He pulled his knees up, plucked at the grass, stared, blushed a little. "You're talking French," said Mr. Mixter.

"La belle découverte!" mocked the Countess. "It's going on ten months," she explained to me, "since I took him in hand. Don't put yourself out not to say he's *la bêtise même,*" she added in fine style. "He won't in the least understand you."

A moment's consideration of Mr. Mixter, awkwardly sporting at our feet, quite assured me that he wouldn't. "I hope your other pupils do you more honour," I then remarked to my entertainer.

"I have no others. They don't know what French—or what anything else—is in this place; they don't want to know. You may therefore imagine the pleasure it is to me to meet a person who speaks it like yourself." I could but reply that my own pleasure wasn't less, and she continued to draw the stitches through her embroidery with an elegant curl of her little finger. Every few moments she put her eyes, near-sightedly, closer to her work—this as if for elegance too. She inspired me with no more confidence than her late husband, if husband he was, had done, years before, on the occasion with which this one so detestably matched: she was coarse, common, affected, dishonest—no more a Countess than I was a Caliph. She had an assurance—based clearly on experience; but this couldn't have been the experience of "race." Whatever it was indeed it did now, in a yearning fashion, flare out of her. "Talk to me of Paris, *mon beau Paris* that I'd give my eyes to see. The very name of it *me fait languir*. How long since you were there?"

"A couple of months ago."

"*Vous avez de la chance!* Tell me something about it. What were they doing? Oh for an hour of the Boulevard!"

"They were doing about what they're always doing—amusing themselves a good deal."

"At the theatres, *hein*?" sighed the Countess. "At the cafés-concerts? *sous ce beau ciel*—at the little tables before the doors? *Quelle existence!* You know I'm a Parisienne, monsieur," she added, "to my finger-tips."

"Miss Spencer was mistaken then," I ventured to return, "in telling me you're a Provençale."

She stared a moment, then put her nose to her embroidery, which struck me as having acquired even while we sat a dingier and more desultory air. "Ah I'm a Provençale by birth, but a Parisienne by—inclination." After which she pursued: "And by the saddest events of my life—as well as by some of the happiest, hélas!"

"In other words by a varied experience!" I now at last smiled.

She questioned me over it with her hard little salient eyes. "Oh experience!—I could talk of that, no doubt, if I wished. *On en a de toutes les sortes*—and I never dreamed that mine, for example, would ever have *this* in store for me." And she indicated with her large bare elbow and with a jerk of her head all surrounding objects; the little white house, the pair of quince-trees, the rickety paling, even the rapt Mr. Mixter.

I took them all bravely in. "Ah if you mean you're decidedly in exile—!"

"You may imagine what it is. These two years of my *épreuve—elles m'en ont données, des heures, des heures!* One gets used to things"—and she raised her shoulders to the highest shrug ever accomplished at North Verona; "so that I sometimes think I've got used to this. But there are some things that are always beginning again. For example my coffee."

I so far again lent myself. "Do you always have coffee at this hour?"

Her eyebrows went up as high as her shoulders had done. "At what hour would you propose to me to have it? I must have my little cup after breakfast."

"Ah you breakfast at this hour?"

"At mid-day—*comme cela se fait*. Here they breakfast at a quarter past seven. That 'quarter past' is charming!"

"But you were telling me about your coffee," I observed sympathetically.

"My *cousine* can't believe in it; she can't understand it. *C'est une fille charmante,* but that little cup of black coffee with a drop of '*fine,*' served at this hour—they exceed her comprehension. So I have to break the ice each day, and it takes the coffee the time you see to arrive. And when it does arrive, monsieur—! If I don't press it on *you*—though monsieur here sometimes joins me!—it's because you've drunk it on the Boulevard."

I resented extremely so critical a view of my poor friend's exertions, but I said nothing at all—the only way to be sure of my civility. I dropped my eyes on Mr. Mixter, who, sitting cross-legged and nursing his knees, watched my companion's foreign graces with an interest that familiarity had apparently done little to restrict. She became aware, naturally, of my mystified view of him and faced the question with all her boldness. "He adores me, you know," she murmured with her nose again in her tapestry—"he dreams of becoming *mon amoureux*. Yes, *il me fait une cour acharnée*—such as you see him. That's what we've come to. He has read some French novel—it took him six months. But ever since that he has thought himself a hero and me—such as I am, monsieur—*je ne sais quelle dévergondée!*"

Mr. Mixter may have inferred that he was to that extent the object of our reference; but of the manner in which he was handled he must have had small suspicion—preoccupied as he was, as to my companion, with the ecstasy of contemplation. Our hostess moreover at this moment came out of the house, bearing a coffee-pot and three cups on a neat little tray. I took from her eyes, as she approached us, a brief but intense appeal—the mute expression, as I felt, conveyed in the hardest little look she had yet addressed me, of her longing to know what, as a man of the world in general and of the French world in particular, I thought of these allied forces now so encamped on the stricken field of her life. I could only "act" however, as they said at North Verona, quite impenetrably—only make no answering sign. I couldn't intimate, much less could I frankly utter, my inward sense of the Countess's probable past, with its measure of her virtue, value and accomplishments, and of the limits of the consideration to which she could properly pretend. I couldn't give my friend a hint of how I myself personally "saw" her interesting pensioner—whether as the runaway wife of a too-jealous hair-dresser or of a too-morose pastry-cook, say; whether as a very small bourgeoise, in fine, who had vitiated her case beyond patching up, or even as some character, of the nomadic sort, less edifying still. I couldn't let in, by the jog of a shutter, as it were, a hard informing ray and then, washing my hands of the business, turn my back for ever. I could on the contrary but save the situation, my own at least, for the moment, by pulling myself together with a master hand and appearing to ignore everything but that the dreadful person between us *was* a "grande dame." This effort was possible indeed but as a retreat in good order and with all the forms of courtesy. If I couldn't speak, still less could I stay, and I think I must, in spite of everything, have turned black with disgust to see Caroline Spencer stand there like a waiting-maid. I therefore won't answer for the shade of success that may have attended my saying to the Countess, on my feet and as to leave her: "You expect to remain some time in these *parages*?"

What passed between us, as from face to face, while she looked up at me, *that* at least our companion may have caught, that at least may have sown, for the after-time, some seed of revelation. The Countess repeated her terrible shrug. "Who knows? I don't see my way—! It isn't an existence, but when one's in misery—! *Chère belle,*" she added as an appeal to Miss Spencer, "you've gone and forgotten the '*fine*'!"

I detained that lady as, after considering a moment in silence the small array, she was about to turn off in quest of this article.

I held out my hand in silence—I had to go. Her wan set little face, severely mild and with the question of a moment before now quite cold in it, spoke of extreme fatigue, but also of something else strange and conceived—whether a desperate patience still, or at last some other desperation, being more than I can say. What was clearest on the whole was that she was glad I was going. Mr. Mixter had risen to his feet and was pouring out the Countess's coffee. As I went back past the Baptist church I could feel how right my poor friend had been in her conviction at the other, the still intenser, the now historic crisis, that she should still see something of that dear old Europe.

A NOTE ON

FOUR MEETINGS

(1877)

OUR American eagerness for the new and the slick sooner or later breeds its own antibody, an eagerness for the old and the weathered. At times the two drives collide within a single heart. More often we deputize, as it were, a special minority and enjoin it to experience for the community as a whole the thirst and the slaking of the thirst for the traditional, which is the unlimited in time, and the cosmopolitan, which is the unlimited in space.

Here, in this first of James's fictions to display mastery, Caroline Spencer represents that minority group, as Carol Kennicott was to represent it for a later generation. The little spinster is able to feel the passion for Europe in only a limited way, as a longing for "the picturesque." It is a colored postcard, a museum Europe for which her frail Puritan arms reach out. It is for this rather anemic Europe (where she finally spends but thirteen hours of her life) that she suffers. She is willing, as the narrator remarks, "to be ruined for picturesqueness' sake." It is her narrow conception of "Europe" that cruelly betrays her into her cousin's trap. She is fascinated by his fake Bohemianism, by the atmosphere of the foreign he exudes. It is for him, the counterfeit, that she sacrifices her chance to experience the reality. And this counterfeit Europe pursues her to the end of her dun-colored days, taking the form of the vulgar and spurious Countess, whom she is too weak, too mesmerized to reject, and too sensitive to accept.

In "The American" (published, like this story, in 1877) James measured the Europe-America opposition of forces with more delicate instruments. In "The Ambassadors" (1903) and "The Golden Bowl" (1904) these instruments were still further refined. But, masterpieces or near-masterpieces as these novels may be, they still connect with the fragile yet trenchant "Four Meetings," being but the calculated and absolute exhaustion of the theme here tentatively announced.

A BUNDLE OF LETTERS

I

FROM MISS MIRANDA HOPE IN PARIS TO MRS. ABRAHAM C. HOPE AT BANGOR, MAINE

September 5, 1879.

MY DEAR MOTHER.

I've kept you posted as far as Tuesday week last, and though my letter won't have reached you yet I'll begin another before my news accumulates too much. I'm glad you show my letters round in the family, for I like them all to know what I'm doing, and I can't write to everyone, even if I do try to answer all reasonable expectations. There are a great many unreasonable ones, as I suppose you know—not yours, dear mother, for I'm bound to say that you never required of me more than was natural. You see you're reaping your reward: I write to you before I write to any one else.

There's one thing I hope—that you don't show any of my letters to William Platt. If he wants to see any of my letters he knows the right way to go to work. I wouldn't have him see one of these letters, written for circulation in the family, for anything in the world. If he wants one for himself he has got to write to me first. Let him write to me first and then I'll see about answering him. You can show him this if you like; but if you show him anything more, I'll never write to you again.

I told you in my last about my farewell to England, my crossing the Channel and my first impressions of Paris. I've thought a great deal about that lovely England since I left it, and all the famous historic scenes I visited; but I've come to the conclusion that it's not a country in which I should care to reside. The position of woman doesn't seem to me at all satisfactory, and that's a point, you know, on which I feel very strongly. It seems to me that in England they play a very faded-out part, and those with whom I conversed had a kind of downtrodden tone, a spiritless and even benighted air, as if they were used to being snubbed and bullied *and as if they liked it,* which made me want to give them a good shaking. There are a great many people—and a great many things too—over here that I should like to get at for that purpose. I should like to shake the starch out of some of them and the dust out of the others. I know fifty girls in Bangor that come much more up to my notion of the stand a truly noble woman should take than those young ladies in England. But they had the sweetest way of speaking, as if it were a second nature, and the men are *remarkably handsome.* (You can show *that* to William Platt if you like.)

I gave you my first impressions of Paris, which quite came up to my expectations, much as I had heard and read about it. The objects of interest are extremely numerous, and the climate remarkably cheerful and sunny. I should say the position of woman here was considerably higher, though by no means up to the American standard. The manners of the people are in some respects extremely peculiar, and I feel at last that I'm indeed in *foreign parts.* It is, however, a truly elegant city (much more majestic than New York) and I've spent a great deal of time in visiting the various monuments and palaces. I won't give you an account of all my wanderings, though I've been most indefatigable; for I'm keeping, as I told you before, a most *exhaustive* journal, which I'll allow you the *privilege* of reading on my return to Bangor. I'm getting on remarkably well, and I must say I'm sometimes surprised at my universal good fortune. It only shows what a little Bangor energy and gumption will accomplish wherever applied. I've discovered none of those objections to a young lady travelling in Europe by herself of which we heard so much before I left, and I don't expect I ever shall, for I certainly don't mean to look for them. I know what I want and I always go straight for it.

I've received a great deal of politeness—some of it really most pressing, and have experienced no drawbacks whatever. I've made a great many pleasant acquaintances in travelling round —both ladies and gentlemen—and had a great many interesting and open-hearted, if quite informal, talks. I've collected a great many remarkable facts—I guess we don't know quite *everything* at Bangor—for which I refer you to my journal. I assure you my journal's going to be a splendid picture of an earnest young life. I do just exactly as I do in Bangor, and I find I do perfectly right. At any rate I don't care if I don't. I didn't come to Europe to lead a merely conventional society life: I could do that at Bangor. You know I never *would* do it at Bangor, so it isn't likely I'm going to worship false gods over here. So long as I accomplish what I desire and make my money hold out I shall regard the thing as a success. Sometimes I feel rather lonely, especially evenings; but I generally manage to interest myself in something or in some one. I mostly read up, evenings, on the objects of interest I've visited during the day, or put in time on my journal. Sometimes I go to the theatre or else play the piano in the public parlour. The public parlour at the hotel isn't much; but the piano's better than that fearful old thing at the Sebago House. Sometimes I go downstairs and talk to the lady who keeps the books—a real French lady, who's remarkably polite. She's very handsome, though in the peculiar French way, and always wears a black dress of the most beautiful fit. She speaks a little English; she tells me she had to learn it in order to converse with the Americans who come in such numbers to this hotel. She has given me lots of points on the position of woman in France, and seems to think that on the whole there's hope. But she has told me at the same time some things I shouldn't like to write to you—I'm hesitating even about putting them into my journal—especially if my letters are to be handed round in the family. I assure you they appear to talk about things here that we never think of mentioning at Bangor, even to ourselves or to our very closest; and it has struck me that people are closer—to each other—down in Maine than seems mostly to be expected here. This bright-minded lady appears at any rate to think she can tell me everything because I've told her I'm travelling for general culture. Well, I *do* want to know so much that it seems sometimes as if I wanted to know most everything; and yet I guess there are some things that don't count for improvement. But as a general thing everything's intensely interesting; I don't mean only everything this charming woman tells me, but everything I see and hear for myself. I guess I'll come out where I want.

I meet a great many Americans who, as a general thing, I must say, are not so polite to me as the people over here. The people over here—especially the gentlemen—are much more what I should call almost oppressively attentive. I don't know whether Americans are more truly sincere; I haven't yet made up my mind about that. The only drawback I experience is when Americans sometimes express surprise that I should be travelling round alone; so you see it doesn't come from Europeans. I always have my answer ready: "For general culture, to acquire the languages and to see Europe for myself"; and that generally seems to calm them. Dear mother, my money holds out very well, and it *is* real interesting.

II

FROM THE SAME TO THE SAME

September 16.

SINCE I last wrote to you I've left that nice hotel and come to live in a French family—which however is nice too. This place is a kind of boarding-house that's at the same time a kind of school; only it's not like an American boarding-house, nor like an American school either. There are four or five people here that have come to learn the language—not to take lessons, but to have an opportunity for conversation. I was very glad to come to such a place, for I had begun to realise that I wasn't pressing onward quite as I had dreamed with the French. Wasn't I going to feel ashamed to have spent two months in Paris and not to have acquired more insight into the language? I had always heard so much of French conversation, and I found I wasn't having much more opportunity to practise it than if I had remained at Bangor. In fact I used to hear a great deal more at Bangor from those French-Canadians who came down to cut the ice than I saw I should ever hear at that nice hotel where there was no struggle—*some* fond struggle being my real atmosphere. The lady who kept the books seemed to want so much to talk to me in English (for the sake of practice, too, I suppose—she kind of yearned to struggle too: we don't yearn *only* down in Maine—) that I couldn't bear to show her I didn't like it. The chambermaid was Irish and all the waiters German, so I never heard a word of French spoken. I suppose you might hear a great deal in the shops; but as I don't buy anything—I prefer to spend my money for purposes of culture—I don't have that advantage.

I've been thinking some of taking a teacher, but am well acquainted with the grammar already, and over here in Europe teachers don't seem to think it's *really* in their interest to let you press forward. The more you strike out and realise your power the less they've got to teach you. I was a good deal troubled anyhow, for I felt as if I didn't want to go away without having at least got a general idea of French conversation. The theatre gives you a good deal of insight, and as I told you in my last I go a good deal to the brightest places of amusement. I find no difficulty whatever in going to such places alone, and am always treated with the politeness which, as I've mentioned—for I want you to feel happy about that—I encounter everywhere from the best people. I see plenty of other ladies alone (mostly French) and they generally seem to be enjoying themselves as much as I. Only on the stage every one talks so fast that I can scarcely make out what they say; and, besides, there are a great many vulgar expressions which it's unnecessary to learn. But it was this experience nevertheless that put me on the track. The very next day after I wrote to you last I went to the Palais Royal, which is one of the principal theatres in Paris. It's very small but very celebrated, and in my guide-book it's marked with *two stars,* which is a sign of importance attached only to *first-class* objects of interest. But after I had been there half an hour I found I couldn't understand a single word of the play, they gabbled it off so fast and made use of such peculiar expressions. I felt a good deal disappointed and checked—I saw I wasn't going to come out where I had dreamed. But while I was thinking it over —thinking what I *would* do—I heard two gentlemen talking behind me. It was between the acts, and I couldn't help listening to what they said. They were talking English, but I guess they were Americans.

"Well," said one of them, "it all depends on what you're after. I'm after French; that's what I'm after."

"Well," said the other, "I'm after Art."

"Well," said the first, "I'm after Art too; but I'm after French most."

Then, dear mother, I'm sorry to say the second one swore a little. He said "Oh damn French!"

"No, I won't damn French," said his friend. "I'll acquire it —that's what I'll do with it. I'll go right into a family."

"What family'll you go into?"

"Into some nice French family. That's the only way to do— to go to some place where you can talk. If you're after Art you want to stick to the galleries; you want to go right through the Louvre, room by room; you want to take a room a day, or something of that sort. But if you want to acquire French the thing is to look out for some family that has got—and they mostly have—more of it than they've use for themselves. How *can* they have use for so much as they seem to *have* to have? They've got to work it off. Well, they work it off on *you*. There are lots of them that take you to board and teach you. My second cousin —that young lady I told you about—she got in with a crowd like that, and they posted her right up in three months. They just took her right in and let her have it—the full force. That's what they do to you; they set you right down and they talk *at* you. You've got to understand them or perish—so you strike out in self-defence; you can't help yourself. That family my cousin was with has moved away somewhere, or I should try and get in with them. They were real live people, that family; after she left my cousin corresponded with them in French. You've got to do *that* too, to make much real head. But I mean to find some other crowd, if it takes a lot of trouble!"

I listened to all this with great interest, and when he spoke about his cousin I was on the point of turning around to ask him the address of the family she was with; but the next moment he said they had moved away, so I sat still. The other gentleman, however, didn't seem to be affected in the same way as I was.

"Well," he said, "you may follow up that if you like; I mean to follow up the pictures. I don't believe there's ever going to be any considerable demand in the United States for French; but I can promise you that in about ten years there'll be a big demand for Art! And it won't be temporary either."

That remark may be very true, but I don't care anything about the demand; I want to know French for its own sake. "Art for art," they say; but I say French for French. I don't want to think I've been all this while without having gained an insight. . . . The very next day, I asked the lady who kept the books at the hotel whether she knew of any family that could take me to board and give me the benefit of their conversation. She instantly threw up her hands with little shrill cries—in their wonderful French way, you know—and told me that her dearest friend kept a regular place of that kind. If she had known I was looking out for such a place she would have told me before; she hadn't spoken of it herself because she didn't wish to injure the hotel by working me off on another house. She told me this was a charming family who had often received American ladies—and others, including three Tahitians—who wished to follow up the language, and she was sure I'd fall in love with them. So she gave me their address and offered to go with me to introduce me. But I was in such a hurry that I went off by myself and soon found them all right. They were sitting there as if they kind of expected me, and wouldn't scarcely let me come round again for my baggage. They seemed to have right there on hand, as those gentlemen of the theatre said, plenty of what I was after, and I now feel there'll be no trouble about *that.*

I came here to stay about three days ago, and by this time I've quite worked in. The price of board struck me as rather high, but I must remember what a chance to press onward it includes. I've a very pretty little room—without any carpet, but with seven mirrors, two clocks and five curtains. I was rather disappointed, however, after I arrived, to find that there are several other Americans here—all also bent on pressing onward. At least there are three American and two English pensioners, as they call them, as well as a German gentleman—and there seems nothing backward about *him.* I shouldn't wonder if we'd make a regular class, with "moving up" and "moving down"; anyhow I guess I won't be at the foot, but I've not yet time to judge. I try to talk with Madame de Maisonrouge all I can—she's the lady of the house, and the *real* family consists only of herself and her two daughters. They're bright enough to give points to our own brightest, and I guess we'll become quite intimate. I'll write you more about everything in my next. Tell William Platt I don't care a speck *what* he does.

III

FROM MISS VIOLET RAY IN PARIS TO MISS AGNES RICH IN NEW YORK

September 21.

WE had hardly got here when father received a telegram saying he would have to come right back to New York. It was for something about his business—I don't know exactly what; you know I never understand those things and never want to. We had just got settled at the hotel, in some charming rooms, and mother and I, as you may imagine, were greatly annoyed.

Father's extremely fussy, as you know, and his first idea, as soon as he found he should have to go back, was that we should go back with him. He declared he'd never leave us in Paris alone and that we must return and come out again. I don't know what he thought would happen to us; I suppose he thought we should be too extravagant. It's father's theory that we're always running up bills, whereas a little observation would show him that we wear the same old *rags* FOR MONTHS. But father has no observation; he has nothing but blind theories. Mother and I, however, have fortunately a great deal of *practice,* and we succeeded in making him understand that we wouldn't budge from Paris and that we'd rather be chopped into small pieces than cross that squalid sea again. So at last he decided to go back alone and to leave us here for three months. Only, to show you how fussy he is, he refused to let us stay at the hotel and insisted that we should go into a *family*. I don't know what put such an idea into his head unless it was some advertisement that he saw in one of the American papers that are published here. Don't think you can escape from them anywhere.

There are families here who receive American and English people to live with them under the pretence of teaching them French. You may imagine what people they are—I mean the families themselves. But the Americans who choose this peculiar manner of seeing Paris must be actually just as bad. Mother and I were horrified—we declared that *main force* shouldn't remove us from the hotel. But father has a way of arriving at his ends which is more effective than violence. He worries and goes on; he "nags," as we used to say at school; and when mother and I are quite worn to the bone his triumph is assured. Mother's more quickly ground down than I, and she ends by siding with father; so that at last when they combine their forces against poor little me I've naturally to succumb. You should have heard the way father went on about this "family" plan; he talked to every one he saw about it; he used to go round to the banker's and talk to the people there—the people in the post-office; he used to try and exchange ideas about it with the waiters at the hotel. He said it would be more safe, more respectable, more economical; that I should pick up more French; that mother would learn how a French household's conducted; that he should feel more easy, and that we ourselves should enjoy it when we came to see. All this meant nothing, but that made no difference. It's positively cruel his harping on our pinching and saving when every one knows that business in America has completely recovered, that the prostration's all over and that *immense fortunes* are being made. We've been depriving ourselves of the commonest necessities for the last five years, and I supposed we came abroad to reap the benefits of it.

As for my French it's already much better than that of most of our helpless compatriots, who are all unblushingly destitute of the very rudiments. (I assure you I'm often surprised at my own fluency, and when I get a little more practice in the circumflex accents and the genders and the idioms I shall quite hold my own.) To make a long story short, however, father carried his point as usual; mother basely deserted me at the last moment, and after holding out alone for three days I told them to do with me what they would. Father lost three steamers in succession by remaining in Paris to argue with me. You know he's like the schoolmaster in Goldsmith's "Deserted Village"—"e'en though vanquished" he always argues still. He and mother went to look at some seventeen families—they had got the addresses somewhere—while I retired to my sofa and would have nothing to do with it. At last they made arrangements and I was transported, as in chains, to the establishment from which I now write you. I address you from the bosom of a Parisian ménage—from the depths of a second-rate boarding-house.

Father only left Paris after he had seen us what he calls comfortably settled here and had informed Madame de Maisonrouge—the mistress of the establishment, the head of the "family"—that he wished my French pronunciation especially attended to. The pronunciation, as it happens, is just what I'm most at home in; if he had said my genders or my subjunctives or my idioms there would have been some sense. But poor father has no native tact, and this deficiency has become flagrant since we've been in Europe. He'll be absent, however, for three months, and mother and I shall breathe more freely; the situation will be less tense. I must confess that we breathe more freely than I expected in this place, where we've been about a week. I was sure before we came that it would prove to be an establishment of the *lowest description;* but I must say that in this respect I'm agreeably disappointed. The French spirit is able to throw a sort of grace even over a swindle of this general order. Of course it's very disagreeable to live with strangers, but as, after all, if I weren't staying with Madame de Maisonrouge I shouldn't be *vautrée* in the Faubourg Saint-Germain, I don't know that from the point of view of exclusiveness I'm much the loser.

Our rooms are very prettily arranged and the table's remarkably good. Mamma thinks the whole thing—the place and the people, the manners and customs—very amusing; but mamma can be put off with any imposture. As for me, you know, all that I ask is to be let alone and not to have people's society *forced upon me.* I've never wanted for society of my own choosing, and, so long as I retain possession of my faculties, I don't suppose I ever shall. As I said, however, the place seems to scramble along, and I succeed in doing as I please, which, you know, is my most cherished pursuit. Madame de Maisonrouge has a great deal of tact—much more than poor floundering father. She's what they call here a *grande belle femme,* which means that she's high-shouldered and short-necked and literally hideous, but with a certain quantity of false type. She has a good many clothes, some rather bad; but a very good manner—only one, and worked to death, but intended to be of the best. Though she's a very good imitation of a *femme du monde* I never see her behind the dinner-table in the evening, never see her smile and bow and duck as the people come in, really glaring all the while at the dishes and the servants, without thinking of a *dame de comptoir* blooming in a corner of a shop or a restaurant. I'm sure that in spite of her *beau nom* she was once a paid book-keeper. I'm also sure that in spite of her smiles and the pretty things she says to every one, she hates us all and would like to murder us. She is a hard clever Frenchwoman who would like to amuse herself and enjoy her Paris, and she must be furious at having to pass her time grinning at specimens of the stupid races who mumble broken French at her. Some day she'll poison the soup or the *vin rouge,* but I hope that won't be until after mother and I shall have left her. She has two daughters who, except that one's decidedly pretty, are meagre imitations of herself.

The "family," for the rest, consists altogether of our beloved compatriots and of still more beloved Englanders. There's an Englander with his sister, and they seem rather decent. He's remarkably handsome, but excessively affected and patronising, especially to us Americans; and I hope to have a chance of biting his head off before long. The sister's very pretty and apparently very nice, but in costume Britannia incarnate. There's a very pleasant little Frenchman—when they're nice they're charming—and a German doctor, a big blond man who looks like a great white bull; and two Americans besides mother and me. One of them's a young man from Boston—an æsthetic young man who talks about its being "a real Corot day," and a young woman—a girl, a female, I don't know what to call her—from Vermont or Minnesota or some such place. This young woman's the most extraordinary specimen of self-complacent provinciality that I've ever encountered; she's really too horrible and too humiliating. I've been three times to Clémentine about your underskirt etc.

IV

FROM LOUIS LEVERETT IN PARIS TO HARVARD TREMONT IN BOSTON

September 25.

MY DEAR HARVARD.

I've carried out my plan, of which I gave you a hint in my last, and I only regret I shouldn't have done it before. It's human nature, after all, that's the most interesting thing in the world, and it only reveals itself to the truly earnest seeker. There's a want of earnestness in that life of hotels and railroad-trains which so many of our countrymen are content to lead in this strange rich elder world, and I was distressed to find how far I myself had been led along the dusty beaten track. I had, however, constantly wanted to turn aside into more unfrequented ways—to plunge beneath the surface and see what I should discover. But the opportunity had always been missing; somehow I seem never to meet those opportunities that we hear about and read about—the things that happen to people in novels and biographies. And yet I'm always on the watch to take advantage of any opening that may present itself; I'm always looking out for experiences, for sensations—I might almost say for adventures.

The great thing is to *live,* you know—to feel, to be conscious of one's possibilities; not to pass through life mechanically and insensibly, even as a letter through the post-office. There are times, my dear Harvard, when I feel as if I were really capable of everything—*capable de tout,* as they say here—of the greatest excesses as well as the greatest heroism. Oh to be able to say that one has lived—*qu'on a vécu,* as they say here—that idea exercises an indefinable attraction for me. You'll perhaps reply that nothing's easier than to say it! Only the thing's to make people believe you—to make above all one's self. And then I don't want any second-hand spurious sensations; I want the knowledge that leaves a trace—that leaves strange scars and stains, ineffable reveries and aftertastes, behind it! But I'm afraid I shock you, perhaps even frighten you.

If you repeat my remarks to any of the West Cedar Street circle be sure you tone them down as your discretion will suggest. For yourself you'll know that I have always had an intense desire to see something of *real French life*. You're acquainted with my great sympathy with the French; with my natural tendency to enter into their so supremely fine exploitation of the whole personal consciousness. I sympathise with the artistic temperament; I remember you used sometimes to hint to me that you thought my own temperament *too* artistic. I don't consider that in Boston there's any real sympathy with the artistic temperament; we tend to make everything a matter of right and wrong. And in Boston one can't *live—on ne peut pas vivre,* as they say here. I don't mean one can't reside—for a great many people manage that; but one can't live æsthetically—I almost venture to say one can't live sensuously. This is why I've always been so much drawn to the French, who are so æsthetic, so sensuous, so *entirely* living. I'm so sorry dear Théophile Gautier has passed away; I should have liked so much to go and see him and tell him all I owe him. He was living when I was here before; but, you know, at that time I was travelling with the Johnsons, who are not æsthetic and who used to make me feel rather ashamed of my love and my need of beauty. If I had gone to see the great apostle of that religion I should have had to go clandestinely—*en cachette,* as they say here; and that's not my nature; I like to do everything frankly, freely, *naïvement, au grand jour*. That's the great thing—to be free, to be frank, to be *naïf*. Doesn't Matthew Arnold say that somewhere—or is it Swinburne or Pater?

When I was with the Johnsons everything was superficial, and, as regards life, everything was brought down to the question of right and wrong. They were eternally didactic; art should never be didactic; and what's life but the finest of arts? Pater has said that so well somewhere. With the Johnsons I'm afraid I lost many opportunities; the whole outlook or at least the whole medium—of feeling, of appreciation—was grey and cottony, I might almost say woolly. Now, however, as I tell you, I've determined to take right hold for myself; to look right into European life and judge it without Johnsonian prejudices. I've taken up my residence in a French family, in a real Parisian house. You see I've the courage of my opinions; I don't shrink from carrying out my theory that the great thing is to *live*.

You know I've always been intensely interested in Balzac, who never shrank from the reality and whose almost *lurid* pictures of Parisian life have often haunted me in my wanderings through the old wicked-looking streets on the other side of the river. I'm only sorry that my new friends—my French family—don't live in the old city, *au cœur du vieux Paris,* as they say here. They live only on the Boulevard Haussmann, which is a compromise, but in spite of this they have a great deal of the Balzac tone. Madame de Maisonrouge belongs to one of the oldest and proudest families in France, but has had reverses which have compelled her to open an establishment in which a limited number of travellers, who are weary of the beaten track, who shun the great caravanseries, who cherish the tradition of the old French sociability—she explains it herself, she expresses it so well—in short to open a "select" boarding-house. I don't see why I shouldn't after all use that expression, for it's the correlative of the term pension bourgeoise, employed by Balzac in "Le Père Goriot." Do you remember the pension bourgeoise of Madame Vauquer née de Conflans? But this establishment isn't at all like that, and indeed isn't bourgeois at all; I don't quite know how the machinery of selection operates, but we unmistakably feel we're select. The Pension Vauquer was dark, brown, sordid, *graisseuse*; but this is in quite a different tone, with high, clear lightly-draped windows and several rather good Louis Seize pieces—family heirlooms, Madame de Maisonrouge explains. She recalls to me Madame Hulot—do you remember "la belle Madame Hulot"?—in "Les Parents Pauvres."

She has a great charm—though a little artificial, a little jaded and faded, with a suggestion of hidden things in her life. But I've always been sensitive to the seduction of an ambiguous fatigue.

I'm rather disappointed, I confess, in the society I find here; it isn't so richly native, of so indigenous a note, as I could have desired. Indeed, to tell the truth, it's not native at all; though on the other hand it *is* furiously cosmopolite, and that speaks to me too at my hours. We're French *and* we're English; we're American *and* we're German; I believe too there are some Spaniards and some Hungarians expected. I'm much interested in the study of racial types; in comparing, contrasting, seizing the strong points, the weak points, in identifying, however muffled by social hypocrisy, the sharp keynote of each. It's interesting to shift one's point of view, to despoil one's self of one's idiotic prejudices, to enter into strange exotic ways of looking at life.

The American types don't, I much regret to say, make a strong, or rich affirmation, and, excepting my own (and what *is* my own, dear Harvard, I ask you?) are wholly negative and feminine. We're *thin*—that I should have to say it! we're pale, we're poor, we're flat. There's something meagre about us; our line is wanting in roundness, our composition in richness. We lack temperament; we don't know how to live; *nous ne savons pas vivre,* as they say here. The American temperament is represented—putting myself aside, and I often think that my temperament isn't at all American—by a young girl and her mother and by another young girl without her mother, without either parent or any attendant or appendage whatever. These inevitable creatures are more or less in the picture; they have a certain interest, they have a certain stamp, but they're disappointing too: they don't go far; they don't keep all they promise; they don't satisfy the imagination. They are cold, slim, sexless; the physique's not generous, not abundant; it's only the drapery, the skirts and furbelows—that is I mean in the young lady wh has her mother—that are abundant. They're rather different—we *have* our little differences, thank God: one of them all elegance, all "paid bills" and extra-fresh *gants de Suède,* from New York; the other a plain pure clear-eyed narrow-chested straight-stepping maiden from the heart of New England. And yet they're very much alike too—more alike than they would care to think themselves; for they face each other with scarcely disguised opposition and disavowal. They're both specimens of the practical positive passionless young thing as we let her loose on the world—and yet with a certain fineness and knowing, as you please, either too much or too little. With all of which, as I say, they have their spontaneity and even their oddity; though no more mystery, either of them, than the printed circular thrust into your hand on the street-corner.

The little New Yorker's sometimes very amusing; she asks me if every one in Boston talks like me—if every one's as "intellectual" as your poor correspondent. She's for ever throwing Boston up at me; I can't get rid of poor dear little Boston. The other one rubs it into me too; but in a different way; she seems to feel about it as a good Mohammedan feels toward Mecca, and regards it as a focus of light for the whole human race. Yes, poor little Boston, what nonsense is talked in thy name! But this New England maiden is in her way a rare white flower: she's travelling all over Europe alone—"to see it," she says, "for herself." For herself! What can that strangely serene self of hers do with such sights, such depths! She looks at everything, goes everywhere, passes her way with her clear quiet eyes wide open; skirting the edge of obscene abysses without suspecting them; pushing through brambles without tearing her robe; exciting, without knowing it, the most injurious suspicions; and always holding her course—without a stain, without a sense, without a fear, without a charm!

Then by way of contrast there's a lovely English girl with eyes as shy as violets and a voice as sweet!—the difference between the printed, the distributed, the gratuitous hand-bill and the shy scrap of a *billet-doux* dropped where you may pick it up. She has a sweet Gainsborough head and a great Gainsborough hat with a mighty plume in front of it that makes a shadow over her quiet English eyes. Then she has a sage-green robe, "mystic wonderful," all embroidered with subtle devices and flowers, with birds and beasts of tender tint; very straight and tight in front and adorned behind, along the spine, with large strange iridescent buttons. The revival of taste, of the sense of beauty, in England, interests me deeply; what is there in a simple row of spinal buttons to make one dream—to *donner à rêver,* as they say here? I believe a grand æsthetic renascence to be at hand and that a great light will be kindled in England for all the world to see. There are spirits there I should like to commune with; I think they'd understand me.

This gracious English maiden, with her clinging robes, her amulets and girdles, with something quaint and angular in her step, her carriage, something mediæval and Gothic in the details of her person and dress, this lovely Evelyn Vane (isn't it a beautiful name?) exhales association and implication. She's so much a woman—*elle est bien femme,* as they say here; simpler softer rounder richer than the easy products I spoke of just now. Not much talk—a great sweet silence. Then the violet eye—the very eye itself seems to blush; the great shadowy hat making the brow so quiet; the strange clinging clutched pictured raiment! As I say, it's a very gracious tender type. She has her brother with her, who's a beautiful fair-haired grey-eyed young Englishman. He's purely objective, but he too is very plastic.

V

FROM MIRANDA HOPE TO HER MOTHER

September 26.

You mustn't be frightened at not hearing from me oftener; it isn't because I'm in any trouble, but because I'm getting on so well. If I were in any trouble I don't think I'd write to you; I'd just keep quiet and see it through myself. But that's not the case at present; and if I don't write to you it's because I'm so deeply interested over here that I don't seem to find time. It was a real providence that brought me to this house, where, in spite of all obstacles, I *am* able to press onward. I wonder how I find time for all I do, but when I realise I've only got about a year left, all told, I feel as if I wouldn't sacrifice a single hour.

The obstacles I refer to are the disadvantages I have in acquiring the language, there being so many persons round me speaking English, and that, as you may say, in the very bosom of a regular French family. It seems as if you heard English everywhere; but I certainly didn't expect to find it in a place like this. I'm not discouraged, however, and I exercise all I can, even with the other English boarders. Then I've a lesson every day from Mademoiselle—the elder daughter of the lady of the house and the intellectual one; she has a wonderful fearless mind, almost like my friend at the hotel—and French give-and-take every evening in the salon, from eight to eleven, with Madame herself and some friends of hers who often come in. Her cousin, Mr. Verdier, a young French gentleman, is fortunately staying with her, and I make a point of talking with him as much as possible. I have *extra-private lessons* from him, and I often ramble round with him. Some night soon he's to accompany me to the comic opera. We've also a most interesting plan of visiting the galleries successively together and taking the schools in their order—for they mean by "the schools" here something quite different from what we do. Like most of the

French Mr. Verdier converses with great fluency, and I feel I may really gain from him. He's remarkably handsome, in the French style, and extremely polite—making a great many speeches which I'm afraid it wouldn't always do to pin one's faith on. When I get down in Maine again I guess I'll tell you some of the things he has said to me. I think you'll consider them extremely curious—very beautiful *in their French way.*

The conversation in the parlour (from eight to eleven) ranges over many subjects—I sometimes feel as if it really avoided *none;* and I often wish you or some of the Bangor folks could be there to enjoy it. Even though you couldn't understand it I think you'd like to hear the way they go on; they seem to express so much. I sometimes think that at Bangor they don't express enough—except that it seems as if over there they've less *to* express. It seems as if at Bangor there were things that folks never *tried* to say; but I seem to have learned here from studying French that you've no idea what you *can* say before you try. At Bangor they kind of give it up beforehand; they don't make any effort. (I don't say this in the least for William Platt *in particular.*)

I'm sure I don't know what they'll think of me when I get back anyway. It seems as if over here I had learned to come out with everything. I suppose they'll think I'm not sincere; but isn't it more sincere to come right out with things than just to keep feeling of them in your mind—without giving any one the benefit? I've become very good friends with every one in the house—that is (you see I *am* sincere) with *almost* every one. It's the most interesting circle I ever was in. There's a girl here, an American, that I don't like so much as the rest; but that's only because she won't let me. I should like to like her, ever so much, because she's most lovely and most attractive; but she doesn't seem to want to know me or to take to me. She comes from New York and she's remarkably pretty, with beautiful eyes and the most delicate features; she's also splendidly stylish —in this respect would bear comparison with any one I've seen over here. But it seems as if she didn't want to recognise me or associate with me, as if she wanted to make a difference between us. It is like people they call "haughty" in books. I've never seen any one like that before—any one that wanted to make a difference; and at first I was right down interested, she seemed to me so like a proud young lady in a novel. I kept saying to myself all day "haughty, haughty," and I wished she'd keep on so. But she did keep on—she kept on too long; and then I began to feel it in a different way, to feel as if it kind of wronged me. I couldn't think what I've done, and I can't think yet. It's as if she had got some idea about me or had heard some one say something. If some girls should behave like that I wouldn't make any account of it; but this one's so refined, and looks as if she might be so fascinating if I once got to know her, that I think about it a good deal. I'm bound to find out what her reason is—for of course she has got some reason; I'm right down curious to know.

I went up to her to ask her the day before yesterday; I thought that the best way. I told her I wanted to know her better and would like to come and see her in her room—they tell me she has got a lovely one—and that if she had heard anything against me perhaps she'd tell me when I came. But she was more distant than ever and just turned it off; said she had never heard me mentioned and that her room was too small to receive visitors. I suppose she spoke the truth, but I'm sure she has some peculiar ground, all the same. She has got some idea; which I'll die if I don't find out soon—if I have to ask every one in the house. I never *could* be happy under an appearance of wrong. I wonder if she doesn't think me refined—or if she had ever heard anything against Bangor? I can't think it's that. Don't you remember when Clara Barnard went to visit in New York, three years ago, how much attention she received? And you know Clara *is* Bangor, to the soles of her shoes. Ask William Platt—so long as he isn't native—if he doesn't consider Clara Barnard refined.

Apropos, as they say here, of refinement, there's another American in the house—a gentleman from Boston—who's just crammed with it. His name's Mr. Louis Leverett (such a beautiful name I think) and he's about thirty years old. He's rather small and he looks pretty sick; he suffers from some affection of the liver. But his conversation leads you right on—they *do* go so far over here: even our people seem to strain ahead in Europe, and perhaps when I get back it may strike you I've learned to keep up with them. I delight to listen to him anyhow—he has such beautiful ideas. I feel as if these moments were hardly right, not being in French; but fortunately he uses a great many French expressions. It's in a different style from the dazzle of Mr. Verdier—not so personal, but much more earnest: he says the only earnestness left in the world now is French. He's intensely fond of pictures and has given me a great many ideas about them that I'd never have gained without him; I shouldn't have known how to go to work to strike them. He thinks everything of pictures; he thinks we don't make near enough of them. They seem to make a good deal of them here, but I couldn't help telling him the other day that in Bangor I really don't think we do.

If I had any money to spend I'd buy some and take them back to hang right up. Mr. Leverett says it would do them good—not the pictures, but the Bangor folks (though sometimes he seems to want to hang *them* up too). He thinks everything of the French, anyhow, and says we don't make nearly enough of them. I couldn't help telling him the other day that they certainly make enough of *themselves*. But it's very interesting to hear him go on about the French, and it's so much gain to me, since it's about the same as what I came for. I talk to him as much as I dare about Boston, but I do feel as if this were right down wrong—a stolen pleasure.

I can get all the Boston culture I want when I go back, if I carry out my plan, my heart's secret, of going there to reside. I ought to direct all my efforts to European culture now, so as to keep Boston to finish off. But it seems as if I couldn't help taking a peep now and then in advance—with a real Bostonian. I don't know when I may meet one again; but if there are many others like Mr. Leverett there I shall be certain not to lack when I carry out my dream. He's just as full of culture as he can live. But it seems strange how many different sorts there are.

There are two of the English who I suppose are very cultivated too; but it doesn't seem as if I could enter into theirs so easily, though I try all I can. I do love their way of speaking, and sometimes I feel almost as if it would be right to give up going for French and just try to get the hang of English as these people have got it. It doesn't come out in the things they say so much, though these are often rather curious, but in the sweet way they say them and in their kind of making so much, such an easy lovely effect, of saying almost anything. It seems as if they must *try* a good deal to sound like that; but these English who are here don't seem to try at all, either to speak or do anything else. They're a young lady and her brother, who belong, I believe, to some noble family. I've had a good deal of intercourse with them, because I've felt more free to talk to them than to the Americans—on account of the language. They often don't understand mine, and then it's as if I had to learn theirs to explain.

I never supposed when I left Bangor that I was coming to Europe to improve in *our* old language—and yet I feel I can. If I do get where I *may* in it I guess you'll scarcely understand me when I get back, and I don't think you'll particularly see the point. I'd be a good deal criticised if I spoke like that at Bangor. However, I verily believe Bangor's the most critical place on earth; I've seen nothing like it over here. Well, tell them I'll give them about all they can do. But I was speaking about this English young lady and her brother; I wish I could put them before you. She's lovely just to see; she seems so modest and retiring. In spite of this, however, she dresses in a way that attracts great attention, as I couldn't help noticing when one day I went out to walk with her. She was ever so much more looked at than what I'd have thought she'd like; but she didn't seem to care, till at last I couldn't help calling attention to it. Mr. Leverett thinks everything of it; he calls it the "costume of the future." I'd call it rather the costume of the past—you know the English have such an attachment to the past. I said this the other day to Madame de Maisonrouge—that Miss Vane dressed in the costume of the past. *De l'an passé, vous voulez dire?* she asked in her gay French way. (You can get William Platt to translate this; he used to tell me he knows so much French.)

You know I told you, in writing some time ago, that I had tried to get some insight into the position of woman in England, and, being here with Miss Vane, it has seemed to me to be a good opportunity to get a little more. I've asked her a great deal about it, but she doesn't seem able to tell me much. The first time I asked her she said the position of a lady depended on the rank of her father, her eldest brother, her husband—all on somebody else; and they, as to their position, on something quite else (than themselves) as well. She told me her own position was very good because her father was some relation—I forget what—to a lord. She thinks everything of this; and that proves to me their standing can't be *really* good, because if it were it wouldn't be involved in that of your relations, even your nearest. I don't know much about lords, and it does try my patience—though she's just as sweet as she can live—to hear her talk as if it were a matter of course I should.

I feel as if it were right to ask her as often as I can if she doesn't consider every one equal; but she always says she doesn't, and she confesses that she doesn't think *she's* equal to Lady Something-or-Other, who's the wife of that relation of her father. I try and persuade her all I can that she *is;* but it seems as if she didn't want to be persuaded, and when I ask her if that superior being is of the same opinion—that Miss Vane isn't her equal—she looks so soft and pretty with her eyes and says "How can she not be?" When I tell her that this is right down bad for the other person it seems as if she wouldn't believe me, and the only answer she'll make is that the other person's "awfully nice." I don't believe she's nice at all; if she were nice she wouldn't have such ideas as that. I tell Miss Vane that at Bangor we think such ideas vulgar, but then she looks as though she had never heard of Bangor. I often want to shake her, though she *is* so sweet. If she isn't angry with the people who make her feel that way, at least I'm angry *for* her. I'm angry with her brother too, for she's evidently very much afraid of him, and this gives me some further insight into the subject. She thinks everything of her brother; she thinks it natural she should be afraid of him not only physically—for that *is* natural, as he's enormously tall and strong and has very big fists—but morally and intellectually. She seems unable, however, to take in any argument, and she makes me realise what I've often heard—that if you're timid nothing will reason you out of it.

Mr. Vane also, the brother, seems to have the same prejudices, and when I tell him, as I often think it right to do, that his sister's not his subordinate, even if she does think so, but his equal, and perhaps in some respects his superior, and that if my brother in Bangor were to treat me as he treats this charming but abject creature, who has not spirit enough to see the question in its true light, there would be an indignation-meeting of the citizens to protest against such an outrage to the sanctity of womanhood—when I tell him all this, at breakfast or dinner, he only bursts out laughing so loud that all the plates clatter on the table.

But at such a time as this there's always one person who seems interested in what I say—a German gentleman, a professor, who sits next to me at dinner and whom I must tell you more about another time. He's very learned, but wants to push further and further all the time; he appreciates a great many of my remarks, and after dinner, in the salon, he often comes to me to ask me questions about them. I have to think a little sometimes to know what I did say or what I do think. He takes you right up where you left off, and he's most as fond of discussing things as William Platt ever was. He's splendidly educated, in the German style, and he told me the other day that he was an "intellectual broom." Well, if he is he sweeps clean; I told him that. After he has been talking to me I feel as if I hadn't got a speck of dust left in my mind anywhere. It's a most delightful feeling. He says he's a remorseless observer, and though I don't know about remorse—for a bright mind isn't a crime, is it?—I'm sure there's plenty over here to observe. But I've told you enough for today. I don't know how much longer I shall stay here; I'm getting on now so fast that it has come to seem sometimes as if I shouldn't need all the time I've laid out. I suppose your cold weather has promptly begun, as usual; it sometimes makes me envy you. The fall weather here is very dull and damp, and I often suffer from the want of bracing.

VI

FROM MISS EVELYN VANE IN PARIS TO THE LADY AUGUSTA FLEMING AT BRIGHTON

Paris September 30.

DEAR LADY AUGUSTA,

I'm afraid I shall not be able to come to you on January 7th, as you kindly proposed at Homburg. I'm so very very sorry; it's an immense disappointment. But I've just heard that it has been settled that mamma and the children come abroad for a part of the winter, and mamma wishes me to go with them to Hyères, where Georgina has been ordered for her lungs. She has not been at all well these three months, and now that the damp weather has begun she's very poorly indeed; so that last week papa decided to have a consultation, and he and mamma went with her up to town and saw some three or four doctors. They all of them ordered the south of France, but they didn't agree about the place; so that mamma herself decided for Hyères, because it's the most economical. I believe it's very dull, but I hope it will do Georgina good. I'm afraid, however, that nothing will do her good until she consents to take more care of herself; I'm afraid she's very wild and wilful, and mamma tells me that all this month it has taken papa's positive orders to make her stop indoors. She's very cross (mamma writes me) about coming abroad, and doesn't seem at all to mind the expense papa has been put to—talks very ill-naturedly about her loss of the hunting and even perhaps of the early spring meetings. She expected to begin to hunt in December and wants to know whether anybody keeps hounds at Hyères. Fancy that rot when she's too ill to sit a horse or to go anywhere. But I dare say that when she gets there she'll be glad enough to keep quiet, as they say the heat's intense. It may cure Georgina, but I'm sure it will make the rest of us very ill.

Mamma, however, is only going to bring Mary and Gus and Fred and Adelaide abroad with her: the others will remain at Kingscote till February (about the 3d) when they'll go to Eastbourne for a month with Miss Turnover, the new governess, who has proved such a very nice person. She's going to take Miss Travers, who has been with us so long, but is only qualified for the younger children, to Hyères, and I believe some of the Kingscote servants. She has perfect confidence in Miss T.; it's only a pity the poor woman has such an odd name. Mamma thought of asking her if she would mind taking another when she came; but papa thought she might object. Lady Battledown makes all her governesses take the same name; she gives £5 more a year for the purpose. I forget what it is she calls them; I think it's Johnson (which to me always suggests a lady's maid). Governesses shouldn't have too pretty a name—they shouldn't have a nicer name than the family.

I suppose you heard from the Desmonds that I didn't go back to England with them. When it began to be talked about that Georgina should be taken abroad mamma wrote to me that

I had better stop in Paris for a month with Harold, so that she could pick me up on their way to Hyères. It saves the expense of my journey to Kingscote and back, and gives me the opportunity to "finish" a little in French.

You know Harold came here six weeks ago to get up his French for those dreadful exams that he has to pass so soon. He came to live with some French people that take in young men (and others) for this purpose; it's a kind of coaching-place, only kept by women. Mamma had heard it was very nice, so she wrote to me that I was to come and stop here with Harold. The Desmonds brought me and made the arrangement or the bargain or whatever you call it. Poor Harold was naturally not at all pleased, but he has been very kind and has treated me like an angel. He's getting on beautifully with his French, for though I don't think the place is so good as papa supposed, yet Harold is so immensely clever that he can scarcely help learning. I'm afraid I learn much less, but fortunately I haven't to go up for anything—unless perhaps to mamma if she takes it into her head to examine me. But she'll have so much to think of with Georgina that I hope this won't occur to her. If it does I shall be, as Harold says, in a dreadful funk.

This isn't such a nice place for a girl as for a gentleman, and the Desmonds thought it *exceedingly odd* that mamma should wish me to come here. As Mrs. Desmond said, it's because she's so very unconventional. But you know Paris is so very amusing, and if only Harold remains good-natured about it I shall be content to wait for the caravan—which is what he calls mamma and the children. The person who keeps the establishment, or whatever they call it, is rather odd and *exceedingly foreign;* but she's wonderfully civil and is perpetually sending to my door to see if I want anything. She's tremendously pretentious and of course isn't a lady. The servants are not at all like English ones and come bursting in, the footman—they've only one —and the maids alike, at all sorts of hours, in the *most sudden way*. Then when one rings it takes ages. Some of the food too is rather nasty. All of which is very uncomfortable, and I dare say will be worse at Hyères. There, however, fortunately, we shall have our own people.

There are some very odd Americans here who keep throwing Harold into fits of laughter. One's a dreadful little man whom indeed he also wants to kick and who's always sitting over the fire and talking about the colour of the sky. I don't believe he ever saw the sky except through the window-pane. The other day he took off my frock—that green one you thought so nice at Homburg—and told me that it reminded him of the texture of the Devonshire turf. And then he talked for half an hour about the Devonshire turf, which I thought such a very extraordinary subject. Harold firmly believes him mad. It's rather horrid to be living in this way with people one doesn't know—I mean doesn't know as one knows them in England.

The other Americans, besides the madman, are two girls about my own age, one of whom is rather nice. She has a mother; but the mother always sits in her bedroom, which seems so very odd. I should like mamma to ask them to Kingscote, but I'm afraid mamma wouldn't like the mother, who's awfully vulgar. The other girl is awfully vulgar herself—she's travelling about quite alone. I think she's a middle-class schoolmistress—sacked perhaps for some irregularity; but the other girl (I mean the nicer one, with the objectionable mother) tells me she's more respectable than she seems. She has, however, the most extraordinary opinions—wishes to do away with the aristocracy, thinks it wrong that Arthur should have Kingscote when papa dies, etc. I don't see what it signifies to her that poor Arthur should come into the property, which will be so delightful—except for papa dying. But Harold says she's mad too. He chaffs her tremendously about her radicalism, and he's so immensely clever that she can't answer him, though she has a supply of the most extraordinary big words.

There's also a Frenchman, a nephew or cousin or something of the person of the house, who's a horrid low cad; and a German professor or doctor who eats with his knife and is a great bore. I'm so very sorry about giving up my visit. I'm afraid you'll never ask me again.

VII

FROM LÉON VERDIER IN PARIS TO PROSPER GOBAIN AT LILLE

September 28.

MON GROS VIEUX.

It's a long time since I've given you of my news, and I don't know what puts it into my head tonight to recall myself to your affectionate memory. I suppose it is that when we're happy the mind reverts instinctively to those with whom formerly we shared our vicissitudes, and *je t'en ai trop dit dans le bon temps, cher vieux,* and you always listened to me too imperturbably, with your pipe in your mouth and your waistcoat unbuttoned, for me not to feel that I can count on your sympathy today. *Nous en sommes-nous flanquées, des confidences?* —in those happy days when my first thought in seeing an adventure *poindre à l'horizon* was of the pleasure I should have in relating it to the great Prosper. As I tell thee, I'm happy; decidedly *j'ai de la chance,* and from that avowal I trust thee to construct the rest. Shall I help thee a little? Take three adorable girls—three, my good Prosper, the mystic number, neither more, nor less. Take them and place in the midst of them thy insatiable little Léon. Is the situation sufficiently indicated, or does the scene take more doing?

You expected perhaps I was going to tell thee I had made my fortune, or that the Uncle Blondeau had at last decided to recommit himself to the breast of nature after having constituted me his universal legatee. But I needn't remind you for how much women have always been in any happiness of him who thus overflows to you—for how much in any happiness and for how much more in any misery. But don't let me talk of misery now; time enough when it comes, when *ces demoiselles* shall have joined the serried ranks of their amiable predecessors. Ah I comprehend your impatience. I must tell you of whom *ces demoiselles* consist.

You've heard me speak of my *cousine* de Maisonrouge, that *grande belle femme* who, after having married, *en secondes noces*—there had been, to tell the truth, some irregularity about her first union—a venerable relic of the old noblesse of Poitou, was left, by the death of her husband, complicated by the crash of expensive tastes against an income of 17,000 francs, on the pavement of Paris with two little demons of daughters to bring up in the path of virtue. She managed to bring them up; my little cousins are ferociously *sages*. If you ask me how she managed it I can't tell you; it's no business of mine, and *a fortiori* none of yours. She's now fifty years old—she confesses to thirty-eight—and her daughters, whom she has never been able to place, are respectively twenty-seven and twenty-three (they confess to twenty and to seventeen). Three years ago she had the thrice-blest idea of opening a well-upholstered and otherwise attractive *asile* for the blundering barbarians who come to Paris in the hope of picking up a few stray pearls from the *écrin* of Voltaire—or of Zola. The idea has brought her luck; the house does an excellent business. Until within a few months ago it was carried on by my cousins alone; but lately the need of a few extensions and improvements has caused itself to be felt. My cousin has undertaken them, regardless of expense; in other words she has asked me to come and stay with her—board and lodging gratis—and correct the conversational exercises of her *pensionnaire*-pupils. I'm the extension, my good Prosper; I'm the improvement. She has enlarged the *personnel*—I'm the enlargement. I form the exemplary sounds that the prettiest English lips are invited to imitate. The English lips are not all pretty, heaven knows, but enough of them are so to make it a good bargain for me.

Just now, as I told you, I'm in daily relation with three separate pairs. The owner of one of them has private lessons; she pays extra. My cousin doesn't give me a sou of the money, but I consider nevertheless that I'm not a loser by the arrangement. Also I'm well, very very well, with the proprietors of the two other pairs. One of these is a little Anglaise of twenty—a *figure de keepsake;* the most adorable miss you ever, or at least I ever, beheld. She's hung all over with beads and bracelets and amulets, she's embroidered all over like a sampler or a vestment; but her principal decoration consists of the softest and almost the hugest grey eyes in the world, which rest upon you with a profundity of confidence—a confidence I really feel some compunction in betraying. She has a tint as white as this sheet of paper, except just in the middle of each cheek, where it passes into the purest and most transparent, most liquid, carmine. Occasionally this rosy fluid overflows into the rest of her face —by which I mean that she blushes—as softly as the mark of your breath on the window-pane.

Like every Anglaise she's rather pinched and prim in public; but it's easy to see that when no one's looking *elle ne demande qu'à se laisser aller!* Whenever she wants it I'm always there, and I've given her to understand she can count upon me. I've reason to believe she appreciates the assurance, though I'm bound in honesty to confess that with her the situation's a little less advanced than with the others. *Que voulez-vous?* The English are heavy and the Anglaises move slowly, that's all. The movement, however, is perceptible, and once this fact's established I can let the soup simmer, I can give her time to arrive, for I'm beautifully occupied with her competitors. *They* don't keep me waiting, please believe.

These young ladies are Americans, and it belongs to that national character to move fast. "All right—go ahead!" (I'm learning a great deal of English, or rather a great deal of American.) They go ahead at a rate that sometimes makes it difficult for me to keep up. One of them's prettier than the other; but this latter—the one that takes the extra-private lessons—is really *une fille étonnante. Ah par exemple, elle brûle ses vaisseaux, celle-là!* She threw herself into my arms the very first day, and I almost owed her a grudge for having deprived me of that pleasure of gradation, of carrying the defences one by one, which is almost as great as that of entering the place. For would you believe that at the end of exactly twelve minutes she gave me a rendezvous? In the Galerie d'Apollon at the Louvre I admit; but that was respectable for a beginning, and since then we've had them by the dozen; I've ceased to keep the account. *Non, c'est une fille qui me dépasse.*

The other, the slighter but "smarter" little person—she has a mother somewhere out of sight, shut up in a closet or a trunk—is a good deal prettier, and perhaps on that account *elle y met plus de façons.* She doesn't knock about Paris with me by the hour; she contents herself with long interviews in the *petit salon,* with the blinds half-drawn, beginning at about three o'clock, when every one is *à la promenade.* She's admirable, cette petite, a little too immaterial, with the bones rather over-accentuated, yet of a detail, on the whole, most satisfactory. And you can say anything to her. She takes the trouble to appear not to understand, but her conduct, half an hour afterwards, reassures you completely—oh completely!

However, it's the big bouncer of the extra-private lessons who's the most remarkable. These private lessons, my good Prosper, are the most brilliant invention of the age, and a real stroke of genius on the part of Miss Miranda! They also take place in the *petit salon,* but with the doors tightly closed and with explicit directions to every one in the house that we are not to be disturbed. And we're not, *mon gros,* we're not! Not a sound, not a shadow, interrupts our felicity. My cousins are on the right track—such a house must make its fortune. Miss Miranda's too tall and too flat, with a certain want of coloration; she hasn't the transparent *rougeurs* of the little Anglaise. But she has wonderful far-gazing eyes, superb teeth, a nose modelled by a sculptor, and a way of holding up her head and looking every one in the face, which combines apparent innocence with complete assurance in a way I've never seen equalled. She's making the *tour du monde,* entirely alone, without even a soubrette to carry the ensign, for the purpose of seeing for herself, seeing *à quoi s'en tenir sur les hommes et les choses*—on *les hommes* particularly. *Dis donc, mon vieux,* it must be a *drôle de pays* over there, where such a view of the right thing for the aspiring young bourgeoises is taken. If we should turn the tables some day, thou and I, and go over and see it for ourselves? Why isn't it as well we should go and find them *chez elles,* as that they should come out here after us? *Dis donc, mon gros Prosper . . . !*

VIII

FROM DR. RUDOLPH STAUB IN PARIS TO DR. JULIUS HIRSCH AT GÖTTINGEN

MY DEAR BROTHER IN SCIENCE.

I resume my hasty notes, of which I sent you the first instalment some weeks ago. I mentioned that I intended to leave my hotel, not finding in it real matter. It was kept by a Pomeranian and the waiters without exception were from the Fatherland. I might as well have sat down with my note-book Unter den Linden, and I felt that, having come here for documentation, or to put my finger straight upon the social pulse, I should project myself as much as possible into the circumstances which are in part the consequence and in part the cause of its activities and intermittences. I saw there could be no well-grounded knowledge without this preliminary operation of my getting a near view, as slightly as possible modified by elements proceeding from a different combination of forces, of the spontaneous home-life of the nation.

I accordingly engaged a room in the house of a lady of pure French extraction and education, who supplements the shortcomings of an income insufficient to the ever-growing demands of the Parisian system of sense-gratification by providing food and lodging for a limited number of distinguished strangers. I should have preferred to have my room here only, and to take my meals in a brewery, of very good appearance, which I speedily discovered in the same street; but this arrangement, though very clearly set out by myself, was not acceptable to the mistress of the establishment—a woman with a mathematical head—and I have consoled myself for the extra expense by fixing my thoughts upon the great chance that conformity to the customs of the house gives me of studying the table-manners of my companions, and of observing the French nature at a peculiarly physiological moment, the moment when the satisfaction of the *taste,* which is the governing quality in its composition, produces a kind exhalation, an intellectual transpiration, which, though light and perhaps invisible to a superficial spectator, is nevertheless appreciable by a properly adjusted instrument. I've adjusted my instrument very satisfactorily—I mean the one I carry in my good square German head—and I'm not afraid of losing a single drop of this valuable fluid as it condenses itself upon the plate of my observation. A prepared surface is what I need, and I've prepared my surface.

Unfortunately here also I find the individual native in the minority. There are only four French persons in the house—the individuals concerned in its management, three of whom are women, and one a man. Such a preponderance of the *Weibliche* is, however, in itself characteristic, as I needn't remind you what an abnormally-developed part this sex has played in French history. The remaining figure is ostensibly that of a biped, and apparently that of a man, but I hesitate to allow him the whole benefit of the higher classification. He strikes me as less human than simian, and whenever I hear him talk I seem to myself to have paused in the street to listen to the shrill clatter of a hand-organ, to which the gambols of a hairy *homunculus* form an accompaniment.

I mentioned to you before that my expectation of rough usage in consequence of my unattenuated even if not frivolously aggressive, Teutonism was to prove completely unfounded. No one seems either unduly conscious or affectedly unperceiving of my so rich Berlin background; I'm treated on the contrary with the positive civility which is the portion of every traveller who pays the bill without scanning the items too narrowly. This, I confess, has been something of a surprise to me, and I've not yet made up my mind as to the fundamental cause of the anomaly. My determination to take up my abode in a French interior was largely dictated by the supposition that I should be substantially disagreeable to its inmates. I wished to catch in the fact the different forms taken by the irritation I should naturally produce; for it is under the influence of irritation that the French character most completely expresses itself. My presence, however, operates, as I say, less than could have been hoped as a stimulus, and in this respect I'm materially disappointed. They treat me as they treat every one else; whereas, in order to be treated differently, I was resigned in advance to being treated worse. A further proof, if any were needed, of that vast and, as it were, fluid *waste* (I have so often dwelt on to you) which attends the process of philosophic secretion. I've not, I repeat, fully explained to myself this logical contradiction; but this is the explanation to which I tend. The French are so exclusively occupied with the idea of themselves that in spite of the very definite image the German personality presented to them by the war of 1870 they have at present no distinct apprehension of its existence. They are not very sure that there *are,* concretely, any Germans; they have already forgotten the convincing proofs presented to them nine years ago. A German was something disagreeable and disconcerting, an irreducible mass, which they determined to keep out of their conception of things. I therefore hold we're wrong to govern ourselves upon the hypothesis of the *revanche;* the French nature is too shallow for that large and powerful plant to bloom in it.

The English-speaking specimens, too, I've not been willing to neglect the opportunity to examine; and among these I've paid special attention to the American varieties, of which I find here several singular examples. The two most remarkable are a young man who presents all the characteristics of a period of national decadence; reminding me strongly of some diminutive Hellenised Roman of the third century. He's an illustration of the period of culture in which the faculty of appreciation has obtained such a preponderance over that of production that the latter sinks into a kind of rank sterility, and the mental condition becomes analogous to that of a malarious bog. I hear from him of the existence of an immense number of Americans exactly resembling him, and that the city of Boston indeed is almost exclusively composed of them. (He communicated this fact very proudly, as if it were greatly to the credit of his native country; little perceiving the truly sinister impression it made on me.)

What strikes one in it is that it is a phenomenon to the best of my knowledge—and you know what my knowledge is—unprecedented and unique in the history of mankind; the arrival of a nation at an ultimate stage of evolution without having passed through the mediate one; the passage of the fruit, in other words, from crudity to rottenness, without the interposition of a period of useful (and ornamental) ripeness. With the Americans indeed the crudity and the rottenness are identical and simultaneous; it is impossible to say, as in the conversation of this deplorable young man, which is the one and which the other: they're inextricably confused. Homunculus for homunculus I prefer that of the Frenchman; he's at least more amusing.

It's interesting in this manner to perceive, so largely developed, the germs of extinction in the so-called powerful Anglo-Saxon family. I find them in almost as recognisable a form in a young woman from the State of Maine, in the province of

New England, with whom I have had a good deal of conversation. She differs somewhat from the young man I just mentioned in that the state of affirmation, faculty of production and capacity for action are things, in her, less inanimate; she has more of the freshness and vigour that we suppose to belong to a young civilisation. But unfortunately she produces nothing but evil, and her tastes and habits are similarly those of a Roman lady of the lower Empire. She makes no secret of them and has in fact worked out a complete scheme of experimental adventure, that is of personal license, which she is now engaged in carrying out. As the opportunities she finds in her own country fail to satisfy her she has come to Europe "to try," as she says, "for herself." It's the doctrine of universal "unprejudiced" experience professed with a cynicism that is really most extraordinary, and which, presenting itself in a young woman of considerable education, appears to me to be the judgement of a society.

Another observation which pushes me to the same deduction—that of the premature vitiation of the American population—is the attitude of the Americans whom I have before me with regard to each other. I have before me a second flower of the same huge so-called democratic garden, who is less abnormally developed than the one I have just described, but who yet bears the stamp of this peculiar combination of the barbarous and, to apply to them one of their own favourite terms, the *ausgespielt,* the "played-out." These three little persons look with the greatest mistrust and aversion upon each other; and each has repeatedly taken me apart and assured me secretly, that he or she only is the real, the genuine, the typical American. A type that has lost itself before it has been fixed—what can you look for from this?

Add to this that there are two young Englanders in the house who hate all the Americans in a lump, making between them none of the distinctions and favourable comparisons which they insist upon, and for which, as involving the recognition of shades and a certain play of the critical sense, the still quite primitive insular understanding is wholly inept, and you will, I think, hold me warranted in believing that, between precipitate decay and internecine enmities, the English-speaking family is destined to consume itself, and that with its decline the prospect of successfully-organised conquest and unarrested incalculable expansion, to which I alluded above, will brighten for the deep-lunged children of the Fatherland!

IX

MIRANDA HOPE TO HER MOTHER

October 22.

DEAR MOTHER.

I'm off in a day or two to visit some new country; I haven't yet decided which. I've satisfied myself with regard to France, and obtained a good knowledge of the language. I've enjoyed my visit to Madame de Maisonrouge deeply, and feel as if I were leaving a circle of real friends. Everything has gone on beautifully up to the end, and every one has been as kind and attentive as if I were their own sister, especially Mr. Verdier, the French gentleman, from whom I have gained more than I ever expected (in six weeks) and with whom I have promised to *correspond*. So you can imagine me dashing off the liveliest and yet the most elegant French letters; and if you don't believe in them I'll keep the rough drafts to show you when I go back.

The German gentleman is also more interesting the more you know him; it seems sometimes as if I could fairly drink in his ideas. I've found out why the young lady from New York doesn't like me! It's because I said one day at dinner that I *admired* to go to the Louvre. Well, when I first came it seemed as if I *did* admire everything! Tell William Platt his letter has come. I knew he'd have to write, and I was bound I'd make him! I haven't decided what country I'll visit next; it seems as if there were so many to choose from. But I must take care to pick out a good one and to meet plenty of fresh experiences. Dearest mother, my money holds out, and it *is* most interesting!

A NOTE ON

A BUNDLE OF LETTERS

(1879)

In one of his many stories about super-sensitive artists, "The Next Time," James dramatized the plight of a silk purse that was unable to make itself into a sow's ear. We watch Ralph Limbert, the novelist-hero, trying hard to vulgarize his superb but commercially unprofitable talent. The point of the tale is that he cannot help remaining a genius.

Ralph Limbert is commonly taken for an aspect of James. This is a plausible enough assumption, for, with all his horror of the second-rate, James, inconsistent human being that he was, had a rather comical itch for "success." Occasionally this itch drove him to turn out stories intended for the market. Perhaps "A Bundle of Letters" is such a one. He called it "a mere ingenious and more or less effective" pleasantry and, though more than that, it is surely the most casually readable, most easily penetrated of his shorter fictions. Neither subtle nor blunt, the satire is something delectably in-between. The types (they are not intended to be characters) are at once recognizable. The mere interweaving of a strand or two of plot would have transformed the story into a popular article of literary commerce. In fact it furnishes an example of the versatility with which James is all too rarely credited.

But I have other reasons for admiring "A Bundle of Letters." For one thing, it strikes me as quite funny. The colloquy of the two Americans in Paris, for example, is the very perfection of gentle kidding:

"Well," said one of them, "it all depends on what you're after. I'm after French; that's what I'm after."

"Well," said the other, "I'm after Art."

"Well," said the first, "I'm after Art too; but I'm after French most."

To which, a little later in the dialogue, the other replies: "I don't believe there is ever going to be any considerable demand in the United States for French; but I can promise you that in about ten years there'll be a big demand for Art! And it won't be temporary, either."

Note that, though its level barely rises above that of persiflage, this story touches another side of the theme announced in "Four Meetings." Any national trait, if it be both wide and deep, is bound to have its ludicrous aspect. The hunger for ultra-provincial experience, for the past, for the wider horizon, handled with incisive pathos in "Four Meetings," is treated with amiable satire in "A Bundle of Letters." The pert, downright, independent, doubtless somewhat angular Yankee miss, alert in her quest of "conversation"; the snappish, snobbish New York heiress, whose European tour is less a quest for culture than an obeisance to the conventions of her class; the sensitive young man from Boston, with his French phrases, his Corot evenings, and his niminy-piminy temperament: these familiar types show James gently laughing at his and our countrymen.

But the laughter is not directed solely at Americans. James invites us also to a general grin in the direction of the little boulevardier, Léon, the wolf of the Pension Maisonrouge; and no less in the direction of the Rossettian young Englishwoman, so beautifully bare of brains, so proudly subordinate to her males, so total in her insularity. She stands as one among a hundred instances showing us how clearly James saw through the British upper classes of which in other moods he seems so foolish-fond.

Even more clearly, to my mind, he sees through the eternal German. Dr. Staub, in keeping with the light tone of the story, is presented as a ridiculous character. But we can perceive now (as James was to perceive in 1914) that the end-product of this ridiculousness is the slaughterhouse and torture-factory into which Dr. Staub has systematically converted the European continent. For Dr. Staub the Pension Maisonrouge is merely a stimulus to the barbaric race-thinking that has done duty for rational reflection among his countrymen ever since Tacitus described them for all time. Henry James disliked the Germans; indeed his dislike is the first proof of his understanding of them. In 1879 he knew what after two German Wars Against Mankind we have refused to learn—that the German means exactly what he says: that he does not like civilization and will murder wholesale in order to destroy it.

"It is interesting," comments Dr. Staub, ". . . to perceive, so largely developed, the germs of extinction in the so-called powerful Anglo-Saxon family. . . . You will, I think, hold me warranted in believing that between precipitate decay and internecine enmities, the English-speaking family is destined to consume itself, and that with its decline the prospect of general pervasiveness . . . will brighten for the deep-lunged children of the Fatherland!"

Today we know what that "general pervasiveness" means to the German man and woman: the enslavement of mankind. James—there are other instances in his work of the same insight—saw back of the ludicrous pedantry of the German, back, back, back, to the paranoia on which it rests. In Dr. Rudolph Staub (remember, this was 1879) lies the germ of the First German War Against Mankind and of the Second.

This is not an irrelevant comment. One of the crucial, character-revealing gestures of James's life came toward its close when, at the age of 71, he renounced his American citizenship and became a British subject. He did this not because he was more comfortable in England—that he had been for years—but because he recognized what 1914 meant. It meant the first great showdown between two views of mankind. One view—I am putting it at its simplest—held that mankind in general had some worth. The other view held that only Germans had worth. Because England, for all its inconsistent and often questionable history, held more or less firmly to the first view, James, the apostle of sentient man, threw in his lot with her. He knew that the struggle, underneath all the superficialities of power politics, was between civilization and Dr. Staub. For him the choice was clear, and he made it. We have not yet done so.

LOUISA PALLANT

I

Never say you know the last word about any human heart! I was once treated to a revelation which startled and touched me in the nature of a person with whom I had been acquainted —well, as I supposed—for years, whose character I had had good reasons, heaven knows, to appreciate and in regard to whom I flattered myself I had nothing more to learn.

It was on the terrace of the Kursaal at Homburg, nearly ten years ago, one beautiful night toward the end of July. I had come to the place that day from Frankfort, with vague intentions, and was mainly occupied in waiting for my young nephew, the only son of my sister, who had been entrusted to my care by a very fond mother for the summer—I was expected to show him Europe, only the very best of it—and was on his way from Paris to join me. The excellent band discoursed music not too abstruse, while the air was filled besides with the murmur of different languages, the smoke of many cigars, the creak on the gravel of the gardens of strolling shoes and the thick tinkle of beer-glasses. There were a hundred people walking about, there were some in clusters at little tables and many on benches and rows of chairs, watching the others as if they had paid for the privilege and were rather disappointed. I was among these last; I sat by myself, smoking my cigar and thinking of nothing very particular while families and couples passed and repassed me.

I scarce know how long I had sat when I became aware of a recognition which made my meditations definite. It was on my own part, and the object of it was a lady who moved to and fro, unconscious of my observation, with a young girl at her side. I hadn't seen her for ten years, and what first struck me was the fact not that she was Mrs. Henry Pallant, but that the girl who was with her was remarkably pretty—or rather first of all that every one who passed appeared extremely to admire. This led me also to notice the young lady myself, and her charming face diverted my attention for some time from that of her companion. The latter, moreover, though it was night, wore a thin light veil which made her features vague. The couple slowly walked and walked, but though they were very quiet and decorous, and also very well dressed, they seemed to have no friends. Every one observed but no one addressed them; they appeared even themselves to exchange very few words. Moreover they bore with marked composure and as if they were thoroughly used to it the attention they excited. I am afraid it occurred to me to take for granted that they were of an artful intention and that if they hadn't been the elder lady would have handed the younger over a little less to public valuation and not have sought so to conceal her own face. Perhaps this question came into my mind too easily just then—in view of my prospective mentorship to my nephew. If I was to show him only the best of Europe I should have to be very careful about the people he should meet—especially the ladies—and the relations he should form. I suspected him of great innocence and was uneasy about my office. Was I completely relieved and reassured when I became aware that I simply had Louisa Pallant before me and that the girl was her daughter Linda, whom I had known as a child—Linda grown up to charming beauty?

The question was delicate and the proof that I was not very sure is perhaps that I forbore to speak to my pair at once. I watched them a while—I wondered what they would do. No great harm assuredly; but I was anxious to see if they were really isolated. Homburg was then a great resort of the English—the London season took up its tale there toward the first of August—and I had an idea that in such a company as that Louisa would naturally know people. It was my impression that she "cultivated" the English, that she had been much in London and would be likely to have views in regard to a permanent settlement there. This supposition was quickened by the sight of Linda's beauty, for I knew there is no country in which such attractions are more appreciated. You will see what time I took, and I confess that as I finished my cigar I thought it all over. There was no good reason in fact why I should have rushed into Mrs. Pallant's arms. She had not treated me well and we had never really made it up. Somehow even the circumstance that—after the first soreness—I was glad to have lost her had never put us quite right with each other; nor, for herself, had it made her less ashamed of her heartless behaviour that poor Pallant proved finally no great catch. I had forgiven her; I hadn't felt it anything but an escape not to have married a girl who had in her to take back her given word and break a fellow's heart for mere flesh-pots—or the shallow promise, as it pitifully turned out, of flesh-pots. Moreover we had met since then—on the occasion of my former visit to Europe; had looked each other in the eyes, had pretended to be easy friends and had talked of the wickedness of the world as composedly as if we were the only just, the only pure. I knew by that time what she had given out—that I had driven her off by my insane jealousy before she ever thought of Henry Pallant, before she had ever seen him. This hadn't been before and couldn't be today a ground of real reunion, especially if you add to it that she knew perfectly what I thought of her. It seldom ministers to friendship, I believe, that your friend shall know your real opinion, for he knows it mainly when it's unfavourable, and this is especially the case if—let the solecism pass!—he be a woman. I hadn't followed Mrs. Pallant's fortunes; the years went by for me in my own country, whereas she led her life, which I vaguely believed to be difficult after her husband's death—virtually that of a bankrupt—in foreign lands. I heard of her from time to time; always as "established" somewhere, but on each occasion in a different place. She drifted from country to country, and if she had been of a hard composition at the beginning it could never occur to me that her struggle with society, as it might be called, would have softened the paste. Whenever I heard a woman spoken of as "horribly worldly" I thought immediately of the object of my early passion. I imagined she had debts, and when I now at last made up my mind to recall myself to her it was present to me that she might ask me to lend her money. More than anything else, however, at this time of day, I was sorry for her, so that such an idea didn't operate as a deterrent.

She pretended afterwards that she hadn't noticed me—expressing as we stood face to face great surprise and wishing to know where I had dropped from; but I think the corner of her eye had taken me in and she had been waiting to see what I would do. She had ended by sitting down with her girl on the same row of chairs with myself, and after a little, the seat next to her becoming vacant, I had gone and stood before her. She had then looked up at me a moment, staring as if she couldn't imagine who I was or what I wanted; after which, smiling and extending her hands, she had broken out: "Ah my dear old friend—what a delight!" If she had waited to see what I would do in order to choose her own line she thus at least carried out this line with the utmost grace. She was cordial, friendly, artless, interested, and indeed I'm sure she was very glad to see me. I may as well say immediately, none the less, that she gave me neither then nor later any sign of a desire to contract a loan. She had scant means—that I learned—yet seemed for the moment able to pay her way. I took the empty chair and we remained in talk for an hour. After a while she made me sit at her other side, next her daughter, whom she wished to know me—to love me—as one of their oldest friends. "It goes back, back, back, doesn't it?" said Mrs. Pallant; "and of course she remembers you as a child." Linda smiled all sweetly and blankly, and I saw she remembered me not a whit. When her mother threw out that they had often talked about me she failed to take it up, though she looked extremely nice. Looking nice was her strong point; she was prettier even than her mother had been.

She was such a little lady that she made me ashamed of having doubted, however vaguely and for a moment, of her position in the scale of propriety. Her appearance seemed to say that if she had no acquaintances it was because she didn't want them—because nobody there struck her as attractive: there wasn't the slightest difficulty about her choosing her friends. Linda Pallant, young as she was, and fresh and fair and charming, gentle and sufficiently shy, looked somehow exclusive—as if the dust of the common world had never been meant to besprinkle her. She was of thinner consistency than her mother and clearly not a young woman of professions—except in so far as she was committed to an interest in you by her bright pure candid smile. No girl who had such a lovely way of parting her lips could pass for designing.

As I sat between the pair I felt I had been taken possession of and that for better or worse my stay at Homburg would be intimately associated with theirs. We gave each other a great deal of news and expressed unlimited interest in each other's history since our last meeting. I mightn't judge of what Mrs. Pallant kept back, but for myself I quite overflowed. She let me see at any rate that her life had been a good deal what I supposed, though the terms she employed to describe it were less crude than those of my thought. She confessed they had drifted, she and her daughter, and were drifting still. Her narrative rambled and took a wrong turn, a false flight, or two, as I thought Linda noted, while she sat watching the passers, in a manner that betrayed no consciousness of their attention, without coming to her mother's aid. Once or twice Mrs. Pallant made me rather feel a cross-questioner, which I had had no intention of being. I took it that if the girl never put in a word it was because she had perfect confidence in her parent's ability to come out straight. It was suggested to me, I scarcely knew how, that this confidence between the two ladies went to a great length; that their union of thought, their system of reciprocal divination, was remarkable, and that they probably seldom needed to resort to the clumsy and in some cases dangerous expedient of communicating by sound. I suppose I made this reflection not all at once—it was not wholly the result of that first meeting. I was with them constantly for the next several days and my impressions had time to clarify.

I do remember, however, that it was on this first evening that Archie's name came up. She attributed her own stay at Homburg to no refined nor exalted motive—didn't put it that she was there from force of habit or because a high medical authority had ordered her to drink the waters; she frankly admitted the reason of her visit to have been simply that she didn't know where else to turn. But she appeared to assume that my behaviour rested on higher grounds and even that it required explanation, the place being frivolous and modern—devoid of that interest of antiquity which I had ever made so much of. "Don't you remember—ever so long ago—that you wouldn't look at anything in Europe that wasn't a thousand years old? Well, as we advance in life I suppose we don't think that quite such a charm." And when I mentioned that I had arrived because the place was as good as another for awaiting my nephew she exclaimed: "Your nephew—what nephew? He must have come up of late." I answered that his name was Archie Parker and that he was modern indeed; he was to attain legal manhood in a few months and was in Europe for the first time. My last news of him had been from Paris and I was expecting to hear further from one day to the other. His father was dead, and though a selfish bachelor, little versed in the care of children, I was considerably counted on by his mother to see that he didn't smoke nor flirt too much, nor yet tumble off an Alp.

Mrs. Pallant immediately guessed that his mother was my sister Charlotte, whom she spoke of familiarly, though I knew she had scarce seen her. Then in a moment it came to her which of the Parkers Charlotte had married; she remembered the family perfectly from the old New York days—"that disgustingly rich set." She said it was very nice having the boy come out that way to my care; to which I replied that it was very nice for the boy. She pronounced the advantage rather mine—I ought to have had children; there was something so parental about me and I would have brought them up so well. She could make an allusion like that—to all that might have been and had not been—without a gleam of guilt in her eye; and I foresaw that before I left the place I should have confided to her that though I detested her and was very glad we had fallen out, yet our old relations had left me no heart for marrying another woman. If I had remained so single and so sterile the fault was nobody's but hers. She asked what I meant to do with my nephew—to which I replied that it was much more a question of what he would do with me. She wished to know if he were a nice young man and had brothers and sisters and any particular profession. I assured her I had really seen little of him; I believed him to be six feet high and of tolerable parts. He was an only son, but there was a little sister at home, a delicate, rather blighted child, demanding all the mother's care.

"So that makes your responsibility greater, as it were, about the boy, doesn't it?" said Mrs. Pallant.

"Greater? I'm sure I don't know."

"Why if the girl's life's uncertain he may become, some moment, all the mother has. So that being in your hands—"

"Oh I shall keep him alive, I suppose, if you mean that," I returned.

"Well, *we* won't kill him, shall we, Linda?" my friend went on with a laugh.

"I don't know—perhaps we shall!" smiled the girl.

II

I CALLED on them the next day at their lodgings, the modesty of which was enhanced by a hundred pretty feminine devices—flowers and photographs and portable knick-knacks and a hired piano and morsels of old brocade flung over angular sofas. I took them to drive; I met them again at the Kursaal; I arranged that we should dine together, after the Homburg fashion, at the same *table d'hôte;* and during several days this revived familiar intercourse continued, imitating intimacy if not quite achieving it. I was pleased, as my companions passed the time for me and the conditions of our life were soothing—the feeling of summer and shade and music and leisure in the German gardens and woods, where we strolled and sat and gossiped; to which may be added a vague sociable sense that among people whose challenge to the curiosity was mainly not irresistible we kept quite to ourselves. We were on the footing of old friends who still had in regard to each other discoveries to make. We knew each other's nature but didn't know each other's experience; so that when Mrs. Pallant related to me what she had been "up to," as I called it, for so many years, the former knowledge attached a hundred interpretative footnotes—as if I had been editing an author who presented difficulties—to the interesting page. There was nothing new to me in the fact that I didn't esteem her, but there was relief in my finding that this wasn't necessary at Homburg and that I could like her in spite of it. She struck me, in the oddest way, as both improved and degenerate; the two processes, in her nature, might have gone on together. She was battered and world-worn and, spiritually speaking, vulgarised; something fresh had rubbed off her—it even included the vivacity of her early desire to do the best thing for herself—and something rather stale had rubbed on. At the same time she betrayed a scepticism, and that was rather becoming, for it had quenched the eagerness of her prime, the mercenary principle I had so suffered from. She had grown weary and detached, and since she affected me as more impressed with the evil of the world than with the good, this was a gain; in other words her accretion of indifference, if not of cynicism, showed a softer surface than that of her old ambitions. Furthermore I had to recognise that her devotion to her daughter was a kind of religion; she had done the very best possible for Linda.

Linda was curious, Linda was interesting; I've seen girls I

liked better—charming as this one might be—but have never seen one who for the hour you were with her (the impression passed somehow when she was out of sight) occupied you so completely. I can best describe the attention she provoked by saying that she struck you above all things as a felicitous *final* product—after the fashion of some plant or some fruit, some waxen orchid or some perfect peach. She was clearly the result of a process of calculation, a process patiently educative, a pressure exerted, and all artfully, so that she should reach a high point. This high point had been the star of her mother's heaven—it hung before her so unquenchably—and had shed the only light (in default of a better) that was to shine on the poor lady's path. It stood her instead of every other ideal. The very most and the very best—that was what the girl had been led on to achieve; I mean of course, since no real miracle had been wrought, the most and the best she was capable of. She was as pretty, as graceful, as intelligent, as well-bred, as well-informed, as well-dressed, as could have been conceived for her; her music, her singing, her German, her French, her English, her step, her tone, her glance, her manner, everything in her person and movement, from the shade and twist of her hair to the way you saw her finger-nails were pink when she raised her hand, had been carried so far that one found one's self accepting them as the very measure of young grace. I regarded her thus as a model, yet it was a part of her perfection that she had none of the stiffness of a pattern. If she held the observation it was because you wondered where and when she would break down; but she never broke down, either in her French accent or in her rôle of educated angel.

After Archie had come the ladies were manifestly his greatest resource, and all the world knows why a party of four is more convenient than a party of three. My nephew had kept me waiting a week, with a serenity all his own; but this very coolness was a help to harmony—so long, that is, as I didn't lose my temper with it. I didn't, for the most part, because my young man's unperturbed acceptance of the most various forms of good fortune had more than anything else the effect of amusing me. I had seen little of him for the last three or four years; I wondered what his impending majority would have made of him—he didn't at all carry himself as if the wind of his fortune were rising—and I watched him with a solicitude that usually ended in a joke. He was a tall fresh-coloured youth, with a candid circular countenance and a love of cigarettes, horses and boats which had not been sacrificed to more strenuous studies. He was reassuringly natural, in a supercivilised age, and I soon made up my mind that the formula of his character was in the clearing of the inward scene by his so preordained lack of imagination. If he was serene this was still further simplifying. After that I had time to meditate on the line that divides the serene from the inane, the simple from the silly. He wasn't clever; the fonder theory quite defied our cultivation, though Mrs. Pallant tried it once or twice; but on the other hand it struck me his want of wit might be a good defensive weapon. It wasn't the sort of density that would let him in, but the sort that would keep him out. By which I don't mean that he had shortsighted suspicions, but that on the contrary imagination would never be needed to save him, since she would never put him in danger. He was in short a well-grown well-washed muscular young American, whose extreme salubrity might have made him pass for conceited. If he looked pleased with himself it was only because he was pleased with life—as well he might be, with the fortune that awaited the stroke of his twenty-first year—and his big healthy independent person was an inevitable part of that. I am bound to add that he was accommodating—for which I was grateful. His habits were active, but he didn't insist on my adopting them and he made numerous and generous sacrifices for my society. When I say he made them for mine I must duly remember that mine and that of Mrs. Pallant and Linda were now very much the same thing. He was willing to sit and smoke for hours under the trees or, adapting his long legs to the pace of his three companions, stroll through the nearer woods of the charming little hill-range of the Taunus to those rustic *Wirthschaften* where coffee might be drunk under a trellis.

Mrs. Pallant took a great interest in him; she made him, with his easy uncle, a subject of discourse; she pronounced him a delightful specimen, as a young gentleman of his period and country. She even asked me the sort of "figure" his fortune might really amount to, and professed a rage of envy when I told her what I supposed it to be. While we were so occupied Archie, on his side, couldn't do less than converse with Linda, nor to tell the truth did he betray the least inclination for any different exercise. They strolled away together while their elders rested; two or three times, in the evening, when the ballroom of the Kursaal was lighted and dance-music played, they whirled over the smooth floor in a waltz that stirred my memory. Whether it had the same effect on Mrs. Pallant's I know not: she held her peace. We had on certain occasions our moments, almost our half-hours, of unembarrassed silence while our young companions disported themselves. But if at other times her enquiries and comments were numerous on this article of my ingenuous charge, that might very well have passed for a courteous recognition of the frequent admiration I expressed for Linda—an admiration that drew from her, I noticed, but scant direct response. I was struck thus with her reserve when I spoke of her daughter—my remarks produced so little of a maternal flutter. Her detachment, her air of having no fatuous illusions and not being blinded by prejudice, seemed to me at times to savour of affectation. Either she answered me with a vague and impatient sigh and changed the subject, or else she said before doing so: "Oh yes, yes, she's a very brilliant creature. She ought to be: God knows what I've done for her!"

The reader will have noted my fondness, in all cases, for the explanations of things; as an example of which I had my theory here that she was disappointed in the girl. Where then had her special calculation failed? As she couldn't possibly have wished her prettier or more pleasing, the pang must have been for her not having made a successful use of her gifts. Had she expected her to "land" a prince the day after leaving the schoolroom? There was after all plenty of time for this, with Linda but two-and-twenty. It didn't occur to me to wonder if the source of her mother's tepidity was that the young lady had not turned out so nice a nature as she had hoped, because in the first place Linda struck me as perfectly innocent, and because in the second I wasn't paid, in the French phrase, for supposing Louisa Pallant much concerned on that score. The last hypothesis I should have invoked was that of private despair at bad moral symptoms. And in relation to Linda's nature I had before me the daily spectacle of her manner with my nephew. It was as charming as it could be without betrayal of a desire to lead him on. She was as familiar as a cousin, but as a distant one—a cousin who had been brought up to observe degrees. She was so much cleverer than Archie that she couldn't help laughing at him, but she didn't laugh enough to exclude variety, being well aware, no doubt, that a woman's cleverness most shines in contrast with a man's stupidity when she pretends to take that stupidity for her law. Linda Pallant moreover was not a chatterbox; as she knew the value of many things she knew the value of intervals. There were a good many in the conversation of these young persons; my nephew's own speech, to say nothing of his thought, abounding in comfortable lapses; so that I sometimes wondered how their association was kept at that pitch of continuity of which it gave the impression. It was friendly enough, evidently, when Archie sat near her—near enough for low murmurs, had such risen to his lips—and watched her with interested eyes and with freedom not to try too hard to make himself agreeable. She had always something in hand—a flower in her tapestry to finish, the leaves of a magazine to cut, a button to sew on her glove (she carried a little work-bag in her pocket and was a person of the daintiest habits), a pencil to ply ever so neatly in the sketchbook which she rested on her knee. When we were indoors—mainly then at her mother's modest rooms—she had always the resource of her piano, of which she was of course a perfect mistress. These pursuits supported her, they helped her to an assurance under such narrow inspection —I ended by rebuking Archie for it; I told him he stared the poor girl out of countenance—and she sought further relief in smiling all over the place. When my young man's eyes shone at her those of Miss Pallant addressed themselves brightly to the trees and clouds and other surrounding objects, including her mother and me. Sometimes she broke into a sudden embarrassed happy pointless laugh. When she wandered off with him she looked back at us in a manner that promised it wasn't for long and that she was with us still in spirit. If I liked her I had therefore my good reason: it was many a day since a pretty girl had had the air of taking me so much into account. Sometimes when they were so far away as not to disturb us she read aloud a little to Mr. Archie. I don't know where she got her books—I never provided them, and certainly he didn't. He was no reader and I fear he often dozed.

III

I REMEMBER well the first time—it was at the end of about ten days of this—that Mrs. Pallant remarked to me: "My dear friend, you're quite amazing! You behave for all the world as if you were perfectly ready to accept certain consequences." She nodded in the direction of our young companions, but I nevertheless put her at the pains of saying what consequences she meant. "What consequences? Why the very same consequences that ensued when you and I first became acquainted."

I hesitated, but then, looking her in the eyes, said: "Do you mean she'd throw him over?"

"You're not kind, you're not generous," she replied with a quick colour. "I'm giving you a warning."

"You mean that my boy may fall in love with your girl?"

"Certainly. It looks even as if the harm might be already done."

"Then your warning comes too late," I significantly smiled. "But why do you call it a harm?"

"Haven't you any sense of the rigour of your office?" she asked. "Is that what his mother has sent him out to you for: that you shall find him the first wife you can pick up, that you shall let him put his head into the noose the day after his arrival?"

"Heaven forbid I should do anything of the kind! I know moreover that his mother doesn't want him to marry young. She holds it the worst of mistakes, she feels that at that age a man never really chooses. He doesn't choose till he has lived a while, till he has looked about and compared."

"And what do you think then yourself?"

"I should like to say I regard the fact of falling in love, at whatever age, as in itself an act of selection. But my being as I am at this time of day would contradict me too much."

"Well then, you're too primitive. You ought to leave this place tomorrow."

"So as not to see Archie fall—?"

"You ought to fish him out now—from where he *has* fallen —and take him straight away."

I wondered a little. "Do you think he's in very far?"

"If I were his mother I know what I should think. I can put myself in her place—I'm not narrow-minded. I know perfectly well how she must regard such a question."

"And don't you know," I returned, "that in America that's not thought important—the way the mother regards it?"

Mrs. Pallant had a pause—as if I mystified or vexed her. "Well, we're not in America. We happen to be here."

"No; my poor sister's up to her neck in New York."

"I'm almost capable of writing to her to come out," said Mrs. Pallant.

"You *are* warning me," I cried, "but I hardly know of what!

It seems to me my responsibility would begin only at the moment your daughter herself should seem in danger."

"Oh you needn't mind that—I'll take care of Linda."

But I went on. "If you think she's in danger already I'll carry him off tomorrow."

"It would be the best thing you could do."

"I don't know—I should be very sorry to act on a false alarm. I'm very well here; I like the place and the life and your society. Besides, it doesn't strike me that—on her side—there's any real symptom."

She looked at me with an air I had never seen in her face, and if I had puzzled her she repaid me in kind. "You're very annoying. You don't deserve what I'd fain do for you."

What she'd fain do for me she didn't tell me that day, but we took up the subject again. I remarked that I failed to see why we should assume that a girl like Linda—brilliant enough to make one of the greatest matches—would fall so very easily into my nephew's arms. Might I enquire if her mother had won a confession from her, if she had stammered out her secret? Mrs. Pallant made me, on this, the point that they had no need to tell each other such things—they hadn't lived together twenty years in such intimacy for nothing. To which I returned that I had guessed as much, but that there might be an exception for a great occasion like the present. If Linda had shown nothing it was a sign that for *her* the occasion wasn't great; and I mentioned that Archie had spoken to me of the young lady only to remark casually and rather patronisingly, after his first encounter with her, that she was a regular little flower. (The little flower was nearly three years older than himself.) Apart from this he hadn't alluded to her and had taken up no allusion of mine. Mrs. Pallant informed me again—for which I was prepared—that I was quite too primitive; after which she said: "We needn't discuss the case if you don't wish to, but I happen to know—how I obtained my knowledge isn't important—that the moment Mr. Parker should propose to my daughter she'd gobble him down. Surely it's a detail worth mentioning to you."

I sought to defer then to her judgement. "Very good. I'll sound him. I'll look into the matter tonight."

"Don't, don't; you'll spoil everything!" she spoke as with some finer view. "Remove him quickly—that's the only thing."

I didn't at all like the idea of removing him quickly; it seemed too summary, too extravagant, even if presented to him on specious grounds; and moreover, as I had told Mrs. Pallant, I really had no wish to change my scene. It was no part of my promise to my sister that, with my middle-aged habits, I should duck and dodge about Europe. So I temporised. "Should you really object to the boy so much as a son-in-law? After all he's a good fellow and a gentleman."

"My poor friend, you're incredibly superficial!" she made answer with an assurance that struck me.

The contempt in it so nettled me in fact that I exclaimed: "Possibly! But it seems odd that a lesson in consistency should come from *you*."

I had no retort from her on this, rather to my surprise, and when she spoke again it was all quietly. "I think Linda and I had best withdraw. We've been here a month—it will have served our purpose."

"Mercy on us, that will be a bore!" I protested; and for the rest of the evening, till we separated—our conversation had taken place after dinner at the Kursaal—she said little, preserving a subdued and almost injured air. This somehow didn't appeal to me, since it was absurd that Louisa Pallant, of all women, should propose to put me in the wrong. If ever a woman had been in the wrong herself—! I had even no need to go into that. Archie and I, at all events, usually attended the ladies back to their own door—they lived in a street of minor accommodation at a certain distance from the Rooms—where we parted for the night late, on the big cobblestones, in the little sleeping German town, under the closed windows of which, suggesting stuffy interiors, our cheerful English partings resounded. On this occasion indeed they rather languished; the question that had come up for me with Mrs. Pallant appeared —and by no intention of mine—to have brushed the young couple with its chill. Archie and Linda too struck me as conscious and dumb.

As I walked back to our hotel with my nephew I passed my hand into his arm and put to him, by no roundabout approach, the question of whether he were in serious peril of love.

"I don't know, I don't know—really, uncle, I don't know!" was, however, all the satisfaction I could extract from the youth, who hadn't the smallest vein of introspection. He mightn't know, but before we reached the inn—we had a few more words on the subject—it seemed to me that *I* did. His mind wasn't formed to accommodate at one time many subjects of thought, but Linda Pallant certainly constituted for the moment its principal furniture. She pervaded his consciousness, she solicited his curiosity, she associated herself, in a manner as yet informal and undefined, with his future. I could see that she held, that she beguiled him as no one had ever done. I didn't betray to him, however, that perception, and I spent my night a prey to the consciousness that, after all, it had been none of my business to provide him with the sense of being captivated. To put him in relation with a young enchantress was the last thing his mother had expected of me or that I had expected of myself. Moreover it was quite my opinion that he himself was too young to be a judge of enchantresses. Mrs. Pallant was right and I had given high proof of levity in regarding her, with her beautiful daughter, as a "resource." There were other resources —one of which *would* be most decidedly to clear out. What did I know after all about the girl except that I rejoiced to have escaped from marrying her mother? That mother, it was true, was a singular person, and it was strange her conscience should have begun to fidget in advance of my own. It was strange she should so soon have felt Archie's peril, and even stranger that she should have then wished to "save" him. The ways of women were infinitely subtle, and it was no novelty to me that one never knew where they would turn up. As I haven't hesitated in this report to expose the irritable side of my own nature I shall confess that I even wondered if my old friend's solicitude hadn't been a deeper artifice. Wasn't it possibly a plan of her own for making sure of my young man—though I didn't quite see the logic of it? If she regarded him, which she might in view of his large fortune, as a great catch, mightn't she have arranged this little comedy, in their personal interest, with the girl?

That possibility at any rate only made it a happier thought that I should win my companion to some curiosity about other places. There were many of course much more worth his attention than Homburg. In the course of the morning—it was after our early luncheon—I walked round to Mrs. Pallant's to let her know I was ready to take action; but even while I went I again felt the unlikelihood of the part attributed by my fears and by the mother's own, so far as they had been roused, to Linda. Certainly if she was such a girl as these fears represented her she would fly at higher game. It was with an eye to high game, Mrs. Pallant had frankly admitted to me, that she had been trained, and such an education, to say nothing of such a performer, justified a hope of greater returns. A young American, the fruit of scant "modelling," who could give her nothing but pocket-money, was a very moderate prize, and if she had been prepared to marry for ambition—there was no such hardness in her face or tone, but then there never is—her mark would be inevitably a "personage" *quelconque*. I was received at my friend's lodging with the announcement that she had left Homburg with her daughter half an hour before. The good woman who had entertained the pair professed to know nothing of their movements beyond the fact that they had gone to Frankfort, where, however, it was her belief that they didn't intend to remain. They were evidently travelling beyond. Sudden, their decision to move? Oh yes, the matter of a moment.

They must have spent the night in packing, they had so many things and such pretty ones; and their poor maid, all the morning, had scarce had time to swallow her coffee. But they clearly were ladies accustomed to come and go. It didn't matter—with such rooms as hers she never wanted: there was a new family coming in at three.

IV

THIS piece of strategy left me staring and made me, I confess, quite furious. My only consolation was that Archie, when I told him, looked as blank as myself, and that the trick touched him more nearly, for I was not now in love with Louisa. We agreed that we required an explanation and we pretended to expect one the next day in the shape of a letter satisfactory even to the point of being apologetic. When I say "we" pretended I mean that I did, for my suspicion that he knew what had been on foot—through an arrangement with Linda—lasted only a moment. If his resentment was less than my own his surprise was equally great. I had been willing to bolt, but I felt slighted by the ease with which Mrs. Pallant had shown she could part with us. Archie professed no sense of a grievance, because in the first place he was shy about it and because in the second it was evidently not definite to him that he had been encouraged—equipped as he was, I think, with no very particular idea of what constituted encouragement. He was fresh from the wonderful country in which there may between the ingenuous young be so little question of "intentions." He was but dimly conscious of his own and could by no means have told me whether he had been challenged or been jilted. I didn't want to exasperate him, but when at the end of three days more we were still without news of our late companions I observed that it was very simple: they must have been just hiding from us; they thought us dangerous; they wished to avoid entanglements. They had found us too attentive and wished not to raise false hopes. He appeared to accept this explanation and even had the air—so at least I inferred from his asking me no questions—of judging the matter might be delicate for myself. The poor youth was altogether much mystified, and I smiled at the image in his mind of Mrs. Pallant fleeing from his uncle's importunities.

We decided to leave Homburg, but if we didn't pursue our fugitives it wasn't simply that we were ignorant of where they were. I could have found that out with a little trouble, but I was deterred by the reflexion that this would be Louisa's reasoning. She was a dreadful humbug and her departure had been a provocation—I fear it was in that stupid conviction that I made out a little independent itinerary with Archie. I even believed we should learn where they were quite soon enough, and that our patience—even my young man's—would be longer than theirs. Therefore I uttered a small private cry of triumph when three weeks later—we happened to be at Interlaken—he reported to me that he had receievd a note from Miss Pallant. The form of this confidence was his enquiring if there were particular reasons why we should longer delay our projected visit to the Italian lakes. Mightn't the fear of the hot weather, which was moreover at that season our native temperature, cease to operate, the middle of September having arrived? I answered that we would start on the morrow if he liked, and then, pleased apparently that I was so easy to deal with, he revealed his little secret. He showed me his letter, which was a graceful natural document—it covered with a few flowing strokes but a single page of note-paper—not at all compromising to the young lady. If, however, it was almost the apology I had looked for—save that this should have come from the mother—it was not ostensibly in the least an invitation. It mentioned casually—the mention was mainly in the words at the head of her paper—that they were on the Lago Maggiore, at Baveno; but it consisted mainly of the expression of a regret that they had had so abruptly to leave Homburg. Linda failed to say under what necessity they had found themselves; she only hoped we hadn't judged them too harshly and would accept "this hasty line" as a substitute for the omitted good-bye. She also hoped our days were passing pleasantly and with the same lovely weather that prevailed south of the Alps; and she remained very sincerely and with the kindest remembrances—!

The note contained no message from her mother, and it was open to me to suppose, as I should prefer, either that Mrs. Pallant hadn't known she was writing or that they wished to make us think she hadn't known. The letter might pass as a common civility of the girl's to a person with whom she had been on easy terms. It was, however, for something more than this that my nephew took it; so at least I gathered from the touching candour of his determination to go to Baveno. I judged it idle to drag him another way; he had money in his own pocket and was quite capable of giving me the slip. Yet—such are the sweet incongruities of youth—when I asked him to what tune he had been thinking of Linda since they left us in the lurch he replied: "Oh I haven't been thinking at all! Why should I?" This fib was accompanied by an exorbitant blush. Since he was to obey his young woman's signal I must equally make out where it would take him, and one splendid morning we started over the Simplon in a post-chaise.

I represented to him successfully that it would be in much better taste for us to alight at Stresa, which as every one knows is a resort of tourists, also on the shore of the major lake, at about a mile's distance from Baveno. If we stayed at the latter place we should have to inhabit the same hotel as our friends, and this might be awkward in view of a strained relation with them. Nothing would be easier than to go and come between the two points, especially by the water, which would give Archie a chance for unlimited paddling. His face lighted up at the vision of a pair of oars; he pretended to take my plea for discretion very seriously, and I could see that he had at once begun to calculate opportunities for navigation with Linda. Our post-chaise—I had insisted on easy stages and we were three days on the way—deposited us at Stresa toward the middle of the afternoon, and it was within an amazingly short time that I found myself in a small boat with my nephew, who pulled us over to Baveno with vigorous strokes. I remember the sweetness of the whole impression. I had had it before, but to my companion it was new, and he thought it as pretty as the opera: the enchanting beauty of the place and hour, the stillness of the air and water, with the romantic fantastic Borromean Islands set as great jewels in a crystal globe. We disembarked at the steps by the garden-foot of the hotel, and somehow it seemed a perfectly natural part of the lovely situation that I should immediately become conscious of Mrs. Pallant and her daughter seated on the terrace and quietly watching us. They had the air of expectation, which I think we had counted on. I hadn't even asked Archie if he had answered Linda's note; this was between themselves and in the way of supervision I had done enough in coming with him.

There is no doubt our present address, all round, lacked a little the easiest grace—or at least Louisa's and mine did. I felt too much the appeal of her exhibition to notice closely the style of encounter of the young people. I couldn't get it out of my head, as I have sufficiently indicated, that Mrs. Pallant was playing a game, and I'm afraid she saw in my face that this suspicion had been the motive of my journey. I had come there to find her out. The knowledge of my purpose couldn't help her to make me very welcome, and that's why I speak of our meeting constrainedly. We observed none the less all the forms, and the admirable scene left us plenty to talk about. I made no reference before Linda to the retreat from Homburg. This young woman looked even prettier than she had done on the eve of that manœuvre and gave no sign of an awkward consciousness. She again so struck me as a charming clever girl that I was freshly puzzled to know why we should get—or should have got—into tangle about her. People had to want to complicate a situation to do it on so simple a pretext as that Linda was in every way beautiful. This was the clear fact: so why shouldn't the presumptions be in favour of every result of it? One of the effects of that cause, on the spot, was that at the end of a very short time Archie proposed to her to take a turn with him in his boat, which awaited us at the foot of the steps. She looked at her mother with a smiling "May I, mamma?" and Mrs. Pallant answered "Certainly, darling, if you're not afraid." At this—I scarcely knew why—I sought the relief of laughter: it must have affected me as comic that the girl's general competence should suffer the imputation of that particular flaw. She gave me a quick slightly sharp look as she turned away with my nephew; it appeared to challenge me a little— "Pray what's the matter with *you*?" It was the first expression of the kind I had ever seen in her face. Mrs. Pallant's attention, on the other hand, rather strayed from me; after we had been left there together she sat silent, not heeding me, looking at the lake and mountains—at the snowy crests crowned with the flush of evening. She seemed not even to follow our young companions as they got into their boat and pushed off. For some minutes I respected her mood; I walked slowly up and down the terrace and lighted a cigar, as she had always permitted me to do at Homburg. I found in her, it was true, rather a new air of weariness; her fine cold well-bred face was pale; I noted in it new lines of fatigue, almost of age. At last I stopped in front of her and—since she looked so sad—asked if she had been having bad news.

"The only bad news was when I learned—through your nephew's note to Linda—that you were coming to us."

"Ah then he wrote?"

"Certainly he wrote."

"You take it all harder than I do," I returned as I sat down beside her. And then I added, smiling: "Have you written to his mother?"

Slowly at last, and more directly, she faced me. "Take care, take care, or you'll have been more brutal than you'll afterwards like," she said with an air of patience before the inevitable.

"Never, never! Unless you think me brutal if I ask whether you knew when Linda wrote."

She had an hesitation. "Yes, she showed me her letter. She wouldn't have done anything else. I let it go because I didn't know what course was best. I'm afraid to oppose her to her face."

"Afraid, my dear friend, with that girl?"

"That girl? Much you know about her! It didn't follow you'd come. I didn't take that for granted."

"I'm like you," I said—"I too am afraid of my nephew. I don't venture to oppose him to his face. The only thing I could do—once he wished it—was to come with him."

"I see. Well, there are grounds, after all, on which I'm glad," she rather inscrutably added.

"Oh I was conscientious about that! But I've no authority; I can neither drive him nor stay him—I can use no force," I explained. "Look at the way he's pulling that boat and see if you can fancy me."

"You could tell him she's a bad, hard girl—one who'd poison any good man's life!" my companion broke out with a passion that startled me.

At first I could only gape. "Dear lady, what do you mean?"

She bent her face into her hands, covering it over with them, and so remained a minute; then she continued a little differently, though as if she hadn't heard my question: "I hoped you were too disgusted with us—after the way we left you planted."

"It was disconcerting assuredly, and it might have served if Linda hadn't written. That patched it up," I gaily professed. But my gaiety was thin, for I was still amazed at her violence of a moment before. "Do you really mean that she won't do?" I added.

She made no direct answer; she only said after a little that it didn't matter whether the crisis should come a few weeks sooner or a few weeks later, since it was destined to come at the first chance, the favouring moment. Linda had marked my young man—and when Linda had marked a thing!

"Bless my soul—how very grim!" But I didn't understand. "Do you mean she's in love with him?"

"It's enough if she makes him think so—though even that isn't essential."

Still I was at sea. "If she makes him think so? Dear old friend, what's your idea? I've observed her, I've watched her, and when all's said what has she done? She has been civil and pleasant to him, but it would have been much more marked if she hadn't. She has really shown him, with her youth and her natural charm, nothing more than common friendliness. Her note was nothing; he let me see it."

"I don't think you've heard every word she has said to him," Mrs. Pallant returned with an emphasis that still struck me as perverse.

"No more have you, I take it!" I promptly cried. She evidently meant more than she said; but if this excited my curiosity it also moved, in a different connexion, my indulgence.

"No, but I know my own daughter. She's a most remarkable young woman."

"You've an extraordinary tone about her," I declared—"such a tone as I think I've never before heard on a mother's lips. I've had the same impression from you—that of a disposition to 'give her away,' but never yet so strong."

At this Mrs. Pallant got up; she stood there looking down at me. "You make my reparation—my expiation—difficult!" And leaving me still more astonished she moved along the terrace.

I overtook her presently and repeated her words. "Your reparation—your expiation? What on earth are you talking about?"

"You know perfectly what I mean—it's too magnanimous of you to pretend you don't."

"Well, at any rate," I said, "I don't see what good it does me, or what it makes up to me for, that you should abuse your daughter."

"Oh I don't care; I shall save him!" she cried as we went, and with an extravagance, as I felt, of sincerity. At the same moment two ladies, apparently English, came toward us—scattered groups had been sitting there and the inmates of the hotel were moving to and fro—and I observed the immediate charming transition, the fruit of such years of social practice, by which, as they greeted us, her tension and her impatience dropped to recognition and pleasure. They stopped to speak to her and she enquired with sweet propriety as to the "continued improvement" of their sister. I strolled on and she presently rejoined me; after which she had a peremptory note. "Come away from this—come down into the garden." We descended to that blander scene, strolled through it and paused on the border of the lake.

V

THE charm of the evening had deepened, the stillness was like a solemn expression on a beautiful face and the whole air of the place divine. In the fading light my nephew's boat was too far out to be perceived. I looked for it a little and then, as I gave it up, remarked that from such an excursion as that, on such a lake and at such an hour, a young man and a young woman of common sensibility could only come back doubly pledged to each other.

To this observation Mrs. Pallant's answer was, superficially at least, irrelevant; she said after a pause: "With you, my dear man, one has certainly to dot one's 'i's.' Haven't you discovered, and didn't I tell you at Homburg, that we're miserably poor?"

"Isn't 'miserably' rather too much—living as you are at an expensive hotel?"

Well, she promptly met this. "They take us *en pension,* for ever so little a day. I've been knocking about Europe long enough to learn all sorts of horrid arts. Besides, don't speak of hotels; we've spent half our life in them and Linda told me only last night that she hoped never to put her foot into one again. She feels that when she comes to such a place as this she ought, if things were decently right, to find a villa of her own."

"Then her companion there's perfectly competent to give her one. Don't think I've the least desire to push them into each other's arms—I only ask to wash my hands of them. But I should like to know why you want, as you said just now, to save him. When you speak as if your daughter were a monster I take it you're not serious."

She was facing me in the rich short twilight, and to describe herself as immeasurably more serious perhaps than she had ever been in her life she had only to look at me without protestation. "It's Linda's standard. God knows I myself could get on! She's ambitious, luxurious, determined to have what she wants—more 'on the make' than any one I've ever seen. Of course it's open to you to tell me it's my own fault, that I was so before her and have made her so. But does that make me like it any better?"

"Dear Mrs. Pallant, you're wonderful, you're terrible," I could only stammer, lost in the desert of my thoughts.

"Oh yes, you've made up your mind about me; you see me in a certain way and don't like the trouble of changing. *Votre siège est fait.* But you'll *have* to change—if you've any generosity!" Her eyes shone in the summer dusk and the beauty of her youth came back to her.

"Is this a part of the reparation, of the expiation?" I demanded. "I don't see what you ever did to Archie."

"It's enough that he belongs to you. But it isn't for you I do it—it's for myself," she strangely went on.

"Doubtless you've your own reasons—which I can't penetrate. But can't you sacrifice something else? Must you sacrifice your only child?"

"My only child's my punishment, my only child's my stigma!" she cried in her exaltation.

"It seems to me rather that you're hers."

"Hers? What does *she* know of such things?—what can she ever feel? She's cased in steel; she has a heart of marble. It's true—it's true," said Louisa Pallant. "She appalls me!"

I laid my hand on my poor friend's; I uttered, with the intention of checking and soothing her, the first incoherent words that came into my head and I drew her toward a bench a few steps away. She dropped upon it; I placed myself near her and besought her to consider well what she said. She owed me nothing and I wished no one injured, no one denounced or exposed for my sake.

"For your sake? Oh I'm not thinking of you!" she answered; and indeed the next moment I thought my words rather fatuous. "It's a satisfaction to my own conscience—for I *have* one, little as you may think I've a right to speak of it. I've been punished by my sin itself. I've been hideously worldly, I've thought only of that, and I've taught her to be so—to do the same. That's the only instruction I've ever given her, and she has learned the lesson so well that now I see it stamped there in all her nature, on all her spirit and on all her form, I'm horrified at my work. For years we've lived that way; we've thought of nothing else. She has profited so well by my beautiful influence that she has gone far beyond the great original. I say I'm horrified," Mrs. Pallant dreadfully wound up, "because she's horrible."

"My poor extravagant friend," I pleaded, "isn't it still more so to hear a mother say such things?"

"Why so, if they're abominably true? Besides, I don't care what I say if I save him."

I could only gape again at this least expected of all my adventures. "Do you expect me then to repeat to him—"

"Not in the least," she broke in; "I'll do it myself." At this I uttered some strong inarticulate protest, but she went on with the grimmest simplicity: "I was very glad at first, but it would have been better if we hadn't met."

"I don't agree to that, for you interest me," I rather ruefully professed, "immensely."

"I don't care if I do—so I interest *him*."

"You must reflect then that your denunciation can only strike me as, for all its violence, vague and unconvincing. Never had a girl less the appearance of bearing such charges out. You know how I've admired her."

"You know nothing about her! *I* do, you see, for she's the work of my hand!" And Mrs. Pallant laughed for bitterness. "I've watched her for years, and little by little, for the last two or three, it has come over me. There's not a tender spot in her whole composition. To arrive at a brilliant social position, if it were necessary, she would see me drown in this lake without lifting a finger, she would stand there and see it—she would push me in—and never feel a pang. That's my young lady!" Her lucidity chilled me to the soul—it seemed to shine so flawlessly. "To climb up to the top and be splendid and envied there," she went on—"to do that at any cost or by any meanness and cruelty is the only thing she has a heart for. She'd lie for it, she'd steal for it, she'd kill for it!" My companion brought out these words with a cold confidence that had evidently behind it some occult past process of growth. I watched her pale face and glowing eyes; she held me breathless and frowning, but her strange vindictive, or at least retributive, passion irresistibly imposed itself. I found myself at last believing her, pitying her more than I pitied the subject of her dreadful analysis. It was as if she had held her tongue for longer than she could bear, suffering more and more the importunity of the truth. It relieved her thus to drag that to the light, and still she kept up the high and most unholy sacrifice. "God in his mercy has let me see it in time, but his ways are strange that he has let me see it in my daughter. It's myself he has let me see—myself as I was for years. But she's worse—she *is,* I assure you; she's worse than I intended or dreamed." Her hands were clasped tightly together in her lap; her low voice quavered and her breath came short; she looked up at the southern stars as if *they* would understand.

"Have you ever spoken to her as you speak to me?" I finally asked. "Have you ever put before her this terrible arraignment?"

"Put it before her? How can I put it before her when all she would have to say would be: 'You, *you,* you base one, who made me—?'"

"Then why do you want to play her a trick?"

"I'm not bound to tell you, and you wouldn't see my point if I did. I should play that boy a far worse one if I were to stay my hand."

Oh I had my view of this. "If he loves her he won't believe a word you say."

"Very possibly, but I shall have done my duty."

"And shall you say to him," I asked, "simply what you've said to me?"

"Never mind what I shall say to him. It will be something that will perhaps helpfully affect him. Only," she added with her proud decision, "I must lose no time."

"If you're so bent on gaining time," I said, "why did you let her go out in the boat with him?"

"Let her? How could I prevent it?"

"But she asked your permission."

"Ah that," she cried, "is all a part of all the comedy!"

It fairly hushed me to silence, and for a moment more she said nothing. "Then she doesn't know you hate her?" I resumed.

"I don't know what she knows. She has depths and depths, and all of them bad. Besides, I don't hate her in the least; I just pity her for what I've made of her. But I pity still more the man who may find himself married to her."

"There's not much danger of there being any such person," I wailed, "at the rate you go on."

"I beg your pardon—there's a perfect possibility," said my companion. "She'll marry—she'll marry 'well.' She'll marry a title as well as a fortune."

"It's a pity my nephew hasn't a title," I attempted the grimace of suggesting.

She seemed to wonder. "I see you think I want that, and that I'm acting a part. God forgive you! Your suspicion's perfectly natural. How can any one *tell*," asked Louisa Pallant—"with people like us?"

Her utterance of these words brought tears to my eyes. I laid my hand on her arm, holding her a while, and we looked at each other through the dusk. "You couldn't do more if he were my son."

"Oh if he had been your son he'd have kept out of it! I like him for himself. He's simple and sane and honest—he needs affection."

"He would have quite the most remarkable of mothers-in-law!" I commented.

Mrs. Pallant gave a small dry laugh—she wasn't joking. We lingered by the lake while I thought over what she had said to me and while she herself apparently thought. I confess that even close at her side and under the strong impression of her sincerity, her indifference to the conventional graces, my imagination, my constitutional scepticism began to range. Queer ideas came into my head. Was the comedy on *her* side and not on the girl's, and was she posturing as a magnanimous woman at poor Linda's expense? Was she determined, in spite of the young lady's preference, to keep her daughter for a grander personage than a young American whose dollars were not numerous enough—numerous as they were—to make up for his want of high relationships, and had she invented at once the boldest and the subtlest of games in order to keep the case in her hands? If she was prepared really to address herself to

Archie she would have to go very far to overcome the mistrust he would be sure to feel at a proceeding superficially so sinister? Was she prepared to go far enough? The answer to these doubts was simply the way I had been touched—it came back to me the next moment—when she used the words "people like us." Their effect was to wring my heart. She seemed to kneel in the dust, and I felt in a manner ashamed that I had let her sink to it. She said to me at last that I must wait no longer, I must go away before the young people came back. They were staying long, too long; all the more reason then she should deal with my nephew that night. I must drive back to Stresa, or if I liked I could go on foot: it wasn't far—for an active man. She disposed of me freely, she was so full of her purpose; and after we had quitted the garden and returned to the terrace above she seemed almost to push me to leave her—I felt her fine consecrated hands fairly quiver on my shoulders. I was ready to do as she prescribed; she affected me painfully, she had given me a "turn," and I wanted to get away from her. But before I went I asked her why Linda should regard my young man as such a *parti;* it didn't square after all with her account of the girl's fierce ambitions. By that account these favours to one so graceless were a woeful waste of time.

"Oh she has worked it all out; she has regarded the question in every light," said Mrs. Pallant. "If she has made up her mind it's because she sees what she can do."

"Do you mean that she has talked it over with you?"

My friend's wonderful face pitied my simplicity. "Lord! for what do you take us? We don't talk things over today. We know each other's point of view and only have to act. We observe the highest proprieties of speech. We never for a moment name anything ugly—we only just go at it. We can take definitions, which are awkward things, for granted."

"But in this case," I nevertheless urged, "the poor thing can't possibly be aware of your point of view."

"No," she conceded—"that's because I haven't played fair. Of course she couldn't expect I'd cheat. There ought to be honour among thieves. But it was open to her to do the same."

"What do you mean by the same?"

"She might have fallen in love with a poor man. Then I should have been 'done.'"

"A rich one's better; he can do more," I replied with conviction.

At this she appeared to have, in the oddest way, a momentary revulsion. "So you'd have reason to know if you had led the life that we have! Never to have had really enough—I mean to do just the few simple thinge we've wanted; never to have had the sinews of war, I suppose you'd call them, the funds for a campaign; to have felt every day and every hour the hard eternal pinch and found the question of dollars and cents—and so horridly few of them—mixed up with every experience, with every impulse: that *does* make one mercenary, does make money seem a good beyond all others; which it's quite natural it should! And it's why Linda's of the opinion that a fortune's always a fortune. She knows all about that of your nephew, how it's invested, how it may be expected to increase, exactly on what sort of footing it would enable her to live. She has decided that it's enough, and enough is as good as a feast. She thinks she could lead him by the nose, and I dare say she could. She'll of course make him live in these countries; she hasn't the slightest intention of casting her pearls—but *basta*!" said my friend. "I think she has views upon London, because in England he can hunt and shoot, and that will make him leave her more or less to herself."

"I don't know about his leaving her to herself, but it strikes me that he would like the rest of that matter very much," I returned. "That's not at all a bad programme even from Archie's point of view."

"It's no use thinking of princes," she pursued as if she hadn't heard me. "They're most of them more in want of money even than we. Therefore 'greatness' is out of the question—we really recognised that at an early stage. Your nephew's exactly the sort of young man we've always built upon—if he wasn't, so impossibly, your nephew. From head to foot he was made on purpose. Dear Linda was her mother's own daughter when she recognised him on the spot! One's enough of a prince today when one's the right American: such a wonderful price is set on one's not being the wrong! It does as well as anything and it's a great simplification. If you don't believe me go to London and see."

She had come with me out to the road. I had said I would walk back to Stresa and we stood there in the sweet dark warmth. As I took her hand, bidding her good-night, I couldn't but exhale a compassion. "Poor Linda, poor Linda!"

"Oh she'll live to do better," said Mrs. Pallant.

"How can she do better—since you've described all she finds Archie as perfection?"

She knew quite what she meant. "Ah better for *him*!"

I still had her hand—I still sought her eyes. "How came it you could throw me over—such a woman as you?"

"Well, my friend, if I hadn't thrown you over how could I do this for you?" On which, disengaging herself, she turned quickly away.

VI

I DON'T know how deeply she flushed as she made, in the form of her question, this avowal, which was a retraction of a former denial and the real truth, as I permitted myself to believe; but was aware of the colour of my own cheeks while I took my way to Stresa—a walk of half an hour—in the attenuating night. The new and singular character in which she had appeared to me produced in me an emotion that would have made sitting still in a carriage impossible. This same stress kept me up after I had reached my hotel; as I knew I shouldn't sleep it was useless to go to bed. Long, however, as I deferred this ceremony, Archie had not reappeared when the inn-lights began here and there to be dispensed with. I felt even slightly anxious for him, wondering at possible mischances. Then I reflected that in case of an accident on the lake, that is of his continued absence from Baveno—Mrs. Pallant would already have dispatched me a messenger. It was foolish moreover to suppose anything could have happened to him after putting off from Baveno by water to rejoin me, for the evening was absolutely windless and more than sufficiently clear and the lake as calm as glass. Besides I had unlimited confidence in his power to take care of himself in a much tighter place. I went to my room at last; his own was at some distance, the people of the hotel not having been able—it was the height of the autumn season—to make us contiguous. Before I went to bed I had occasion to ring for a servant, and I then learned by a chance enquiry that my nephew had returned an hour before and had gone straight to his own quarters. I hadn't supposed he could come in without my seeing him—I was wandering about the saloons and terraces—and it had not occurred to me to knock at his door. I had half a mind to do so now—I was so anxious as to how I should find him; but I checked myself, for evidently he had wanted to dodge me. This didn't diminish my curiosity, and I slept even less than I had expected. His so markedly shirking our encounter—for if he hadn't perceived me downstairs he might have looked for me in my room—was a sign that Mrs. Pallant's interview with him would really have come off. What had she said to him? What strong measures had she taken? That almost morbid resolution I still seemed to hear the ring of pointed to conceivable extremities that I shrank from considering. She had spoken of these things while we parted there as something she would do for me; but I had made the mental comment in walking away from her that she hadn't done it yet. It wouldn't truly be done till Archie had truly backed out. Perhaps it was done by this time; his avoiding me seemed almost a proof. That was what I thought of most of the night. I spent a considerable part of it at my window, looking out to the couchant Alps. *Had* he thought better of it?—was he making up his mind to think better of it? There was a strange contradiction in the matter; there were in fact more contradictions than ever. I had taken from Louisa what she told me of Linda, and yet that other idea made me ashamed of my nephew. I was sorry for the girl; I regretted her loss of a great chance, if loss it was to be; and yet I hoped her mother's grand treachery—I didn't know what to call it—had been at least, to her lover, thoroughgoing. It would need strong action in that lady to justify his retreat. For him too I was sorry—if she had made on him the impression she desired. Once or twice I was on the point of getting into my dressing-gown and going forth to condole with him. I was sure he too had jumped up from his bed and was looking out of his window at the everlasting hills.

But I am bound to say that when we met in the morning for breakfast he showed few traces of ravage. Youth is strange; it has resources that later experience seems only to undermine. One of these is the masterly resource of beautiful blankness. As we grow older and cleverer we think that too simple, too crude; we dissimulate more elaborately, but with an effect much less baffling. My young man looked not in the least as if he had lain awake or had something on his mind; and when I asked him what he had done after my premature departure—I explained this by saying I had been tired of waiting for him; fagged with my journey I had wanted to go to bed—he replied: "Oh nothing in particular. I hung about the place; I like it better than this one. We had an awfully jolly time on the water. *I* wasn't in the least fagged." I didn't worry him with questions; it struck me as gross to try to probe his secret. The only indication he gave was on my saying after breakfast that I should go over again to see our friends and my appearing to take for granted he would be glad to come too. Then he let fall that he'd stop at Stresa—he had paid them such a tremendous visit; also that he had arrears of letters. There was a freshness in his scruples about the length of his visits, and I knew something about his correspondence, which consisted entirely of twenty pages every week from his mother. But he soothed my anxiety so little that it was really this yearning that carried me back to Baveno. This time I ordered a conveyance, and as I got into it he stood watching me from the porch of the hotel with his hands in his pockets. Then it was for the first time that I saw in the poor youth's face the expression of a person slightly dazed, slightly foolish even, to whom something disagreeable has happened. Our eyes met as I observed him, and I was on the point of saying "You had really better come with me" when he turned away. He went into the house as to escape my call. I said to myself that he had been indeed warned off, but that it wouldn't take much to bring him back.

The servant to whom I spoke at Baveno described my friends as in a summer-house in the garden, to which he led the way. The place at large had an empty air; most of the inmates of the hotel were dispersed on the lake, on the hills, in picnics, excursions, visits to the Borromean Islands. My guide was so far right as that Linda was in the summer-house, but she was there alone. On finding this the case I stopped short, rather awkwardly—I might have been, from the way I suddenly felt, an unmasked hypocrite, a proved conspirator against her security and honour. But there was no embarrassment in lovely Linda; she looked up with a cry of pleasure from the book she was reading and held out her hand with engaging frankness. I felt again as if I had no right to that favour, which I pretended not to have noticed. This gave no chill, however, to her pretty manner; she moved a roll of tapestry off the bench so that I might sit down; she praised the place as a delightful shady corner. She had never been fresher, fairer, kinder; she made her mother's awful talk about her a hideous dream. She told me her mother was coming to join her; she had remained indoors to write a letter. One couldn't write out there, though it was so nice in other respects: the table refused to stand firm. They too then had pretexts of letters between them—I judged this a token that the situation was tense. It was the only one nevertheless that Linda gave: like Archie she was young enough to carry it off. She had been used to seeing us always together, yet she made no comment on my having come over without him. I waited in vain for her to speak of this—it would only be natural; her omission couldn't but have a sense. At last I remarked that my nephew was very unsociable that morning; I had expected him to join me, but he hadn't seemed to see the attraction.

"I'm very glad. You can tell him that if you like," said Linda Pallant.

I wondered at her. "If I tell him he'll come at once."

"Then don't tell him; I don't want him to come. He stayed too long last night," she went on, "and kept me out on the water till I don't know what o'clock. That sort of thing isn't done here, you know, and every one was shocked when we came back—or rather, you see, when we didn't! I begged him to bring me in, but he wouldn't. When we did return—I almost had to take the oars myself—I felt as if every one had been sitting up to time us, to stare at us. It was awfully awkward."

These words much impressed me; and as I have treated the reader to most of the reflexions—some of them perhaps rather morbid—in which I indulged on the subject of this young lady and her mother, I may as well complete the record and let him know that I now wondered whether Linda—candid and accomplished maiden—entertained the graceful thought of strengthening her hold of Archie by attempting to prove he had "compromised" her. "Ah no doubt that was the reason he had a bad conscience last evening!" I made answer. "When he came back to Stresa he sneaked off to his room; he wouldn't look me in the face."

But my young lady was not to be ruffled. "Mamma was so vexed that she took him apart and gave him a scolding. And to punish *me* she sent me straight to bed. She has very old-fashioned ideas—haven't you, mamma?" she added, looking over my head at Mrs. Pallant, who had just come in behind me.

I forget how her mother met Linda's appeal; Louisa stood there with two letters, sealed and addressed, in her hand. She greeted me gaily and then asked her daughter if she were possessed of postage-stamps. Linda consulted a well-worn little pocket-book and confessed herself destitute; whereupon her mother gave her the letters with the request that she would go into the hotel, buy the proper stamps at the office, carefully affix them and put the letters into the box. She was to pay for the stamps, not have them put on the bill—a preference for which Mrs. Pallant gave reasons. I had bought some at Stresa that morning and was on the point of offering them when, apparently having guessed my intention, the elder lady silenced me with a look. Linda announced without reserve that she hadn't money and Louisa then fumbled for a franc. When she had found and bestowed it the girl kissed her before going off with the letters.

"Darling mother, you haven't any too many of them, have you?" she murmured; and she gave me, sidelong, as she left us, the prettiest half-comical, half-pitiful smile.

"She's amazing—she's amazing," said Mrs. Pallant as we looked at each other.

"Does she know what you've done?"

"She knows I've done something and she's making up her mind what it is. She'll satisfy herself in the course of the next twenty-four hours—if your nephew doesn't come back. I think I can promise you he won't."

"And won't she ask you?"

"Never!"

"Shan't you tell her? Can you sit down together in this summer-house, this divine day, with such a dreadful thing as that between you?"

My question found my friend quite ready. "Don't you remember what I told you about our relations—that everything was implied between us and nothing expressed? The ideas we have had in common—our perpetual worldliness, our always looking out for chances—are not the sort of thing that can be uttered conveniently between persons who like to keep up forms, as we both do: so that, always, if we've understood each other it has been enough. We shall understand each other now, as we've always done, and nothing will be changed. There has always been something between us that couldn't be talked about."

"Certainly, she's amazing—she's amazing," I repeated; "but so are you." And then I asked her what she had said to my boy.

She seemed surprised. "Hasn't he told you?"

"No, and he never will."

"I'm glad of that," she answered simply.

"But I'm not sure he won't come back. He didn't this morning, but he had already half a mind to."

"That's your imagination," my companion said with her fine authority. "If you knew what I told him you'd be sure."

"And you won't let me know?"

"Never, dear friend."

"And did he believe you?"

"Time will show—but I think so."

"And how did you make it plausible to him that you should take so unnatural a course?"

For a moment she said nothing, only looking at me. Then at last: "I told him the truth."

"The truth?"

"Take him away—take him away!" she broke out. "That's why I got rid of Linda, to tell you you mustn't stay—you must leave Stresa tomorrow. This time it's you who must do it. I can't fly from you again—it costs too much!" And she smiled strangely.

"Don't be afraid; don't be afraid. We'll break camp again tomorrow—ah me! But I want to go myself," I added. I took her hand in farewell, but spoke again while I held it. "The way you put it, about Linda, was very bad?"

"It was horrible."

I turned away—I felt indeed that I couldn't stay. She kept me from going to the hotel, as I might meet Linda coming back, which I was far from wishing to do, and showed me another way into the road. Then she turned round to meet her daughter and spend the rest of the morning there with her, spend it before the bright blue lake and the snowy crests of the Alps. When I reached Stresa again I found my young man had gone off to Milan—to see the cathedral, the servant said—leaving a message for me to the effect that, as he shouldn't be back for a day or two, though there were numerous trains, he had taken a few clothes. The next day I received telegram-notice that he had determined to go on to Venice and begged I would forward the rest of his luggage. "Please don't come after me," this missive added; "I want to be alone; I shall do no harm." That sounded pathetic to me, in the light of what I knew, and I was glad to leave him to his own devices. He proceeded to Venice and I recrossed the Alps. For several weeks after this I expected to discover that he had rejoined Mrs. Pallant; but when we met that November in Paris I saw he had nothing to hide from me save indeed the secret of what our extraordinary friend had said to him. This he concealed from me then and has concealed ever since. He returned to America before Christmas—when I felt the crisis over. I've never again seen the wronger of my youth. About a year after our more recent adventure her daughter Linda married, in London, a young Englishman, the heir to a large fortune, a fortune acquired by his father in some prosaic but flourishing industry. Mrs. Gimingham's admired photographs—such is Linda's present name—may be obtained from the principal stationers. I am convinced her mother was sincere. My nephew has not even yet changed his state, my sister at last thinks it high time. I put before her as soon as I next saw her the incidents here recorded, and—such is the inconsequence of women—nothing can exceed her reprobation of Louisa Pallant.

A NOTE ON

LOUISA PALLANT
(1888)

WITH "Louisa Pallant" we begin to dig a little deeper into human motives. "Four Meetings" and "A Bundle of Letters" are intended to touch or amuse, but hardly to stir us. "Louisa Pallant," however, despite the surface smoothness of its worldly —one might almost say gossipy—style, cuts into life's quick tissue. In Jamesian fashion it does so by means of a narrative in which nothing violent—indeed, hardly anything very definite —occurs. A rather silly young man is attracted to a young woman, and then, warned off by her mother, flees from her: such is the ostensible action. The true action takes the form of a moral crisis, the story being a bitter tragi-comedy of conscience.

We encounter here two new Jamesian themes that are to be worked and reworked in dozens of his fictions. Theme number one is that of the money-marriage, theme number two that of the nature of evil. The first theme, depending for its relevance on the structure of a particular society, is mundane and evanescent. The second theme, depending for its relevance on the moral structure of man, is spiritual and permanent. (The interlocking of two themes of broadly differing intensities characterizes James.) It is the second that really interests him, the first being used in part for its decoy value, its power to engage the reader's immediate interest.

I do not mean to imply that James was not genuinely concerned with the problem of the money-marriage. On the contrary, it fascinated him to a point where he often overworked it. But in his defense we must remember that his concern was with a reality, if with one perhaps less salient in our day than in his. Further, we must remember that his concern was not frivolous or worldly, but deeply moral. The same critic who will praise Theodore Dreiser for his monumental novels that show how modern man makes money (*The Titan, The Financier*) may fail to perceive that the stories of Henry James often devote themselves with no less conscientiousness to the reverse of the picture. They show how modern woman, in the only way permitted by our diseased society, makes money—that is, by marrying it. I have vaguely felt that those who find disagreeable James's obsessive interest in the marriage of economic convenience are displeased less by the theme itself than by the fact that the sums of money involved are large rather than small. The story of the poor typist who marries the bookkeeper because, tired of insecurity, she covets his forty weekly dollars—this is searching realism. But the story of the fortune-hunting, predatory female who sinks her talons into an American millionaire—this is cynical snobbery. In truth, however, the stories may be of equal value (depending on the intensity of the author's insight) and they testify in much the same way to one of the sicknesses of an acquisitive society.

Through a number of James's larger works runs "Louisa Pallant's" major theme: the existence and operation of evil. Here the evil lives not so much in a person (Linda Pallant) as in the relation between Linda and her mother, Louisa. Louisa is a Frankenstein who, having created a monster, repents of her creature.

The story is one of desperate expiation. While it seems to narrate an episode in the life of Linda, it really opens up the whole bitter meaning of the life of her mother. Louisa's motivations are not transparent; there lies part of the tale's fascination. It is only after the reader has himself done some mental work that he perceives what they are. It is only on reflection that the full meaning of Louisa's anguished cry—"Ah, my friend, if I hadn't thrown you over I couldn't do this for you."—breaks on the reader. That cry is the center of the story, and everything else but a preparation for it. It is Louisa's rebellion against the evil in herself. Note, however, that James never relaxes in the direction of mere moral optimism. The wicked irony of the story's concluding sentence bids us remain aware that the world is, for the most part, still incapable of understanding the purity of Louisa's expiatory gesture.

Finally, "Louisa Pallant" exhibits another of James's interests —the character that we may call "the finished product." Linda is the result of training, of calculation, as is Christina Light in "Roderick Hudson," as is the Prince in "The Golden Bowl." Perhaps in portraying these finished products James consciously merged two of his dominating obsessions—his obsession with people, his obsession with works of art.

THE LIAR

I

The train was half an hour late and the drive from the station longer than he had supposed, so that when he reached the house its inmates had dispersed to dress for dinner and he was conducted straight to his room. The curtains were drawn in this asylum, the candles lighted, the fire bright, and when the servant had quickly put out his clothes the comfortable little place might have been one of the minor instruments in a big orchestra—seemed to promise a pleasant house, a various party, talk, acquaintances, affinities, to say nothing of very good cheer. He was too occupied with his profession often to pay country visits, but he had heard people who had more time for them speak of establishments where "they do you very well." He foresaw that the proprietors of Stayes would do him very well. In his bedroom on such occasions he always looked first at the books on the shelf and the prints on the walls; these things would give in a sort the social, the conversational value of his hosts. Though he had but little time to devote to them on this occasion a cursory inspection assured him that if the literature, as usual, was mainly American and humorous the art consisted neither of the water-colour studies of the children nor of "goody" engravings. The walls were adorned with old-fashioned lithographs, mostly portraits of country gentlemen with high collars and riding-gloves: this suggested—and it was encouraging—that the tradition of portraiture was held in esteem. There was the customary novel of Mr. Le Fanu for the bedside, the ideal reading in a country house for the hours after midnight. Oliver Lyon could scarcely forbear beginning it while he buttoned his shirt.

Perhaps that is why he not only found every one assembled in the hall when he went down, but saw from the way the move to dinner was instantly made that they had been waiting for him. There was no delay to introduce him to a lady, for he went out unimportant and in a group of unmated men. The men, straggling behind, sidled and edged as usual at the door of the dining-room, and the *dénouement* of this little comedy was that he came to his place last of all. This made him suppose himself in a sufficiently distinguished company, for if he had been humiliated—which he was not—he couldn't have consoled himself with the reflection that such a fate was natural to an obscure and struggling young artist. He could no longer think of himself as notably young, alas, and if his position wasn't so brilliant as it ought to be he could no longer justify it by calling it a struggle. He was appreciably "known" and was now apparently in a society of the known if not of the knowing. This idea added to the curiosity with which he looked up and down the long table as he settled himself in his place.

It was a numerous party—five-and-twenty people; rather an odd occasion to have proposed to him, as he thought. He wouldn't be surrounded by the quiet that ministers to good work; however, it had never interfered with his work to feel the human scene enclose it as a ring. And though he didn't know this, it was never quiet at Stayes. When he was working well he found himself in that happy state—the happiest of all for an artist—in which things in general interweave with his particular web and make it thicker and stronger and more many-coloured. Moreover there was an exhilaration (he had felt it before) in the rapid change of scene—the jump, in the dusk of the afternoon, from foggy London and his familiar studio to a centre of festivity in the middle of Hertfordshire and a drama half-acted, a drama of pretty women and noted men and wonderful orchids in silver jars. He observed as a not unimportant fact that one of the pretty women was beside him: a gentleman sat on his other hand. But he appraised his neighbours little as yet: he was busy with the question of Sir David, whom he had never seen and about whom he naturally was curious.

Evidently, however, Sir David was not at dinner, a circumstance sufficiently explained by the other circumstance forming our friend's principal knowledge of him—his being ninety years of age. Oliver Lyon had looked forward with pleasure to painting a picked nonagenarian, so that though the old man's absence from table was something of a disappointment—it was an opportunity the less to observe him before going to work—it seemed a sign that he was rather a sacred and perhaps therefore an impressive relic. Lyon looked at his son with the greater interest—wondered if the glazed bloom of such a cheek had been transmitted from Sir David. That would be jolly to paint in the old man—the withered ruddiness of a winter apple, especially if the eye should be still alive and the white hair carry out the frosty look. Arthur Ashmore's hair had a midsummer glow, but Lyon was glad his call had been for the great rather than the small bearer of the name, in spite of his never having seen the one and of the other's being seated there before him now in the very highest relief of impersonal hospitality.

Arthur Ashmore was a fresh-coloured thick-necked English gentleman, but he was just not a subject; he might have been a farmer and he might have been a banker; you could scarcely paint him in character. His wife didn't make up the amount; she was a large bright negative woman who had the same air as her husband of being somehow tremendously new; an appearance as of fresh varnish—Lyon could scarcely tell whether it came from her complexion or from her clothes—so that one felt she ought to sit in a gilt frame and be dealt with by reference to a catalogue or a price-list. It was as if she were already rather a bad though expensive portrait, knocked off by an eminent hand, and Lyon had no wish to copy that work. The pretty woman on his right was engaged with her neighbour, while the gentleman on his other side looked detached and desperate, so that he had time to lose himself in his favourite diversion of watching face after face. This amusement gave him the greatest pleasure he knew, and he often thought it a mercy the human mask did interest him and that it had such a need, frequently even in spite of itself, to testify, since he was to make his living by reproducing it. Even if Arthur Ashmore wouldn't be inspiring to paint (a certain anxiety rose in him lest, should he make a hit with her father-in-law, Mrs. Arthur should take it into her head that he had now proved himself worthy to handle her husband); even if he had looked a little less like a page—fine as to print and margin—without punctuation, he would still be a refreshing iridescent surface. But the gentleman four persons off—what was he? Would he be a subject, or was his face only the legible door-plate of his identity, burnished with punctual washing and shaving—the least thing that was decent you might know him by?

This face arrested Oliver Lyon, striking him at first as very handsome. The gentleman might still be called young, and his features were regular: he had a plentiful fair moustache that curled up at the ends, a brilliant gallant almost adventurous air, together with a big shining breastpin in the middle of his shirt. He appeared a fine satisfied soul, and Lyon perceived that wherever he rested his friendly eye there fell an influence as pleasant as the September sun—as if he could make grapes and pears or even human affection ripen by looking at them. What was odd in him was a certain mixture of the correct and the extravagant: as if he were an adventurer imitating a gentleman with rare perfection, or a gentleman who had taken a fancy to go about with hidden arms. He might have been a dethroned prince or the war-correspondent of a newspaper: he represented both enterprise and tradition, good manners and bad taste. Lyon at length fell into conversation with the lady beside him—they dispensed, as he had had to dispense at dinner-parties before, with an introduction—by asking who this personage might be.

"Oh Colonel Capadose, don't you know?" Lyon didn't know and asked for further information. His neighbour had a sociable manner and evidently was accustomed to quick transitions; she turned from her other interlocutor with the promptness of a good cook who lifts the cover of the next saucepan. "He has been a great deal in India—isn't he rather celebrated?" she put it. Lyon confessed he had never heard of him, and she went on: "Well, perhaps he isn't; but he says he is, and if you think it that's just the same, isn't it?"

"If *you* think it?"

"I mean if he thinks it—that's just as good, I suppose."

"Do you mean if he thinks he has done things he hasn't?"

"Oh dear no; because I never really know the difference between what people say—! He's exceedingly clever and amusing—quite the cleverest person in the house, unless indeed you're more so. But that I can't tell yet, can I? I only know about the people I know; I think that's celebrity enough!"

"Enough for them?"

"Oh I see you're clever. Enough for me! But I've heard of you," the lady went on. "I know your pictures; I admire them. But I don't think you look like them."

"They're mostly portraits," Lyon said; "and what I usually try for is not my own resemblance."

"I see what you mean. But they've much more colour. Don't you suppose Vandyke's things tell a lot about him? And now you're going to do some one here?"

"I've been invited to do Sir David. I'm rather disappointed at not seeing him this evening."

"Oh he goes to bed at some unnatural hour—eight o'clock, after porridge and milk. You know he's rather an old mummy."

"An old mummy?" Oliver Lyon repeated.

"I mean he wears half a dozen waistcoats and sits by the fire. He's always cold."

"I've never seen him and never seen any portrait or photograph of him," Lyon said. "I'm surprised at his never having had anything done—at their waiting all these years."

"Ah that's because he was afraid, you know; it was his pet superstition. He was sure that if anything were done he would die directly afterwards. He has only consented today."

"He's ready to die then?"

"Oh now he's so old he doesn't care."

"Well, I hope I shan't kill him," said Lyon. "It was rather unnatural of his son to send for me."

"Oh they've nothing to gain—everything is theirs already!" his companion rejoined, as if she took this speech quite literally. Her talkativeness was systematic—she fraternised as seriously as she might have played whist. "They do as they like—they fill the house with people—they have *carte blanche*."

"I see—but there's still the 'title.' "

"Yes, but what's the tuppenny title?"

Our artist broke into laughter at this, whereat his companion stared. Before he had recovered himself she was scouring the plain with her other neighbour. The gentleman on his left at last risked an observation as if it had been a move at chess, exciting in Lyon however a comparative wantonness. This personage played his part with difficulty: he uttered a remark as a lady fires a pistol, looking the other way. To catch the ball Lyon had to bend his ear, and this movement led to his observing a handsome creature who was seated on the same side, beyond his interlocutor. Her profile was presented to him and at first he was only struck with its beauty; then it produced an impression still more agreeable—a sense of undimmed remembrance and intimate association. He had not recognised her on the instant only because he had so little expected to see her there; he had not seen her anywhere for so long, and no news of her now ever came to him. She was often in his thoughts, but she had passed out of his life. He thought of her twice a week; that may be called often, even for fidelity, when it has been kept up a dozen years. The moment after he recognised her he felt how true it was that only she could carry that head, the most charming head in the world and of which there could never be a replica. She was leaning forward a little; she remained in profile, slightly turned to some further neighbour. She was listening, but her eyes moved, and after a moment Lyon followed their direction. They rested on the gentleman who had been described to him as Colonel Capadose—rested, he made out, as with an habitual visible complacency. This was not strange, for the Colonel was unmistakably formed to attract the sympathetic gaze of woman; but Lyon felt it as the source of an ache that she could let *him* look at her so long without giving him a glance. There was nothing between them today and he had no rights, but she must have known he was coming—it was of course no such tremendous event, but she couldn't have been staying in the house without some echo of it—and it wasn't natural this should absolutely fail to affect her.

She was looking at Colonel Capadose as if she had been in love with him—an odd business for the proudest, most reserved of women. But doubtless it was all right if her husband was satisfied: he had heard indefinitely, years before, that she was married, and he took for granted—as he had not heard—the presence of the happy man on whom she had conferred what she had refused to a poor art-student at Munich. Colonel Capadose seemed aware of nothing, and this fact, incongruously enough, rather annoyed Lyon than pleased him. Suddenly the lady moved her head, showing her full face to our hero. He was so prepared with a greeting that he instantly smiled, as a shaken jug overflows; but she made no response, turned away again and sank back in her chair. All her face said in that instant was "You see I'm as handsome as ever." To which he mentally subjoined: "Yes, and as much good as ever it does me!" He asked the young man beside him if he knew who that beautiful being was—the fourth person beyond him. The young man leaned forward, considered and then said: "I think she's Mrs. Capadose."

"Do you mean his wife—that fellow's?" And Lyon indicated the subject of the information given him by his other neighbour.

"Oh is *he* Mr. Capadose?" said the young man, to whom it appeared to mean little. He admitted his ignorance of these values and explained it by saying that there were so many people and he had come but the day before. What was definite to our friend was that Mrs. Capadose was in love with her husband—so that he wished more than ever he might have married her.

"She's very fond and true," he found himself saying three minutes later, with a small ironic ring, to the lady on his right. He added that he meant Mrs. Capadose.

"Ah you know her then?"

"I knew her once upon a time—when I was living abroad."

"Why then were you asking me about her husband?"

"Precisely for that reason." Lyon was clear. "She married after that—I didn't even know her present name."

"How then do you know it now?"

"This gentleman has just told me—he appears to know."

"I didn't know he knew anything," said the lady with a crook that took him in.

"I don't think he knows anything but that."

"Then you've found out for yourself that she's—what do you call it?—tender and true? What do you mean by that?"

"Ah you mustn't question me—I want to put things to *you,*" Lyon said. "How do you all like her here?"

"You ask too much! I can only speak for myself. I think she's hard."

"That's only because she's honest and straightforward."

"Do you mean I like people in proportion as they deceive?"

"I think we all do, so long as we don't find them out," Lyon said. "And then there's something in her face—a sort of nobleness of the Roman type, in spite of her having such English eyes. In fact she's English down to the ground; but her complexion, her low forehead and that beautiful close little wave in her dark hair make her look like a transfigured Trasteverina."

"Yes, and she always sticks pins and daggers into her head, to bring out that effect. I must say I like her husband better: he *gives* so much."

"Well, when I knew her there was no comparison that could injure her," Lyon richly sighed. "She was altogether the most delightful thing in Munich."

"In Munich?"

"Her people lived there; they weren't rich—in pursuit of economy in fact, and Munich was very cheap. Her father was the younger son of some noble house; he had married a second time and had a lot of little mouths to feed. She was the child of the first wife and didn't like her stepmother, but she was charming to her little brothers and sisters. I once made a sketch of her as Werther's Charlotte cutting bread and butter while the children clustered round her. All the artists in the place were in love with her, but she wouldn't look at 'the likes' of us. She was too proud—I grant you that, but not stuck up nor young-ladyish, only perfectly simple and frank about it. She used to remind me of Thackeray's Ethel Newcome. She told me she must marry well: it was the one thing she could do for her family. I suppose you'd say she *has* married well."

"She told *you*?" smiled Lyon's neighbour.

"Oh of course I proposed to her too. But she evidently thinks so herself!" he added. "I mean that it's no mistake."

When the ladies left the table the host as usual bade the gentlemen draw together, so that Lyon found himself opposite to Colonel Capadose. The conversation was mainly about the "run," for it had apparently been a great day in the hunting-field. Most of the men had a comment or an anecdote, several had many; but the Colonel's pleasant voice was the most audible in the chorus. It was a bright and fresh but masculine organ, just such a voice as, to Lyon's sense, such a "fine man" ought to have had. It appeared from his allusions that he was a very straight rider, which was also very much what Lyon would have expected. Not that he swaggered, for his points were all quietly and casually made; but they had all to do with some dangerous experiment or close shave. Lyon noted after a little that the attention paid by the company to the Colonel's remarks was not in direct proportion to the interest they seemed to offer; the result of which was that the speaker, who noticed that *he* at least was listening, began to treat him as his particular auditor and to fix his eyes on him as he talked. Lyon had nothing to do but to look sympathetic and assent—the narrator building on the tribute so rendered. A neighbouring squire had had an accident; he had come a cropper in an awkward place—just at the finish—with consequences that looked grave. He had struck his head; he remained insensible up to the last accounts: there had evidently been concussion of the brain. There was some exchange of views as to his recovery, how soon it would take place or whether it would take place at all; which led the Colonel to confide to our artist across the table that *he* shouldn't despair of a fellow even if he didn't come round for weeks—for weeks and weeks and weeks—for months, almost for years. He leaned forward (Lyon leaned forward to listen) and mentioned that he knew from personal experience how little limit there really was to the time a fellah might lie like a stone without being the worse for it. It had happened to him in Ireland years before; he had been pitched out of a dogcart, had turned a sheer somersault and landed on his head. They had thought he was dead, but he wasn't; they had carried him first to the nearest cabin, where he lay for some days with the pigs, and then to an inn in a neighbouring town—it was a near thing they hadn't put him underground. He had been completely insensible—without a ray of recognition of any human thing—for three whole months; hadn't had a glimmer of consciousness of any blessed thing. It had been touch and go to that degree that they couldn't come near him, couldn't feed him, could scarcely look at him. Then one day he had opened his eyes—as fit as a flea!

"I give you my honour it had done me good—it rested my brain." He conveyed, though without excessive emphasis, that with an intelligence so active as his these periods of repose were providential. Lyon was struck by his story, but wanted to ask if he hadn't shammed a little; not in relating it, only in keeping so quiet. He hesitated however, in time, to betray a doubt—he was so impressed with the tone in which Colonel Capadose pronounced it the turn of a hair that they hadn't buried him alive. That had happened to a friend of his in India—a fellow who was supposed to have died of jungle-fever and whom they clapped into a coffin. He was going on to recite the further fate of this unfortunate gentleman when Mr. Ashmore said a word and every one rose for the move to the drawing-room. Lyon noticed that by this time no one was heeding his new friend's prodigies. These two came round on either side of the table and met while their companions hung back for each other.

"And do you mean your comrade was literally buried alive?" asked Lyon in some suspense.

The Colonel looked at him as with the thread of the conversation already lost. Then his face brightened—and when it brightened it was doubly handsome. "Upon my soul he was shoved into the ground!"

"And left there?"

"Left there till I came and hauled him out."

"*You* came?"

"I dreamed about him—it's the most extraordinary story: I heard him calling to me in the night. I took on myself to dig him up. You know there are people in India—a kind of beastly race, the ghouls—who violate graves. I had a sort of presentiment that they would get at him first. I rode straight, I can tell you; and, by Jove, a couple of them had just broken ground! Crack—crack from a couple of barrels, and they showed me their heels as you may believe. Would you credit that I took him out myself? The air brought him round and he was none the worse. He has got his pension—he came home the other day. He'd do anything for me," the narrator added.

"He called to you in the night?" said Lyon, much thrilled.

"That's the interesting point. Now *what was it?* It wasn't his ghost, because he wasn't dead. It wasn't himself, because he couldn't. It was some confounded brain-wave or other! You see India's a strange country—there's an element of the mysterious: the air's full of things you can't explain."

They passed out of the dining-room, and this master of anecdote, who went among the first, was separated from his newest victim; but a minute later, before they reached the drawing-room, he had come back. "Ashmore tells me who you are. Of course I've often heard of you. I'm very glad to make your acquaintance. My wife used to know you."

"I'm glad she remembers me. I recognised her at dinner and was afraid she didn't."

"Ah I dare say she was ashamed," said the Colonel with genial ease.

"Ashamed of me?" Lyon replied in the same key.

"Wasn't there something about a picture? Yes; you painted her portrait."

"Many times," Lyon said; "and she may very well have been ashamed of what I made of her."

"Well, *I* wasn't, my dear sir; it was the sight of that picture, which you were so good as to present to her, that made me first fall in love with her."

Our friend lived over again for a few seconds a lost felicity. "Do you mean one with the children—cutting bread and butter?"

"Bread and butter? Bless me, no—vine-leaves and a leopard-skin. A regular Bacchante."

"Ah yes," said Lyon; "I remember. It was the first decent portrait I painted. I should be curious to see it today."

"Don't ask her to show it to you—she'll feel it awkward," the Colonel went on.

"Awkward?"—our artist wondered.

"We parted with it—in the most disinterested manner," the other laughed. "An old friend of my wife's—her family had known him intimately when they lived in Germany—took the most extraordinary fancy to it: the Grand Duke of Silberstadt-Schreckenstein, don't you know? He came out to Bombay while we were there and he spotted your picture (you know he's one of the greatest collectors in Europe) and made such eyes at it that, upon my word—it happened to be his birthday—she told him he might have it to get rid of him. He was perfectly enchanted—but we miss the picture."

"It's very good of you," Lyon said. "If it's in a great collection—a work of my incompetent youth—I'm infinitely honoured."

"Oh he keeps it in one of his castles; I don't know which—you know he has so many. He sent us, before he left India—to return the compliment—a magnificent old vase."

"That was more than the thing was worth," Lyon modestly urged.

Colonel Capadose gave no heed to this observation; his thoughts now seemed elsewhere. After a moment, however, he said: "If you'll come and see us in town she'll show you the vase." And as they passed into the drawing-room he gave his fellow visitor a friendly propulsion. "Go and speak to her; there she is. She'll be delighted."

Oliver Lyon took but a few steps into the wide saloon; he stood there a moment looking at the bright composition of the lamplit group of fair women, the single figures, the great setting of white and gold, the panels of old damask, in the centre of each of which was a single celebrated picture. There was a subdued lustre in the scene and an air as of the shining trains of dresses tumbled over the carpet. At the furthest end of the room sat Mrs. Capadose, rather isolated; she was on a small sofa with an empty place beside her. Lyon couldn't flatter himself she had been keeping it for him; her failure to take up his shy signal at table contradicted this, but his desire to join her was too strong. Moreover he had her husband's sanction; so he crossed the room, stepping over the tails of gowns, and stood before her with his appeal. "I hope you don't mean to repudiate me."

She looked up at him with frank delight. "I'm so glad to see you. I was charmed when I heard you were coming."

"I tried to get a smile from you at dinner—but I couldn't," Lyon returned.

"I didn't see—I didn't understand. Besides, I hate smirking and telegraphing. Also I'm very shy—you won't have forgotten that. Now we can communicate comfortably." And she made a better place for him on her sofa. He sat down and they had a talk that smote old chords in him; the sense of what he had loved her for came back to him, as well as not a little of the actual effect of that cause. She was still the least spoiled beauty he had ever seen, with an absence of the "wanton" or of any insinuating art that resembled an omitted faculty: she affected him at moments as some fine creature from an asylum—a surprising deaf-mute or one of the operative blind. Her noble pagan head gave her privileges that she neglected, and when people were admiring her brow she was wondering if there were a good fire in her bedroom, or at the very most in theirs. She was simple, kind and good; inexpressive but not inhuman, not stupid. Now and again she dropped something, some small fruit of discrimination, that might have come from a mind, have been an impression at first hand. She had no imagination and only the simpler feelings, but several of these had grown up to full size. Lyon talked of the old days in Munich, reminded her of incidents, pleasures and pains, asked her about her father and the others; and she spoke in return of her being so impressed with his own fame, his brilliant position in the world, that she hadn't felt sure he would notice her or that his mute appeal at table was meant for her. This was plainly a perfectly truthful speech—she was incapable of any other—and he was affected by such humility on the part of a woman whose grand line was unique. Her father was dead; one of her brothers was in the navy and the other on a ranch in America; two of her sisters were married and the youngest just coming out and very pretty. She didn't mention her stepmother. She questioned him on his own story, and he described it mainly as his not having married.

"Oh you ought to," she answered. "It's the best thing."

"I like that—from you!"

"Why not from me? I'm very happy."

"That's just why I can't be," he returned. "It's cruel of you to praise your state. But I've had the pleasure of making the acquaintance of your husband. We had a good bit of talk in the other room."

"You must know him better—you must know him really well," said Mrs. Capadose.

"I'm sure that the further you go the more you find. But he makes a fine show too."

She rested her good grey eyes on this recovered "backer." "Don't you think he's handsome?"

"Handsome and clever and entertaining. You see I'm generous."

"Yes; you must know him well," Mrs. Capadose repeated.

"He has seen a great deal of life," said her companion.

"Ah we've been in so many situations. You must see my little girl. She's nine years old—she's too beautiful."

Lyon rose fully to the occasion. "You must bring her to my studio some day—I should like to paint her."

"Oh don't speak of that," said Mrs. Capadose. "It reminds me of something so distressing."

"I hope you don't mean of when *you* used to sit to me—though that may well have bored you."

"It's not what you did—it's what we've done. It's a confession I must make—it's a weight on my mind! I mean on the subject of the lovely picture you gave me—it used to be so much admired. When you come to see me in London—and I count on your doing that very soon—I shall see you looking all round. I can't tell you I keep it in my own room because I love it so, for the simple reason—" It fairly pulled her up.

"Because you can't tell wicked lies," said Lyon.

"No, I can't. So before you ask for it—"

"Oh I know you parted with it—the blow has already fallen," Lyon interrupted.

"Ah then you've heard? I was sure you would! But do you know what we got for it? Two hundred pounds."

"You might have got much more," the artist smiled.

"That seemed a great deal at the time. We were in want of the money—it was a good while ago, when we first married. Our means were very small then, but fortunately that has changed rather for the better. We had the chance; it really seemed a big sum, and I'm afraid we jumped at it. My husband had expectations which have partly come into effect, so that now we do well enough. But meanwhile the picture went."

"Fortunately the original remained. But do you mean that two hundred was the value of the vase?" Lyon asked.

"Of the vase?"

"The beautiful old Indian vase—the Grand Duke's offering."

"The Grand Duke?"

"What's his name?—Silberstadt-Schreckenstein. Your husband mentioned the transaction."

"Oh my husband!" said Mrs. Capadose; and Lyon now saw her change colour.

Not to add to her embarrassment, but to clear up the ambiguity, which he perceived the next moment he had better have left alone, he went on: "He tells me it's now in his collection."

"In the Grand Duke's? Ah you know its reputation? I believe it contains treasures." She was bewildered, but she recovered herself, and Lyon made the mental reflection that for some reason which would seem good when he knew it the husband and the wife had prepared different versions of the same incident. It was true that he didn't exactly see Everina Brant preparing a version; that wasn't her line of old, and indeed there was no such subterfuge in her eyes today. At any rate they both had the matter too much on their conscience. He changed the subject—said Mrs. Capadose must really bring the little girl. He sat with her some time longer and imagined—perhaps too freely—her equilibrium slightly impaired, as if she were annoyed at their having been even for a moment at cross-purposes. This didn't prevent his saying to her at the last, just as the ladies began to gather themselves for bed: "You seem much impressed, from what you say, with my renown and my prosperity, and you are so good as greatly to exaggerate them. Would you have married me if you had known I was destined to success?"

"I did know it."

"*I* didn't, then!"

"You were too modest."

"You didn't think so when I proposed to you."

"Well, if I had married you I couldn't have married *him*—and he's so awfully nice," Mrs. Capadose said. Lyon knew this was her faith—he had learned that at dinner—but it vexed him a little to hear her proclaim it. The gentleman designated by the pronoun came up, amid the prolonged handshaking for good-night, and Mrs. Capadose remarked to her husband as she turned away, "He wants to paint Amy."

"Ah she's a charming child, a most interesting little creature," the Colonel said to Lyon. "She does the most remarkable things."

Mrs. Capadose stopped in the rustling procession that followed the hostess out of the room. "Don't tell him, please don't," she said.

"Don't tell him what?"

"Why, what she does. Let him find out for himself." And she passed on.

"She thinks I swagger about the child—that I bore people," said the Colonel. "I hope you smoke." He appeared ten minutes later in the smoking-room, brilliantly equipped in a suit of crimson foulard covered with little white spots. He gratified Lyon's eye, made him feel that the modern age has its splendour too and its opportunities for costume. If his wife was an antique he was a fine specimen of the period of colour: he might have passed for a Venetian of the sixteenth century. They were a remarkable couple, Lyon thought, and as he looked at the Colonel standing in bright erectness before the chimney-piece and emitting great smoke-puffs he didn't wonder Everina couldn't regret she hadn't married *him*. All the men collected at Stayes were not smokers and some of them had gone to bed. Colonel Capadose remarked that there probably would be a smallish muster, they had had such a hard day's work. That was the worst of a hunting-house—the men were so sleepy after dinner; it was a great sell for the ladies, even for those who hunted themselves, women being so tough that they never showed it. But most fellows revived under the stimulating influences of the smoking-room, and some of them, in this confidence, would turn up yet. Some of the grounds of their confidence—not all—might have been seen in a cluster of glasses and bottles on a table near the fire, which made the great salver and its contents twinkle sociably. The others lurked as yet in various improper corners of the minds of the most loquacious. Lyon was alone with Colonel Capadose for some moments before their companions, in varied eccentricities of uniform, straggled in, and he felt how little loss of vital tissue this wonderful man had to repair.

They talked about the house, Lyon having noticed an oddity of construction in the smoking-room; and the Colonel explained that it consisted of two distinct parts, one of very great antiquity. They were two complete houses in short, the old and the new, each of great extent and each very fine in its way. The two formed together an enormous structure—Lyon must make a point of going all over it. The modern piece had been erected by the old man when he bought the property; oh yes, he had bought it forty years before—it hadn't been in the family: there hadn't been any particular family for it to be in. He had had the good taste not to spoil the original house—he had not touched it beyond what was just necessary for joining it on. It was very curious indeed—a most irregular rambling mysterious pile, where they now and then discovered a walled-up room or a secret staircase. To his mind it was deadly depressing, however; even the modern additions, splendid as they were, failed to make it cheerful. There was some story of how a skeleton had been found years before, during some repairs, under a stone slab of the floor of one of the passages; but the family were rather shy of its being talked about. The place they were in was of course in the old part, which contained after all some of the best rooms: he had an idea it had been the primitive kitchen, half-modernised at some intermediate period.

"My room is in the old part too then—I'm very glad," Lyon said. "It's very comfortable and contains all the latest conveniences, but I observed the depth of the recess of the door and the evident antiquity of the corridor and staircase—the first short one—after I came out. That panelled corridor is admirable; it looks as if it stretched away, in its brown dimness (the lamps didn't seem to me to make much impression on it) for half a mile."

"Oh don't go to the end of it!" the Colonel warningly smiled.

"Does it lead to the haunted room?" Lyon asked.

His companion looked at him a moment. "Ah you know about that?"

"No, I don't speak from knowledge, only from hope. I've never had any luck—I've never stayed in a spooky house. The places I go to are always as safe as Charing Cross. I want to see—whatever there is, the regular thing. *Is* there a ghost here?"

"Of course there is—a rattling good one."

"And have you seen him?"

"Oh don't ask me what *I've* seen—I should tax your credulity. I don't like to talk of these things. But there are two or three as bad—that is, as good!—rooms as you'll find anywhere."

"Do you mean in my corridor?" Lyon asked.

"I believe the worst is at the far end. But you'd be ill-advised to sleep there."

"Ill-advised?"

"Until you've finished your job. You'll get letters of importance the next morning and take the 10.20."

"Do you mean I shall invent a pretext for running away?"

"Unless you're braver than almost any one has ever been. They don't often put people to sleep there, but sometimes the house is so crowded that they have to. The same thing always happens—ill-concealed agitation at the breakfast-table and letters of the greatest importance. Of course it's a bachelor's room, and my wife and I are at the other end of the house. But we saw the comedy three days ago—the day after we got here. A young fellow had been put there—I forget his name—the house was so full; and the usual consequence followed. Letters at breakfast—an awfully queer face—an urgent call to town—so sorry his visit was cut short. Ashmore and his wife looked at each other and off the poor devil went."

"Ah that wouldn't suit me; I must do my job," said Lyon. "But do they mind your speaking of it? Some people who've a good ghost are very proud of it, you know."

What answer Colonel Capadose was on the point of making to this query our hero was not to learn, for at that moment their host had walked into the room accompanied by three or four of their fellow guests. Lyon was conscious that he was partly answered by the Colonel's not going on with the subject. This on the other hand was rendered natural by the fact that one of the gentlemen appealed to him for an opinion on a point under discussion, something to do with the everlasting history of the day's run. To Lyon himself Mr. Ashmore began to talk, expressing his regret for the delay of this pleasure. The topic that suggested itself was naturally that most closely connected with the motive of the artist's visit. The latter observed that it was a great disadvantage to him not to have had some preliminary acquaintance with Sir David—in most cases he found this so important. But the present sitter was so far advanced in life that there was doubtless no time to lose. "Oh I can tell you all about him," said Mr. Ashmore; and for half an hour he told him a good deal. It was very interesting as well as a little extravagant, and Lyon felt sure he was a fine old boy to have endeared himself so to a son who was evidently not a gusher. At last he got up—he said he must go to bed if he wished to be fresh for his work in the morning. To which his host replied "Then you must take your candle; the lights are out; past this hour I don't keep my servants up."

In a moment Lyon had his glimmering taper in hand, and as he was leaving the room—he didn't disturb the others with a good-night, they were absorbed in the lemon-squeezer and the soda-water cork—he remembered other occasions on which he had made his way to bed alone through a darkened country-house: such occasions had not been rare, for he was almost always the first to leave the smoking-room. If he hadn't stayed at places of markedly evil repute he had, none the less—having too much imagination—sometimes found the great black halls and staircases rather "creepy": there had been often a sinister effect for his nerves in the sound of his tread through the long passages or the way the winter moon peeped into tall windows on landings. It occurred to him that if houses without supernatural pretensions could look so wicked at night the old corridors of Stayes would certainly give him a sensation. He didn't know whether the proprietors were sensitive; very often, as he had said to Colonel Capadose, people enjoyed the impeachment. What determined him to speak despite the risk was a need that had suddenly come to him to measure the Colonel's accuracy. As he had his hand on the door he said to his host: "I hope I shan't meet any ghosts."

"Any ghosts?"

"You ought to have some—in this fine old part."

"We do our best, but they're difficult to raise," said Mr. Ashmore. "I don't think they like the hot-water pipes."

"They remind them too much of their own climate? But haven't you a haunted room—at the end of my passage?"

"Oh there are stories—we try to keep them up."

"I should like very much to sleep there," Lyon said.

"Well, you can move there tomorrow if you like."

"Perhaps I had better wait," Lyon smiled, "till I've done my work." But he was to have presently the slightly humiliated sense of having been "arch" about nothing.

"Very good; but you won't work there, you know. My father will sit to you in his own apartments."

"Oh it isn't that; it's the fear of running away—like that gentleman three days ago."

"Three days ago? What gentleman?" Mr. Ashmore asked.

"The one who got urgent letters at breakfast and fled by the 10.20. Did he stand more than one night?"

"I don't know what you're talking about"—the son of Stayes was sturdy and blank. "There was no such gentleman—three days ago."

"Ah so much the better," said Lyon, nodding good-night and departing. He took his course, as he remembered it, with his wavering candle, and, though he encountered a great many gruesome objects, safely reached the passage out of which his room opened. In the complete darkness it seemed to stretch away still further, but he followed it, for the curiosity of the thing, to the end. He passed several doors with the name of the room painted up, but found nothing else. He was tempted to try the last door, to look into the room his friend had incriminated; but he felt this would be indiscreet, that gentleman's warrant was somehow a document of too many flourishes. There might be apparitions or other uncanny things and there mightn't; but there was surely nothing in the house so odd as Colonel Capadose.

II

LYON found Sir David Ashmore a beautiful subject as well as the serenest and blandest of sitters. Moreover he was a very informing old man, tremendously puckered but not in the least dim; and he wore exactly the furred dressing-gown his portrayer would have chosen. He was proud of his age but ashamed of his infirmities, which however he greatly exaggerated and which didn't prevent his submitting to the brush as bravely as he might have to the salutary surgical knife. He sat there with the firm eyes and set smile of "Well, do your worst!" He demolished the legend of his having feared the operation would be fatal, giving an explanation which pleased our friend much better. He held that a gentleman should be painted but once in his life—that it was eager and fatuous to be hung up all over the place. That was good for women, who made a pretty wall-pattern; but the male face didn't lend itself to decorative repetition. The proper time for the likeness was at the last, when the whole man was there, when you got the sum of his experience. Lyon couldn't reply, as he would have done in many a case, that this was not a real synthesis—you had to allow so for leakage; since there had been no crack in Sir David's crystallisation. He spoke of his portrait as a plain map of the country, to be consulted by his children in a case of uncertainty. A proper map could be drawn up only when the country had been travelled. He gave Lyon his mornings, till luncheon, and they talked of many things, not neglecting, as a stimulus to gossip, the company at Stayes. Now that he didn't "go out," as he said, he saw much less of the people in his house—processions that came and went, that he knew nothing about and that he liked to hear Lyon describe. The artist sketched with a fine point and didn't caricature, and it usually befell that when Sir David didn't know the sons and daughters he had known the fathers and mothers. He was one of those terrible old persons who keep the book of antecedents. But in the case of the Capadose family, at whom they arrived by an easy stage, his knowledge embraced two, or even three, generations. General Capadose was an old crony, and he remembered his father before him. The General was rather a smart soldier, but in private life of too speculative a turn—always sneaking into the City to put his money into some rotten thing. He had married a girl who brought him something—and with it half a dozen children. He scarcely knew what had become of the rest of them, except that one was in the Church and had found preferment—wasn't he Dean of Rockingham? Clement, the fellow who was at Stayes, had apparently some gift for arms; he had served in the East and married a pretty girl. He had been at Eton with Arthur and used them to come to Stayes in his holidays. Lately, back in England, he had turned up with his wife again; that was before he—the old man—had been put to grass. He was a taking dog but had a monstrous foible.

"A monstrous foible?" Lyon echoed.

"He pulls the long bow—the longest that ever was."

Lyon's brush stopped short, while he repeated, for somehow the words both startled him and brought light: " 'The longest that ever was'?"

"You're very lucky not to have had to catch him."

Lyon debated. "Well, I think I *have* rather caught him. He revels in the miraculous."

"Oh it isn't always the miraculous. He'll lie about the time of day, about the name of his hatter. It's quite disinterested."

"Well, it's very base," Lyon declared, feeling rather sick for what Everina Brant had done with herself.

"Oh it's an extraordinary trouble to take," said the old man, "but this fellow isn't in himself at all base. There's no harm in him and no bad intention; he doesn't steal nor cheat nor gamble nor drink; he's very kind—he sticks to his wife, is fond of his children. He simply can't give you a straight answer."

"Then everything he told me last night, I now see, was tarred with that brush: he delivered himself of a series of the steepest statements. They stuck when I tried to swallow them, yet I never thought of so simple an explanation."

"No doubt he was in the vein," Sir David went on. "It's a natural peculiarity—as you might limp or stutter or be left-handed. I believe it comes and goes with changes of the wind. My son tells me that his friends quite allow for it and don't pin him down—for the sake of his wife, whom every one likes."

"Oh his wife—his wife!" Lyon murmured, painting fast.

"I dare say she's used to it."

"Never in the world, Sir David. How can she be used to it?"

"Why, my dear sir, when a woman's fond—! And don't they mostly rather handle that instrument themselves? They're connoisseurs in the business," Sir David cackled with a harmless old-time cynicism. "They've a sympathy for a fellow performer."

Lyon wondered; he had no ground for denying that Mrs. Capadose was attached to her husband. But after a little he rejoined: "Oh not this one! I knew her years ago—before her marriage; knew her well and admired her. She was as clear as a bell."

"I like her very much," Sir David said, "but I've seen her back him up."

Lyon considered his host a moment not in the light of a sitter. "Are you very sure?"

The old man grinned and brought out: "My dear sir, you're in love with her."

"Very likely. God knows I used to be!"

"She must help him out—she can't expose him."

"She can hold her tongue," Lyon returned.

"Well, before you probably she will."

"That's what I'm curious to see." And he added privately:

"Mercy on us, what he must have made of her!" He kept this reflexion to himself, for he considered that he had sufficiently betrayed his state of mind with regard to Mrs. Capadose. None the less it occupied him now immensely, the question of how such a woman would arrange herself in such a position. He watched her with an interest deeply quickened when he mingled with the company; he had had his own troubles in life, but had rarely been so anxious about anything as about this question of what the loyalty of a wife and the infection of an example would have made of a perfectly candid mind. Oh he would answer for it that whatever other women might be prone to do she, of old, had stuck to the truth as a bather who can't swim sticks to shallow water. Even if she hadn't been too simple for deviations she would have been too proud, and if she hadn't had too much conscience would have had too little eagerness. The lie was the last thing she would have endured or condoned —the particular thing she wouldn't have forgiven. Did she sit in torment while her husband gave the rein, or was she now too so perverse that she thought it a fine thing to be striking at the expense—Lyon would have been ready to say—of one's decency? It would have taken a wondrous alchemy—working backwards, as it were—to produce this latter result. Besides these alternatives—that she suffered misery in silence and that she was so much in love that her husband's exorbitance seemed to her but an added richness, a proof of life and talent—there was still the possibility that she hadn't found him out, that she took his false coinage at his own valuation. A little reflexion rendered this hypothesis untenable; it was too evident that the account he gave of things must repeatedly have contradicted her own knowledge. Within an hour or two of his meeting them Lyon had seen her confronted with that perfectly gratuitous invention about the profit they had made of his early picture. Even then indeed she had not, so far as he could see, smarted, and—but for the present he could only stare at the mystery!

Even if it hadn't been interfused, through his uneradicated interest in Mrs. Capadose, with an element of suspense, the question would still have been attaching and worrying; since, truly, he hadn't painted portraits so many years without becoming curious of queer cases. His attention was limited for the moment to the opportunity the following three days might yield, as the Colonel and his wife were going on to another house. It fixed itself largely of course upon the Colonel too—the fellow was *so* queer a case. Moreover it had to go on very quickly. Lyon was at once too discreet and too fond of his own intimate inductions to ask other people how they answered his conundrum—too afraid also of exposing the woman he once had loved. It was probably indeed that light would come to him from the talk of their companions; the Colonel's idiosyncrasy, both as it affected his own situation and as it affected his wife, would be a familiar theme in any house in which he was in the habit of staying. Lyon hadn't observed in the circles in which he visited any marked abstention from comment on the singularities of their members. It interfered with his progress that the Colonel hunted all day, while he plied his brushes and chatted with Sir David; but a Sunday intervened and that partly made it up. Mrs. Capadose fortunately didn't hunt and, his work done, was not inaccessible. He took a couple of good walks with her—she was fond of good walks—and beguiled her at tea into a friendly nook in the hall. Regard her as he might he couldn't make out to himself that she was consumed by a hidden shame; the sense of being married to a man whose word had no worth was not, in her spirit, so far as he could guess, the canker within the rose. Her mind appeared to have nothing on it but its own placid frankness, and when he sounded her eyes—with the long plummet he occasionally permitted himself to use—they had no uncomfortable consciousness. He talked to her again and still again of the dear old days—reminded her of things he hadn't had (before this reunion) any sense of himself remembering. Then he spoke to her of her husband, praised his appearance, his talent for conversation, professed to have felt a quick friendship for him and asked, with an amount of "cheek" for which he almost blushed, what manner of man he was. "What manner?" she echoed. "Dear me, how can one describe one's husband? I like him very much."

"Ah you've insisted on that to me already!" Lyon growled to exaggeration.

"Then why do you ask me again?" She added in a moment, as if she were so happy that she could aflord to take pity on him: "He's everything that's good and true and kind. He's a soldier and a gentleman and a dear! He hasn't a fault. And he has great, great ability."

"Yes, he strikes one as having great, great ability. But of course I can't think him a dear."

"I don't care what you think him!" Everina laughed, looking still handsomer in the act than he had ever seen her. She was either utterly brazen or of a contrition quite impenetrable, and he had little prospect of extorting from her what he somehow so longed for—some avowal that she had after all better have married a man who was not a by-word for the most contemptible, the least heroic of vices. Hadn't she seen, hadn't she felt, the smile, the cold faded smile of complete depreciation, go round when her husband perjured himself to some particularly characteristic blackness? How could a woman of her quality live with that day after day, year after year, except by her quality's altering? But he would believe in the alteration only when he should have heard *her* lie. He was held by his riddle and yet impatient of it, he asked himself all kinds of questions. Didn't she lie, after all, when she let *his* lies pass without turning a hair? Wasn't her life a perpetual complicity, and didn't she aid and abet him by the simple fact that she wasn't disgusted with him? Then again perhaps she *was* disgusted and it was the mere desperation of her pride that had given her an inscrutable mask. Perhaps she protested in private, passionately; perhaps every night, in their own apartments, after the day's low exhibition, she had things out with him in a manner known only to the pair themselves. But if such scenes were of no avail and he took no more trouble to cure himself, how could she regard him, and after so many years of marriage too, with the perfectly artless complacency that Lyon had surprised in her in the course of the first day's dinner? If our friend hadn't been in love with her he would surely have taken the Colonel's delinquencies less to heart. As the case stood they fairly turned to the tragical for him, even while he was sharply aware of how merely "his funny way" they were to others—and of how funny his, Oliver Lyon's, own way of regarding them would have seemed to every one.

The observation of these three days showed him that if Capadose was an abundant he was not a malignant liar and that his fine faculty exercised itself mainly on subjects of small direct importance. "He's the liar platonic," he said to himself; "he's disinterested, as Sir David said, he doesn't operate with a hope of gain or with a desire to injure. It's art for art—he's prompted by some love of beauty. He has an inner vision of what might have been, of what ought to be, and he helps on the good cause by the simple substitution of a shade. He lays on colour, as it were, and what less do I do myself?" His disorder had a wide range, but a family likeness ran through all its forms, which consisted mainly of their singular futility. It was this that made them an affliction; they encumbered the field of conversation, took up valuable space, turned it into the desert of a perpetual shimmering mirage. For the falsehood uttered under stress a convenient place can usually be found, as for a person who presents himself with an author's order at the first night of a play. But the mere luxurious lie is the gentleman without a voucher or a ticket who accommodates himself with a stool in the passage.

Of one possible charge Lyon acquitted his successful rival; it had puzzled him that, irrepressible as he was, he had never got into a mess in the Service. But it was to be made out that he drew the line at the Service—over that august institution he never flapped his wings. Moreover, for all the personal pretension in his talk it rarely came, oddly enough, to swagger about his military exploits. He had a passion for the chase, he had followed it in far countries, and some of his finest flowers were reminiscences of what he had prodigiously done and miraculously escaped when off by himself. The more by himself he had been of course the bigger the commemorative nosegay bloomed. A new acquaintance always received from him, in honour of their meeting, one of the most striking of these tributes—that generalisation Lyon very promptly made. And the extraordinary man had inconsistencies and unexpected lapses—lapses into the very commonplace of the credible. Lyon recognised what Sir David had told him, that he flourished and drooped by an incalculable law and would sometimes keep the truce of God for a month at a time. The muse of improvisation breathed on him at her pleasure and appeared sometimes quite to avert her face. He would neglect the finest openings and then set sail with everything against him. As a general thing he affirmed the impossible rather than denied the certain, though this too had lively exceptions. Very often, when it was loud enough—for he liked a noise about him—he joined in the reprobation that cast him out, he allowed he was trying it on and that one didn't know what had happened to one till one *had* tried. Still, he never completely retracted nor retreated—he dived and came up in another place. Lyon guessed him capable on occasion of defending his position with violence, though only when it was very bad. Then he might easily be dangerous—then he would hit out and not care whom he touched. Such moments as those would test his wife's philosophy—Lyon would have liked to see her there. In the smoking-room and elsewhere the company, so far as it was composed of his familiars, had an hilarious protest always at hand; but among the men who had known him long his big brush was an old story, so old that they had ceased to talk about it, and Lyon didn't care, as I have said, to bring to a point those impatiences that might have resembled his own.

The oddest thing of all was that neither surprise nor familiarity prevented the Colonel's being liked; his largest appeals even to proved satiety passed for an overflow of life and high spirits—almost of simple good looks. If he was fond of treating his gallantry with a flourish he was none the less unmistakably gallant. He was a first-rate rider and shot, in spite of his fund of anecdote illustrating these accomplishments: in short he was very nearly as clever and brave, and his adventures and observations had been very nearly as numerous and wonderful, as the list he unrolled. His best quality however remained that indiscriminate sociability which took interest and favour for granted and about which he bragged least. It made him cheap, it made him even in a manner vulgar; but it was so contagious that his listener was more or less on his side as against the probabilities. It was a private reflexion of Oliver Lyon's that he not only was mendacious but made any charmed converser feel as much so by the very action of the charm—of a certain guilty submission of which no intention of ridicule could yet purge you. In the evening, at dinner and afterwards, our friend, better placed for observation than the first night, watched his wife's face to see if some faint shade or spasm never passed over it. But she continued to show nothing, and the wonder was that when he spoke she almost always listened. That was her pride: she wished not to be even suspected of not facing the music. Lyon had none the less an importunate vision of a veiled figure coming the next day in the dusk to certain places to repair the Colonel's ravages, as the relatives of kleptomaniacs punctually call at the shops that have suffered from their depredations.

"I must apologise; of course it wasn't true; I hope no harm is done; it's only his incorrigible—" oh to hear that woman's voice in that deep abasement! Lyon had no harsh design, no conscious wish to practise on her sensibility or her loyalty; but he did say to himself that he should have liked to bring her round, liked to see her *show* him that a vision of the dignity of not being married to a mountebank sometimes haunted her dreams. He even imagined the hour when, with a burning face, she might ask *him* not to take the question up. Then he should be almost consoled—he would be magnanimous.

He finished his picture and took his departure, after having worked in a glow of interest which made him believe in his success, until he found he had pleased every one, especially Mr. and Mrs. Ashmore, when he began to be sceptical. The party at any rate changed: Colonel and Mrs. Capadose went their way. He was able to say to himself however that his parting with Everina wasn't so much an end as a beginning, and he called on her soon after his return to town. She had told him the hours she was at home—she seemed to like him. If she liked him why hadn't she married him, or at any rate why wasn't she sorry she hadn't? If she was sorry she concealed it too well. The point he made of some visible contrition in her on this head may strike the reader as extravagant, but something must be allowed so disappointed a man. He didn't ask much after all; not that she should love him today or that she should allow him to tell her that he loved her, but only that she should give him some sign she didn't feel her choice as *all* gain. Instead of this, for the present, she contented herself with exhibiting her small daughter to him. The child was beautiful and had the prettiest eyes of innocence he had ever seen: which didn't prevent his wondering if she told horrid fibs. This idea much occupied and rather darkly amused him—the picture of the anxiety with which her mother would watch as she grew older for symptoms of the paternal strain. That was a pleasant care for such a woman as Everina Brant! Did she lie to the child herself about her father—was that necessary when she pressed her daughter to her bosom to cover up his tracks? Did he control himself before the little girl—so that she mightn't hear him say things she knew to be other than his account of them? Lyon scarcely thought that probable: his genius would be ever too strong for him, and the only guard for Amy would be in her being too simple for criticism. One couldn't judge yet—she was too young to show. If she should grow up clever she would be sure to tread in his steps—a delightful improvement in her mother's situation! Her little face was not shifty, but neither was her father's big one; so that proved nothing.

Lyon reminded his friends more than once of their promise that Amy should sit to him, and it was now only a question of his own leisure. The desire grew in him to paint the Colonel also—an operation from which he promised himself a rich private satisfaction. He would draw him out, he would set him up in that totality about which he had talked with Sir David, and none but the initiated would know. They, however, would rank the picture high, and it would be indeed six rows deep—a masterpiece of fine characterisation, of legitimate treachery. He had dreamed for years of some work that should show the master of the deeper vision as well as the mere reporter of the items, and here at last was his subject. It was a pity it wasn't better, but that wasn't *his* fault. It was his impression that already no one "drew" the Colonel in the social sense more effectively than he, and he did this not only by instinct but on a plan. There were moments when he almost winced at the success of his plan—the poor gentleman went so terribly far. He would pull up some day, look at his critic between the eyes and guess he was being played upon—which would lead to his wife's guessing it also. Not that Lyon cared much for that however, so long as she failed to suppose—and she couldn't divine it—that *she* was a part of his joke. He formed such a habit now of going to see her of a Sunday afternoon that he was angry when she went out of town. This occurred often, as the couple were great visitors and the Colonel was always looking for sport, which he liked best when it could be had at the expense of others. Lyon would have supposed the general gregarious life, the constant presence of a gaping "gallery," particularly little to her taste, for it was naturally in country-houses that her husband came out strongest. To let him go off without her, not to see him expose himself—that ought properly to have been her relief and her nearest approach to a luxury. She mentioned to her friend in fact that she preferred staying at home, but she didn't say it was because in other people's houses she was on the rack: the reason she gave was that she liked so to be with the child. It wasn't perhaps criminal to deal in such "whoppers," but it was damned vulgar: poor Lyon was delighted when he arrived at that formula. Certainly some day too he would cross the line—he would practise the fraud to which his talked "rot" had the same relation as the experiments of the forger have to the signed cheque. And in the meantime, yes, he was vulgar, in spite of his facility, his impunity, his so remarkably fine person. Twice, by exception, toward the end of the winter, when he left town for a few days' hunting, his wife remained at home. Lyon hadn't yet reached the point of asking himself if the wish not to miss two of his visits might have had something to do with this course. That enquiry would perhaps have been more in place later, when he began to paint her daughter and she made a rule of coming with her. But it wasn't in her to give the wrong name, to affect motives, and Lyon could see she had the maternal passion in spite of the bad blood in the little girl's veins.

She came inveterately, though Lyon multiplied the sittings: Amy was never entrusted to the governess or the maid. He had knocked off poor old Sir David in ten days, but the simple face of the child held him and worried him and gave him endless work. He asked for sitting after sitting, and it might have struck a solicitous spectator that he was wearing the little girl out. He knew better, however, and Mrs. Capadose also knew: they were present together at the long intermissions he gave her, when she left her pose and roamed about the great studio, amusing herself with its curiosities, playing with the old draperies and costumes, having unlimited leave to handle. Then her mother and their so patient friend—much more patient than her piano-mistress—sat and talked; he laid aside his brushes and leaned back in his chair; he always gave her tea. What Mrs. Capadose couldn't suspect was the rate at which, during these weeks, he neglected other orders: women have no faculty of imagination with regard to a man's work beyond a vague idea that it doesn't matter. Lyon in fact put off everything and made high celebrities wait. There were half-hours of silence, when he plied his brushes, during which he was mainly conscious that Everina was sitting there. She easily fell into that if he didn't insist on talking, and she wasn't embarrassed nor bored by any lapse of communication. Sometimes she took up a book—there were plenty of them about; sometimes, a little way off in her chair, she watched his progress—though without in the least advising or correcting—as if she cared for every stroke that was to contribute to his result. These strokes were occasionally a little wild; he was thinking so much more of his heart than of his hand. He wasn't more embarrassed than she, but he was more agitated: it was as if in the sittings (for the child too was admirably quiet) something had beautifully settled itself between them or had already grown—a tacit confidence, an inexpressible secret. He at least felt it that way, but he after all couldn't be sure she did. What he wanted her to do for him was very little; it wasn't even to allow that she was unhappy. She would satisfy him by letting him know even by some quite silent sign that she could imagine her happiness with him—well, more unqualified. Perhaps indeed—his presumption went so far—that was what she did mean by contentedly sitting there.

III

At last he broached the question of painting the Colonel: it was now very late in the season—there would be little time before the common dispersal. He said they must make the most of it; the great thing was to begin; then in the autumn, with the resumption of their London life, they could go forward.

Mrs. Capadose objected to this that she really couldn't consent to accept another present of such value. Lyon had sacrificed to her the portrait of herself of old—he knew what they had had the indelicacy to do with it. Now he had offered her this wondrous memorial of the child—wondrous it would evidently be when he should be able to bring it to a finish; a precious possession that, this time, they would cherish for ever. But his generosity and their indiscretion must stop there—they couldn't be so tremendously "beholden" to him. They couldn't order the picture, which of course he would understand without her explaining: it was a luxury beyond their reach, since they knew the great prices he received. Besides, what had they ever done—what above all had *she* ever done, that he should overload them with benefits? No, he was too dreadfully good; it was really impossible that Clement should sit. Lyon listened to her without protest, without interruption, while he bent forward at his work; and at last returned: "Well, if you won't take it why not let him sit just for my own pleasure and profit? Let it be a favour, a service I ask of him. All the generosity and charity will so be on your side. It will do me a lot of good to paint him and the picture will remain in my hands."

"How will it do you a lot of good?" Mrs. Capadose asked.

"Why he's such a rare model—such an interesting subject. He has such an expressive face. It will teach me no end of things."

"Expressive of what?" said Mrs. Capadose.

"Why of his inner man."

"And you want to paint his inner man?"

"Of course I do. That's what a great portrait gives you, and with a splendid comment on it thrown in for the money. I shall make the Colonel's a great one. It will put me up high. So you see my request is eminently interested."

"How can you be higher than you are?"

"Oh I'm an insatiable climber. So don't stand in my way," said Lyon.

"Well, everything in him is very noble," Mrs. Capadose gravely contended.

"Ah trust me to bring everything out!" Lyon returned, feeling a little ashamed of himself.

Mrs. Capadose, before she went, humoured him to the point of saying that her husband would probably comply with his invitation; but she added: "Nothing would induce me to let you pry into *me* that way!"

"Oh you," her friend laughed—"I could do you in the dark!"

The Colonel shortly afterwards placed his leisure at the painter's disposal and by the end of July had paid him several visits. Lyon was disappointed neither in the quality of his sitter nor in the degree to which he himself rose to the occasion; he felt really confident of producing what he had conceived. He was in the spirit of it, charmed with his motive and deeply interested in his problem. The only point that troubled him was the idea that when he should send his picture to the Academy he shouldn't be able to inscribe it in the catalogue under the simple rubric to which all propriety pointed. He couldn't in short send in the title as "The Liar"—more was the pity. However, this little mattered, for he had now determined to stamp that sense on it as legibly—and to the meanest intelligence—as it was stamped for his own vision on the living face. As he saw nothing else in the Colonel today, so he gave himself up to the joy of "rendering" nothing else. How he did it he couldn't have told you, but he felt a miracle of method freshly revealed to him every time he sat down to work. It was in the eyes and it was in the mouth, it was in every line of the face and every fact of the attitude, in the indentation of the chin, in the way the hair was planted, the moustache was twisted, the smile came and went, the breath rose and fell. It was in the way he looked out at a bamboozled world in short—the way he would look out for ever. There were half a dozen portraits in Europe that Lyon rated as supreme; he thought of them always as immortal things, for they were as perfectly preserved as they were consummately painted. It was to this small exemplary group that he aspired to attach the canvas on which he was now engaged. One of the productions that helped to compose it was the magnificent Moroni of the National Gallery—the young tailor in the white jacket at his board with his shears. The Colonel was not a tailor, nor was Moroni's model, unlike many tailors, a liar; the very man, body and soul, should bloom into life under his hand with just that assurance of no loss of a drop of the liquor. The Colonel, as it turned out, liked to sit, and liked to talk while sitting: which was very fortunate, as his talk was half the inspiration of his artist. Lyon applied without mercy his own gift of provocation; he couldn't possibly have been in a better relation to him for the purpose. He encouraged, beguiled, excited him, manifested an unfathomable credulity, and his own sole lapses were when the Colonel failed, as he called it, to "act." He had his intermissions, his hours of sterility, and then Lyon knew that the picture also drooped. The higher his companion soared, the more he circled and sang in the blue, the better he felt himself paint; he only couldn't make the flights and the evolutions last. He lashed his victim on when he flagged; his one difficulty was his fear again that his game might be suspected. The Colonel, however, was easily beguiled; he basked and expanded in the fine steady light of the painter's attention. In this way the picture grew very fast, astonishingly faster, in spite of its so much greater "importance," than the simple-faced little girl's. By the fifth of August it was pretty well finished: that was the date of the last sitting the Colonel was for the present able to give—he was leaving town the next day with his wife. Lyon was amply content—he saw his way so clear: he should be able to do at leisure the little that remained, in respect to which his friend's attendance would be a minor matter. As there was no hurry, in any case, he would let the thing stand over till his own return to London, in November, when he should come back to it with a fresh eye. On the Colonel's asking him if Everina might have a sight of it next day, should she find a minute—this being so greatly her desire—Lyon begged as a special favour that she would wait: what he had yet to do was small in amount, but it would make all the difference. This was the repetition of a proposal Mrs. Capadose had made on the occasion of his last visit to her, and he had then recommended her not coming till he should be himself better pleased. He had really never been, at a corresponding stage, better pleased; and he blushed a little for his subtlety.

By the fifth of August the weather was very warm, and on that day, while the Colonel sat at his usual free practice Lyon opened for the sake of ventilation a little subsidiary door which led directly from his studio into the garden and sometimes served as an entrance and an exit for models and for visitors of the humbler sort, and as a passage for canvases, frames, packing-boxes and other professional gear. The main entrance was through the house and his own apartments, and this approach had the charming effect of admitting you first to a high gallery, from which a winding staircase, happily disposed, dropped to the wide decorated encumbered room. The view of this room beneath them, with all its artistic ingenuities and the objects of value that Lyon had collected, never failed to elicit exclamations of delight from persons stepping into the gallery. The way from the garden was plainer and at once more practicable and more private. Lyon's domain, in Saint John's Wood, was not vast, but when the door stood open of a summer's day it offered a glimpse of flowers and trees, there was a sweetness in the air and you heard the birds. On this particular morning the side-door had been found convenient by an unannounced visitor, a youngish woman who stood in the room before the Colonel was aware of her, but whom he was then the first to see. She was very quiet—she looked from one of the men to the other. "Oh, dear, here's another!" Lyon exclaimed as soon as his eyes rested on her. She belonged in fact to the somewhat importunate class of the model in search of employment, and she explained that she had ventured to come straight in, that way, because very often when she went to call upon gentlemen the servants played her tricks, turned her off and wouldn't take in her name.

"But how did you get into the garden?" Lyon asked.

"The gate was open, sir—the servants' gate. The butcher's cart was there."

"The butcher ought to have closed it," said Lyon.

"Then you don't require me, sir?" the lady continued.

Lyon continued to paint; he had given her a sharp look at first, but now his eyes were only for his work. The Colonel, however, examined her with interest. She was a person of whom you could scarcely say whether being young she looked old or old looked young; she had at any rate clearly rounded several of the corners of life; she had a face that was rosy, yet that failed to suggest freshness. She was nevertheless rather pretty and even looked as if at one time she might have sat for the complexion. She wore a hat with many feathers, a dress with many bugles, long black gloves encircled with silver bracelets, and very bad shoes. There was something about her not exactly of the governess out of place nor completely of the actress seeking an engagement, but that savoured of a precarious profession, perhaps even of a blighted career. She was perceptibly soiled and tarnished, and after she had been in the room a few moments the air, or at any rate the nostril, became acquainted with a vague alcoholic waft. She was unpractised in the *h,* and when Lyon at last thanked her and said he didn't want her —he was doing nothing for which she could be useful—she replied in rather a wounded manner: "Well, you know you *'ave* 'ad me!"

"I don't remember you," Lyon protested.

"Well, I dare say the people who saw your pictures do! I haven't much time, but I thought I'd look in."

"I'm much obliged to you."

"If ever you should require me and just send me a postcard—"

"I never send postcards," said Lyon.

"Oh well, I should value a private letter! Anything to Miss Geraldine, Mortimer Terrace Mews, Notting 'ill—"

"Very good; I'll remember," said Lyon.

Miss Geraldine lingered. "I thought I'd just stop on the chance."

"I'm afraid I can't hold out hopes, I'm so busy with portraits," Lyon continued.

"Yes; I see you are. I wish I was in the gentleman's place."

"I'm afraid in that case it wouldn't look like the gentleman," the Colonel sociably laughed.

"Oh of course it couldn't compare—it wouldn't be so 'andsome! But I do hate them portraits!" Miss Geraldine declared. "It's so much bread out of our mouths."

"Well, there are many who can't paint them," Lyon suggested for comfort.

"Oh I've sat to the very first—and only to the first! There's many that couldn't do anything without me."

"I'm glad you're in such demand." Lyon's amusement had turned to impatience and he added that he wouldn't detain her—he would send for her in case of need.

"Very well; remember it's the Mews—more's the pity! You don't sit so well as *us*!" Miss Geraldine pursued, looking at the Colonel. "If *you* should require me, sir—"

"You put him out; you embarrass him," said Lyon.

"Embarrass him, oh gracious!" the visitor cried with a laugh that diffused a fragrance. "Perhaps *you* send postcards, eh?" she went on to the Colonel; but she retreated with a wavering step. She passed out into the garden as she had come.

"How very dreadful—she's drunk!" said Lyon. He was painting hard, but looked up, checking himself: Miss Geraldine, in the open doorway, had thrust in her head again.

"Yes, I do hate it—that sort of thing!" she cried with an explosion of mirth which confirmed Lyon's charge. On which she disappeared.

"What sort of thing—what does she mean?" the Colonel asked.

"Oh my painting you when I might be painting her."

"And have you ever painted her?"

"Never in the world; I've never seen her. She's quite mistaken."

The Colonel just waited; then he remarked: "She was very pretty—ten years ago."

"I dare say, but she's quite ruined. For me the least 'drop too much' spoils them; I shouldn't care for her at all."

"My dear fellow, she's not a model," the Colonel laughed.

"Today, no doubt, she's not worthy of the name; but she has done her time."

"*Jamais de la vie!* That's all a pretext."

"A pretext?" Lyon pricked up his ears—he wondered what now would come.

"She didn't want you—she wanted *me*."

"I noticed she paid you some attention. What then does she want of you?"

"Oh to do me an ill turn. She hates me—lots of women do. She's watching me—she follows me."

Lyon leaned back in his chair—without a single grain of faith. He was all the more delighted with what he heard and with the Colonel's bright and candid manner. The story had shot up and bloomed, from the dropped seed, on the spot. "My dear Colonel!" he murmured with friendly interest and commiseration.

"I was vexed when she came in—but I wasn't upset," his sitter continued.

"You concealed it very well if you were."

"Ah when one has been through what I have! Today, however, I confess I was half-prepared. I've noticed her hanging about—she knows my movements. She was near my house this morning—she must have followed me."

"But who is she then—with such charming 'cheek'?"

"Yes, she has plenty of cheek," said the Colonel; "but as you observe she was primed. Still, she carried it off as a cool hand. Oh she's a bad 'un! She isn't a model and never was; no doubt she has known some of those women and picked up their form. She had hold of a friend of mine ten years ago—a young jackanapes who might have been left to be plucked but whom I was obliged to take an interest in for family reasons. It's a long story—I had really forgotten all about it. She's thirty-seven if she's a day. I was able to make a diversion and let him get off—after which I sent her about her business. She knew it was me she had to thank. She has never forgiven me—I think she's off her head. Her name isn't Geraldine at all and I doubt very much if that's her address."

"Ah what *is* her name?" Lyon was all participation. He had always noted that when once his friend was launched there was no danger in asking; the more you asked the more abundantly you were served.

"It's Pearson—Harriet Pearson; but she used to call herself Grenadine—wasn't that a rum notion? Grenadine—Geraldine—the jump was easy." Lyon was charmed with this flow of facility, and his interlocutor went on: "I hadn't thought of her for years—I had quite lost sight of her. I don't know what her idea is, but practically she's harmless. As I came in I thought I saw her a little way up the road. She must have found out I come here and have arrived before me. I dare say—or rather I'm sure—she's waiting for me there now."

"Hadn't you better have protection?" Lyon asked with amusement.

"The best protection's five shillings—I'm willing to go that length. Unless indeed she has a bottle of vitriol. But they only throw vitriol on the fellows who have 'undone' them, and I never undid her—I told her the first time I saw her that it wouldn't do. Oh if she's there we'll walk a little way together and talk it over, and, as I say, I'll go as far as five shillings."

"Well," said Lyon, "I'll contribute another five." He felt this little to pay for what he was getting.

That entertainment was interrupted, however, for the time, by the Colonel's departure. Lyon hoped for some sequel to match—a report, by note, of the next scene in the drama as his friend had met it, but this genius apparently didn't operate with the pen. At any rate he left town without writing—they had taken a tryst for three months later. Oliver Lyon always passed the holidays in the same way; during the first weeks he paid a visit to his elder brother, the happy possessor, in the south of England, of a rambling old house with formal gardens, in which he delighted, and then he went abroad—usually to Italy or Spain. This year he carried out his custom after taking a last look at his all but finished work and feeling as nearly pleased with it as decency permitted, the translation of the idea by the hand appearing always to him at the best a pitiful compromise. One yellow afternoon in the country, as he smoked his pipe on one of the old terraces, he was taken with a fancy for another look at what he had lately done, and with that in particular of doing two or three things more to it: he had been much haunted with this unrest while he lounged there. The provocation was not to be resisted, and though he was at any rate so soon to be back in London he was unable to brook delay. Five minutes with his view of the Colonel would be enough—it would clear up questions that hummed in his brain; so that the next morning, to give himself this luxury, he took the train for town. He sent no word in advance; he would lunch at his club and probably return into Sussex by the 5.45.

In Saint John's Wood the tide of human life flows at no time very fast, and in the first days of September Lyon found mere desolation in the straight sunny roads where the little plastered garden-walls, with their incommunicative doors, looked feebly Oriental. There was definite stillness in his own house, to which he admitted himself by his pass-key, it being a matter of conscience with him sometimes to take his servants unawares. The good woman set in authority over them and who cumulated the functions of cook and housekeeper was, however, quickly summoned by his step, and—as he cultivated frankness of intercourse with his domestics—received him without the confusion of surprise. He reassured her as to any other effect of unpreparedness—he had come up but for a few hours and should be busy in the studio. She announced that he was just in time to see a lady and a gentleman who were there at the moment—they had arrived five minutes before. She had told them he was absent but they said it was all right; they only wanted to look at a picture and would be very careful of everything. "I hope it's all right, sir," this informant concluded. "The gentleman says he's a sitter and he gave me his name—rather an odd name; I think it's military. The lady's a very fine lady, sir; at any rate there they are."

"Oh it's all right"—Lyon read the identity of his visitors. The good woman couldn't know, having when he was at home so little to do with the comings and goings; his man, who showed people in and out, had accompanied him to the country. He was a good deal surprised at the advent of Mrs. Capadose, who knew how little he wished her to see the portrait unfinished, but it was a familiar truth to him that she was a woman of a high spirit. Besides, perhaps the lady wasn't Everina; the Colonel might well have brought some inquisitive friend, a person who perhaps wanted a portrait of *her* husband. What were they doing in town, in any case, at that moment? Lyon made his way to the studio with a certain curiosity; he wondered vaguely what his friends were "up to." He laid his hand upon the curtain draping the door of communication, the door opening upon the gallery constructed for relief at the time the studio was added to the house; but with his motion to slide the tapestry on its rings arrested in the act. A singular startling sound reached him from the room beneath; it had the appearance of a passionate wail, or perhaps rather a smothered shriek, accompanied by a violent burst of tears. Oliver Lyon listened intently and then passed in to the balcony, which was covered with an old thick Moorish rug. His step was noiseless without his trying to keep it so, and after that first instant he found himself profiting irresistibly by the accident of his not having attracted the attention of the two persons in the studio, who were some twenty feet below him. They were in truth so deeply and strangely engaged that their unconsciousness of observation was explained. The scene that took place before Lyon's eyes was more extraordinary than any he had ever felt free to overlook. Delicacy and the failure to understand kept him at first from interfering—what he saw was a woman who had thrown herself in a flood of tears on her companion's bosom; after which surprise and discretion gave way to a force that made him step back behind the curtain. This same force, further—the force of a *need* to know—caused him to avail himself for better observation of a crevice formed by his gathering together the two halves of his swinging tapestry. He was perfectly aware of what he was about—he was for the moment an eavesdropper and a spy; but he was also aware that something irregular, as to which his confidence had been trifled with, was on foot, and that he was as much concerned with the reasons of it as he might be little concerned with the taken form. His observation, his reflexions, accomplished themselves in a flash.

His visitors were in the middle of the room; Mrs. Capadose clung to her husband, weeping; she sobbed as if her heart would break. Her distress was horrible to Oliver Lyon, but his astonishment was greater than his horror when he heard the Colonel respond to it by the vehement imprecation "Damn him, damn him, damn him!" What in the world had happened? why was she sobbing and whom was he damning? What had happened, Lyon saw the next instant, was that the Colonel had finally rummaged out the canvas before which he had been sitting—he knew the corner where the artist usually placed it, out of the way and its face to the wall—and had set it up for his wife on an empty easel. She had looked at it a few moments and then—apparently—what she saw in it had produced an explosion of dismay and resentment. She was too overcome, and the Colonel too busy holding her and re-expressing his wrath, to look round or look up. The scene was so unexpected to Lyon that all impulse failed in him on the spot for a proof of the triumph of his hand—of a tremendous hit: he could only wonder what on earth was the matter. The idea of the triumph was yet to come. He could see his projected figure, however, from where he stood; he was startled with its look of life—he hadn't supposed the force of the thing could so prevail. Mrs. Capadose flung herself away from her husband—she dropped into the nearest chair, leaned against a table, buried her face in her arms. The sound of her woe diminished, but she shuddered there as if overwhelmed with anguish and shame. Her husband stood a moment glaring at the picture, then went to her, bent over her, took hold of her again, soothed her. "What is it, darling—what the devil is it?"

Lyon fairly drank in her answer. "It's cruel—oh it's too cruel!"

"Damn him, damn him, damn him!" the Colonel repeated.

"It's all there—it's all there!" Mrs. Capadose went on.

"Hang it, what's all there?"

"Everything there oughtn't to be—everything he has seen. It's too dreadful!"

"Everything he has seen? Why, ain't I a good-looking fellow? I'll be bound to say he has made me handsome."

Mrs. Capadose had sprung up again; she had darted another glance at the painted betrayal. "Handsome? Hideous, hideous! Not that—never, never!"

"Not *what,* in heaven's name?" the Colonel almost shouted. Lyon could see his flushed bewildered face.

"What he has made of you—what you know! *He* knows—he has seen. Every one will, every one know and see. Fancy that thing in the Academy!"

"You're going wild, darling; but if you hate it so it needn't go," the poor branded man declared.

"Ah he'll send it—it's so good! Come away—come away!" Mrs. Capadose wailed, seizing her husband.

"It's so good?" the victim cried.

"Come away—come away," she only repeated, and she turned toward the staircase that ascended to the gallery.

"Not that way—not through the house in the state you're in," Lyon heard her companion object. "This way—we can pass," he added; and he drew his wife to the small door that opened into the garden. It was bolted, but he pushed the bolt and opened the door. She passed out quickly, but he stood there looking back into the room. "Wait for me a moment!" he cried out to her; and with an excited stride he re-entered the studio. He came up to the picture again—again he covered it with his baffled glare. "Damn him—damn him—damn him!" he broke out once more. Yet it wasn't clear to Lyon whether this malediction had for object the guilty original or the guilty painter. The Colonel turned away and moved about as if looking for something; Lyon for the moment wondered at his intentions; saying to himself the next, however, below his breath: "He's going to do it a harm!" His first impulse was to raise a preventive cry, but he paused with the sound of Everina Brant's sobs still in his ears. The Colonel found what he was looking for—found it among some odds and ends on a small table and strode back with it to the easel. At one and the same moment Lyon recognised the object seized as a small Eastern dagger and saw that he had plunged it into the canvas. Animated as with a sudden fury and exercising a rare vigour of hand, he dragged the instrument down—Lyon knew it to have no very fine edge—making a long and abominable gash. Then he plucked it out and dashed it again several times into the face of the likeness, exactly as if he were stabbing a human victim: it had the most portentous effect—that of some act of prefigured or rehearsed suicide. In a few seconds more the Colonel had tossed the dagger away

—he looked at it in this motion as for the sight of blood—and hurried out of the place with a bang of the door.

The strangest part of all was—as will doubtless appear—that Oliver Lyon lifted neither voice nor hand to save his picture. The point is that he didn't feel as if he were losing it or didn't care if he were, so much more was he conscious of gaining a certitude. His old friend *was* ashamed of her husband, and he had made her so, and he had scored a great success, even at the sacrifice of his precious labour. The revelation so excited him—as indeed the whole scene did—that when he came down the steps after the Colonel had gone he trembled with his happy agitation; he was dizzy and had to sit down a moment. The portrait had a dozen jagged wounds—the Colonel literally had hacked himself to death. Lyon left it there where it grimaced, never touched it, scarcely looked at it; he only walked up and down his studio with a sense of such achieved success as nothing finished and framed, varnished and delivered and paid for had ever given him. At the end of this time his good woman came to offer him luncheon; there was a passage under the staircase from the offices.

"Ah the lady and gentleman have gone, sir? I didn't hear them."

"Yes; they went by the garden."

But she had stopped, staring at the picture on the easel. "Gracious, how you *'ave* served it, sir!"

Lyon imitated the Colonel. "Yes, I cut it up—in a fit of disgust."

"Mercy, after all your trouble! Because they weren't pleased, sir?"

"Yes; they weren't pleased."

"Well, they must be very grand! Blest if I would!"

"Have it chopped up; it will do to light fires," Lyon magnificently said.

He returned to the country by the 3.30 and a few days later passed over to France. There was something he found himself looking for during these two months on the Continent; he had an expectation—he could hardly have said of what; of some characteristic sign or other on the Colonel's part. Wouldn't he write, wouldn't he explain, wouldn't he take for granted Lyon had discovered the way he had indeed been "served" and hold it only decent to show some form of pity for his mystification? Would he plead guilty or would he repudiate suspicion? The latter course would be difficult, would really put his genius to the test, in view of the ready and responsible witness who had admitted the visitors the day of the ravage and would establish the connexion between their presence and that perpetration. Would the Colonel proffer some apology or some amends, or would any word from him be only a further expression of that exasperated wonder which our friend had seen his wife so suddenly and so fatally communicate? He would have either to take oath that he hadn't touched the picture or to admit that he had, and in either case would be at costs for a difficult version. Lyon was impatient for this probably remarkable story, and as no letter came was disappointed at the failure of the exhibition. His impatience however was much greater in respect to Mrs. Capadose's inevitable share in the report, if report there was to be; for certainly that would be the real test, would show how far she would go for her husband on the one side or for himself on the other. He could scarcely wait to see what line she would take—whether she would simply adopt the Colonel's, whatever it might be. It would have met his impatience most to draw her out without waiting, to get an idea in advance. He wrote to her, to this end, from Venice, in the tone of their established friendship, asking for news, telling her of his movements, hoping for their reunion in London and not saying a word about the picture. Day followed day, after the time, and he received no answer; on which he reflected that she couldn't trust herself to write—was still too deeply ruffled, too disconcerted, by his "betrayal." Her husband had espoused her resentment and she had espoused the action he had taken in consequence of it; the rupture was therefore complete and everything at an end. Lyon was frankly rueful over this prospect, at the same time that he thought it deplorable such charming people should have put themselves so grossly in the wrong. He was at last cheered, though little further enlightened, by the arrival of a letter, brief but breathing good humour and hinting neither at a grievance nor at a bad conscience. The most interesting part of it to him was the postscript, which ran as follows: "I have a confession to make to you. We were in town for a couple of days, early in September, and I took the occasion to defy your authority: this was very bad of me but I couldn't help it. I made Clement take me to your studio—I wanted so dreadfully to see what you had done with him, your wishes to the contrary notwithstanding. We made your servants let us in and I took a good look at the picture. It is really wonderful!" "Wonderful" was non-committal, but at least with this letter there was no rupture.

The third day after his return was a Sunday, so that he could go and ask Mrs. Capadose for luncheon. She had given him in the spring a general invitation to do so and he had several times profited by it. These had been the occasions, before his sittings, when he saw the Colonel most familiarly. Directly after the meal his host disappeared (went out, as he said, to call on *his* women) and the second half-hour was the best, even when there were other people. Now, in the first days of December, Lyon had the luck to find the pair alone, without even Amy, who appeared but little in public. They were in the drawing-room waiting for the repast to be announced, and as soon as he came in the Colonel broke out: "My dear fellow, I'm delighted to see you! I'm so keen to begin again."

"Oh do go on; it's so beautiful," Mrs. Capadose said as she gave him her hand.

Lyon looked from one to the other; he didn't know what he had expected, but he hadn't expected this. "Ah then you think I've got something?"

"You've got everything." And Mrs. Capadose smiled from her golden-brown eyes.

"She wrote you of our little crime?" her husband asked. "She dragged me there—I had to go." Lyon wondered for a moment whether he meant by their little crime the assault on the canvas; but his friend's next words made this impossible. "You know I like to sit—you want me animated, and it leaves me so to wag my tongue. And just now I've time."

"You must remember how near I had got to the end," Lyon returned.

"So you had. More's the pity. I should like you to begin again."

"My dear fellow, I shall have to begin again!" laughed the painter with his eyes on Mrs. Capadose. She didn't meet them —she had got up to ring for luncheon. "The picture has been smashed," Lyon continued.

"Smashed? Ah what did you do that for?" cried Everina, standing there before him in all her clear rich beauty. Now that she did look at him she was impenetrable.

"I didn't—I found it so—with a dozen holes punched in it!"

"I say!" cried the Colonel—"what a jolly shame!"

Lyon took him in with a wide smile. "I hope *you* didn't go for it?"

"Is it done for?" the Colonel earnestly asked. He was as brightly true as his wife and he looked simply as if Lyon's question couldn't be serious. "For the love of sitting to you? My dear fellow, if I had thought of it I would!"

"Nor you either?" the painter demanded of Mrs. Capadose.

Before she had time to reply her husband had seized her arm as if a lurid light had come to him. "I say, my dear, that woman—that woman!"

"That woman?" Mrs. Capadose repeated; and Lyon too wondered what woman he meant.

"Don't you remember when we came out, she was at the door—or a little way from it? I spoke to you of her—I told you about her. Geraldine—Grenadine—the one who burst in that day," he explained to Lyon. "We saw her hanging about—I called Everina's attention to her."

"Do you mean she got at my picture?"

"Ah yes, I remember," said Mrs. Capadose with a vague recovery.

"She burst in again—she had learned the way—she was waiting for her chance," the Colonel continued. "Ah the horrid little brute!"

Lyon looked down; he felt himself colouring. This was what he had been waiting for—the day the Colonel should wantonly sacrifice some innocent person. And could his wife be a party to that final atrocity? He had reminded himself repeatedly during the previous weeks that when her husband perpetrated his misdeed she had already quitted the room; but he had argued none the less—it was a virtual certainty—that he had on rejoining her at once mentioned his misdeed. He was in the flush of performance; and even if he hadn't reported what he had done she would have guessed it. Lyon didn't for an instant believe poor Miss Geraldine to have been hovering about his door, nor had the account given by the Colonel the summer before of his relations with this lady affected him as in the least convincing. Lyon had never seen her till the day she planted herself in his studio, but he knew her and classified her as if he had made her. He was acquainted with the London model in all her feminine varieties—in every phase of her development and every step of her decay. When he entered his house that September morning just after the arrival of his two friends there had been no symptoms whatever, up and down the road, of Miss Geraldine's reappearance. That fact had been fixed in his mind by his recollecting the vacancy of the prospect when his cook told him that a lady and a gentleman were in his studio: he had wondered there was neither carriage nor cab at his door. Then he had reflected that they would have come by the underground railway; he was near the Marlborough

Road station and he knew the Colonel, repeating his pilgrimage so often, habitually made use of that convenience. "How in the world did she get in?" He addressed the question to his companions indifferently.

"Let us go down to luncheon," said Mrs. Capadose, passing out of the room.

"We went by the garden—without troubling your servant—I wanted to show my wife." Lyon followed his hostess with her husband, and the Colonel stopped him at the top of the stairs. "My dear fellow, I *can't* have been guilty of the folly of not fastening the door?"

"I'm sure I don't know, Colonel," Lyon said as they went down. "It was a very determined hand that did the deed—in the spirit of a perfect wild-cat."

"Well, she *is* a wild-cat—confound her! That's why I wanted to get him away from her."

"But I don't understand her motive."

"Well, she's practically off her head—and she hates me. That was her motive."

"But she doesn't hate me, my dear fellow!" Lyon amusedly urged.

"She hated the picture—don't you remember she said so? The more portraits, the less employment for such as her."

"Yes; but if she's not really the model she pretends to be, how can that hurt her?" Lyon asked.

The question baffled the Colonel an instant—but only an instant. "Ah she's so bad she goes it blind. She doesn't know where she is."

They passed into the dining-room, where Mrs. Capadose was taking her place. "It's too low; it's too horrid!" she said. "You see the fates are against you. Providence won't let you be so disinterested—throwing off masterpieces for nothing."

"Did *you* see the woman?" Lyon put to her with something like a sternness he couldn't mitigate.

She seemed not to feel it, or not to heed it if she did. "There was a person, not far from your door, whom Clement called my attention to. He told me something about her, but we were going the other way."

"And do you think she did it?"

"How can I tell? If she did she was mad, poor wretch."

"I should like very much to get hold of her," said Lyon. This was a false plea for the truth: he had no desire for any further conversation with Miss Geraldine. He had exposed his friends to his own view, but without wish to expose them to others, and least of all to themselves.

"Oh depend upon it she'll never show again. You're all right *now!*" the Colonel guaranteed.

"But I remember her address—Mortimer Terrace Mews, Notting Hill."

"Oh that's pure humbug. There isn't any such place."

"Lord, what a practised deceiver!" said Lyon.

"Is there any one else you suspect?" his host went on.

"Not a creature."

"And what do your servants say?"

"They say it wasn't *them,* and I reply that I never said it was. That's about the substance of our interviews."

"And when did they discover the havoc?"

"They never discovered it at all. I noticed it first—when I came back."

"Well, she could easily have stepped in," said the subject of Miss Geraldine's pursuit. "Don't you remember how she turned up that day like the clown in the ring?"

"Yes, yes; she could have done the job in three seconds, except that the picture wasn't out."

"Ah my dear fellow," the Colonel groaned, "don't utterly curse me!—but of course I dragged it out."

"You didn't put it *back?*" Lyon tragically cried.

"Ah Clement, Clement, didn't I tell you to?" Mrs. Capadose reproachfully wailed.

The Colonel almost howled for compunction; he covered his face with his hands. His wife's words were for Lyon the finishing touch; they made his whole vision crumble—his theory that she had secretly kept herself true. Even to her old lover she wouldn't be so! He was sick; he couldn't eat; he knew how strange he must have looked. He attempted some platitude about spilled milk and the folly of crying over it—he tried to turn the talk to other things. But it was a horrid effort and he wondered how it pressed upon *them*. He wondered all sorts of things: whether they guessed he disbelieved them—that he had seen them of course they would never guess; whether they had arranged their story in advance or it was only an inspiration of the moment; whether she had resisted, protested, when the Colonel proposed it to her, and then had been borne down by him; whether in short she didn't loathe herself as she sat there. The cruelty, the cowardice of fastening their unholy act upon the wretched woman struck him as monstrous—no less monstrous indeed than the levity that could make them run the risk of her giving them, in her righteous indignation, the lie. Of course that risk could only exculpate her and not inculpate them—the probabilities protected them so perfectly; and what the Colonel counted on—what he would have counted upon the day he delivered himself, after first seeing her, at the studio, if he had thought about the matter then at all and not spoken from the pure spontaneity of his genius—was simply that Miss Geraldine must have vanished for ever into her native unknown. Lyon wanted so much to cut loose, in his disgust, that when after a little Mrs. Capadose said to him "But can nothing be done, can't the picture be repaired? You know they do such wonders in that way now," he only made answer: "I don't know, I don't care, it's all over, *n'en parlons plus!*" Her hypocrisy revolted him. And yet by way of plucking off the last veil of her shame he broke out to her again, shortly afterwards: "And you *did* like it, really?" To which she returned, looking him straight in his face, without a blush, a pallor, an evasion: "Oh *cher grand maître,* I loved it!" Truly her husband had trained her well. After that Lyon said no more, and his companions forbore temporarily to insist, like people of tact and sympathy aware that the odious accident had made him sore.

When they quitted the table the Colonel went away without coming upstairs; but Lyon returned to the drawing-room with his hostess, remarking to her however on the way that he could remain but a moment. He spent that moment—it prolonged itself a little—standing with her before the chimney-piece. She neither sat down nor asked him to; her manner betrayed some purpose of going out. Yes, her husband had trained her well; yet Lyon dreamed for a moment that now he was alone with her she would perhaps break down, retract, apologise, confide, say to him: "My dear old friend, forgive this hideous comedy—you understand!" And then how he would have loved her and pitied her, guarded her, helped her always! If she weren't ready to do something of that sort why had she treated him so as a dear old friend; why had she let him for months suppose certain things—or almost; why had she come to his studio day after day to sit near him on the pretext of her child's portrait, as if she liked to think what might have been? Why had she come so near a tacit confession if she wasn't willing to go an inch further? And she wasn't willing—she wasn't; he could see that as he lingered there. She moved about the room a little, rearranging two or three objects on the tables, but she did nothing more. Suddenly he said to her: "Which way was she going when you came out?"

"She—the woman we saw?"

"Yes, your husband's strange friend. It's a clue worth following." He didn't want to scare or to shake her; he only wanted to communicate the impulse that would make her say: "Ah spare me—and spare *him*! There was no such person."

Instead of this Everina replied: "She was going away from us—she crossed the road. We were coming toward the station."

"And did she appear to recognise the Colonel—did she look round?"

"Yes; she looked round, but I didn't notice much. A hansom came along and we got into it. It wasn't till then that Clement told me who she was: I remember he said that she was there for no good. I suppose we ought to have gone back."

"Yes; you'd have saved the picture."

For a moment she said nothing; then she smiled. "For you, *cher maître,* I'm very sorry. But you must remember I possess the original!"

At this he turned away. "Well, I must go," he said; and he left her without any other farewell and made his way out of the house. As he went slowly up the street the sense came back to him of that first glimpse of her he had had at Stayes—of how he had seen her gaze across the table at her husband. He stopped at the corner, looking vaguely up and down. He would never go back—he couldn't. Nor should he ever sound her abyss. He believed in her absolute straightness where she and her affairs alone might be concerned, but she was still in love with the man of her choice, and since she couldn't redeem him she would adopt and protect him. So he had trained her.

A NOTE ON

THE LIAR

(1888)

I come back, for "The Liar," as for so many of its fellows, to holding my personal experience, poor thing though it may have been, immediately accountable. For by what else in the world but by fatal design had I been placed at dinner one autumn evening of old London days face to face with a gentleman, met for the first time, though favorably known to me by name and fame, in whom I recognized the most unbridled colloquial romancer the "joy of life" had ever found occasion to envy? Under what other conceivable coercion had I been invited to reckon, through the evening, with the type, with the character, with the countenance, of this magnificent master's wife, who, veracious, serene and charming, yet not once meeting straight the eyes of one of us, did her duty by each, and by her husband most of all, without so much as, in the vulgar phrase, turning a hair? It was long ago, but I have never, to this hour, forgotten the evening itself—embalmed for me now in an old-time sweetness beyond any aspect of my reproduction. I made but a fifth person, the other couple our host and hostess; between whom and one of the company, while we listened to the woven wonders of a summer holiday, the exploits of a salamander, among Mediterranean isles, were exchanged, dimly and discreetly, ever so guardedly, but all expressively, imperceptible lingering looks. It was exquisite, it *could* but become, inevitably, some "short story" or other, which it clearly pre-fitted as the hand the glove.

So runs James's account of the germ of "The Liar." Again and again we shall note that he requires no more than such a mild encounter to set him off. The story itself, in all its elaboration, lies ready within him, awaiting but the touch of the spring, as the dream of Phidias sleeps within the rough block.

"The Liar" is more complex than at first appears. But complexity is of no interest in itself. It may be—indeed, it is, when James is at his feeblest—the mere conjunction of difficulties. In this story, however, complexity is an instrument for grasping Proteus, Proteus who is the nature of man.

At first reading we are diverted by the ingenuity of the plot, its sly twists and turns, the adroit complication, for example, of the episode of Miss Geraldine. Then, as we re-read, or reflect, the character of Colonel Capadose emerges as "The Liar's" center of gravity. Here is Munchausen analyzed by a psychologist, skilfully, almost professionally, yet with a continuous play of sympathetic humor. We perceive that this is not in the least so banal a thing as a story about lying as a vice but rather so imaginative a thing as a story about lying as a passion. Passion is an old-fashioned term; if you prefer a more up-to-date metaphor, you may substitute compulsive neurosis. (James's anticipations of modern psychiatry deserve a chapter to themselves.) The passion, or neurosis, is interesting enough, but James does not remain satisfied with the unconditioned portrayal of it. What excites him, here as everywhere, is relation, reaction, the effect of one passion upon another. The Colonel is an ingenious enough study, yet what makes the story remarkable is not the Colonel's weakness (or forte, if you wish) but his wife's iron will to protect and defend it. Her passion for the Colonel is so intense that, honorable though she is, she will lie, deceive, and even connive in a criminal act so that he may remain unexposed.

Finally, it dawns upon us that "The Liar," at its deepest level, is a love story. The love between Capadose and his wife is complicated. It even contains an element of sadism-masochism, signpointed by the recurrent phrase—humorous on the surface, grim at the base—"Her husband had trained her well."

Hardly one of James's greatest tales, "The Liar" suggests his greatest in this theme-within-theme quality, like a nest of Chinese boxes. It is illuminating, as we have seen, on at least three levels of insight.

It is also one of his wittiest tales; indeed, the whole narrative is a unified piece of wit. The Jamesian wit is of the sort decidedly out of fashion at the moment, for it is untouched by vulgarity, it does not call names, it does not invite attention to itself, and it is intellectual. By "intellectual" I mean that it connects and opens out, rather than encloses. Each witty sentence, being part of James's mind (which was extensive) seems part of a larger and for the moment unverbalized field of reflection. It makes a playful but by no means trivial judgment on human character. It is intellectual also in that his wit requires some corresponding wit in the reader. Our contemporary satirists do all the work for the reader, or auditor; if we "get the point" we have got all. James makes our minds work; he assumes that we are reflective human beings.

Here, picked almost at random, are five sentences from "The

Liar." They are not intended to be profound on the one hand or highly laughable on the other. They are bits and pieces of acute observation, parts of an unformulated moral system. They may or may not seem witty to you. If they do not it is probably because the culture of our time has so blunted us that genuine wit appears anemic and only gags appear effective.

She was a large, bright, negative woman, who had the same air as her husband of being somehow tremendously new.

Her talkativeness was systematic—she fraternised as seriously as she might have played whist.

Her noble head gave her privileges that she neglected, and when people were admiring her brow she was wondering whether there were a good fire in her bedroom.

He spoke of his portrait as a plain map of the country, to be consulted by his children in a case of uncertainty. A proper map could be drawn up only when the country had been travelled.

Women have no faculty of imagination with regard to a man's work beyond a vague idea that it doesn't matter.

A final note: the point on which the action hinges—the narrator's ability to expose in oils the true character of Capadose is, I am assured by a competent portrait painter of my acquaintance, quite implausible. It is interesting, however, to reflect on how little this admitted improbability, or impossibility, detracts from the value of the story.

THE REAL THING

I

When the porter's wife, who used to answer the house-bell, announced "A gentleman and a lady, sir," I had, as I often had in those days—the wish being father to the thought—an immediate vision of sitters. Sitters my visitors in this case proved to be; but not in the sense I should have preferred. There was nothing at first however to indicate that they mightn't have come for a portrait. The gentleman, a man of fifty, very high and very straight, with a moustache slighlty grizzled and a dark grey walking-coat admirably fitted, both of which I noted professionally—I don't mean as a barber or yet as a tailor—would have struck me as a celebrity if celebrities often were striking. It was a truth of which I had for some time been conscious that a figure with a good deal of frontage was, as one might say, almost never a public institution. A glance at the lady helped to remind me of this paradoxical law: she also looked too distinguished to be a "personality." Moreover one would scarcely come across two variations together.

Neither of the pair immediately spoke—they only prolonged the preliminary gaze suggesting that each wished to give the other a chance. They were visibly shy; they stood there letting me taken them in—which, as I afterwards perceived, was the most practical thing they could have done. In this way their embarrassment served their cause. I had seen people painfully reluctant to mention that they desired anything so gross as to be represented on canvas; but the scruples of my new friends appeared almost insurmountable. Yet the gentleman might have said "I should like a portrait of my wife," and the lady might have said "I should like a portrait of my husband." Perhaps they weren't husband and wife—this naturally would make the matter more delicate. Perhaps they wished to be done together—in which case they ought to have brought a third person to break the news.

"We come from Mr. Rivet," the lady finally said with a dim smile that had the effect of a moist sponge passed over a "sunk" piece of painting, as well as of a vague allusion to vanished beauty. She was as tall and straight, in her degree, as her companion, and with ten years less to carry. She looked as sad as a woman could look whose face was not charged with expression; that is her tinted oval mask showed waste as an exposed surface shows friction. The hand of time had played over her freely, but to an effect of elimination. She was slim and stiff, and so well-dressed, in dark blue cloth, with lappets and pockets and buttons, that it was clear she employed the same tailor as her husband. The couple had an indefinable air of prosperous thrift—they evidently got a good deal of luxury for their money. If I was to be one of their luxuries it would behoove me to consider my terms.

"Ah Claude Rivet recommended me?" I echoed; and I added that it was very kind of him, though I could reflect that, as he only painted landscape, this wasn't a sacrifice.

The lady looked very hard at the gentleman, and the gentleman looked round the room. Then staring at the floor a moment and stroking his moustache, he rested his pleasant eyes on me with the remark: "He said you were the right one."

"I try to be, when people want to sit."

"Yes, we should like to," said the lady anxiously.

"Do you mean together?"

My visitors exchanged a glance. "If you could do anything with *me* I suppose it would be double," the gentleman stammered.

"Oh yes, there's naturally a higher charge for two figures than for one."

"We should like to make it pay," the husband confessed.

"That's very good of you," I returned, appreciating so unwonted a sympathy—for I supposed he meant pay the artist.

A sense of strangeness seemed to dawn on the lady. "We mean for the illustrations—Mr. Rivet said you might put one in."

"Put in—an illustration?" I was equally confused.

"Sketch her off, you know," said the gentleman, colouring.

It was only then that I understood the service Claude Rivet had rendered me; he had told them how I worked in black-and-white, for magazines, for storybooks, for sketches of contemporary life, and consequently had copious employment for models. These things were true, but it was not less true—I may confess it now; whether because the aspiration was to lead to everything or to nothing I leave the reader to guess—that I couldn't get the honours, to say nothing of the emoluments, of a great painter of portraits out of my head. My "illustrations" were my pot-boilers; I looked to a different branch of art—far and away the most interesting it had always seemed to me—to perpetuate my fame. There was no shame in looking to it also to make my fortune; but that fortune was by so much further from being made from the moment my visitors wished to be "done" for nothing. I was disappointed; for in the pictorial sense I had immediately *seen* them. I had seized their type—I had already settled what I would do with it. Something that wouldn't absolutely have pleased them, I afterwards reflected.

"Ah you're—you're—a?" I began as soon as I had mastered my surprise. I couldn't bring out the dingy word "models": it seemed so little to fit the case.

"We haven't had much practice," said the lady.

"We've got to *do* something, and we've thought that an artist in your line might perhaps make something of us," her husband threw off. He further mentioned that they didn't know many artists and that they had gone first, on the off-chance—he painted views of course, but sometimes put in figures; perhaps I remembered—to Mr. Rivet, whom they had met a few years before at a place in Norfolk where he was sketching.

"We used to sketch a little ourselves," the lady hinted.

"It's very awkward, but we absolutely *must* do something," her husband went on.

"Of course we're not so *very* young," she admitted with a wan smile.

With the remark that I might as well know something more about them the husband had handed me a card extracted from a neat new pocket-book—their appurtenances were all of the freshest—and inscribed with the words "Major Monarch." Impressive as these words were they didn't carry my knowledge much further; but my visitor presently added: "I've left the army and we've had the misfortune to lose our money. In fact our means are dreadfully small."

"It's awfully trying—a regular strain," said Mrs. Monarch.

They evidently wished to be discreet—to take care not to swagger because they were gentlefolk. I felt them willing to recognise this as something of a drawback, at the same time that I guessed at an underlying sense—their consolation in adversity—that they *had* their points. They certainly had; but these advantages struck me as preponderantly social; such for instance as would help to make a drawing-room look well. However, a drawing-room was always, or ought to be, a picture.

In consequence of his wife's allusion to their age Major Monarch observed: "Naturally it's more for the figure that we thought of going in. We can still hold ourselves up." On the instant I saw that the figure was indeed their strong point. His "naturally" didn't sound vain, but it lighted up the question. "*She* has the best one," he continued, nodding at his wife with a pleasant after-dinner absence of circumlocution. I could only reply, as if we were in fact sitting over our wine, that this didn't prevent his own from being very good; which led him in turn to make answer: "We thought that if you ever have to do people like us we might be something like it. *She* particularly—for a lady in a book, you know."

I was so amused by them that, to get more of it, I did my best to take their point of view; and thought it was an embarrassment to find myself appraising physically, as if they were animals on hire or useful blacks, a pair whom I should have expected to meet only in one of the relations in which criticism is tacit, I looked at Mrs. Monarch judicially enough to be able to exclaim after a moment with conviction: "Oh yes, a lady in a book!" She was singularly like a bad illustration.

"We'll stand up, if you like," said the Major; and he raised himself before me with a really grand air.

I could take his measure at a glance—he was six feet two and a perfect gentleman. It would have paid any club in process of formation and in want of a stamp to engage him at a salary to stand in the principal window. What struck me at once was that in coming to me they had rather missed their vocation; they could surely have been turned to better account for advertising purposes. I couldn't of course see the thing in detail, but I could see them make somebody's fortune—I don't mean their own. There was something in them for a waistcoat-maker, an hotel-keeper or a soap-vendor. I could imagine "We always use it" pinned on their bosoms with the greatest effect; I had a vision of the brilliancy with which they would launch a table d'hôte.

Mrs. Monarch sat still, not from pride but from shyness, and presently her husband said to her: "Get up, my dear, and show how smart you are." She obeyed, but she had no need to get up to show it. She walked to the end of the studio and then came back blushing, her fluttered eyes on the partner of her appeal. I was reminded of an incident I had accidentally had a glimpse of in Paris—being with a friend there, a dramatist about to produce a play, when an actress came to him to ask to be entrusted with a part. She went through her paces before him, walked up and down as Mrs. Monarch was doing. Mrs. Monarch did it quite as well, but I abstained from applauding. It was very odd to see such people apply for such poor pay. She looked as if she had ten thousand a year. Her husband had used the word that described her: she was in the London current jargon essentially and typically "smart." Her figure was, in the same order of ideas, conspicuously and irreproachably "good." For a woman of her age her waist was surprisingly small; her elbow moreover had the orthodox crook. She held her head at the conventional angle, but why did she come to *me*? She ought to have tried on jackets at a big shop. I feared my visitors were not only destitute but "artistic"—which would be a great complication. When she sat down again I thanked her, observing that what a draughtsman most valued in his model was the faculty of keeping quiet.

"Oh *she* can keep quiet," said Major Monarch. Then he added jocosely: "I've always kept her quiet."

"I'm not a nasty fidget, am I?" It was going to wring tears from me, I felt, the way she hid her head, ostrich-like, in the other broad bosom.

The owner of this expanse addressed his answer to me. "Perhaps it isn't out of place to mention—because we ought to be quite business-like, oughtn't we?—that when I married her she was known as the Beautiful Statue."

"Oh dear!" said Mrs. Monarch ruefully.

"Of course I should want a certain amount of expression," I rejoined.

"Of *course!*"—and I had never heard such unanimity.

"And then I suppose you know that you'll get awfully tired."

"Oh we *never* get tired!" they eagerly cried.

"Have you had any kind of practice?"

They hesitated—they looked at each other. "We've been photographed—*immensely,*" said Mrs. Monarch.

"She means the fellows have asked us themselves," added the Major.

"I see—because you're so good-looking."

"I don't know what they thought, but they were always after us."

"We always got our photographs for nothing," smiled Mrs. Monarch.

"We might have brought some, my dear," her husband remarked.

"I'm not sure we have any left. We've given quantities away," she explained to me.

"With our autographs and that sort of thing," said the Major.

"Are they to be got in the shops?" I enquired as a harmless pleasantry.

"Oh yes, *hers*—they used to be."

"Not now," said Mrs. Monarch with her eyes on the floor.

II

I COULD fancy the "sort of thing" they put on the presentation copies of their photographs, and I was sure they wrote a beautiful hand. It was odd how quickly I was sure of everything that concerned them. If they were now so poor as to have to earn shillings and pence they could never have had much of a margin. Their good looks had been their capital, and they had good-humouredly made the most of the career that this resource marked out for them. It was in their faces, the blankness, the deep intellectual repose of the twenty years of country-house visiting that had given them pleasant intonations. I could see the sunny drawing-rooms, sprinkled with periodicals she didn't read, in which Mrs. Monarch had continuously sat; I could see the wet shrubberies in which she had walked, equipped to admiration for either exercise. I could see the rich covers the Major had helped to shoot and the wonderful garments in which, late at night, he repaired to the smoking-room to talk about them. I could imagine their leggings and waterproofs, their knowing tweeds and rugs, their rolls of sticks and cases of tackle and neat umbrellas; and I could evoke the exact appearance of their servants and the compact variety of their luggage on the platforms of country stations.

They gave small tips, but they were liked; they didn't do anything themselves, but they were welcome. They looked so well everywhere; they gratified the general relish for stature, complexion and "form." They knew it without fatuity or vulgarity, and they respected themselves in consequence. They weren't superficial; they were thorough and kept themselves up—it had been their line. People with such a taste for activity had to have some line. I could feel how even in a dull house they could have been counted on for the joy of life. At present something had happened—it didn't matter what, their little income had grown less, it had grown least—and they had to do something for pocket-money. Their friends could like them, I made out, without liking to support them. There was something about them that represented credit—their clothes, their manners, their type; but if credit is a large empty pocket in which an occasional chink reverberates, the chink at least must be audible. What they wanted of me was to help to make it so. Fortunately they had no children—I soon divined that. They would also perhaps wish our relations to be kept secret: this was why it was "for the figure"—the reproduction of the face would betray them.

I liked them—I felt, quite as their friends must have done—they were so simple; and I had no objection to them if they would suit. But somehow with all their perfections I didn't easily believe in them. After all they were amateurs, and the ruling passion of my life was the detestation of the amateur. Combined with this was another perversity—an innate preference for the represented subject over the real one: the defect of the real one was so apt to be a lack of representation. I like things that appeared; then one was sure. Whether they *were* or not was a subordinate and almost always a profitless question. There were other considerations, the first of which was that I already had two or three recruits in use, notably a young person with big feet, in alpaca, from Kilburn, who for a couple of years had come to me regularly for my illustrations and with whom I was still—perhaps ignobly—satisfied. I frankly explained to my visitors how the case stood, but they had taken more precautions than I supposed. They had reasoned out their opportunity, for Claude Rivet had told them of the projected *édition de luxe* of one of the writers of our day—the rarest of the novelists—who, long neglected by the multitudinous vulgar and dearly prized by the attentive (need I mention Philip Vincent?) had had the happy fortune of seeing, late in life, the dawn and then the full light of a higher criticism; an estimate in which on the part of the public there was something really of expiation. The edition preparing, planned by a publisher of taste, was practically an act of high reparation; the wood-cuts with which it was to be enriched were the homage of English art to one of the most independent representatives of English letters. Major and Mrs. Monarch confessed to me they had hoped I might be able to work *them* into my branch of the enterprise. They knew I was to do the first of the books, "Rutland Ramsay," but I had to make clear to them that my participation in the rest of the affair—this first book was to be a test—must depend on the satisfaction I should give. If this should be limited my employers would drop me with scarce common forms. It was therefore a crisis for me, and naturally I was making special preparations, looking about for new people, should they be necessary, and securing the best types. I admitted however that I should like to settle down to two or three good models who would do for everything.

"Should we have often to—a—put on special clothes?" Mrs. Monarch timidly demanded.

"Dear yes—that's half the business."

"And should we be expected to supply our own costumes?"

"Oh no; I've got a lot of things. A painter's models put on—or put off—anything he likes."

"And you mean—a—the same?"

"The same?"

Mrs. Monarch looked at her husband again.

"Oh she was just wondering," he explained, "if the costumes are in *general* use." I had to confess that they were, and I mentioned further that some of them—I had a lot of genuine greasy last-century things—had served their time, a hundred years ago, on living world-stained men and women; on figures not perhaps so far removed, in that vanished world, from *their* type, the Monarchs', *quoi!* of a breeched and bewigged age. "We'll put on anything that *fits,*" said the Major.

"Oh I arrange that—they fit in the pictures."

"I'm afraid I should do better for the modern books. I'd come as you like," said Mrs. Monarch.

"She has got a lot of clothes at home: they might do for contemporary life," her husband continued.

"Oh I can fancy scenes in which you'd be quite natural." And indeed I could see the slipshod rearrangements of stale properties—the stories I tried to produce pictures for without the exasperation of reading them—whose sandy tracts the good lady might help to people. But I had to return to the fact that for this sort of work—the daily mechanical grind—I was already equipped: the people I was working with were fully adequate.

"We only thought we might be more like *some* characters," said Mrs. Monarch mildly, getting up.

Her husband also rose; he stood looking at me with a dim wistfulness that was touching in so fine a man. "Wouldn't it be rather a pull sometimes to have—a—to have—?" He hung fire; he wanted me to help him by phrasing what he meant. But I couldn't—I didn't know. So he brought it out awkwardly: "The *real* thing; a gentleman, you know, or a lady." I was quite ready to give a general assent—I admitted that there was a great deal in that. This encouraged Major Monarch to say, following up his appeal with an unacted gulp: "It's awfully hard—we've tried everything." The gulp was communicative; it proved too much for his wife. Before I knew it Mrs. Monarch had dropped again upon a divan and burst into tears. Her husband sat down beside her, holding one of her hands; whereupon she quickly dried her eyes with the other, while I felt embarrassed as she looked up at me. "There isn't a confounded job I haven't applied for—waited for—prayed for. You can fancy we'd be pretty bad first. Secretaryships and that sort of thing? You might as well ask for a peerage. I'd be *anything*—I'm strong; a messenger or a coalheaver. I'd put on a gold-laced cap and open carriage-doors in front of the haberdasher's; I'd hang about a station to carry portmanteaux; I'd be a postman. But they won't *look* at you; there are thousands as good as yourself already on the ground. *Gentlemen,* poor beggars, who've drunk their wine, who've kept their hunters!"

I was as reassuring as I knew how to be, and my visitors were presently on their feet again while, for the experiment, we agreed on an hour. We were discussing it when the door opened and Miss Churm came in with a wet umbrella. Miss Churm had to take the omnibus to Maida Vale and then walk half a mile. She looked a trifle blowsy and slightly splashed. I scarcely ever saw her come in without thinking afresh how odd it was that, being so little in herself, she should yet be so much in others. She was a meagre little Miss Churm, but was such an ample heroine of romance. She was only a freckled cockney, but she could represent everything, from a fine lady to a shepherdess; she had the faculty as she might have had a fine voice or long hair. She couldn't spell and she loved beer, but she had two or three "points," and practice, and a knack, and mother-wit, and a whimsical sensibility, and a love of the theatre, and seven sisters, and not an ounce of respect, especially for the *h*. The first thing my visitors saw was that her umbrella was wet, and in their spotless perfection they visibly winced at it. The rain had come on since their arrival.

"I'm all in a soak; there *was* a mess of people in the 'bus. I wish you lived near a stytion," said Miss Churm. I requested her to get ready as quickly as possible, and she passed into the room in which she always changed her dress. But before going out she asked me what she was to get into this time.

"It's the Russian princess, don't you know?" I answered;

"the one with the 'golden eyes,' in black velvet, for the long thing in the *Cheapside*."

"Golden eyes? I *say!*" cried Miss Churm, while my companions watched her with intensity as she withdrew. She always arranged herself, when she was late, before I could turn round; and I kept my visitors a little on purpose, so that they might get an idea, from seeing her, what would be expected of themselves. I mentioned that she was quite my notion of an excellent model—she was really very clever.

"Do you think she looks like a Russian princess?" Major Monarch asked with lurking alarm.

"When I make her, yes."

"Oh if you have to *make* her—!" he reasoned, not without point.

"That's the most you can ask. There are so many who are not makeable."

"Well now, *here's* a lady"—and with a persuasive smile he passed his arm into his wife's—"who's already made!"

"Oh I'm not a Russian princess," Mrs. Monarch protested a little coldly. I could see she had known some and didn't like them. There at once was a complication of a kind I never had to fear with Miss Churm.

This young lady came back in black velvet—the gown was rather rusty and very low on her lean shoulders—and with a Japanese fan in her red hands. I reminded her that in the scene I was doing she had to look over some one's head. "I forget whose it is; but it doesn't matter. Just look over a head."

"I'd rather look over a stove," said Miss Churm; and she took her station near the fire. She fell into position, settled herself into a tall attitude, gave a certain backward inclination to her head and a certain forward droop to her fan, and looked, at least to my prejudiced sense, distinguished and charming, foreign and dangerous. We left her looking so while I went downstairs with Major and Mrs. Monarch.

"I believe I could come about as near it as that," said Mrs. Monarch.

"Oh you think she's shabby, but you must allow for the alchemy of art."

However, they went off with an evident increase of comfort founded on their demonstrable advantage in being the real thing. I could fancy them shuddering over Miss Churm. She was very droll about them when I went back, for I told her what they wanted.

"Well, if *she* can sit I'll tyke to book-keeping," said my model.

"She's very ladylike," I replied as an innocent form of aggravation.

"So much the worse for *you.* That means she can't turn round."

"She'll do for the fashionable novels."

"Oh yes, she'll *do* for them!" my model humorously declared. "Ain't they bad enough without her?" I had often sociably denounced them to Miss Churm.

III

It was for the elucidation of a mystery in one of these works that I first tried Mrs. Monarch. Her husband came with her, to be useful if necessary—it was sufficiently clear that as a general thing he would prefer to come with her. At first I wondered if this were for "propriety's" sake—if he were going to be jealous and meddling. The idea was too tiresome, and if it had been confirmed it would speedily have brought our acquaintance to a close. But I soon saw there was nothing in it and that if he accompanied Mrs. Monarch it was—in addition to the chance of being wanted—simply because he had nothing else to do. When they were separate his occupation was gone and they never *had* been separate. I judged rightly that in their awkward situation their close union was their main comfort and that this union had no weak spot. It was a real marriage, an encouragement to the hesitating, a nut for pessimists to crack. Their address was humble—I remember afterwards thinking it had been the only thing about them that was really professional—and I could fancy the lamentable lodgings in which the Major would have been left alone. He could sit there more or less grimly with his wife—he couldn't sit there anyhow without her.

He had too much tact to try and make himself agreeable when he couldn't be useful; so when I was too absorbed in my work to talk he simply sat and waited. But I liked to hear him talk—it made my work, when not interrupting it, less mechanical, less special. To listen to him was to combine the excitement of going out with the economy of staying at home. There was only one hindrance—that I seemed not to know any of the people this brilliant couple had known. I think he wondered extremely, during the term of our intercourse, whom the deuce I *did* know. He hadn't a stray sixpence of an idea to fumble for, so we didn't spin it very fine; we confined ourselves to questions of leather and even of liquor—saddlers and breeches-makers and how to get excellent claret cheap—and matters like "good trains" and the habits of small game. His lore on these last subjects was astonishing—he managed to interweave the station-master with the ornithologist. When he couldn't talk about greater things he could talk cheerfully about smaller, and since I couldn't accompany him into reminiscences of the fashionable world he could lower the conversation without a visible effort to my level.

So earnest a desire to please was touching in a man who could so easily have knocked one down. He looked after the fire and had an opinion on the draught of the stove without my asking him, and I could see that he thought many of my arrangements not half knowing. I remember telling him that if I were only rich I'd offer him a salary to come and teach me how to live. Sometimes he gave a random sigh of which the essence might have been: "Give me even such a bare old barrack as *this,* and I'd do something with it!" When I wanted to use him he came alone; which was an illustration of the superior courage of women. His wife could bear her solitary second floor, and she was in general more discreet; showing by various small reserves that she was alive to the propriety of keeping our relations markedly professional—not letting them slide into sociability. She wished it to remain clear that she and the Major were employed, not cultivated, and if she approved of me as a superior, who could be kept in his place, she never thought me quite good enough for an equal.

She sat with great intensity, giving the whole of her mind to it, and was capable of remaining for an hour almost as motionless as before a photographer's lens. I could see she had been photographed often, but somehow the very habit that made her good for that purpose unfitted her for mine. At first I was extremely pleased with her ladylike air, and it was a satisfaction, on coming to follow her lines, to see how good they were and how far they could lead the pencil. But after a little skirmishing I began to find her too insurmountably stiff; do what I would with it my drawing looked like a photograph or a copy of a photograph. Her figure had no variety of expression—she herself had no sense of variety. You may say that this was my business and was only a question of placing her. Yet I placed her in every conceivable position and she managed to obliterate their differences. She was always a lady certainly, and into the bargain was always the same lady. She was the real thing, but always the same thing. There were moments when I rather writhed under the serenity of her confidence that she *was* the real thing. All her dealings with me and all her husband's were an implication that this was lucky for *me*. Meanwhile I found myself trying to invent types that approached her own, instead of making her own transform itself—in the clever way that was not impossible for instance to poor Miss Churm. Arrange as I would and take the precautions I would, she always came out, in my pictures, too tall—landing me in the dilemma of having represented a fascinating woman as seven feet high, which (out of respect perhaps to my own very much scantier inches) was far from my idea of such a personage.

The case was worse with the Major—nothing I could do would keep *him* down, so that he became useful only for the representation of brawny giants. I adored variety and range, I cherished human accidents, the illustrative note; I wanted to characterise closely, and the thing in the world I most hated was the danger of being ridden by a type. I had quarrelled with some of my friends about it; I had parted company with them for maintaining that one *had* to be, and that if the type was beautiful—witness Raphael and Leonardo—the servitude was only a gain. I was neither Leonardo nor Raphael—I might only be a presumptuous young modern searcher; but I held that everything was to be sacrificed sooner than character. When they claimed that the obsessional form could easily *be* character I retorted, perhaps superficially, "Whose?" It couldn't be everybody's—it might end in being nobody's.

After I had drawn Mrs. Monarch a dozen times I felt surer even than before that the value of such a model as Miss Churm resided precisely in the fact that she had no positive stamp, combined of course with the other fact that what she did have was a curious and inexplicable talent for imitation. Her usual appearance was like a curtain which she could draw up at request for a capital performance. This performance was simply suggestive; but it was a word to the wise—it was vivid and pretty. Sometimes even I thought it, though she was plain herself, too insipidly pretty; I made it a reproach to her that the figures drawn from her were monotonously (*bêtement,* as we used to say) graceful. Nothing made her more angry; it was so much her pride to feel she could sit for characters that had nothing in common with each other. She would accuse me at such moments of taking away her "reputytion."

It suffered a certain shrinkage, this queer quantity, from the repeated visits of my new friends. Miss Churm was greatly in demand, never in want of employment, so I had no scruple in putting her off occasionally, to try them more at my ease. It was certainly amusing at first to do the real thing—it was amusing to do Major Monarch's trousers. They *were* the real thing, even if he did come out colossal. It was amusing to do his wife's back hair—it was so mathematically neat—and the particular "smart" tension of her tight stays. She lent herself especially to positions in which the face was somewhat averted or blurred; she abounded in ladylike back views and *profils perdus*. When she stood erect she took naturally one of the attitudes in which court-painters represent queens and princesses; so that I found myself wondering whether, to draw out this accomplishment, I couldn't get the editor of the *Cheapside* to publish a really royal romance, "A Tale of Buckingham Palace." Sometimes however the real thing and the make-believe came into contact; by which I mean that Miss Churm, keeping an appointment or coming to make one on days when I had much work in hand, encountered her invidious rivals. The encounter was not on their part, for they noticed her no more than if she had been the housemaid; not from intentional loftiness, but simply because as yet, professionally, they didn't know how to fraternise, as I could imagine they would have liked—or at least that the Major would. They couldn't talk about the omnibus—they always walked; and they didn't know what else to try—she wasn't interested in good trains or cheap claret. Besides, they must have felt—in the air—that she was amused at them, secretly derisive of their ever knowing how. She wasn't a person to conceal the limits of her faith if she had had a chance to show them. On the other hand Mrs. Monarch didn't think her tidy; for why else did she take pains to say to me—it was going out of the way, for Mrs. Monarch—that she didn't like dirty women?

One day when my young lady happened to be present with my other sitters—she even dropped in, when it was convenient, for a chat—I asked her to be so good as to lend a hand in getting tea, a service with which she was familiar and which was one of a class that, living as I did in a small way, with slender domestic resources, I often appealed to my models to render. They liked to lay hands on my property, to break the sitting, and sometimes the china—it made them feel Bohemian. The next time I saw Miss Churm after this incident she surprised me greatly by making a scene about it—she accused me of having wished to humiliate her. She hadn't resented the outrage at the time, but had seemed obliging and amused, enjoying the comedy of asking Mrs. Monarch, who sat vague and silent, whether she would have cream and sugar, and putting an exaggerated simper into the question. She had tried intonations—as if she too wished to pass for the real thing—till I was afraid my other visitors would take offence.

Oh they were determined not to do this, and their touching patience was the measure of their great need. They would sit by the hour, uncomplaining, till I was ready to use them; they would come back on the chance of being wanted and would walk away cheerfully if it failed. I used to go to the door with them to see in what magnificent order they retreated. I tried to find other employment for them—I introduced them to several artists. But they didn't "take," for reasons I could appreciate, and I became rather anxiously aware that after such disappointments they fell back upon me with a heavier weight. They did me the honour to think me most *their* form. They weren't romantic enough for the painters, and in those days there were few serious workers in black-and-white. Besides, they had an eye to the great job I had mentioned to them—they had secretly set their hearts on supplying the right essence for my pictorial vindication of our fine novelist. They knew that for this undertaking I should want no costume-effects, none of the frippery of past ages—that it was a case in which everything would be contemporary and satirical and presumably genteel. If I could work them into it their future would be assured, for the labour would of course be long and the occupation steady.

One day Mrs. Monarch came without her husband—she explained his absence by his having had to go to the City. While she sat there in her usual relaxed majesty there came at the door a knock which I immediately recognised as the subdued appeal of a model out of work. It was followed by the entance of a young man whom I at once saw to be a foreigner and who proved in fact an Italian acquainted with no English word but my name, which he uttered in a way that made it seem to include all others. I hadn't then visited his country, nor was I proficient in his tongue; but as he was not so meanly constituted —what Italian is?—as to depend only on that member for expression he conveyed to me, in familiar but graceful mimicry, that he was in search of exactly the employment in which the lady before me was engaged. I was not struck with him at first, and while I continued to draw I dropped few signs of interest or encouragement. He stood his ground however—not importunately, but with a dumb dog-like fidelity in his eyes that amounted to innocent impudence, the manner of a devoted servant—he might have been in the house for years—unjustly suspected. Suddenly it struck me that this very attitude and expression made a picture; whereupon I told him to sit down and wait till I should be free. There was another picture in the way he obeyed me, and I observed as I worked that there were others still in the way he looked wonderingly, with his head thrown back, about the high studio. He might have been crossing himself in Saint Peter's. Before I finished I said to myself "The fellow's a bankrupt orange-monger, but a treasure."

When Mrs. Monarch withdrew he passed across the room like a flash to open the door for her, standing there with the rapt pure gaze of the young Dante spellbound by the young Beatrice. As I never insisted, in such situations, on the blankness of the British domestic, I reflected that he had the making of a servant—and I needed one, but couldn't pay him to be only that—as well as of a model; in short I resolved to adopt my bright adventurer if he would agree to officiate in the double capacity. He jumped at my offer, and in the event my rashness —for I had really known nothing about him—wasn't brought home to me. He proved a sympathetic though a desultory ministrant, and had in a wonderful degree the *sentiment de la pose.* It was uncultivated, instinctive, a part of the happy instinct that had guided him to my door and helped him to spell out my name on the card nailed to it. He had had no other introduction to me than a guess, from the shape of my high north window, seen outside, that my place was a studio and that as a studio it would contain an artist. He had wandered to England in search of fortune, like other itinerants, and had embarked, with a partner and a small green hand-cart, on the sale of penny ices. The ices had melted away and the partner had dissolved in their train. My young man wore tight yellow trousers with reddish stripes and his name was Oronte. He was sallow but fair, and when I put him into some old clothes of my own he looked like an Englishman. He was as good as Miss Churm, who could look, when requested, like an Italian.

IV

I THOUGHT Mrs. Monarch's face slightly convulsed when, on her coming back with her husband, she found Oronte installed. It was strange to have to recognise in a scrap of a lazzarone a competitor to her magnificent Major. It was she who scented danger first, for the Major was anecdotically unconscious. But Oronte gave us tea, with a hundred eager confusions—he had never been concerned in so queer a process—and I think she thought better of me for having at last an "establishment." They saw a couple of drawings that I had made of the establishment, and Mrs. Monarch hinted that it never would have struck her he had sat for them. "Now the drawings you make from *us,* they look exactly like us," she reminded me, smiling in triumph; and I recognised that this was indeed just their defect. When I drew the Monarchs I couldn't anyhow get away from them—get into the character I wanted to represent; and I hadn't the least desire my model should be discoverable in my picture. Miss Churm never was, and Mrs. Monarch thought I hid her, very properly, because she was vulgar; whereas if she was lost it was only as the dead who go to heaven are lost—in the gain of an angel the more.

By this time I had got a certain start with "Rutland Ramsay," the first novel in the great projected series; that is I had produced a dozen drawings, several with the help of the Major and his wife, and I had sent them in for approval. My understanding with the publishers, as I have already hinted, had been that I was to be left to do my work, in this particular case, as I liked, with the whole book committed to me; but my connexion with the rest of the series was only contingent. There were moments when, frankly, it *was* a comfort to have the real thing under one's hand; for there were characters in "Rutland Ramsay" that were very much like it. There were people presumably as erect as the Major and women of as good a fashion as Mrs. Monarch. There was a great deal of country-house life—treated, it is true, in a fine fanciful ironical generalised way—and there was a considerable implication of knickerbockers and kilts. There were certain things I had to settle at the outset; such things for instance as the exact appearance of the hero and the particular bloom and figure of the heroine. The author of course gave me a lead, but there was a margin for interpretation. I took the Monarchs into my confidence, I told them frankly what I was about, I mentioned my embarrassments and alternatives. "Oh take *him*!" Mrs. Monarch murmured sweetly, looking at her husband; and "What could you want better than my wife?" the Major enquired with the comfortable candour that now prevailed between us.

I wasn't obliged to answer these remarks—I was only obliged to place my sitters. I wasn't easy in mind, and I postponed a little timidly perhaps the solving of my question. The book was a large canvas, the other figures were numerous, and I worked off at first some of the episodes in which the hero and the heroine were not concerned. When once I had set *them* up I should have to stick to them—I couldn't make my young man seven feet high in one place and five feet nine in another. I inclined on the whole to the latter measurement, though the Major more than once reminded me that *he* looked about as young as any one. It was indeed quite possible to arrange him, for the figure, so that it would have been difficult to detect his age. After the spontaneous Oronte had been with me a month, and after I had given him to understand several times over that his native exuberance would presently constitute an insurmountable barrier to our further intercourse, I waked to a sense of his heroic capacity. He was only five feet seven, but the remaining inches were latent. I tried him almost secretly at first, for I was really rather afraid of the judgement my other models would pass on such a choice. If they regarded Miss Churm as little better than a snare what would they think of the representation by a person so little the real thing as an Itailian street-vendor of a protagonist formed by a public school?

If I went a little in fear of them it wasn't because they bullied me, because they had got an oppressive foothold, but because in their really pathetic decorum and mysteriously permanent newness they counted on me so intensely. I was therefore very glad when Jack Hawley came home: he was always of such good counsel. He painted badly himself, but there was no one like him for putting his finger on the place. He had been absent from England for a year; he had been somewhere—I don't remember where—to get a fresh eye. I was in a good deal of dread of any such organ, but we were old friends; he had been away for months and a sense of emptiness was creeping into my life. I hadn't dodged a missile for a year.

He came back with a fresh eye, but with the same old black velvet blouse, and the first evening he spent in my studio we smoked cigarettes till the small hours. He had done no work himself, he had only got the eye; so the field was clear for the production of my little things. He wanted to see what I had produced for the *Cheapside,* but he was disappointed in the exhibition. That at least seemed the meaning of two or three comprehensive groans which, as he lounged on my big divan, his leg folded under him, looking at my latest drawings, issued from his lips with the smoke of the cigarette.

"What's the matter with you?" I asked.

"What's the matter with *you*?"

"Nothing save that I'm mystified."

"You are indeed. You're quite off the hinge. What's the meaning of this new fad?" And he tossed me, with visible irreverence, a drawing in which I happened to have depicted both my elegant models. I asked if he didn't think it good, and he replied that it struck him as execrable, given the sort of thing I had always represented myself to him as wishing to arrive at; but I let that pass—I was so anxious to see exactly what he meant. The two figures in the picture looked colossal, but I supposed this was *not* what he meant, inasmuch as, for aught he knew to the contrary, I might have been trying for some such effect. I maintained that I was working exactly in the same way as when he last had done me the honour to tell me I might do something some day. "Well, there's a screw loose somewhere," he answered; "wait a bit and I'll discover it." I depended upon him to do so: where else was the fresh eye? But he produced at last nothing more luminous than "I don't know—I don't like your types." This was lame for a critic who had never consented to discuss with me anything but the question of execution, the direction of strokes and the mystery of values.

"In the drawings you've been looking at I think my types are very handsome."

"Oh they won't do!"

"I've been working with new models."

"I see you have. *They* won't do."

"Are you very sure of that?"

"Absolutely—they're stupid."

"You mean *I* am—for I ought to get round that."

"You *can't*—with such people. Who are they?"

I told him, so far as was necessary, and he concluded heartlessly: "Ce sont des gens qu'il faut mettre à la porte."

"You've never seen them; they're awfully good"—I flew to their defence.

"Not seen them? Why all this recent work of yours drops to pieces with them. It's all I want to see of them."

"No one else has said anyting against it—the *Cheapside* people are pleased."

"Every one else is an ass, and the *Cheapside* people the biggest asses of all. Come, don't pretend at this time of day to have pretty illusions about the public, especially about publishers and editors. It's not for *such* animals you work—it's for those who know, *coloro che sanno;* so keep straight for *me* if you can't keep straight for yourself. There was a certain sort of thing you used to try for—and a very good thing it was. But this twaddle isn't *in* it." When I talked with Hawley later about "Rutland Ramsay" and its possible successors he declared that I must get back into my boat again or I should go to the bottom. His voice in short was the voice of warning.

I noted the warning, but I didn't turn my friends out of doors. They bored me a good deal; but the very fact that they bored me admonished me not to sacrifice them—if there was anything to be done with them—simply to irritation. As I look back at this phase they seem to me to have pervaded my life not a little. I have a vision of them as most of the time in my studio, seated against the wall on an old velvet bench to be out of the way, and resembling the while a pair of patient courtiers in a royal antechamber. I'm convinced that during the coldest weeks of the winter they held their ground because it saved them fire. Their newness was losing its gloss, and it was impossible not to feel them objects of charity. Whenever Miss Churm arrived they went away, and after I was fairly launched in "Rutland Ramsay" Miss Churm arrived pretty often. They managed to express to me tacitly that they supposed I wanted her for the low life of the book, and I let them suppose it, since they had attempted to study the work—it was lying about the studio—without discovering that it dealt only with the highest circles.

They had dipped into the most brilliant of our novelists without deciphering many passages. I still took an hour from them, now and again, in spite of Jack Hawley's warning: it would be time enough to dismiss them, if dismissal should be necesssary, when the rigour of the season was over. Hawley had made their acquaintance—he had met them at my fireside—and thought them a ridiculous pair. Learning that he was a painter they tried to approach him, to show him too that they were the real thing; but he looked at them, across the big room, as if they were miles away: they were a compendium of everything he most objected to in the social system of his country. Such people as that, all convention and patent-leather, with ejaculations that stopped conversation, had no business in a studio. A studio was a place to learn to see, and how could you see through a pair of feather-beds?

The main inconvenience I suffered at their hands was that at first I was shy of letting it break upon them that my artful little servant had begun to sit to me for "Rutland Ramsay." They knew I had been odd enough—they were prepared by this time to allow oddity to artists—to pick a foreign vagabond out of the streets when I might have had a person with whiskers and credentials; but it was some time before they learned how high I rated his accomplishments. They found him in an attitude more than once, but they never doubted I was doing him as an organ-grinder. There were several things they never guessed, and one of them was that for a striking scene in the novel, in which a footman briefly figured, it occurred to me to make use of Major Monarch as the menial. I kept putting this off, I didn't like to ask him to don the livery—besides the difficulty of finding a livery to fit him. At last, one day late in the winter, when I was at work on the despised Oronte, who caught one's idea on the wing, and was in the glow of feeling myself go very straight, they came in, the Major and his wife, with their society laugh about nothing (there was less and less to laugh at); came in like country-callers—they always reminded me of that—who have walked across the park after church and are presently persuaded to stay to luncheon. Luncheon was over, but they could stay to tea—I knew they wanted it. The fit was on me, however, and I couldn't let my ardour cool and my work wait, with the fading daylight, while my model prepared it. So I asked Mrs. Monarch if she would mind laying it out—a request which for an instant brought all the blood to her face. Her eyes were on her husband's for a second, and some mute telegraphy passed between them. Their folly was over the next instant; his cheerful shrewdness put an end to it. So far from pitying their wounded pride, I must add, I was moved to give it as complete a lesson as I could. They bustled about together and got out the cups and saucers and made the kettle boil. I know they felt as if they were waiting on my servant, and when the tea was prepared I said: "He'll have a cup, please—he's tired." Mrs. Monarch brought him one where he stood, and he took it from her as if he had been a gentleman at a party squeezing a crush-hat with an elbow.

Then it came over me that she had made a great effort for me—made it with a kind of nobleness—and that I owed her a compensation. Each time I saw her after this I wondered what the compensation could be. I couldn't go on doing the wrong thing to oblige them. Oh it *was* the wrong thing, the stamp of the work for which they sat—Hawley was not the only person to say it now. I sent in a large number of the drawings I had made for "Rutland Ramsay," and I received a warning that was more to the point than Hawley's. The artistic adviser of the house for which I was working was of opinion that many of my illustrations were not what had been looked for. Most of these illustrations were the subjects in which the Monarchs had figured. Without going into the question of what *had* been looked for, I had to face the fact that at this rate I shouldn't get the other books to do. I hurled myself in despair on Miss Churm—I put her through all her paces. I not only adopted Oronte publicly as my hero, but one morning when the Major looked in to see if I didn't require him to finish a *Cheapside* figure for which he had begun to sit the week before, I told him I had changed my mind—I'd do the drawing from my man. At this my visitor turned pale and stood looking at me. "Is *he* your idea of an English gentleman?" he asked.

I was disappointed, I was nervous, I wanted to get on with my work; so I replied with irritation: "Oh my dear Major—I can't be ruined for *you*!"

It was a horrid speech, but he stood another moment—after which, without a word, he quitted the studio. I drew a long breath, for I said to myself that I shouldn't see him again. I hadn't told him definitely that I was in danger of having my work rejected, but I was vexed at his not having felt the catastrophe in the air, read with me the moral of our fruitless collaboration, the lesson that in the deceptive atmosphere of art even the highest respectability may fail of being plastic.

I didn't owe my friends money, but I did see them again. They reappeared together three days later, and, given all the other facts, there was something tragic in that one. It was a clear proof they could find nothing else in life to do. They had threshed the matter out in a dismal conference—they had digested the bad news that they were not in for the series. If they weren't useful to me even for the *Cheapside* their function seemed difficult to determine, and I could only judge at first that they had come, forgivingly, decorously, to take a last leave. This made me rejoice in secret that I had little leisure for a scene; for I had placed both my other models in position together and I was pegging away at a drawing from which I hoped to derive glory. It had been suggested by the passage in which Rutland Ramsay, drawing up a chair to Artemisia's piano-stool, says extraordinary things to her while she ostensibly fingers out a difficult piece of music. I had done Miss Churm at the piano before—it was an attitude in which she knew how to take on an absolutely poetic grace. I wished the two figures to "compose" together with intensity, and my little Italian had entered perfectly into my conception. The pair were vividly before me, the piano had been pulled out; it was a charming show of blended youth and murmured love, which I had only to catch and keep. My visitors stood and looked at it, and I was friendly to them over my shoulder.

They made no response, but I was used to silent company and went on with my work, only a little disconcerted—even though exhilarated by the sense that *this* was at least the ideal thing—at not having got rid of them after all. Presently I heard Mrs. Monarch's sweet voice beside or rather above me: "I wish her hair were a little better done." I looked up and she was staring with a strange fixedness at Miss Churm, whose back was turned to her. "Do you mind my just touching it?" she went on—a question which made me spring up for an instant as with the instinctive fear that she might do the young lady a harm. But she quieted me with a glance I shall never forget—I confess I should like to have been able to paint *that*—and went for a moment to my model. She spoke to her softly, laying a hand on her shoulder and bending over her; and as the girl, understanding, gratefully assented, she disposed her rough curls, with a few quick passes, in such a way as to make Miss Churm's head twice as charming. It was one of the most heroic personal services I've ever seen rendered. Then Mrs. Monarch turned away with a low sigh and, looking about her as if for something to do, stooped to the floor with a noble humility and picked up a dirty rag that had dropped out of my paint-box.

The Major meanwhile had also been looking for something to do, and, wandering to the other end of the studio, saw before him my breakfast-things neglected, unremoved. "I say, can't I be useful *here*?" he called out to me with an irrepressible quaver. I assented with a laugh that I fear was awkward, and for the next ten minutes, while I worked, I heard the light clatter of china and the tinkle of spoons and glass. Mrs. Monarch assisted her husband—they washed up my crockery, they put it away. They wandered off into my little scullery, and I afterwards found that they had cleaned my knives and that my slender stock of plate had an unprecedented surface. When it came over me, the latent eloquence of what they were doing, I confess that my drawing was blurred for a moment—the picture swam. They had accepted their failure, but they couldn't accept their fate. They had bowed their heads in bewilderment to the perverse and cruel law in virtue of which the real thing could be so much less precious than the unreal; but they didn't want to starve. If my servants were my models, then my models might be my servants. They would reverse the parts—the others would sit for the ladies and gentlemen and *they* would do the work. They would still be in the studio—it was an intense dumb appeal to me not to turn them out. "Take us on," they wanted to say—"we'll do *anything*."

My pencil dropped from my hand; my sitting was spoiled and I got rid of my sitters, who were also evidently rather mystified and awestruck. Then, alone with the Major and his wife I had a most uncomfortable moment. He put their prayer into a single sentence: "I say, you know—just let *us* do for you, can't you?" I couldn't—it was dreadful to see them emptying my slops; but I pretended I could, to oblige them, for about a week. Then I gave them a sum of money to go away, and I never saw them again. I obtained the remaining books, but my friend Hawley repeats that Major and Mrs. Monarch did me a permanent harm, got me into false ways. If it be true I'm content to have paid the price—for the memory.

A NOTE ON

THE REAL THING

(1890)

WITH "The Real Thing" we meet the first James story—the first in this collection—concerned specifically with the dilemmas of the artist class. (I do not count "The Liar," where the painter is more important as observer than as artist.) "The Real Thing," thought its key is that of light comedy, deals with the most serious problem any artist can pose to himself: the nature of reality. James's conclusion is not in the least original. Every writer, painter, sculptor who has the root of the matter in him has come to it. Goethe expresses it with lucidity when he says something to the effect that Life and Art are two different things, and that is why we call one Life and the other Art. It is a truth which the journalists writing our modern novels deny.

James came to write "The Real Thing" very much as he came to write "The Liar." He was talking one day to George du Maurier (at that time "Punch" was du Maurier). The artist told him about a couple whose reduced circumstances had compelled them to propose themselves as models for his weekly illustrations of upper-class English life. They were impeccable in background and appearance. They wouldn't have to pose to "make believe." They were "the real thing." But hiring them would have meant the dismissal of his two professional models. These had not a drop of blue blood in their veins but they nevertheless "had had, for dear life, to *know how* (which was to have learned how) to do something." "The question," James goes on to recall, "struck me as exquisite, and out of a momentary fond consideration of it 'The Real Thing' sprang at a bound."

The story, then, expresses amusingly (and no more than that) the old truth that art is a *transformation* of reality, not a mere reflection of the thing itself. Mrs. Monarch is a true lady, but for that very reason she cannot be a fine model of a true lady. "She was the real thing, but always the same thing." The vulgar Miss Churm, on the other hand, can represent anything, including the gentility she lacks. The Monarchs are amateurs; Miss Churm and the little Italian are professionals.

James's sympathy for his shabby-elegant pair precludes his making the point too explicitly, but it soon becomes apparent to the attentive reader, I think, that the real trouble with the Monarchs is that they are dead. They have not enough life in them to furnish a base on which the transforming power of art may work. James says it amiably enough, but he says it: "It was in their faces, the blankness, the deep intellectual repose of the twenty years of country-house visiting which had given them pleasant intonations." Whereas Miss Churm and the Italian, though social outsiders, obviously have the principle of life active in them. They cannot be lady and gentleman for twenty years, but it is within the scope of their talent to be lady and gentleman, if need be, for half an hour. It is not alone their faculty of mimesis the artist draws on; it is their vitality, their flexibility, their humor, their understanding, crude as it may be, of the sinuous, protean, evasive nature of human character.

Thus "The Real Thing" can be seen, like all of James's stories, to be a moral, as well as esthetic, comment. Or, as he would maintain, the two are one and the same.

THE PUPIL

I

THE poor young man hesitated and procrastinated: it cost him such an effort to broach the subject of terms, to speak of money to a person who spoke only of feelings and, as it were, of the aristocracy. Yet he was unwilling to take leave, treating his engagement as settled, without some more conventional glance in that direction than he could find an opening for in the manner of the large affable lady who sat there drawing a pair of soiled *gants de Suède* through a fat jewelled hand and, at once pressing and gliding, repeated over and over everything but the thing he would have liked to hear. He would have liked to hear the figure of his salary; but just as he was nervously about to sound that note the little boy came back—the little boy Mrs. Moreen had sent out of the room to fetch her fan. He came back without the fan, only with the casual observation that he couldn't find it. As he dropped this cynical confession he looked straight and hard at the candidate for the honour of taking his education in hand. This personage reflected somewhat grimly that the first thing he should have to teach his little charge would be to appear to address himself to his mother when he spoke to her—especially not to make her such an improper answer as that.

When Mrs. Moreen bethought herself of this pretext for getting rid of their companion Pemberton supposed it was precisely to approach the delicate subject of his remuneration. But it had been only to say some things about her son that it was better a boy of eleven shouldn't catch. They were extravagantly to his advantage save when she lowered her voice to sigh, tapping her left side familiarly, "And all overclouded by *this,* you know; all at the mercy of a weakness—!" Pemberton gathered that the weakness was in the region of the heart. He had known the poor child was not robust: this was the basis on which he had been invited to treat, through an English lady, an Oxford acquaintance, then at Nice, who happened to know both his needs and those of the amiable American family looking out for something really superior in the way of a resident tutor.

The young man's impression of his prospective pupil, who had come into the room as if to see for himsef the moment Pemberton was admitted, was not quite the soft solicitation the visitor had taken for granted. Morgan Moreen was somehow sickly without being "delicate," and that he looked intelligent —it is true Pemberton wouldn't have enjoyed his being stupid —only added to the suggestion that, as with his big mouth and big ears he really couldn't be called pretty, he might too utterly fail to please. Pemberton was modest, was even timid; and the chance that his small scholar would prove cleverer than himself had quite figured, to his anxiety, among the dangers of an untried experiment. He reflected, however, that these were risks one had to run when one accepted a position, as it was called, in a private family; when as yet one's university honours had, pecuniarily speaking, remained barren. At any rate when Mrs. Moreen got up as to intimate that, since it was understood he would enter upon his duties within the week she would let him off now, he succeeded, in spite of the presence of the child, in squeezing out a phrase about the rate of payment. It was not the fault of the conscious smile which seemed a reference to the lady's expensive identity, it was not the fault of this demonstration, which had, in a sort, both vagueness and point, if the allusion didn't sound rather vulgar. This was exactly because she became still more gracious to reply: "Oh I can assure you that all that will be quite regular."

Pemberton only wondered, while he took up his hat, what "all that" was to amount to—people had such different ideas. Mrs. Moreen's words, however, seemed to commit the family to a pledge definite enough to elicit from the child a strange little comment in the shape of the mocking foreign ejaculation "Oh la-la!"

Pemberton, in some confusion, glanced at him as he walked slowly to the window with his back turned, his hands in his pockets and the air in his elderly shoulders of a boy who didn't play. The young man wondered if he should be able to teach him to play, though his mother had said it would never do and that this was why school was impossible. Mrs. Moreen exhibited no discomfiture; she only continued blandly: "Mr. Moreen will be delighted to meet your wishes. As I told you, he has been called to London for a week. As soon as he comes back you shall have it out with him."

This was so frank and friendly that the young man could only reply, laughing as his hostess laughed: "Oh I don't imagine we shall have much of a battle."

"They'll give you anything you like," the boy remarked unexpectedly, returning from the window. "We don't mind what anything costs—we live awfully well."

"My darling, you're too quaint!" his mother exclaimed, putting out to caress him a practised but ineffectual hand. He slipped out of it, but looked with intelligent innocent eyes at Pemberton, who had already had time to notice that from one moment to the other his small satiric face seemed to change its time of life. At this moment it was infantine, yet it appeared also to be under the influence of curious intuitions and knowledges. Pemberton rather disliked precocity and was disappointed to find gleams of it in a disciple not yet in his teens. Nevertheless he divined on the spot that Morgan wouldn't prove a bore. He would prove on the contrary a source of agitation. This idea held the young man, in spite of a certain repulsion.

"You pompous little person! We're not extravagant!" Mrs. Moreen gaily protested, making another unsuccessful attempt to draw the boy to her side. "You must know what to expect," she went on to Pemberton.

"The less you expect the better!" her companion interposed. "But we *are* people of fashion."

"Only so far as *you* make us so!" Mrs. Moreen tenderly

mocked. "Well then, on Friday—don't tell me you're superstitious—and mind you don't fail us. Then you'll see us all. I'm so sorry the girls are out. I guess you'll like the girls. And, you know, I've another son, quite different from this one."

"He tries to imitate me," Morgan said to their friend.

"He tries? Why he's twenty years old!" cried Mrs. Moreen.

"You're very witty," Pemberton remarked to the child—a proposition his mother echoed with enthusiasm, declaring Morgan's sallies to be the delight of the house.

The boy paid no heed to this; he only enquired abruptly of the visitor, who was surprised afterwards that he hadn't struck him as offensively forward: "Do you *want* very much to come?"

"Can you doubt it after such a description of what I shall hear?" Pemberton replied. Yet he didn't want to come at all; he was coming because he had to go somewhere, thanks to the collapse of his fortune at the end of a year abroad spent on the system of putting his scant patrimony into a single full wave of experience. He had had his full wave but couldn't pay the score at his inn. Moreover he had caught in the boy's eyes the glimpse of a far-off appeal.

"Well, I'll do the best I can for you," said Morgan; with which he turned away again. He passed out of one of the long windows; Pemberton saw him go and lean on the parapet of the terrace. He remained there while the young man took leave of his mother, who, on Pemberton's looking as if he expected a farewell from him, interposed with: "Leave him, leave him; he's so strange!" Pemberton supposed her to fear something he might say. "He's a genius—you'll love him," she added. "He's much the most interesting person in the family." And before he could invent some civility to oppose to this she wound up with: "But we're all good, you know!"

"He's a genius—you'll love him!" were words that recurred to our aspirant before the Friday, suggesting among many things that geniuses were not invariably loveable. However, it was all the better if there was an element that would make tutorship absorbing: he had perhaps taken too much for granted it would only disgust him. As he left the villa after his interview he looked up at the balcony and saw the child leaning over it. "We shall have great larks!" he called up.

Morgan hung fire a moment and then gaily returned: "By the time you come back I shall have thought of something witty!"

This made Pemberton say to himself "After all he's rather nice."

II

On the Friday he saw them all, as Mrs. Moreen had promised, for her husband had come back and the girls and the other son were at home. Mr. Moreen had a white moustache, a confiding manner and, in his buttonhole, the ribbon of a foreign order—bestowed, as Pemberton eventually learned, for services. For what services he never clearly ascertained: this was a point—one of a larger number—that Mr. Moreen's manner never confided. What it emphatically did confide was that he was even more a man of the world than you might first make out. Ulick, the firstborn, was in visible training for the same profession—under the disadvantage as yet, however, of a buttonhole but feebly floral and a moustache with no pretensions to type. The girls had hair and figures and manners and small fat feet, but had never been out alone. As for Mrs. Moreen, Pemberton saw on a nearer view that her elegance was intermittent and her parts didn't always match. Her husband, as she had promised, met with enthusiasm Pemberton's ideas in regard to a salary. The young man had endeavoured to keep these stammerings modest, and Mr. Moreen made it no secret that *he* found them wanting in "style." He further mentioned that he aspired to be intimate with his children, to be their best friend, and that he was always looking out for them. That was what he went off for, to London and other places—to look out; and this vigilance was the theory of life, as well as the real occupation, of the whole family. They all looked out, for they were very frank on the subject of its being necessary. They desired it to be understood that they were earnest people, and also that their fortune, though quite adequate for earnest people, required the most careful administration. Mr. Moreen, as the parent bird, sought sustenance for the nest. Ulick invoked support mainly at the club, where Pemberton guessed that it was usually served on green cloth. The girls used to do up their hair and their frocks themselves, and our young man felt appealed to to be glad, in regard to Morgan's education, that, though it must naturally be of the best, it didn't cost too much. After a little he *was* glad, forgetting at times his own needs in the interest inspired by the child's character and culture and the pleasure of making easy terms for him.

During the first weeks of their acquaintance Morgan had been as puzzling as a page in an unknown language—altogether different from the obvious little Anglo-Saxons who had misrepresented childhood to Pemberton. Indeed the whole mystic volume in which the boy had been amateurishly bound demanded some practice in translation. Today, after a considerable interval, there is something phantasmagoric, like a prismatic reflexion or a serial novel, in Pemberton's memory of the queerness of the Moreens. If it were not for a few tangible tokens—a lock of Morgan's hair cut by his own hand, and the half-dozen letters received from him when they were disjoined—the whole episode and the figures peopling it would seem too inconsequent for anything but dreamland. Their supreme quaintness was their success—as it appeared to him for a while at the time; since he had never seen a family so brilliantly equipped for failure. Wasn't it success to have kept him so hatefully long? Wasn't it success to have drawn him in that first morning at *déjeuner,* the Friday he came—it was enough to *make* one superstitious—so that he utterly committed himself, and this not by calculation or on a signal, but from a happy instinct which made them, like a band of gipsies, work so neatly together? They amused him as much as if they had really been a band of gipsies. He was still young and had not seen much of the world—his English years had been properly arid; therefore the reversed conventions of the Moreens—for they had *their* desperate properties—struck him as topsy-turvy. He had encountered nothing like them at Oxford; still less had any such note been struck to his younger American ear during the four years at Yale in which he had richly supposed himself to be reacting against a Puritan strain. The reaction of the Moreens, at any rate, went ever so much further. He had thought himself very sharp that first day in hitting them all off in his mind with the "cosmopolite" label. Later it seemed feeble and colourless—confessedly helplessly provisional.

He yet when he first applied it felt a glow of joy—for an instructor he was still empirical—rise from the apprehension that living with them would really be to see life. Their sociable strangeness was an imitation of that—their chatter of tongues, their gaiety and good humour, their infinite dawdling (they were always getting themselves up, but it took for ever, and Pemberton had once found Mr. Moreen shaving in the drawing-room), their French, their Italian and, cropping up in the foreign fluencies, their cold tough slices of American. They lived on maccaroni and coffee—they had these articles prepared in perfection—but they knew recipes for a hundred other dishes. They overflowed with music and song, were always humming and catching each other up, and had a sort of professional acquaintance with Continental cities. They talked of "good places" as if they had been pickpockets or strolling players. They had at Nice a villa, a carriage, a piano and a banjo, and they went to official parties. They were a perfect calendar of the "days" of their friends, which Pemberton knew them, when they were indisposed, to get out of bed to go to, and which made the week larger than life when Mrs. Moreen talked of them with Paula and Amy. Their initiations gave their new inmate at first an almost dazzling sense of culture. Mrs. Moreen had translated something at some former period—an author whom it made Pemberton feel *borné* never to have heard of. They could imitate Venetian and sing Neapolitan, and when they wanted to say something very particular communicated with each other in an ingenious dialect of their own, an elastic spoken cipher which Pemberton at first took for some *patois* of one of their countries, but which he "caught on to" as he would not have grasped provincial development of Spanish or German.

"It's the family language—Ultramoreen," Morgan explained to him drolly enough; but the boy rarely condescended to use it himself, though he dealt in colloquial Latin as if he had been a little prelate.

Among all the "days" with which Mrs. Moreen's memory was taxed she managed to squeeze in one of her own, which her friends sometimes forgot. But the house drew a frequented air from the number of fine people who were freely named there and from several mysterious men with foreign titles and English clothes whom Morgan called the Princes and who, on sofas with the girls, talked French very loud—though sometimes with some oddity of accent—as if to show they were saying nothing improper. Pemberton wondered how the Princes could ever propose in that tone and so publicly: he took for granted cynically that this was what was desired of them. Then he recognised that even for the chance of such an advantage Mrs. Moreen would never allow Paula and Amy to receive alone. These young ladies were not at all timid, but it was just the safeguards that made them so candidly free. It was a houseful of Bohemians who wanted tremendously to be Philistines.

In one respect, however, certainly, they achieved no rigour—they were wonderfully amiable and ecstatic about Morgan. It was a genuine tenderness, an artless admiration, equally strong in each. They even praised his beauty, which was small, and were as afraid of him as if they felt him of finer clay. They spoke of him as a little angel and a prodigy—they touched on his want of health with long, vague faces. Pemberton feared at first an extravagance that might make him hate the boy, but before this happened he had become extravagant himself. Later, when he had grown rather to hate the others, it was a bribe to patience for him that they were at any rate nice about Morgan, going on tiptoe if they fancied he was showing symptoms, and even giving up somebody's "day" to procure him a pleasure. Mixed with this too was the oddest wish to make him independent, as if they had felt themselves not good enough for him. They passed him over to the new members of their circle very much as if wishing to force some charity of adoption on so free an agent and get rid of their own charge. They were delighted when they saw Morgan take so to his kind playfellow, and could think of no higher praise for the young man. It was strange how they contrived to reconcile the appearance, and indeed the essential fact, of adoring the child with their eagerness to wash their hands of him. Did they want to get rid of him before he should find them out? Pemberton was finding them out month by month. The boy's fond family, however this might be, turned their backs with exaggerated delicacy, as if to avoid the reproach of interfering. Seeing in time how little he had in common with them—it was by *them* he first observed it; they proclaimed it with complete humility—his companion was moved to speculate on the mysteries of transmission, the far jumps of heredity. Where his detachment from most of the things they represented had come from was more than an observer could say—it certainly had burrowed under two or three generations.

As for Pemberton's own estimate of his pupil, it was a good while before he got the point of view, so little had he been prepared for it by the smug young barbarians to whom the tradition of tutorship, as hitherto revealed to him, had been adjusted. Morgan was scrappy and surprising, deficient in many properties supposed common to the *genus* and abounding in others that were the portion only of the supernaturally clever. One day his friend made a great stride: it cleared up the question to perceive that Morgan *was* supernaturally clever and that, though the formula was temporarily meagre, this would be the only assumption on which one could successfully deal with him. He had the general quality of a child for whom life had not been simplified by school, a kind of homebred sensibility which might have been bad for himself but was charming for others, and a whole range of refinement and perception—little musical vibrations as taking as picked-up airs—begotten by wandering about Europe at the tail of his migratory tribe. This might not have been an education to recommend in advance, but its results with so special a subject were as appreciable as the marks on a piece of fine porcelain. There was at the same time in him a small strain of stoicism, doubtless the fruit of having had to begin early to bear pain, which counted for pluck and made it of less consequence that he might have been thought at school rather a polyglot little beast. Pemberton indeed quickly found himself rejoicing that school was out of the question: in any million of boys it was probably good for all but one, and Morgan was that millionth. It would have made him comparative and superior—it might have made him really require kicking. Pemberton would try to be school himself—a bigger seminary than five hundred grazing donkeys, so that, winning no prizes, the boy would remain unconscious and irresponsible and amusing—amusing, because, though life was already intense in his childish nature, freshness still made there a strong draught for jokes. It turned out that even in the still air of Morgan's various disabilities jokes flourished greatly. He was a pale lean acute undeveloped little cosmopolite, who liked intellectual gymnastics and who also, as regards the behaviour of mankind, had noticed more things than you might suppose, but who nevertheless had his proper playroom of superstitions, where he smashed a dozen toys a day.

III

At Nice once, toward evening, as the pair rested in the open air after a walk, and looked over the sea at the pink western lights, he said suddenly to his comrade: "Do you like it, you know—being with us all in this intimate way?"

"My dear fellow, why should I stay if I didn't?"

"How do I know you'll stay? I'm almost sure you won't, very long."

"I hope you don't mean to dismiss me," said Pemberton.

Morgan debated, looking at the sunset. "I think if I did right I ought to."

"Well, I know I'm supposed to instruct you in virtue; but in that case don't do right."

"You're very young—fortunately," Morgan went on, turning to him again.

"Oh yes, compared with you!"

"Therefore it won't matter so much if you do lose a lot of time."

"That's the way to look at it," said Pemberton accommodatingly.

They were silent a minute; after which the boy asked: "Do you like my father and my mother very much?"

"Dear me, yes. Charming people."

Morgan received this with another silence; then unexpectedly, familiarly, but at the same time affectionately, he remarked: "You're a jolly old humbug!"

For a particular reason the words made our young man change colour. The boy noticed in an instant that he had turned red, whereupon he turned red himself and pupil and master exchanged a longish glance in which there was a consciousness of many more things than are usually touched upon, even tacitly, in such a relation. It produced for Pemberton an embarrassment; it raised in a shadowy form a question—this was the first glimpse of it—destined to play a singular and, as he imagined, owing to the altogether peculiar conditions, an unprecedented part in his intercourse with his little companion. Later, when he found himself talking with the youngster in a way in which few youngsters could ever have been talked with, he thought of that clumsy moment on the bench at Nice as the dawn of an understanding that had broadened. What had added to the clumsiness then was that he thought it his duty to declare to Morgan that he might abuse him, Pemberton, as much as he liked, but must never abuse his parents. To this Morgan had the easy retort that he hadn't dreamed of abusing them; which appeared to be true: it put Pemberton in the wrong.

"Then why am I a humbug for saying *I* think them charming?" the young man asked, conscious of a certain rashness.

"Well—they're not your parents."

"They love you better than anything in the world—never forget that," said Pemberton.

"Is that why you like them so much?"

"They're very kind to me," Pemberton replied evasively.

"You *are* a humbug!" laughed Morgan, passing an arm into his tutor's. He leaned against him looking off at the sea again and swinging his long thin legs.

"Don't kick my shins," said Pemberton while he reflected "Hang it, I can't complain of them to the child!"

"There's another reason too," Morgan went on, keeping his legs still.

"Another reason for what?"

"Besides their not being your parents."

"I don't understand you," said Pemberton.

"Well, you will before long. All right!"

He did understand fully before long, but he made a fight even with himself before he confessed it. He thought it the oddest thing to have a struggle with the child about. He wondered he didn't hate the hope of the Moreens for bringing the struggle on. But by the time it began any such sentiment for that scion was closed to him. Morgan was a special case, and to know him was to accept him on his own odd terms. Pemberton had spent his aversion to special cases before arriving at knowledge. When at last he did arrive his quandary was great. Against every interest he had attached himself. They would have to meet things together. Before they went home that evening at Nice the boy had said, clinging to his arm:

"Well, at any rate you'll hang on to the last."

"To the last?"

"Till you're fairly beaten."

"*You* ought to be fairly beaten!" cried the young man, drawing him closer.

IV

A YEAR after he had come to live with them Mr. and Mrs. Moreen suddenly gave up the villa at Nice. Pemberton had got used to suddenness, having seen it practised on a considerable scale during two jerky little tours—one in Switzerland the first summer, and the other late in the winter, when they all ran down to Florence and then, at the end of ten days, liking it much less than they had intended, straggled back in mysterious depression. They had returned to Nice "for ever," as they said; but this didn't prevent their squeezing, one rainy muggy May night, into a second-class railway-carriage—you could never tell by which class they would travel—where Pemberton helped them to stow away a wonderful collection of bundles and bags. The explanation of this manœuvre was that they had determined to spend the summer "in some bracing place"; but in Paris they dropped into a small furnished apartment—a fourth floor in a third-rate avenue, where there was a smell on the staircase and the *portier* was hateful—and passed the next four months in blank indigence.

The better part of this baffled sojourn was for the preceptor and his pupil, who, visiting the Invalides and Notre Dame, the Conciergerie and all the museums, took a hundred remunerative rambles. They learned to know their Paris, which was useful, for they came back another year for a longer stay, the general character of which in Pemberton's memory today mixes pitiably and confusedly with that of the first. He sees Morgan's shabby knickerbockers—the everlasting pair that didn't match his blouse and that as he grew longer could only grow faded. He remembers the particular holes in his three or four pair of coloured stockings.

Morgan was dear to his mother, but he never was better dressed than was absolutely necessary—partly, no doubt, by his own fault, for he was as indifferent to his appearance as a German philosopher. "My dear fellow, you *are* coming to pieces," Pemberton would say to him in sceptical remonstrance; to which the child would reply, looking at him serenely up and down: "My dear fellow, so are you! I don't want to cast you in the shade." Pemberton could have no rejoinder for this—the assertion so closely represented the fact. If however the deficiencies of his own wardrobe were a chapter by themselves he didn't like his little charge to look too poor. Later he used to say "Well, if we're poor, why, after all, shouldn't we look it?" and he consoled himself with thinking there was something rather elderly and gentlemanly in Morgan's disrepair—it differed from the untidiness of the urchin who plays and spoils his things. He could trace perfectly the degrees by which, in proportion as her little son confined himself to his tutor for society, Mrs. Moreen shrewdly forbore to renew his garments. She did nothing that didn't show, neglected him because he escaped notice, and then, as he illustrated this clever policy, discouraged at home his public appearances. Her position was logical enough—those members of her family who did show had to be showy.

During this period and several others Pemberton was quite aware of how he and his comrade might strike people; wandering languidly through the Jardin des Plantes as if they had nowhere to go, sitting on the winter days in the galleries of the Louvre, so splendidly ironical to the homeless, as if for the advantage of the *calorifère*. They joked about it sometimes: it was the sort of joke that was perfectly within the boy's compass. They figured themselves as part of the vast vague hand-to-mouth multitude of the enormous city and pretended they were proud of their position in it—it showed them "such a lot of life" and made them conscious of a democratic brotherhood. If Pemberton couldn't feel a sympathy in destitution with his small companion—for after all Morgan's fond parents would never have let him really suffer—the boy would at least feel it with him, so it came to the same thing. He used sometimes to wonder what people would think they were—to fancy they were looked askance at, as if it might be a suspected case of kidnapping. Morgan wouldn't be taken for a young patrician with a preceptor—he wasn't smart enough; though he might pass for his companion's sickly little brother. Now and then he had a five-franc piece, and except once, when they bought a couple of lovely neckties, one of which he made Pemberton accept, they laid it out scientifically in old books. This was sure to be a great day, always spent on the quays, in a rummage of the dusty boxes that garnish the parapets. Such occasions helped them to live, for their books ran low very soon after the beginning of their acquaintance. Pemberton had a good many in England, but he was obliged to write to a friend and ask him kindly to get some fellow to give him something for them.

If they had to relinquish that summer the advantage of the bracing climate the young man couldn't but suspect this failure of the cup when at their very lips to have been the effect of a rude jostle of his own. This had represented his first blow-out, as he called it, with his patrons; his first successful attempt—though there was little other success about it—to bring them to a consideration of his impossible position. As the ostensible eve of a costly journey the moment had struck him as favourable to an earnest protest, the presentation of an ultimatum. Ridiculous as it sounded, he had never yet been able to compass an uninterrupted private interview with the elder pair or with either of them singly. They were always flanked by their elder children, and poor Pemberton usually had his own little charge at his side. He was conscious of its being a house in which the surface of one's delicacy got rather smudged; nevertheless he had preserved the bloom of his scruple against announcing to Mr. and Mrs. Moreen with publicity that he shouldn't be able to go on longer without a little money. He was still simple enough to suppose Ulick and Paula and Amy might not know that since his arrival he had only had a hundred and forty francs; and he was magnanimous enough to wish not to compromise their parents in their eyes. Mr. Moreen now listened to him, as he listened to every one and to every thing, like a man of the world, and seemed to appeal to him—though not of course too grossly—to try and be a little more of one himself. Pemberton recognised in fact the importance of the character—from the advantage it gave Mr. Moreen. He was not even confused or embarrassed, whereas the young man in his service was more so than there was any reason for. Neither was he surprised—at least any more than a gentleman had to be who freely confessed himself a little shocked—though not perhaps strictly at Pemberton.

"We must go into this, mustn't we, dear?" he said to his wife. He assured his young friend that the matter should have his very best attention; and he melted into space as elusively as if, at the door, he were taking an inevitable but deprecatory precedence. When, the next moment, Pemberton found himself alone with Mrs. Moreen it was to hear her say "I see, I see"—stroking the roundness of her chin and looking as if she were only hesitating between a dozen easy remedies. If they didn't make their push Mr. Moreen could at least disappear for several days. During his absence his wife took up the subject again spontaneously, but her contribution to it was merely that she had thought all the while they were getting on so beautifully. Pemberton's reply to this revelation was that unless they immediately put down something on account he would leave them on the spot and for ever. He knew she would wonder how he would get away, and for a moment expected her to enquire. She didn't for which he was almost grateful to her, so little was he in a position to tell.

"You won't, you *know* you won't—you're too interested," she said. "You *are* interested, you know you are, you dear kind man!" She laughed with almost condemnatory archness, as if it were a reproach—though she wouldn't insist; and flirted a soiled pocket-handkerchief at him.

Pemberton's mind was fully made up to take his step the following week. This would give him time to get an answer to a letter he had dispatched to England. If he did in the event nothing of the sort—that is if he stayed another year and then went away only for three months—it was not merely because before the answer to his letter came (most unsatisfactory when it did arrive) Mr. Moreen generously counted out to him, and again with the sacrifice to "form" of a marked man of the world, three hundred francs in elegant ringing gold. He was irritated to find that Mrs. Moreen was right, that he couldn't at the pinch bear to leave the child. This stood out clearer for the very reason that, the night of his desperate appeal to his patrons, he had seen fully for the first time where he was. Wasn't it another proof of the success with which those patrons practised their arts that they had managed to avert for so long the illuminating flash? It descended on our friend with a breadth of effect which perhaps would have struck a spectator as comical, after he had returned to his little servile room, which looked into a close court where a bare dirty opposite wall took, with the sound of shrill clatter, the reflexion of lighted back windows. He had simply given himself away to a band of adventurers. The idea, the word itself, wore a romantic horror for him—he had always lived on such safe lines. Later it assumed a more interesting, almost a soothing, sense: it pointed a moral, and Pemberton could enjoy a moral. The Moreens were adventurers not merely because they didn't pay their debts, because they lived on society, but because their whole view of life, dim and confused and instinctive, like that of clever colour-blind animals, was speculative and rapacious and mean. Oh they were "respectable," and that only made them more *immondes*! The young man's analysis, while he brooded, put it at last very simply—they were adventurers because they were toadies and snobs. That was the completest account of them—it was the law of their being. Even when this truth became vivid to their ingenious inmate he remained unconscious of how much his mind had been prepared for it by the extraordinary little boy who had now become such a complication in his life. Much less could he then calculate on the information he was still to owe the extraordinary little boy.

V

But it was during the ensuing time that the real problem came up—the problem of how far it was excusable to discuss the turpitude of parents with a child of twelve, of thirteen, of fourteen. Absolutely inexcusable and quite impossible it of course at first appeared; and indeed the question didn't press for some time after Pemberton had received his three hundred francs. They produced a temporary lull, a relief from the sharpest pressure. The young man frugally amended his wardrobe and even had a few francs in his pocket. He thought the Moreens looked at him as if he were almost too smart, as if they ought to take care not to spoil him. If Mr. Moreen hadn't been such a man of the world he would perhaps have spoken of the freedom of such neckties on the part of a subordinate. But Mr. Moreen was always enough a man of the world to let things pass—he had certainly shown that. It was singular how Pemberton guessed that Morgan, though saying nothing about it, knew something had happened. But three hundred francs, especially when one owed money, couldn't last for ever; and when the treasure was gone—the boy knew when it had failed—Morgan did break ground. The party had returned to Nice at the beginning of the winter, but not to the charming villa. They went to an hotel, where they stayed three months, and then moved to another establishment, explaining that they had left the first because, after waiting and waiting, they couldn't get the rooms they wanted. These apartments, the rooms they wanted, were generally very splendid; but fortunately they never *could* get them—fortunately, I mean, for Pemberton, who reflected always that if they had got them there would have been a still scanter educational fund. What Morgan said at last was said suddenly, irrelevantly, when the moment came, in the middle of a lesson, and consisted of the apparently unfeeling words: "You ought to *filer,* you know—you really ought."

Pemberton stared. He had learnt enough French slang from Morgan to know that to *filer* meant to cut sticks. "Ah my dear fellow, don't turn me off!"

Morgan pulled a Greek lexicon toward him—he used a Greek-German—to look out a word, instead of asking it of Pemberton. "You can't go on like this, you know."

"Like what, my boy?"

"You know they don't pay you up," said Morgan, blushing and turning his leaves.

"Don't pay me?" Pemberton stared again and feigned amazement. "What on earth put that into your head?"

"It has been there a long time," the boy replied rummaging his book.

Pemberton was silent, then he went on: "I say, what are you hunting for? They pay me beautifully."

"I'm hunting for the Greek for awful whopper," Morgan dropped.

"Find that rather for gross impertinence and disabuse your mind. What do I want of money?"

"Oh that's another question!"

Pemberton wavered—he was drawn in different ways. The severely correct thing would have been to tell the boy that such a matter was none of his business and bid him go on with his lines. But they were really too intimate for that; it was not the way he was in the habit of treating him; there had been no reason it should be. On the other hand Morgan had quite lighted on the truth—he really shouldn't be able to keep it up much longer; therefore why not let him know one's real motive for forsaking him? At the same time it wasn't decent to abuse to one's pupil the family of one's pupil; it was better to misrepresent than to do that. So in reply to his comrade's last exclamation he just declared, to dismiss the subject, that he had received several payments.

"I say—I say!" the boy ejaculated, laughing.

"That's all right," Pemberton insisted. "Give me your written rendering."

Morgan pushed a copybook across the table, and he began to read the page, but with something running in his head that made it no sense. Looking up after a minute or two he found the child's eyes fixed on him and felt in them something strange. Then Morgan said: "I'm not afraid of the stern reality."

"I haven't yet seen the thing you *are* afraid of—I'll do you that justice!"

This came out with a jump—it was perfectly true—and evidently gave Morgan pleasure. "I've thought of it a long time," he presently resumed.

"Well, don't think of it any more."

The boy appeared to comply, and they had a comfortable and even an amusing hour. They had a theory that they were very thorough, and yet they seemed always to be in the amusing part of lessons, the intervals between the dull dark tunnels, where there were waysides and jolly views. Yet the morning was brought to a violent end by Morgan's suddenly leaning his arms on the table, burying his head in them and bursting into tears: at which Pemberton was the more startled that, as it then came over him, it was the first time he had ever seen the boy cry and that the impression was consequently quite awful.

The next day, after much thought, he took a decision and, believing it to be just, immediately acted on it. He cornered Mr.

and Mrs. Moreen again and let them know that if on the spot they didn't pay him all they owed him he wouldn't only leave their house but would tell Morgan exactly what had brought him to it.

"Oh you *haven't* told him?" cried Mrs. Moreen with a pacifying hand on her well-dressed bosom.

"Without warning you? For what do you take me?" the young man returned.

Mr. and Mrs. Moreen looked at each other; he could see that they appreciated, as tending to their security, his superstition of delicacy, and yet that there was a certain alarm in their relief. "My dear fellow," Mr. Moreen demanded, "what use *can* you have, leading the quiet life we all do, for such a lot of money?" —a question to which Pemberton made no answer, occupied as he was in noting that what passed in the mind of his patrons was something like: "Oh then, if we've felt that the child, dear little angel, has judged us and how he regards us, and we haven't been betrayed, he must have guessed—and in short it's *general*!" an inference that rather stirred up Mr. and Mrs. Moreen, as Pemberton had desired it should. At the same time, if he had supposed his threat would do something towards bringing them round, he was disappointed to find them taking for granted—how vulgar their perception *had* been!—that he had already given them away. There was a mystic uneasiness in their parental breasts, and that had been the inferior sense of it. None the less, however, his threat did touch them; for if they had escaped it was only to meet a new danger. Mr. Moreen appealed to him, on every precedent, as a man of the world; but his wife had recourse, for the first time since his domestication with them, to a fine *hauteur,* reminding him that a devoted mother, with her child, had arts that protected her against gross misrepresentation.

"I should misrepresent you grossly if I accused you of common honesty!" our friend replied; but as he closed the door behind him sharply, thinking he had not done himself much good, while Mr. Moreen lighted another cigarette, he heard his hostess shout after him more touchingly:

"Oh you do, you *do,* put the knife to one's throat!"

The next morning, very early, she came to his room. He recognised her knock, but had no hope she brought him money; as to which he was wrong, for she had fifty francs in her hand. She squeezed forward in her dressing-gown, and he received her in his own, between his bath-tub and his bed. He had been tolerably schooled by this time to the "foreign ways" of his hosts. Mrs. Moreen was ardent, and when she was ardent she didn't care what she did; so she now sat down on his bed, his clothes being on the chairs, and, in her preoccupation, forgot, as she glanced round, to be ashamed of giving him such a horrid room. What Mrs. Moreen's ardour now bore upon was the design of persuading him that in the first place she was very good-natured to bring him fifty francs, and that in the second, if he would only see it, he was really too absurd to expect to be *paid*. Wasn't he paid enough without perpetual money—wasn't he paid by the comfortable luxurious home he enjoyed with them all, without a care, an anxiety, a solitary want? Wasn't he sure of his position, and wasn't that everything to a young man like him, quite unknown, with singularly little to show, the ground of whose exorbitant pretensions it had never been easy to discover? Wasn't he paid above all by the sweet relation he had established with Morgan—quite ideal as from master to pupil—and by the simple privilege of knowing and living with so amazingly gifted a child; than whom really (and she meant literally what she said) there was no better company in Europe? Mrs. Moreen herself took to appealing to him as a man of the world; she said "Voyons, mon cher," and "My dear man, look here now"; and urged him to be reasonable, putting it before him that it was truly a chance for him. She spoke as if, according as he *should* be reasonable, he would prove himself worthy to be her son's tutor and of the extraordinary confidence they had placed in him.

After all, Pemberton reflected, it was only a difference of theory and the theory didn't matter much. They had hitherto gone on that of remunerated, as now they would go on that of gratuitous, service; but why should they have so many words about it? Mrs. Moreen at all events continued to be convincing; sitting there with her fifty francs she talked and reiterated as women reiterate, and bored and irritated him, while he leaned against the wall with his hands in the pockets of his wrapper, drawing it together round his legs and looking over the head of his visitor at the grey negations of his window. She wound up with saying: "You see I bring you a definite proposal."

"A definite proposal?"

"To make our relations regular, as it were—to put them on a comfortable footing."

"I see—it's a system," said Pemberton. "A kind of organised blackmail."

Mrs. Moreen bounded up, which was exactly what he wanted. "What do you mean by that?"

"You practise on one's fears—one's fears about the child if one should go away."

"And pray what would happen to him in that event?" she demanded with majesty.

"Why he'd be alone with *you*."

"And pray with whom *should* a child be but with those whom he loves most?"

"If you think that, why don't you dismiss me?"

"Do you pretend he loves you more than he loves *us*?" cried Mrs. Moreen.

"I think he ought to. I make sacrifices for him. Though I've heard of those *you* make I don't see them."

Mrs. Moreen stared a moment; then with emotion she grasped her inmate's hand. "*Will* you make it—the sacrifice?"

He burst out laughing. "I'll see. I'll do what I can. I'll stay a little longer. Your calculation's just—I *do* hate intensely to give him up; I'm fond of him and he thoroughly interests me, in spite of the inconvenience I suffer. You know my situation perfectly. I haven't a penny in the world and, occupied as you see me with Morgan, am unable to earn money."

Mrs. Moreen tapped her undressed arm with her folded bank-note. "Can't you write articles? Can't you translate as *I* do?"

"I don't know about translating; it's wretchedly paid."

"I'm glad to earn what I can," said Mrs. Moreen with prodigious virtue.

"You ought to tell me who you do it for." Pemberton paused a moment, and she said nothing; so he added: "I've tried to turn off some little sketches, but the magazines won't have them—they're declined with thanks."

"You see then you're not such a phœnix," his visitor pointedly smiled—"to pretend to abilities you're sacrificing for our sake."

"I haven't time to do things properly," he ruefully went on. Then as it came over him that he was almost abjectly good-natured to give these explanations he added: "If I stay on longer it must be on one condition—that Morgan shall know distinctly on what footing I am."

Mrs. Moreen demurred. "Surely you don't want to show off to a child?"

"To show *you* off, do you mean?"

Again she cast about, but this time it was to produce a still finer flower. "And *you* talk of blackmail!"

"You can easily prevent it," said Pemberton.

"And *you* talk of practising on fears!" she bravely pushed on.

"Yes, there's no doubt I'm a great scoundrel."

His patroness met his eyes—it was clear she was in straits. Then she thrust out her money at him. "Mr. Moreen desired me to give you this on account."

"I'm much obliged to Mr. Moreen, but we *have* no account."

"You won't take it?"

"That leaves me more free," said Pemberton.

"To poison my darling's mind?" groaned Mrs. Moreen.

"Oh your darling's mind—!" the young man laughed.

She fixed him a moment, and he thought she was going to break out tormentedly, pleadingly: "For God's sake, tell me what *is* in it!" But she checked this impulse—another was stronger. She pocketed the money—the crudity of the alternative was comical—and swept out of the room with the desperate concession: "You may tell him any horror you like!"

VI

A COUPLE of days after this, during which he had failed to profit by so free a permission, he had been for a quarter of an hour walking with his charge in silence when the boy became sociable again with the remark: "I'll tell you how I know it; I know it through Zénobie."

"Zénobie? Who in the world is *she*?"

"A nurse I used to have—ever so many years ago. A charming woman. I liked her awfully, and she liked me."

"There's no accounting for tastes. What is it you know through her?"

"Why what their idea is. She went away because they didn't fork out. She did like me awfully, and she stayed two years. She told me all about it—that at last she could never get her wages. As soon as they saw how much she liked me they stopped giving her anything. They thought she'd stay for nothing—just *because,* don't you know?" And Morgan had a queer little conscious lucid look. "She did stay ever so long—as long as she could. She was only a poor girl. She used to send money to her mother. At last she couldn't afford it any longer, and went away in a fearful rage one night—I mean of course in a rage against *them*. She cried over me tremendously, she hugged me nearly to death. She told me all about it," the boy repeated. "She told me it was their idea. So I guessed, ever so long ago, that they have had the same idea with you."

"Zénobie was very sharp," said Pemberton. "And she made you so."

"Oh that wasn't Zénobie; that was nature. And experience!" Morgan laughed.

"Well, Zénobie was a part of your experience."

"Certainly I was a part of hers, poor dear!" the boy wisely sighed. "And I'm part of yours."

"A very important part. But I don't see how you know I've been treated like Zénobie."

"Do you take me for the biggest dunce you've known?" Morgan asked. "Haven't I been conscious of what we've been through together?"

"What we've been through?"

"Our privations—our dark days."

"Oh our days have been bright enough."

Morgan went on in silence for a moment. Then he said: "My dear chap, you're a hero!"

"Well, you're another!" Pemberton retorted.

"No I'm not, but I ain't a baby. I won't stand it any longer. You must get some occupation that pays. I'm ashamed, I'm ashamed!" quavered the boy with a ring of passion, like some high silver note from a small cathedral chorister, that deeply touched his friend.

"We ought to go off and live somewhere together," the young man said.

"I'll go like a shot if you'll take me."

"I'd get some work that would keep us both afloat," Pemberton continued.

"So would I. Why shouldn't *I* work? I ain't such a beastly little muff as *that* comes to."

"The difficulty is that your parents wouldn't hear of it. They'd never part with you; they worship the ground you tread on. Don't you see the proof of it?" Pemberton developed. "They don't dislike me; they wish me no harm; they're very amiable people; but they're perfectly ready to expose me to any awkwardness in life for your sake."

The silence in which Morgan received his fond sophistry struck Pemberton somehow as expressive. After a moment the child repeated: "You *are* a hero!" Then he added: "They leave me with you altogether. You've all the responsibility. They put me off on you from morning till night. Why then should they object to my taking up with you completely? I'd help you."

"They're not particularly keen about my being helped, and they delight in thinking of you as *theirs*. They're tremendously proud of you."

"I'm not proud of *them*. But you know that," Morgan returned.

"Except for the little matter we speak of they're charming people," said Pemberton, not taking up the point made for his intelligence, but wondering greatly at the boy's own, and especially at this fresh reminder of something he had been conscious of from the first—the strangest thing in his friend's large little composition, a temper, a sensibility, even a private ideal, which made him as privately disown the stuff his people were made of. Morgan had in secret a small loftiness which made him acute about betrayed meanness; as well as a critical sense for the manners immediately surrounding him that was quite without precedent in a juvenile nature, especially when one noted that it had not made this nature "old-fashioned," as the word is of children—quaint or wizened or offensive. It was as if he had been a little gentleman and had paid the penalty by discovering that he was the only such person in his family. This comparison didn't make him vain, but it could make him melancholy and a trifle austere. While Pemberton guessed at these dim young things, shadows of shadows, he was partly drawn on and partly checked, as for a scruple, by the charm of attempting to sound the little cool shallows that were so quickly growing deeper. When he tried to figure to himself the morning twilight of childhood, so as to deal with it safely, he saw it was never fixed, never arrested, that ignorance, at the instant he touched it, was already flushing faintly into knowledge, that there was nothing that at a given moment you could say an intelligent child didn't know. It seemed to him that he himself knew too much to imagine Morgan's simplicity and too little to disembroil his tangle.

The boy paid no heed to his last remark; he only went on: "I'd have spoken to them about their idea, as I call it, long ago, if I hadn't been sure what they'd say."

"And what would they say?"

"Just what they said about what poor Zénobie told me—that it was a horrid dreadful story, that they had paid her every penny they owed her."

"Well, perhaps they had," said Pemberton.

"Perhaps they've paid you!"

"Let us pretend they have, and *n'en parlons plus.*"

"They accused her of lying and cheating"—Morgan stuck to historic truth. "That's why I don't want to speak to them."

"Lest they should accuse me too?" To this Morgan made no answer, and his companion, looking down at him—the boy turned away his eyes, which had filled—saw that he couldn't have trusted himself to utter. "You're right. Don't worry them," Pemberton pursued. "Except for that, they *are* charming people."

"Except for *their* lying and *their* cheating?"

"I say—I say!" cried Pemberton, imitating a little tone of the lad's which was itself an imitation.

"We must be frank, at the last; we *must* come to an understanding," said Morgan with the importance of the small boy who lets himself think he is arranging great affairs—almost playing at shipwreck or at Indians. "I know all about everything."

"I dare say your father has his reasons," Pemberton replied, but too vaguely, as he was aware.

"For lying and cheating?"

"For saving and managing and turning his means to the best account. He has plenty to do with his money. You're an expensive family."

"Yes, I'm very expensive," Morgan concurred in a manner that made his preceptor burst out laughing.

"He's saving for *you,*" said Pemberton. "They think of you in everything they do."

"He might, while he's about it, save a little—" The boy paused, and his friend waited to hear what. Then Morgan brought out oddly: "A little reputation."

"Oh there's plenty of that. That's all right!"

"Enough of it for the people they know, no doubt. The people they know are awful."

"Do you mean the princes? We mustn't abuse the princes."

"Why not? They haven't married Paula—they haven't married Amy. They only clean out Ulick."

"You *do* know everything!" Pemberton declared.

"No I don't after all. I don't know what they live on, or how they live, or *why* they live! What have they got and how did they get it? Are they rich, are they poor, or have they a *modeste aisance?* Why are they always chiveying me about—living one year like ambassadors and the next like paupers? Who are they, anyway, and what are they? I've thought of all that—I've thought of a lot of things. They're so beastly worldly. That's what I hate most—oh I've *seen* it! All they care about is to make an appearance and to pass for something or other. What the dickens do they want to pass for? What *do* they, Mr. Pemberton?"

"You pause for a reply," said Pemberton, treating the question as a joke, yet wondering too and greatly struck with his mate's intense if imperfect vision. "I haven't the least idea."

"And what good does it do? Haven't I seen the way people treat them—the 'nice' people, the ones they want to know? They'll take anything from them—they'll lie down and be trampled on. The nice ones hate that—they just sicken them. You're the only really nice person we know."

"Are you sure? They don't lie down for me!"

"Well, you shan't lie down for them. You've got to go—that's what you've got to do," said Morgan.

"And what will become of you?"

"Oh I'm growing up. I shall get off before long. I'll see you later."

"You had better let me finish you," Pemberton urged, lending himself to the child's strange superiority.

Morgan stopped in their walk, looking up at him. He had to look up much less than a couple of years before—he had grown, in his loose leanness, so long and high. "Finish me?" he echoed.

"There are such a lot of jolly things we can do together yet. I want to turn you out—I want you to do me credit."

Morgan continued to look at him. "To give you credit—do you mean?"

"My dear fellow, you're too clever to live."

"That's just what I'm afraid you think. No, no; it isn't fair—I can't endure it. We'll separate next week. The sooner it's over the sooner to sleep."

"If I hear of anything—any other chance—I promise to go," Pemberton said.

Morgan consented to consider this. "But you'll be honest," he demanded; "you won't pretend you haven't heard?"

"I'm much more likely to pretend I have."

"But what can you hear of, this way, stuck in a hole with us? You ought to be on the spot, to go to England—you ought to go to America."

"One would think you were *my* tutor!" said Pemberton.

Morgan walked on and after a little had begun again: "Well, now that you know I know and that we look at the facts and keep nothing back—it's much more comfortable, isn't it?"

"My dear boy, it's so amusing, so interesting, that it will surely be quite impossible for me to forego such hours as these."

This made Morgan stop once more. "You *do* keep something back. Oh you're not straight—*I* am!"

"How am I not straight?"

"Oh you've got your idea!"

"My idea?"

"Why that I probably shan't make old—make older—bones, and that you can stick it out till I'm removed."

"You *are* too clever to live!" Pemberton repeated.

"I call it a mean idea," Morgan pursued. "But I shall punish you by the way I hang on."

"Look out or I'll poison you!" Pemberton laughed.

"I'm stronger and better every year. Haven't you noticed that there hasn't been a doctor near me since you came?"

"*I'm* your doctor," said the young man, taking his arm and drawing him tenderly on again.

Morgan proceeded and after a few steps gave a sigh of mingled weariness and relief. "Ah now that we look at the facts it's all right!"

VII

THEY looked at the facts a good deal after this; and one of the first consequences of their doing so was that Pemberton stuck it out, in his friend's parlance, for the purpose. Morgan made the facts so vivid and so droll, and at the same time so bald and so ugly, that there was fascination in talking them over with him, just as there would have been heartlessness in leaving him alone with them. Now that the pair had such perceptions in common it was useless for them to pretend they didn't judge such people; but the very judgement and the exchange of perceptions created another tie. Morgan had never been so interesting as now that he himself was made plainer by the sidelight of these confidences. What came out in it most was the small fine passion of his pride. He had plenty of that, Pemberton felt—so much that one might perhaps wisely wish for it some early bruises. He would have liked his people to have a spirit and had waked up to the sense of their perpetually eating humble-pie. His mother would consume any amount, and his father would consume even more than his mother. He had a theory that Ulick had wriggled out of an "affair" at Nice: there had once been a flurry at home, a regular panic, after which they all went to bed and took medicine, not to be accounted for on any other supposition. Morgan had a romantic imagination, fed by poetry and history, and he would have liked those who "bore his name"—as he used to say to Pemberton with the humour that made his queer delicacies manly—to carry themselves with an air. But their one idea was to get in with people who didn't want them and to take snubs as if they were honourable scars. Why people didn't want them more he didn't know—that was people's own affair; after all they weren't superficially repulsive, they were a hundred times cleverer than most of the dreary grandees, the "poor swells" they rushed about Europe to catch up with. "After all they *are* amusing—they are!" he used to pronounce with the wisdom of the ages. To which Pemberton always replied: "Amusing—the great Moreen troupe? Why they're altogether delightful; and if it weren't for the hitch that you and I (feeble performers!) make in the *ensemble* they'd carry everything before them."

What the boy couldn't get over was the fact that this particular blight seemed, in a tradition of self-respect, so undeserved and so arbitrary. No doubt people had a right to take the line they liked; but why should *his* people have liked the line of pushing and toadying and lying and cheating? What had their forefathers—all decent folk, so far as he knew—done to them, or what had *he* done to them? Who had poisoned their blood with the fifth-rate social ideal, the fixed idea of making smart acquaintances and getting into the *monde chic,* especially when it was foredoomed to failure and exposure? They showed so what they were after; that was what made the people they wanted not want *them*. And never a wince for dignity, never a throb of shame at looking each other in the face, never any independence or resentment or disgust. If his father or his brother would only knock some one down once or twice a year! Clever as they were they never guessed the impression they made. They were good-natured, yes—as good-natured as Jews at the doors of clothing-shops! But was that the model one wanted one's family to follow? Morgan had dim memories of an old grandfather, the maternal, in New York, whom he had been taken across the ocean at the age of five to see: a gentleman with a high neck-cloth and a good deal of pronunciation, who wore a dress-coat in the morning, which made one wonder what he wore in the evening, and had, or was supposed to have, "property" and something to do with the Bible Society. It couldn't have been but that *he* was a good type. Pemberton himself remembered Mrs. Clancy, a widowed sister of Mr. Moreen's, who was as irritating as a moral tale and had paid a fortnight's visit to the family at Nice shortly after he came to live with them. She was "pure and refined," as Amy said over the banjo, and had the air of not knowing what they meant when they talked, and of keeping something rather important back. Pemberton judged that what she kept back was an approval of many of their ways; therefore it was to be supposed that she too was of a good type, and that Mr. and Mrs. Moreen and Ulick and Paula and Amy might easily have been of a better one if they would.

But that they wouldn't was more and more perceptible from day to day. They continued to "chivey," as Morgan called it, and in due time became aware of a variety of reasons for proceeding to Venice. They mentioned a great many of them—they were always strikingly frank and had the brightest friendly chatter, at the late foreign breakfast in especial, before the ladies had made up their faces, when they leaned their arms on the table, had something to follow the *demi-tasse,* and, in the heat of familiar discussion as to what they "really ought" to do, fell inevitably into the languages in which they could *tutoyer*. Even Pemberton liked them then; he could endure even Ulick when he heard him give his little flat voice for the "sweet sea-city." That was what made him have a sneaking kindness for them—that they were so out of the workaday world and kept him so out of it. The summer had waned when, with cries of ecstasy, they all passed out on the balcony that overhung the Grand Canal. The sunsets then were splendid and the Dorringtons had arrived. The Dorringtons were the only reason they hadn't talked of at breakfast; but the reasons they didn't talk of at breakfast always came out in the end. The Dorringtons on the other hand came out very little; or else when they did they stayed—as was natural—for hours, during which periods Mrs. Moreen and the girls sometimes called at their hotel (to see if they had returned) as many as three times running. The gondola was for the ladies, as in Venice too there were "days," which Mrs. Moreen knew in their order an hour after she arrived. She immediately took one herself, to which the Dorringtons never came, though on a certain occasion when Pemberton and his pupil were together at Saint Mark's—where, taking the best walks they had ever had and haunting a hundred churches, they spent a great deal of time—they saw the old lord turn up with Mr. Moreen and Ulick, who showed him the dim basilica as if it belonged to them. Pemberton noted how much less, among its curiosities, Lord Dorrington carried himself as a man of the world; wondering too whether, for such services, his companions took a fee from him. The autumn at any rate waned, the Dorringtons departed, and Lord Verschoyle, the eldest son, had proposed neither for Amy nor for Paula.

One sad November day, while the wind roared round the old palace and the rain lashed the lagoon, Pemberton, for exercise and even somewhat for warmth—the Moreens were horribly frugal about fires; it was a cause of suffering to their inmate—walked up and down the big bare *sala* with his pupil. The scagliola floor was cold, the high battered casements shook in the storm, and the stately decay of the place was unrelieved by a particle of furniture. Pemberton's spirits were low, and it came over him that the fortune of the Moreens was now even lower. A blast of desolation, a portent of disgrace and disaster, seemed to draw through the comfortless hall. Mr. Moreen and Ulick were in the Piazza, looking out for something, strolling drearily, in mackintoshes, under the arcades; but still, in spite of mackintoshes, unmistakeable men of the world. Paula and Amy were in bed—it might have been thought they were staying there to keep warm. Pemberton looked askance at the boy at his side, to see to what extent he was conscious of these dark omens. But Morgan, luckily for him, was now mainly conscious of growing taller and stronger and indeed of being in his fifteenth year. This fact was intensely interesting to him and the basis of a private theory—which, however, he had imparted to his tutor—that in a little while he should stand on his own feet. He considered that the situation would change—that in short he should be "finished," grown up, producible in the world of affairs and ready to prove himself of sterling ability. Sharply as he was capable at times of analysing, as he called it, his life, there were happy hours when he remained, as he also called it —and as the name, really, of their right ideal—"jolly" superficial; the proof of which was his fundamental assumption that he should presently go to Oxford, to Pemberton's college, and aided and abetted by Pemberton, do the most wonderful things. It depressed the young man to see how little in such a project he took account of ways and means: in other connexions he mostly kept to the measure. Pemberton tried to imagine the Moreens at Oxford and fortunately failed; yet unless they were to adopt it as a residence there would be no *modus vivendi* for Morgan. How could he live without an allowance, and where was the allowance to come from? He, Pemberton, might live on Morgan; but how could Morgan live on *him*? What was to become of him anyhow? Somehow the fact that he was a big boy now, with better prospects of health, made the question of his future more difficult. So long as he was markedly frail the great consideration he inspired seemed enough of an answer to it. But at the bottom of Pemberton's heart was the recognition of his probably being strong enough to live and not yet strong enough to struggle or to thrive. Morgan himself at any rate was in the first flush of the rosiest consciousness of adolescence, so that the beating of the tempest seemed to him after all but the voice of life and the challenge of fate. He had on his shabby little overcoat, with the collar up, but was enjoying his walk.

It was interrupted at last by the appearance of his mother at the end of the *sala*. She beckoned him to come to her, and while Pemberton saw him, complaisant, pass down the long vista and over the damp false marble, he wondered what was in the air. Mrs. Moreen said a word to the boy and made him go into the room she had quitted. Then, having closed the door after him, she directed her steps swiftly to Pemberton. There *was* something in the air, but his wildest flight of fancy wouldn't have suggested what it proved to be. She signified that she had made a pretext to get Morgan out of the way, and then she enquired —without hesitation—if the young man could favour her with the loan of three louis. While, before bursting into a laugh, he stared at her with surprise, she declared that she was awfully pressed for the money; she was desperate for it—it would save her life.

"Dear lady, *c'est trop fort!*" Pemberton laughed in the manner and with the borrowed grace of idiom that marked the best colloquial, the best anecdotic, moments of his friends themselves. "Where in the world do you suppose I should get three louis, *du train dont vous allez*?"

"I thought you worked—wrote things. Don't they pay you?"

"Not a penny."

"Are you such a fool as to work for nothing?"

"You ought surely to know that."

Mrs. Moreen stared, then she coloured a little. Pemberton

saw she had quite forgotten the terms—if "terms" they could be called—that he had ended by accepting from herself; they had burdened her memory as little as her conscience. "Oh yes, I see what you mean—you've been very nice about that; but why drag it in so often?" She had been perfectly urbane with him ever since the rough scene of explanation in his room the morning he made her accept *his* "terms"—the necessity of his making his case known to Morgan. She had felt no resentment after seeing there was no danger Morgan would take the matter up with her. Indeed, attributing this immunity to the good taste of his influence with the boy, she had once said to Pemberton "My dear fellow, it's an immense comfort you're a gentleman." She repeated this in substance now. "Of course you're a gentleman—that's a bother the less!" Pemberton reminded her that he had not "dragged in" anything that wasn't already in as much as his foot was in his shoe; and she also repeated her prayer that, somewhere and somehow, he would find her sixty francs. He took the liberty of hinting that if he could find them it wouldn't be to lend them to *her*—as to which he consciously did himself injustice, knowing that if he had them he would certainly put them at her disposal. He accused himself, at bottom and not unveraciously, of a fantastic, a demoralised sympathy with her. If misery made strange bedfellows it also made strange sympathies. It was moreover a part of the abasement of living with such people that one had to make vulgar retorts, quite out of one's own tradition of good manners. "Morgan, Morgan, to what pass have I come for you?" he groaned while Mrs. Moreen floated voluminously down the *sala* again to liberate the boy, wailing as she went that everything was too odious.

Before their young friend was liberated there came a thump at the door communicating with the staircase, followed by the apparition of a dripping youth who poked in his head. Pemberton recognised him as the bearer of a telegram and recognised the telegram as addressed to himself. Morgan came back as, after glancing at the signature—that of a relative in London —he was reading the words: "Found jolly job for you, engagement to coach opulent youth on own terms. Come at once." The answer happily was paid and the messenger waited. Morgan, who had drawn near, waited too and looked hard at Pemberton; and Pemberton, after a moment, having met his look, handed him the telegram. It was really by wise looks—they knew each other so well now—that, while the telegraph-boy, in his waterproof cape, made a great puddle on the floor, the thing was settled between them. Pemberton wrote the answer with a pencil against the frescoed wall, and the messenger departed. When he had gone the young man explained himself.

"I'll make a tremendous charge; I'll earn a lot of money in a short time, and we'll live on it."

"Well, I hope the opulent youth will be a dismal dunce—he probably will," Morgan parenthesised—"and keep you a long time a-hammering of it in."

"Of course the longer he keeps me the more we shall have for our old age."

"But suppose *they* don't pay you!" Morgan awfully suggested.

"Oh there are not two such—!" But Pemberton pulled up; he had been on the point of using too invidious a term. Instead of this he said "Two such fatalities."

Morgan flushed—the tears came to his eyes. "*Dites toujours* two such rascally crews!" Then in a different tone he added: "Happy opulent youth!"

"Not if he's a dismal dunce."

"Oh they're happier then. But you can't have everything, can you?" the boy smiled.

Pemberton held him fast, hands on his shoulders—he had never loved him so. "What will become of *you*, what will you do?" He thought of Mrs. Moreen, desperate for sixty francs.

"I shall become an *homme fait*." And then as if he recognised all the bearings of Pemberton's allusion: "I shall get on with them better when you're not here."

"Ah don't say that—it sounds as if I set you against them!"

"You do—the sight of you. It's all right; you know what I mean. I shall be beautiful. I'll take their affairs in hand; I'll marry my sisters."

"You'll marry yourself!" joked Pemberton; as high, rather tense pleasantry would evidently be the right, or the safest, tone for their separation.

It was, however, not purely in this strain that Morgan suddenly asked: "But I say—how will you get to your jolly job? You'll have to telegraph to the opulent youth for money to come on."

Pemberton bethought himself. "They won't like that, will they?"

"Oh look out for them!"

Then Pemberton brought out his remedy. "I'll go to the American Consul; I'll borrow some money of him—just for the few days, on the strength of the telegram."

Morgan was hilarious. "Show him the telegram—then collar the money and stay!"

Pemberton entered into the joke sufficiently to reply that for Morgan he was really capable of that; but the boy, growing more serious, and to prove he hadn't meant what he said, not only hurried him off to the Consulate—since he was to start that evening, as he had wired to his friend—but made sure of their affair by going with him. They splashed through the tortuous perforations and over the humpbacked bridges, and they passed through the Piazza, where they saw Mr. Moreen and Ulick go into a jeweller's shop. The Consul proved accommodating—Pemberton said it wasn't the letter, but Morgan's grand air—and on their way back they went into Saint Mark's for a hushed ten minutes. Later they took up and kept up the fun of it to the very end; and it seemed to Pemberton a part of that fun that Mrs. Moreen, who was very angry when he had announced her his intention, should charge him, grotesquely and vulgarly and in reference to the loan she had vainly endeavoured to effect, with bolting lest they should "get something out" of him. On the other hand he had to do Mr. Moreen and Ulick the justice to recognise that when on coming in *they* heard the cruel news they took it like perfect men of the world.

VIII

When he got at work with the opulent youth, who was to be taken in hand for Balliol, he found himself unable to say if this aspirant had really such poor parts or if the appearance were only begotten of his own long association with an intensely living little mind. From Morgan he heard half a dozen times: the boy wrote charming young letters, a patchwork of tongues, with indulgent postscripts in the family Volapuk and, in little squares and rounds and crannies of the text, the drollest illustrations—letters that he was divided between the impulse to show his present charge as a vain, a wasted incentive, and the sense of something in them that publicity would profane. The opulent youth went up in due course and failed to pass; but it seemed to add to the presumption that brilliancy was not expected of him all at once that his parents, condoning the lapse, which they good-naturedly treated as little as possible as if it were Pemberton's, should have sounded the rally again, begged the young coach to renew the siege.

The young coach was now in a position to lend Mrs. Moreen three louis, and he sent her a post-office order even for a larger amount. In return for his favour he received a frantic scribbled line from her: "Implore you to come back instantly—Morgan dreadfully ill." They were on the rebound, once more in Paris—often as Pemberton had seen them depressed he had never seen them crushed—and communication was therefore rapid. He wrote to the boy to ascertain the state of his health, but awaited the answer in vain. He accordingly, after three days, took an abrupt leave of the opulent youth and, crossing the Channel, alighted at the small hotel, in the quarter of the Champs Élysées, of which Mrs. Moreen had given him the address. A deep if dumb dissatisfaction with this lady and her companions bore him company: they couldn't be vulgarly honest, but they could live at hotels, in velvety *entresols,* amid a smell of burnt pastilles, surrounded by the most expensive city in Europe. When he had left them in Venice it was with an irrepressible suspicion that something was going to happen; but the only thing that could have taken place was again their masterly retreat. "How is he? where is he?" he asked of Mrs. Moreen; but before she could speak these questions were answered by the pressure round his neck of a pair of arms, in shrunken sleeves, which still were perfectly capable of an effusive young foreign squeeze.

"Dreadfully ill—I don't see it!" the young man cried. And then to Morgan: "Why on earth didn't you relieve me? Why didn't you answer my letter?"

Mrs. Moreen declared that when she wrote he was very bad, and Pemberton learned at the same time from the boy that he had answered every letter he had received. This led to the clear inference that Pemberton's note had been kept from him so that the game to be practised should not be interfered with. Mrs. Moreen was prepared to see the fact exposed, as Pemberton saw the moment he faced her that she was prepared for a good many other things. She was prepared above all to maintain that she had acted from a sense of duty, that she was enchanted she had got him over, whatever they might say, and that it was useless of him to pretend he didn't know in all his bones that his place at such a time was with Morgan. He had taken the boy away from them and now had no right to abandon him. He had created for himself the gravest responsibilities and must at least abide by what he had done.

"Taken him away from you?" Pemberton exclaimed indignantly.

"Do it—do it for pity's sake; that's just what I want. I can't stand *this*—and such scenes. They're awful frauds—poor dears!" These words broke from Morgan, who had intermitted his embrace, in a key which made Pemberton turn quickly to him and see that he had suddenly seated himself, was breathing in great pain and was very pale.

"*Now* do you say he's not in a state, my precious pet?" shouted his mother, dropping on her knees before him with clasped hands, but touching him no more than if he had been a gilded idol. "It will pass—it's only for an instant; but don't say such dreadful things!"

"I'm all right—all right," Morgan panted to Pemberton, whom he sat looking up at with a strange smile, his hands resting on either side on the sofa.

"Now do you pretend I've been dishonest, that I've deceived?" Mrs. Moreen flashed at Pemberton as she got up.

"It isn't *he* says it, it's I!" the boy returned, apparently easier but sinking back against the wall; while his restored friend, who had sat down beside him, took his hand and bent over him.

"Darling child, one does what one can; there are so many things to consider," urged Mrs. Moreen. "It's his *place*—his only place. You see *you* think it is now."

"Take me away—take me away," Morgan went on, smiling to Pemberton with his white face.

"Where shall I take you, and how—oh *how,* my boy?" the young man stammered, thinking of the rude way in which his friends in London held that, for his convenience, with no assurance of prompt return, he had thrown them over; of the just resentment with which they would already have called in a successor, and of the scant help to finding fresh employment that resided for him in the grossness of his having failed to pass his pupil.

"Oh we'll settle that. You used to talk about it," said Morgan. "If we can only go all the rest's a detail."

"Talk about it as much as you like, but don't think you can attempt it. Mr. Moreen would never consent—it would be so *very* hand-to-mouth," Pemberton's hostess beautifully explained to him. Then to Morgan she made it clearer: "It would destroy our peace, it would break our hearts. Now that he's back it will be all the same again. You'll have your life, your work and your freedom, and we'll all be happy as we used to be. You'll bloom and grow perfectly well, and we won't have any more silly experiments, will we? They're too absurd. It's Mr. Pemberton's place—every one in his place. You in yours, your papa in his, me in mine—*n'est-ce pas, chéri*? We'll all forget how foolish we've been and have lovely times."

She continued to talk and to surge vaguely about the little draped stuffy salon while Pemberton sat with the boy, whose colour gradually came back; and she mixed up her reasons, hinting that there were going to be changes, that the other children might scatter (who knew?—Paula had her ideas) and that then it might be fancied how much the poor old parent-birds would want the little nestling. Morgan looked at Pemberton, who wouldn't let him move; and Pemberton knew exactly how he felt at hearing himself called a little nestling. He admitted that he had had one or two bad days, but he protested afresh against the wrong of his mother's having made them the ground of an appeal to poor Pemberton. Poor Pemberton could laugh now, apart from the comicality of Mrs. Moreen's mustering so much philosophy for her defence—she seemed to shake it out of her agitated petticoats, which knocked over the light gilt chairs—so little did their young companion, *marked,* unmistakably marked at the best, strike him as qualified to repudiate any advantage.

He himself was in for it at any rate. He should have Morgan on his hands again indefinitely; though indeed he saw the lad had a private theory to produce which would be intended to smooth this down. He was obliged to him for it in advance; but the suggested amendment didn't keep his heart rather from sinking, any more than it prevented him from accepting the prospect on the spot, with some confidence moreover that he should do even better if he could have a little supper. Mrs. Moreen threw out more hints about the changes that were to be looked for, but she was such a mixture of smiles and shudders—she confessed she was very nervous—that he couldn't tell if she were in high feather or only in hysterics. If the family was really at last going to pieces why shouldn't she recognise the necessity of pitching Morgan into some sort of lifeboat? This presumption was fostered by the fact that they were established in luxurious quarters in the capital of pleasure; that was exactly where they naturally *would* be established in view of going to pieces. Moreover didn't she mention that Mr. Moreen and the others were enjoying themselves at the opera with Mr. Granger, and wasn't *that* also precisely where one would look for them on the eve of a smash? Pemberton gathered that Mr. Granger was a rich vacant American—a big bill with a flourishy heading and no items; so that one of Paula's "ideas" was probably that this time she hadn't missed fire—by which straight shot indeed she would have shattered the general cohesion. And if the cohesion was to crumble what would become of poor Pemberton? He felt quite enough bound up with them to figure to his alarm as a dislodged block in the edifice.

It was Morgan who eventually asked if no supper had been ordered for him; sitting with him below, later, at the dim delayed meal, in the presence of a great deal of corded green plush, a plate of ornamental biscuit and an aloofness marked on the part of the waiter. Mrs. Moreen had explained that they had been obliged to secure a room for the visitor out of the house; and Morgan's consolation—he offered it while Pemberton reflected on the nastiness of luke-warm sauces—proved to be, largely, that this circumstance would facilitate their escape. He talked of their escape—recurring to it often afterwards—as if they were making up a "boy's book" together. But he likewise expressed his sense that there was something in the air, that the Moreens couldn't keep it up much longer. In point of fact, as Pemberton was to see, they kept it up for five or six months. All the while, however, Morgan's contention was designed to cheer him. Mr. Moreen and Ulick, whom he had met the day after his return, accepted that return like perfect men of the world. If Paula and Amy treated it even with less formality an allowance was to be made for them, inasmuch as Mr. Granger hadn't come to the opera after all. He had only placed his box at their service, with a bouquet for each of the party; there was even one apiece, embittering the thought of his profusion, for Mr. Moreen and Ulick. "They're all like that," was Morgan's comment; "at the very last, just when we think we've landed them they're back in the deep sea!"

Morgan's comments in these days were more and more free; they even included a large recognition of the extraordinary tenderness with which he had been treated while Pemberton was away. Oh yes, they couldn't do enough to be nice to him, to show him they had him on their mind and make up for his loss. That was just what made the whole thing so sad and caused him to rejoice after all in Pemberton's return—he had to keep thinking of their affection less, had less sense of obligation. Pemberton laughed out at this last reason, and Morgan blushed and said "Well, dash it, you know what I mean." Pemberton knew perfectly what he meant; but there were a good many things that—dash it too!—it didn't make any clearer. This episode of his second sojourn in Paris stretched itself out wearily, with their resumed readings and wanderings and maunderings, their potterings on the quays, their hauntings of the museums, their occasional lingerings in the Palais Royal when the first sharp weather came on and there was a comfort in warm emanations, before Chevet's wonderful succulent window. Morgan wanted to hear all about the opulent youth—he took an immense interest in him. Some of the details of his opulence—Pemberton could spare him none of them—evidently fed the boy's appreciation of all his friend had given up to come back to him; but in addition to the greater reciprocity established by that heroism he had always his little brooding theory, in which there was a frivolous gaiety too, that their long probation was drawing to a close. Morgan's conviction that the Moreens couldn't go on much longer kept pace with the unexpended impetus with which, from month to month, they did go on. Three weeks after Pemberton had rejoined them they went on to another hotel, a dingier one than the first; but Morgan rejoiced that his tutor had at least still not sacrificed the advantage of a room outside. He clung to the romantic utility of this when the day, or rather the night, should arrive for their escape.

For the first time, in this complicated connexion, our friend felt his collar gall him. It was, as he had said to Mrs. Moreen in Venice, *trop fort*—everything was *trop fort*. He could neither really throw off his blighting burden nor find in it the benefit of a pacified conscience or of a rewarded affection. He had spent all the money accruing to him in England, and he saw his youth going and that he was getting nothing back for it. It was all very well of Morgan to count it for reparation that he should now settle on him permanently—there was an irritating flaw in such a view. He saw what the boy had in his mind; the conception that as his friend had had the generosity to come back he must show his gratitude by giving him his life. But the poor friend didn't desire the gift—what could he do with Morgan's dreadful little life? Of course at the same time that Pemberton was irritated he remembered the reason, which was very honourable to Morgan and which dwelt simply in his making one so forget that he was no more than a patched urchin. If one dealt with him on a different basis one's misadventures were one's own fault. So Pemberton waited in a queer confusion of yearning and alarm for the catastrophe which was held to hang over the house of Moreen, of which he certainly at moments felt the symptoms brush his cheek and as to which he wondered much in what form it would find its liveliest effect.

Perhaps it would take the form of sudden dispersal—a frightened *sauve qui peut,* a scuttling into selfish corners. Certainly they were less elastic than of yore; they were evidently looking for something they didn't find. The Dorringtons hadn't re-appeared, the princes had scattered; wasn't that the beginning of the end? Mrs. Moreen had lost her reckoning of the famous "days"; her social calendar was blurred—it had turned its face to the wall. Pemberton suspected that the great, the cruel discomfiture had been the unspeakable behaviour of Mr. Granger, who seemed not to know what he wanted, or, what was much worse, what *they* wanted. He kept sending flowers, as if to bestrew the path of his retreat, which was never the path of a return. Flowers were all very well, but—Pemberton could complete the proposition. It was now positively conspicuous that in the long run the Moreens were a social failure; so that the young man was almost grateful the run had not been short. Mr. Moreen indeed was still occasionally able to get away on business and, what was more surprising, was likewise able to get back. Ulick had no club, but you couldn't have discovered it from his appearance, which was as much as ever that of a person looking at life from the window of such an institution; therefore Pemberton was doubly surprised at an answer he once heard him make his mother in the desperate tone of a man familiar with the worst privations. Her question Pemberton had not quite caught; it appeared to be an appeal for a suggestion as to whom they might get to take Amy. "Let the Devil take her!" Ulick snapped; so that Pemberton could see that they had not only lost their amiability but had ceased to believe in themselves. He could also see that if Mrs. Moreen was trying to get people to take her children she might be regarded as closing the hatches for the storm. But Morgan would be the last she would part with.

One winter afternoon—it was a Sunday—he and the boy

walked far together in the Bois de Boulogne. The evening was so splendid, the cold lemon-coloured sunset so clear, the stream of carriages and pedestrians so amusing and the fascination of Paris so great, that they stayed out later than usual and became aware that they should have to hurry home to arrive in time for dinner. They hurried accordingly, arm-in-arm, good-humoured and hungry, agreeing that there was nothing like Paris after all and that after everything too that had come and gone they were not yet sated with innocent pleasures. When they reached the hotel they found that, though scandalously late, they were in time for all the dinner they were likely to sit down to. Confusion reigned in the apartments of the Moreens—very shabby ones this time, but the best in the house—and before the interrupted service of the table, with objects displaced almost as if there had been a scuffle and a great wine-stain from an overturned bottle, Pemberton couldn't blink the fact that there had been a scene of the last proprietary firmness. The storm had come—they were all seeking refuge. The hatches were down, Paula and Amy were invisible—they had never tried the most casual art upon Pemberton, but he felt they had enough of an eye to him not to wish to meet him as young ladies whose frocks had been confiscated—and Ulick appeared to have jumped overboard. The host and his staff, in a word, had ceased to "go on" at the pace of their guests, and the air of embarrassed detention, thanks to a pile of gaping trunks in the passage, was strangely commingled with the air of indignant withdrawal.

When Morgan took all this in—and he took it in very quickly—he coloured to the roots of his hair. He had walked from his infancy among difficulties and dangers, but he had never seen a public exposure. Pemberton noticed in a second glance at him that the tears had rushed into his eyes and that they were tears of a new and untasted bitterness. He wondered an instant, for the boy's sake, whether he might successfully pretend not to understand. Not successfully, he felt, as Mr. and Mrs. Moreen dinnerless by their extinguished hearth, rose before him in their little dishonoured salon, casting about with glassy eyes for the nearest port in such a storm. They were not prostrate but were horribly white, and Mrs. Moreen had evidently been crying. Pemberton quickly learned however that her grief was not for the loss of her dinner, much as she usually enjoyed it, but the fruit of a blow that struck even deeper, as she made all haste to explain. He would see for himself, so far as that went, how the great change had come, the dreadful bolt had fallen, and how they would now all have to turn themselves about. Therefore cruel as it was to them to part with their darling she must look to him to carry a little further the influence he had so fortunately acquired with the boy—to induce his young charge to follow him into some modest retreat. They depended on him —that was the fact—to take their delightful child temporarily under his protection: it would leave Mr. Moreen and herself so much more free to give the proper attention (too little, alas! had been given) to the readjustment of their affairs.

"We trust you—we feel we *can,*" said Mrs. Moreen, slowly rubbing her plump white hands and looking with compunction hard at Morgan, whose chin, not to take liberties, her husband stroked with a tentative paternal forefinger.

"Oh yes—we feel that we *can*. We trust Mr. Pemberton fully, Morgan," Mr. Moreen pursued.

Pemberton wondered again if he might pretend not to understand; but everything good gave way to the intensity of Morgan's understanding. "Do you mean he may take me to live with him for ever and ever?" cried the boy. "May take me away, away, anywhere he likes?"

"For ever and ever? *Comme vous-y-allez!*" Mr. Moreen laughed indulgently. "For as long as Mr. Pemberton may be so good."

"We've struggled, we've suffered," his wife went on; "but you've made him so your own that we've already been through the worst of the sacrifice."

Morgan had turned away from his father—he stood looking at Pemberton with a light in his face. His sense of shame for their common humiliated state had dropped; the case had another side—the thing was to clutch at *that*. He had a moment of boyish joy, scarcely mitigated by the reflexion that with this unexpected consecration of his hope—too sudden and too violent; the turn taken was away from a *good* boy's book—the "escape" was left on their hands. The boyish joy was there an instant, and Pemberton was almost scared at the rush of gratitude and affection that broke through his first abasement. When he stammered "My dear fellow, what do you say to *that*?" how could one not say something enthusiastic? But there was more need for courage at something else that immediately followed and that made the lad sit down quickly on the nearest chair. He had turned quite livid and had raised his hand to his left side. They were all three looking at him, but Mrs. Moreen suddenly bounded forward. "Ah his darling little heart!" she broke out; and this time, on her knees before him and without respect for the idol, she caught him ardently in her arms. "You walked him too far, you hurried him too fast!" she hurled over her shoulder at Pemberton. Her son made no protest, and the next instant, still holding him, she sprang up with her face convulsed and with the terrified cry "Help, help! he's going, he's gone!" Pemberton saw with equal horror, by Morgan's own stricken face, that he was beyond their wildest recall. He pulled him half out of his mother's hands, and for a moment, while they held him together, they looked all their dismay into each other's eyes. "He couldn't stand it with his weak organ," said Pemberton—"the shock, the whole scene, the violent emotion."

"But I thought he *wanted* to go to you!" wailed Mrs. Moreen.

"I *told* you he didn't, my dear," her husband made answer. Mr. Moreen was trembling all over and was in his way as deeply affected as his wife. But after the very first he took his bereavement as a man of the world.

A NOTE ON

THE PUPIL

(1891)

Now that you have finished this story (which is a masterpiece) I suggest you re-read, drawn from its context on page 228, a scrap of dialogue. (James not only bears re-reading, he requires it: a mark of the master.)

"I hope you don't mean to dismiss me," said Pemberton.
Morgan considered a moment, looking at the sunset. "I think if I did right I ought to."
"Well, I know I'm supposed to instruct you in virtue; but in that case don't do right."
"You're very young—fortunately," Morgan went on, turning to him again.
"Oh yes, compared with you!"
"Therefore, it won't matter so much if you do lose a lot of time."
"That's the way to look at it," said Pemberton accommodatingly.

When first read, the passage seemed casual enough, almost trivial, did it not? Now, however, that we are acquainted with Morgan Moreen and his fate, how much heavier is the burden of meaning of these lines. We understand that Morgan speaks as he does because, though aware of the corruption of his family and the degradation they intend to visit upon Pemberton, he cannot communicate this knowledge. For one thing, he is too young—Pemberton may not accept his statements as responsible. For another, he likes Pemberton; he doesn't want to lose him. Finally—for, after all, he is a child—he cannot quite bring himself to denounce his own family by an explicit indictment. Being intellectually conscientious, however, he does go so far as to murmur, with an ambiguousness whose subtlety we can now perceive, that if he "did right" he "ought to" dismiss Pemberton. Then, his intuitive foresight urging him to qualify the statement, he continues, "You're very young—fortunately." Why "fortunately"? Because he knows—and we know too now—that Pemberton has let himself in for an experience that will have its good points as well as its bad. When the tutor replies lightly, "Oh yes, compared with you!", the boy does not pick up the gambit of humor. He is quite serious as he goes on, "Therefore, it won't matter so much if you do lose a lot of time."

Morgan sees all round the situation, partly because he is so intelligent, partly because he has been in it before. The central actor, he is also the observer. He understands his own rôle, the rôle of his family, the rôle of Pemberton. He even, I think—though this is debatable—has a dim foreknowledge of the tragic *dénouement* of the situation. For the implied contrast he draws seriously (Pemberton does so jokingly) between the tutor's youth and his own—what shall we call it? agelessness?—seems a feather-light allusion to his own early death. Pemberton will have time in which to be young, but not young Morgan.

All this in half a dozen lines! The heavy load they bear is made possible only by the absolute control James enjoys over his material. This control is the most magical thing about him. It is his hallmark; there is never any doubt as to who is in charge. Control, of course, is another word for understanding. Morgan is clear to himself and clear to us because in the beginning he was clear to James.

In his account of how "The Pupil" came about, James tells us that a friend, one summer's day, happened to speak of "a wonderful American family, an odd, adventurous, extravagant band" and of their "small boy, acute and precocious . . . who saw their prowling, precarious life exactly as it was." James goes on to tell us—we are familiar with the process from reading "The Liar"—"I *saw,* on the spot, little Morgan Moreen, I saw all the rest of the Moreens. . . ." Then he reflects, "The whole cluster of items forming the image is on these occasions born at once; the parts are not pieced together, they conspire and interdepend; but what it really comes to, no doubt, is that at a simple touch an old latent and dormant impression, a buried germ, implanted by experience and then forgotten, flashes to the surface as a fish, with a single 'squirm,' rises to the baited hook, and there meets instantly the vivifying ray." *

Thus, "with a single squirm," a character rises to the surface and is caught. Only after being thus caught in James's mind is he permitted to make his appearance on paper. The character is fully created before we glimpse him. He may be, he often is, complex. Morgan, despite or, more likely, because of his youth, is such a complex character. He is apt to say things, as in the dialogue we were reading, that seem ambiguous, that are part of a frame of private reference with which the reader only becomes familiar as he reads the whole story. The reader is not given too much of a break. He may have to work (read *think*, read *feel*) in order to grasp the character. He may have to read the story several times. Very well, says James; that's not asking too much.

Virtually all our current novelists—there are a few exceptions—exert their talents to "interest the reader." James exerts his genius to create a character. It is this attitude toward his job that makes James a writer. It is the lack of this attitude that makes most of our novelists merely men and women who write. James wants to *make* characters; the others want to *sell* characters. Both succeed, but in the difference lies the chasm between art and advertisement.

The more one reflects on "The Pupil" the greater seem its depths. There is something Greek in the tragedy it recites. Morgan is the noble hero; his speech and actions, making due allowance for his youth, are those of a superior man. But this

* The reader who would like to read a complete and absorbing analysis of this creative process is directed to John Livingston Lowes' *The Road to Xanadu*. It happens to deal with Coleridge but Lowes and James are talking about the same miracle.

hero is the prisoner of a world inferior to himself, symbolized by his family. Between Morgan and the unheroic world Pemberton acts as a kind of intercessor. But his mediation is vain, because the relation between his pupil and the Moreen family is fatally flawed. Morgan's frailty and the Moreens' egotism are both too great. It is their egotism that takes the last advantage of his weakness. It is their egotism that taxes his overjoyed, frail heart, their selfishness that in the very moment of his "liberation" kills him.

He is betrayed by what is false without, by the external forces of mediocrity, snobbery, vulgarity. But, in a curious way, he is betrayed also by himself. Morgan's weakness arises in part from the very circumstance that he understands these external forces so well. He understands them so well that he cannot, except with the inefficient weapon of irony, oppose them. It is hard to rebel successfully against what one understands perfectly. In the end, then, Morgan's tragedy is the tragedy of excessive sensibility: the typical Jamesian tragedy.

The poignance, the sorrowfulness of "The Pupil" does not lend itself easily to explanation. Yet I cannot help feeling that part of its quality derives from the feeling all of us have had, observing certain families, that the children are superior to the parents—but only for a time. They seem purer, they seem to see things more clearly, they seem, for all their "inexperience" (experience is the term we use to cover up the fact that we have not really lived) to be wiser. This superiority they do not long retain. With the onset of adolescence they begin slowly to sink into that morass of grown-upness in which you and I, their elders, have for years been supinely imbedded. But those few radiant years are often enough to make adulthood seem merely an involved form of degeneration.

Morgan is the very type and figure of this superiority, just as his family is the very type and figure of spurious "maturity," worldliness without wisdom. One feels that his sisters, waiting like spiders for their hapless millionaires, have never had even a fleeting moment of that crystalline youthful vision that is Morgan's. They and their parents are what James calls "the fools"; they are unaware. The contrast between the almost febrile awareness of the boy and the basic stupidity (despite their shrewdness) of his family is a contrast between two kinds of human beings, between two universes of feeling.

Not the least interesting aspect of this reverberant story is presented by the relation between tutor and pupil. It is extraordinarily complex, all the more so because, as it shifts and alters its balance, Morgan seems at times to become the elder and Pemberton the younger. (James plays the alternation for comedy as well as pathos; he doesn't miss a trick.)

The relation between them goes beyond mutual respect and affection. Its roots reach deep into the dark soil of their emotional under-lives. The conventions of his day (which James, through his subtle magic, both obeyed and evaded) prevented him from making any more explicit the perfectly unconscious homosexual love—of a type that could never ripen into overt action—binding Morgan and Pemberton. Yet we feel it, and perhaps with added force just because it is touched upon with such delicate restraint. It adds still another dimension to this rich narrative, endowing it with a troubling beauty whose parallel is perhaps to be found nowhere else save in Thomas Mann's "Death in Venice."

BROOKSMITH

We are scattered now, the friends of the late Mr. Oliver Offord; but whenever we chance to meet I think we are conscious of a certain esoteric respect for each other. "Yes, you too have been in Arcadia," we seem not too grumpily to allow. When I pass the house in Mansfield Street I remember that Arcadia was there. I don't know who has it now, and don't want to know; it's enough to be so sure that if I should ring the bell there would be no such luck for me as that Brooksmith should open the door. Mr. Offord, the most agreeable, the most attaching of bachelors, was a retired diplomatist, living on his pension and on something of his own over and above; a good deal confined, by his infirmities, to his fireside and delighted to be found there any afternoon in the year, from five o'clock on, by such visitors as Brooksmith allowed to come up. Brooksmith was his butler and his most intimate friend, to whom we all stood, or I should say sat, in the same relation in which the subject of the sovereign finds himself to the prime minister. By having been for years, in foreign lands, the most delightful Englishman any one had ever known, Mr. Offord had in my opinion rendered signal service to his country. But I suppose he had been too much liked—liked even by those who didn't like *it*—so that as people of that sort never get titles or dotations for the horrid things they've *not* done, his principal reward was simply that we went to see him.

Oh we went perpetually, and it was not our fault if he was not overwhelmed with this particular honour. Any visitor who came once came again; to come merely once was a slight nobody, I'm sure, had ever put upon him. His circle therefore was essentially composed of habitués, who were habitués for each other as well as for him, as those of a happy salon should be. I remember vividly every element of the place, down to the intensely Londonish look of the grey opposite houses, in the gap of the white curtains of the high windows, and the exact spot where, on a particular afternoon, I put down my tea-cup for Brooksmith, lingering an instant, to gather it up as if he were plucking a flower. Mr. Offord's drawing-room was indeed Brooksmith's garden, his pruned and tended human parterre, and if we all flourished there and grew well in our places it was largely owing to his supervision.

Many persons have heard much, though most have doubtless seen little, of the famous institution of the salon, and many are born to the depression of knowing that this finest flower of social life refuses to bloom where the English tongue is spoken. The explanation is usually that our women have not the skill to cultivate it—the art to direct through a smiling land, between suggestive shores, a sinuous stream of talk. My affectionate, my pious memory of Mr. Offord contradicts this induction only, I fear, more insidiously to confirm it. The sallow and slightly smoked drawing-room in which he spent so large a portion of the last years of his life certainly deserved the distinguished name; but on the other hand it couldn't be said at all to owe its stamp to any intervention throwing into relief the fact that there was no Mrs. Offord. The dear man had indeed, at the most, been capable of one of those sacrifices to which women are deemed peculiarly apt: he had recognised—under the influence, in some degree, it is true, of physical infirmity—that if you wish people to find you at home you must manage not to be out. He had in short accepted the truth which many dabblers in the social art are slow to learn, that you must really, as they say, take a line, and that the only way as yet discovered of being at home is to stay at home. Finally his own fireside had become a summary of his habits. Why should he ever have left it?—since this would have been leaving what was notoriously pleasantest in London, the compact charmed cluster (thinning away indeed into casual couples) round the fine old last-century chimney-piece which, with the exception of the remarkable collection of miniatures, was the best thing the place contained. Mr. Offord wasn't rich; he had nothing but his pension and the use for life of the somewhat superannuated house.

When I'm reminded by some opposed discomfort of the present hour how perfectly we were all handled there, I ask myself once more what had been the secret of such perfection. One had taken it for granted at the time, for anything that is supremely good produces more acceptance than surprise. I felt we were all happy, but I didn't consider how our happiness was managed. And yet there were questions to be asked, questions that strike me as singularly obvious now that there's nobody to answer them. Mr. Offord had solved the insoluble; he had, without feminine help—save in the sense that ladies were dying to come to him and that he saved the lives of several—established a salon; but I might have guessed that there was a method in his madness, a law in his success. He hadn't hit it off by a mere fluke. There was an art in it all, and how was the art so hidden? Who indeed if it came to that was the occult artist? Launching this enquiry the other day I had already got hold of the tail of my reply. I was helped by the very wonder of some of the conditions that came back to me—those that used to seem as natural as sunshine in a fine climate.

How was it for instance that we never were a crowd, never either too many or too few, always the right people *with* the right people—there must really have been no wrong people at all—always coming and going, never sticking fast nor overstaying, yet never popping in or out with an indecorous familiarity? How was it that we all sat where we wanted and moved when we wanted and met whom we wanted and escaped whom we wanted; joining, according to the accident of inclination, the general circle or falling in with a single talker on a convenient sofa? Why were all the sofas so convenient, the accidents so happy, the talkers so ready, the listeners so willing, the subjects presented to you in a rotation as quickly foreordained as the courses at dinner? A dearth of topics would have been as unheard of as a lapse in the service. These speculations couldn't fail to lead me to the fundamental truth that Brooksmith had been somehow at the bottom of the mystery. If he hadn't established the salon at least he had carried it on. Brooksmith in short was the artist!

We felt this covertly at the time, without formulating it, and were conscious, as an ordered and prosperous community, of his evenhanded justice, all untainted with flunkeyism. He had none of that vulgarity—his touch was infinitely fine. The delicacy of it was clear to me on the first occasion my eyes rested, as they were so often to rest again, on the domestic revealed, in the turbid light of the street, by the opening of the house-door. I saw on the spot that though he had plenty of school he carried it without arrogance—he had remained articulate and human. *L'École Anglaise* Mr. Offord used laughingly to call him when, later on, it happened more than once that we had some conversation about him. But I remember accusing Mr. Offord of not doing him quite ideal justice. That he wasn't one of the giants of the school, however, was admitted by my old friend, who really understood him perfectly and was devoted to him, as I shall show; which doubtless poor Brooksmith had himself felt, to his cost, when his value in the market was originally determined. The utility of his class in general is estimated by the foot and the inch, and poor Brooksmith had only about five feet three to put into circulation. He acknowledged the inadequacy of this provision, and I'm sure was penetrated with the everlasting fitness of the relation between service and stature. If *he* had been Mr. Offord he certainly would have found Brooksmith wanting, and indeed the laxity of his employer on this score was one of many things he had had to condone and to which he had at last indulgently adapted himself.

I remember the old man's saying to me: "Oh my servants, if they can live with me a fortnight they can live with me for ever.

But it's the first fortnight that tries 'em." It was in the first fortnight for instance that Brooksmith had had to learn that he was exposed to being addressed as "my dear fellow" and "my poor child." Strange and deep must such a probation have been to him, and he doubtless emerged from it tempered and purified. This was written to a certain extent in his appearance; in his spare brisk little person, in his cloistered white face and extraordinarily polished hair, which told of responsibility, looked as if it were kept up to the same high standard as the plate; in his small clear anxious eyes, even in the permitted, though not exactly encouraged, tuft on his chin. "He thinks me rather mad, but I've broken him in, and now he likes the place, he likes the company," said the old man. I embraced this fully after I had become aware that Brooksmith's main characteristic was a deep and shy refinement, though I remember I was rather puzzled when, on another occasion, Mr. Offord remarked: "What he likes is the talk—mingling in the conversation." I was conscious I had never seen Brooksmith permit himself this freedom, but I guessed in a moment that what Mr. Offord alluded to was a participation more intense than any speech could have represented—that of being perpetually present on a hundred legitimate pretexts, errands, necessities, and breathing the very atmosphere of criticism, the famous criticism of life. "Quite an education, sir, isn't it, sir?" he said to me one day at the foot of the stairs when he was letting me out; and I've always remembered the words and the tone as the first sign of the quickening drama of poor Brooksmith's fate. It was indeed an education, but to what was this sensitive young man of thirty-five, of the servile class, being educated?

Practically and inevitably, for the time, to companionship, to the perpetual, the even exaggerated reference and appeal of a person brought to dependence by his time of life and his infirmities and always addicted moreover—this was the exaggeration—to the art of giving you pleasure by letting you do things for him. There were certain things Mr. Offord was capable of pretending he liked you to do even when he didn't—this, I mean, if he thought *you* liked them. If it happened that you didn't either—which was rare, yet might be—of course there were cross-purposes; but Brooksmith was there to prevent their going very far. This was precisely the way he acted as moderator; he averted misunderstandings or cleared them up. He had been capable, strange as it may appear, of acquiring for this purpose an insight into the French tongue, which was often used at Mr. Offord's; for besides being habitual to most of the foreigners, and they were many, who haunted the place or arrived with letters—letters often requiring a little worried consideration, of which Brooksmith always had cognisance—it had really become the primary language of the master of the house. I don't know if all the *malentendus* were in French, but almost all the explanations were, and this didn't a bit prevent Brooksmith's following them. I know Mr. Offord used to read passages to him from Montaigne and Saint-Simon, for he read perpetually when alone—when *they* were alone, that is—and Brooksmith was always about. Perhaps you'll say no wonder Mr. Offord's butler regarded him as "rather mad." However, if I'm not sure what he thought about Montaigne I'm convinced he admired Saint-Simon. A certain feeling for letters must have rubbed off on him from the mere handling of his master's books, which he was always carrying to and fro and putting back in their places.

I often noticed that if an anecdote or a quotation, much more a lively discussion, was going forward, he would, if busy with the fire or the curtains, the lamp or the tea, find a pretext for remaining in the room till the point should be reached. If his purpose was to catch it you weren't discreet, you were in fact scarce human, to call him off, and I shall never forget a look, a hard stony stare—I caught it in its passage—which, one day when there were a good many people in the room, he fastened upon the footman who was helping him in the service and who, in an undertone, had asked him some irrelevant question.

It was the only manifestation of harshness I ever observed on Brooksmith's part, and I at first wondered what was the matter. Then I became conscious that Mr. Offord was relating a very curious anecdote, never before perhaps made so public, and imparted to the narrator by an eye-witness of the fact, bearing on Lord Byron's life in Italy. Nothing would induce me to reproduce it here, but Brooksmith had been in danger of losing it. If I ever should venture to reproduce it I shall feel how much I lose in not having my fellow auditor to refer to.

The first day Mr. Offord's door was closed was therefore a dark date in contemporary history. It was raining hard and my umbrella was wet, but Brooksmith received it from me exactly as if this were a preliminary for going upstairs. I observed however that instead of putting it away he held it poised and trickling over the rug, and I then became aware that he was looking at me with deep acknowledging eyes—his air of universal responsibility. I immediately understood—there was scarce need of question and answer as they passed between us. When I took in that our good friend had given up as never before, though only for the occasion, I exclaimed dolefully: "What a difference it will make—and to how many people!"

"I shall be one of them, sir!" said Brooksmith; and that was the beginning of the end.

Mr. Offord came down again, but the spell was broken, the great sign being that the conversation was for the first time not directed. It wandered and stumbled, a little frightened, like a lost child—it had let go the nurse's hand. "The worst of it is that now we shall talk about my health—*c'est la fin de tout,*" Mr. Offord said when he reappeared; and then I recognised what a note of change that would be—for he had never tolerated anything so provincial. We "ran" to each other's health as little as to the daily weather. The talk became ours, in a word—not his; and as ours, even when *he* talked, it could only be inferior. In this form it was a distress to Brooksmith, whose attention now wandered from it altogether: he had so much closer a vision of his master's intimate conditions than our superficialities represented. There were better hours, and he was more in and out of the room, but I could see he was conscious of the decline, almost of the collapse, of our great institution. He seemed to wish to take counsel with me about it, to feel responsible for its going on in some form or other. When for the second period—the first had lasted several days—he had to tell me that his employer didn't receive, I half-expected to hear him say after a moment "Do you think I ought to, sir, in his place?"—as he might have asked me, with the return of autumn, if I thought he had better light the drawing-room fire.

He had a resigned philosophic sense of what his guests—our guests, as I came to regard them in our colloquies—would expect. His feeling was that he wouldn't absolutely have approved of himself as a substitute for Mr. Offord; but he was so saturated with the religion of habit that he would have made, for our friends, the necessary sacrifice to the divinity. He would take them on a little further and till they could look about them. I think I saw him also mentally confronted with the opportunity to deal—for once in his life—with some of his own dumb preferences, his limitations of sympathy, *weeding* a little in prospect and returning to a purer tradition. It was not unknown to me that he considered that toward the end of our host's career a certain laxity of selection had crept in.

At last it came to be the case that we all found the closed door more often than the open one; but even when it was closed Brooksmith managed a crack for me to squeeze through; so that practically I never turned away without having paid a visit. The difference simply came to be that the visit was to Brooksmith. It took place in the hall, at the familiar foot of the stairs, and we didn't sit down, at least Brooksmith didn't; moreover it was devoted wholly to one topic and always had the air of being already over—beginning, so to say, at the end. But it was always interesting—it always gave me something to think about. It's true that the subject of my meditation was ever the same—ever "It's all very well, but what *will* become of Brooksmith?" Even my private answer to this question left me still unsatisfied. No doubt Mr. Offord would provide for him, but *what* would he provide?—that was the great point. He couldn't provide society; and society had become a necessity of Brooksmith's nature. I must add that he never showed a symptom of what I may call sordid solicitude—anxiety on his own account. He was rather livid and intensely grave, as befitted a man before whose eyes the "shade of that which once was great" was passing away. He had the solemnity of a person winding up, under depressing circumstances, a long-established and celebrated business; he was a kind of social executor or liquidator. But his manner seemed to testify exclusively to the uncertainty of *our* future. I couldn't in those days have afforded it—I lived in two rooms in Jermyn Street and didn't "keep a man"; but even if my income had permitted I shouldn't have ventured to say to Brooksmith (emulating Mr. Offord) "My dear fellow, I'll take you on." The whole tone of our intercourse was so much more an implication that it was *I* who should now want a lift. Indeed there was a tacit assurance in Brooksmith's whole attitude that he should have me on his mind.

One of the most assiduous members of our circle had been Lady Kenyon, and I remember his telling me one day that her ladyship had in spite of her own infirmities, lately much aggravated, been in person to inquire. In answer to this I remarked that she would feel it more than any one. Brooksmith had a pause before saying in a certain tone—there's no reproducing some of his tones—"I'll go and see her." I went to see her myself and learned he had waited on her; but when I said to her, in the form of a joke but with a core of earnest, that when all was over some of us ought to combine, to club together, and set Brooksmith up on his own account, she replied a trifle disappointingly: "Do you mean in a public-house?" I looked at her in a way that I think Brooksmith himself would have approved, and then I answered: "Yes, the Offord Arms." What

I had meant of course was that for the love of art itself we ought to look to it that such a peculiar faculty and so much acquired experience shouldn't be wasted. I really think that if we had caused a few black-edged cards to be struck off and circulated —"Mr. Brooksmith will continue to receive on the old premises from four to seven; business carried on as usual during the alterations"—the greater number of us would have rallied.

Several times he took me upstairs—always by his own proposal—and our dear old friend, in bed (in a curious flowered and brocaded casaque which made him, especially as his head was tied up in a handkerchief to match, look, to my imagination, like the dying Voltaire) held for ten minutes a sadly shrunken little salon. I felt indeed each time as if I were attending the last *coucher* of some social sovereign. He was royally whimsical about his sufferings and not at all concerned—quite as if the Constitution provided for the case—about his successor. He glided over *our* sufferings charmingly, and none of his jokes—it was a gallant abstention, some of them would have been so easy—were at our expense. Now and again, I confess, there was one at Brooksmith's, but so pathetically sociable as to make the excellent man look at me in a way that seemed to say: "Do exchange a glance with me, or I shan't be able to stand it." What he wasn't able to stand was not what Mr. Offord said about him, but what he wasn't able to say in return. His idea of conversation for himself was giving you the convenience of speaking to him; and when he went to "see" Lady Kenyon for instance it was to carry her the tribute of his receptive silence. Where would the speech of his betters have been if proper service had been a manifestation of sound? In that case the fundamental difference would have had to be shown by *their* dumbness, and many of them, poor things, were dumb enough without that provision. Brooksmith took an unfailing interest in the preservation of the fundamental difference; it was the thing he had most on his conscience.

What had become of it however when Mr. Offord passed

away like any inferior person—was relegated to eternal stillness after the manner of a butler above-stairs? His aspect on the event—for the several successive days—may be imagined, and the multiplication by funereal observance of the things he didn't say. When everything was over—it was late the same day—I knocked at the door of the house of mourning as I so often had done before. I could never call on Mr. Offord again, but I had come literally to call on Brooksmith. I wanted to ask him if there was anything I could do for him, tainted with vagueness as this enquiry could only be. My presumptuous dream of taking him into my own service had died away: my service wasn't worth his being taken into. My offer could only be to help him to find another place, and yet there was an indelicacy, as it were, in taking for granted that his thoughts would immediately be fixed on another. I had a hope that he would be able to give his life a different form—though certainly not the form, the frequent result of such bereavements, of his setting up a little shop. That would have been dreadful; for I should have wished to forward any enterprise he might embark in, yet how could I have brought myself to go and pay him shillings and take back coppers over a counter? My visit then was simply an intended compliment. He took it as such, gratefully and with all the tact in the world. He knew I really couldn't help him and that I knew he knew I couldn't; but we discussed the situation—with a good deal of elegant generality—at the foot of the stairs, in the hall already dismantled, where I had so often discussed other situations with him. The executors were in possession, as was still more apparent when he made me pass for a few minutes into the dining-room, where various objects were muffled up for removal.

Two definite facts, however, he had to communicate; one being that he was to leave the house for ever that night (servants, for some mysterious reason, seem always to depart by night), and the other—he mentioned it only at the last and with hesitation—that he was already aware his late master had left him a legacy of eighty pounds. "I'm very glad," I said, and Brooksmith was of the same mind: "It was so like him to think of me." This was all that passed between us on the subject, and I know nothing of his judgement of Mr. Offord's memento. Eighty pounds are always eighty pounds, and no one has ever left *me* an equal sum; but, all the same, for Brooksmith, I was disappointed. I don't know what I had expected, but it was almost a shock. Eighty pounds might stock a small shop—a *very* small shop; but, I repeat, I couldn't bear to think of that. I asked my friend if he had been able to save a little, and he replied: "No, sir; I've had to do things." I didn't enquire what things they might have been; they were his own affair, and I took his word for them as assentingly as if he had had the greatness of an ancient house to keep up; especially as there was something in his manner that seemed to convey a prospect of further sacrifice.

"I shall have to turn round a bit, sir—I shall have to look about me," he said; and then he added indulgently, magnanimously: "If you should happen to hear of anything for me—"

I couldn't let him finish; this was, in its essence, too much in the really grand manner. It would be a help to my getting him off my mind to be able to pretend I *could* find the right place, and that help he wished to give me, for it was doubtless painful to him to see me in so false a position. I interposed with a few words to the effect of how well aware I was that wherever he should go, whatever he should do, he would miss our old friend terribly—miss him even more than I should, having been with him so much more. This led him to make the speech that has remained with me as the very text of the whole episode.

"Oh sir, it's sad for *you,* very sad indeed, and for a great many gentlemen and ladies; that it is, sir. But for me, sir, it is, if I may say so, still graver even than that: it's just the loss of something that was everything. For me, sir," he went on with rising tears, "he was just *all,* if you know what I mean, sir. You have others, sir, I dare say—not that I would have you understand me to speak of them as in any way tantamount. But you have the pleasures of society, sir; if it's only in talking about him, sir, as I dare say you do freely—for all his blest memory has to fear from it—with gentlemen and ladies who have had the same honour. That's not for me, sir, and I've to keep my associations to myself. Mr. Offord was *my* society, and now, you see, I just haven't any. You go back to conversation, sir, after all, and I go back to my place," Brooksmith stammered, without exaggerated irony or dramatic bitterness, but with a flat unstudied veracity and his hand on the knob of the street-door. He turned it to let me out and then he added: "I just go downstairs, sir, again, and I stay there."

"My poor child," I replied in my emotion, quite as Mr. Offord used to speak, "my dear fellow, leave it to me: *we'll* look after you, we'll all do something for you."

"Ah if you could give me some one *like* him! But there ain't two such in the world," Brooksmith said as we parted.

He had given me his address—the place where he would be to be heard of. For a long time I had no occasion to make use of the information: he proved on trial so very difficult a case. The people who knew him and had known Mr. Offord didn't want to take him, and yet I couldn't bear to try to thrust him among strangers—strangers to his past when not to his present. I spoke to many of our old friends about him and found them all governed by the odd mixture of feelings of which I myself was conscious—as well as disposed, further, to entertain a suspicion that he was "spoiled," with which I then would have nothing to do. In plain terms a certain embarrassment, a sensible awkwardness when they thought of it, attached to the idea of using him as a menial: they had met him so often in society. Many of them would have asked him, and did ask him, or rather did ask me to ask him, to come and see them; but a mere visiting-list was not what I wanted for him. He was too short for people who were very particular; nevertheless I heard of an opening in a diplomatic household which led me to write him a note, though I was looking much less for something grand than for something human. Five days later I heard from him. The secretary's wife had decided, after keeping him waiting till then, that she couldn't take a servant out of a house in which there hadn't been a lady. The note had a P.S.: "It's a good job there wasn't, sir, such a lady as some."

A week later he came to see me and told me he was "suited," committed to some highly respectable people—they were something quite immense in the City—who lived on the Bayswater side of the Park. "I dare say it will be rather poor, sir," he admitted; "but I've seen the fireworks, haven't I, sir?—it can't be fireworks *every* night. After Mansfield Street there ain't much choice." There was a certain amount, however, it seemed; for the following year, calling one day on a country cousin, a lady of a certain age who was spending a fortnight in town with some friends of her own, a family unknown to me and resident in Chester Square, the door of the house was opened, to my surprise and gratification, By Brooksmith in person. When I came out I had some conversation with him from which I gathered that he had found the large City people too dull for endurance, and I guessed, though he didn't say it, that he had found them vulgar as well. I don't know what judgement he would have passed on his actual patrons if my relative hadn't been their friend; but in view of that connexion he abstained from comment.

None was necessary, however, for before the lady in question brought her visit to a close they honoured me with an invitation to dinner, which I accepted. There was a largeish party on the occasion, but I confess I thought of Brooksmith rather more than of the seated company. They required no depth of attention—they were all referable to usual irredeemable inevitable types. It was the world of cheerful commonplace and conscious gentility and prosperous density, a full-fed material insular world, a world of hideous florid plate and ponderous order and thin conversation. There wasn't a word said about Byron, or even about a minor bard then much in view. Nothing would have induced me to look at Brooksmith in the course of the repast, and I felt sure that not even my overturning the wine would have induced him to meet my eye. We were in intellectual sympathy—we felt, as regards each other, a degree of social responsibility. In short we had been in Arcadia together, and we had both come to *this*! No wonder we were ashamed to be confronted. When he had helped on my overcoat, as I was going away, we parted, for the first time since the earliest days of Mansfield Street, in silence. I thought he looked lean and wasted, and I guessed that his new place wasn't more "human" than his previous one. There was plenty of beef and beer, but there was no reciprocity. The question for him to have asked before accepting the position wouldn't have been "How many footmen are kept?" but "How much imagination?"

The next time I went to the house—I confess it wasn't very soon—I encountered his successor, a personage who evidently enjoyed the good fortune of never having quitted his natural level. Could any be higher? he seemed to ask—over the heads of three footmen and even of some visitors. He made me feel as if Brooksmith were dead; but I didn't dare to enquire—I couldn't have borne his "I haven't the least idea, sir." I dispatched a note to the address that worthy had given me after Mr. Offord's death, but I received no answer. Six months later however I was fovoured with a visit from an elderly dreary dingy person who introduced herself to me as Mr. Brooksmith's aunt and from whom I learned that he was out of place and out of health and had allowed her to come and say to me that if I could spare half an hour to look in at him he would take it as a rare honour.

I went the next day—his messenger had given me a new address—and found my friend lodged in a short sordid street in Marylebone, one of those corners of London that wear the last expression of sickly meanness. The room into which I was shown was above the small establishment of a dyer and cleaner who had inflated kid gloves and discoloured shawls in his shop-front. There was a great deal of grimy infant life up and down the place, and there was a hot moist smell within, as of the "boiling" of dirty linen. Brooksmith sat with a blanket over his legs at a clean little window where, from behind stiff bluish-white curtains, he could look across at a huckster's and a tinsmith's and a small greasy public-house. He had passed through an illness and was convalescent, and his mother, as well as his aunt, was in attendance on him. I liked the nearer relative, who was bland and intensely humble, but I had my doubts of the remoter, whom I connected perhaps unjustly with the opposite public-house—she seemed somehow greasy with the same grease—and whose furtive eye followed every movement of my hand as if to see if it weren't going into my pocket. It didn't take this direction—I couldn't, unsolicited, put myself at that sort of ease with Brooksmith. Several times the door of the room opened and mysterious old women peeped in and shuffled back again. I don't know who they were; poor Brooksmith seemed encompassed with vague prying beery females.

He was vague himself, end evidently weak, and much embarrassed, and not an allusion was made between us to Mansfield Street. The vision of the salon of which he had been an ornament hovered before me however, by contrast, sufficiently. He assured me he was really getting better, and his mother remarked that he would come round if he could only get his spirits up. The aunt echoed this opinion, and I became more sure that in her own case she knew where to go for such a purpose. I'm afraid I was rather weak with my old friend, for I neglected the opportunity, so exceptionally good, to rebuke the levity which had led him to throw up honourable positions—fine stiff steady berths in Bayswater and Belgravia, with morning prayers, as I knew, attached to one of them. Very likely his reasons had been profane and sentimental; he didn't want morning prayers, he wanted to be somebody's dear fellow; but I couldn't be the person to rebuke him. He shuffled these episodes out of sight—I saw he had no wish to discuss them. I noted further, strangely enough, that it would probably be a questionable pleasure for him to see me again: he doubted now even of my power to condone his aberrations. He didn't wish to have to explain; and his behaviour was likely in future to need explanation. When I bade him farewell he looked at me a moment with eyes that said everything: "How can I talk about those exquisite years in this place, before these people, with the old women poking their heads in? It was very good of you to come to see me; it wasn't my idea—*she* brought you. We've said everything; it's over; you'll lose all patience with me, and I'd rather you shouldn't see the rest." I sent him some money in a letter the next day, but I saw the rest only in the light of a barren sequel.

A whole year after my visit to him I became aware once, in dining out, that Brooksmith was one of the several servants who hovered behind our chairs. He hadn't opened the door of the house to me, nor had I recognised him in the array of retainers in the hall. This time I tried to catch his eye, but he never gave me a chance, and when he handed me a dish I could only be careful to thank him audibly. Indeed I partook of two *entrées* of which I had my doubts, subsequently converted into certainties, in order not to snub him. He looked well enough in health, but much older, and wore in an exceptionally marked degree the glazed and expressionless mask of the British domestic *de race*. I saw with dismay that if I hadn't known him I should have taken him, on the showing of his countenance, for an extravagant illustration of irresponsive servile gloom. I said to myself that he had become a reactionary, gone over to the Philistines, thrown himself into religion, the religion of his "place," like a foreign lady *sur le retour*. I divined moreover that he was only engaged for the evening—he had become a mere waiter, had joined the band of the white-waistcoated who "go out." There was something pathetic in this fact—it was a terrible vulgarisation of Brooksmith. It was the mercenary prose of butlerhood; he had given up the struggle for the poetry. If reciprocity was what he had missed where was the reciprocity now? Only in the bottoms of the wine-glasses and the five shillings—or whatever they get—clapped into his hand by the permanent man. However, I supposed he had taken up a precarious branch of his profession because it after all sent him less downstairs. His relations with London society were more superficial, but they were of course more various. As I went away on this occasion I looked out for him eagerly among the four or five attendants whose perpendicular persons, fluting the walls of London passages, are supposed to lubricate the process of departure; but he was not on duty. I asked one of the others if he were not in the house, and received the prompt answer: "Just left, sir. Anything I can do for you, sir?" I wanted to say "Please give him my kind regards"; but I abstained—I didn't want to compromise him; and I never came across him again.

Often and often, in dining out, I looked for him, sometimes accepting invitations on purpose to multiply the chances of my meeting him. But always in vain; so that as I met many other members of the casual class over and over again I at last adopted the theory that he always procured a list of expected guests beforehand and kept away from the banquets which he thus learned I was to grace. At last I gave up hope, and one day at the end of three years I received another visit from his aunt. She was drearier and dingier, almost squalid, and she was in great tribulation and want. Her sister, Mrs. Brooksmith, had been dead a year, and three months later her nephew had disappeared. He had always looked after her a bit—since her troubles; I never knew what her troubles had been—and now she hadn't so much as a petticoat to pawn. She had also a niece, to whom she had been everything before her troubles, but the niece had treated her most shameful. These were details; the great and romantic fact was Brooksmith's final evasion of his fate. He had gone out to wait one evening as usual, in a white waistcoat she had done up for him with her own hands—being due at a large party up Kensington way. But he had never come home again and had never arrived at the large party, nor at any party that any one could make out. No trace of him had come to light—no gleam of the white waistcoat had pierced the obscurity of his doom. This news was a sharp shock to me, for I had my ideas about his real destination. His aged relative had promptly, as she said, guessed the worst. Somehow and somewhere he had got out of the way altogether, and now I trust that, with characteristic deliberation, he is changing the plates of the immortal gods. As my depressing visitant also said, he never *had* got his spirits up. I was fortunately able to dismiss her with her own somewhat improved. But the dim ghost of poor Brooksmith is one of those that I see. He had indeed been spoiled.

A NOTE ON

BROOKSMITH

(1891)

THIS tale is virtually all tone, bearing a frail minimum of content. Max Beerbohm might have written it, or the Harold Nicolson of *Some People;* but they would have striven to make it wittier, and succeeded, perhaps unfortunately. James is content with a light touch on the keys of sentiment.

Many of James's stories about professional artists seem to me to have a tincture of self-pity. I prefer "Brooksmith" to most of them. It is more original in its handling of one of James's perennial themes: the unwillingness or inability of society to sustain the artist. The tragedy of Brooksmith is that the passing of his master means also the passing of the setting in which he can exercise his art. That is why nothing can be done for him. As the narrator in honest bewilderment says about the artist-butler, "My service was not worth his being taken into." It is one of the guilts of our society (James would never have put it that way) that we provide no place for the Brooksmiths of this world. Brooksmith is a little, limited man; but his trouble is not little, not limited. On a reduced scale it is the same trouble that afflicts the hearts of all those sensitives who must somehow make do with a world in which imagination is rare. Do not say that Brooksmith killed himself, though he did. Say rather that he died of hunger—of hunger for good conversation.

The symbiotic relationship between master and man is one of the staple motifs in literature. The relationship is interesting because, though it is partly a function of a class system, it is largely independent of it. The bond between Don Quixote and Sancho Panza will bring laughter and tears to those natives of a future Utopia who may have no personal experience of any social inequality. And so, when Mr. Offord died, we know how Brooksmith felt, for we know how Sancho Panza felt when his master died.

It is quite true that the scaffolding of this tale rests upon the existence of a class-stratified society. James does not question—at least, not here—the value of that society. He accepts it as it is, and then asks himself, what will happen in such a society to a man like little Brooksmith. This society, whatever its shortcomings, is complete, consistent, and possessed of a certain beauty. It is also flexible enough to afford a place to an outsider, to a butler. For a brief moment it nourishes and sustains Brooksmith; it endows him with a decisive character; and when it falls apart, he falls apart with it. The tragedy of the life and death of Brooksmith, for all the lightness and charm with which James treats it, is linked to the general tragedy of the artist who has been born into a world in which he never can be thoroughly at home.

THE MIDDLE YEARS

I

THE April day was soft and bright, and poor Dencombe, happy in the conceit of reasserted strength, stood in the garden of the hotel, comparing, with a deliberation in which however there was still something of languor, the attractions of easy strolls. He liked the feeling of the south so far as you could have it in the north, he liked the sandy cliffs and the clustered pines, he liked even the colourless sea. "Bournemouth as a health-resort" had sounded like a mere advertisement, but he was thankful now for the commonest conveniences. The sociable country postman, passing through the garden, had just given him a small parcel which he took out with him, leaving the hotel to the right and creeping to a bench he had already haunted, a safe recess in the cliff. It looked to the south, to the tinted walls of the Island, and was protected behind by the sloping shoulder of the down. He was tired enough when he reached it, and for a moment was disappointed; he was better of course, but better, after all, than what? He should never again, as at one or two great moments of the past, be better than himself. The infinite of life was gone, and what remained of the dose a small glass scored like a thermometer by the apothecary. He sat and stared at the sea, which appeared all surface and twinkle, far shallower than the spirit of man. It was the abyss of human illusion that was the real, the tideless deep. He held his packet, which had come by book-post, unopened on his knee, liking, in the lapse of so many joys—his illness had made him feel his age—to know it was there, but taking for granted there could be no complete renewal of the pleasure, dear to young experience, of seeing one's self "just out." Dencombe, who had a reputation, had come out too often and knew too well in advance how he should look.

His postponement associated itself vaguely, after a little, with a group of three persons, two ladies and a young man, whom, beneath him, straggling and seemingly silent, he could see move slowly together along the sands. The gentleman had his head bent over a book and was occasionally brought to a stop by the charm of this volume, which, as Dencombe could perceive even at a distance, had a cover alluringly red. Then his companions, going a little further, waited for him to come up, poking their parasols into the beach, looking around them at the sea and sky and clearly sensible of the beauty of the day. To these things the young man with the book was still more clearly indifferent; lingering, credulous, absorbed, he was an object of envy to an observer from whose connexion with literature all such artlessness had faded. One of the ladies was large and mature; the other had the spareness of comparative youth and of a social situation possibly inferior. The large lady carried back Dencombe's imagination to the age of crinoline; she wore a hat of the shape of a mushroom, decorated with a blue veil, and had the air, in her aggressive amplitude, of clinging to a vanished fashion or even a lost cause. Presently her companion produced from under the folds of a mantle a limp portable chair which she stiffened out and of which the large lady took possession. This act, and something in the movement of either party, at once characterised the performers—they performed for Dencombe's recreation—as opulent matron and humble dependent. Where moreover was the virtue of an approved novelist if one couldn't establish a relation between such figures? the clever theory for instance that the young man was the son of the opulent matron and that the humble dependent, the daughter of a clergyman or an officer, nourished a secret passion for him. Was that not visible from the way she stole behind her protectress to look back at him?—back to where he had let himself come to a full stop when his mother sat down to rest. His book was a novel, it had the catchpenny binding; so that while the romance of life stood neglected at his side he lost himself in that of the circulating library. He moved mechanically to where the sand was softer and ended by plumping down in it to finish his chapter at his ease. The humble dependent, discouraged by his remoteness, wandered with a martyred droop of the head in another direction, and the exorbitant lady, watching the waves, offered a confused resemblance to a flying-machine that had broken down.

When his drama began to fail Dencombe remembered that he had after all another pastime. Though such promptitude on the part of the publisher was rare he was already able to draw from its wrapper his "latest," perhaps his last. The cover of "The Middle Years" was duly meretricious, the smell of the fresh pages the very odour of sanctity; but for the moment he went no further—he had become conscious of a strange alienation. He had forgotten what his book was about. Had the assault of his old ailment, which he had so fallaciously come to Bournemouth to ward off, interposed utter blankness as to what had preceded it? He had finished the revision of proof before quitting London, but his subsequent fortnight in bed had passed the sponge over colour. He couldn't have chanted to himself a single sentence, couldn't have turned with curiosity or confidence to any particular page. His subject had already gone from him, leaving scarce a superstition behind. He uttered a low moan as he breathed the chill of this dark void, so desperately it seemed to represent the completion of a sinister process. The tears filled his mild eyes; something precious had passed away. This was the pang that had been sharpest during the last few years—the sense of ebbing time, of shrinking opportunity; and now he felt not so much that his last chance was going as that it was gone indeed. He had done all he should ever do, and yet hadn't done what he wanted. This was the laceration—that practically his career was over: it was as violent as a grip at his throat. He rose from his seat nervously—a creature hunted by a dread; then he fell back in his weakness and nervously opened his book. It was a single volume; he preferred single volumes and aimed at a rare compression.

He began to read and, little by little, in this occupation, was pacified and reassured. Everything came back to him, but came back with a wonder, came back above all with a high and magnificent beauty. He read his own prose, he turned his own leaves, and had as he sat there with the spring sunshine on the page an emotion peculiar and intense. His career was over, no doubt, but it was over, when all was said, with *that*.

He had forgotten during his illness the work of the previous year; but what he had chiefly forgotten was that it was extraordinarily good. He dived once more into his story and was drawn down, as by a siren's hand, to where, in the dim underworld of fiction, the great glazed tank of art, strange silent subjects float. He recognised his motive and surrendered to his talent. Never probably had that talent, such as it was, been so fine. His difficulties were still there, but what was also there, to his perception, though probably, alas! to nobody's else, was the art that in most cases had surmounted them. In his surprised enjoyment of this ability he had a glimpse of a possible reprieve. Surely its force wasn't spent—there was life and service in it yet. It hadn't come to him easily, it had been backward and roundabout. It was the child of time, the nursling of delay; he had struggled and suffered for it, making sacrifices not to be counted, and now that it was really mature was it to cease to yield, to confess itself brutally beaten? There was an infinite charm for Dencombe in feeling as he had never felt before that diligence *vincit omnia*. The result produced in his little book was somehow a result beyond his conscious intention: it was as if he had planted his genius, had trusted his method, and they had grown up and flowered with this sweetness. If the achievement had been real, however, the process had been painful enough. What he saw so intensely today, what he felt as a nail driven in, was that only now, at the very last, had he come into possession. His development had been abnormally slow, almost grotesquely gradual. He had been hindered and retarded by experience, he had for long periods only groped his way. It had taken too much of his life to produce too little of his art. The art had come, but it had come after everything else. At such a rate a first existence was too short—long enough only to collect material; so that to fructify, to use the material, one should have a second age, an extension. This extension was what poor Dencombe sighed for. As he turned the last leaves of his volume he murmured "Ah for another go, ah for a better chance!"

The three persons drawing his attention to the sands had vanished and then reappeared; they had now wandered up a path, an artificial and easy ascent, which led to the top of the cliff. Dencombe's bench was halfway down, on a sheltered ledge, and the large lady, a massive heterogeneous person with bold black eyes and kind red cheeks, now took a few moments to rest. She wore dirty gauntlets and immense diamond ear-rings; at first she looked vulgar, but she contradicted this announcement in an agreeable off-hand tone. While her companions stood waiting for her she spread her skirts on the end of Dencombe's seat. The young man had gold spectacles, through which, with his finger still in his red-covered book, he glanced at the volume, bound in the same shade of the same colour, lying on the lap of the original occupant of the bench. After an instant Dencombe felt him struck with a resemblance; he had recognised the gilt stamp on the crimson cloth, was reading "The Middle Years" and now noted that somebody else had kept pace with him. The stranger was startled, possibly even a little ruffled, to find himself not the only person favoured with an early copy. The eyes of the two proprietors met a moment, and Dencombe borrowed amusement from the expression of those of his competitor, those, it might even be inferred, of his admirer. They confessed to some resentment—they seemed to say: "Hang it, has he got it *already*? Of course he's a brute of a reviewer!" Dencombe shuffled his copy out of sight while the opulent matron, rising from her repose, broke out: "I feel already the good of this air!"

"I can't say I do," said the angular lady. "I find myself quite let down."

"I find myself horribly hungry. At what time did you order luncheon?" her protectress pursued.

The young person put the question by. "Doctor Hugh always orders it."

"I ordered nothing today—I'm going to make you diet," said their comrade.

"Then I shall go home and sleep. *Qui dort dine!*"

"Can I trust you to Miss Vernham?" asked Doctor Hugh of his elder companion.

"Don't I trust *you*?" she archly enquired.

"Not too much!" Miss Vernham, with her eyes on the ground, permitted herself to declare. "You must come with us at least to the house," she went on while the personage on whom they appeared to be in attendance began to mount higher. She had got a little out of ear-shot; nevertheless Miss Vernham became, so far as Dencombe was concerned, less distinctly audible to murmur to the young man: "I don't think you realise all you owe the Countess!"

Absently, a moment, Doctor Hugh caused his gold-rimmed spectacles to shine at her. "Is that the way I strike you? I see—I see!"

"She's awfully good to us," continued Miss Vernham, compelled by the lapse of the other's motion to stand there in spite of his discussion of private matters. Of what use would it have been that Dencombe should be sensitive to shades hadn't he detected in that arrest a strange influence from the quiet old convalescent in the great tweed cape? Miss Vernham appeared suddenly to become aware of some such connexion, for she added in a moment: "If you want to sun yourself here you can come back after you've seen us home."

Doctor Hugh, at this, hesitated, and Dencombe, in spite of a desire to pass for unconscious, risked a covert glance at him. What his eyes met this time, as happened, was, on the part of the young lady, a queer stare, naturally vitreous, which made her remind him of some figure—he couldn't name it—in a play or a novel, some sinister governess or tragic old maid. She seemed to scan him, to challenge him, to say out of general spite: "What have you got to do with us?" At the same instant the rich humour of the Countess reached them from above: "Come, come, my little lambs; you should follow your old *bergère*!" Miss Vernham turned away for it, pursuing the ascent, and Doctor Hugh, after another mute appeal to Dencombe and a minute's evident demur, deposited his book on the bench as if to keep his place, or even as a gage of earnest return, and bounded without difficulty up the rougher part of the cliff.

Equally innocent and infinite are the pleasures of observation and the resources engendered by the trick of analysing life. It amused poor Dencombe, as he dawdled in his tepid air-bath, to believe himself awaiting a revelation of something at the back of a fine young mind. He looked hard at the book on the end of the bench, but wouldn't have touched it for the world. It served his purpose to have a theory that shouldn't be exposed to refutation. He already felt better of his melancholy; he had, according to his old formula, put his head at the window. A passing Countess could draw off the fancy when, like the elder of the ladies who had just retreated, she was as obvious as the giantess of a caravan. It was indeed general views that were terrible; short ones, contrary to an opinion sometimes expressed, were the refuge, were the remedy. Doctor Hugh couldn't possibly be anything but a reviewer who had understandings for early copies with publishers or with newspapers. He reappeared in a quarter of an hour with visible relief at finding Dencombe on the spot and the gleam of white teeth in an embarrassed but generous smile. He was perceptibly disappointed at the eclipse of the other copy of the book; it made a pretext the less for speaking to the quiet gentleman. But he spoke notwithstanding; he held up his own copy and broke out pleadingly: "*Do* say, if you have occasion to speak of it, that it's the best thing he has done yet!"

Dencombe responded with a laugh: "Done yet" was so amusing to him, made such a grand avenue of the future. Better still, the young man took *him* for a reviewer. He pulled out "The Middle Years" from under his cape, but instinctively concealed any telltale look of fatherhood. This was partly because a person was always a fool for insisting to others on his work. "Is that what you're going to say yourself?" he put to his visitor.

"I'm not quite sure I shall write anything. I don't, as a regular thing—I enjoy in peace. But it's awfully fine."

Dencombe just debated. If the young man had begun to abuse him he would have confessed on the spot to his identity, but there was no harm in drawing out any impulse to praise. He drew it out with such success that in a few moments his new acquaintance, seated by his side, was confessing candidly that the works of the author of the volumes before them were the only ones he could read a second time. He had come the day before from London, where a friend of his, a journalist, had lent him his copy of the last, the copy sent to the office of the journal and already the subject of a "notice" which, as was pretended there—but one had to allow for "swagger"—it had taken a full quarter of an hour to prepare. He intimated that he was ashamed for his friend, and in the case of a work demanding and repaying study, of such inferior manners; and, with his fresh appreciation and his so irregular wish to express it, he speedily became for poor Dencombe a remarkable, a delightful apparition. Chance had brought the weary man of letters face to face with the greatest admirer in the new generation of whom it was supposable he might boast. The admirer in truth was mystifying, so rare a case was it to find a bristling young doctor—he looked like a German physiologist—enamoured of literary form. It was an accident, but happier than most accidents, so that Dencombe, exhilarated as well as confounded, spent half an hour in making his visitor talk while he kept himself quiet. He explained his premature possession of "The Middle Years" by an allusion to the friendship of the publisher, who, knowing he was at Bournemouth for his health, had paid him this graceful attention. He allowed he had been ill, for Doctor Hugh would infallibly have guessed it; he even went so far as to wonder if he mightn't look for some hygienic "tip" from a personage combining so bright an enthusiasm with a presumable knowledge of the remedies now in vogue. It would shake his faith a little perhaps to have to take a doctor seriously who could take *him* so seriously, but he enjoyed this gushing modern youth and felt with an acute pang that there would still be work to do in a world in which such odd combinations were presented. It wasn't true, what he had tried for renunciation's sake to believe, that all the combinations were exhausted. They weren't by any means—they were infinite: the exhaustion was in the miserable artist.

Doctor Hugh, an ardent physiologist, was saturated with the spirit of the age—in other words he had just taken his degree; but he was independent and various, he talked like a man who would have preferred to love literature best. He would fain have made fine phrases, but nature had denied him the trick. Some of the finest in "The Middle Years" had struck him inordinately, and he took the liberty of reading them to Dencombe in support of his plea. He grew vivid, in the balmy air, to his companion, for whose deep refreshment he seemed to have been sent; and was particularly ingenuous in describing how recently he had become acquainted, and how instantly infatuated, with the only man who had put flesh between the ribs of an art that was starving on superstitions. He hadn't yet written to him—he was deterred by a strain of respect. Dencombe at this moment rejoiced more inwardly than ever that he had never answered the photographers. His visitor's attitude promised him a luxury of intercourse, though he was sure a due freedom for Doctor Hugh would depend not a little on the Countess. He learned without delay what type of Countess was involved, mastering as well the nature of the tie that united the curious trio. The large lady, an Englishwoman by birth and the daughter of a celebrated baritone, whose taste *minus* his talent she had inherited, was the widow of a French nobleman and mistress of all that remained of the handsome fortune, the fruit of her father's earnings, that had constituted her dower. Miss Vernham, an odd creature but an accomplished pianist, was attached to her person at a salary. The Countess was generous, independent, eccentric; she travelled with her minstrel and her medical man. Ignorant and passionate she had nevertheless moments in which she was almost irresistible. Dencombe saw her sit for her portrait in Doctor Hugh's free sketch, and felt the picture of his young friend's relation to her frame itself in his mind. This young friend, for a representative of the new psychology, was himself easily hypnotised, and if he became abnormally communicative it was only a sign of his real subjection. Dencombe did accordingly what he wanted with him, even without being known as Dencombe.

Taken ill on a journey in Switzerland the Countess had picked him up at an hotel, and the accident of his happening to please her had made her offer him, with her imperious liberality, terms that couldn't fail to dazzle a practitioner without patients and whose resources had been drained dry by his studies. It wasn't the way he would have proposed to spend his time, but it was time that would pass quickly, and meanwhile she was wonderfully kind. She exacted perpetual attention, but it was impossible not to like her. He gave details about his queer patient, a "type" if there ever was one, who had in connexion with her flushed obesity, and in addition to the morbid strain of a violent and aimless will, a grave organic disorder; but he came back to his loved novelist, whom he was so good as to pronounce more essentially a poet than many of those who went in for verse, with a zeal excited, as all his indiscretion had been excited, by the happy chance of Dencombe's sympathy and the coincidence of their occupation. Dencombe had confessed to a slight personal acquaintance with the author of "The Middle Years," but had not felt himself as ready as he could have wished when his companion, who had never yet encountered a being so privileged, began to be eager for particulars. He even divined in Doctor Hugh's eye at that moment a glimmer of suspicion. But the young man was too inflamed to be shrewd and repeatedly caught up the book to exclaim: "Did you notice this?" or "Weren't you immensely struck with that?" "There's a beautiful passage toward the end," he broke out; and again he laid his hand on the volume. As he turned the pages he came upon something else, while Dencombe saw him suddenly change colour. He had taken up as it lay on the bench Dencombe's copy instead of his own, and his neighbour at once guessed the reason of his start. Doctor Hugh looked grave an instant; then he said: "I see you've been altering the text!" Dencombe was a passionate corrector, a fingerer of style; the last thing he ever arrived at was a form final for himself. His ideal would have been to publish secretly, and then, on the published text, treat himself to the terrified revise, sacrificing always a first edition and beginning for posterity and even for the collectors, poor dears, with a second. This morning, in "The Middle Years," his pencil had pricked a dozen lights. He was amused at the effect of the young man's reproach; for an instant it made him change colour. He stammered at any rate ambiguously, then through a blur of ebbing consciousness saw Doctor Hugh's mystified eyes. He only had time to feel he was about to be ill again—that emotion, excitement, fatigue, the heat of the sun, the solicitation of the air, had combined to play him a trick, before, stretching out a hand to his visitor with a plaintive cry, he lost his senses altogether.

Later he knew he had fainted and that Doctor Hugh had got him home in a Bath-chair, the conductor of which, prowling within hail for custom, had happened to remember seeing him in the garden of the hotel. He had recovered his perception on the way, and had, in bed that afternoon, a vague recollection of Doctor Hugh's young face, as they went together, bent over him in a comforting laugh and expressive of something more than a suspicion of his identity. That identity was ineffaceable now, and all the more that he was rueful and sore. He had been rash, been stupid, had gone out too soon, stayed out too long. He oughtn't to have exposed himself to strangers, he ought to have taken his servant. He felt as if he had fallen into a hole too deep to descry any little patch of heaven. He was confused about the time that had passed—he pieced the fragments together. He had seen his doctor, the real one, the one who had treated him from the first and who had again been very kind. His servant was in and out on tiptoe, looking very wise after the fact. He said more than once something about the sharp young gentleman. The rest was vagueness in so far as it wasn't despair. The vagueness, however, justified itself by dreams, dozing anxieties from which he finally emerged to the consciousness of a dark room and a shaded candle.

"You'll be all right again—I know all about you now," said a voice near him that he felt to be young. Then his meeting with Doctor Hugh came back. He was too discouraged to joke about it yet, but made out after a little that the interest was intense for his visitor. "Of course I can't attend you professionally—you've got your own man, with whom I've talked and who's excellent," Doctor Hugh went on. "But you must let me come to see you as a good friend. I've just looked in before going to bed. You're doing beautifully, but it's a good job I was with you on the cliff. I shall come in early tomorrow. I want to do something for you. I want to do everything. You've done a tremendous lot for me." The young man held his hand, hanging over him, and poor Dencombe, weakly aware of this living pressure, simply lay there and accepted his devotion. He couldn't do anything less—he needed help too much.

The idea of the help he needed was very present to him that night, which he spent in a lucid stillness, an intensity of thought that constituted a reaction from his hours of stupor. He was lost, he was lost— he was lost if he couldn't be saved. He wasn't afraid of suffering, of death, wasn't even in love with life; but he had had a deep demonstration of desire. It came over him in the long quiet hours that only with "The Middle Years" had he taken his flight; only on that day, visited by soundless processions, had he recognised his kingdom. He had had a revelation of his range. What he dreaded was the idea that his reputation should stand on the unfinished. It wasn't with his past but with his future that it should properly be concerned. Illness and age rose before him like spectres with pitiless eyes: how was he to bribe such fates to give him the second chance? He had had the one chance that all men have—he had had the chance of life. He went to sleep again very late, and when he awoke Doctor Hugh was sitting at hand. There was already by this time something beautifully familiar in him.

"Don't think I've turned out your physician," he said; "I'm acting with his consent. He has been here and seen you. Somehow he seems to trust me. I told him how we happened to come together yesterday, and he recognises that I've a peculiar right."

Dencombe felt his own face pressing. "How have you squared the Countess?"

The young man blushed a little, but turned it off. "Oh never mind the Countess!"

"You told me she was very exacting."

Doctor Hugh had a wait. "So she is."

"And Miss Vernham's an *intrigante*."

"How do you know that?"

"I know everything. One *has* to, to write decently!"

"I think she's mad," said limpid Doctor Hugh.

"Well, don't quarrel with the Countess—she's a present help to you."

"I don't quarrel," Doctor Hugh returned. "But I don't get on with silly women." Presently he added: "You seem very much alone."

"That often happens at my age. I've outlived, I've lost by the way."

Doctor Hugh faltered; then surmounting a soft scruple: "Whom have you lost?"

"Every one."

"Ah no," the young man breathed, laying a hand on his arm.

"I once had a wife—I once had a son. My wife died when my child was born, and my boy, at school, was carried off by typhoid."

"I wish I'd been there!" cried Doctor Hugh.

"Well—if you're here!" Dencombe answered with a smile that, in spite of dimness, showed how he valued being sure of his companion's whereabouts.

"You talk strangely of your age. You're not old."

"Hypocrite—so early!"

"I speak physiologically."

"That's the way I've been speaking for the last five years, and it's exactly what I've been saying to myself. It isn't till we *are* old that we begin to tell ourselves we're not."

"Yet I know I myself am young," Doctor Hugh returned.

"Not so well as I!" laughed his patient, whose visitor indeed would have established the truth in question by the honesty with which he changed the point of view, remarking that it must be one of the charms of age—at any rate in the case of high distinction—to feel that one has laboured and achieved. Doctor Hugh employed the common phrase about earning one's rest, and it made poor Dencombe for an instant almost angry. He recovered himself, however, to explain, lucidly enough, that if, ungraciously, he knew nothing of such a balm, it was doubtless because he had wasted inestimable years. He had followed literature from the first, but he had taken a lifetime to get abreast of her. Only today at last had he begun to *see,* so that all he had hitherto shown was a movement without a direction. He had ripened too late and was so clumsily constituted that he had had to teach himself by mistakes.

"I prefer your flowers then to other people's fruit, and your mistakes to other people's successes," said gallant Doctor Hugh. "It's for your mistakes I admire you."

"You're happy—you don't know," Dencombe answered.

Looking at his watch the young man had got up; he named the hour of the afternoon at which he would return. Dencombe warned him against committing himself too deeply, and expressed again all his dread of making him neglect the Countess—perhaps incur her displeasure.

"I want to be like you—I want to learn by mistakes!" Doctor Hugh laughed.

"Take care you don't make too grave a one! But do come back," Dencombe added with the glimmer of a new idea.

"You should have had more vanity!" His friend spoke as if he knew the exact amount required to make a man of letters normal.

"No, no—I only should have had more time. I want another go."

"Another go?"

"I want an extension."

"An extension?" Again Doctor Hugh repeated Dencombe's words, with which he seemed to have been struck.

"Don't you know?—I want to what they call 'live.'"

The young man, for good-bye, had taken his hand, which closed with a certain force. They looked at each other hard. "You *will live,*" said Doctor Hugh.

"Don't be superficial. It's too serious!"

"You *shall* live!" Dencombe's visitor declared, turning pale.

"Ah that's better!" And as he retired the invalid, with a troubled laugh, sank gratefully back.

All that day and all the following night he wondered if it mightn't be arranged. His doctor came again, his servant was attentive, but it was to his confident young friend that he felt himself mentally appeal. His collapse on the cliff was plausibly explained and his liberation, on a better basis, promised for the morrow; meanwhile, however, the intensity of his meditations kept him tranquil and made him indifferent. The idea that occupied him was none the less absorbing because it was a morbid fancy. Here was a clever son of the age, ingenious and ardent, who happened to have set him up for connoisseurs to worship. This servant of his altar had all the new learning in science and all the old reverence in faith; wouldn't he therefore put his knowledge at the disposal of his sympathy, his craft at the disposal of his love? Couldn't he be trusted to invent a remedy for a poor artist to whose art he had paid a tribute? If he couldn't the alternative was hard: Dencombe would have to surrender to silence unvindicated and undivined. The rest of the day and all the next he toyed in secret with this sweet futility. Who would work the miracle for him but the young man who could combine such lucidity with such passion? He thought of the fairy-tales of science and charmed himself into forgetting that he looked for a magic that was not of this world. Doctor Hugh was an apparition, and that placed him above the law. He came and went while his patient, who now sat up, followed him with supplicating eyes. The interest of knowing the great author had made the young man begin "The Middle Years" afresh and would help him to find a richer sense between its covers. Dencombe had told him what he "tried for"; with all his intelligence, on a first perusal, Doctor Hugh had failed to guess it. The baffled celebrity wondered then who in the world *would* guess it: he was amused once more at the diffused massive weight that could be thrown into the missing of an intention. Yet he wouldn't rail at the general mind today—consoling as that ever had been: the revelation of his own slowness had seemed to make all stupidity sacred.

Doctor Hugh, after a little, was visibly worried, confessing, on enquiry, to a source of embarrassment at home. "Stick to the Countess—don't mind me," Dencombe said repeatedly; for his companion was frank enough about the large lady's attitude. She was so jealous that she had fallen ill—she resented such a breach of allegiance. She paid so much for his fidelity that she must have it all: she refused him the right to other sympathies, charged him with scheming to make her die alone, for it was needless to point out how little Miss Vernham was a resource in trouble. When Doctor Hugh mentioned that the Countess would already have left Bournemouth if he hadn't kept her in bed, poor Dencombe held his arm tighter and said with decision: "Take her straight away." They had gone out together, walking back to the sheltered nook in which, the other day, they had met. The young man, who had given his companion a personal support, declared with emphasis that his conscience was clear—he could ride two horses at once. Didn't he dream for his future of a time when he should have to ride five hundred? Longing equally for virtue, Dencombe replied that in that golden age no patient would pretend to have contracted with him for his whole attention. On the part of the Countess wasn't such an avidity lawful? Doctor Hugh denied it, said there was no contract, but only a free understanding, and that a sordid servitude was impossible to a generous spirit; he liked moreover to talk about art, and that was the subject on which, this time, as they sat together on the sunny bench, he tried most to engage the author of "The Middle Years." Dencombe, soaring again a little on the weak wings of convalescence and still haunted by that happy notion of an organised rescue, found another strain of eloquence to plead the cause of a certain splendid "last manner," the very citadel, as it would prove, of his reputation, the stronghold into which his real treasure would be gathered. While his listener gave up the morning and the great still sea ostensibly waited he had a wondrous explanatory hour. Even for himself he was inspired as he told what his treasure would consist of; the precious metals he would dig from the mine, the jewels rare, strings of pearls, he would hang between the columns of his temple. He was wondrous for himself, so thick his convictions crowded, but still more wondrous for Doctor Hugh, who assured him none the less that the very pages he had just published were already encrusted with gems. This admirer, however, panted for the combinations to come and, before the face of the beautiful day, renewed to Dencombe his guarantee that his profession would hold itself responsible for such a life. Then he suddenly clapped his hand upon his watch-pocket and asked leave to absent himself for half an hour. Dencombe waited there for his return, but was at last recalled to the actual by the fall of a shadow across the ground. The shadow darkened into that of Miss Vernham, the young lady in attendance on the Countess; whom Dencombe, recognising her, perceived so clearly to have come to speak to him that he rose from his bench to acknowledge the civility. Miss Vernham indeed proved not particularly civil; she looked strangely agitated, and her type was now unmistakeable.

"Excuse me if I do ask," she said, "whether it's too much to hope that you may be induced to leave Doctor Hugh alone." Then before our poor friend, greatly disconcerted, could protest: "You ought to be informed that you stand in his light—that you may do him a terrible injury."

"Do you mean by causing the Countess to dispense with his services?"

"By causing her to disinherit him." Dencombe stared at this, and Miss Vernham pursued, in the gratification of seeing she could produce an impression: "It has depended on himself to come into something very handsome. He has had a grand prospect, but I think you've succeeded in spoiling it."

"Not intentionally, I assure you. Is there no hope the accident may be repaired?" Dencombe asked.

"She was ready to do anything for him. She takes great fancies, she lets herself go—it's her way. She has no relations, she's free to dispose of her money, and she's very ill," said Miss Vernham for a climax.

"I'm very sorry to hear it," Dencombe stammered.

"Wouldn't it be possible for you to leave Bournemouth? That's what I've come to see about."

He sank to his bench. "I'm very ill myself, but I'll try!"

Miss Vernham still stood there with her colourless eyes and the brutality of her good conscience. "Before it's too late, please!" she said; and with this she turned her back, in order, quickly, as if it had been a business to which she could spare but a precious moment, to pass out of his sight.

Oh yes, after this Dencombe was certainly very ill. Miss Vernham had upset him with her rough fierce news; it was the sharpest shock to him to discover what was at stake for a penniless young man of fine parts. He sat trembling on his bench, staring at the waste of waters, feeling sick with the directness of the blow. He was indeed too weak, too unsteady, too alarmed; but he would make the effort to get away, for he couldn't accept the guilt of interference and his honour was really involved. He would hobble home, at any rate, and then think what was to be done. He made his way back to the hotel and, as he went, had a characteristic vision of Miss Vernham's great motive. The Countess hated women of course—Dencombe was lucid about that; so the hungry pianist had no personal hopes and could only console herself with the bold conception of helping Doctor Hugh in order to marry him after he should get his money or else induce him to recognise her claim for compensation and buy her off. If she had befriended him at a fruitful crisis he would really, as a man of delicacy—and she knew what to think of that point—have to reckon with her.

At the hotel Dencombe's servant insisted on his going back to bed. The invalid had talked about catching a train and had begun with orders to pack; after which his racked nerves had yielded to a sense of sickness. He consented to see his physician, who immediately was sent for, but he wished it to be understood that his door was irrevocably closed to Doctor Hugh. He had his plan, which was so fine that he rejoiced in it after getting back to bed. Doctor Hugh, suddenly finding himself snubbed without mercy, would, in natural disgust and to the joy of Miss Vernham, renew his allegiance to the Countess. When his physician arrived Dencombe learned that he was feverish and that this was very wrong: he was to cultivate calmness and try, if possible, not to think. For the rest of the day he wooed stupidity; but there was an ache that kept him sentient, the probable sacrifice of his "extension," the limit of his course. His medical adviser was anything but pleased; his successive relapses were ominous. He charged this personage to put out a strong hand and take Doctor Hugh off his mind—it would contribute so much to his being quiet. The agitating name, in his room, was not mentioned again, but his security was a smothered fear, and it was not confirmed by the receipt, at ten o'clock that evening, of a telegram which his servant opened and read him and to which, with an address in London, the signature of Miss Vernham was attached. "Beseech you to use all influence to make our friend join us here in the morning. Countess much the worse for dreadful journey, but everything may still be saved." The two ladies had gathered themselves up and had been capable in the afternoon of a spiteful revolution. They had started for the capital, and if the elder one, as Miss Vernham had announced, was very ill, she had wished to make it clear that she was proportionately reckless. Poor Dencombe, who was not reckless and who only desired that everything should indeed be "saved," sent this missive straight off to the young man's lodging and had on the morrow the pleasure of knowing that he had quitted Bournemouth by an early train.

Two days later he pressed in with a copy of a literary journal in his hand. He had returned because he was anxious and for the pleasure of flourishing the great review of "The Middle

Years." Here at least was something adequate—it rose to the occasion; it was an acclamation, a reparation, a critical attempt to place the author in the niche he had fairly won. Dencombe accepted and submitted; he made neither objection nor enquiry, for old complications had returned and he had had two dismal days. He was convinced not only that he should never again leave his bed, so that his young friend might pardonably remain, but that the demand he should make on the patience of beholders would be of the most moderate. Doctor Hugh had been to town, and he tried to find in his eyes some confession that the Countess was pacified and his legacy clinched; but all he could see there was the light of his juvenile joy in two or three of the phrases of the newspaper. Dencombe couldn't read them, but when his visitor had insisted on repeating them more than once he was able to shake an unintoxicated head. "Ah no—but they would have been true of what I *could* have done!"

"What people 'could have done' is mainly what they've in fact done," Doctor Hugh contended.

"Mainly, yes; but I've been an idiot!" Dencombe said.

Doctor Hugh did remain; the end was coming fast. Two days later his patient observed to him, by way of the feeblest of jokes, that there would now be no question whatever of a second chance. At this the young man stared; then he exclaimed: "Why it has come to pass—it has come to pass! The second chance has been the public's—the chance to find the point of view, to pick up the pearl!"

"Oh the pearl!" poor Dencombe uneasily sighed. A smile as cold as a winter sunset flickered on his drawn lips as he added: "The pearl is the unwritten—the pearl is the unalloyed, the *rest,* the lost!"

From that hour he was less and less present, heedless to all appearance of what went on round him. His disease was definitely mortal, of an action as relentless, after the short arrest that had enabled him to fall in with Doctor Hugh, as a leak in a great ship. Sinking steadily, though this visitor, a man of rare resources, now cordially approved by his physician, showed endless art in guarding him from pain, poor Dencombe kept no reckoning of favour or neglect, betrayed no symptom of regret or speculation. Yet toward the last he gave a sign of having noticed how for two days Doctor Hugh hadn't been in his room, a sign that consisted of his suddenly opening his eyes to put a question. Had he spent those days with the Countess?

"The Countess is dead," said Doctor Hugh. "I knew that in a particular contingency she wouldn't resist. I went to her grave."

Dencombe's eyes opened wider. "She left you 'something handsome'?"

The young man gave a laugh almost too light for a chamber of woe. "Never a penny. She roundly cursed me."

"Cursed you?" Dencombe wailed.

"For giving her up. I gave her up for *you*. I had to choose," his companion explained.

"You chose to let a fortune go?"

"I chose to accept, whatever they might be, the consequences of my infatuation," smiled Doctor Hugh. Then as a larger pleasantry: "The fortune be hanged! It's your own fault if I can't get your things out of my head."

The immediate tribute to his humour was a long bewildered moan; after which, for many hours, many days, Dencombe lay motionless and absent. A response so absolute, such a glimpse of a definite result and such a sense of credit, worked together in his mind and, producing a strange commotion, slowly altered and transfigured his despair. The sense of cold submersion left him—he seemed to float without an effort. The incident was extraordinary as evidence, and it shed an intenser light. At the last he signed to Doctor Hugh to listen and, when he was down on his knees by the pillow, brought him very near. "You've made me think it all a delusion."

"Not your glory, my dear friend," stammered the young man.

"Not my glory—what there is of it! It *is* glory—to have been tested, to have had our little quality and cast our little spell. The thing is to have made somebody care. You happen to be crazy of course, but that doesn't affect the law."

"You're a great success!" said Doctor Hugh, putting into his young voice the ring of a marriage-bell.

Dencombe lay taking this in; then he gathered strength to speak once more. "A second chance—*that's* the delusion. There never was to be but one. We work in the dark—we do what we can—we give what we have. Our doubt is our passion and our passion is our task. The rest is the madness of art."

"If you've doubted, if you've despaired, you've always 'done' it," his visitor subtly argued.

"We've done something or other," Dencombe conceded.

"Something or other is everything. It's the feasible. It's *you*!"

"Comforter!" poor Dencombe ironically sighed.

"But it's true," insisted his friend.

"It's true. It's frustration that doesn't count."

"Frustration's only life," said Doctor Hugh.

"Yes, it's what passes." Poor Dencombe was barely audible, but he had marked with the words the virtual end of his first and only chance.

A NOTE ON

THE MIDDLE YEARS

(1893)

INTO "The Middle Years" is worked one of James's favorite themes—that of the relation between master and disciple. "Brooksmith" and "The Pupil" display other, somewhat more original, mutations of the same motive. It is one, it may be, that afforded a special and private gratification to the mind of Henry James. Many of his stories—and this is one—dramatize a relationship lacking in his life. He had a few imitators and a few who, like Edith Wharton, thought of themselves as his disciples; but, with respect to their books, his sights were set too high to permit him to distribute more than affectionate praise. Though he hungered for it, I do not think he ever experienced true discipleship. Silently, wistfully he pleaded for understanding, for an audience, but was compelled to satisfy himself with what to any real artist is but a galling compensation—a coterie. "The Middle Years," then, embodies one of the recurrent visions of James's dream life.

Most of James's tales of writers are diluted by a certain infusion of self-pity, self-pity arising precisely from James's constant sense that he was spending his life dropping masterpieces into a void of indifference. With an irony that often sharpened into mere irritation he wrote of the vulgarity of "success." Yet he never quite succeeded in refining out of himself a hankering for that very success. The consequence of this impurity of attitude is that many of his stories about novelists are a bit sentimental, deficient in the Socratic detachment of his finer work. In these stories, despite all his theories about the need for preserving "the point of view," the point of view remains that of

Henry James in person, and a rather querulous Henry James at that.

This stricture does not apply to "The Middle Years." It is true that the novelist Dencombe is James. But he is a James who has risen beyond his own parochial frustrations into a region where the life of the artist may be contemplated, if with sorrow, also with philosophy. "The Middle Years" has altitude.

The plot is a makeshift. Dr. Hugh's sacrifice, whereby in order to pay homage to a master he cheerfully surrenders the chance of a fortune, is but a symbolical device. Call it the lever with which James uprears in Dencombe's mind his final vision of himself, the meaning of his life, of the lives of all creators. Up to the time of this vision Dencombe is tormented, as are you and I, by "the sense of ebbing time, of shrinking opportunity." He, too, like every terrified mortal who has ever squirmed out his little life on the hook of nature, cries, "Ah, for another go! ah, for a better chance!" It is what we all want, the second chance, the "extension." Life is always around the corner.

The desire for another chance is not too tragic a thing in most of us, for the probability is that few of us would be capable, on a second try, of improvement. But Dencombe's case seems, to him and to us, at first, quite different. Perhaps he, a genius, might make real use of the "extension." We, the rest of us, merely live; he grows. "Only today, at last, had he begun to *see,* so that what he had hitherto done was a movement without a direction."

But Dencombe, aided by his disciple, comes to perceive, in the very hour of his death, the meaninglessness of the cry for a second chance. "He had had the one chance that all men have—he had had the chance of life." Anything more is a delusion. "There never was to be but one," murmurs Dencombe, in one of the classic expressions of the creed of the creator. "We work in the dark—we do what we can—we give what we have. Our doubt is our passion, and our passion is our task. The rest is the madness of art." What passes, as Dr. Hugh gently points out, is mere living, which is frustration. This frustration doesn't count. What counts is what does not pass, the residue of the doubt and the passion—"the madness of art."

THE ALTAR OF THE DEAD

I

He had a mortal dislike, poor Stransom, to lean anniversaries, and loved them still less when they made a pretence of a figure. Celebrations and suppressions were equally painful to him, and but one of the former found a place in his life. He had kept each year in his own fashion the date of Mary Antrim's death. It would be more to the point perhaps to say that this occasion kept *him:* it kept him at least effecutally from doing anything else. It took hold of him again and again with a hand of which time had softened but never loosened the touch. He waked to his feast of memory as consciously as he would have waked to his marriage-morn. Marriage had had of old but too little to say to the matter: for the girl who was to have been his bride there had been no bridal embrace. She had died of a malignant fever after the wedding-day had been fixed, and he had lost before fairly tasting it an affection that promised to fill his life to the brim.

Of that benediction, however, it would have been false to say this life could really be emptied: it was still ruled by a pale ghost, still ordered by a sovereign presence. He had not been a man of numerous passions, and even in all these years no sense had grown stronger with him than the sense of being bereft. He had needed no priest and no altar to make him for ever widowed. He had done many things in the world—he had done almost all but one: he had never, never forgotten. He had tried to put into his existence whatever else might take up room in it, but had failed to make it more than a house of which the mistress was eternally absent. She was most absent of all on the recurrent December day that his tenacity set apart. He had no arranged observance of it, but his nerves made it all their own. They drove him forth without mercy, and the goal of his pilgrimage was far. She had been buried in a London suburb, a part then of Nature's breast, but which he had seen lose one after another every feature of freshness. It was in truth during the moments he stood there that his eyes beheld the place least. They looked at another image, they opened to another light. Was it a credible future? Was it an incredible past? Whatever the answer it was an immense escape from the actual.

It's true that if there weren't other dates than this there were other memories; and by the time George Stransom was fifty-five such memories had greatly multiplied. There were other ghosts in his life than the ghost of Mary Antrim. He had perhaps not had more losses than most men, but he had counted his losses more; he hadn't seen death more closely, but had in a manner felt it more deeply. He had formed little by little the habit of numbering his Dead: it had come to him early in life that there was something one had to do for them. They were there in their simplified intensified essence, their conscious absence and expressive patience, as personally there as if they had only been stricken dumb. When all sense of them failed, all sound of them ceased, it was if their purgatory were really still on earth; they asked so little that they got, poor things, even less, and died again, died every day, of the hard usage of life. They had no organised service, no reserved place, no honour, no shelter, no safety. Even ungenerous people provided for the living, but even those who were called most generous did nothing for the others. So on George Stransom's part had grown up with the years a resolve that he at least would do something, do it, that is, for his own—would perform the great charity without reproach. Every man *had* his own, and every man had, to meet this charity, the ample resources of the soul.

It was doubtless the voice of Mary Antrim that spoke for them best; as the years at any rate went by he found himself in regular communion with these postponed pensioners, those whom indeed he always called in his thoughts the Others. He spared them the moments, he organised the charity. Quite how it had risen he probably never could have told you, but what came to pass was that an altar, such as was after all within everybody's compass, lighted with perpetual candles and dedicated to these secret rites, reared itself in his spiritual spaces. He had wondered of old, in some embarrassment, whether he had a religion; being very sure, and not a little content, that he hadn't at all events the religion some of the people he had known wanted him to have. Gradually this question was straightened out for him: it became clear to him that the religion instilled by his earliest consciousness had been simply the religion of the Dead. It suited his inclination, it satisfied his spirit, it gave employment to his piety. It answered his love of great offices, of a solemn and splendid ritual; for no shrine could be more bedecked and no ceremonial more stately than those to which his worship was attached. He had no imagination about these things but that they were accessible to any who should feel the need of them. The poorest could build such temples of the spirit—could make them blaze with candles and smoke with incense, make them flush with pictures and flowers. The cost, in the common phrase, of keeping them up fell wholly on the generous heart.

II

He had this year, on the eve of his anniversary, as happened, an emotion not unconnected with that range of feeling. Walking home at the close of a busy day he was arrested in the London street by the particular effect of a shop-front that lighted the dull brown air with its mercenary grin and before which several persons were gathered. It was the window of a jeweller whose diamonds and sapphires seemed to laugh, in flashes like high notes of sound, with the mere joy of knowing how much more they were "worth" than most of the dingy pedestrians staring at them from the other side of the pane. Stransom lingered long enough to suspend, in a vision, a string of pearls about the white neck of Mary Antrim, and then was kept an instant longer by the sound of a voice he knew. Next him was a mumbling old woman, and beyond the old woman a gentleman with a lady on his arm. It was from him, from Paul Creston, the voice had proceeded: he was talking with the lady of some precious object in the window. Stransom had no sooner recognised him than the old woman turned away; but just with this growth of opportunity came a felt strangeness that stayed him in the very act of laying his hand on his friend's arm. It lasted but the instant, only that space sufficed for the flash of a wild question. Was *not* Mrs. Creston dead?—the ambiguity met him there in the short drop of her husband's voice, the drop conjugal, if it ever was, and in the way the two figures leaned to each other. Creston, making a step to look at something else, came nearer, glanced at him, started and exclaimed—behaviour the effect of which was at first only to leave Stransom staring, staring back across the months at the different face, the wholly other face, the poor man had shown him last, the blurred ravaged mask bent over the open grave by which they had stood together. That son of affliction wasn't in mourning now; he detached his arm from his companion's to grasp the hand of the older friend. He coloured as well as smiled in the strong light of the shop when Stransom raised a tentative hat to the lady. Stransom had just time to see she was pretty before he found himself gaping at a fact more portentous. "My dear fellow, let me make you acquainted with my wife."

Creston had blushed and stammered over it, but in half a minute, at the rate we live in polite society, it had practically become, for our friend, the mere memory of a shock. They stood there and laughed and talked; Stransom had instantly whisked the shock out of the way, to keep it for private consumption. He felt himself grimace, he heard himself exaggerate the proper, but was conscious of turning not a little faint. That new woman, that hired performer Mrs. Creston? Mrs. Creston had been more living for him than any woman but one. This lady had a face that shone as publicly as the jeweller's window, and in the happy candour with which she wore her monstrous character was an effect of gross immodesty. The character of Paul Creston's wife thus attributed to her was monstrous for reasons Stransom could judge his friend to know perfectly that he knew. The happy pair had just arrived from America, and Stransom hadn't needed to be told this to guess the nationality of the lady. Somehow it deepened the foolish air that her husband's confused cordiality was unable to conceal. Stransom recalled that he had heard of poor Creston's having, while his bereavement was still fresh, crossed the sea for what people in such predicaments call a little change. He had found little change indeed, he had brought the little change back; it was the little change that stood there and that, do what he would, he couldn't, while he showed those high front teeth of his, look other than a conscious ass about. They were going into the shop, Mrs. Creston said, and she begged Mr. Stransom to come with them and help to decide. He thanked her, opening his watch and pleading an engagement for which he was already late, and they parted while she shrieked into the fog "Mind now you come to see me right away!" Creston had had the delicacy not to suggest that, and Stransom hoped it hurt him somewhere to hear her scream it to all the echoes.

He felt quite determined, as he walked away, never in his life to go near her. She was perhaps a human being, but Creston oughtn't to have shown her without precautions, oughtn't indeed to have shown her at all. His precautions should have been those of a forger or a murderer, and the people at home would never have mentioned extradition. This was a wife for foreign service or purely external use; a decent consideration would have spared her the injury of comparisons. Such was the first flush of George Stransom's reaction; but as he sat alone that night—there were particular hours he always passed alone—the harshness dropped from it and left only the pity. *He* could spend an evening with Kate Creston, if the man to whom she had given everything couldn't. He had known her twenty years, and she was the only woman for whom he might perhaps have been unfaithful. She was all cleverness and sympathy and charm; her house had been the very easiest in all the world and her friendship the very firmest. Without accidents he had loved her, without accidents every one had loved her: she had made the passions about her as regular as the moon makes the tides. She had been also of course far too good for her husband, but he never suspected it, and in nothing had she been more admirable than in the exquisite art with which she tried to keep every one else (keeping Creston was no trouble) from finding it out. Here was a man to whom she had devoted her life and for whom she had given it up—dying to bring into the world a child of his bed; and she had had only to submit to her fate to have, ere the grass was green on her grave, no more existence for him than a domestic servant he had replaced. The frivolity, the indecency of it made Stransom's eyes fill; and he had that evening a sturdy sense that he alone, in a world without delicacy, had a right to hold up his head. While he smoked, after dinner, he had a book in his lap, but he had no eyes for his page: his eyes, in the swarming void of things, seemed to have caught Kate Creston's, and it was into their sad silences he looked. It was to him her sentient spirit had turned, knowing it to be of her he would think. He thought for a long time of how the closed eyes of dead women could still live—how they could open again, in a quiet lamplit room, long after they had looked their last. They had looks that survived—had them as great poets had quoted lines.

The newspaper lay by his chair—the thing that came in the afternoon and the servants thought one wanted; without sense for what was in it he had mechanically unfolded and then dropped it. Before he went to bed he took it up, and this time, at the top of a paragraph, he was caught by five words that made him start. He stood staring, before the fire, at the "Death of Sir Acton Hague, K.C.B.," the man who ten years earlier had been the nearest of his friends and whose deposition from this eminence had practically left it without an occupant. He had seen him after their rupture, but hadn't now seen him for years.

Standing there before the fire he turned cold as he read what had befallen him. Promoted a short time previous to the governorship of the Westward Islands, Acton Hague had died, in the bleak honour of this exile, of an illness consequent on the bite of a poisonous snake. His career was compressed by the newspaper into a dozen lines, the perusal of which excited on George Stransom's part no warmer feeling than one of relief at the absence of any mention of their quarrel, an incident accidentally tainted at the time, thanks to their joint immersion in large affairs, with a horrible publicity. Public indeed was the wrong Stransom had, to his own sense, suffered, the insult he had blankly taken from the only man with whom he had ever been intimate; the friend, almost adored, of his University years, the subject, later, of his passionate loyalty: so public that he had never spoken of it to a human creature, so public that he had completely overlooked it. It had made the difference for him that friendship too was all over, but it had only made just that one. The shock of interests had been private, intensely so; but the action taken by Hague had been in the face of men. Today it all seemed to have occurred merely to the end that George Stransom should think of him as "Hague" and measure exactly how much he himself could resemble a stone. He went cold, suddenly and horribly cold, to bed.

III

The next day, in the afternoon, in the great grey suburb, he knew his long walk had tired him. In the dreadful cemetery alone he had been on his feet an hour. Instinctively, coming back, they had taken him a devious course, and it was a desert in which no circling cabman hovered over possible prey. He paused on a corner and measured the dreariness; then he made out through the gathered dusk that he was in one of those tracts of London which are less gloomy by night than by day, because, in the former case, of the civil gift of light. By day there was nothing, but by night there were lamps, and George Stransom was in a mood that made lamps good in themselves. It wasn't that they could show him anything, it was only that they could burn clear. To his surprise, however, after a while, they did show him something: the arch of a high doorway approached by a low terrace of steps, in the depth of which—it formed a dim vestibule—the raising of a curtain at the moment he passed gave him a glimpse of an avenue of gloom with a glow of tapers at the end. He stopped and looked up, recognising the place as a church. The thought quickly came to him that since he was tired he might rest there; so that after a moment he had in turn pushed up the leathern curtain and gone in. It was a temple of the old persuasion, and there had evidently been a function—perhaps a service for the dead; the high altar was still a blaze of candles. This was an exhibition he always liked, and he dropped into a seat with relief. More than it had ever yet come home to him it struck him as good there should be churches.

This one was almost empty and the other altars were dim; a verger shuffled about, an old woman coughed, but it seemed to Stransom there was hospitality in the thick sweet air. Was it only the savour of the incense or was it something of larger intention? He had at any rate quitted the great grey suburb and come nearer to the warm centre. He presently ceased to feel intrusive, gaining at last even a sense of community with the only worshipper in his neighbourhood, the sombre presence of a woman, in mourning unrelieved, whose back was all he could see of her and who had sunk deep into prayer at no great distance from him. He wished he could sink, like her, to the very bottom, be as motionless, as rapt in prostration. After a few moments he shifted his seat; it was almost indelicate to be so aware of her. But Stransom subsequently quite lost himself, floating away on the sea of light. If occasions like this had been more frequent in his life he would have had more present the great original type, set up in myriad temples, of the unapproachable shrine he had erected in his mind. That shrine had begun in vague likeness to church pomps, but the echo had ended by growing more distinct than the sound. The sound now rang out, the type blazed at him with all its fires and with a mystery of radiance in which endless meanings could glow. The thing became as he sat there his appropriate altar and each starry candle an appropriate vow. He numbered them, named them, grouped them—it was the silent roll-call of his Dead. They made together a brightness vast and intense, a brightness in which the mere chapel of his thoughts grew so dim that as it faded away he asked himself if he shouldn't find his real comfort in some material act, some outward worship.

This idea took possession of him while, at a a distance, the black-robed lady continued prostrate; he was quietly thrilled with his conception, which at last brought him to his feet in the sudden excitement of a plan. He wandered softly through the aisles, pausing in the different chapels, all save one applied to a special devotion. It was in this clear recess, lampless and unapplied, that he stood longest—the length of time it took him fully to grasp the conception of gilding it with his bounty. He should snatch it from no other rites and associate it with nothing profane; he would simply take it as it should be given up to him and make it a masterpiece of splendour and a mountain of fire. Tended sacredly all the year, with the sanctifying church round it, it would always be ready for his offices. There would be difficulties, but from the first they presented themselves only as difficulties surmounted. Even for a person so little affiliated the thing would be a matter of arrangement. He saw it all in advance, and how bright in especial the place would become to him in the intermissions of toil and the dusk of afternoons; how rich in assurance at all times, but especially in the indifferent world. Before withdrawing he drew nearer again to the spot where he had first sat down, and in the movement he met the lady whom he had seen praying and who was now on her way to the door. She passed him quickly, and he had only a glimpse of her pale face and her unconscious, almost sightless eyes. For that instant she looked faded and handsome.

This was the origin of the rites more public, yet certainly esoteric, that he at last found himself able to establish. It took a long time, it took a year, and both the process and the result would have been—for any who knew—a vivid picture of his good faith. No one did know, in fact—no one but the bland ecclesiastics whose acquaintance he had promptly sought, whose objections he had softly overridden, whose curiosity and sympathy he had artfully charmed, whose assent to his eccentric munificence he had eventually won, and who had asked for concessions in exchange for indulgences. Stransom had of course at an early stage of his enquiry been referred to the Bishop, and the Bishop had been delightfully human, the Bishop had been almost amused. Success was within sight, at any rate, from the moment the attitude of those whom it concerned became liberal in response to liberality. The altar and the sacred shell that half-encircled it, consecrated to an ostensible and customary worship, were to be splendidly maintained; all that Stransom reserved to himself was the number of his lights and the free enjoyment of his intention. When the intention had taken complete effect the enjoyment became even greater than he had ventured to hope. He liked to think of this effect when far from it, liked to convince himself of it yet again when near. He was not often indeed so near as that a visit to it hadn't perforce something of the patience of a pilgrimage; but the time he gave to his devotion came to seem to him more a contribution to his other interests than a betrayal of them. Even a loaded life might be easier when one had added a new necessity to it.

How much easier was probably never guessed by those who simply knew there were hours when he disappeared and for many of whom there was a vulgar reading of what they used to call his plunges. These plunges were into depths quieter than the deep sea-caves, and the habit had at the end of a year or two become the one it would have cost him most to relinquish. Now they had really, his Dead, something that was indefeasibly theirs; and he liked to think that they might in cases be the

Dead of others, as well as that the Dead of others might be invoked there under the protection of what he had done. Whoever bent a knee on the carpet he had laid down appeared to him to act in the spirit of his intention. Each of his lights had a name for him, and from time to time a new light was kindled. This was what he had fundamentally agreed for, that there should always be room for them all. What those who passed or lingered saw was simply the most resplendent of the altars called suddenly into vivid usefulness, with a quiet elderly man, for whom it evidently had a fascination, often seated there in a maze or a doze; but half the satisfaction of the spot for this mysterious and fitful worshipper was that he found the years of his life there, and the ties, the affections, the struggles, the submissions, the conquests, if there had been such, a record of that adventurous journey in which the beginnings and the endings of human relations are the lettered mile-stones. He had in general little taste for the past as a part of his own history; at other times and in other places it mostly seemed to him pitiful to consider and impossible to repair; but on these occasions he accepted it with something of that positive gladness with which one adjusts one's self to an ache that begins to succumb to treatment. To the treatment of time the malady of life begins at a given moment to succumb; and these were doubtless the hours at which that truth most came home to him. The day was written for him there on which he had first become acquainted with death, and the successive phases of the acquaintance were marked each with a flame.

The flames were gathering thick at present, for Stransom had entered that dark defile of our earthly descent in which some one dies every day. It was only yesterday that Kate Creston had flashed out her white fire; yet already there were younger stars ablaze on the tips of the tapers. Various persons in whom his interest had not been intense drew closer to him by entering this company. He went over it, head by head, till he felt like the shepherd of a huddled flock, with all a shepherd's vision of differences imperceptible. He knew his candles apart, up to the colour of the flame, and would still have known them had their positions all been changed. To other imaginations they might stand for other things—that they should stand for something to be hushed before was all he desired; but he was intensely conscious of the personal note of each and of the distinguishable way it contributed to the concert. There were hours at which he almost caught himself wishing that certain of his friends would now die, that he might establish with them in this manner a connexion more charming than, as it happened, it was possible to enjoy with them in life. In regard to those from whom one was separated by the long curves of the globe such a connexion could only be an improvement: it brought them instantly within reach. Of course there were gaps in the constellation, for Stransom knew he could only pretend to act for his own, and it wasn't every figure passing before his eyes into the great obscure that was entitled to a memorial. There was a strange sanctification in death, but some characters were more sanctified by being forgotten than by being remembered. The greatest blank in the shining page was the memory of Acton Hague, of which he inveterately tried to rid himself. For Acton Hague no flame could ever rise on any altar of his.

IV

EVERY year, the day he walked back from the great graveyard, he went to church as he had done the day his idea was born. It was on this occasion, as it happened, after a year had passed, that he began to observe his altar to be haunted by a worshipper at least as frequent as himself. Others of the faithful, and in the rest of the church, came and went, appealing sometimes, when they disappeared, to a vauge or to a particular recognition; but this unfailing presence was always to be observed when he arrived and still in possession when he departed. He was surprised, the first time, at the promptitude with which it assumed an identity for him—the identity of the lady whom two years before, on his anniversary, he had seen so intensely bowed, and of whose tragic face he had had so flitting a vision. Given the time that had passed, his recollection of her was fresh enough to make him wonder. Of himself she had of course no impression, or rather had had none at first: the time came when her manner of transacting her business suggested her having gradually guessed his call to be of the same order. She used his altar for her own purpose—he could only hope that, sad and solitary as she always struck him, she used it for her own Dead. There were interruptions, infidelities, all on his part, calls to other associations and duties; but as the months went on he found her whenever he returned, and he ended by taking pleasure in the thought that he had given her almost the contentment he had given himself. They worshipped side by side so often that there were moments when he wished he might be sure, so straight did their prospect stretch away of growing old together in their rites. She was younger than he, but she looked as if her Dead were at least as numerous as his candles. She had no colour, no sound, no fault, and another of the things about which he had made up his mind was that she had no fortune. Always black-robed, she must have had a succession of sorrows. People weren't poor, after all, whom so many losses could overtake; they were positively rich when they had had so much to give up. But the air of this devoted and indifferent woman, who always made, in any attitude, a beautiful accidental line, conveyed somehow to Stransom that she had known more kinds of trouble than one.

He had a great love of music and little time for the joy of it; but occasionally, when workaday noises were muffled by Saturday afternoons, it used to come back to him that there were glories. There were moreover friends who reminded him of this and side by side with whom he found himself sitting out concerts. On one of these winter evenings, in Saint James's Hall, he became aware after he had seated himself that the lady he had so often seen at church was in the place next him and was evidently alone, as he also this time happened to be. She was at first too absorbed in the consideration of the programme to heed him, but when she at last glanced at him he took advantage of the movement to speak to her, greeting her with the remark that he felt as if he already knew her. She smiled as she said "Oh yes, I recognise you"; yet in spite of this admission of long acquaintance it was the first he had seen of her smile. The effect of it was suddenly to contribute more to that acquaintance than all the previous meetings had done. He hadn't "taken in," he said to himself, that she was so pretty. Later, that evening—it was while he rolled along in a hansom on his way to dine out—he added that he hadn't taken in that she was so interesting. The next morning in the midst of his work he quite suddenly and irrelevantly reflected that his impression of her, beginning so far back, was like a winding river that had at last reached the sea.

His work in fact was blurred a little all that day by the sense of what had now passed between them. It wasn't much, but it had just made the difference. They had listened together to Beethoven and Schumann; they had talked in the pauses, and at the end, when at the door, to which they moved together, he had asked her if he could help her in the matter of getting away. She had thanked him and put up her umbrella, slipping into the crowd without an allusion to their meeting yet again and leaving him to remember at leisure that not a word had been exchanged about the usual scene of that coincidence. This omission struck him now as natural and then again as perverse. She mightn't in the least have allowed his warrant for speaking to her, and yet if she hadn't he would have judged her an underbred woman. It was odd that when nothing had really ever brought them together he should have been able successfully to assume they were in a manner old friends—that this negative quantity was somehow more than they could express. His success, it was true, had been qualified by her quick escape, so that there grew up in him an absurd desire to put it to some better test. Save in so far as some other poor chance might help him, such a test could be only to meet her afresh at church. Left to himself he would have gone to church the very next afternoon, just for the curiosity of seeing if he should find her there. But he wasn't left to himself, a fact he discovered quite at the last, after he had virtually made up his mind to go. The influence that kept him away really revealed to him how little to himself his Dead *ever* left him. He went only for *them*—for nothing else in the world.

The force of this revulsion kept him away ten days: he hated to connect the place with anything but his offices or to give a glimpse of the curiosity that had been on the point of moving him. It was absurd to weave a tangle about a matter so simple as a custom of devotion that might with ease have been daily or hourly; yet the tangle got itself woven. He was sorry, he was disappointed: it was as if a long happy spell had been broken and he had lost a familiar security. At the last, however, he asked himself if he was to stay away for ever from the fear of this muddle about motives. After an interval neither longer nor shorter than usual he re-entered the church with a clear conviction that he should scarcely heed the presence or the absence of the lady of the concert. This indifference didn't prevent his at once noting that for the only time since he had first seen her she wasn't on the spot. He had now no scruple about giving her time to arrive, but she didn't arrive, and when he went away still missing her he was profanely and consentingly sorry. If her absence made the tangle more intricate, that was all her own doing. By the end of another year it was very intricate indeed; but by that time he didn't in the least care, and it was only his cultivated consciousness that had given him scruples. Three times in three months he had gone to church without finding her, and he felt he hadn't needed these occasions to show him his suspense had dropped. Yet it was, incongruously, not indifference, but a refinement of delicacy that had kept him from asking the sacristan, who would of course immediately have recognised his description of her, whether she had been seen at other hours. His delicacy had kept him from asking any question about her at any time, and it was exactly the same virtue that had left him so free to be decently civil to her at the concert.

This happy advantage now served him anew, enabling him when she finally met his eyes—it was after a fourth trial—to predetermine quite fixedly his awaiting her retreat. He joined her in the street as soon as she had moved, asking her if he might accompany her a certain distance. With her placid permission he went as far as a house in the neighbourhood at which she had business: she let him know it was not where she lived. She lived, as she said, in a mere slum, with an old aunt, a person in connexion with whom she spoke of the engrossment of humdrum duties and regular occupations. She wasn't, the mourning niece, in her first youth, and her vanished freshness had left something behind that, for Stransom, represented the proof it had been tragically sacrificed. Whatever she gave him the assurance of she gave without references. She might have been a divorced duchess—she might have been an old maid who taught the harp.

V

THEY fell at last into the way of walking together almost every time they met, though for a long time still they never met but at church. He couldn't ask her to come and see him, and as if she hadn't a proper place to receive him she never invited her friend. As much as himself she knew the world of London, but from an undiscussed instinct of privacy they haunted the region not mapped on the social chart. On the return she always made him leave her at the same corner. She looked with him, as a pretext for a pause, at the depressed things in suburban shop-fronts; and there was never a word he had said to her that she hadn't beautifully understood. For long ages he never knew her name, any more than she had ever pronounced his own; but it was not their names that mattered, it was only their perfect practice and their common need.

These things made their whole relation so impersonal that they hadn't the rules or reasons people found in ordinary friendships. They didn't care for the things it was supposed necessary to care for in the intercourse of the world. They ended one day —they never knew which of them expressed it first—by throwing out the idea that they didn't care for each other. Over this idea they grew quite intimate; they rallied to it in a way that marked a fresh start in their confidence. If to feel deeply together about certain things wholly distinct from themselves didn't constitute a safety, where was safety to be looked for? Not lightly nor often, not without occasion nor without emotion, any more than in any other reference by serious people to a mystery of their faith; but when something had happened to warm, as it were, the air for it, they came as near as they could come to calling their Dead by name. They felt it was coming very near to utter their thought at all. The word "they" expressed enough; it limited the mention, it had a dignity of its own, and if, in their talk, you had heard our friends use it, you might have taken them for a pair of pagans of old alluding decently to the domesticated gods. They never knew—at least Stransom never knew—how they had learned to be sure about each other. If it had been with each a question of what the other was there for, the certitude had come in some fine way of its own. Any faith, after all, has the instinct of propagation, and it was as natural as it was beautiful that they should have taken pleasure on the spot in the imagination of a following. If the following was for each but a following of one it had proved in the event sufficient. Her debt, however, of course, was much greater than his, because while she had only given him a worshipper he had given her a splendid temple. Once she said she pitied him for the length of his list—she had counted his candles almost as often as himself—and this made him wonder what could have been the length of hers. He had wondered before at the coincidence of their losses, especially as from time to time a new candle was set up. On some occasion some accident led him to express this curiosity, and she answered as if in surprise that he hadn't already understood. "Oh for me, you know, the more there are the better—there could never be too many. I should like hundreds and hundreds—I should like thousands; I should like a great mountain of light."

Then of course in a flash he understood. "Your Dead are only One?"

She hung back at this as never yet. "Only One," she answered, colouring as if now he knew her guarded secret. It really made him feel he knew less than before, so difficult was it for him to reconstitute a life in which a single experience had so belittled all others. His own life, round its central hollow, had been packed close enough. After this she appeared to have regretted her confession, though at the moment she spoke there had been pride in her very embarrassment. She declared to him that his own was the larger, the dearer possession—the portion one would have chosen if one had been able to choose; she assured him she could perfectly imagine some of the echoes with which his silences were peopled. He knew she couldn't: one's relation to what one had loved and hated had been a relation too distinct from the relations of others. But this didn't affect the fact that they were growing old together in their piety. She was a feature of that piety, but even at the ripe stage of acquaintance in which they occasionally arranged to meet at a concert or to go together to an exhibition she was not a feature of anything else. The most that happened was that his worship became paramount. Friend by friend dropped away till at last there were more emblems on his altar than houses left him to enter. She was more than any other the friend who remained, but she was unknown to all the rest. Once when she had discovered, as they called it, a new star, she used the expression that the chapel at last was full.

"Oh no," Stransom replied, "there's a great thing wanting for that! The chapel will never be full till a candle is set up before which all the others will pale. It will be the tallest candle of all."

Her mild wonder rested on him. "What candle do you mean?"

"I mean, dear lady, my own."

He had learned after a long time that she earned money by her pen, writing under a pseudonym she never disclosed in magazines he never saw. She knew too well what he couldn't read and what she couldn't write, and she taught him to cultivate indifference with a success that did much for their good relations. Her invisible industry was a convenience to him; it helped his contented thought of her, the thought that rested in the dignity of her proud obscure life, her little remunerated art and her little impenetrable home. Lost, with her decayed relative, in her dim suburban world, she came to the surface for him in distant places. She was really the priestess of his altar, and whenever he quitted England he committed it to her keeping. She proved to him afresh that women have more of the spirit of religion than men; he felt his fidelity pale and faint in comparison with hers. He often said to her that since he had so little time to live he rejoiced in her having so much; so glad was he to think she would guard the temple when he should have been called. He had a great plan for that, which of course he told her too, a bequest of money to keep it up in undiminished state. Of the administration of this fund he would appoint her superintendent, and if the spirit should move her she might kindle a taper even for him.

"And who will kindle one even for me?" she then seriously asked.

VI

SHE was always in mourning, yet the day he came back from the longest absence he had yet made her appearance immediately told him she had lately had a bereavement. They met on this occasion as she was leaving the church, so that postponing his own entrance he instantly offered to turn round and walk away with her. She considered, then she said: "Go in now, but come and see me in an hour." He knew the small vista of her street, closed at the end and as dreary as an empty pocket, where the pairs of shabby little houses, semi-detached but indissolubly united, were like married couples on bad terms. Often, however, as he had gone to the beginning he had never gone beyond. Her aunt was dead—that he immediately guessed, as well as that it made a difference; but when she had for the first time mentioned her number he found himself, on her leaving him, not a little agitated by this sudden liberality. She wasn't a person with whom, after all, one got on so very fast: it had taken him months and months to learn her name, years and years to learn her address. If she had looked, on this reunion, so much older to him, how in the world did he look to her? She had reached the period of life he had long since reached, when, after separations, the marked clock-face of the friend we meet announces the hour we have tried to forget. He couldn't have said what he expected as, at the end of his waiting, he turned the corner where for years he had always paused; simply not to pause was a sufficient cause for emotion. It was an event, somehow; and in all their long acquaintance there had never been an event. This one grew larger when, five minutes later, in the faint elegance of her little drawing-room, she quavered out a greeting that showed the measure she took of it. He had a strange sense of having come for something in particular; strange because literally there was nothing particular between them, nothing save that they were at one on their great point, which had long ago become a magnificent matter of course. It was true that after she had said "You can always come now, you know," the thing he was there for seemed already to have happened. He asked her if it was the death of her aunt that made the difference; to which she replied: "She never knew I knew you. I wished her not to." The beautiful clearness of her candour—her faded beauty was like a summer twilight—disconnected the words from any image of deceit. They might have struck him as the record of a deep dissimulation, but she had always given him a sense of noble reasons. The vanished aunt was present, as he looked about him, in the small complacencies of the room, the beaded velvet and the fluted moreen; and though, as we know, he had the worship of the Dead, he found himself not definitely regretting this lady. If she wasn't in his long list, however, she was in her niece's short one, and Stransom presently observed to the latter that now at least, in the place they haunted together, she would have another object of devotion.

"Yes, I shall have another. She was very kind to me. It's that that's the difference."

He judged, wondering a good deal before he made any motion to leave her, that the difference would somehow be very great and would consist of still other things than her having let him come in. It rather chilled him, for they had been happy together as they were. He extracted from her at any rate an intimation that she should now have means less limited, that her aunt's tiny fortune had come to her, so that there was henceforth only one to consume what had formerly been made to suffice for two. This was a joy to Stransom, because it had hitherto been equally impossible for him either to offer her presents or contentedly to stay his hand. It was too ugly to be at her side that way, abounding himself and yet not able to overflow—a demonstration that would have been signally a false note. Even her better situation too seemed only to draw out in a sense the loneliness of her future. It would merely help her to live more and more for their small ceremonial, and this at a time when he himself had begun wearily to feel that, having set it in motion, he might depart. When they had sat a while in the pale parlour she got up—"This isn't *my* room: let us go into mine." They had only to cross the narrow hall, as he found, to pass quite into another air. When she had closed the door of the second room, as she called it, he felt at last in real possession of her. The place had the flush of life—it was expressive; its dark red walls were articulate with memories and relics. These were simple things—photographs and water-colours, scraps of writing framed and ghosts of flowers embalmed; but a moment sufficed to show him they had a common meaning. It was here she had lived and worked, and she had already told him she would make no change of scene. He read the reference in the objects about her—the general one to places and times; but after a minute he distinguished among them a small portrait of a gentleman. At a distance and without their glasses his eyes were only so caught by it as to feel a vague curiosity. Presently this impulse carried him nearer, and in another moment he was staring at the picture in stupefaction and with the sense that some sound had broken from him. He was further conscious that he showed his companion a white face when he turned round on her gasping: "Acton Hague!"

She matched his great wonder. "Did you know him?"

"He was the friend of all my youth—of my early manhood. And *you* knew him?"

She coloured at this and for a moment her answer failed; her eyes embraced everything in the place, and a strange irony reached her lips as she echoed: "Knew him?"

Then Stransom understood, while the room heaved like the cabin of a ship, that its whole contents cried out with him, that it was a museum in his honour, that all her later years had been addressed to him and that the shrine he himself had reared had been passionately converted to this use. It was all for Acton Hague that she had kneeled every day at his altar. What need had there been for a consecrated candle when he was present in the whole array? The revelation so smote our friend in the face that he dropped into a seat and sat silent. He had quickly felt her shaken by the force of his shock, but as she sank on the sofa beside him and laid her hand on his arm he knew almost as soon that she mightn't resent it as much as she'd have liked.

VII

He learned in that instant two things: one being that even in so long a time she had gathered no knowledge of his great intimacy and his great quarrel; the other that in spite of this ignorance, strangely enough, she supplied on the spot a reason for his stupor. "How extraordinary," he presently exclaimed, "that we should never have known!"

She gave a wan smile which seemed to Stransom stranger even than the fact itself. "I never, never spoke of him."

He looked again about the room. "Why then, if your life had been so full of him?"

"Mayn't I put you that question as well? Hadn't your life also been full of him?"

"Any one's, every one's life who had the wonderful experience of knowing him. *I* never spoke of him," Stransom added in a moment, "because he did me—years ago—an unforgettable wrong." She was silent, and with the full effect of his presence all about them it almost startled her guest to hear no protest escape her. She accepted his words; he turned his eyes to her again to see in what manner she accepted them. It was with rising tears and a rare sweetness in the movement of putting out her hand to take his own. Nothing more wonderful had ever appeared to him than, in that little chamber of remembrance and homage, to see her convey with such exquisite mildness that as from Acton Hague any injury was credible. The clock ticked in the stillness—Hague had probably given it to her—and while he let her hold his hand with a tenderness that was almost an assumption of responsibility for his old pain as well as his new, Stransom after a minute broke out: "Good God, how he must have used *you*!"

She dropped his hand at this, got up and, moving across the room, made straight a small picture to which, on examining it, he had given a slight push. Then turning round on him with her pale gaiety recovered, "I've forgiven him!" she declared.

"I know what you've done," said Stransom; "I know what you've done for years." For a moment they looked at each other through it all with their long community of service in their eyes. This short passage made, to his sense, for the woman before him, an immense, an absolutely naked confession; which was presently, suddenly blushing red and changing her place again, what she appeared to learn he perceived in it. He got up and "How you must have loved him!" he cried.

"Women aren't like men. They can love even where they've suffered."

"Women are wonderful," said Stransom. "But I assure you I've forgiven him too."

"If I had known of anything so strange I wouldn't have brought you here."

"So that we might have gone on in our ignorance to the last?"

"What do you call the last?" she asked, smiling still.

At this he could smile back at her. "You'll see—when it comes."

She thought of that. "This is better perhaps; but as we were—it was good."

He put her the question. "Did it never happen that he spoke of me?"

Considering more intently she made no answer, and he then knew he should have been adequately answered by her asking how often he himself had spoken of their terrible friend. Suddenly a brighter light broke in her face and an excited idea sprang to her lips in the appeal: "You *have* forgiven him?"

"How, if I hadn't, could I linger here?"

She visibly winced at the deep but unintended irony of this; but even while she did so she panted quickly: "Then in the lights on your altar—?"

"There's never a light for Acton Hague!"

She stared with a dreadful fall. "But if he's one of your Dead?"

"He's one of the world's, if you like—he's one of yours. But he's not one of mine. Mine are only the Dead who died possessed of me. They're mine in death because they were mine in life."

"*He* was yours in life then, even if for a while he ceased to be. If you forgave him you went back to him. Those whom we've once loved—"

"Are those who can hurt us most," Stransom broke in.

"Ah it's not true—you've *not* forgiven him!" she wailed with a passion that startled him.

He looked at her as never yet. "What was it he did to you?"

"Everything!" Then abruptly she put out her hand in farewell. "Good-bye."

He turned as cold as he had turned that night he read the man's death. "You mean that we meet no more?"

"Not as we've met—not *there*!"

He stood aghast at this snap of their great bond, at the renouncement that rang out in the word she so expressively sounded. "But what's changed—for you?"

She waited in all the sharpness of a trouble that for the first time since he had known her made her splendidly stern. "How can you understand now when you didn't understand before?"

"I didn't understand before only because I didn't know. Now that I know, I see what I've been living with for years," Stransom went on very gently.

She looked at him with a larger allowance, doing this gentleness justice. "How can I then, on this new knowledge of my own, ask you to continue to live with it?"

"I set up my altar, with its multiplied meanings," Stransom began; but she quickly interrupted him.

"You set up your altar, and when I wanted one most I found it magnificently ready. I used it with the gratitude I've always shown you, for I knew it from of old to be dedicated to Death.

I told you long ago that my Dead weren't many. Yours were, but all you had done for them was none too much for *my* worship! You had placed a great light for Each—I gathered them together for One!"

"We had simply different intentions," he returned. "That, as you say, I perfectly knew, and I don't see why your intention shouldn't still sustain you."

"That's because you're generous—you can imagine and think. But the spell's broken."

It seemed to poor Stransom, in spite of his resistance, that it really was, and the prospect stretched grey and void before him. All he could say, however, was: "I hope you'll try before you give up."

"If I had known you had ever known him I should have taken for granted he had his candle," she presently answered. "What's changed, as you say, is that on making the discovery I find he never has had it. That makes *my* attitude"—she paused as thinking how to express it, then said simply—"all wrong."

"Come once again," he pleaded.

"Will you give him his candle?" she asked.

He waited, but only because it would sound ungracious; not because of a doubt of his feeling. "I can't do that!" he declared at last.

"Then good-bye." And she gave him her hand again.

He had got his dismissal; besides which, in the agitation of everything that had opened out to him, he felt the need to recover himself as he could only do in solitude. Yet he lingered—lingered to see if she had no compromise to express, no attenuation to propose. But he only met her great lamenting eyes, in which indeed he read that she was as sorry for him as for any one else. This made him say: "At least, in any case, I may see you here."

"Oh yes, come if you like. But I don't think it will do."

He looked round the room once more, knowing how little he was sure it would do. He felt also stricken and more and more cold, and his chill was like an ague in which he had to make an effort not to shake. Then he made doleful reply: "I must try on my side—if you can't try on yours." She came out with him to the hall and into the doorway, and here he put her the question he held he could least answer from his own wit. "Why have you never let me come before?"

"Because my aunt would have seen you, and I should have had to tell her how I came to know you."

"And what would have been the objection to that?"

"It would have entailed other explanations; there would at any rate have been that danger."

"Surely she knew you went every day to church," Stransom objected.

"She didn't know what I went for."

"Of me then she never even heard?"

"You'll think I was deceitful. But I didn't need to be!"

He was now on the lower door-step, and his hostess held the door half-closed behind him. Through what remained of the opening he saw her framed face. He made a supreme appeal. "What *did* he do to you?"

"It would have come out—*she* would have told you. That fear at my heart—that was my reason!" And she closed the door, shutting him out.

VIII

He had ruthlessly abandoned her—that of course was what he had done. Stransom made it all out in solitude, at leisure, fitting the unmatched pieces gradually together and dealing one by one with a hundred obscure points. She had known Hague only after her present friend's relations with him had wholly terminated; obviously indeed a good while after; and it was natural enough that of his previous life she should have ascertained only what he had judged good to communicate. There were passages it was quite conceivable that even in moments of the tenderest expansion he should have withheld. Of many facts in the career of a man so in the eye of the world there was of course a common knowledge; but this lady lived apart from public affairs, and the only time perfectly clear to her would have been the time following the dawn of her own drama. A man in her place would have "looked up" the past—would even have consulted old newspapers. It remained remarkable indeed that in her long contact with the partner of her retrospect no accident had lighted a train; but there was no arguing about that; the accident had in fact come: it had simply been that security had prevailed. She had taken what Hague had given her, and her blankness in respect of his other connexions was only a touch in the picture of that plasticity Stransom had supreme reason to know so great a master could have been trusted to produce.

This picture was for a while all our friend saw; he caught his breath again and again as it came over him that the woman with whom he had had for years so fine a point of contact was a woman whom Acton Hague, of all men in the world, had more or less fashioned. Such as she sat there today she was ineffaceably stamped with him. Beneficent, blameless as Stransom held her, he couldn't rid himself of the sense that he had been, as who should say, swindled. She had imposed upon him hugely, though she had known it as little as he. All this later past came back to him as a time grotesquely misspent. Such at least were his first reflexions; after a while he found himself more divided and only, as the end of it, more troubled. He imagined, recalled, reconstituted, figured out for himself the truth she had refused to give him; the effect of which was to make her seem to him only more saturated with her fate. He felt her spirit, through the whole strangeness, finer than his own to the very degree in which she might have been, in which she certainly had been, more wronged. A woman, when wronged, was always more wronged than a man, and there were conditions when the least she could have got off with was more than the most he could have to bear. He was sure this rare creature wouldn't have got off with the least. He was awestruck at the thought of such a surrender—such a prostration. Moulded indeed she had been by powerful hands, to have converted her injury into an exaltation so sublime. The fellow had only had to die for everything that was ugly in him to be washed out in a torrent. It was vain to try to guess what had taken place, but nothing could be clearer than that she had ended by accusing herself. She absolved him at every point, she adored her very wounds. The passion by which he had profited had rushed back after its ebb, and now the tide of tenderness, arrested for ever at flood, was too deep even to fathom. Stransom sincerely considered that he had forgiven him; but how little he had achieved the miracle that she had achieved! His forgiveness was silence, but hers was mere unuttered sound. The light she had demanded for his altar would have broken his silence with a blare; whereas all the lights in the church were for her too great a hush.

She had been right about the difference—she had spoken the truth about the change: Stransom was soon to know himself as perversely but sharply jealous. *His* tide had ebbed, not flowed; if he had "forgiven" Acton Hague, that forgiveness was a motive with a broken spring. The very fact of her appeal for a material sign, a sign that should make her dead lover equal there with the others, presented the concession to her friend as too handsome for the case. He had never thought of himself as hard, but an exorbitant article might easily render him so. He moved round and round this one, but only in widening circles—the more he looked at it the less acceptable it seemed. At the same time he had no illusion about the effect of his refusal; he perfectly saw how it would make for a rupture. He left her alone a week, but when at last he again called this conviction was cruelly confirmed. In the interval he had kept away from the church, and he needed no fresh assurance from her to know she hadn't entered it. The change was complete enough: it had broken up her life. Indeed it had broken up his, for all the fires of his shrine seemed to him suddenly to have been quenched. A great indifference fell upon him, the weight of which was in itself a pain; and he never knew what his devotion had been for him till in that shock it ceased like a dropped watch. Neither did he know with how large a confidence he had counted on the final service that had now failed: the mortal deception was that in this abandonment the whole future gave way.

These days of her absence proved to him of what she was capable; all the more that he never dreamed she was vindictive or even resentful. It was not in anger she had forsaken him; it was in simple submission to hard reality, to the stern logic of life. This came home to him when he sat with her again in the room in which her late aunt's conversation lingered like the tone of a cracked piano. She tried to make him forget how much they were estranged, but in the very presence of what they had given up it was impossible not to be sorry for her. He had taken from her so much more than she had taken from him. He argued with her again, told her she could now have the altar to herself; but she only shook her head with pleading sadness, begging him not to waste his breath on the impossible, the extinct. Couldn't he see that in relation to her private need the rites he had established were practically an elaborate exclusion? She regretted nothing that had happened; it had all been right so long as she didn't know, and it was only that now she knew too much and that from the moment their eyes were open they would simply have to conform. It had doubtless been happiness enough for them to go on together so long. She was gentle, grateful, resigned; but this was only the form of a deep immoveability. He saw he should never more cross the threshold of the second room, and he felt how much this alone would make a stranger of him and give a conscious stiffness to his visits. He would have hated to plunge again into that well of reminders, but he enjoyed quite as little the vacant alternative.

After he had been with her three or four times it struck him that to have come at last into her house had had the horrid effect of diminishing their intimacy. He had known her better, had liked her in greater freedom, when they merely walked together or kneeled together. Now they only pretended; before they had been nobly sincere. They began to try their walks again, but it proved a lame imitation, for these things, from the first, beginning or ending, had been connected with their visits to the church. They had either strolled away as they came out or gone in to rest on the return. Stransom, besides, now faltered; he couldn't walk as of old. The omission made everything false; it was a dire mutilation of their lives. Our friend was frank and monotonous, making no mystery of his remonstrance and no secret of his predicament. Her response, whatever it was, always came to the same thing—an implied invitation to him to judge, if he spoke of predicaments, of how much comfort she had in hers. For him indeed was no comfort even in complaint, since every allusion to what had befallen them but made the author of their trouble more present. Acton Hague was between them—that was the essence of the matter, and never so much between them as when they were face to face. Then Stransom, while still wanting to banish him, had the strangest sense of striving for an ease that would involve having accepted him. Deeply disconcerted by what he knew, he was still worse tormented by really not knowing. Perfectly aware that it would have been horribly vulgar to abuse his old friend or to tell his companion the story of their quarrel, it yet vexed him that her depth of reserve should give him no opening and should have the effect of a magnanimity greater even than his own.

He challenged himself, denounced himself, asked himself if he were in love with her that he should care so much what adventures she had had. He had never for a moment allowed he was in love with her; therefore nothing could have surprised him more than to discover he was jealous. What but jealousy could give a man that sore contentious wish for the detail of what would make him suffer? Well enough he knew indeed that he should never have it from the only person who today could give it to him. She let him press her with his sombre eyes, only smiling at him with an exquisite mercy and breathing equally little the word that would expose her secret and the word that would appear to deny his literal right to bitterness. She told nothing, she judged nothing; she accepted everything but the possibility of her return to the old symbols. Stransom divined that for her too they had been vividly individual, had stood for particular hours or particular attributes—particular links in her chain. He made it clear to himself, as he believed, that his difficulty lay in the fact that the very nature of the plea for his faithless friend constituted a prohibition; that it happened to have come from *her* was precisely the vice that attached to it. To the voice of impersonal generosity he felt sure he would have listened; he would have deferred to an advocate who, speaking from abstract justice, knowing of his denial without having known Hague, should have had the imagination to say: "Ah remember only the best of him; pity him; provide for him." To provide for him on the very ground of having discovered another of his turpitudes was not to pity but to glorify him. The more Stransom thought the more he made out that whatever this relation of Hague's it could only have been a deception more or less finely practised. Where had it come into the life that all men saw? Why had one never heard of it if it had had the frankness of honourable things? Stransom knew enough of his other ties, of his obligations and appearances, not to say enough of his general character, to be sure there had been some infamy. In one way or another this creature had been coldly sacrificed. That was why at the last as well as the first he must still leave him out and out.

IX

And yet this was no solution, especially after he had talked again to his friend of all it had been his plan she should finally do for him. He had talked in the other days, and she had responded with a frankness qualified only by a courteous reluctance, a reluctance that touched him, to linger on the question of his death. She had then practically accepted the charge, suffered him to feel he could depend upon her to be the eventual guardian of his shrine; and it was in the name of what had so passed between them that he appealed to her not to forsake him in his age. She listened at present with shining coldness and all her habitual forbearance to insist on her terms; her deprecation was even still tenderer, for it expressed the compassion of her own sense that he was abandoned. Her terms, however, remained the same, and scarcely the less audible for not being uttered; though he was sure that secretly even more than he she felt bereft of the satisfaction his solemn trust was to have provided her. They both missed the rich future, but she missed it most, because after all it was to have been entirely hers; and it was her acceptance of the loss that gave him the full measure of her preference for the thought of Acton Hague over any other thought whatever. He had humour enough to laugh rather grimly when he said to himself: "Why the deuce does she like him so much more than she likes me?"—the reasons being really so conceivable. But even his faculty of analysis left the irritation standing, and this irritation proved perhaps the greatest misfortune that had ever overtaken him. There had been nothing yet that made him so much want to give up. He had of course by this time well reached the age of renouncement; but it had not hitherto been vivid to him that it was time to give up everything.

Practically, at the end of six months, he had renounced the friendship once so charming and comforting. His privation had two faces, and the face it had turned to him on the occasion of his last attempt to cultivate that friendship was the one he could look at least. This was the privation he inflicted; the other was the privation he bore. The conditions she never phrased he used to murmur to himself in solitude: "One more, one more—only just one." Certainly he was going down; he often felt it when he caught himself, over his work, staring at vacancy and giving voice to that inanity. There was proof enough besides in his being so weak and so ill. His irritation took the form of melancholy, and his melancholy that of the conviction that his health had quite failed. His altar moreover had ceased to exist; his chapel, in his dreams, was a great dark cavern. All the lights had gone out—all his Dead had died again. He couldn't exactly see at first how it had been in the power of his late companion to extinguish them, since it was neither for her nor by her that they had been called into being. Then he understood that it was essentially in his own soul the revival had taken place, and that in the air of this soul they were now unable to breathe. The candles might mechanically burn, but each of them had lost its lustre. The church had become a void; it was his presence, her presence, their common presence, that had made the indispensable medium. If anything was wrong everything was—her silence spoiled the tune.

Then when three months were gone he felt so lonely that he went back; reflecting that as they had been his best society for years his Dead perhaps wouldn't let him forsake them without doing something more for him. They stood there, as he had left them, in their tall radiance, the bright cluster that had already made him, on occasions when he was willing to compare small things with great, liken them to a group of sea-lights on the edge of the ocean of life. It was a relief to him, after a while, as he sat there, to feel they had still a virtue. He was more and more easily tired, and he always drove now; the action of his heart was weak and gave him none of the reassurance conferred by the action of his fancy. None the less he returned yet again, returned several times, and finally, during six months, haunted the place with a renewal of frequency and a strain of impatience. In winter the church was unwarmed and exposure to cold forbidden him, but the glow of his shrine was an influence in which he could almost bask. He sat and wondered to what he had reduced his absent associate and what she now did with the hours of her absence. There were other churches, there were other altars, there were other candles; in one way or another her piety would still operate; he couldn't absolutely have deprived her of her rites. So he argued, but without contentment; for he well enough knew there was no other such rare semblance of the mountain of light she had once mentioned to him as the satisfaction of her need. As this semblance again gradually grew great to him and his pious practice more regular, he found a sharper and sharper pang in the imagination of her darkness; for never so much as in these weeks had his rites been real, never had his gathered company seemed so to respond and even to invite. He lost himself in the large lustre, which was more and more what he had from the first wished it to be—as dazzling as the vision of heaven in the mind of a child. He wandered in the fields of light; he passed, among the tall tapers, from tier to tier, from fire to fire, from name to name, from the white intensity of one clear emblem, of one saved soul, to another. It was in the quiet sense of having saved his souls that his deep strange instinct rejoiced. This was no dim theological rescue, no boon of a contingent world; they were saved better than faith or works could save them, saved for the warm world they had shrunk from dying to, for actuality, for continuity, for the certainty of human remembrance.

By this time he had survived all his friends; the last straight flame was three years old, there was no one to add to the list. Over and over he called his roll, and it appeared to him compact and complete. Where should he put in another, where, if there were no other objection, would it stand in its place in the rank? He reflected, with a want of sincerity of which he was quite conscious, that it would be difficult to determine that place. More and more, besides, face to face with his little legion, reading over endless histories, handling the empty shells and playing with the silence—more and more he could see that he had never introduced an alien. He had had his great compassions, his indulgences—there were cases in which they had been immense; but what had his devotion after all been if it hadn't been at bottom a respect? He was, however, himself surprised at his stiffness; by the end of the winter the responsibility of it was what was uppermost in his thoughts. The refrain had grown old to them, that plea for just one more. There came a day when, for simple exhaustion, if symmetry should demand just one he was ready so far to meet symmetry. Symmetry was harmony, and the idea of harmony began to haunt him; he said to himself that harmony was of course everything. He took, in fancy, his composition to pieces, redistributing it into other lines, making other juxtapositions and contrasts. He shifted this and that candle, he made the spaces different, he effaced the disfigurement of a possible gap. There were subtle and complex relations, a scheme of cross-reference, and moments in which he seemed to catch a glimpse of the void so sensible to the woman who wandered in exile or sat where he had seen her with the portrait of Acton Hague. Finally, in this way, he arrived at a conception of the total, the ideal, which left a clear opportunity for just another figure. "Just one more —to round it off; just one more, just one," continued to hum in his head. There was a strange confusion in the thought, for he felt the day to be near when he too should be one of the Others. What in this event would the Others matter to him, since they only mattered to the living? Even as one of the Dead what would his altar matter to him, since his particular dream of keeping it up had melted away? What had harmony to do with the case if his lights were all to be quenched? What he had hoped for was an instituted thing. He might perpetuate it on some other pretext, but his special meaning would have dropped. This meaning was to have lasted with the life of the one other person who understood it.

In March he had an illness during which he spent a fortnight in bed, and when he revived a little he was told of two things that had happened. One was that a lady whose name was not known to the servants (she left none) had been three times to ask about him; the other was that in his sleep and on an occasion when his mind evidently wandered he was heard to murmur again and again: "Just one more—just one." As soon as he found himself able to go out, and before the doctor in attendance had pronounced him so, he drove to see the lady who had come to ask about him. She was not at home; but this gave him the opportunity, before his strength should fail again, to take his way to the church. He entered it alone; he had declined, in a happy manner he possessed of being able to decline effectively, the company of his servant or of a nurse. He knew now perfectly what these good people thought; they had discovered his clandestine connexion, the magnet that had drawn him for so many years, and doubtless attached a significance of their own to the odd words they had repeated to him. The nameless lady was the clandestine connexion—a fact nothing could have made clearer than his indecent haste to rejoin her. He sank on his knees before his altar while his head fell over on his hands. His weakness, his life's weariness overtook him. It seemed to him he had come for the great surrender. At first he asked himself how he should get away; then, with the failing belief in the power, the very desire to move gradually left him. He had come, as he always came, to lose himself; the fields of light were still there to stray in; only this time, in straying, he would never come back. He had given himself to his Dead, and it was good: this time his Dead would keep him. He couldn't rise from his knees; he believed he should never rise again; all he could do was to lift his face and fix his eyes on his lights. They looked unusually, strangely splendid, but the one that always drew him most had an unprecedented lustre. It was the central voice of the choir, the glowing heart of the brightness, and on this occasion it seemed to expand, to spread great wings of flame. The whole altar flared—dazzling and blinding; but the source of the vast radiance burned clearer than the rest, gathering itself into form, and the form was human beauty and human charity, was the far-off face of Mary

Antrim. She smiled at him from the glory of heaven—she brought the glory down with her to take him. He bowed his head in submission and at the same moment another wave rolled over him. Was it the quickening of joy to pain? In the midst of his joy at any rate he felt his buried face grow hot as with some communicated knowledge that had the force of a reproach. It suddenly made him contrast that very rapture with the bliss he had refused to another. This breath of the passion immortal was all that other had asked; the descent of Mary Antrim opened his spirit with a great compunctious throb for the descent of Acton Hague. It was as if Stransom had read what her eyes said to him.

After a moment he looked round in a despair that made him feel as if the source of life were ebbing. The church had been empty—he was alone; but he wanted to have something done, to make a last appeal. This idea gave him strength for an effort; he rose to his feet with a movement that made him turn, supporting himself by the back of a bench. Behind him was a prostrate figure, a figure he had seen before; a woman in deep mourning, bowed in grief or in prayer. He had seen her in other days—the first time of his entrance there, and he now slightly wavered, looking at her again till she seemed aware he had noticed her. She raised her head and met his eyes: the partner of his long worship had come back. She looked across at him an instant with a face wondering and scared; he saw he had made her afraid. Then quickly rising she came straight to him with both hands out.

"Then you *could* come? God sent you!" he murmured with a happy smile.

"You're very ill—you shouldn't be here," she urged in anxious reply.

"God sent me too, I think. I was ill when I came, but the sight of you does wonders." He held her hands, which steadied and quickened him. "I've something to tell you."

"Don't tell me!" she tenderly pleaded; "let me tell you. This afternoon, by a miracle, the sweetest of miracles, the sense of our difference left me. I was out—I was near, thinking, wandering alone, when, on the spot, something changed in my heart. It's my confession—there it is. To come back, to come back on the instant—the idea gave me wings. It was as if I suddenly saw something—as if it all became possible. I could come for what you yourself came for: that was enough. So here I am. It's not for my own—that's over. But I'm here for *them*." And breathless, infinitely relieved by her low precipitate explanation, she looked with eyes that reflected all its splendour at the magnificence of their altar.

"They're here for you," Stransom said, "they're present tonight as they've never been. They speak for you—don't you see? —in a passion of light; they sing out like a choir of angels. Don't you hear what they say?—they offer the very thing you asked of me."

"Don't talk of it—don't think of it; forget it!" She spoke in hushed supplication, and while the alarm deepened in her eyes she disengaged one of her hands and passed an arm round him to support him better, to help him to sink into a seat.

He let himself go, resting on her; he dropped upon the bench and she fell on her knees beside him, his own arm round her shoulder. So he remained an instant, staring up at his shrine. "They say there's a gap in the array—they say it's not full, complete. Just one more," he went on, softly—"isn't that what you wanted? Yes, one more, one more."

"Ah no more—no more!" she wailed, as with a quick new horror of it, under her breath.

"Yes, one more," he repeated, simply; "just one!" And with this his head dropped on her shoulder; she felt that in his weakness he had fainted. But alone with him in the dusky church a great dread was on her of what might still happen, for his face had the whiteness of death.

A NOTE ON

THE ALTAR OF THE DEAD

(1895)

We living are a meager handful whose pathways briefly intersect in a flash of time, before we join the larger population of The Dead. Are we not but the rim, the outer edge, transiently illumined, of the world's people, the little passing as against the great passed? We choose to believe that we alone exist and that we exist alone, just as we choose to call the thin crust beneath our feet "the earth," ignoring the enormous, deep-extending mass under it. That the dead are alive in us, logic, psychology and genetics agree. But how few of us feel it to be true! Tacitly we throttle in ourselves the sense of the dead—or relegate that sense to what we may not improperly call the dead files; to our imagined hells and heavens, Valhallas, and Happy Hunting Grounds.

By letting the dead die we have killed a certain part of the life in us. Our idiot worship of the "career," of "achievement," of the measurable, the boundable in human experience is helping to wither in us that piety of the imagination which springs from an awareness of our links with the past. Marcus Aurelius, who was a mature man, began his book by making grave obeisance to those, many of them dead, who had formed his mind—his tutors and friends and family. How many of the bright children of all ages who in the past twenty-five years have offered us their autobiographies would think of thus beginning their narratives? The powerful magazine and newspaper publishers who direct our thinking frown upon the sense of continuity. Today for them is unarguably more interesting than yesterday simply because it is more recent. The headline is truer than the proposition. The fact is all.

Against this pitiful, childish, time-bound egoism, this Caliban-religion of modern journalism Henry James set his subtle mind. His weapons were too elegant for effectiveness. His words of warning—you will find them at their most explicit in "The American Scene"—fell on ears thickened by the wax of materialism. And just such a word of warning, or, if you prefer, of lament, comprises the substance of this curious story, "The Altar of the Dead."

"The sense of the state of the dead," remarks James, "is but part of the sense of the state of the living." For James, therefore, the cultivation of this sense may provide a legitimate theme for the novelist, whose business is to deal with human life completely. "What sort of free intelligence," he inquires, "would it be that, addressed to the human scene, should propose to itself, all vulgarly, never to be waylaid or averted, never effectively inspired, by some imaged appeal of the lost Dead?" His, at any rate, was not that sort of intelligence. He knew how much rich life, if of a rarefied order, walks and breathes in a proper sense of the dead, in the dark, shadow-thick valleys of memory.

"The Altar of the Dead" is far removed from the ghostly or the morbid. The homage its two characters pay to their dead comes out of a sense of the fullness of life, rather than out of any perverse interest in the smell of mortality. The story is crowded, not with terror, but with love. Indeed it *is* a love story, the death of Stransom being a true *Liebestod*. The plot, however, with its rather artificial spring of action (the mortmain of Acton Hague) is less impressive than the theme itself, less dominating than the absoluteness with which James builds up our belief in this strange man and woman, creates in us a willingness to accept as beautiful and interesting their cult of the dead.

Stransom, we are told, "had done almost all things but one: he had never forgotten." It is a miracle of James's art that he makes us quite willing to forego all knowledge of the many things Stransom had done in order that we may know fully only one thing he had done: his never forgetting.

Of all the short stories of Henry James, "The Altar of the Dead" administers the quietest and gravest rebuke to whatever is spurious, whatever is quotidian, whatever is vulgar, in the reigning taste of our time. For that reason, among others, I have thought it proper to include it in this collection.

"EUROPE"

I

"OUR feeling is, you know, that Becky should go." The earnest little remark comes back to me, even after long years, as the first note of something that began, for my observation, the day I went with my sister-in-law to take leave of her good friends. It's a memory of the American time, which revives so at present—under some touch that doesn't signify—that it rounds itself off as an anecdote. That walk to say good-bye was the beginning; and the end, so far as I enjoyed a view of it, was not till long after; yet even the end also appears to me now as of the old days. I went, in those days, on occasion, to see my sister-in-law, in whose affairs, on my brother's death, I had had to take a helpful hand. I continued to go indeed after these little matters were straightened out, for the pleasure, periodically, of the impression—the change to the almost pastoral sweetness of the good Boston suburb from the loud longitudinal New York. It was another world, with other manners, a different tone, a different taste; a savour nowhere so mild, yet so distinct, as in the square white house—with the pair of elms, like gigantic wheat-sheaves, in front, the rustic orchard not far behind, the old-fashioned door-lights, the big blue-and-white jars in the porch, the straight bricked walk from the high gate—that enshrined the extraordinary merit of Mrs. Rimmle and her three daughters.

These ladies were so much of the place and the place so much of themselves that from the first of their being revealed to me I felt that nothing else at Brookbridge much mattered. They were what, for me, at any rate, Brookbridge had most to give: I mean in the way of what it was naturally strongest in, the thing we called in New York the New England expression, the air of Puritanism reclaimed and refined. The

Rimmles had brought this down to a wonderful delicacy. They struck me even then—all four almost equally—as very ancient and very earnest, and I think theirs must have been the house in all the world in which "culture" first came to the aid of morning calls. The head of the family was the widow of a great public character—as public characters were understood at Brookbridge—whose speeches on anniversaries formed a part of the body of national eloquence spouted in the New England schools by little boys covetous of the most marked, though perhaps the easiest, distinction. He was reported to have been celebrated, and in such fine declamatory connexions that he seemed to gesticulate even from the tomb. He was understood to have made, in his wife's company, the tour of Europe at a date not immensely removed from that of the battle of Waterloo. What was the age then of the bland firm antique Mrs. Rimmle at the period of her being first revealed to me? That's a point I'm not in a position to determine—I remember mainly that I was young enough to regard her as having reached the limit. And yet the limit for Mrs. Rimmle must have been prodigiously extended; the scale of its extension is in fact the very moral of this reminiscence. She was old, and her daughters were old, but I was destined to know them all as older. It was only by comparison and habit that—however much I recede—Rebecca, Maria and Jane were the "young ladies."

I think it was felt that, though their mother's life, after thirty years of widowhood, had had a grand backward stretch, her blandness and firmness—and this in spite of her extreme physical frailty—would be proof against any surrender not overwhelmingly justified by time. It had appeared, years before, at a crisis of which the waves had not even yet quite subsided, a surrender not justified by anything nameable that she should go to Europe with her daughters and for her health. Her health was supposed to require constant support; but when it had at that period tried conclusions with the idea of Europe it was not the idea of Europe that had been insidious enough to prevail.

She hadn't gone, and Becky, Maria and Jane hadn't gone, and this was long ago. They still merely floated in the air of the visit achieved, with such introductions and such acclamations, in the early part of the century; they still, with fond glances at the sunny parlour-walls, only referred, in conversation, to divers pictorial and other reminders of it. The Misses Rimmles had quite been brought up on it, but Becky, as the most literary, had most mastered the subject. There were framed letters—tributes to their eminent father—suspended among the mementoes, and of two or three of these, the most foreign and complimentary, Becky had executed translations that figured beside the text. She knew already, through this and other illumination, so much about Europe that it was hard to believe for her in that limit of adventure which consisted only of her having been twice to Philadelphia. The others hadn't been to Philadelphia, but there was a legend that Jane had been to Saratoga. Becky was a short stout fair person with round serious eyes, a high forehead, the sweetest neatest enunciation, and a miniature of her father—"done in Rome"—worn as a breastpin. She had written the life, she had edited the speeches, of the original of this ornament, and now at last, beyond the seas, she was really to tread in his footsteps.

Fine old Mrs. Rimmle, in the sunny parlour and with a certain austerity of cap and chair—though with a gay new "front" that looked like rusty brown plush—had had so unusually good a winter that the question of her sparing two members of her family for an absence had been threshed as fine, I could feel, as even under that Puritan roof any case of conscience had ever been threshed. They were to make their dash while the coast, as it were, was clear, and each of the daughters had tried—heroically, angelically and for the sake of each of her sisters—not to be one of the two. What I encountered that first time was an opportunity to concur with enthusiasm in the general idea that Becky's wonderful preparation would be wasted if she were the one to stay with their mother. Their talk of Becky's preparation (they had a sly old-maidish humour that was as mild as milk) might have been of some mixture, for application somewhere, that she kept in a precious bottle. It had been settled at all events that, armed with this concoction and borne aloft by their introductions, she and Jane were to start. They were wonderful on their introductions, which proceeded naturally from their mother and were addressed to the charming families that in vague generations had so admired vague Mr. Rimmle. Jane, I found at Brookbridge, had to be described, for want of other description, as the pretty one, but it wouldn't have served to identify her unless you had seen the others. *Her* preparation was only this figment of her prettiness—only, that is, unless one took into account something that, on the spot, I silently divined: the lifelong secret passionate ache of her little rebellious desire. They were all growing old in the yearning to go, but Jane's yearning was the sharpest. She struggled with it as people at Brookbridge mostly struggled with what they liked, but fate, by threatening to prevent what she *dis*liked and what was therefore duty—which was to stay at home instead of Maria—had bewildered her, I judged, not a little. It was she who, in the words I have quoted, mentioned to me Becky's case and Becky's affinity as the clearest of all. Her mother moreover had on the general subject still more to say.

"I positively desire, I really quite insist that they shall go," the old lady explained to us from her stiff chair. "We've talked about it so often, and they've had from me so clear an account—I've amused them again and again with it—of what's to be seen and enjoyed. If they've had hitherto too many duties to leave, the time seems to have come to recognise that there are also many duties to *seek*. Wherever we go we find them—I always remind the girls of that. There's a duty that calls them to those wonderful countries, just as it called, at the right time, their father and myself—if it be only that of laying-up for the years to come the same store of remarkable impressions, the same wealth of knowledge and food for conversation as, since my return, I've found myself so happy to possess." Mrs. Rimmle spoke of her return as of something of the year before last, but the future of her daughters was somehow, by a different law, to be on the scale of great vistas, of endless aftertastes. I think that, without my being quite ready to say it, even this first impression of her was somewhat upsetting; there was a large placid perversity, a grim secrecy of intention, in her estimate of the ages.

"Well, I'm so glad you don't delay it longer," I said to Miss Becky before we withdrew. "And whoever should go," I continued in the spirit of the sympathy with which the good sisters had already inspired me, "I quite feel, with your family, you know, that *you* should. But of course I hold that every one should." I suppose I wished to attenuate my solemnity; there was, however, something in it I couldn't help. It must have been a faint foreknowledge.

"Have you been a great deal yourself?" Miss Jane, I remembered, enquired.

"Not so much but that I hope to go a good deal more. So perhaps we shall meet," I encouragingly suggested.

I recall something—something in the nature of susceptibility to encouragement—that this brought into the more expressive brown eyes to which Miss Jane mainly owed it that she was the pretty one. "Where, do you think?"

I tried to think. "Well, on the Italian lakes—Como, Bellaggio, Lugano." I liked to say the names to them.

"'Sublime, but neither bleak nor bare—nor misty are the mountains there!'" Miss Jane softly breathed, while her sister looked at her as if her acquaintance with the poetry of the subject made her the most interesting feature of the scene she evoked.

But Miss Becky presently turned to me. "Do you know everything—?"

"Everything?"

"In Europe."

"Oh yes," I laughed, "and one or two things even in America."

The sisters seemed to me furtively to look at each other. "Well, you'll have to be quick—to meet *us*," Miss Jane resumed.

"But surely when you're once there you'll stay on."

"Stay on?"—they murmured it simultaneously and with the oddest vibration of dread as well as of desire. It was as if they had been in presence of a danger and yet wished me, who "knew everything," to torment them with still more of it.

Well, I did my best. "I mean it will never do to cut it short."

"No, that's just what I keep saying," said brilliant Jane. "It would be better in that case not to go."

"Oh, don't talk about not going—at this time!" It was none of my business, but I felt shocked and impatient.

"No, not at *this* time!" broke in Miss Maria, who, very red in the face, had joined us. Poor Miss Maria was known as the flushed one; but she was not flushed—she only had an unfortunate surface. The third day after this was to see them embark.

Miss Becky, however, desired as little as any one to be in any way extravagant. "It's only the thought of our mother," she explained.

I looked a moment at the old lady, with whom my sister-in-law was engaged. "Well—your mother's magnificent."

"*Isn't* she magnificent?"—they eagerly took it up.

She *was*—I could reiterate it with sincerity, though I perhaps mentally drew the line when Miss Maria again risked, as a fresh ejaculation: "I think she's better than Europe!"

"Maria!" they both, at this, exclaimed with a strange emphasis: it was as if they feared she had suddenly turned cynical over the deep domestic drama of their casting of lots. The innocent laugh with which she answered them gave the measure of her cynicism.

We separated at last, and my eyes met Mrs. Rimmle's as I

held for an instant her aged hand. It was doubtless only my fancy that her calm cold look quietly accused me of something. Of what *could* it accuse me? Only, I thought, of thinking.

II

I LEFT Brookbridge the next day, and for some time after that had no occasion to hear from my kinswoman; but when she finally wrote there was a passage in her letter that affected me more than all the rest. "Do you know the poor Rimmles never, after all, 'went'? The old lady, at the eleventh hour, broke down; everything broke down, and all of *them* on top of it, so that the dear things are with us still. Mrs. Rimmle, the night after our call, had, in the most unexpected manner, a turn for the worse—something in the nature (though they're rather mysterious about it) of a seizure; Becky and Jane felt it—dear devoted stupid angels that they are—heartless to leave her at such a moment, and Europe's indefinitely postponed. However, they think they're still going—or *think* they think it—when she's better. They also think—or think they think—that she *will* be better. I certainly pray she may." So did I—quite fervently. I was conscious of a real pang—I didn't know how much they had made me care.

Late that winter my sister-in-law spent a week in New York; when almost my first enquiry on meeting her was about the health of Mrs. Rimmle.

"Oh she's rather bad—she really is, you know. It's not surprising that at her age she should be infirm."

"Then what the deuce *is* her age?"

"I can't tell you to a year—but she's immensely old."

"That of course I saw," I replied—"unless you literally mean so old that the records have been lost."

My sister-in-law thought. "Well, I believe she wasn't positively young when she married. She lost three or four children before these women were born."

We surveyed together a little, on this, the "dark backward."

"And they were born, I gather, *after* the famous tour? Well then, as the famous tour was in a manner to celebrate—wasn't it?—the restoration of the Bourbons—" I considered, I gasped. "My dear child, what on earth do you make her out?"

My relative, with her Brookbridge habit, transferred her share of the question to the moral plane—turned it forth to wander, by implication at least, in the sandy desert of responsibility. "Well, you know, we all immensely admire her."

"You can't admire her more than I do. She's awful."

My converser looked at me with a certain fear. "She's *really* ill."

"Too ill to get better?"

"Oh no—we hope not. Because then they'll be able to go."

"And *will* they go if she should?"

"Oh the moment they should be quite satisfied. I mean *really*," she added.

I'm afraid I laughed at her—the Brookbridge "really" was a thing so by itself. "But if she shouldn't get better?" I went on.

"Oh don't speak of it! They want so to go."

"It's a pity they're so infernally good," I mused.

"No—don't say that. It's what keeps them up."

"Yes, but isn't it what keeps *her* up too?"

My visitor looked grave. "Would you like them to kill her?"

I don't know that I was then prepared to say I should—though I believe I came very near it. But later on I burst all bounds, for the subject grew and grew. I went again before the good sisters ever did—I mean I went to Europe. I think I went twice, with a brief interval, before my fate again brought round for me a couple of days at Brookbridge. I had been there repeatedly, in the previous time, without making the acquaintance of the Rimmles; but now that I had had the revelation I couldn't have it too much, and the first request I preferred was to be taken again to see them. I remember well indeed the scruple I felt—the real delicacy—about betraying that *I* had, in the pride of my power, since our other meeting, stood as their phrase went, among romantic scenes; but they were themselves the first to speak of it, and what moreover came home to me was that the coming and going of their friends in general—Brookbridge itself having even at that period one foot in Europe—was such as to place constantly before them the pleasure that was only postponed. They were thrown back after all on what the situation, under a final analysis, had most to give—the sense that, as every one kindly said to them and they kindly said to every one, Europe would keep. Every one felt for them so deeply that their own kindness in alleviating every one's feeling was really what came out most. Mrs. Rimmle was still in her stiff chair and in the sunny parlour, but if *she* made no scruple of introducing the Italian lakes my heart sank to observe that she dealt with them, as a topic, not in the least in the leave-taking manner in which Falstaff babbled of green fields.

I'm not sure that after this my pretexts for a day or two with my sister-in-law weren't apt to be a mere cover for another glimpse of these particulars: I at any rate never went to Brookbridge without an irrepressible eagerness for our customary call. A long time seems to me thus to have passed, with glimpses and lapses, considerable impatience and still more pity. Our visits indeed grew shorter, for, as my companion said, they were more and more of a strain. It finally struck me that the good sisters even shrank from me a little as from one who penetrated their consciousness in spite of himself. It was as if they knew where I thought they ought to be, and were moved to deprecate at last, by a systematic silence on the subject of that hemisphere, the criminality I fain would fix on them. They were full instead—as with the instinct of throwing dust in my eyes—of little pathetic hypocrisies about Brookbridge interests and delights. I dare say that as time went on my deeper sense of their situation came practically to rest on my companion's report of it. I certainly think I recollect every word we ever exchanged about them, even if I've lost the thread of the special occasions. The impression they made on me after each interval always broke out with extravagance as I walked away with her.

"*She* may be as old as she likes—I don't care. It's the fearful age the 'girls' are reaching that constitutes the scandal. One shouldn't pry into such matters, I know; but the years and the chances are really going. They're all growing old together—it will presently be too late; and their mother meanwhile perches over them like a vulture—what shall I call it?—calculating. Is she waiting for them successively to drop off? She'll survive them each and all. There's something too remorseless in it."

"Yes, but what do you want her to do? If the poor thing *can't* die she can't. Do you want her to take poison or to open a blood-vessel? I dare say she'd prefer to go."

"I beg your pardon," I must have replied; "you daren't say anything of the sort. If she'd prefer to go she *would* go. She'd feel the propriety, the decency, the necessity of going. She just prefers *not* to go. She prefers to stay and keep up the tension, and her calling them 'girls' and talking of the good time they'll still have is the mere conscious mischief of a subtle old witch. They won't have *any* time—there isn't any time to have! I mean there's, on her own part, no real loss of measure or of perspective in it. She *knows* she's a hundred and ten, and she takes a cruel pride in it."

My sister-in-law differed with me about this; she held that the old woman's attitude was an honest one and that her magnificent vitality, so great in spite of her infirmities, made it inevitable she should attribute youth to persons who had come into the world so much later. "Then suppose she should die?"—so my fellow student of the case always put it to me.

"Do you mean while her daughters are away? There's not the least fear of that—not even if at the very moment of their departure she should be *in extremis.* They'd find her all right on their return."

"But think how they'd feel not to have been with her!"

"That's only, I repeat, on the unsound assumption. If they'd only go tomorrow—literally make a good rush for it—they'll be with her when they come back. That will give them plenty of time." I'm afraid I even heartlessly added that if she *should,* against every probability, pass away in their absence they wouldn't have to come back at all—which would be just the compensation proper to their long privation. And then Maria would come out to join the two others, and they would be—though but for the too scanty remnant of their career—as merry as the day is long.

I remained ready, somehow, pending the fulfilment of that vision, to sacrifice Maria; it was only over the urgency of the case for the others respectively that I found myself balancing. Sometimes it was for Becky I thought the tragedy deepest—sometimes, and in quite a different manner, I thought it most dire for Jane. It was Jane after all who had most sense of life. I seemed in fact dimly to descry in Jane a sense—as yet undescried by herself or by any one—of all sorts of queer things. Why didn't *she* go? I used desperately to ask; why didn't she make a bold personal dash for it, strike up a partnership with some one or other of the travelling spinsters in whom Brookbridge more and more abounded? Well, there came a flash for me at a particular point of the grey middle desert: my correspondent was able to let me know that poor Jane at last *had* sailed. She had gone of a sudden—I liked my sister-in-law's view of suddenness—with the kind Hathaways, who had made an irresistible grab at her and lifted her off her feet. They were going for the summer and for Mr. Hathaway's health, so that the opportunity was perfect and it was impossible not to be glad that something very like physical force had finally prevailed. This was the general feeling at Brookbridge, and I might imagine what Brookbridge had been brought to from the fact that, at the very moment she was hustled off, the doctor, called to her mother at the peep of dawn, had considered that *he* at least must stay. There had been real alarm—greater than ever before; it actually did seem as if this time the end had come. But it was

Becky, strange to say, who, though fully recognising the nature of the crisis, had kept the situation in hand and insisted upon action. This, I remember, brought back to me a discomfort with which I had been familiar from the first. One of the two had sailed, and I was sorry it wasn't the other. But if it had been the other I should have been equally sorry.

I saw with my eyes that very autumn what a fool Jane would have been if she had again backed out. Her mother had of course survived the peril of which I had heard, profiting by it indeed as she had profited by every other; she was sufficiently better again to have come downstairs. It was there that, as usual, I found her, but with a difference of effect produced somehow by the absence of one of the girls. It was as if, for the others, though they hadn't gone to Europe, Europe had come to them: Jane's letters had been so frequent and so beyond even what could have been hoped. It was the first time, however, that I perceived on the old woman's part a certain failure of lucidity. Jane's flight was clearly the great fact with her, but she spoke of it as if the fruit had now been plucked and the parenthesis closed. I don't know what sinking sense of still further physical duration I gathered, as a menace, from this first hint of her confusion of mind.

"My daughter has been; my daughter has been—" She kept saying it, but didn't say where; that seemed unnecessary, and she only repeated the words to her visitors with a face that was all puckers and yet now, save in so far as it expressed an ineffaceable complacency, all blankness. I think she rather wanted us to know how little she had stood in the way. It added to something—I scarce knew what—that I found myself desiring to extract privately from Becky. As our visit was to be of the shortest my opportunity—for one of the young ladies always came to the door with us—was at hand. Mrs. Rimmle, as we took leave, again sounded her phrase, but she added this time: "I'm so glad she's going to have always—"

I knew so well what she meant that, as she again dropped,

looking at me queerly and becoming momentarily dim, I could help her out. "Going to have what *you* have?"

"Yes, yes—my privilege. Wonderful experience," she mumbled. She bowed to me a little as if I would understand. "She has things to tell."

I turned, slightly at a loss, to Becky. "She has then already arrived?"

Becky was at that moment looking a little strangely at her mother, who answered my question. "She reached New York this morning—she comes on today."

"Oh then—!" But I let the matter pass as I met Becky's eye—I saw there was a hitch somewhere. It was not she but Maria who came out with us; on which I cleared up the question of their sister's reappearance.

"Oh no, not tonight," Maria smiled; "that's only the way mother puts it. We shall see her about the end of November—the Hathaways are so indulgent. They kindly extend their tour."

"For *her* sake? How sweet of them!" my sister-in-law exclaimed.

I can see our friend's plain mild old face take on a deeper mildness, even though a higher colour, in the light of the open door. "Yes, it's for Jane they prolong it. And do you know what they write?" She gave us time, but it was too great a responsibility to guess. "Why that it has brought her out."

"Oh, I knew it *would*!" my companion sympathetically sighed.

Maria put it more strongly still. "They say we wouldn't know her."

This sounded a little awful, but it was after all what I had expected.

III

My correspondent in Brookbridge came to me that Christmas, with my niece, to spend a week; and the arrangement had of course been prefaced by an exchange of letters, the first of which from my sister-in-law scarce took space for acceptance of my invitation before going on to say: "The Hathaways are back—but without Miss Jane!" She presented in a few words the situation thus created at Brookbridge, but was not yet, I gathered, fully in possession of the other one—the situation created in "Europe" by the presence there of that lady. The two together, however that might be, demanded, I quickly felt, all my attention, and perhaps my impatience to receive my relative was a little sharpened by my desire for the whole story. I had it at last, by the Christmas fire, and I may say without reserve that it gave me all I could have hoped for. I listened eagerly, after which I produced the comment: "Then she simply refused—"

"To budge from Florence? Simply. She had it out there with the poor Hathaways, who felt responsible for her safety, pledged to restore her to her mother's, to her sisters' hands, and showed herself in a light, they mention under their breath, that made their dear old hair stand on end. Do you know what, when they first got back, they said of her—at least it was *his* phrase—to two or three people?"

I thought a moment. "That she had 'tasted blood'?"

My visitor fairly admired me. "How clever of you to guess! It's exactly what he did say. She appeared—she continues to appear, it seems—in a new character."

I wondered a little. "But that's exactly—don't you remember?—what Miss Maria reported to us from them; that we 'wouldn't know her.'"

My sister-in-law perfectly remembered. "Oh yes—she broke out from the first. But when they left her she was worse."

"Worse?"

"Well, different—different from anything she ever *had* been or—for that matter—had had a chance to be." My reporter hung fire a moment, but presently faced me. "Rather strange and free and obstreperous."

"Obstreperous?" I wondered again.

"Peculiarly so, I inferred, on the question of not coming away. She wouldn't hear of it and, when they spoke of her mother, said she had given her mother up. She had thought she should like Europe, but didn't know she should like it so much. They had been fools to bring her if they expected to take her away. She was going to see what she could—she hadn't yet seen half. The end of it at any rate was that they had to leave her alone."

I seemed to see it all—to see even the scared Hathaways. "So she *is* alone?"

"She told them, poor thing, it appears, and in a tone they'll never forget, that she was in any case quite old enough to be. She cried—she quite went on—over not having come sooner. That's why the only way for her," my companion mused, "*is,* I suppose, to stay. They wanted to put her with some people or other—to find some American family. But she says she's on her own feet."

"And she's still in Florence?"

"No—I believe she was to travel. She's bent on the East."

I burst out laughing. "Magnificent Jane! It's most interesting. Only I feel that I distinctly *should* 'know' her. To my sense, always, I must tell you, she had it in her."

My relative was silent a little. "So it now appears Becky always felt."

"And yet pushed her off? Magnificent Becky!"

My companion met my eyes a moment. "You don't know the queerest part. I mean the way it has *most* brought her out."

I turned it over; I felt I should like to know—to that degree indeed that, oddly enough, I jocosely disguised my eagerness. "You don't mean she has taken to drink?"

My visitor had a dignity—and yet had to have a freedom. "She has taken to flirting."

I expressed disappointment. "Oh she took to *that* long ago. Yes," I declared at my kinswoman's stare, "she positively flirted—with *me*!"

The stare perhaps sharpened. "Then you flirted with *her*?"

"How else could I have been as sure as I wanted to be? But has she means?"

"Means to flirt?"—my friend looked an instant as if she spoke literally. "I don't understand about the means—though of course they have something. But I have my impression," she went on. "I think that Becky—" It seemed almost too grave to say.

But *I* had no doubts. "That Becky's backing her?"

She brought it out. "Financing her."

"Stupendous Becky! So that morally then—"

"Becky's quite in sympathy. But isn't it too odd?" my sister-in-law asked.

"Not in the least. Didn't we know, as regards Jane, that Europe was to bring her out? Well, it has also brought out Rebecca."

"It has indeed!" my companion indulgently sighed. "So what would it do if she were there?"

"I should like immensely to see. And we *shall* see."

"Do you believe then she'll still go?"

"Certainly. She *must*."

But my friend shook it off. "She won't."

"She shall!" I retorted with a laugh. But the next moment I said: "And what does the old woman say?"

"To Jane's behaviour? Not a word—never speaks of it. She talks now much less than she used—only seems to wait. But it's my belief she thinks."

"And—do you mean—knows?"

"Yes, knows she's abandoned. In her silence there she takes it in."

"It's her way of making Jane pay?" At this, somehow, I felt more serious. "Oh dear, dear—she'll disinherit her!"

When in the following June I went on to return my sister-in-law's visit the first object that met my eyes in her little white parlour was a figure that, to my stupefaction, presented itself for the moment as that of Mrs. Rimmle. I had gone to my room after arriving and had come down when dressed; the apparition I speak of had arisen in the interval. Its ambiguous character lasted, however, but a second or two—I had taken Becky for her mother because I knew no one but her mother of that extreme age. Becky's age was quite startling; it had made a great stride, though, strangely enough, irrecoverably seated as she now was in it, she had a wizened brightness that I had scarcely yet seen in her. I remember indulging on this occasion in two silent observations: one on the article of my not having hitherto been conscious of her full resemblance to the old lady, and the other to the effect that, as I had said to my sister-in-law at Christmas, "Europe," even as reaching her only through Jane's sensibilities, had really at last brought her out. She was in fact "out" in a manner of which this encounter offered to my eyes a unique example: it was the single hour, often as I had been at Brookbridge, of my meeting her elsewhere than in her mother's drawing-room. I surmise that, besides being adjusted to her more marked time of life, the garments she wore abroad, and in particular her little plain bonnet, presented points of resemblance to the close sable sheath and the quaint old head-gear that, in the white house behind the elms, I had from far back associated with the eternal image in the stiff chair. Of course I immediately spoke of Jane, showing an interest and asking for news; on which she answered me with a smile, but not at all as I had expected.

"*Those* are not really the things you want to know—where she is, whom she's with, how she manages and where she's going next—oh no!" And the admirable woman gave a laugh that was somehow both light and sad—sad, in particular, with a strange long weariness. "What you do want to know is when she's coming back."

I shook my head very kindly, but out of a wealth of experience that, I flattered myself, was equal to Miss Becky's. "I do know it. Never."

Miss Becky exchanged with me at this a long deep look. "Never."

We had, in silence, a little luminous talk about it, at the end of which she seemed to have told me the most interesting things. "And how's your mother?" I then enquired.

She hesitated, but finally spoke with the same serenity. "My mother's all right. You see she's not alive."

"Oh Becky!" my sister-in-law pleadingly interjected.

But Becky only addressed herself to me. "Come and see if she is. *I* think she isn't—but Maria perhaps isn't so clear. Come at all events and judge and tell me."

It was a new note, and I was a little bewildered. "Ah but I'm not a doctor!"

"No, thank God—you're not. That's why I ask you." And now she said good-bye.

I kept her hand a moment. "*You're* more alive than ever!"

"I'm very tired." She took it with the same smile, but for Becky it was much to say.

IV

"Not alive," the next day, was certainly what Mrs. Rimmle looked when, arriving in pursuit of my promise, I found her, with Miss Maria, in her usual place. Though wasted and shrunken she still occupied her high-backed chair with a visible theory of erectness, and her intensely aged face—combined with something dauntless that belonged to her very presence and that was effective even in this extremity—might have been that of some immemorial sovereign, of indistinguishable sex, brought forth to be shown to the people in disproof of the rumour of extinction. Mummified and open-eyed she looked at me, but I had no impression that she made me out. I had come this time without my sister-in-law, who had frankly pleaded to me—which also, for a daughter of Brookbridge, was saying much—that the house had grown too painful. Poor Miss Maria excused Miss Becky on the score of her not being well—and that, it struck me, was saying most of all. The absence of the others gave the occasion a different note; but I talked with Miss Maria for five minutes and recognised that—save for her saying, of her own movement, anything about Jane—she now spoke as if her mother had lost hearing or sense, in fact both, alluding freely and distinctly, though indeed favourably, to her condition. "She has expected your visit and much enjoys it," my entertainer said, while the old woman, soundless and motionless, simply fixed me without expression. Of course there was little to keep me; but I became aware as I rose to go that there was more than I had supposed.

On my approaching her to take leave Mrs. Rimmle gave signs of consciousness. "Have you heard about Jane?"

I hesitated, feeling a responsibility, and appealed for direction to Maria's face. But Maria's face was troubled, was turned altogether to her mother's. "About her life in Europe?" I then rather helplessly asked.

The old lady fronted me on this in a manner that made me feel silly. "Her life?"—and her voice, with this second effort, came out stronger. "Her death, if you please."

"Her death?" I echoed, before I could stop myself, with the accent of deprecation.

Miss Maria uttered a vague sound of pain, and I felt her turn away, but the marvel of her mother's little unquenched spark still held me. "Jane's dead. We've heard," said Mrs. Rimmle. "We've heard from—where is it we've heard from?" She had quite revived—she appealed to her daughter.

The poor old girl, crimson, rallied to her duty. "From Europe."

Mrs. Rimmle made at us both a little grim inclination of the head. "From Europe." I responded, in silence, by a deflexion from every rigour, and, still holding me, she went on: "And now Rebecca's going."

She had gathered by this time such emphasis to say it that

again, before I could help myself, I vibrated in reply. "To Europe—now?" It was as if for an instant she had made me believe it.

She only stared at me, however, from her wizened mask; then her eyes followed my companion. "Has she gone?"

"Not yet, mother." Maria tried to treat it as a joke, but her smile was embarrassed and dim.

"Then where is she?"

"She's lying down."

The old woman kept up her hard queer gaze, but directing it after a minute to me. "She's going."

"Oh some day!" I foolishly laughed; and on this I got to the door, where I separated from my younger hostess, who came no further.

Only, as I held the door open, she said to me under cover of it and very quietly: "It's poor mother's idea."

I saw—it was her idea. Mine was—for some time after this, even after I had returned to New York and to my usual occupations—that I should never again see Becky. I had seen her for the last time, I believed, under my sister-in-law's roof, and in the autumn it was given to me to hear from that fellow admirer that she had succumbed at last to the situation. The day of the call I have just described had been a date in the process of her slow shrinkage—it was literally the first time she had, as they said at Brookbridge, given up. She had been ill for years, but the other state of health in the contemplation of which she had spent so much of her life had left her till too late no margin for heeding it. The power of attention came at last simply in the form of the discovery that it *was* too late; on which, naturally, she had given up more and more. I had heard indeed, for weeks before, by letter, how Brookbridge had watched her do so; in consequence of which the end found me in a manner prepared. Yet in spite of my preparation there remained with me a soreness, and when I was next—it was some six months later—on the scene of her martyrdom I fear I replied with an almost rabid negative to the question put to me in due course by my kinswoman. "Call on them? Never again!"

I went none the less the very next day. Everything was the same in the sunny parlour—everything that most mattered, I mean: the centenarian mummy in the high chair and the tributes, in the little frames on the walls, to the celebrity of its late husband. Only Maria Rimmle was different: if Becky, on my last seeing her, had looked as old as her mother, Maria—save that she moved about—looked older. I remember she moved about, but I scarce remember what she said; and indeed what was there to say? When I risked a question, however, she found a reply.

"But *now* at least—?" I tried to put it to her suggestively.

At first she was vague. " 'Now'?"

"Won't Miss Jane come back?"

Oh the headshake she gave me! "Never." It positively pictured to me, for the instant, a well-preserved woman, a rich ripe *seconde jeunesse* by the Arno.

"Then that's only to make more sure of your finally joining her."

Maria Rimmle repeated her headshake. "Never."

We stood so a moment bleakly face to face; I could think of no attenuation that would be particularly happy. But while I heard a hoarse gasp that fortunately relieved me—a signal strange and at first formless from the occupant of the high-backed chair. "Mother wants to speak to you," Maria then said.

So it appeared from the drop of the old woman's jaw, the expression of her mouth opened as if for the emission of sound. It was somehow difficult to me to seem to sympathise without hypocrisy, but, so far as a step nearer could do that, I invited communication. "Have you heard where Becky's gone?" the wonderful witch's white lips then extraordinarily asked.

It drew from Maria, as on my previous visit, an uncontrollable groan, and this in turn made me take time to consider.

As I considered, however, I had an inspiration. "To Europe?"

I must have adorned it with a strange grimace, but my inspiration had been right. "To Europe," said Mrs. Rimmle.

A NOTE ON

"EUROPE"

(1899)

MANY of the shorter short stories of James are trivial and artificial. " 'Europe,' " however, does not fall into this group. It is quite apparent here that James knew he had under his hand a theme charged with extensive meaning. Hence he has dramatized it with all the solicitude that he devoted to his novels.

His conception of the short story is so remote from the standards laid down by our popular magazines that it is fair to say that the only thing a tale such as " 'Europe' " has in common with the short fiction we currently read is that both use English words. Reflecting on this story in later years, James wrote, "The merit of the thing is in the feat of the transfusion; the receptacle (of form) being so exiguous, the brevity imposed so great. I undertook the brevity, so often undertaken on a like scale before, and again arrived at it by the innumerable repeated chemical reductions and condensations that tend to make of the very short story . . . one of the costliest, even if, like the hard shining sonnet, one of the most indestructible, forms of compositions in general use. I accepted the rigour of its having, all sternly, in this case, to treat so many of its most appealing values as waste; and I now seek my comfort perforce in the mere exhibited result, the union of whatever fullness with whatever clearness."

It would be hard to find many short tales comparable, in

their combination of "fullness" and "clearness," to this story of "'Europe.'" By "clearness" James does not mean what we call "readability," which is merely what modern journalism prefers to anything that taxes the intelligence. By "clearness" he would have us understand that he has so told his tale that the attentive reader—and for James there is no other kind—should be able to perceive the variety and extent of its meanings; and that these meanings are expressed or implied with the maximum economy. By "fullness" he would say that the meanings have depth and that these depths are explored as completely as the limitations of the story's form permit.

Among other things, for example, "'Europe'" is a variation on a theme: the uneasy but perennially dynamic relationship between Europe and America. We encountered slighter variations on this same theme in "Four Meetings" and "A Bundle of Letters." "Four Meetings" was wistful with a touch of bitterness; "A Bundle of Letters" lightly satirical; "'Europe'" is tragic, and has more than a touch of the horrible. And yet, so dexterous is James in his handling of contrasting tones, that it is also humorous. The Europe-mania of the Rimmles has its grotesque side, and as types they display a quaint, faded quality at which James bids us gently smile.

On another level "'Europe'" is a quiet study of the life-denying power of American Puritanism. Puritanism, for James, is only superficially understood when we conceive of it merely as rigorous morality. At its base—and the base lies deep—Puritanism is what, almost by reflex action, works against the expansive forces in human life. Wherever minds, bodies, emotions, wills are tight, taut, or grimly passive, there is Puritanism.

Mrs. Rimmle is the central symbol here. She has had one experience—"Europe." It was her life. Nothing happened to her after it. As Puritanism is always emotionally dominating, she must enslave her daughters to her own religion of contraction. She does not dare deny them "Europe" in form but she is capable of using a functional nervous breakdown to deny it to them in fact. When Jane, representing the expansive, non-Puritan forces of American life, finally achieves a successful revolt, "the bland, firm, antique Mrs. Rimmle," the vulture-mother, prefers to consider her dead. In a sense Mrs. Rimmle murders Jane; she murders Jane in her own mind. As for Rebecca, Mrs. Rimmle kills her in a more obvious sense, by constricting her life so that the poor woman has nothing left but to die. Then comes the queerest turn of all. For Mrs. Rimmle, wishing to shift from herself any sense of guilt or remorse Rebecca's death may have caused her, ingeniously reverses her attitude toward Jane. She refuses to believe that Rebecca is dead. Instead she announces that Rebecca has gone "to Europe." Alone and hopeless, Maria is left to take care of the old witch whose power to deny life to others as well as herself has in a way enabled her to triumph over three human beings.

This story provides an example of James's perfection of narrative tone. Note how easy and familiar the tale is, with what naturalness it is told. This is generally the effect James strives for—that of conversation or monologue. Of course, the monologist is extremely cultivated, perceptive, a genius at interpretation; but he is perfectly acceptable as a real character. His voice, his accent are always true.

THE GREAT GOOD PLACE

I

George Dane had opened his eyes to a bright new day, the face of nature well washed by last night's downpour and shining as with high spirits, good resolutions, lively intentions—the great glare of recommencement in short fixed in his patch of sky. He had sat up late to finish work—arrears overwhelming, then at last had gone to bed with the pile but little reduced. He was now to return to it after the pause of the night; but he could only look at it, for the time, over the bristling hedge of letters planted by the early postman an hour before and already, on the customary table by the chimney-piece, formally rounded and squared by his systematic servant. It was something too merciless, the domestic perfection of Brown. There were newspapers on another table, ranged with the same rigour of custom, newspapers too many—what could any creature want of so much news?—and each with its hand on the neck of the other, so that the row of their bodiless heads was like a series of decapitations. Other journals, other periodicals of every sort, folded and in wrappers, made a huddled mound that had been growing for several days and of which he had been wearily, helplessly aware. There were new books, also in wrappers as well as disenveloped and dropped again—books from publishers, books from authors, books from friends, books from enemies, books from his own bookseller, who took, it sometimes struck him, inconceivable things for granted. He touched nothing, approached nothing, only turned a heavy eye over the work, as it were, of the night—the fact, in his high wide-windowed room, where duty shed its hard light into every corner, of the still unashamed admonitions. It was the old rising tide, and it rose and rose even under a minute's watching. It had been up to his shoulders last night—it was up to his chin now.

Nothing had *gone,* had passed on while he slept—everything had stayed; nothing, that he could yet feel, had died—so naturally, one would have thought; many things on the contrary had been born. To let them alone, these things, the new things, let them utterly alone and see if that, by chance, wouldn't somehow prove the best way to deal with them: this fancy brushed his face for a moment as a possible solution, just giving it, as so often before, a cool wave of air. Then he knew again as well as ever that leaving was difficult, leaving impossible—that the only remedy, the true soft effacing sponge, would be to *be* left, to be forgotten. There was no footing on which a man who had ever liked life—liked it at any rate as *he* had—could now escape it. He must reap as he had sown. It was a thing of meshes; he had simply gone to sleep under the net and had simply waked up there. The net was too fine; the cords crossed each other at spots too near together, making at each a little tight hard knot that tired fingers were this morning too limp and too tender to touch. Our poor friend's touched nothing—only stole significantly into his pockets as he wandered over to the window and faintly gasped at the energy of nature. What was most overwhelming was that she herself was so ready. She had soothed him rather, the night before, in the small hours by the lamp. From behind the drawn curtain of his study the rain had been audible and in a manner merciful; washing the window in a steady flood, it had seemed the right thing, the retarding interrupting thing, the thing that, if it would only last, might clear the ground by floating out to a boundless sea the innumerable objects among which his feet stumbled and strayed. He had positively laid down his pen as on a sense of friendly pressure from it. The kind full swish had been on the glass when he turned out his lamp; he had left his phrase unfinished and his papers lying quite as for the flood to bear them away in its rush. But there still on the table were the bare bones of the sentence—and not all of those; the single thing borne away and that he could never recover was the missing half that might have paired with it and begotten a figure.

Yet he could at last only turn back from the window; the world was everywhere, without and within, and the great staring egotism of its health and strength wasn't to be trusted for tact or delicacy. He faced about precisely to meet his servant and the absurd solemnity of two telegrams on a tray. Brown ought to have kicked them into the room—then he himself might have kicked them out.

"And you told me to remind you, sir—"

George Dane was at last angry. "Remind me of nothing!"

"But you insisted, sir, that I was to insist!"

He turned away in despair, using a pathetic quaver at absurd variance with his words: "If you insist, Brown, I'll kill you!" He found himself anew at the window, whence, looking down from his fourth floor, he could see the vast neighbourhood, under the trumpet-blare of the sky, beginning to rush about. There was a silence, but he knew Brown hadn't left him—knew exactly how straight and serious and stupid and faithful he stood there. After a minute he heard him again.

"It's only because, sir, you know, sir, you can't remember—"

At this Dane did flash round; it was more than at such a moment he could bear. "Can't remember, Brown? I can't forget. That's what's the matter with me."

Brown looked at him with the advantage of eighteen years of consistency. "I'm afraid you're not well, sir."

Brown's master thought. "It's a shocking thing to say, but I wish to heaven I weren't! It would be perhaps an excuse."

Brown's blankness spread like the desert. "To put them off?"

"Ah!" The sound was a groan; the plural pronoun, *any* pronoun, so mistimed. "Who is it?"

"Those ladies you spoke of—to luncheon."

"Oh!" The poor man dropped into the nearest chair and stared a while at the carpet. It was very complicated.

"How many will there be, sir?" Brown asked.

"Fifty!"

"Fifty, sir?"

Our friend, from his chair, looked vaguely about; under his hand were the telegrams, still unopened, one of which he now tore asunder. "'Do hope you sweetly won't mind, today, 1.30, my bringing poor dear Lady Mullet, who's so awfully bent,'" he read to his companion.

His companion weighed it. "How many does *she* make, sir?"

"Poor dear Lady Mullet? I haven't the least idea."

"Is she—a—deformed, sir?" Brown enquired, as if in this case she might make more.

His master wondered, then saw he figured some personal curvature. "No; she's only bent on coming!" Dane opened the other telegram and again read out: "'So sorry it's at eleventh hour impossible, and count on you here, as very greatest favour, at two sharp instead.'"

"How many does *that* make?" Brown imperturbably continued.

Dane crumpled up the two missives and walked with them to the waste-paper basket, into which he thoughtfully dropped them. "I can't say. You must do it all yourself. I shan't be there."

It was only on this that Brown showed an expression. "You'll go instead—"

"I'll go instead!" Dane raved.

Brown, however, had had occasion to show before that *he* would never desert their post. "Isn't that rather sacrificing the three?" Between respect and reproach he paused.

"*Are* there three?"

"I lay for four in all."

His master had at any rate caught his thought. "Sacrificing the three to the one, you mean? Oh I'm not going to *her*!"

Brown's famous "thoroughness"—his great virtue—had never been so dreadful. "Then where *are* you going?"

Dane sat down to his table and stared at his ragged phrase. "'*There* is a happy land—far far away!'" He chanted it like a sick child and knew that for a minute Brown never moved. During this minute he felt between his shoulders the gimlet of criticism.

"Are you quite sure you're all right?"

"It's my certainty that overwhelms me, Brown. Look about you and judge. Could anything be more 'right,' in the view of the envious world, than everything that surrounds us here: that immense array of letters, notes, circulars; that pile of printers' proofs, magazines and books; these perpetual telegrams, these impending guests, this retarded, unfinished and interminable work? What could a man want more?"

"Do you mean there's too much, sir?"—Brown had sometimes these flashes.

"There's too much. There's too much. But *you* can't help it, Brown."

"No, sir," Brown assented. "Can't *you*?"

"I'm thinking—I must see. There are hours—!" Yes, there were hours, and this was one of them: he jerked himself up for another turn in his labyrinth, but still not touching, not even again meeting, his admonisher's eye. If he was a genius for any one he was a genius for Brown; but it was terrible what that meant, being a genius for Brown. There had been times when he had done full justice to the way it kept him up; now, however, it was almost the worst of the avalanche. "Don't trouble about me," he went on insincerely and looking askance through his window again at the bright and beautiful world. "Perhaps it will rain—that *may* not be over. I do love the rain," he weakly pursued. "Perhaps, better still, it will snow."

Brown now had indeed a perceptible expression, and the expression was of fear. "Snow, sir—the end of May?" Without pressing this point he looked at his watch. "You'll feel better when you've had breakfast."

"I dare say," said Dane, whom breakfast struck in fact as a pleasant alternative to opening letters. "I'll come in immediately."

"But without waiting—?"

"Waiting for what?"

Brown at last, under his apprehension, had his first lapse from logic, which he betrayed by hesitating in the evident hope his companion might by a flash of remembrance relieve him of an invidious duty. But the only flashes now were the good man's own. "You say you can't forget, sir; but you do forget—"

"Is it anything very horrible?" Dane broke in.

Brown hung fire. "Only the gentleman you told me you had asked—"

Dane again took him up; horrible or not it came back—indeed its mere coming back classed it. "To breakfast today? It *was* today; I see." It came back, yes, came back; the appointment with the young man—he supposed him young—whose letter, the letter about—what was it?—had struck him. "Yes, yes; wait, wait."

"Perhaps he'll do you good, sir," Brown suggested.

"Sure to—sure to. All right!" Whatever he might do he would at least prevent some other doing: that was present to our friend as, on the vibration of the electric bell at the door of the flat, Brown moved away. Two things in the short interval that followed were present to Dane: his having utterly forgotten the connexion, the whence, whither and why of his guest; and his continued disposition not to touch—no, not with the finger. Ah if he might *never* again touch! All the unbroken seals and neglected appeals lay there while, for a pause he couldn't measure, he stood before the chimney-piece with his hands still in his pockets. He heard a brief exchange of words in the hall, but never afterwards recovered the time taken by Brown to reappear, to precede and announce another person—a person whose name somehow failed to reach Dane's ear. Brown went off again to serve breakfast, leaving host and guest confronted. The duration of this first stage also, later on, defied measurement; but that little mattered, for in the train of what happened came promptly the second, the third, the fourth, the rich succession of the others. Yet what happened was but that Dane took his hand from his pocket, held it straight out and felt it taken. Thus indeed, if he had wanted never again to touch, it was already done.

II

HE might have been a week in the place—the scene of his new consciousness—before he spoke at all. The occasion of it then was that one of the quiet figures he had been idly watching drew at last nearer and showed him a face that was the highest expression—to his pleased but as yet slightly confused perception—of the general charm. What *was* the general charm? He couldn't, for that matter, easily have phrased it; it was such an abyss of negatives, such an absence of positives and of everything. The oddity was that after a minute he was struck as by the reflexion of his own very image in this first converser seated with him, on the easy bench, under the high clear portico and above the wide far-reaching garden, where the things that most showed in the greenness were the surface of still water and the white note of old statues. The absence of everything was, in the aspect of the Brother who had thus informally joined him—a man of his own age, tired distinguished modest kind—really, as he could soon see, but the absence of what he didn't want. He didn't want, for the time, anything but just to *be* there, to steep in the bath. He was in the bath yet, the broad deep bath of stillness. They sat in it together now with the water up to their chins. He hadn't had to talk, he hadn't had to think, he had scarce even had to feel. He had been sunk that way before, sunk —when and where?—in another flood; only a flood of rushing waters in which bumping and gasping were all. *This* was a current so slow and so tepid that one floated practically without motion and without chill. The break of silence was not immediate, though Dane seemed indeed to feel it begin before a sound passed. It could pass quite sufficiently without words that he and his mate were Brothers, and what that meant.

He wondered, but with no want of ease—for want of ease was impossible—if his friend found in *him* the same likeness, the proof of peace, the gage of what the place could do. The long afternoon crept to its end; the shadows fell further and the sky glowed deeper; but nothing changed—nothing *could* change—in the element itself. It was a conscious security. It was wonderful! Dane had lived into it, but he was still immensely aware. He would have been sorry to lose that, for just this fact as yet, the blest fact of consciousness, seemed the greatest thing of all. Its only fault was that, being in itself such an occupation, so fine an unrest in the heart of gratitude, the life of the day all went to it. But what even then was the harm? He had come only to come, to take what he found. This was the part where the great cloister, enclosed externally on three sides and probably the largest lightest fairest effect, to his charmed sense, that human hands could ever have expressed in dimensions of length and breadth, opened to the south its splendid fourth quarter, turned to the great view an outer gallery that combined with the rest of the portico to form a high dry loggia, such as he a little pretended to himself he had, in the Italy of old days, seen in old cities, old convents, old villas. This recalled disposition of some great abode of an Order, some mild Monte Cassino, some Grande Chartreuse more accessible, was his main term of comparison; but he knew he had really never anywhere beheld anything at once so calculated and so generous.

Three impressions in particular had been with him all the week, and he could but recognise in silence their happy effect on his nerves. How it was all managed he couldn't have told—he had been content moreover till now with his ignorance of cause and pretext; but whenever he chose to listen with a certain intentness he made out as from a distance the sound of slow sweet bells. How could they be so far and yet so audible? How could they be so near and yet so faint? How above all could they, in such an arrest of life, be, to *time* things, so frequent? The very essence of the bliss of Dane's whole change had been precisely that there was nothing now to time. It was the same with the slow footsteps that, always within earshot to the vague attention, marked the space and the leisure, seemed, in long cool arcades, lightly to fall and perpetually to recede. This was the second impression, and it melted into the third, as, for that matter, every form of softness, in the great good place, was but a further turn, without jerk or gap, of the endless roll of serenity. The quiet footsteps were quiet figures; the quiet figures that, to the eye, kept the picture human and brought its perfection within reach. This perfection, he felt on the bench by his friend, was now more within reach than ever. His friend at last turned to him a look different from the looks of friends in London clubs.

"The thing was to find it out!"

It was extraordinary how this remark fitted into his thought. "Ah wasn't it? And when I think," said Dane, "of all the people who haven't and who never will!" He sighed over these unfortunates with a tenderness that, in its degree, was practically new to him, feeling too how well his companion would know the people he meant. He only meant some, but they were all who'd want it; though of these, no doubt—well, for reasons, for things that, in the world, he had observed—there would never be too many. Not all perhaps who wanted would really find; but none at least would find who didn't really want. And then what the need would have to have been first! What it at first had had to be for himself! He felt afresh, in the light of his companion's face, what it might still be even when deeply satisfied, as well as what communication was established by the mere common knowledge of it.

"Every man must arrive by himself and on his own feet—isn't that so? We're Brothers here for the time, as in a great monastery, and we immediately think of each other and recognise each other as such; but we must have first got here as we can, and we meet after long journeys by complicated ways. Moreover we meet—don't we?—with closed eyes."

"Ah don't speak as if we were dead!" Dane laughed.

"I shan't mind death if it's like this," his friend replied.

It was too obvious, as Dane gazed before him, that one wouldn't; but after a moment he asked with the first articulation as yet of his most elementary wonder: "Where is it?"

"I shouldn't be surprised if it were much nearer than one ever suspected."

"Nearer 'town,' do you mean?"

"Nearer everything—nearer every one."

George Dane thought. "Would it be somewhere for instance down in Surrey?"

His Brother met him on this with a shade of reluctance. "Why should we call it names? It must have a climate, you see."

"Yes," Dane happily mused; "without that—!" All it so securely did have overwhelmed him again, and he couldn't help breaking out: "*What* is it?"

"Oh it's positively a part of our ease and our rest and our change, I think, that we don't at all know and that we may really call it, for that matter, anything in the world we like—the thing for instance we love it most for being."

"I know what *I* call it," said Dane after a moment. Then as his friend listened with interest: "Just simply 'The Great Good Place.' "

"I see—what can you say more? I've put it to myself perhaps a little differently." They sat there as innocently as small boys confiding to each other the names of toy animals. " 'The Great Want Met.' "

"Ah yes—that's it!"

"Isn't it enough for us that it's a place carried on for our benefit so admirably that we strain our ears in vain for a creak of the machinery? Isn't it enough for us that it's simply a thorough hit?"

"Ah a hit!" Dane benignantly murmured.

"It does for us what it pretends to do," his companion went on; "the mystery isn't deeper than that. The thing's probably simple enough in fact, and on a thoroughly practical basis; only it has had its origin in a splendid thought, in a real stroke of genius."

"Yes," Dane returned, "in a sense—on somebody or other's part—so exquisitely personal!"

"Precisely—it rests, like all good things, on experience. The 'great want' comes home—that's the great thing it does! On the day it came home to the right mind this dear place was constituted. It always moreover in the long run *has* been met—it always must be. How can it not require to be, more and more, as pressure of every sort grows?"

Dane, with his hands folded in his lap, took in these words of wisdom. "Pressure of every sort *is* growing!" he placidly observed.

"I see well enough what that fact has done to *you*," his Brother declared.

Dane smiled. "I couldn't have borne it longer. I don't know what would have become of me."

"I know what would have become of *me*."

"Well, it's the same thing."

"Yes," said Dane's companion, "it's doubtless the same thing." On which they sat in silence a little, seeming pleasantly to follow, in the view of the green garden, the vague movements of the monster—madness, surrender, collapse—they had escaped. Their bench was like a box at the opera. "And I may perfectly, you know," the Brother pursued, "have seen you before. I may even have known you well. We don't know."

They looked at each other again serenely enough, and at last Dane said: "No, we don't know."

"That's what I meant by our coming with our eyes closed. Yes—there's something out. There's a gap, a link missing, the great hiatus!" the Brother laughed. "It's as simple a story as the old, old rupture—the break that lucky Catholics have always been able to make, that they're still, with their innumerable religious houses, able to make, by going into 'retreat.' I don't speak of the pious exercises—I speak only of the material simplification. I don't speak of the putting off of one's self; I speak only—if one has a self worth sixpence—of the getting it back. The place, the time, the way were, for those of the old persuasion, always there—are indeed practically there for them as much as ever. They can always get off—the blessed houses receive. So it was high time that we—we of the great Protestant peoples, still more, if possible, in the sensitive individual case, overscored and overwhelmed, still more congested with mere quantity and prostituted, through our 'enterprise,' to mere profanity—should learn how to get off, should find somewhere *our* retreat and remedy. There was such a huge chance for it!"

Dane laid his hand on his companion's arm. "It's charming how when we speak for ourselves we speak for each other. That was exactly what I said!" He had fallen to recalling from over the gulf the last occasion.

The Brother, as if it would do them both good, only desired to draw him out. "What you 'said'—?"

"To *him*—that morning." Dane caught a far bell again and heard a slow footstep. A quiet presence passed somewhere—neither of them turned to look. What was little by little more present to him was the perfect taste. It was supreme—it was everywhere. "I just dropped my burden—and he received it."

"And was it very great?"

"Oh such a load!" Dane said with gaiety.

"Trouble, sorrow, doubt?"

"Oh no—worse than that!"

"Worse?"

" 'Success'—the vulgarest kind!" He mentioned it now as with amusement.

"Ah I know that too! No one in future, as things are going, will be able to face success."

"Without something of this sort—never. The better it is the worse—the greater the deadlier. But my one pain here," Dane continued, "is in thinking of my poor friend."

"The person to whom you've already alluded?"

He tenderly assented. "My substitute in the world. Such an unutterable benefactor. He turned up that morning when everything had somehow got on my nerves, when the whole great globe indeed, nerves or no nerves, seemed to have appallingly squeezed itself into my study and to be bent on simply swelling there. It wasn't a question of nerves, it was a mere question of the dislodgement and derangement of everything—of a general submersion by our eternal too much. I didn't know *où donner de la tête*—I couldn't have gone a step further."

The intelligence with which the Brother listened kept them as children feeding from the same bowl. "And then you got the tip?"

"I got the tip!" Dane happily sighed.

"Well, we all get it. But I dare say differently."

"Then how did *you*—?"

The Brother hesitated, smiling. "You tell me first."

III

"Well," said George Dane, "it was a young man I had never seen—a man at any rate much younger than myself—who had written to me and sent me some article, some book. I read the stuff, was much struck with it, told him so and thanked him—on which of course I heard from him again. Ah *that*—!" Dane comically sighed. "He asked me things—his questions were interesting; but to save time and writing I said to him: 'Come to see me—we can talk a little; but all I can give you is half an hour at breakfast.' He arrived to the minute on a day when more than ever in my life before I seemed, as it happened, in the endless press and stress, to have lost possession of my soul and to be surrounded only with the affairs of other people, smothered in mere irrelevant importunity. It made me literally ill—made me feel as I had never felt that should I once really for an hour lose hold of the thing itself, the thing that did matter and that I was trying for, I should never recover it again. The wild waters would close over me and I should drop straight to the dark depths where the vanquished dead lie."

"I follow you every step of your way," said the friendly Brother. "The wild waters, you mean, of our horrible time."

"Of our horrible time precisely. Not of course—as we sometimes dream—of any other."

"Yes, any other's only a dream. We really know none but our own."

"No, thank God—that's enough," Dane contentedly smiled. "Well, my young man turned up, and I hadn't been a minute in his presence before making out that practically it would be in him somehow or other to help me. He came to me with envy, envy extravagant—really passionate. I was, heaven save us, the great 'success' for him; he himself was starved and broken and beaten. How can I say what passed between us?—it was so strange, so swift, so much a matter, from one to the other, of instant perception and agreement. He was so clever and haggard and hungry!"

"Hungry?" the Brother asked.

"I don't mean for bread, though he had none too much, I think, even of that. I mean for—well, what *I* had and what I was a monument of to him as I stood there up to my neck in preposterous evidence. He, poor chap, had been for ten years serenading closed windows and had never yet caused a shutter to show that it stirred. *My* dim blind was the first raised to him an inch; my reading of his book, my impression of it, my note and my invitation, formed literally the only response ever dropped into his dark alley. He saw in my littered room, my shattered day, my bored face and spoiled temper—it's embarrassing, but I must tell you—the very proof of my pudding, the very blaze of my glory. And he saw in my repletion and my 'renown'—deluded innocent!—what he had yearned for in vain."

"What he had yearned for was to *be* you," said the Brother. Then he added: "I see where you're coming out."

"At my saying to him by the end of five minutes: 'My dear

fellow, I wish you'd just try it—wish you'd for a while just *be* me!' You go straight to the mark, good Brother, and that was exactly what occurred—extraordinary though it was that we should both have understood. I saw what he could give, and he did too. He saw moreover what I could take; in fact what he saw was wonderful."

"He must be very remarkable!" Dane's converser laughed.

"There's no doubt of it whatever—far more remarkable than I. That's just the reason why what I put to him in joke—with a fantastic desperate irony—became, in his hands, with his vision of his chance, the blessed means and measure of my sitting on this spot in your company. 'Oh if I could just *shift* it all—make it straight over for an hour to other shoulders! If there only *were* a pair!'—that's the way I put it to him. And then at something in his face, 'Would *you*, by a miracle, undertake it?' I asked. I let him know all it meant—how it meant that he should at that very moment step in. It meant that he should finish my work and open my letters and keep my engagements and be subject, for better or worse, to my contacts and complications. It meant that he should live with my life and think with my brain and write with my hand and speak with my voice. It meant above all that I should get off. He accepted with greatness—rose to it like a hero. Only he said: 'What will become of *you*?' "

"There was the rub!" the Brother admitted.

"Ah but only for a minute. He came to my help again," Dane pursued, "when he saw I couldn't quite meet that, could at least only say that I wanted to think, wanted to cease, wanted to do the thing itself—the thing that mattered and that I was trying for, miserable me, and that thing only—and therefore wanted first of all really to *see* it again, planted out, crowded out, frozen out as it now so long had been. 'I know what you want,' he after a moment quietly remarked to me. 'Ah what I want doesn't exist!' 'I know what you want,' he repeated. At that I began to believe him."

"Had you any idea yourself?" the Brother's attention breathed.

"Oh yes," said Dane, "and it was just my idea that made me despair. There it was as sharp as possible in my imagination and my longing—there it was so utterly *not* in the fact. We were sitting together on my sofa as we waited for breakfast. He presently laid his hand on my knee—showed me a face that the sudden great light in it had made, for me, indescribably beautiful. 'It exists—it exists,' he at last said. And so I remember we sat a while and looked at each other, with the final effect of my finding that I absolutely believed him. I remember we weren't at all solemn—we smiled with the joy of discoverers. He was as glad as I—he was tremendously glad. That came out in the whole manner of his reply to the appeal that broke from me: 'Where is it then in God's name? Tell me without delay where it is!'"

The Brother had bent such a sympathy! "He gave you the address?"

"He was thinking it out—feeling for it, catching it. He has a wonderful head of his own and must be making of the whole thing, while we sit here patching and gossiping, something much better than ever *I* did. The mere sight of his face, the sense of his hand on my knee, made me, after a little, feel that he not only knew what I wanted but was getting nearer to it than I could have got in ten years. He suddenly sprang up and went over to my study-table—sat straight down there as if to write me my prescription or my passport. Then it was—at the mere sight of his back, which was turned to me—that I felt the spell work. I simply sat and watched him with the queerest deepest sweetest sense in the world—the sense of an ache that had stopped. All life was lifted; I myself at least was somehow off the ground. He was already where I had been."

"And where were you?" the Brother amusedly asked.

"Just on the sofa always, leaning back on the cushion and feeling a delicious ease. He was already me."

"And who were *you*?" the Brother continued.

"Nobody. That was the fun."

"That *is* the fun," said the Brother with a sigh like soft music.

Dane echoed the sigh, and, as nobody talking with nobody, they sat there together still and watched the sweet wide picture darken into tepid night.

IV

AT the end of three weeks—so far as time was distinct—Dane began to feel there was something he had recovered. It was the thing they never named—partly for want of the need and partly for lack of the word; for what indeed was the description that would cover it all? The only real need was to know it, to see it in silence. Dane had a private practical sign for it, which, however, he had appropriated by theft—"the vision and the faculty divine." That doubtless was a flattering phrase for his idea of his genius; the genius was at all events what he had been in danger of losing and had at last held by a thread that might at any moment have broken. The change was that little by little his hold had grown firmer, so that he drew in the line—more and more each day—with a pull he was delighted to find it would bear. The mere dream-sweetness of the place was superseded; it was more and more a world of reason and order, of sensible visible arrangement. It ceased to be strange—it was high triumphant clearness. He cultivated, however, but vaguely the question of where he was, finding it near enough the mark to be almost sure that if he wasn't in Kent he was then probably in Hampshire. He paid for everything but that—that wasn't one of the items. Payment, he had soon learned, was definite; it consisted of sovereigns and shillings—just like those of the world he had left, only parted with more ecstatically—that he committed, in his room, to a fixed receptacle and that were removed in his absence by one of the unobtrusive effaced agents (shadows projected on the hours like the noiseless march of the sundial) that were always at work. The scene had whole sides that reminded and resembled, and a pleased resigned perception of these things was at once the effect and the cause of its grace.

Dane picked out of his dim past a dozen halting similes. The sacred silent convent was one; another was the bright country-house. He did the place no outrage to liken it to an hotel; he permitted himself on occasion to feel it suggest a club. Such images, however, but flickered and went out—they lasted only long enough to light up the difference. An hotel without noise, a club without newspapers—when he turned his face to what it was "without" the view opened wide. The only approach to a real analogy was in himself and his companions. They were brothers, guests, members; they were even, if one liked—and they didn't in the least mind what they were called—"regular boarders." It wasn't they who made the conditions, it was the conditions that made them. These conditions found themselves accepted, clearly, with an appreciation, with a rapture, it was rather to be called, that proceeded, as the very air that pervaded them and the force that sustained, from their quiet and noble assurance. They combined to form the large simple idea of a general refuge—an image of embracing arms, of liberal accommodation. What was the effect really but the poetisation by perfect taste of a type common enough? There was no daily miracle; the perfect taste, with the aid of space, did the trick. What underlay and overhung it all, better yet, Dane mused, was some original inspiration, but confirmed, unquenched, some happy thought of an individual breast. It had been born somehow and somewhere—it had had to insist on being—the blest conception. The author might remain in the obscure for that was part of the perfection: personal service so hushed and regulated that you scarce caught it in the act and only knew it by its results. Yet the wise mind was everywhere—the whole thing infallibly centred at the core in a consciousness. And what a consciousness it had been, Dane thought, a consciousness how like his own! The wise mind had felt, the wise mind had suffered; then, for all the worried company of minds, the wise mind had seen a chance. Of the creation thus arrived at you could none the less never have said if it were the last echo of the old or the sharpest note of the modern.

Dane again and again, among the far bells and the soft footfalls, in cool cloister and warm garden, found himself wanting not to know more and yet liking not to know less. It was part of the high style and the grand manner that there was no personal publicity, much less any personal reference. Those things were in the world—in what he had left; there was no vulgarity here of credit or claim or fame. The real exquisite was to be without the complication of an identity, and the greatest boon of all, doubtless, the solid security, the clear confidence one could feel in the keeping of the contract. That was what had been most in the wise mind—the importance of the absolute sense, on the part of its beneficiaries, that what was offered was guaranteed. They had no concern but to pay—the wise mind knew what they paid for. It was present to Dane each hour that he could never be overcharged. Oh the deep deep bath, the soft cool plash in the stillness!—this, time after time, as if under regular treatment, a sublimated German "cure," was the vivid name for his luxury. The inner life woke up again, and it was the inner life, for people of his generation, victims of the modern madness, mere maniacal extension and motion, that was returning health. He had talked of independence and written of it, but what a cold flat word it had been! This was the wordless fact itself—the uncontested possession of the long sweet stupid day. The fragrance of flowers just wandered through the void, and the quiet recurrence of delicate plain fare in a high, clean refectory where the soundless simple service was a triumph of art. That, as he analysed, remained the constant explanation: all the sweetness and serenity were created calculated things. He analysed, however, but in a desultory way and with a positive delight in the residuum of mystery that made for the great agent in the background the innermost shrine of the idol of a temple; there were odd moments for it, mild meditations when, in the broad cloister of peace or some garden-nook where the air was light, a special glimpse of beauty or reminder of felicity seemed, in passing, to hover and linger. In the mere ecstasy of change that had at first possessed him he hadn't discriminated—had only let himself sink, as I have mentioned, down to hushed depths. Then had come the slow soft stages of intelligence and notation, more marked and more fruitful perhaps after that long talk with his mild mate in the twilight, and seeming to wind up the process by putting the key into his hand. This key, pure gold, was simply the cancelled list. Slowly and blissfully he read into the general wealth of his comfort all the particular absences of which it was composed. One by one he touched, as it were, all the things it was such rapture to be without.

It was the paradise of his own room that was most indebted to them—a great square fair chamber, all beautified with omissions, from which, high up, he looked over a long valley to a far horizon, and in which he was vaguely and pleasantly reminded of some old Italian picture, some Carpaccio or some early Tuscan, the representation of a world without newspapers and letters, without telegrams and photographs, without the dreadful fatal too much. There, for a blessing, he *could* read and write; there above all he could do nothing—he could live. And there were all sorts of freedoms—always, for the occasion, the particular right one. He could bring a book from the library—he could bring two, he could bring three. An effect produced by the charming place was that for some reason he never wanted to bring more. The library was a benediction—high and clear and plain like everything else, but with something, in all its arched amplitude, unconfused and brave and gay. He should never forget, he knew, the throb of immediate perception with which he first stood there, a single glance round sufficing so to show him that it would give him what for years he had desired. He had not had detachment, but there was detachment here—the sense of a great silver bowl from which he could ladle up the melted hours. He strolled about from wall to wall, too pleasantly in tune on that occasion to sit down punctually or to choose; only recognising from shelf to shelf every dear old book that he had had to put off or never returned to; every deep distinct voice of another time that in the hubbub of the world, he had had to take for lost and unheard. He came back of course soon, came back every day; enjoyed there, of all the rare strange moments, those that were at once most quickened and most caught—moments in which every apprehension counted double and every act of the mind was a lover's embrace. It was the quarter he perhaps, as the days went on, liked best; though indeed it only shared with the rest of the place, with every aspect to which his face happened to be turned, the power to remind him of the masterly general care.

There were times when he looked up from his book to lose himself in the mere tone of the picture that never failed at any moment or at any angle. The picture was always there, yet was made up of things common enough. It was in the way an open window in a broad recess let in the pleasant morning; in the way the dry air pricked into faint freshness the gilt of old bindings; in the way an empty chair beside a table unlittered showed a volume just laid down; in the way a happy Brother—as detached as one's self and with his innocent back presented—lingered before a shelf with the slow sound of turned pages. It was a part of the whole impression that, by some extraordinary law, one's vision seemed less from the facts than the facts from one's vision; that the elements were determined at the moment by the moment's need or the moment's sympathy. What most prompted this reflexion was the degree in which Dane had after a while a consciousness of company. After that talk with the good Brother on the bench there were other good Brothers in other places—always in cloister or garden some figure that stopped if he himself stopped and with which a greeting became, in the easiest way in the world, a sign of the diffused amenity and the consecrating ignorance.

For always, always, in all contacts, was the balm of a happy blank. What he had felt the first time recurred: the friend was always new and yet at the same time—it was amusing, not disturbing—suggested the possibility that he might be but an old one altered. That was only delightful—as positively delightful in the particular, the actual conditions as it might have been the reverse in the conditions abolished. These others, the abolished, came back to Dane at last so easily that he could exactly measure each difference, but with what he had finally been hustled on to hate in them robbed of its terror in consequence of something that had happened. What had happened was that in tranquil walks and talks the deep spell had worked and he had got his soul again. He had drawn in by this time, with his lightened hand, the whole of the long line, and that fact just dangled at the end. He could put his other hand on it, he could unhook it, he was once more in possession. This, as it befell, was exactly what he supposed he must have said to a comrade beside whom, one afternoon in the cloister, he found himself measuring steps.

"Oh it comes—comes of itself, doesn't it, thank goodness?—just by the simple fact of finding room and time!"

The comrade was possibly a novice or in a different stage from his own; there was at any rate a vague envy in the recognition that shone out of the fatigued yet freshened face. "It has come to *you* then?—you've got what you wanted?" That was the gossip and interchange that could pass to and fro. Dane, years before, had gone in for three months of hydropathy, and there was a droll echo, in this scene, of the old questions of the water-cure, the questions asked in the periodical pursuit of the "reaction"—the ailment, the progress of each, the action of the skin and the state of the appetite. Such memories worked in now—all familiar reference, all easy play of mind; and among them our friends, round and round, fraternised ever so softly till, suddenly stopping short, Dane, with a hand on his companion's arm, broke into the happiest laugh he had yet sounded.

V

"Why it's raining!" And he stood and looked at the splash of the shower and the shine of the wet leaves. It was one of the summer sprinkles that bring out sweet smells.

"Yes—but why not?" his mate demanded.

"Well—because it's so charming. It's so exactly right."

"But everything *is*. Isn't that just why we're here?"

"Just exactly," Dane said; "only I've been living in the beguiled supposition that we've somehow or other a climate."

"So have I, so I dare say has every one. Isn't that the blest moral?—that we live in beguiled suppositions. They come so easily here, where nothing contradicts them." The good Brother looked placidly forth—Dane could identify his phase. "A climate doesn't consist in its never raining, does it?"

"No, I dare say not. But somehow the good I've got has been half the great easy absence of all that friction of which the question of weather mostly forms a part—has been indeed largely the great easy perpetual air-bath."

"Ah yes—that's not a delusion; but perhaps the sense comes a little from our breathing an emptier medium. There are fewer things *in* it! Leave people alone, at all events, and the air's what they take to. Into the closed and the stuffy they have to be driven. I've had too—I think we must all have—a fond sense of the south."

"But imagine it," said Dane, laughing, "in the beloved British islands and so near as we are to Bradford!"

His friend was ready enough to imagine. "To Bradford?" he asked, quite unperturbed. "How near?"

Dane's gaiety grew. "Oh it doesn't matter!"

His friend, quite unmystified, accepted it. "There are things to puzzle out—otherwise it would be dull. It seems to me one can puzzle them."

"It's because we're so well disposed," Dane said.

"Precisely—we find good in everything."

"In everything," Dane went on. "The conditions settle that —they determine us."

They resumed their stroll, which evidently represented on the good Brother's part infinite agreement. "Aren't they probably in fact very simple?" he presently enquired. "Isn't simplification the secret?"

"Yes, but applied with a tact!"

"There it is. The thing's so perfect that it's open to as many interpretations as any other great work—a poem of Goethe, a dialogue of Plato, a symphony of Beethoven."

"It simply stands quiet, you mean," said Dane, "and lets us call it names?"

"Yes, but all such loving ones. We're 'staying' with some one —some delicious host or hostess who never shows."

"It's liberty-hall—absolutely," Dane assented.

"Yes—or a convalescent home."

To this, however, Dane demurred. "Ah that, it seems to me, scarcely puts it. You weren't *ill*—were you? I'm very sure *I* really wasn't. I was only, as the world goes, too 'beastly well'!"

The good Brother wondered. "But if we couldn't keep it up—?"

"We couldn't keep it *down*—that was all the matter!"

"I see—I see." The good Brother sighed contentedly; after which he brought out again with kindly humour: "It's a sort of kindergarten!"

"The next thing you'll be saying that we're babes at the breast!"

"Of some great mild invisible mother who stretches away into space and whose lap's the whole valley—?"

"And her bosom"—Dane completed the figure—"the noble eminence of our hill? That will do; anything will do that covers the essential fact."

"And what do you call the essential fact?"

"Why that—as in old days on Swiss lakesides—we're *en pension*."

The good Brother took this gently up. "I remember—I remember: seven francs a day without wine! But alas it's more than seven francs here."

"Yes, it's considerably more," Dane had to confess. "Perhaps it isn't particularly cheap."

"Yet should you call it particularly dear?" his friend after a moment enquired.

George Dane had to think. "How do I know, after all? What practice has one ever had in estimating the inestimable? Particular cheapness certainly isn't the note we feel struck all round; but don't we fall naturally into the view that there *must* be a price to anything so awfully sane?"

The good Brother in his turn reflected. "We fall into the view that it must pay—that it does pay."

"Oh yes; it does pay!" Dane eagerly echoed. "If it didn't it wouldn't last. It has *got* to last of course!" he declared.

"So that we can come back?"

"Yes—think of knowing that we shall be able to!"

They pulled up again at this and, facing each other, thought of it, or at any rate pretended to; for what was really in their eyes was the dread of a loss of the clue. "Oh when we want it again we shall find it," said the good Brother. "If the place really pays it will keep on."

"Yes, that's the beauty; that it isn't, thank goodness, carried on only for love."

"No doubt, no doubt; and yet, thank goodness, there's love in it too." They had lingered as if, in the mild moist air, they were charmed with the patter of the rain and the way the garden drank it. After a little, however, it did look rather as if they were trying to talk each other out of a faint small fear. They saw the increasing rage of life and the recurrent need, and they wondered proportionately whether to return to the front when their hour should sharply strike would be the end of the dream. Was this a threshold perhaps, after all, that could only be crossed one way? They must return to the front sooner or later—that was certain: for each his hour would strike. The flower would have been gathered and the trick played—the sands would in short have run.

There, in its place, *was* life—with all its rage; the vague unrest of the need for action knew it again, the stir of the faculty that had been refreshed and reconsecrated. They seemed each, thus confronted, to close their eyes a moment for dizziness; then they were again at peace and the Brother's confidence rang out. "Oh we shall meet!"

"Here, do you mean?"

"Yes—and I dare say in the world too."

"But we shan't recognise or know," said Dane.

"In the world, do you mean?"

"Neither in the world nor here."

"Not a bit—not the least little bit, you think?"

Dane turned it over. "Well, so is it that it seems to me all best to hang together. But we shall see."

His friend happily concurred. "We shall see." And at this, for farewell, the Brother held out his hand.

"You're going?" Dane asked.

"No, but I thought *you* were."

It was odd, but at this Dane's hour seemed to strike—his consciousness to crystallise. "Well, I am. I've got it. You stay?" he went on.

"A little longer."

Dane hesitated. "You haven't yet got it?"

"Not altogether—but I think it's coming."

"Good!" Dane kept his hand, giving it a final shake, and at that moment the sun glimmered again through the shower, but with the rain still falling on the hither side of it and seeming to patter even more in the brightness. "Hallo—how charming!"

The Brother looked a moment from under the high arch—

then again turned his face to our friend. He gave this time his longest happiest sigh. "Oh it's all right!"

But why was it, Dane after a moment found himself wondering, that in the act of separation his own hand was so long retained? Why but through a queer phenomenon of change, on the spot, in his companion's face—change that gave it another, but an increasing and above all a much more familiar identity, an identity not beautiful, but more and more distinct, an identity with that of his servant, with the most conspicuous, the physiognomic seat of the public propriety of Brown? To this anomaly his eyes slowly opened; it was not his good Brother, it was verily Brown who possessed his hand. If his eyes had to open it was because they had been closed and because Brown appeared to think he had better wake up. So much as this Dane took in, but the effect of his taking it was a relapse into darkness, a recontraction of the lids just prolonged enough to give Brown time, on a second thought, to withdraw his touch and move softly away. Dane's next consciousness was that of the desire to make sure he *was* away, and this desire had somehow the result of dissipating the obscurity. The obscurity was completely gone by the time he had made out that the back of a person writing at his study-table was presented to him. He recognised a portion of a figure that he had somewhere described to somebody—the intent shoulders of the unsuccessful young man who had come that bad morning to breakfast. It was strange, he at last mused, but the young man was still there. How long had he stayed—days, weeks, months? He was exactly in the position in which Dane had last seen him. Everything—stranger still—was exactly in that position; everything at least but the light of the window, which came in from another quarter and showed a different hour. It wasn't after breakfast now; it was after—well, what? He suppressed a gasp—it was after everything. And yet—quite literally—there were but two other differences. One of these was that if he was still on the sofa he was now lying down; the other was the patter on the glass that showed him how the rain—the great rain of the night—had come back. It was the rain of the night, yet when had he last heard it? But two minutes before? Then how many were there before the young man at the table, who seemed intensely occupied, found a moment to look round at him and, on meeting his open eyes, get up and draw near?

"You've slept all day," said the young man.

"All day?"

The young man looked at his watch. "From ten to six. You were extraordinarily tired. I just after a bit let you alone, and you were soon off." Yes, that was it; he had been "off"—off, off, off. He began to fit it together: while he had been off the young man had been on. But there were still some few confusions; Dane lay looking up. "Everything's done," the young man continued.

"Everything?"

"Everything."

Dane tried to take it all in, but was embarrassed and could only say weakly and quite apart from the matter: "I've been so happy!"

"So have I," said the young man. He positively looked so; seeing which George Dane wondered afresh, and then in his wonder read it indeed quite as another face, quite, in a puzzling way, as another person's. Every one was a little some one else. While he asked himself who else then the young man was, this benefactor, struck by his appealing stare, broke again into perfect cheer. "It's all right!" That answered Dane's question; the face was the face turned to him by the good Brother there in the portico while they listened together to the rustle of the shower. It was all queer, but all pleasant and all distinct, so distinct that the last words in his ear—the same from both quarters—appeared the effect of a single voice. Dane rose and looked about his room, which seemed disencumbered, different, twice as large. It *was* all right.

A NOTE ON

THE GREAT GOOD PLACE

(1900)

JAMES's remarks on this beautiful story should, I presume, preclude my own. To its spirit, he thought, "any gloss or comment would be a tactless challenge. It embodies a calculated effect, and to plunge into it, I find, even for a beguiled glance—a course I indeed recommend—is to have left all else outside." This is true enough but it is almost equally true of *any* James story that "embodies a calculated effect." In extenuation of these "tactless challenges," I fear I can plead only that there is no obligation to read them, and that, if read, they will prove harmless.

Like *The Pilgrim's Progress* or *The Divine Comedy* "The Great Good Place" is a criticism of a whole culture, though developed on a miniature scale. Like them, too, it forsakes completely the methods of realism; like them, it invents a world. In this tiny bit of ordered dreamwork James points, however obliquely, to the essential vacuity of modern living. Only those infatuated with the twentieth century, only the gadget-men, the accumulators, will fail to make some response, however feeble, to "The Great Good Place." But it will haunt the others like a dream which, despite its oddity, seems to offer the serene answer to our deepest and most desperate prayer.

One good way to feel this story is to read it, as I chance just to have done, after listening to Mozart. The Mozartian note—perfection achieved with essentials—is precisely *not* the note of our time. We are anti-Mozartian in many ways but primarily in our passion for organizing non-essentials, both material and mental. Dimly conscious that we have lost a few simple things, we cover over our sense of loss by distributing as widely and as ingeniously as possible a million complicated things. Unable to derive satisfaction from stillness we develop speeds of almost cometary order. No longer certain what it is that makes one man better than another, we solve the problem by grading people according to the number and variety of their possessions.

The consequence of what James in this story calls "the modern madness, mere maniacal extension and motion" is a special form of lunacy known as being "under pressure." The sense of pressure has little to do with overwork or specific worries. Rather is it identical with the whole pattern of our lives, based on "getting somewhere" or "getting something." It comes about because we are engaged in doing something unnatural. We are neglecting, we are denying man's rational mind.

"The Great Good Place" is James's try—and a successful one—at putting all these truisms in the form of a fairy tale. His novelist has done what we all do: he has permitted himself to get so "involved" that he no longer knows who or what he is. He has too much of everything—success, friends, guests, work, appointments. His life is "full" or rather crowded. That is to say, it is devoid of any principle of clarity. There is no Mozart in it.

The Great Good Place is the world of Mozart's music, "all beautiful with omissions." It is not—this is the whole point—a mere refuge, an escape-hole. On the contrary it is "real life"—the life of achievement, success, accumulation and motion that is the escape. It is the escape from the mind, the escape from reflection, the escape from a recognition of one's own personality. The Great Good Place is simply ordered reality, stripped truth. Wherever the mind comes into its own, that is the Great Good Place. As the Brother says, "I don't speak of the putting off of one's self; I speak only—if one has a self worth sixpence—of the getting it back."

Note that the Place is no ethereal heaven—James is almost devoid of any religious sense—but a theoretically achievable

Utopia. It is "an hotel without noise, a club without newspapers." You even have to pay for service. The Place is what our civilization could be if we did not persist in taking wrong turnings, if we divested ourselves of things, if our conception of time were not based on the date-pad and the appointment-book, if we had not forgotten the know-thyself of the Greeks, if we could rediscover the private life.

To my mind "The Great Good Place" is, of the seventeen stories in this collection, the one most densely charged with contemporary application.

THE TREE OF KNOWLEDGE

I

It was one of the secret opinions, such as we all have, of Peter Brench that his main success in life would have consisted in his never having committed himself about the work, as it was called, of his friend Morgan Mallow. This was a subject on which it was, to the best of his belief, impossible with veracity to quote him, and it was nowhere on record that he had, in the connexion, on any occasion and in any embarrassment, either lied or spoken the truth. Such a triumph had its honour even for a man of other triumphs—a man who had reached fifty, who had escaped marriage, who had lived within his means, who had been in love with Mrs. Mallow for years without breathing it, and who, last but not least, had judged himself once for all. He had so judged himself in fact that he felt an extreme and general humility to be his proper portion; yet there was nothing that made him think so well of his parts as the course he had steered so often through the shallows just mentioned. It became thus a real wonder that the friends in whom he had most confidence were just those with whom he had most reserves. He couldn't tell Mrs. Mallow—or at least he supposed, excellent man, he couldn't—that she was the one beautiful reason he had never married; any more than he could tell her husband that the sight of the multiplied marbles in that gentleman's studio was an affliction of which even time had never blunted the edge. His victory, however, as I have intimated, in regard to these productions, was not simply in his not having let it out that he deplored them; it was, remarkably, in his not having kept it in by anything else.

The whole situation, among these good people, was verily a marvel, and there was probably not such another for a long way from the spot that engages us—the point at which the soft declivity of Hampstead began at that time to confess in broken accents to Saint John's Wood. He despised Mallow's statues and adored Mallow's wife, and yet was distinctly fond of Mallow, to whom, in turn, he was equally dear. Mrs. Mallow rejoiced in the statues—though she preferred, when pressed, the busts; and if she was visibly attached to Peter Brench it was because of his affection for Morgan. Each loved the other moreover for the love borne in each case to Lancelot, whom the Mallows respectively cherished as their only child and whom the friend of their fireside identified as the third—but decidedly the handsomest—of his godsons. Already in the old years it had come to that—that no one, for such a relation, could possibly have occurred to any of them, even to the baby itself, but Peter. There was luckily a certain independence, of the pecuniary sort, all round: the Master could never otherwise have spent his solemn *Wanderjahre* in Florence and Rome, and continued by the Thames as well as by the Arno and the Tiber to add unpurchased group to group and model, for what was too apt to prove in the event mere love, fancy-heads of celebrities either too busy or too buried—too much of the age or too little of it—to sit. Neither could Peter, lounging in almost daily, have found time to keep the whole complicated tradition so alive by his presence. He was massive but mild, the depositary of these mysteries—large and loose and ruddy and curly, with deep tones, deep eyes, deep pockets, to say nothing of the habit of long pipes, soft hats and brownish greyish weather-faded clothes, apparently always the same.

He had "written," it was known, but had never spoken, never spoken in particular of that; and he had the air (since, as was believed, he continued to write) of keeping it up in order to have something more—as if he hadn't at the worst enough—to be silent about. Whatever his air, at any rate, Peter's occasional unmentioned prose and verse were quite truly the result of an impulse to maintain the purity of his taste by establishing still more firmly the right relation of fame to feebleness. The little green door of his domain was in a garden-wall on which the discoloured stucco made patches, and in the small detached villa behind it everything was old, the furniture, the servants, the books, the prints, the immemorial habits and the new improvements. The Mallows, at Carrara Lodge, were within ten minutes, and the studio there was on their little land, to which they had added, in their happy faith, for building it. This was the good fortune, if it was not the ill, of her having brought him in marriage a portion that put them in a manner at their ease and enabled them thus, on their side, to keep it up. And they did keep it up—they always had—the infatuated sculptor and his wife, for whom nature had refined on the impossible by relieving them of the sense of the difficult. Morgan had at all events everything of the sculptor but the spirit of Phidias—the brown velvet, the becoming *beretto,* the "plastic" presence, the fine fingers, the beautiful accent in Italian and the old Italian factotum. He seemed to make up for everything when he addressed Egidio with the "tu" and waved him to turn one of the rotary pedestals of which the place was full. They were tremendous Italians at Carrara Lodge, and the secret of the part played by this fact in Peter's life was in a large degree that it gave him, sturdy Briton as he was, just the amount of "going abroad" he could bear. The Mallows were all his Italy, but it was in a measure for Italy he liked them. His one worry was that Lance—to which they had shortened his godson—was, in spite of a public school, perhaps a shade too Italian. Morgan meanwhile looked like somebody's flattering idea of somebody's own person as expressed in the great room provided at the Uffizi Museum for the general illustration of that idea by eminent hands. The Master's sole regret that he hadn't been born rather to the brush than to the chisel sprang from his wish that he might have contributed to that collection.

It appeared with time at any rate to be to the brush that Lance had been born; for Mrs. Mallow, one day when the boy was turning twenty, broke it to their friend, who shared, to the last delicate morsel, their problems and pains, that it seemed as if nothing would really do but that he should embrace the career. It had been impossible longer to remain blind to the fact that he was gaining no glory at Cambridge, where Brench's own college had for a year tempered its tone to him as for Brench's own sake. Therefore why renew the vain form of preparing him for the impossible? The impossible—it had become clear—was that he should be anything but an artist.

"Oh dear, dear!" said poor Peter.

"Don't you believe in it?" asked Mrs. Mallow, who still, at more than forty, had her violet velvet eyes, her creamy satin skin and her silken chestnut hair.

"Believe in what?"

"Why in Lance's passion."

"I don't know what you mean by 'believing in it.' I've never been unaware, certainly, of his disposition, from his earliest time, to daub and draw; but I confess I've hoped it would burn out."

"But why should it," she sweetly smiled, "with his wonderful heredity? Passion is passion—though of course indeed *you,* dear Peter, know nothing of that. Has the Master's ever burned out?"

Peter looked off a little and, in his familiar formless way, kept up for a moment, a sound between a smothered whistle and a subdued hum. "Do you think he's going to be another Master?"

She seemed scarce prepared to go that length, yet she had on the whole a marvellous trust. "I know what you mean by that. Will it be a career to incur the jealousies and provoke the machinations that have been at times almost too much for his father? Well—say it may be, since nothing but clap-trap, in these dreadful days, *can,* it would seem, make its way, and since, with the curse of refinement and distinction, one may easily find one's self begging one's bread. Put it at the worst—say he *has* the misfortune to wing his flight further than the vulgar taste of his stupid countrymen can follow. Think, all the same, of the happiness—the same the Master has had. He'll *know*."

Peter looked rueful. "Ah but *what* will he know?"

"Quiet joy!" cried Mrs. Mallow, quite impatient and turning away.

II

HE had of course before long to meet the boy himself on it and to hear that practically everything was settled. Lance was not to go up again, but to go instead to Paris where, since the die was cast, he would find the best advantages. Peter had always felt he must be taken as he was, but had never perhaps found him so much of that pattern as on this occasion. "You chuck Cambridge then altogether? Doesn't that seem rather a pity?"

Lance would have been like his father, to his friend's sense, had he had less humour, and like his mother had he had more beauty. Yet it was a good middle way for Peter that, in the modern manner, he was, to the eye, rather the young stock-broker than the young artist. The youth reasoned that it was a question of time—there was such a mill to go through, such an awful lot to learn. He had talked with fellows and had judged. "One has got, today," he said, "don't you see? to know."

His interlocutor, at this, gave a groan. "Oh hang it, *don't* know!"

Lance wondered. " 'Don't'? Then what's the use—?"

"The use of what?"

"Why of anything. Don't you think I've talent?"

Peter smoked away for a little in silence; then went on: "It isn't knowledge, it's ignorance that—as we've been beautifully told—is bliss."

"Don't you think I've talent?" Lance repeated.

Peter, with his trick of queer kind demonstrations, passed his arm round his godson and held him a moment. "How do I know?"

"Oh," said the boy, "if it's your own ignorance you're defending—!"

Again, for a pause, on the sofa, his godfather smoked. "It isn't. I've the misfortune to be omniscient."

"Oh well," Lance laughed again, "if you know *too* much—!"

"That's what I do, and it's why I'm so wretched."

Lance's gaiety grew. "Wretched? Come, I say!"

"But I forgot," his companion went on—"you're not to know about that. It would indeed for you too make the too much. Only I'll tell you what I'll do." And Peter got up from the sofa. "If you'll go up again I'll pay your way at Cambridge."

Lance stared, a little rueful in spite of being still more amused. "Oh Peter! You disapprove so of Paris?"

"Well, I'm afraid of it."

"Ah I see!"

"No, you don't see—yet. But you will—that is you would. And you mustn't."

The young man thought more gravely. "But one's innocence, already—!"

"Is considerably damaged? Ah that won't matter," Peter persisted—"we'll patch it up here."

"Here? Then you want me to stay at home?"

Peter almost confessed to it. "Well, we're so right—we four together—just as we are. We're so safe. Come, don't spoil it."

The boy, who had turned to gravity, turned from this, on the real pressure in his friend's tone, to consternation. "Then what's a fellow to be?"

"My particular care. Come, old man"—and Peter now fairly pleaded—"*I'll* look out for you."

Lance, who had remained on the sofa with his legs out and his hands in his pockets, watched him with eyes that showed suspicion. Then he got up. "You think there's something the matter with me—that I can't make a success."

"Well, what do you call a success?"

Lance thought again. "Why the best sort, I suppose, is to

please one's self. Isn't that the sort that, in spite of cabals and things, is—in his own peculiar line—the Master's?"

There were so much too many things in this question to be answered at once that they practically checked the discussion, which became particularly difficult in the light of such renewed proof that, though the young man's innocence might, in the course of his studies, as he contended, somewhat have shrunken, the finer essence of it still remained. That was indeed exactly what Peter had assumed and what above all he desired; yet perversely enough it gave him a chill. The boy believed in the cabals and things, believed in the peculiar line, believed, to be brief, in the Master. What happened a month or two later wasn't that he went up again at the expense of his godfather, but that a fortnight after he had got settled in Paris this personage sent him fifty pounds.

He had meanwhile at home, this personage, made up his mind to the worst; and what that might be had never yet grown quite so vivid to him as when, on his presenting himself one Sunday night, as he never failed to do, for supper, the mistress of Carrara Lodge met him with an appeal as to—of all things in the world—the wealth of the Canadians. She was earnest, she was even excited. "Are many of them *really* rich?"

He had to confess he knew nothing about them, but he often thought afterwards of that evening. The room in which they sat was adorned with sundry specimens of the Master's genius, which had the merit of being, as Mrs. Mallow herself frequently suggested, of an unusually convenient size. They were indeed of dimensions not customary in the products of the chisel, and they had the singularity that, if the objects and features intended to be small looked too large, the objects and features intended to be large looked too small. The Master's idea, either in respect to this matter or to any other, had in almost any case, even after years, remained undiscoverable to Peter Brench. The creations that so failed to reveal it stood about on pedestals and brackets, on tables and shelves, a little staring white population, heroic, idyllic, allegoric, mythic, symbolic, in which "scale" had so strayed and lost itself that the public square and the chimney-piece seemed to have changed places, the monumental being all diminutive and the diminutive all monumental; branches at any rate, markedly, of a family in which stature was rather oddly irrespective of function, age and sex. They formed, like the Mallows themselves, poor Brench's own family—having at least to such a degree the note of familiarity. The occasion was one of those he had long ago learnt to know and to name—short flickers of the faint flame, soft gusts of a kinder air. Twice a year regularly the Master believed in his fortune, in addition to believing all the year round in his genius. This time it was to be made by a bereaved couple from Toronto, who had given him the handsomest order for a tomb to three lost children, each of whom they desired to see, in the composition, emblematically and characteristically represented.

Such was naturally the moral of Mrs. Mallow's question: if their wealth was to be assumed, it was clear, from the nature of their admiration, as well as from mysterious hints thrown out (they were a little odd!) as to other possibilities of the same mortuary sort, that their further patronage might be; and not less evident that should the Master become at all known in those climes nothing would be more inevitable than a run of Canadian custom. Peter had been present before at runs of custom, colonial and domestic—present at each of those of which the aggregation had left so few gaps in the marble company round him; but it was his habit never at these junctures to prick the bubble in advance. The fond illusion, while it lasted, eased the wound of elections never won, the long ache of medals and diplomas carried off, on every chance, by every one but the Master; it moreover lighted the lamp that would glimmer through the next eclipse. They lived, however, after all—as it was always beautiful to see—at a height scarce susceptible of ups and downs. They strained a point at times charmingly, strained it to admit that the public was here and there not too bad to buy; but they would have been nowhere without their attitude that the Master was always too good to sell. They were at all events deliciously formed, Peter often said to himself, for their fate; the Master had a vanity, his wife had a loyalty, of which success, depriving these things of innocence, would have diminished the merit and the grace. Any one could be charming under a charm, and as he looked about him at a world of prosperity more void of proportion even than the Master's museum he wondered if he knew another pair that so completely escaped vulgarity.

"What a pity Lance isn't with us to rejoice!" Mrs. Mallow on this occasion sighed at supper.

"We'll drink to the health of the absent," her husband replied, filling his friend's glass and his own and giving a drop to their companion; "but we must hope he's preparing himself for a happiness much less like this of ours this evening—excusable as I grant it to be!—than like the comfort we have always (whatever has happened or has not happened) been able to trust ourselves to enjoy. The comfort," the Master explained, leaning back in the pleasant lamplight and firelight, holding up his glass and looking round at his marble family, quartered more or less, a monstrous brood, in every room—"the comfort of art in itself!"

Peter looked a little shyly at his wine. "Well—I don't care what you may call it when a fellow doesn't—but Lance must learn to *sell,* you know. I drink to his acquisition of the secret of a base popularity!"

"Oh yes, *he* must sell," the boy's mother, who was still more, however, this seemed to give out, the Master's wife, rather artlessly allowed.

"Ah," the sculptor after a moment confidently pronounced, "Lance *will*. Don't be afraid. He'll have learnt."

"Which is exactly what Peter," Mrs. Mallow gaily returned—"why in the world were you so perverse, Peter?—wouldn't when he told him hear of."

Peter, when this lady looked at him with accusatory affection —a grace on her part not infrequent—could never find a word; but the Master, who was always all amenity and tact, helped him out now as he had often helped him before. "That's his old idea, you know—on which we've so often differed: his theory that the artist should be all impulse and instinct. *I* go in of course for a certain amount of school. Not too much—but a due proportion. There's where his protest came in," he continued to explain to his wife, "as against what *might,* don't you see? be in question for Lance."

"Ah well"—and Mrs. Mallow turned the violet eyes across the table at the subject of this discourse—"he's sure to have meant of course nothing but good. Only that wouldn't have prevented him, if Lance *had* taken his advice, from being in effect horribly cruel."

They had a sociable way of talking of him to his face as if he had been in the clay or—at most—in the plaster, and the Master was unfailingly generous. He might have been waving Egidio to make him revolve. "Ah but poor Peter wasn't so wrong as to what it may after all come to that he *will* learn."

"Oh but nothing artistically bad," she urged—still, for poor Peter, arch and dewy.

"Why just the little French tricks," said the Master: on which their friend had to pretend to admit, when pressed by Mrs. Mallow, that these æsthetic vices had been the objects of his dread.

III

"I KNOW now," Lance said to him the next year, "why you were so much against it." He had come back supposedly for a mere interval and was looking about him at Carrara Lodge, where indeed he had already on two or three occasions since his expatriation briefly reappeared. This had the air of a longer holiday. "Something rather awful has happened to me. It *isn't* so very good to know."

"I'm bound to say high spirits don't show in your face," Peter was rather ruefully forced to confess. "Still, are you very sure you do know?"

"Well, I at least know about as much as I can bear." These remarks were exchanged in Peter's den, and the young man, smoking cigarettes, stood before the fire with his back against the mantel. Something of his bloom seemed really to have left him.

Poor Peter wondered. "You're clear then as to what in particular I wanted you not to go for?"

"In particular?" Lance thought. "It seems to me that in particular there can have been only one thing."

They stood for a little sounding each other. "Are you quite sure?"

"Quite sure I'm a beastly duffer? Quite—by this time."

"Oh!"—and Peter turned away as if almost with relief.

"It's *that* that isn't pleasant to find out."

"Oh I don't care for 'that,'" said Peter, presently coming round again. "I mean I personally don't."

"Yet I hope you can understand a little that I myself should!"

"Well, what do you mean by it?" Peter sceptically asked.

And on this Lance had to explain—how the upshot of his studies in Paris had inexorably proved a mere deep doubt of his means. These studies had so waked him up that a new light was in his eyes; but what the new light did was really to show him too much. "Do you know what's the matter with me? I'm too horribly intelligent. Paris was really the last place for me. I've learnt what I can't do."

Poor Peter stared—it was a staggerer; but even after they had had, on the subject, a longish talk in which the boy brought out to the full the hard truth of his lesson, his friend betrayed less pleasure than usually breaks into a face to the happy tune of "I told you so!" Poor Peter himself made now indeed so little a point of having told him so that Lance broke ground in a different place a day or two after. "What was it then that—before I went—you were afraid I should find out?" This, however, Peter refused to tell him—on the ground that if he hadn't yet guessed perhaps he never would, and that in any case nothing at all for either of them was to be gained by giving the thing a name. Lance eyed him on this an instant with the bold curiosity of youth—with the air indeed of having in his mind two or three names, of which one or other would be right. Peter nevertheless, turning his back again, offered no encouragement, and when they parted afresh it was with some show of impatience on the side of the boy. Accordingly on their next encounter Peter saw at a glance that he had now, in the interval, divined and that, to sound his note, he was only waiting till they should find themselves alone. This he had soon arranged and he then broke straight out. "Do you know your conundrum has been keeping me awake? But in the watches of the night the answer came over me—so that, upon my honour, I quite laughed out. Had you been supposing I had to go to Paris to learn *that*?" Even now, to see him still so sublimely on his guard, Peter's young friend had to laugh afresh. "You won't give a sign till you're sure? Beautiful old Peter!" But Lance at last produced it. "Why, hang it, the truth about the Master."

It made between them for some minutes a lively passage, full of wonder for each at the wonder of the other. "Then how long have you understood—"

"The true value of his work? I understood it," Lance recalled, "as soon as I began to understand anything. But I didn't begin fully to do that, I admit, till I got *là-bas*."

"Dear, dear!"—Peter gasped with retrospective dread.

"But for what have you taken me? I'm a hopeless muff—that I *had* to have rubbed in. But I'm not such a muff as the Master!" Lance declared.

"Then why did you never tell me—?"

"That I hadn't, after all"—the boy took him up—"remained such an idiot? Just because I never dreamed *you* knew. But I beg your pardon. I only wanted to spare you. And what I don't now understand is how the deuce then for so long you've managed to keep bottled."

Peter produced his explanation, but only after some delay and with a gravity not void of embarrassment. "It was for your mother."

"Oh!" said Lance.

"And that's the great thing now—since the murder *is* out. I want a promise from you. I mean"—and Peter almost feverishly followed it up—"a vow from you, solemn and such as you owe me here on the spot, that you'll sacrifice anything rather than let her ever guess—"

"That *I've* guessed?"—Lance took it in. "I see." He evidently after a moment had taken in much. "But what is it you've in mind that I may have a chance to sacrifice?"

"Oh one has always something."

Lance looked at him hard. "Do you mean that *you've* had—?" The look he received back, however, so put the question by that he found soon enough another. "Are you really sure my mother doesn't know?"

Peter, after renewed reflexion, was really sure. "If she does she's too wonderful."

"But aren't we all too wonderful?"

"Yes," Peter granted—"but in different ways. The thing's so desperately important because your father's little public consists only, as you know then," Peter developed—"well, of how many?"

"First of all," the Master's son risked, "of himself. And last of all too. I don't quite see of whom else."

Peter had an approach to impatience. "Of your mother, I say —*always*."

Lance cast it all up. "You absolutely feel that?"

"Absolutely."

"Well then with yourself that makes three."

"Oh *me!*"—and Peter, with a wag of his kind old head, modestly excused himself. "The number's at any rate small enough for any individual dropping out to be too dreadfully missed. Therefore, to put it in a nutshell, take care, my boy—that's all—that *you're* not!"

"I've got to keep on humbugging?" Lance wailed.

"It's just to warn you of the danger of your failing of that that I've seized this opportunity."

"And what do you regard in particular," the young man asked, "as the danger?"

"Why this certainty: that the moment your mother, who feels so strongly, should suspect your secret—well," said Peter desperately, "the fat would be on the fire."

Lance for a moment seemed to stare at the blaze. "She'd throw me over?"

"She'd throw *him* over."

"And come round to us?"

Peter, before he answered, turned away. "Come round to *you*." But he had said enough to indicate—and, as he evidently trusted, to avert—the horrid contingency.

IV

WITHIN six months again, none the less, his fear was on more occasions than one all before him. Lance had returned to Paris for another trial; then had reappeared at home and had had, with his father, for the first time in his life, one of the scenes that strike sparks. He described it with much expression to Peter, touching whom (since they had never done so before) it was the sign of a new reserve on the part of the pair at Carrara Lodge that they at present failed, on a matter of intimate interest, to open themselves—if not in joy then in sorrow—to their good friend. This produced perhaps practically between the parties a shade of alienation and a slight intermission of commerce—marked mainly indeed by the fact that to talk at his ease with his old playmate Lance had in general to come to see him. The closest if not quite the gayest relation they had yet known together was thus ushered in. The difficulty for poor Lance was a tension at home—begotten by the fact that his father wished him to be at least the sort of success he himself had been. He hadn't "chucked" Paris—though nothing appeared more vivid to him than that Paris had chucked him: he would go back again because of the fascination in trying, in seeing, in sounding the depths—in learning one's lesson, briefly, even if the lesson were simply that of one's impotence in the presence of one's larger vision. But what did the Master, all aloft in his senseless fluency, know of impotence, and what vision—to be called such—had he in all his blind life ever had? Lance, heated and indignant, frankly appealed to his godparent on this score.

His father, it appeared, had come down on him for having, after so long, nothing to show, and hoped that on his next return this deficiency would be repaired. *The* thing, the Master complacently set forth was—for any artist, however inferior to himself—at least to "do" something. "What can you do? That's all I ask!" *He* had certainly done enough, and there was no mistake about what he had to show. Lance had tears in his eyes when it came thus to letting his old friend know how great the strain might be on the "sacrifice" asked of him. It wasn't so easy to continue humbugging—as from son to parent—after feeling one's self despised for not grovelling in mediocrity. Yet a noble duplicity was what, as they intimately faced the situation, Peter went on requiring; and it was still for a time what his young friend, bitter and sore, managed loyally to comfort him with. Fifty pounds more than once again, it was true, rewarded both in London and in Paris the young friend's loyalty; none the less sensibly, doubtless, at the moment, that the money was a direct advance on a decent sum for which Peter had long since privately prearranged an ultimate function. Whether by these arts or others, at all events, Lance's just resentment was kept for a season—but only for a season—at bay. The day arrived when he warned his companion that he could hold out—or hold in—no longer. Carrara Lodge had had to listen to another lecture delivered from a great height—an infliction really heavier at last than, without striking back or in some way letting the Master have the truth, flesh and blood could bear.

"And what I don't see is," Lance observed with a certain irritated eye for what was after all, if it came to that, owing to himself too; "what I don't see is, upon my honour, how *you,* as things are going, can keep the game up."

"Oh the game for me is only to hold my tongue," said placid Peter. "And I have my reason."

"Still my mother?"

Peter showed a queer face as he had often shown it before—that is by turning it straight away. "What will you have? I haven't ceased to like her."

"She's beautiful—she's a dear of course," Lance allowed; "but what is she to you, after all, and what is it to you that, as to anything whatever, she should or she shouldn't?"

Peter, who had turned red, hung fire a little. "Well—it's all simply what I make of it."

There was now, however, in his young friend a strange, an adopted insistence. "What are you after all to *her*?"

"Oh nothing. But that's another matter."

"She cares only for my father," said Lance the Parisian.

"Naturally—and that's just why."

"Why you've wished to spare her?"

"Because she cares so tremendously much."

Lance took a turn about the room, but with his eyes still on his host. "How awfully—always—you must have liked her!"

"Awfully. Always," said Peter Brench.

The young man continued for a moment to muse—then stopped again in front of him. "Do you know how much she cares?" Their eyes met on it, but Peter, as if his own found something new in Lance's, appeared to hesitate, for the first time in an age, to say he did know. "*I've* only just found out," said Lance. "She came to my room last night, after being present, in silence and only with her eyes on me, at what I had had to take from him: she came—and she was with me an extraordinary hour."

He had paused again and they had again for a while sounded each other. Then something—and it made him suddenly turn pale—came to Peter. "She *does* know?"

"She does know. She let it all out to me—so as to demand of me no more than 'that,' as she said, of which she herself had been capable. She has always, always known," said Lance without pity.

Peter was silent a long time; during which his companion might have heard him gently breathe, and on touching him might have felt within him the vibration of a long low sound suppressed. By the time he spoke at last he had taken everything in. "Then I do see how tremendously much."

"Isn't it wonderful?" Lance asked.

"Wonderful," Peter mused.

"So that if your original effort to keep me from Paris was to keep me from knowledge—!" Lance exclaimed as if with a sufficient indication of this futility.

It might have been at the futility Peter appeared for a little to gaze. "I think it must have been—without my quite at the time knowing it—to keep *me*!" he replied at last as he turned away.

A NOTE ON

THE TREE OF KNOWLEDGE

(1900)

It is partly in an attempt to be fair to the anti-Jacobeans that I have included this little story, of which, by the way, James himself thought rather highly. It is "snobbish"—that is, it deals sympathetically with people who feel themselves superior to most other people. It is "unreal"—that is, the situation on which it turns is statistically rare in human experience. The style is "over-refined"—that is, it is carefully adapted to the extreme tenuity of the theme. The characters do not "matter"—that is, their dilemmas are rarefied mental ones, quite remote from the gross sufferings of average human beings.

"The Tree of Knowledge," true enough, weighs little and decides nothing. Its area is small and it would be silly to claim that its characters are particularly memorable. Yet it seems to me a remarkable story. Whatever final value you assign it, it is impossible to deny that it wrings the last possible droplet of effect out of a theme that to the quick view would seem to have nothing in it.

A lady, speaking to James about the troubles of a certain young painter whose father also had pretentions to the title of artist, said casually, "And then he had found his father out, artistically: having grown up in so happy a personal relation with him only to feel, at last, quite awfully, that he didn't and couldn't believe in him." Out of this sentence came "The Tree of Knowledge," with all its extraordinary complication. Note particularly its clever use of cumulative effect (Peter knows; then Lance reveals that *he* knows; finally it is disclosed that Mrs. Mallow knows, too). There is a subtle twist at the end, which gives us to understand that while Peter had consciously kept the secret out of friendship for the Mallows he had unconsciously done so to prevent himself from ever knowing how deeply and fatally in love with her husband his adored Mrs. Mallow was.

If you are willing to admit into your own universe this small private world of delicate scruples, refined secrets, unexpressed passions, unacknowledged failures, and unlived lives—if you are willing for a half hour to accept all this, the reward is by no means trivial. For it is a fascinating thing to see how densely James can fill this small private world, how much insight into it he has, how completely he renders it up for our examination. Only the exhaustive, Thomas Mann tells us, is truly interesting. "The Tree of Knowledge" is truly interesting, I feel, because it is so exhaustive. It takes something minor and does everything possible with it. It is not important. It is merely perfect.

THE TONE OF TIME

I

I WAS too pleased with what it struck me that, as an old, old friend, I had done for her, not to go to her that very afternoon with the news. I knew she worked late, as in general I also did; but I sacrificed for her sake a good hour of the February daylight. She was in her studio, as I had believed she would be, where her card ("Mary J. Tredick"—not Mary Jane, but Mary Juliana) was manfully on the door; a little tired, a little old and a good deal spotted, but with her ugly spectacles taken off, as soon as I appeared, to greet me. She kept on, while she scraped her palette and wiped her brushes, the big stained apron that covered her from head to foot and that I have often enough before seen her retain in conditions giving the measure of her renunciation of her desire to dazzle. Every fresh reminder of this brought home to me that she had given up everything but her work, and that there had been in her history some reason. But I was as far from the reason as ever. She had given up too much; this was just why one wanted to lend her a hand. I told her, at any rate, that I had a lovely job for her.

"To copy something I do like?"

Her complaint, I knew, was that people only gave orders, if they gave them at all, for things she did not like. But this wasn't a case of copying—not at all, at least, in the common sense. "It's for a portrait—quite in the air."

"Ah, you do portraits yourself!"

"Yes, and you know how. My trick won't serve for this. What's wanted is a pretty picture."

"Then of whom?"

"Of nobody. That is of anybody. Anybody you like."

She naturally wondered. "Do you mean I'm myself to choose my sitter?"

"Well, the oddity is that there is to *be* no sitter."

"Whom then is the picture to represent?"

"Why, a handsome, distinguished, agreeable man, of not more than forty, clean-shaven, thoroughly well-dressed, and a perfect gentleman."

She continued to stare. "And I'm to find him myself?"

I laughed at the term she used. "Yes, as you 'find' the canvas, the colours and the frame." After which I immediately explained. "I've just had the 'rummest' visit, the effect of which was to make me think of you. A lady, unknown to me and unintroduced, turned up at my place at three o'clock. She had come straight, she let me know, without preliminaries, on account of one's high reputation—the usual thing—and of her having admired one's work. Of course I instantly saw—I mean I saw it as soon as she named her affair—that she hadn't understood my work at all. What am I good for in the world but just the impression of the given, the presented case? I can do but the face I see."

"And do you think I can do the face I don't?"

"No, but you see so many more. You see them in fancy and memory, and they've come out, for you, from all the museums you've haunted and all the great things you've studied. I *know* you'll be able to see the one my visitor wants and to give it—what's the *crux* of the business—the tone of time."

She turned the question over. "What does she want it for?"

"Just *for* that—for the tone of time. And, except that it's to hang over her chimney, she didn't tell me. I've only my idea that it's to represent, to symbolise, as it were, her husband, who's not alive and who perhaps never was. This is exactly what will give you a free hand."

"With nothing to go by—no photographs or other portraits?"

"Nothing."

"She only proposes to describe him?"

"Not even; she wants the picture itself to do that. Her only condition is that he be a *très-bel homme*."

She had begun at last, a little thoughtfully, to remove her apron. "Is she French?"

"I don't know. I give it up. She calls herself Mrs. Bridgenorth."

Mary wondered. *"Connais pas!* I never heard of her."

"You wouldn't."

"You mean it's not her real name?"

I hesitated. "I mean that she's a very downright fact, full of the implication that she'll pay a downright price. It's clear to me that you can ask what you like; and it's therefore a chance that I can't consent to your missing." My friend gave no sign either way, and I told my story. "She's a woman of fifty, perhaps of more, who has been pretty, and who still presents herself, with her grey hair a good deal powdered, as I judge, to carry it off, extraordinarily well. She was a little frightened and a little free; the latter because of the former. But she did uncommonly well, I thought, considering the oddity of her wish. This oddity she quite admits; she began indeed by insisting on it so in advance that I found myself expecting I didn't know what. She broke at moments into French, which was perfect, but no better than her English, which isn't vulgar; not more at least than that of everybody else. The things people *do* say, and the way they say them, to artists! She wanted immensely, I could see, not to fail of her errand, not to be treated as absurd; and she was extremely grateful to me for meeting her so far as I did. She was beautifully dressed and she came in a brougham."

My listener took it in; then, very quietly, "Is she respectable?" she inquired.

"Ah, there you are!" I laughed; "and how you always pick the point right out, even when one has endeavoured to diffuse a specious glamour! She's extraordinary," I pursued after an instant; "and just what she wants of the picture, I think, is to make her a little less so."

"Who is she, then? What is she?" my companion simply went on.

It threw me straightway back on one of my hobbies. "Ah, my dear, what is so interesting as life? What is, above all, so stupendous as London? There's everything in it, everything in the world, and nothing too amazing not some day to pop out at you. What is a woman, faded, preserved, pretty, powdered, vague, odd, dropping on one without credentials, but with a carriage and very good lace? What is such a person but a person who *may* have had adventures, and have made them, in one way or another pay? They're, however, none of one's business; it's scarcely on the cards that one should ask her. I should like, with Mrs. Bridgenorth, to see a fellow ask! She goes in for propriety, the real thing. If I suspect her of being the creation of her own talents, she has clearly, on the other hand, seen a lot of life. Will you meet her?" I next demanded.

My hostess waited. "No."

"Then you won't try?"

"Need I meet her to try?" And the question made me guess that, so far as she had understood, she began to feel herself a little taken. "It seems strange," she none the less mused, "to attempt to please her on such a basis. To attempt," she presently added, "to please her at all. It's your idea that she's not married?" she, with this, a trifle inconsequently asked.

"Well," I replied, "I've only had an hour to think of it, but I somehow already see the scene. Not immediately, not the day after, or even perhaps the year after the thing she desires is set up there, but in due process of time and on convenient opportunity, the transfiguration will occur. 'Who is that awfully handsome man?' 'That? Oh, that's an old sketch of my dear dead husband.' Because I told her—insidiously sounding her—that she would want it to look old, and that the tone of time is exactly what you're full of."

"I believe I am," Mary sighed at last.

"Then put on your hat." I had proposed to her on my arrival

to come out to tea with me, and it was when left alone in the studio while she went to her room that I began to feel sure of the success of my errand. The vision that had an hour before determined me grew deeper and brighter for her while I moved about and looked at her things. There were more of them there on her hands than one liked to see; but at least they sharpened my confidence, which was pleasant for me in view of that of my visitor, who had accepted without reserve my plea for Miss Tredick. Four or five of her copies of famous portraits—ornaments of great public and private collections—were on the walls, and to see them again together was to feel at ease about my guarantee. The mellow manner of them was what I had had in my mind in saying, to excuse myself to Mrs. Bridgenorth, "Oh, my things, you know, look as if they had been painted tomorrow!" It made no difference that Mary's Vandykes and Gainsboroughs were reproductions and replicas, for I had known her more than once to amuse herself with doing the thing quite, as she called it, off her own bat. She had copied so bravely so many brave things that she had at the end of her brush an extraordinary bag of tricks. She had always replied to me that such things were mere clever humbug, but mere clever humbug was what our client happened to want. The thing was to let her have it—one could trust her for the rest. And at the same time that I mused in this way I observed to myself that there was already something more than, as the phrase is, met the eye in such response as I felt my friend had made. I had touched, without intention, more than one spring; I had set in motion more than one impulse. I found myself indeed quite certain of this after she had come back in her hat and her jacket. She was different—her idea had flowered; and she smiled at me from under her tense veil, while she drew over her firm, narrow hands a pair of fresh gloves, with a light distinctly new. "Please tell your friend that I'm greatly obliged to both of you and that I take the order."

"Good. And to give him all his good looks?"

"It's just to do *that* that I accept. I shall make him supremely beautiful—and supremely base."

"Base?" I just demurred.

"The finest gentleman you'll ever have seen, and the worst friend."

I wondered, as I was startled; but after an instant I laughed for joy. "Ah well, so long as he's not mine! I see we *shall* have him," I said as we went, for truly I had touched a spring. In fact I had touched *the* spring.

It rang, more or less, I was presently to find, all over the place. I went, as I had promised, to report to Mrs. Bridgenorth on my mission, and though she declared herself much gratified at the success of it I could see she a little resented the apparent absence of any desire on Miss Tredick's part for a preliminary conference. "I only thought she might have liked just to see me, and have imagined I might like to see *her*."

But I was full of comfort. "You'll see her when it's finished. You'll see her in time to thank her."

"And to pay her, I suppose," my hostess laughed, with an asperity that was, after all, not excessive. "Will she take very long?"

I thought. "She's so full of it that my impression would be that she'll do it off at a heat."

"She *is* full of it then?" she asked; and on hearing to what tune, though I told her but half, she broke out with admiration. "You artists are the most extraordinary people!" It was almost with a bad conscience that I confessed we indeed were, and while she said that what she meant was that we seemed to understand everything, and I rejoined that this was also what *I* meant, she took me into another room to see the place for the picture—a proceeding of which the effect was singularly to confirm the truth in question. The place for the picture—in her own room, as she called it, a boudoir at the back, overlooking the general garden of the approved modern row and, as she said, only just wanting that touch—proved exactly the place (the space of a large panel in the white woodwork over the mantel) that I had spoken of to my friend. She put it quite candidly, "Don't you see what it will do?" and looked at me, wonderfully, as for a sign that I could sympathetically take from her what she didn't literally say. She said it, poor woman, so very nearly that I had no difficulty whatever. The portrait, tastefully enshrined there, of the finest gentleman one should ever have seen, would do even more for herself than it would do for the room.

I may as well mention at once that my observation of Mrs. Bridgenorth was not in the least of a nature to unseat me from the hobby I have already named. In the light of the impression she made on me life seemed quite as prodigious and London quite as amazing as I had ever contended, and nothing could have been more in the key of that experience than the manner in which everything was vivid between us and nothing expressed. We remained on the surface with the tenacity of shipwrecked persons clinging to a plank. Our plank was our concentrated gaze at Mrs. Bridgenorth's mere present. We allowed her past to exist for us only in the form of the prettiness that she had gallantly rescued from it and to which a few scraps of its identity still adhered. She was amiable, gentle, consistently proper. She gave me more than anything else the sense, simply of waiting. She was like a house so freshly and successfully "done up" that you were surprised it wasn't occupied. She was waiting for something to happen—for somebody to come. She was waiting, above all, for Mary Tredick's work. She clearly counted that it would help her.

I had foreseen the fact—the picture was produced at a heat; rapidly, directly, at all events, for the sort of thing it proved to be. I left my friend alone at first, left the ferment to work, troubling her with no questions and asking her for no news; two or three weeks passed, and I never went near her. Then at last, one afternoon as the light was failing, I looked in. She immediately knew what I wanted. "Oh yes, I'm doing him."

"Well," I said, "I've respected your intensity, but I *have* felt curious."

I may not perhaps say that she was never so sad as when she laughed, but it's certain that she always laughed when she was sad. When, however, poor dear, for that matter, was she secretly, not? Her little gasps of mirth were the mark of her worst moments. But why should she have one of these just now? "Oh, I know your curiosity!" she replied to me; and the small chill of her amusement scarcely met it. "He's coming out, but I can't show him to you yet. I must muddle it through in my own way. It has insisted on being, after all, a 'likeness,'" she added. "But nobody will ever know."

"Nobody?"

"Nobody *she* sees."

"Ah, she doesn't, poor thing," I returned, "seem to see anybody!"

"So much the better. I'll risk it." On which I felt I should have to wait, though I had suddenly grown impatient. But I still hung about, and while I did so she explained. "If what I've done is really a portrait, the condition itself prescribed it. If I was to do the most beautiful man in the world I could do but one."

We looked at each other; then I laughed. "It can scarcely be *me*! But you're getting," I asked, "the great thing?"

"The infamy? Oh yes, please God."

It took away my breath a little, and I even for the moment scarce felt at liberty to press. But one could always be cheerful. "What I meant is the tone of time."

"Getting it, my dear man? Didn't I get it long ago? Don't I *show* it—the tone of time?" she suddenly, strangely sighed at me, with something in her face I had never yet seen. "I can't give it to him more than—for all these years—he was to have given it to *me*."

I scarce knew what smothered passion, what remembered wrong, what mixture of joy and pain my words had accidentally quickened. Such an effect of them could only become, for me, an instant pity, which, however, I brought out but indirectly. "It's the tone," I smiled, "in which you're speaking now."

This served, unfortunately, as something of a check. "I didn't mean to speak now." Then with her eyes on the picture, "I've said everything there. Come back," she added, "in three days. He'll be all right."

He was indeed when at last I saw him. She had produced an extraordinary thing—a thing wonderful, ideal, for the part it was to play. My only reserve, from the first, was that it was too fine for its part, that something much less "sincere" would equally have served Mrs. Bridgenorth's purpose, and that relegation to that lady's "own room"—whatever charm it was to work there—might only mean for it cruel obscurity. The picture is before me now, so that I could describe it if description availed. It represents a man of about five-and-thirty, seen only as to the head and shoulders, but dressed, the observer gathers, in a fashion now almost antique and which was far from contemporaneous with the date of the work. His high, slightly narrow face, which would be perhaps too aquiline but for the beauty of the forehead and the sweetness of the mouth, has a charm that even, after all these years, still stirs my imagination. His type has altogether a distinction that you feel to have been firmly caught and yet not vulgarly emphasised. The eyes are just too near together, but they are, in a wondrous way, both careless and intense, while lip, cheek, and chin, smooth and clear, are admirably drawn. Youth is still, you see, in all his presence, the joy and pride of life, the perfection of a high spirit and the expectation of a great fortune, which he takes for granted with unconscious insolence. Nothing has ever happened to humiliate or disappoint him, and if my fancy doesn't run away with me the whole presentation of him is a guarantee that he will die without having suffered. He is so handsome in short, that you can scarcely say what he means, and so happy that you can scarcely guess what he feels.

It is of course, I hasten to add, an appreciably feminine rendering, light, delicate, vague, imperfectly synthetic—insistent and evasive, above all, in the wrong places; but the composition, none the less, is beautiful and the suggestion infinite. The grandest air of the thing struck me in fact, when first I saw it, as coming from the high artistic impertinence with which it offered itself as painted about 1850. It would have been a rare flower of refinement for that dark day. The "tone"—that of such a past as it pretended to—was there almost to excess, a brown bloom into which the image seemed mysteriously to retreat. The subject of it looks at me now across more years and more knowledge, but what I felt at the moment was that he managed to be at once a triumphant trick and a plausible evocation. He hushed me, I remember, with so many kinds of awe that I shouldn't have dreamt of asking who he was. All I said, after my first incoherences of wonder at my friend's practised skill, was: "And you've arrived at this truth without documents?"

"It depends on what you call documents."

"Without notes, sketches, studies?"

"I destroyed them years ago."

"Then you once had them?"

She just hung fire. "I once had everything."

It told me both more and less than I had asked; enough at all events to make my next question, as I uttered it, sound even to myself a little foolish. "So that it's all memory?"

From where she stood she looked once more at her work; after which she jerked away and, taking several steps, came back to me with something new—whatever it was I had already seen—in her air and answer. "It's all *hate*!" she threw at me, and then went out of the room. It was not till she had gone that I quite understood why. Extremely affected by the impression visibly made on me, she had burst into tears but had wished me not to see them. She left me alone for some time with her wonderful subject, and I again, in her absence, made things out. He was dead—he had been dead for years; the sole humiliation, as I have called it, that he was to know had come to him in that form. The canvas held and cherished him, in any case, as it only holds the dead. She had suffered from him, it came to me, the worst that a woman can suffer, and the wound he had dealt her, though hidden, had never effectually healed. It had bled again while she worked. Yet when she at last reappeared there was but one thing to say. "The beauty, heaven knows, I see. But I don't see what you call the infamy."

She gave him a last look—again she turned away. "Oh, he was like that."

"Well, whatever he was like," I remember replying, "I wonder you can bear to part with him. Isn't it better to let her see the picture first here?"

As to this she doubted. "I don't think I want her to come."

I wondered. "You continue to object so to meet her?"

"What good will it do? It's quite impossible I should alter him for her."

"Oh, she won't want *that*!" I laughed. "She'll adore him as he is."

"Are you quite sure of your idea?"

"That he's to figure as Mr. Bridgenorth? Well, if I hadn't been from the first, my dear lady, I should be now. Fancy, with the chance, her *not* jumping at him! Yes, he'll figure as Mr. Bridgenorth."

"Mr. Bridgenorth!" she echoed, making the sound, with her small, cold laugh, grotesquely poor for him. He might really have been a prince, and I wondered if he hadn't been. She had, at all events, a new notion. "Do you mind my having it taken to your place and letting her come to see it there?" Which—as I immediately embraced her proposal, deferring to her reasons, whatever they were—was what was speedily arranged.

II

The next day therefore I had the picture in charge, and on the following Mrs. Bridgenorth, whom I had notified, arrived. I had placed it, framed and on an easel, well in evidence, and I have never forgotten the look and the cry that, as she became aware of it, leaped into her face and from her lips. It was an extraordinary moment, all the more that it found me quite unprepared—so extraordinary that I scarce knew at first what had happened. By the time I really perceived, moreover, more things had happened than one, so that when I pulled myself together it was to face the situation as a whole. She had recognised on the instant the subject; that came first and was irrepressibly vivid in her. Her recognition had, for the length of a flash, lighted for her the possibility that the stroke had been directed. That came second, and she flushed with it as with a blow in the face. What came third—and it was what was really most wondrous—was the quick instinct of getting both her strange recognition and her blind suspicion well in hand. She couldn't control, however, poor woman, the strong colour in her face and the quick tears in her eyes. She could only glare at the canvas, gasping, grimacing, and try to gain time. Whether in surprise or in resentment she intensely reflected, feeling more than anything else how little she might prudently show; and I was conscious even at the moment that nothing of its kind could have been finer than her effort to swallow her shock in ten seconds.

How many seconds she took I didn't measure; enough, assuredly, for me also to profit. I gained more time than she, and the greatest oddity doubtless was my own private manœuvre—the quickest calculation that, acting from a mere confused instinct, I had ever made. If she had known the great gentleman represented there and yet had determined on the spot to carry herself as ignorant, all my loyalty to Mary Tredick came to the surface in a prompt counter-move. What gave me opportunity was the red in her cheek. "Why, you've known him!"

I saw her ask herself for an instant if she mightn't successfully make her startled state pass as the mere glow of pleasure—her natural greeting to her acquisition. She was pathetically, yet at the same time almost comically, divided. Her line was so to cover her tracks that every avowal of a past connection was a danger; but it also concerned her safety to learn, in the light of our astounding coincidence, how far she already stood exposed. She meanwhile begged the question. She smiled through her tears. "He's too magnificent!"

But I gave her, as I say, all too little time. "Who is he? Who *was* he?"

It must have been my look still more than my words that determined her. She wavered but an instant longer, panted, laughed, cried again, and then, dropping into the nearest seat, gave herself up so completely that I was almost ashamed. "Do you think I'd tell you his *name*?" The burden of the backward years—all the effaced and ignored—lived again, almost like an accent unlearned but freshly breaking out at a touch, in the very sound of the words. These perceptions she, however, the next thing showed me, were a game at which two could play. She had to look at me but an instant. "Why, you really *don't* know it!"

I judged best to be frank. "I don't know it."

"Then how does *she*?"

"How do you?" I laughed. "I'm a different matter."

She sat a minute turning things round, staring at the picture. "The likeness, the likeness!" It was almost too much.

"It's so true?"

"Beyond everything."

I considered. "But a resemblance to a known individual—that wasn't what you wanted."

She sprang up at this in eager protest. "Ah, no one else would see it."

I showed again, I fear, my amusement. "No one but you and she?"

"It's her doing *him*!" She was held by her wonder. "Doesn't she, on your honour, know?"

"That his is the very head you would have liked if you had dared? Not a bit. How *should* she? She knows nothing—on my honour."

Mrs. Bridgenorth continued to marvel. "She just painted him for the kind of face—?"

"That corresponds with my description of what you wished? Precisely."

"But *how*—after so long? From memory? As a friend?"

"As a reminiscence—yes. Visual memory, you see, in our uncanny race, is wonderful. As the ideal thing, simply, for your purpose. You *are* then suited?" I, after an instant added.

She had again been gazing, and at this turned her eyes on me; but I saw she couldn't speak, couldn't do more at least than sound, unutterably, "Suited!" so that I was positively not surprised when suddenly—just as Mary had done, the power to produce this effect seeming a property of the model—she burst into tears. I feel no harsher in relating it, however I may appear, than I did at the moment, but it is a fact that while she just wept I literally had a fresh inspiration on behalf of Miss Tredick's interests. I knew exactly, moreover, before my companion had recovered herself, what she would next ask me; and I consciously brought this appeal on in order to have it over. I explained that I had not the least idea of the identity of our artist's sitter, to which she had given me no clue. I had nothing but my impression that she had known him—known him well; and, from whatever material she had worked, the fact of his having also been known to Mrs. Bridgenorth was a coincidence pure and simple. It partook of the nature of prodigy, but such prodigies did occur. My visitor listened with avidity and credulity. She was so far reassured. Then I saw her question come. "Well, if she doesn't dream he was ever anything to me—or what he will be now—I'm going to ask you, as a very particular favour, never to tell her. She will want to know of course exactly how I've been struck. You'll naturally say that I'm delighted, but may I exact from you that you say nothing else?"

There was supplication in her face, but I had to think. "There are conditions I must put to you first, and one of them is also a question, only more frank than yours. Was this mysterious personage—frustrated by death—to have married you?"

She met it bravely. "Certainly, if he had lived."

I was only amused at an artlessness in her "certainly." "Very good. But why do you wish the coincidence—"

"Kept from her?" She knew exactly why. "Because if she suspects it she won't let me have the picture. Therefore," she added with decision, "you must let me pay for it on the spot."

"What do you mean by on the spot?"

"I'll send you a cheque as soon as I get home."

"Oh," I laughed, "let us understand. Why do you consider she won't let you have the picture?"

She made me wait a little for this, but when it came it was perfectly lucid. "Because she'll then see how much more I must want it."

"How much less—wouldn't it be rather, since the bargain was, as the more convenient thing, not for a likeness?"

"Oh," said Mrs. Bridgenorth with impatience, "the likeness will take care of itself. She'll put this and that together." Then she brought out her real apprehension. "She'll be jealous."

"Oh!" I laughed. But I was startled.

"She'll hate me!"

I wondered. "But I don't think she liked him."

"Don't think?" She stared at me, with her echo, over all that might be in it, then seemed to find little enough. "I *say*!"

It was almost comically the old Mrs. Bridgenorth. "But I gather from her that he was bad."

"Then what was *she*?"

I barely hesitated. "What were *you*?"

"That's my own business." And she turned again to the picture. "He was good enough for her to do *that* of him."

I took it in once more. "Artistically speaking, for the way it's done, it's one of the most curious things I've ever seen."

"It's a grand treat!" said poor Mrs. Bridgenorth more simply.

It was, it *is* really; which is exactly what made the case so interesting. "Yet I feel somehow that, as I say, it wasn't done with love."

It was wonderful how she understood. "It was done with rage."

"Then what have you to fear?"

She knew again perfectly. "What happened when he made *me* jealous. So such," she declared, "that if you'll give me your word for silence—"

"Well?"

"Why, I'll double the money."

"Oh," I replied, taking a turn about in the excitement of our concurrence, "that's exactly what—to do a still better stroke for her—it had just come to *me* to propose!"

"It's understood then, on your oath, as a gentleman?" She was so eager that practically this settled it, though I moved to and fro a little while she watched me in suspense. It vibrated all round us that she had gone out to the thing in a stifled flare, that a whole close relation had in the few minutes revived. We know it of the truly amiable person that he will strain a point for another that he wouldn't strain for himself. The stroke to put in for Mary was positively prescribed. The work represented really much more than had been covenanted, and if the purchaser chose so to value it this was her own affair. I decided. "If it's understood also on *your* word."

We were so at one that we shook hands on it. "And when may I send?"

"Well, I shall see her this evening. Say early tomorrow."

"Early tomorrow." And I went with her to her brougham,

into which, I remember, as she took leave, she expressed regret that she mightn't then and there have introduced the canvas for removal. I consoled her with remarking that she couldn't have got it in—which was not quite true.

I saw Mary Tredick before dinner, and though I was not quite ideally sure of my present ground with her I instantly brought out my news. "She's so delighted that I felt I must in conscience do something still better for you. She's not to have it on the original terms. I've put up the price."

Mary wondered. "But to what?"

"Well, to four hundred. If you say so, I'll try even for five."

"Oh, she'll never give that."

"I beg your pardon."

"After the agreement?" She looked grave. "I don't like such leaps and bounds."

"But, my dear child, they're yours. You contracted for a decorative trifle, and you've produced a breathing masterpiece."

She thought. "Is that what she calls it?" Then, as having to think too, I hesitated, "What does she know?" she pursued.

"She knows she wants it."

"So much as that?"

At this I had to brace myself a little. "So much that she'll send me the cheque this afternoon, and that you'll have mine by the first post in the morning."

"Before she has even received the picture?"

"Oh, she'll send for it tomorrow." And as I was dining out and had still to dress, my time was up. Mary came with me to the door, where I repeated my assurance. "You shall receive my cheque by the first post." To which I added: "If it's little enough for a lady so much in need to pay for *any* husband, it isn't worth mentioning as the price of such a one as you've given her!"

I was in a hurry, but she held me. "Then you've felt your idea confirmed?"

"My idea?"

"That that's what I *have* given her?"

I suddenly fancied I had perhaps gone too far; but I had kept my cab and was already in it. "Well, put it," I called with excess of humour over the front, "that you've, at any rate, given *him* a wife!"

When on my return from dinner that night I let myself in, my first care, in my dusty studio, was to make light for another look at Mary's subject. I felt the impulse to bid him good night, but, to my astonishment, he was no longer there. His place was a void—he had already disappeared. I saw, however, after my first surprise, what had happened—saw it moreover, frankly, with some relief. As my servants were in bed I could ask no questions, but it was clear that Mrs. Bridgenorth, whose note, containing its cheque, lay on my table, had been after all unable to wait. The note, I found, mentioned nothing but the enclosure; but it had come by hand, and it was her silence that told the tale. Her messenger had been instructed to "act"; he had come with a vehicle, he had transferred to it canvas and frame. The prize was now therefore landed and the incident closed. I didn't altogether, the next morning, know why, but I had slept the better for the sense of these things, and as soon as my attendant came in I asked for details. It was on this that his answer surprised me. "No, sir, there was no man; she came herself. She had only a four-wheeler, but I helped her, and we got it in. It was a squeeze, sir, but she *would* take it."

I wondered. "She had a four-wheeler? and not her servant?"

"No, no, sir. She came, as you may say, single-handed."

"And not even in her brougham, which would have been larger."

My man, with his habit, weighed it. "But *have* she a brougham, sir?"

"Why, the one she was here in yesterday."

Then light broke. "Oh, *that* lady! It wasn't her, sir. It was Miss Tredick."

Light broke, but darkness a little followed it—a darkness

that, after breakfast, guided my steps back to my friend. There, in its own first place, I met her creation; but I saw it would be a different thing meeting *her*. She immediately put down on a table, as if she had expected me, the cheque I had sent her overnight. "Yes, I've brought it away. And I can't take the money."

I found myself in despair. "You want to keep him?"

"I don't understand what has happened."

"You just back out?"

"I don't understand," she repeated, "what has happened." But what I had already perceived was, on the contrary, that she very nearly, that she in fact quite remarkably, did understand. It was as if in my zeal I had given away my case, and I felt that my test was coming. She had been thinking all night with intensity, and Mrs. Bridgenorth's generosity, coupled with Mrs. Bridgenorth's promptitude, had kept her awake. Thence, for a woman nervous and critical, imaginations, visions, questions. "Why, in writing me last night, did you take for granted it was *she* who had swooped down? Why," asked Mary Tredick, "should she swoop?"

Well, if I could drive a bargain for Mary, I felt I could *a fortiori* lie for her. "Because it's her way. She does swoop. She's impatient and uncontrolled. And it's affectation for you to pretend," I said with diplomacy, "that you see no reason for her falling in love—"

"Falling in love?" She took me straight up.

"With that gentleman. Certainly. What woman wouldn't? What woman didn't? I really don't see, you know, your right to back out."

"I won't back out," she presently returned, "if you'll answer me a question. Does she know the man represented?" Then as I hung fire: "It has come to me that she must. It would account for so much. For the strange way I feel," she went on, "and for the extraordinary sum you've been able to extract from her."

It was a pity, and I flushed with it, besides wincing at the word she used. But Mrs. Bridgenorth and I, between us, had clearly made the figure too high. "You think that, if she *had* guessed, I would naturally work it to 'extract' more?"

She turned away from me on this and, looking blank in her trouble, moved vaguely about. Then she stopped. "I see him set up there. I hear her say it. What you said she would make him pass for."

I believe I foolishly tried—though only for an instant—to look as if I didn't remember what I had said. "Her husband?"

"He wasn't."

The next minute I had risked it. "Was he yours?"

I don't know what I had expected, but I found myself surprised at her mere pacific headshake. "No."

"Then why mayn't he have been—?"

"Another woman's? Because he died, to my absolute knowledge, unmarried." She spoke as quietly. "He had known many women, and there was one in particular with whom he became—and too long remained—ruinously intimate. She tried to make him marry her, and he was very near it. Death, however, saved him. But she was the reason—"

"Yes?" I feared again from her a wave of pain, and I went on while she kept it back. "Did you know her?"

"She was one I wouldn't." Then she brought it out. "She was the reason he failed me." Her successful detachment somehow said all, reduced me to a flat, kind "Oh!" that marked my sense of her telling me, against my expectation, more than I knew what to do with. But it was just while I wondered how to turn her confidence that she repeated, in a changed voice, her challenge of a moment before. "Does she know the man represented?"

"I haven't the least idea." And having so acquitted myself I added, with what strikes me now as futility: "She certainly—yesterday—didn't name him."

"Only recognised him?"

"If she did she brilliantly concealed it."

"So that you got nothing from her?"

It was a question that offered me a certain advantage. "I thought you accused me of getting too much."

She gave me a long look, and I now saw everything in her face. "It's very nice—what you're doing for me, and you do it handsomely. It's beautiful—beautiful, and I thank you with all my heart. But I know."

"And what do you know?"

She went about now preparing her usual work. "What he must have been to her."

"You mean she was the person?"

"Well," she said, putting on her old spectacles, "she was one of them."

"And you accept so easily the astounding coincidence—?"

"Of my finding myself, after years, in so extraordinary a relation with her? What do you call easily? I've passed a night of torment."

"But what put it into your head—?"

"That I had so blindly and strangely given him back to her? *You* put it—yesterday."

"And how?"

"I can't tell you. You didn't in the least mean to—on the contrary. But you dropped the seed. The plant, after you had gone," she said with a businesslike pull at her easel, "the plant began to grow. I *saw* them there—in your studio—face to face."

"You were jealous?" I laughed.

She gave me through her glasses another look, and they seemed, from this moment, in their queerness, to have placed her quite on the other side of the gulf of time. She was firm there; she was settled; I couldn't get at her now. "I see she told you I *would* be." I doubtless kept down too little my start at it, and she immediately pursued. "You say I accept the coincidence, which is of course prodigious. But such things happen. Why shouldn't I accept it if you do?"

"*Do* I?" I smiled.

She began her work in silence, but she presently exclaimed: "I'm glad I didn't meet her!"

"I don't yet see why you wouldn't."

"Neither do I. It was an instinct."

"Your instincts"—I tried to be ironic—"are miraculous."

"They *have* to be, to meet such accidents. I must ask you kindly to tell her, when you return her gift, that now I have done the picture I find I must after all keep it for myself."

"Giving no reason?"

She painted away. "She'll know the reason."

Well, by this time I knew it too; I knew so many things that I fear my resistance was weak. If our wonderful client hadn't been his wife in fact, she was not to be helped to become his wife in fiction. I knew almost more than I can say, more at any rate than I could then betray. He had been bound in common mercy to stand by my friend, and he had basely forsaken her. This indeed brought up the obscure, into which I shyly gazed. "Why, even granting your theory, should you grudge her the portrait? It was painted in bitterness."

"Yes. Without that—!"

"It wouldn't have come? Precisely. Is it in bitterness, then, you'll keep it?"

She looked up from her canvas. "In what would *you* keep it?"

It made me jump. "Do you mean I *may*?" Then I had my idea. "I'd give you her price for it!"

Her smile through her glasses was beautiful. "And afterwards make it over to her? You shall have it when I die." With which she came away from her easel, and I saw that I was staying her work and should properly go. So I put out my hand to her. "It took—whatever you will!—to paint it," she said, "but I shall keep it in joy." I could answer nothing now—had to cease to pretend; the thing was in her hands. For a moment we stood there, and I had again the sense, melancholy and final, of her being, as it were, remotely glazed and fixed into what she had done. "He's taken from me, and for all those years he's kept. Then she herself, by a prodigy—!" She lost herself again in the wonder of it.

"Unwittingly gives him back?"

She fairly, for an instant over the marvel, closed her eyes. "Gives him back."

Then it was I saw how he would be kept! But it was the end of my vision. I could only write, ruefully enough, to Mrs. Bridgenorth, whom I never met again, but of whose death—preceding by a couple of years Mary Tredick's—I happened to hear. This is an old man's tale. I have inherited the picture, in the deep beauty of which, however, darkness still lurks. No one, strange to say, has ever recognised the model, but everyone asks his name. I don't even know it.

A NOTE ON

THE TONE OF TIME

(1900)

"THE TONE OF TIME" is the only story here collected that James himself did not deem worthy of inclusion in the New York Edition that represented his winnowed best. I think that in this case his superb powers of discrimination for once failed him. "The Tone of Time" strikes me as a tale in which there is developed, with the most delicate irony, a situation of subtle appeal. The situation is, of course, among the oldest in human experience, being that of two women disputing the possession of a man. The Jamesian difference lies in the fact that this particular man is made up of streaks of pigment and the grain of canvas. It is James's habit to take something non-human (here it is a picture, in his novel "The Spoils of Poynton" a houseful of furniture) and generate around it the most absolute of passions. For all its urbane tone, "The Tone of Time" vibrates with hatred, love, jealousy and despair. It is no less a tale of passion because the begetter of that passion is a painted simulacrum of a dead man. Here, as in many other instances, James demonstrates that a certain removal from reality can produce an atmosphere so dense, so rich that by contrast a faithful naturalism seems anemic.

A persuasive case could be developed in defense of the proposition that, of all nineteenth-century novelists, Balzac and James knew women best—Balzac, the most "masculine" of men, and James, surely among the least. Balzac studied women as he might have studied a language or explored an unknown land; whereas the women in James's stories seem to have flowed perfectly, easily from his mind, through his pen-point, onto paper. James's knowledge seems immediate, or, as we vaguely say, intuitive; it does not appear to be the consequence of direct experience.

Of this immediacy of apprehension there are several dozen great examples in his novels. Mary Tredick and Mrs. Bridgenorth are two small but no less convincing ones. Short as the tale is, and concentrated on the exhaustion of a single, isolated situation, it nevertheless manages to render for us, quite wholly, two women. Their behavior, face to face with what each loves (or hates, it does not matter) best, illuminates, though only for a brief moment, their real characters. The way, for instance, in which Mary Tredick reaches the conclusion that Mrs. Bridgenorth must have known the original of the portrait—a curious exercise in ratiocination—gives us Mary Tredick as an individual at the same time that it gives us Mary Tredick as a woman. Substitute two men for Mary Tredick and Mrs. Bridgenorth and change the portrait into that of a woman: the whole tale collapses. "The Tone of Time" seems to be built merely around an ingenious—some would say tricky—idea. It is only after we have reflected on its subtleties that we perceive the function of the ingenious idea, to serve as a stage on which James may dramatize his insights into the psychology of women.

"The Tone of Time," by the way, is one of many James stories in which portraits play a considerable rôle. I have never been able to convince myself that James had any deep feeling for the art of painting. His taste—he liked Sargent—was that of the upper-class gentleman of his time, class-bound, rather unimaginative. His enthusiasms were confined largely to the traditionally accepted. Of the business and trade of painting he had a considerable knowledge, but the thing itself seems to have eluded him. His judgments, particularly of the Renaissance Italians, are marked by conventionality edged with snobbery, and he was often unable (see his essay on Du Maurier) to separate whatever genuine taste he had from his merely social prejudices. To these strictures, however, at least one exception must be made—his magnificent, startlingly humane and perceptive treatment of Daumier, whose greatness he sensed at a time when Daumier was generally considered little more than a first-rate cartoonist.

When James mentions music—he does so but rarely—he is even more perilously out of his element. In fact, it might be said that men, women, and the art of writing constitute the world in which he knew his way around. It has proved spacious enough.

MRS. MEDWIN

I

"Well, we *are* a pair!" the poor lady's visitor broke out to her at the end of her explanation in a manner disconcerting enough. The poor lady was Miss Cutter, who lived in South Audley Street, where she had an "upper half" so concise that it had to pass boldly for convenient; and her visitor was her half-brother, whom she hadn't seen for three years. She was remarkable for a maturity of which every symptom might have been observed to be admirably controlled, had not a tendency to stoutness just affirmed its independence. Her present, no doubt, insisted too much on her past, but with the excuse, sufficiently valid, that she must certainly once have been prettier. She was clearly not contented with once—she wished to be prettier again. She neglected nothing that could produce that illusion, and, being both fair and fat, dressed almost wholly in black. When she added a little colour it was not, at any rate, to her drapery. Her small rooms had the peculiarity that everything they contained appeared to testify with vividness to her position in society, quite as if they had been furnished by the bounty of admiring friends. They were adorned indeed almost exclusively with objects that nobody buys, as had more than once been remarked by spectators of her own sex, for herself, and would have been luxurious if luxury consisted mainly in photographic portraits slashed across with signatures, in baskets of flowers beribboned with the cards of passing compatriots, and in a neat collection of red volumes, blue volumes, alphabetical volumes, aids to London lucidity, of every sort, devoted to addresses and engagements. To be in Miss Cutter's tiny drawing-room, in short, even with Miss Cutter alone—should you by any chance have found her so—was somehow to be in the world and in a crowd. It was like an agency—it bristled with particulars.

This was what the tall lean loose gentleman lounging there before her might have have appeared to read in the suggestive scene over which, while she talked to him, his eyes moved without haste and without rest. "Oh come, Mamie!" he occasionally threw off; and the words were evidently connected with the impression thus absorbed. His comparative youth spoke of waste even as her positive—her too positive—spoke of economy. There was only one thing, that is, to make up in him for everything he had lost, though it was distinct enough indeed that this thing might sometimes serve. It consisted in the perfection of an indifference, an indifference at the present moment directed to the plea—a plea of inability, of pure destitution—with which his sister had met him. Yet it had even now a wider embrace, took in quite sufficiently all consequences of queerness, confessed in advance to the false note that, in such a setting, he almost excruciatingly constituted. He cared as little that he looked at moments all his impudence as that he looked all his shabbiness, all his cleverness, all his history. These different things were written in him—in his premature baldness, his seamed strained face, the lapse from bravery of his long tawny moustache; above all in his easy friendly universally acquainted eye, so much too sociable for mere conversation. What possible relation with him could be natural enough to meet it? He wore a scant rough Inverness cape and a pair of black trousers, wanting in substance and marked with the sheen of time, that had presumably once served for evening use. He spoke with the slowness helplessly permitted to Americans—as something too slow to be stopped—and he repeated that he found himself associated with Miss Cutter in a harmony calling for wonder. She had been telling him not only that she couldn't possibly give him ten pounds, but that his unexpected arrival, should he insist on being much in view, might seriously interfere with arrangements necessary to her own maintenance; on which he had begun by replying that he of course knew she had long ago spent her money, but that he looked to her now exactly because she had, without the aid of that convenience, mastered the art of life.

"I'd really go away with a fiver, my dear, if you'd only tell me how you do it. It's no use saying only, as you've always said, that 'people are very kind to you.' What the devil are they kind to you *for*?"

"Well, one reason is precisely that no particular inconvenience has hitherto been supposed to attach to me. I'm just what I am," said Mamie Cutter; "nothing less and nothing more. It's awkward to have to explain to you, which moreover I really needn't in the least. I'm clever and amusing and charming." She was uneasy and even frightened, but she kept her temper and met him with a grace of her own. "I don't think you ought to ask me more questions than I ask you."

"Ah my dear," said the odd young man, "*I've* no mysteries. Why in the world, since it was what you came out for and have devoted so much of your time to, haven't you pulled it off? Why haven't you married?"

"Why haven't *you*?" she retorted. "Do you think that if I had it would have been better for you?—that my husband would for a moment have put up with you? Do you mind my asking you if you'll kindly go *now*?" she went on after a glance at the clock. "I'm expecting a friend, whom I must see alone, on a matter of great importance—"

"And my being seen with you may compromise your respectability or undermine your nerve?" He sprawled imperturbably in his place, crossing again, in another sense, his long black legs and showing, above his low shoes, an absurd reach of parti-coloured sock. "I take your point well enough, but mayn't you be after all quite wrong? If you can't do anything for me couldn't you at least do something *with* me? If it comes to that, I'm clever and amusing and charming too! I've been such an ass that you don't appreciate me. But people like me—I assure you they do. They usually don't know what an ass I've been; they only see the surface, which"—and he stretched himself afresh as she looked him up and down—"you *can* imagine them, can't you, rather taken with? *I'm* 'what I am' too; nothing less and nothing more. That's true of us as a family, you see. We *are* a crew!" He delivered himself serenely. His voice was soft and flat, his pleasant eyes, his simple tones tending to the solemn, achieved at moments that effect of quaintness which is, in certain connexions, socially so known and enjoyed. "English people have quite a weakness for me—more than any others. I get on with them beautifully. I've always been with them abroad. They think me," the young man explained, "diabolically American."

"You!" Such stupidity drew from her a sigh of compassion.

Her companion apparently quite understood it. "Are you homesick, Mamie?" he asked, with wondering irrelevance.

The manner of the question made her for some reason, in spite of her preoccupations, break into a laugh. A shade of indulgence, a sense of other things, came back to her. "You *are* funny, Scott!"

"Well," remarked Scott, "that's just what I claim. But *are* you so homesick?" he spaciously enquired, not as to a practical end, but from an easy play of intelligence.

"I'm just dying of it!" said Mamie Cutter.

"Why so am I!" Her visitor had a sweetness of concurrence.

"We're the only decent people," Miss Cutter declared. "And I know. *You* don't—you can't; and I can't explain. Come in," she continued with a return of her impatience and an increase of her decision, "at seven sharp."

She had quitted her seat some time before, and now, to get him into motion, hovered before him while, still motionless, he looked up at her. Something intimate, in the silence, appeared to pass between them—a community of fatigue and failure and, after all, of intelligence. There was a final cynical humour in it. It determined him, in any case, at last, and he slowly rose, taking in again as he stood there the testimony of the room. He might have been counting the photographs, but he looked at the flowers with detachment. "Who's coming?"

"Mrs. Medwin."

"American?"

"Dear no!"

"Then what are you doing for her?"

"I work for every one," she promptly returned.

"For every one who pays? So I suppose. Yet isn't it only we who do pay?"

There was a drollery, not lost on her, in the way his queer presence lent itself to his emphasised plural. "Do you consider that *you* do?"

At this, with his deliberation, he came back to his charming idea. "Only try me, and see if I can't be *made* to. Work me in." On her sharply presenting her back he stared a little at the clock. "If I come at seven may I stay to dinner?"

It brought her round again. "Impossible. I'm dining out."

"With whom?"

She had to think. "With Lord Considine."

"Oh my eye!" Scott exclaimed.

She looked at him gloomily. "Is *that* sort of tone what makes you pay? I think you might understand," she went on, "that if you're to sponge on me successfully you mustn't ruin me. I must have *some* remote resemblance to a lady."

"Yes? But why must *I*?" Her exasperated silence was full of answers, of which however his inimitable manner took no account. "You don't understand my real strength; I doubt if you even understand your own. You're clever, Mamie, but you're not so clever as I supposed. However," he pursued, "it's out of Mrs. Medwin that you'll get it."

"Get what?"

"Why the cheque that will enable you to assist me."

On this, for a moment, she met his eyes. "If you'll come back at seven sharp—not a minute before, and not a minute after, I'll give you two five-pound notes."

He thought it over. "Whom are you expecting a minute after?"

It sent her to the window with a groan almost of anguish, and she answered nothing till she had looked at the street. "If you injure me, you know, Scott, you'll be sorry."

"I wouldn't injure you for the world. What I want to do in fact is really to help you, and I promise you that I won't leave you—by which I mean won't leave London—till I've effected something really pleasant for you. I like you, Mamie, because I like pluck; I like you much more than you like me. I like you very, *very* much." He had at last with this reached the door and opened it, but he remained with his hand on the latch. "What does Mrs. Medwin want of you?" he thus brought out.

She had come round to see him disappear, and in the relief of this prospect she again just indulged him. "The impossible."

He waited another minute. "And you're going to do it?"

"I'm going to do it," said Mamie Cutter.

"Well then that ought to be a haul. Call it *three* fivers!" he laughed. "At seven sharp." And at last he left her alone.

II

Miss Cutter waited till she heard the house-door close; after which, in a sightless mechanical way, she moved about the room readjusting various objects he had not touched. It was as if his mere voice and accent had spoiled her form. But she was not left too long to reckon with these things, for Mrs. Medwin was promptly announced. This lady was not, more than her hostess, in the first flush of her youth; her appearance—the scattered remains of beauty manipulated by taste—resembled one of the light repasts in which the fragments of yesterday's dinner figure with a conscious ease that makes up for the want of presence. She was perhaps of an effect still too immediate to be called interesting, but she was candid, gentle and surprised—not fatiguingly surprised, only just in the right degree; and her white face—it was too white—with the fixed eyes, the somewhat touzled hair and the Louis Seize hat, might at the end of the very long neck have suggested the head of a princess carried on a pike in a revolution. She immediately took up the business that had brought her, with the air however of drawing from the omens then discernible less confidence than she had hoped. The complication lay in the fact that if it was Mamie's part to present the omens, that lady yet had so to colour them as to make her own service large. She perhaps over-coloured, for her friend gave way to momentary despair.

"What you mean is then that it's simply impossible?"

"Oh no," said Mamie with a qualified emphasis. "It's *possible*."

"But disgustingly difficult?"

"As difficult as you like."

"Then what can I do that I haven't done?"

"You can only wait a little longer."

"But that's just what I *have* done. I've done nothing else. I'm always waiting a little longer!"

Miss Cutter retained, in spite of this pathos, her grasp of the subject. "*The* thing, as I've told you, is for you first to be seen."

"But if people won't look at me?"

"They will."

"They *will*?" Mrs. Medwin was eager.

"They shall," her hostess went on. "It's their only having heard—without having seen."

"But if they stare straight the other way?" Mrs. Medwin continued to object. "You can't simply go up to them and twist their heads about."

"It's just what I can," said Mamie Cutter.

But her charming visitor, heedless for the moment of this attenuation, had found the way to put it. "It's the old story. You can't go into the water till you swim, and you can't swim till you go into the water. I can't be spoken to till I'm seen, but I can't be seen till I'm spoken to."

She met this lucidity, Miss Cutter, with but an instant's lapse.

"You say I can't twist their heads about. But I *have* twisted them."

It had been quietly produced, but it gave her companion a jerk. "They say 'Yes'?"

She summed it up. "All but one. *She* says 'No.'"

Mrs. Medwin thought; then jumped. "Lady Wantridge?"

Miss Cutter, as more delicate, only bowed admission. "I shall see her either this afternoon or late tomorrow. But she has written."

Her visitor wondered again. "May I see her letter?"

"No." She spoke with decision. "But I shall square her."

"Then how?"

"Well"—and Miss Cutter, as if looking upward for inspiration, fixed her eyes a while on the ceiling—"well, it will come to me."

Mrs. Medwin watched her—it was impressive. "And will *they* come to you—the others?" This question drew out the fact that they would—so far at least as they consisted of Lady Edward, Lady Bellhouse and Mrs. Pouncer, who had engaged to muster, at the signal of tea, on the 14th—prepared, as it were, for the worst. There was of course always the chance that Lady Wantridge might take the field in such force as to paralyse them, though that danger, at the same time, seemed inconsistent with her being squared. It didn't perhaps all quite ideally hang together; but what it sufficiently came to was that if she was the one who could do most *for* a person in Mrs. Medwin's position she was also the one who could do most against. It would therefore be distinctly what our friend familiarly spoke of as "collar-work." The effect of these mixed considerations was at any rate that Mamie eventually acquiesced in the idea, handsomely thrown out by her client, that she should have an "advance" to go on with. Miss Cutter confessed that it seemed at times as if one scarce *could* go on; but the advance was, in spite of this delicacy, still more delicately made—made in the form of a banknote, several sovereigns, some loose silver and two coppers, the whole contents of her purse, neatly disposed by Mrs. Medwin on one of the tiny tables. It seemed to clear the air for deeper intimacies, the fruit of which was that Mamie, lonely after all in her crowd and always more helpful than helped, eventually brought out that the way Scott had been going on was what seemed momentarily to overshadow her own power to do so.

"I've had a descent from him." But she had to explain. "My half-brother—Scott Homer. A wretch."

"What kind of a wretch?"

"Every kind. I lose sight of him at times—he disappears abroad. But he always turns up again, worse than ever."

"Violent?"

"No."

"Maudlin?"

"No."

"Only unpleasant?"

"No. Rather pleasant. Awfully clever—awfully travelled and easy."

"Then what's the matter with him?"

Mamie mused, hesitated—seemed to see a wide past. "I don't know."

"Something in the background?" Then as her friend was silent, "Something queer about cards?" Mrs. Medwin threw off.

"I don't know—and I don't want to!"

"Ah well, I'm sure *I* don't," Mrs. Medwin returned with spirit. The note of sharpness was perhaps also a little in the observation she made as she gathered herself to go. "Do you mind my saying something?"

Mamie took her eyes quickly from the money on the little stand. "You may say what you like."

"I only mean that anything awkward you may have to keep out of the way does seem to make more wonderful, doesn't it, that you should have got just where you are? I allude, you know, to your position."

"I see." Miss Cutter somewhat coldly smiled. "To my power."

"So awfully remarkable in an American."

"Ah you like us so."

Mrs. Medwin candidly considered. "But we don't, dearest."

Her companion's smile brightened. "Then why do you come to me?"

"Oh I like *you*!" Mrs. Medwin made out.

"Then that's it. There are no 'Americans.' It's always 'you.' "

"Me?" Mrs. Medwin looked lovely, but a little muddled.

"Me!" Mamie Cutter laughed. "But if you like me, you dear thing, you can judge if I like *you*." She gave her a kiss to dismiss her. "I'll see you again when I've seen her."

"Lady Wantridge? I hope so, indeed. I'll turn up late tomorrow, if you don't catch me first. Has it come to you yet?" the visitor, now at the door, went on.

"No; but it will. There's time."

"Oh a little less every day!"

Miss Cutter had approached the table and glanced again at the gold and silver and the note, not indeed absolutely overlooking the two coppers. "The balance," she put it, "the day after?"

"That very night if you like."

"Then count on me."

"Oh if I didn't—!" But the door closed on the dark idea. Yearningly then, and only when it had done so, Miss Cutter took up the money.

She went out with it ten minutes later, and, the calls on her time being many, remained out so long that at half-past six she hadn't come back. At that hour, on the other hand, Scott Homer knocked at her door, where her maid, who opened it with a weak pretense of holding it firm, ventured to announce to him, as a lesson well learnt, that he hadn't been expected till seven. No lesson, none the less, could prevail against his native art. He pleaded fatigue, her, the maid's, dreadful depressing London, and the need to curl up somewhere. If she'd just leave him quiet half an hour that old sofa upstairs would do for it; of which he took quickly such effectual possession that when five minutes later she peeped, nervous for her broken vow, into the drawing-room, the faithless young woman found him extended at his length and peacefully asleep.

III

The situation before Miss Cutter's return developed in other directions still, and when that event took place, at a few minutes past seven, these circumstances were, by the foot of the stair, between mistress and maid, the subject of some interrogative gasps and scared admissions. Lady Wantridge had arrived shortly after the interloper, and wishing, as she said, to wait, had gone straight up in spite of being told he was lying down.

"She distinctly understood he was there?"

"Oh yes ma'am; I thought it right to mention."

"And what did you call him?"

"Well, ma'am, I thought it unfair to *you* to call him anything but a gentleman."

Mamie took it all in, though there might well be more of it than one could quickly embrace. "But if she has had time," she flashed, "to find out he isn't one?"

"Oh ma'am, she had a quarter of an hour."

"Then she isn't with him still?"

"No ma'am; she came down again at last. She rang, and I saw her here, and she said she wouldn't wait longer."

Miss Cutter darkly mused. "Yet had already waited—?"

"Quite a quarter."

"Mercy on us!" She began to mount. Before reaching the top however she had reflected that quite a quarter was long if Lady Wantridge had only been shocked. On the other hand it was short if she had only been pleased. But how *could* she have been pleased? The very essence of their actual crisis was just that there was no pleasing her. Mamie had but to open the drawing-room door indeed to perceive that this was not true at least of Scott Homer, who was horribly cheerful.

Miss Cutter expressed to her brother without reserve her sense of the constitutional, the brutal selfishness that had determined his mistimed return. It had taken place, in violation of their agreement, exactly at the moment when it was most cruel to her that he should be there, and if she must now completely wash her hands of him he had only himself to thank. She had come in flushed with resentment and for a moment had been voluble; but it would have been striking that, though the way he received her might have seemed but to aggravate, it presently justified him by causing their relation really to take a stride. He had the art of confounding those who would quarrel with him by reducing them to the humiliation of a stirred curiosity.

"What *could* she have made of you?" Mamie demanded.

"My dear girl, she's not a woman who's eager to make too much of anything—anything, I mean, that will prevent her from doing as she likes, what she takes into her head. Of course," he continued to explain, "if it's something she doesn't want to do, she'll make as much as Moses."

Mamie wondered if that was the way he talked to her visitor, but felt obliged to own to his acuteness. It was an exact description of Lady Wantridge, and she was conscious of tucking it away for future use in a corner of her miscellaneous little mind. She withheld however all present acknowledgement, only addressing him another question. "Did you really get on with her?"

"Have you still to learn, darling—I can't help again putting it to you—that I get on with everybody? That's just what I don't seem able to drive into you. Only see how I get on with *you*."

She almost stood corrected. "What I mean is of course whether—"

"Whether she made love to me? Shyly, yet—or because—shamefully? She would certainly have liked awfully to stay."

"Then why didn't she?"

"Because, on account of some other matter—and I could see it was true—she hadn't time. Twenty minutes—she was here less—were all she came to give you. So don't be afraid I've frightened her away. She'll come back."

Mamie thought it over. "Yet you didn't go with her to the door?"

"She wouldn't let me, and I know when to do what I'm told—quite as much as what I'm not told. She wanted to find out about me. I mean from your little creature; a pearl of fidelity, by the way."

"But what on earth did she come up for?" Mamie again found herself appealing, and just by that fact showing her need of help.

"Because she always goes up." Then as, in the presence of this rapid generalisation, to say nothing of that of such a relative altogether, Miss Cutter could only show as comparatively blank: "I mean she knows when to go up and when to come down. She has instincts; she didn't know whom you might have up here. It's a kind of compliment to you anyway. Why Mamie," Scott pursued, "you don't know the curiosity we any of us inspire. You wouldn't believe what I've seen. The bigger bugs they are the more they're on the lookout."

Mamie still followed, but at a distance. "The lookout for what?"

"Why for anything that will help them to live. You've been here all this time without making out then, about them, what I've had to pick out as I can? They're dead, don't you see? And *we're* alive."

"You? Oh!"—Mamie almost laughed about it.

"Well, they're a worn-out old lot anyhow; they've used up their resources. They do look out; and I'll do them the justice to say they're not afraid—not even of me!" he continued as his sister again showed something of the same irony. "Lady Wantridge at any rate wasn't; that's what I mean by her having made love to me. She does what she likes. Mind it, you know." He was by this time fairly teaching her to read one of her best friends, and when, after it, he had come back to the great point of his lesson—that of her failure, through feminine inferiority, practically to grasp the truth that their being just as they were, he and she, was the real card for them to play—when he had renewed that reminder he left her absolutely in a state of dependence. Her impulse to press him on the subject of Lady Wantridge dropped; it was as if she had felt that, whatever had taken place, something would somehow come of it. She was to be in a manner disappointed but the impression helped to keep her over to the next morning, when, as Scott had foretold, his new acquaintance did reappear, explaining to Miss Cutter that she had acted the day before to gain time and that she even now sought to gain it by not waiting longer. What, she promptly intimated she had asked herself, could that friend be thinking of? She must show where she stood before things had gone too far. If she had brought her answer without more delay she wished to make it sharp. Mrs. Medwin? Never! "No, my dear—not I. *There* I stop."

Mamie had known it would be "collar-work," but somehow now, at the beginning, she felt her heart sink. It was not that she had expected to carry the position with a rush, but that, as always after an interval, her visitor's defences really loomed—and quite, as it were, to the material vision—too large. She was always planted with them, voluminous, in the very centre of the passage; was like a person accommodated with a chair in some unlawful place at the theatre. She wouldn't move and you couldn't get round. Mamie's calculation indeed had not been on getting round; she was obliged to recognise that, too foolishly and fondly, she had dreamed of inducing a surrender. Her dream had been the fruit of her need; but, conscious that she was even yet unequipped for pressure, she felt, almost for the first time in her life, superficial and crude. She was to be paid—but with what was she, to that end, to pay? She had engaged to find an answer to this question, but the answer had not, according to her promise, "come." And Lady Wantridge meanwhile massed herself, and there was no view of her that didn't show her as verily, by some process too obscure to be traced, the hard depository of the social law. She was no younger, no fresher, no stronger, really, than any of them; she was only, with a kind of haggard fineness, a sharpened taste for life, and with all sorts of things behind and beneath her, more abysmal and more immoral, more secure and more impertinent. The points she made were two in number. One was that she absolutely declined; the other was that she quite doubted if Mamie herself had measured the job. The thing couldn't be done. But say it *could* be; was Mamie quite the person to do it? To this Miss Cutter, with a sweet smile, replied that she quite understood how little she might seem so. "I'm only one of the persons to whom it has appeared that *you* are."

"Then who are the others?"

"Well, to begin with, Lady Edward, Lady Bellhouse and Mrs. Pouncer."

"Do you mean that they'll come to meet her?"

"I've seen them, and they've promised."

"To come, of course," Lady Wantridge said, "if *I* come."

Her hostess cast about. "Oh of course you could prevent them. But I should take it as awfully kind of you not to. *Won't* you do this for me?" Mamie pleaded.

Her friend looked over the room very much as Scott had done. "Do they really understand what it's *for*?"

"Perfectly. So that she may call."

"And what good will that do her?"

Miss Cutter faltered, but she presently brought it out. "Naturally what one hopes is that you'll ask her."

"Ask her to call?"

"Ask her to dine. Ask her, if you'd be so *truly* sweet, for a Sunday, or something of that sort, and even if only in one of your *most* mixed parties, to Catchmore."

Miss Cutter felt the less hopeful after this effort in that her companion only showed a strange good nature. And it wasn't a satiric amiability, though it *was* amusement. "Take Mrs. Medwin into my family?"

"Some day when you're taking forty others."

"Ah but what I don't see is what it does for *you*. You're already so welcome among us that you can scarcely improve your position even by forming for us the most delightful relation."

"Well, I know how dear you are," Mamie Cutter replied; "but one has after all more than one side and more than one sympathy. I like her, you know." And even at this Lady Wantridge wasn't shocked; she showed that ease and blandness which were her way, unfortunately, of being most impossible. She remarked that *she* might listen to such things, because she was clever enough for them not to matter; only Mamie should take care how she went about saying them at large. When she became definite however, in a minute, on the subject of the public facts, Miss Cutter soon found herself ready to make her own concession. Of course she didn't dispute *them:* there they were; they were unfortunately on record, and nothing was to be done about them but to—Mamie found it in truth at this point a little difficult.

"Well, what? Pretend already to have forgotten them?"

"Why not, when you've done it in so many other cases?"

"There *are* no other cases so bad. One meets them at any rate as they come. Some you can manage, others you can't. It's no use, you must give them up. They're past patching; there's nothing to be done with them. There's nothing accordingly to be done with Mrs. Medwin but to put her off." And Lady Wantridge rose to her height.

"Well, you know, I *do* do things," Mamie quavered with a smile so strained that it partook of exaltation.

"You help people? Oh yes, I've known you to do wonders. But stick," said Lady Wantridge with strong and cheerful emphasis, "to your Americans!"

Miss Cutter, gazing, got up. "You don't do justice, Lady Wantridge, to your own compatriots. Some of them are really charming. Besides," said Mamie, "working for mine often strikes me, so far as the interest—the inspiration and excitement, don't you know?—go, as rather too easy. You all, as I constantly have occasion to say, like us so!"

Her companion frankly weighed it. "Yes; it takes that to account for your position. I've always thought of you nevertheless as keeping for their benefit a regular working agency. They come to you, and you place them. There remains, I confess," her ladyship went on in the same free spirit, "the great wonder—"

"Of how I first placed my poor little self? Yes," Mamie bravely conceded, "when *I* began there was no agency. I just worked my passage. I didn't even come to *you,* did I? You never noticed me till, as Mrs. Short Stokes says, 'I was 'way, 'way up!' Mrs. Medwin," she threw in, "can't get over it." Then, as her friend looked vague: "Over my social situation."

"Well, it's no great flattery to you to say," Lady Wantridge good-humouredly returned, "that she certainly can't hope for one resembling it." Yet it really seemed to spread there before them. "You simply *made* Mrs. Short Stokes."

"In spite of her name!" Mamie smiled.

"Oh your 'names'—! In spite of everything."

"Ah I'm something of an artist." With which, and a relapse marked by her wistful eyes into the gravity of the matter, she supremely fixed her friend. She felt how little she minded betraying at last the extremity of her need, and it was out of this extremity that her appeal proceeded. "Have I really had your last word? It means so much to me."

Lady Wantridge came straight to the point. "You mean you depend on it?"

"Awfully!"

"Is it all you have?"

"All. Now."

"But Mrs. Short Stokes and the others—'rolling,' aren't they? Don't they pay up?"

"Ah," sighed Mamie, "if it wasn't for *them*—!"

Lady Wantridge perceived. "You've had so much?"

"I couldn't have gone on."

"Then what do you do with it all?"

"Oh most of it goes back to them. There are all sorts, and it's all help. Some of them have nothing."

"Oh if you feed the hungry," Lady Wantridge laughed, "you're indeed in a great way of business. Is Mrs. Medwin"—her transition was immediate—"really rich?"

"Really. He left her everything."

"So that if I do say 'yes'—"

"It will quite set me up."

"I see—and how much more responsible it makes one! But I'd rather myself give you the money."

"Oh!" Mamie coldly murmured.

"You mean I mayn't suspect your prices? Well, I dare say I don't! But I'd rather give you ten pounds."

"Oh!" Mamie repeated in a tone that sufficiently covered her prices. The question was in every way larger. "Do you *never* forgive?" she reproachfully enquired. The door opened however at the moment she spoke and Scott Homer presented himself.

IV

Scott Homer wore exactly, to his sister's eyes, the aspect he had worn the day before, and it also formed to her sense the great feature of his impartial greeting.

"How d'ye do, Mamie? How d'ye do, Lady Wantridge?"

"How d'ye do again?" Lady Wantridge replied with an equanimity striking to her hostess. It was as if Scott's own had been contagious; it was almost indeed as if she had seen him before. *Had* she ever so seen him—before the previous day? While Miss Cutter put to herself this question her visitor at all events met the one she had previously uttered. "Ever 'forgive'?" this personage echoed in a tone that made as little account as possible of the interruption. "Dear, yes! The people I *have* forgiven!" She laughed—perhaps a little nervously; and she was now looking at Scott. The way she looked at him was precisely what had already had its effect for his sister. "The people I can!"

"Can you forgive *me*?" asked Scott Homer.

She took it so easily. "But—what?"

Mamie interposed; she turned directly to her brother. "Don't try her. Leave it so." She had had an inspiration; it was the most extraordinary thing in the world. "Don't try *him*"—she had turned to their companion. She looked grave, sad, strange. "Leave it so." Yes, it was a distinct inspiration, which she couldn't have explained, but which had come, prompted by something she had caught—the extent of the recognition expressed—in Lady Wantridge's face. It had come absolutely of a sudden, straight out of the opposition of the two figures before her—quite as if a concussion had struck a light. The light was helped by her quickened sense that her friend's silence on the incident of the day before showed some sort of consciousness. She looked surprised. "Do you know my brother?"

"*Do* I know you?" Lady Wantridge asked of him.

"No, Lady Wantridge," Scott pleasantly confessed, "not one little mite!"

"Well then if you *must* go—!" and Mamie offered her a hand. "But I'll go down with you. Not *you!*" she launched at her brother, who immediately effaced himself. His way of doing so —and he had already done so, as for Lady Wantridge, in respect to their previous encounter—struck her even at the moment as an instinctive if slightly blind tribute to her possession of an idea; and as such, in its celerity, made her so admire him, and their common wit, that she on the spot more than forgave him his queerness. He was right. He could be as queer as liked! The queerer the better! It was at the foot of the stairs, when she had got her guest down, that what she had assured Mrs. Medwin would come did indeed come. "*Did* you meet him here yesterday?"

"Dear yes. Isn't he too funny?"

"Yes," said Mamie gloomily. "He *is* funny. But had you ever met him before?"

"Dear no!"

"Oh!"—and Mamie's tone might have meant many things.

Lady Wantridge however, after all, easily overlooked it. "I only knew he was one of your odd Americans. That's why, when I heard yesterday here that he was up there awaiting your return, I didn't let that prevent me. I thought he might be. He certainly," her ladyship laughed, "*is*."

"Yes, he's very American," Mamie went on in the same way.

"As you say, we *are* fond of you! Good-bye," said Lady Wantridge.

But Mamie had not half done with her. She felt more and more—or she hoped at least—that she looked strange. She *was*, no doubt, if it came to that, strange. "Lady Wantridge," she almost convulsively broke out, "I don't know whether you'll understand me, but I seem to feel that I must act with you—I don't know what to call it!—responsibly. He *is* my brother."

"Surely—and why not?" Lady Wantridge stared. "He's the image of you!"

"Thank you!"—and Mamie was stranger than ever.

"Oh he's good-looking. He's handsome, my dear. Oddly—but distinctly!" Her ladyship was for treating it much as a joke.

But Mamie, all sombre, would have none of this. She boldly gave him up. "I think he's awful."

"He is indeed—delightfully. And where *do* you get your ways of saying things? It isn't anything—and the things aren't anything. But it's so droll."

"Don't let yourself, all the same," Mamie consistently pursued, "be carried away by it. The thing can't be done—simply."

Lady Wantridge wondered. "'Done simply'?"

"Done at all."

"But what can't be?"

"Why, what you might think—from his pleasantness. What he spoke of your doing for him."

Lady Wantridge recalled. "Forgiving him?"

"He asked you if you couldn't. But you can't. It's too dreadful for me, as so near a relation, to have, loyally—loyally to *you*—to say it. But he's impossible."

It was so portentously produced that her ladyship had somehow to meet it. "What's the matter with him?"

"I don't know."

"Then what's the matter with *you*?" Lady Wantridge enquired.

"It's because I *won't* know," Mamie—not without dignity—explained.

"Then *I* won't either!"

"Precisely. Don't. It's something," Mamie pursued, with some inconsequence, "that—somewhere or other, at some time or other—he appears to have done. Something that has made a difference in his life."

"'Something'?" Lady Wantridge echoed again. "What kind of thing?"

Mamie looked up at the light above the door, through which the London sky was doubly dim. "I haven't the least idea."

"Then what kind of difference?"

Mamie's gaze was still at the light. "The difference you see."

Lady Wantridge, rather obligingly, seemed to ask herself what she saw. "But I don't see any! It seems, at least," she added, "such an amusing one! And he has such nice eyes."

"Oh *dear* eyes!" Mamie conceded; but with too much sadness, for the moment, about the connexions of the subject, to say more.

It almost forced her companion after an instant to proceed. "Do you mean he can't go home?"

She weighed her responsibility. "I only make out—more's the pity!—that he doesn't."

"Is it then something too terrible—?"

She thought again. "I don't know what—for men—*is* too terrible."

"Well then as you don't know what 'is' for women either—good-bye!" her visitor laughed.

It practically wound up the interview; which, however, terminating thus on a considerable stir of the air, was to give Miss Cutter for several days the sense of being much blown about. The degree to which, to begin with, she had been drawn—or perhaps rather pushed—closer to Scott was marked in the brief colloquy that she on her friend's departure had with him. He had immediately said it. "You'll see if she doesn't ask me down!"

"So soon?"

"Oh I've known them at places—at Cannes, at Pau, at Shanghai—do it sooner still. I always know when they will. You *can't* make out they don't love me!" He spoke almost plaintively, as if he wished she could.

"Then I don't see why it hasn't done you more good."

"Why Mamie," he patiently reasoned, "what more good *could* it? As I tell you," he explained, "it has just been my life."

"Then why do you come to me for money?"

"Oh they don't give me *that*!" Scott returned.

"So that it only means then, after all, that I, at the best, must keep you up?"

He fixed on her the nice eyes Lady Wantridge admired. "Do you mean to tell me that already—at this very moment—I'm not distinctly keeping *you*?"

She gave him back his look. "Wait till she *has* asked you, and then," Mamie added, "decline."

Scott, not too grossly, wondered. "As acting for *you*?"

Mamie's next injunction was answer enough. "But *before*—yes—call."

He took it in. "Call—but decline. Good!"

"The rest," she said, "I leave to you." And she left it in fact with such confidence that for a couple of days she was not only conscious of no need to give Mrs. Medwin another turn of the screw, but positively evaded, in her fortitude, the reappearance of that lady. It was not till the fourth day that she waited upon her, finding her, as she had expected, tense.

"Lady Wantridge *will*—?"

"Yes, though she says she won't."

"She says she won't? O—oh!" Mrs. Medwin moaned.

"Sit tight all the same. I *have* her!"

"But how?"

"Through Scott—whom she wants."

"Your bad brother!" Mrs. Medwin stared. "What does she want of him?"

"To amuse them at Catchmore. Anything for that. And he *would*. But he shan't!" Mamie declared. "He shan't go unless she comes. She must meet you first—you're my condition."

"O—o—oh!" Mrs. Medwin's tone was a wonder of hope and fear. "But doesn't he want to go?"

"He wants what *I* want. She draws the line at *you*. I draw the line at *him*."

"But *she*—doesn't she mind that he's bad?"

It was so artless that Mamie laughed. "No—it doesn't touch her. Besides, perhaps he isn't. It isn't as for *you*—people seem not to know. He has settled everything, at all events, by going to see her. It's before her that he's the thing she'll have to have."

"Have to?"

"For Sundays in the country. A feature—*the* feature."

"So she has asked him?"

"Yes—and he has declined."

"For *me?*" Mrs. Medwin panted.

"For me," said Mamie on the door-step. "But I don't leave him for long." Her hansom had waited. "She'll come."

Lady Wantridge did come. She met in South Audley Street, on the fourteenth, at tea, the ladies whom Mamie had named to her, together with three or four others, and it was rather a master-stroke for Miss Cutter that if Mrs. Medwin was modestly present Scott Homer was as markedly not. This occasion, however, is a medal that would take rare casting, as would also, for that matter, even the minor light and shade, the lower relief, of the pecuniary transaction that Mrs. Medwin's flushed gratitude scarce awaited the dispersal of the company munificently to complete. A new understanding indeed on the spot rebounded from it, the conception of which, in Mamie's mind, had promptly bloomed. "He shan't go *now* unless he takes you." Then, as her fancy always moved quicker for her client than her client's own—"Down with him to Catchmore! When he goes to amuse them *you,*" she serenely developed, "shall amuse them too." Mrs. Medwin's response was again rather oddly divided, but she was sufficiently intelligible when it came to meeting the hint that this latter provision would represent success to the tune of a separate fee. "Say," Mamie had suggested, "the same."

"Very well; the same."

The knowledge that it was to be the same had perhaps something to do also with the obliging spirit in which Scott eventually went. It was all at the last rather hurried—a party rapidly got together for the Grand Duke, who was in England but for the hour, who had good-naturedly proposed himself, and who liked his parties small, intimate and funny. This one was of the smallest and was finally judged to conform neither too little nor too much to the other conditions—after a brief whirlwind of wires and counterwires, and an iterated waiting of hansoms at various doors—to include Mrs. Medwin. It was from Catchmore itself that, snatching a moment on the wondrous Sunday afternoon, this lady had the harmonious thought of sending the new cheque. She was in bliss enough, but her scribble none the less intimated that it was Scott who amused them most. He *was* the feature.

A NOTE ON

MRS. MEDWIN

(1902)

I HAVE included this rather frail and certainly quite cynical story because it throws some light on the question of James's snobbery and Anglomania. The question is as complex and permanently discussable as his art. To call him *tout court* a snob and Anglomaniac is to simplify an unsimplifiable temperament. Just as the typical Jamesian sentence is made up of qualifications rather than of statements (for James the statement is complete only after all possible qualifications have been made), so is his "snobbery" composed of a hundred reservations and modifications. Part of James part of the time was a snob, but in the end this part always gave way to the central, the basic James. The basic James was not a snob, not an Anglomaniac, not a deracinated American, not a gentleman of the leisure class, though he was in part and at times all of these things. The basic James—I do not know how otherwise to put it—was an understander. His insight was so tireless that it was bound to comprehend finally even his own prejudices. In the end he saw through even himself. All things, including his own weaknesses, were soluble finally in the acid of analysis.

This is not to say that James was ever one to protest against what he saw. He understood fully, for example, that the British ruling class rested on a rotten foundation, that it was bound to decay and fall apart, but the knowledge never aroused him to indignation, much less to the gesture of reform. He was too interested in it to attack it, save by the most glancing of blows.

Such a glancing blow is "Mrs. Medwin." The essence of the story lies in a line or two of dialogue between Mamie and her attractive, shiftless, non-gentlemanly American half-brother. "The bigger bugs they are," says the percipient Scott, "the more they're on the lookout." "The lookout for what?" demands Mamie. "Why, for anything," is the reply, "that will help them to live. . . . They're dead, don't you see? And *we're* alive." There is the message, if message there can be in a James story. James knew that by 1900 the current of emotional lend-lease was beginning to reverse its flow. Before that time the American tourist came to Europe to strengthen, to re-invigorate himself by the absorption of a tradition lacking in his own country. But now upper-class Europe and England, its blood-pressure dangerously low, was beginning to live on transfusions from the full, pulsing veins of American energy. Scott and his half-sister represent that energy, just as Lady Wantridge, for all her imperiousness, represents a society on the defensive, badly in need of something beyond a fresh supply of gentlemen.

"Mrs. Medwin" is a humorous—cynical, if you prefer—recognition of this state of things. Even the severest of anti-Jacobeans would be hard put to prove from "Mrs Medwin" that James had a fatuous, drawing-room-floor-licking affection for the British aristocracy. Always he fools you in the end, does James; he fools you because you cannot pin him down to an attitude. For him an attitude and analysis are uncompromisingly in opposition. If you inflexibly choose the first you cannot flexibly practise the second.

THE BIRTHPLACE

I

It seemed to them at first, the offer, too good to be true, and their friend's letter, addressed to them to feel, as he said, the ground, to sound them as to inclinations and possibilities, had almost the effect of a brave joke at their expense. Their friend, Mr. Grant-Jackson, a highly preponderant pushing person, great in discussion and arrangement, abrupt in overture, unexpected, if not perverse, in attitude, and almost equally acclaimed and objected to in the wide midland region to which he had taught, as the phrase was, the size of his foot—their friend had launched his bolt quite out of the blue and had thereby so shaken them as to make them fear almost more than hope. The place had fallen vacant by the death of one of the two ladies, mother and daughter, who had discharged its duties for fifteen years; the daughter was staying on alone, to accommodate, but had found, though extremely mature, an opportunity of marriage that involved retirement, and the question of the new incumbents was not a little pressing. The want thus determined was of a united couple of some sort, of the right sort, a pair of educated and competent sisters possibly preferred, but a married pair having its advantages if other qualifications were marked. Applicants, candidates, besiegers of the door of every one supposed to have a voice in the matter, were already beyond counting, and Mr. Grant-Jackson, who was in his way diplomatic and whose voice, though not perhaps of the loudest, possessed notes of insistence, had found his preference fixing itself on some person or brace of persons who had been decent and dumb. The Gedges appeared to have struck him as waiting in silence—though absolutely, as happened, no busybody had brought them, far away in the North, a hint either of bliss or of danger; and the happy spell, for the rest, had obviously been wrought in him by a remembrance which, though now scarcely fresh, had never before borne any such fruit.

Morris Gedge had for a few years, as a young man, carried on a small private school of the order known as preparatory, and had happened then to receive under his roof the small son of the great man, who was not at that time so great. The little boy, during an absence of his parents from England, had been dangerously ill, so dangerously that they had been recalled in haste, though with inevitable delays, from a far country—they had gone to America, with the whole continent and the great sea to cross again—and had got back to find the child saved, but saved, as couldn't help coming to light, by the extreme devotion and perfect judgement of Mrs. Gedge. Without children of her own she had particularly attached herself to this tiniest and tenderest of her husband's pupils, and they had both dreaded as a dire disaster the injury to their little enterprise that would be caused by their losing him. Nervous anxious sensitive persons, with a pride—as they were for that matter well aware—above their position, never, at the best, to be anything but dingy, they had nursed him in terror and had brought him through in exhaustion. Exhaustion, as befell, had thus overtaken them early and had for one reason and another managed to assert itself as their permanent portion. The little boy's death would, as they said, have done for them, yet his recovery hadn't saved them; with which it was doubtless also part of a shy but stiff candour in them that they didn't regard themselves as having in a more indirect manner laid up treasure. Treasure was not to be, in any form whatever, of their dreams or of their waking sense; and the years that followed had limped under their weight, had now and then rather grievously stumbled, had even barely escaped laying them in the dust. The school hadn't prospered, had but dwindled to a close. Gedge's health had failed and still more every sign in him of a capacity to publish himself as practical. He had tried several things, he had tried many, but the final appearance was of their having tried him not less.

They mostly, at the time I speak of, were trying his successors, while he found himself, with an effect of dull felicity that had come in this case from the mere postponement of change, in charge of the grey town-library of Blackport-on-Dwindle, all granite, fog and female fiction. This was a situation in which his general intelligence—admittedly his strong point—was doubtless imaged, around him, as feeling less of a strain than that mastery of particulars in which he was recognised as weak.

It was at Blackport-on-Dwindle that the silver shaft reached and pierced him; it was as an alternative to dispensing dog-eared volumes the very titles of which, on the lips of innumerable glib girls, were a challenge to his nerves, that the wardenship of so different a temple presented itself. The stipend named exceeded little the slim wage at present paid him, but even had it been less the interest and the honour would have struck him as determinant. The shrine at which he was to preside—though he had always lacked occasion to approach it—figured to him as the most sacred known to the steps of men, the early home of the supreme poet, the Mecca of the English-speaking race. The tears came into his eyes sooner still than into his wife's while he looked about with her at their actual narrow prison, so grim with enlightenment, so ugly with industry, so turned away from any dream, so intolerable to any taste. He felt as if a window had opened into a great green woodland, a woodland that had a name all glorious, immortal, that was peopled with vivid figures, each of them renowned, and that gave out a murmur, deep as the sound of the sea, which was the rustle in forest shade of all the poetry, the beauty, the colour of life. It would be prodigious that of this transfigured world *he* should keep the key. No—he couldn't believe it, not even when Isabel, at sight of his face, came and helpfully kissed him. He shook his head with a strange smile. "We shan't get it. Why should we? It's perfect."

"If we don't he'll simply have been cruel; which is impossible when he has waited all this time to be kind." Mrs. Gedge did believe—she *would;* since the wide doors of the world of poetry had suddenly pushed back for them it was in the form of poetic justice that they were first to know it. She had her faith in their patron; it was sudden, but now complete. "He remembers—that's all; and that's our strength."

"And what's *his*?" Gedge asked. "He may want to put us through, but that's a different thing from being able. What are our special advantages?"

"Well, that we're just the thing." Her knowledge of the needs of the case was as yet, thanks to scant information, of the vaguest, and she had never, more than her husband, stood on the sacred spot; but she saw herself waving a nicely-gloved hand over a collection of remarkable objects and saying to a compact crowd of gaping awestruck persons: "And now, please, *this* way." She even heard herself meeting with promptness and decision an occasional enquiry from a visitor in whom audacity had prevailed over awe. She had once been with a cousin, years before, to a great northern castle, and that was the way the housekeeper had taken them round. And it was not moreover, either, that she thought of herself as a housekeeper: she was well above that, and the wave of her hand wouldn't fail to be such as to show it. This and much else she summed up as she answered her mate. "Our special advantages are that you're a gentleman."

"Oh!" said Gedge as if he had never thought of it, and yet as if too it were scarce worth thinking of.

"I see it all," she went on; "they've *had* the vulgar—they find they don't do. We're poor and we're modest, but any one can see what we are."

Gedge wondered. "Do you mean—?" More modest than she, he didn't know quite what she meant.

"We're refined. We know how to speak."

"Do we?"—he still, suddenly, wondered.

But she was from the first surer of everything than he; so

that when a few weeks more had elapsed and the shade of uncertainty—though it was only a shade—had grown almost to sicken him, her triumph was to come with the news that they were fairly named. "We're on poor pay, though we manage"—she had at the present juncture contended for her point. "But we're highly cultivated, and for them to get *that,* don't you see? without getting too much with it in the way of pretensions and demands, must be precisely their dream. We've no social position, but we don't *mind* that we haven't, do we? a bit; which is because we know the difference between realities and shams. We hold to reality, and that gives us common sense, which the vulgar have less than anything and which yet must be wanted there, after all, as well as anywhere else."

Her companion followed her, but musingly, as if his horizon had within a few moments grown so great that he was almost lost in it and required a new orientation. The shining spaces surrounded him; the association alone gave a nobler arch to the sky. "Allow that we hold also a little to the romance. It seems to me that that's the beauty. We've missed it all our life, and now it's come. We shall be at headquarters for it. We shall have our fill of it."

She looked at his face, at the effect in it of these prospects, and her own lighted as if he had suddenly grown handsome. "Certainly—we shall live as in a fairy-tale. But what I mean is that we shall give, in a way—and so gladly—quite as much as we get. With all the rest of it we're for instance neat." Their letter had come to them at breakfast, and she picked a fly out of the butter-dish. "It's the way we'll *keep* the place"—with which she removed from the sofa to the top of the cottage-piano a tin of biscuits that had refused to squeeze into the cupboard. At Blackport they were in lodgings—of the lowest description, she had been known to declare with a freedom felt by Blackport to be slightly invidious. The Birthplace—and that itself, after such a life, was exaltation—wouldn't be lodgings, since a house close beside it was set apart for the warden, a house joining on to it as a sweet old parsonage is often annexed to a quaint old church. It would all together be their home, and such a home as would make a little world that they would never want to leave. She dwelt on the gain, for that matter, to their income; as obviously, though the salary was not a change for the better, the house given them would make all the difference. He assented to this, but absently, and she was almost impatient at the range of his thoughts. It was as if something, for him—the very swarm of them—veiled the view; and he presently of himself showed what it was.

"What I can't get over is its being such a man—!" He almost, from inward emotion, broke down.

"Such a man—?"

"Him, *him,* HIM—!" It was too much.

"Grant-Jackson? Yes, it's a surprise, but one sees how he has been meaning, all the while, the right thing by us."

"I mean *Him,*" Gedge returned more coldly; "our becoming familiar and intimate—for that's what it will come to. We shall just live with Him."

"Of course—it *is* the beauty." And she added quite gaily: "The more we do the more we shall love Him."

"No doubt—but it's rather awful. The more we *know* Him," Gedge reflected, "the more we shall love Him. We don't as yet, you see, know Him so very tremendously."

"We do so quite as well, I imagine, as the sort of people they've had. And that probably isn't—unless you care, as we do—so awfully necessary. For there are the facts."

"Yes—there are the facts."

"I mean the principal ones. They're all that the people—the people who come—want."

"Yes—they must be all *they* want."

"So that they're all that those who've been in charge have needed to know."

"Ah," he said as if it were a question of honour, "*we* must know everything."

She cheerfully acceded: she had the merit, he felt, of keeping the case within bounds. "Everything. But about him personally," she added, "there isn't, is there? so very very much."

"More, I believe, than there used to be. They've made discoveries."

It was a grand thought. "Perhaps *we* shall make some!"

"Oh I shall be content to be a little better up in what has been done." And his eyes rested on a shelf of books, half of which, little worn but much faded, were of the florid "gift" order and belonged to the house. Of those among them that were his own most were common specimens of the reference sort, not excluding an old Bradshaw and a catalogue of the town-library. "We've not even a Set of our own. Of the Works," he explained in quick repudiation of the sense, perhaps more obvious, in which she might have taken it.

As a proof of their scant range of possessions this sounded almost abject, till the painful flush with which they met on the admission melted presently into a different glow. It was just for that kind of poorness that their new situation was, by its intrinsic charm, to console them. And Mrs. Gedge had a happy thought. "Wouldn't the Library more or less have them?"

"Oh no, we've nothing of that sort: for what do you take us?" This, however, was but the play of Gedge's high spirits: the form both depression and exhilaration most frequently took with him being a bitterness on the subject of the literary taste of Blackport. No one was so deeply acquainted with it. It acted with him in fact as so lurid a sign of the future that the charm of the thought of removal was sharply enhanced by the prospect of escape from it. The institution he served didn't of course deserve the particular reproach into which his irony had flowered; and indeed if the several Sets in which the Works were present were a trifle dusty, the dust was a little his own fault. To make up for that now he had the vision of immediately giving his time to the study of them; he saw himself indeed, inflamed with a new passion, earnestly commenting and collating. Mrs. Gedge, who had suggested that, till their move should come, they ought to read Him regularly of an evening—certain as they were to do it still more when in closer quarters with Him—Mrs. Gedge felt also, in her degree, the spell; so that the very happiest time of their anxious life was perhaps to have been the series of lamp-light hours, after supper, in which, alternately taking the book, they declaimed, they almost performed, their beneficent author. He became speedily more than their author—their personal friend, their universal light, their final authority and divinity. Where in the world, they were already asking themselves, would they have been without Him? By the time their appointment arrived in form their relation to Him had immensely developed. It was amusing to Morris Gedge that he had so lately blushed for his ignorance, and he made this remark to his wife during the last hour they were able to give their study before proceeding, across half the country, to the scene of their romantic future. It was as if, in deep close throbs, in cool after-waves that broke of a sudden and bathed his mind, all possession and comprehension and sympathy, all the truth and the life and the story, had come to him, and come, as the newspapers said, to stay. "It's absurd," he didn't hesitate to say, "to talk of our not 'knowing.' So far as we don't it's because we're dunces. He's *in* the thing, over His ears, and the more [illegible] into it the more we're with Him. I seem to myself at any rate," he declared, "to *see* Him in it as if He were painted on the wall."

"Oh *doesn't* one rather, the dear thing? And don't you feel where it is?" Mrs. Gedge finely asked. "We see Him because we love Him—that's what we do. How can we not, the old darling—with what He's doing for us? There's no light"—she had a sententious turn—"like true affection."

"Yes, I suppose that's it. And yet," her husband mused, "I see, confound me, the faults."

"That's because you're so critical. You see them, but you don't mind them. You see them, but you forgive them. You mustn't mention them *there*. We shan't, you know, be there for *that*."

"Dear no!" he laughed: "we'll chuck out any one who hints at them."

II

If the sweetness of the preliminary months had been great, great too, though almost excessive as agitation, was the wonder of fairly being housed with Him, of treading day and night in the footsteps He had worn, of touching the objects, or at all events the surfaces, the substances, over which His hands had played, which His arms, His shoulders had rubbed, of breathing the air—or something not too unlike it—in which His voice had sounded. They had had a little at first their bewilderments, their disconcertedness; the place was both humbler and grander than they had exactly prefigured, more at once of a cottage and of a museum, a little more archaically bare and yet a little more richly official. But the sense was strong with them that the point of view, for the inevitable ease of the connexion, patiently, indulgently awaited them; in addition to which, from the first evening, after closing-hour, when the last blank pilgrim had gone, the mere spell, the mystic presence—as if they had had it quite to themselves—were all they could have desired. They had received, at Grant-Jackson's behest and in addition to a table of instructions and admonitions by the number and in some particulars by the nature of which they found themselves slightly depressed, various little guides, manuals, travellers' tributes, literary memorials and other catch-penny publications; which, however, were to be for the moment swallowed up in the interesting episode of the induction or initiation appointed for them in advance at the hands of several persons whose relation to the establishment was, as superior to their own, still more official, and at those in especial of one of the ladies who had for so many years borne the brunt. About the instructions from above, about the shilling books and the well-known facts and the full-blown legend, the supervision, the subjection, the submission, the view as of a cage in which he should circulate and a groove in which he should slide, Gedge had preserved a certain play of mind; but all power of reaction appeared suddenly to desert him in the presence of his so visibly competent predecessor and as an effect of her good offices. He had not the resource, enjoyed by his wife, of seeing himself, with impatience, attired in black silk of a make characterised by just the right shade of austerity; so that this firm smooth expert and consummately respectable middle-aged person had him somehow, on the whole ground, completely at her mercy.

It was evidently something of a rueful moment when, as a lesson—she being for the day or two still in the field—he accepted Miss Putchin's suggestion of "going round" with her and with the successive squads of visitors she was there to deal with. He appreciated her method—he saw there had to *be* one; he admired her as succinct and definite; for there were the facts, as his wife had said at Blackport, and they were to be disposed of in the time; yet he felt a very little boy as he dangled, more than once, with Mrs. Gedge, at the tail of the human comet. The idea had been that they should by this attendance more fully embrace the possible accidents and incidents, so to put it, of the relation to the great public in which they were to find themselves; and the poor man's excited perception of the great public rapidly became such as to resist any diversion meaner than that of the admirable manner of their guide. It wandered from his gaping companions to that of the priestess in black silk, whom he kept asking himself if either he or Isabel could hope by any possibility ever remotely to resemble; then it bounded restlessly back to the numerous persons who revealed to him as it had never yet been revealed the happy power of the simple to hang upon the lips of the wise. The great thing seemed to be—and quite surprisingly—that the business was easy and the strain, which as a strain they had feared, moderate; so that he might have been puzzled, had he fairly caught himself in the act, by his recognising as the last effect of the impression an odd absence of the power really to rest in it, an agitation deep within him that vaguely threatened to grow. "It isn't, you see, so very complicated," the black silk lady seemed to throw off, with everything else, in her neat crisp cheerful way; in spite of which he already, the very first time—that is after several parties had been in and out and up and down—went so far as to wonder if there weren't more in it than she imagined. She was, so to speak, kindness itself—was all encouragement and reassurance; but it was just her slightly coarse redolence of these very things that, on repetition, before they parted, dimmed a little, as he felt, the light of his acknowledging smile. This again she took for a symptom of some pleading weakness in him—he could never be as brave as she; so that she wound up with a few pleasant words from the very depth of her experience. "You'll get into it, never fear—it will *come;* and then you'll feel as if you had never done anything else." He was afterwards to know that, on the spot, at this moment, he must have begun to wince a little at such a menace; that he might come to feel as if he had never done anything but what Miss Putchin did loomed for him, in germ, as a penalty to pay. The support she offered, none the less, continued to strike him; she put the whole thing on so sound a basis when she said: "You see they're so nice about it—they take such an interest. And they never do a thing they shouldn't. That was always everything to mother and me." "They," Gedge had already noticed, referred constantly and hugely, in the good woman's talk, to the millions who shuffled through the house; the pronoun in question was for ever on her lips, the hordes it represented filled her consciousness, the addition of their numbers ministered to her glory. Mrs. Gedge promptly fell in. "It must be indeed delightful to see the effect on so many and to feel that one may perhaps do something to make it—well, permanent." But he was kept silent by his becoming more sharply aware that this was a new view, for him, of the reference made, that he had never thought of the quality of the place as derived from Them, but from Somebody

Else, and that They, in short, seemed to have got into the way of crowding Him out. He found himself even a little resenting this for Him—which perhaps had something to do with the slightly invidious cast of his next enquiry.

"And are They always, as one might say—a—stupid?"

"Stupid!" She stared, looking as if no one *could* be such a thing in such a connexion. No one had ever been anything but neat and cheerful and fluent, except to be attentive and unobjectionable and, so far as was possible, American.

"What I mean is," he explained, "is there any perceptible proportion that take an interest in Him?"

His wife stepped on his toe; she deprecated levity. But his mistake fortunately was lost on their friend. "That's just why they come, that they take such an interest. I sometimes think they take more than about anything else in the world." With which Miss Putchin looked about at the place. "It *is* pretty, don't you think, the way they've got it now?" This, Gedge saw, was a different "They"; it applied to the powers that were—the people who had appointed him, the governing, visiting Body, in respect to which he was afterwards to remark to Mrs. Gedge that a fellow—it was the difficulty—didn't know "where to have her." His wife, at a loss, questioned at that moment the necessity of having her anywhere, and he said, good-humouredly "Of course; it's all right." He was in fact content enough with the last touches their friend had given the picture. "There are many who know all about it when they come, and the Americans often are tremendously up. Mother and me really enjoyed"—it was her only slip—"the interest of the Americans. We've sometimes had ninety a day, and all wanting to see and hear everything. But you'll work them off; you'll see the way—it's all experience." She came back for his comfort to that. She came back also to other things: she did justice to the considerable class who arrived positive and primed. "There are those who know more about it than you do. But *that* only comes from their interest."

"Who know more about what?" Gedge enquired.

"Why about the place. I mean they have their ideas—of what everything is, and *where* it is, and what it isn't and where it *should* be. They do ask questions," she said, yet not so much in warning as in the complacency of being herself seasoned and sound; "and they're down on you when you think you go wrong. As if you ever could! You know too much," she astutely smiled; "or you *will*."

"Oh you mustn't know *too* much, must you?" And Gedge now smiled as well. He knew, he thought, what he meant.

"Well, you must know as much as anybody else. I claim at any rate that I do," Miss Putchin declared. "They never really caught me out."

"I'm very certain of *that*"—and Mrs. Gedge had an elation almost personal.

"Surely," he said, "I don't want to be caught out." She rejoined that in such a case he would have *Them* down on him, and he saw that this time she meant the powers above. It quickened his sense of all the elements that were to reckon with, yet he felt at the same time that the powers above were not what he should most fear. "I'm glad," he observed, "that they ever ask questions; but I happened to notice, you know, that no one did today."

"Then you missed several—and no loss. There were three or four put to me too silly to remember. But of course they mostly *are* silly."

"You mean the questions?"

She laughed with all her cheer. "Yes, sir; I don't mean the answers."

Whereupon, for a moment snubbed and silent, he felt like one of the crowd. Then it made him slightly vicious. "I didn't know but you meant the people in general—till I remembered that I'm to understand from you that *they're* wise, only occasionally breaking down."

It wasn't really till then, he thought, that she lost patience;

and he had had, much more than he meant no doubt, a cross-questioning air. "You'll see for yourself." Of which he was sure enough. He was in fact so ready to take this that she came round to full accommodation, put it frankly that every now and then they broke out—not the silly, oh no, the intensely enquiring. "We've had quite lively discussions, don't you know, about well-known points. They want it all *their* way, and I know the sort that are going to as soon as I see them. That's one of the things you do—you get to know the sorts. And if it's what you're afraid of—their taking you up," she was further gracious enough to say, "you needn't mind a bit. What *do* they know, after all, when for us it's our life? I've never moved an inch, because, you see, I shouldn't have been here if I didn't know what I was. No more will *you* be a year hence—you know what I mean, putting it impossibly—if *you* don't. I expect you do, in spite of your fancies." And she dropped once more to bed-rock. "There are the facts. Otherwise where would any of us be? That's all you've got to go upon. A person, however cheeky, can't have them *his* way just because he takes it into his head. There can only be *one* way, and," she gaily added as she took leave of them, "I'm sure it's quite enough!"

III

GEDGE not only assented eagerly—one way *was* quite enough if it were the right one—but repeated it, after this conversation, at odd moments, several times over to his wife. "There can only be one way, one way," he continued to remark—though indeed much as if it were a joke; till she asked him how many more he supposed she wanted. He failed to answer this question, but resorted to another repetition. "There are the facts, the facts," which perhaps, however, he kept a little more to himself, sounding it at intervals in different parts of the house. Mrs. Gedge was full of comment on their clever introductress, though not restrictively save in the matter of her speech, "Me and mother," and a general tone—which certainly was not their sort of thing. "I don't know," he said, "perhaps it comes with the place, since speaking in immortal verse doesn't seem to come. It must be, one seems to see, one thing or the other. I dare say that in a few months I shall also be at it—'me and the wife.' "

"Why not 'me and the missus' at once?" Mrs. Gedge resentfully enquired. "I don't think," she observed at another time, "that I quite know what's the matter with you."

"It's only that I'm excited, awfully excited—as I don't see how one can't be. You wouldn't have a fellow drop into this berth as into an appointment at the Post Office. Here on the spot it goes to my head—how can that be helped? But we shall live into it, and perhaps," he said with an implication of the other possibility that was doubtless but part of his fine ecstasy, "we shall live through it." The place acted on his imagination—how, surely, shouldn't it? And his imagination acted on his nerves, and these things together, with the general vividness and the new and complete immersion, made rest for him almost impossible, so that he could scarce go to bed at night and even during the first week more than once rose in the small hours to move about, up and down, with his lamp—standing, sitting, listening, wondering, in the stillness, as if positively to recover some echo, to surprise some secret, of the *genius loci*. He couldn't have explained it—and didn't in fact need to explain it, at least to himself, since the impulse simply held him and shook him; but the time after closing, the time above all after the people—Them, as he felt himself on the way habitually to put it, predominant, insistent, all in the foreground—brought him, or ought to have brought him, he seemed to see, nearer to the enshrined Presence, enlarging the opportunity for communion and intensifying the sense of it. These nightly prowls, as he called them, were disquieting to his wife, who had no disposition to share in them, speaking with decision of the whole place as just the place to be forbidding after dark. She rejoiced in the distinctness, contiguous though it was, of their own little residence, where she trimmed the lamp and stirred the fire and heard the kettle sing, repairing the while the omissions of the small domestic who slept out; she foresaw herself, with some promptness, drawing rather sharply the line between her own precinct and that in which the great spirit might walk. It would be with them, the great spirit, all day—even if indeed on her making that remark, and in just that form, to her husband, he replied with a queer "But will he though?" And she vaguely imaged the development of a domestic antidote after a while, precisely, in the shape of curtains more markedly drawn and everything most modern and lively, tea, "patterns," the newspapers, the female fiction itself that they had reacted against at Blackport, quite defiantly cultivated.

These possibilities, however, were all right, as her companion said it was, all the first autumn—they had arrived at summer's end; and he might have been more than content with a special set of his own that he had access to from behind, passing out of their low door for the few steps between it and the Birthplace. With his lamp ever so carefully guarded and his nursed keys that made him free of treasures, he crossed the dusky interval so often that she began to qualify it as a habit that "grew." She spoke of it almost as if he had taken to drink, and he humoured that view of it by allowing the cup to be strong. This had been in truth altogether his immediate sense of it; strange and deep for him the spell of silent sessions before familiarity and, to some small extent, disappointment had set in. The exhibitional side of the establishment had struck him, even on arrival, as qualifying too much its character; he scarce knew what he might best have looked for, but the three or four rooms bristled overmuch, in the garish light of day, with busts and relics, not even ostensibly always *His,* old prints and old editions, old objects fashioned in His likeness, furniture "of the time" and autographs of celebrated worshippers. In the quiet hours and the deep dusk, none the less, under the play of the shifted lamp and that of his own emotion, these things too recovered their advantage, ministered to the mystery, or at all events to the impression, seemed consciously to offer themselves as personal to the poet. Not one of them was really or unchallengeably so, but they had somehow, through long association, got, as Gedge always phrased it, into the secret, and it was about the secret he asked them while he restlessly wandered. It wasn't till months had elapsed that he found how little they had to tell him, and he was quite at his ease with them when he knew they were by no means where his sensibility had first placed them. They were as out of it as he; only, to do them justice, they had made him immensely feel. And still, too, it was not they who had done that most, since his sentiment had gradually cleared itself to deep, to deeper refinements.

The Holy of Holies of the Birthplace was the low, the sublime Chamber of Birth, sublime because, as the Americans usually said—unlike the natives they mostly found words—it was so pathetic; and pathetic because it was—well, really nothing else in the world that one could name, number or measure. It was as empty as a shell of which the kernel has withered, and contained neither busts nor prints nor early copies; it contained only the Fact—*the* Fact itself—which, as he stood sentient there at midnight, our friend, holding his breath, allowed to sink into him. He *had* to take it as the place where the spirit would most walk and where He would therefore be most to be met, with possibilities of recognition and reciprocity. He hadn't, most probably—*He* hadn't—much inhabited the room, as men weren't apt, as a rule, to convert to their later use and involve in their wider fortune the scene itself of their nativity. But as there were moments when, in the conflict of theories, the sole certainty surviving for the critic threatened to be that He had not—unlike other successful men—*not* been born, so Gedge, though little of a critic, clung to the square feet of space that connected themselves, however feebly, with the positive appearance. He was little of a critic—he was nothing of one; he hadn't pretended to the character before coming, nor come to pretend to it; also, luckily for him, he was seeing day by day how little use he could possibly have for it. It would be to him, the attitude of a high expert, distinctly a stumbling-block, and that he rejoiced, as the winter waned, in his ignorance, was one of the propositions he betook himself, in his odd manner, to enunciating to his wife. She denied it, for hadn't she in the first place been present, wasn't she still present, at his pious, his tireless study of everything connected with the subject?—so present that she had herself learned more about it than had ever seemed likely. Then in the second place he wasn't to proclaim on the house-tops any point at which he might be weak, for who knew, if it should get abroad that they were ignorant, what effect might be produced—?

"On the attraction"—he took her up—"of the Show?"

He had fallen into the harmless habit of speaking of the place as the "Show"; but she didn't mind this so much as to be diverted by it. "No; on the attitude of the Body. You know they're pleased with us, and I don't see why you should want to spoil it. We got in by a tight squeeze—you know we've had evidence of that, and that it was about as much as our backers could manage. But we're proving a comfort to them, and it's absurd of you to question your suitability to people who were content with the Putchins."

"I don't, my dear," he returned, "question anything; but if I should do so it would be precisely because of the greater advantage constituted for the Putchins by the simplicity of their spirit. They were kept straight by the quality of their ignorance—which was denser even than mine. It was a mistake in us from the first to have attempted to correct or to disguise ours. We should have waited simply to become good parrots, to learn our lesson—all on the spot here, so little of it is wanted—and squawk it off."

"Ah 'squawk,' love—what a word to use about Him!"

"It isn't about Him—nothing's about Him. None of Them care tuppence about Him. The only thing They care about is this empty shell—or rather, for it isn't empty, the extraneous preposterous stuffing of it."

"Preposterous?" he made her stare with this as he hadn't yet done.

At sight of her look, however—the gleam, as it might have been, of a queer suspicion—he bent to her kindly and tapped her cheek. "Oh it's all right. We *must* fall back on the Putchins. Do you remember what she said?—'They've made it so pretty now.' They *have* made it pretty, and it's a first-rate show. It's a first-rate show and a first-rate billet, and He was a first-rate poet, and you're a first-rate woman—to put up so sweetly, I mean, with my nonsense."

She appreciated his domestic charm and she justified that part of his tribute which concerned herself. "I don't care how much of your nonsense you talk to me, so long as you *keep* it all for me and don't treat *Them* to it."

"The pilgrims? No," he conceded—"it isn't fair to Them. They mean well."

"What complaint have we after all to make of Them so long as They don't break off bits—as They used, Miss Putchin told us, so awfully—in order to conceal them about Their Persons? She broke Them at least of that."

"Yes," Gedge mused again; "I wish awfully she hadn't!"

"You'd like the relics destroyed, removed? That's all that's wanted!"

"There *are* no relics."

"There won't be any *soon*—unless you take care." But he was already laughing, and the talk wasn't dropped without his having patted her once more. An impression or two nevertheless remained with her from it, as he saw from a question she asked him on the morrow. "What did you mean yesterday about Miss Putchin's simplicity—it's keeping her 'straight'? Do you mean mentally?"

Her "mentally" was rather portentous, but he practically

confessed. "Well, it kept her up. I mean," he amended, laughing, "it kept her down."

It was really as if she had been a little uneasy. "You consider there's a danger of your being affected? You know what I mean—of its going to your head. You do know," she insisted as he said nothing. "Through your caring for him so. You'd certainly be right in that case about its having been a mistake for you to plunge so deep." And then as his listening without reply, though with his look a little sad for her, might have denoted that, allowing for extravagance of statement, he saw there was something in it: "Give up your prowls. Keep it for daylight. Keep it for *Them*."

"Ah," he smiled, "if one could! My prowls," he added, "are what I most enjoy. They're the only time, as I've told you before, that I'm really with *Him*. Then I don't see the place. He isn't the place."

"I don't care for what you 'don't see,'" she returned with vivacity; "the question is of what you do see."

Well, if it was, he waited before meeting it. "Do you know what I sometimes do?" And then as she waited too: "In the Birthroom there, when I look in late, I often put out my light. That makes it better."

"Makes what—?"

"Everything."

"What is it then you see in the dark?"

"Nothing!" said Morris Gedge.

"And what's the pleasure of that?"

"Well, what the American ladies say. It's so fascinating!"

IV

THE autumn was brisk, as Miss Putchin had told them it would be, but business naturally fell off with the winter months and the short days. There was rarely an hour indeed without a call of some sort, and they were never allowed to forget that they kept the shop in all the world, as they might say, where custom was least fluctuating. The seasons told on it, as they tell on travel, but no other influence, consideration or convulsion to which the population of the globe is exposed. This population, never exactly in simultaneous hordes, but in a full swift and steady stream, passed through the smoothly-working mill and went, in its variety of degrees duly impressed and edified, on its artless way. Gedge gave himself up, with much ingenuity of spirit, to trying to keep in relation with it; having even at moments, in the early time, glimpses of the chance that the impressions gathered from so rare an opportunity for contact with the general mind might prove as interesting as anything else in the connexion. Types, classes, nationalities, manners, diversities of behaviour, modes of seeing, feeling, of expression, would pass before him and become for him, after a fashion, the experience of an untravelled man. His journeys had been short and saving, but poetic justice again seemed inclined to work for him in placing him just at the point in all Europe perhaps where the confluence of races was thickest. The theory at any rate carried him on, operating helpfully for the term of his anxious beginnings and gilding in a manner—it was the way he characterised the case to his wife—the somewhat stodgy gingerbread of their daily routine. They hadn't known many people and their visiting-list was small—which made it again poetic justice that they should be visited on such a scale. They dressed and were at home, they were under arms and received, and except for the offer of refreshment—and Gedge had his view that there would eventually be a *buffet* farmed out to a great firm—their hospitality would have made them princely if mere hospitality ever did. Thus they were launched, and it was interesting; so that from having been ready to drop, originally, with fatigue they emerged as even-winded and strong in the legs as if they had had an Alpine holiday. This experience, Gedge opined, also represented, as a gain, a like seasoning of the spirit—by which he meant a certain command of impenetrable patience.

The patience was needed for the particular feature of the ordeal that, by the time the lively season was with them again, had disengaged itself as the sharpest—the immense assumption of veracities and sanctities, of the general soundness of the legend, with which every one arrived. He was well provided certainly for meeting it, and he gave all he had, yet he had sometimes the sense of a vague resentment on the part of his pilgrims at his not ladling out their fare with a bitter spoon. An irritation had begun to grumble in him during the comparatively idle months of winter when a pilgrim would turn up singly. The pious individual, entertained for the half-hour, had occasionally seemed to offer him the promise of beguilement or the semblance of a personal relation; it came back again to the few pleasant calls he had received in the course of a life almost void of social amenity. Sometimes he liked the person, the face, the speech: an educated man, a gentleman, not one of the herd; a graceful woman, vague, accidental, unconscious of him, but making him wonder, while he hovered, who she was. These chances represented for him light yearnings and faint flutters; they acted indeed within him to a special, an extraordinary tune. He would have liked to talk with such stray companions, to talk with them *really,* to talk with them as he might have talked had he met them where he couldn't meet them—at dinner, in the "world," on a visit at a country-house. Then he could have said—and about the shrine and the idol always—things he couldn't say now. The form in which his irritation first came to him was that of his feeling obliged to say to them—to the single visitor, even when sympathetic, quite as to the gaping group—the particular things, a dreadful dozen or so, that they expected. If he had thus arrived at characterising these things as dreadful the reason touched the very point that, for a while turning everything over, he kept dodging, not facing, trying to ignore. The point was that he was on his way to become two quite different persons, the public and the private—as to which it would somehow have to be managed that these persons should live together. He was splitting into halves, unmistakably—he who, whatever else he had been, had at least always been so entire and in his way so solid. One of the halves, or perhaps even, since the split promised to be rather unequal, one of the quarters, was the keeper, the showman, the priest of the idol; the other piece was the poor unsuccessful honest man he had always been.

There were moments when he recognised this primary character as he had never done before; when he in fact quite shook in his shoes at the idea that it perhaps had in reserve some supreme assertion of its identity. It was honest, verily, just by reason of the possibility. It was poor and unsuccessful because here it was just on the verge of quarrelling with its bread and butter. Salvation would be of course—the salvation of the showman—rigidly to *keep* it on the verge; not to let it, in other words, overpass by an inch. He might count on this, he said to himself, if there weren't any public—if there weren't thousands of people demanding of him what he was paid for. He saw the approach of the stage at which they would affect him, the thousands of people—and perhaps even more the earnest individual—as coming really to see if he were earning his wage. Wouldn't he soon begin to fancy them in league with the Body, practically deputed by it—given, no doubt, a kindled suspicion—to look in and report observations? It was the way he broke down with the lonely pilgrim that led to his first heart-searchings—broke down as to the courage required for damping an uncritical faith. What they all most wanted was to feel that everything was "just as it was"; only the shock of having to part with that vision was greater than any individual could bear unsupported. The bad moments were upstairs in the Birthroom, for here the forces pressing on the very edge assumed a dire intensity. The mere expression of eye, all-credulous, omnivorous and fairly moistening in the act, with which many persons gazed about, might eventually make it difficult for him to remain fairly civil. Often they came in pairs

—sometimes one had come before—and then they explained to each other. He in that case never corrected; he listened, for the lesson of listening: after which he would remark to his wife that there was no end to what he was learning. He saw that if he should really ever break down it would be with her he would begin. He had given her hints and digs enough, but she was so inflamed with appreciation that she either didn't feel them or pretended not to understand.

This was the greater complication that, with the return of the spring and the increase of the public, her services were more required. She took the field with him from an early hour; she was present with the party above while he kept an eye, and still more an ear, on the party below; and how could he know, he asked himself, what she might say to them and what she might suffer *Them* to say—or in other words, poor wretches, to believe—while removed from his control? Some day or other, and before too long, he couldn't but think, he must have the matter out with her—the matter, namely, of the *morality* of their position. The morality of women was special—he was getting lights on that. Isabel's conception of her office was to cherish and enrich the legend. It was already, the legend, very taking, but what was she there for but to make it more so? She certainly wasn't there to chill any natural piety. If it was all in the air—all in their "eye," as the vulgar might say—that He *had* been born in the Birthroom, where was the value of the sixpences they took? where the equivalent they had engaged to supply? "Oh dear, yes—just about *here*"; and she must tap the place with her foot. "Altered? Oh dear, no—save in a few trifling particulars; you see the place—and isn't that just the charm of it?—quite as *He* saw it. Very poor and homely, no doubt; but that's just what's so wonderful." He didn't want to hear her, and yet he didn't want to give her her head; he didn't want to make difficulties or to snatch the bread from her mouth. But he must none the less give her a warning before they had gone *too* far. That was the way, one evening in June, he put it to her; the affluence, with the finest weather, having lately been of the largest and the crowd all day fairly gorged with the story. "We mustn't, you know, go *too* far."

The odd thing was that she had now ceased even to be conscious of what troubled him—she was so launched in her own career. "Too far for what?"

"To save our immortal souls. We mustn't, love, tell too many lies."

She looked at him with dire reproach. "Ah now are you going to begin again?"

"I never *have* begun; I haven't wanted to worry you. But, you know, we don't know anything about it." And then as she stared, flushing: "About His having been born up there. About anything really. Not the least little scrap that would weigh in any other connexion as evidence. So don't rub it in so."

"Rub it in how?"

"That He *was* born—" But at sight of her face he only sighed. "Oh dear, oh dear!"

"Don't you think," she replied cuttingly, "that He was born anywhere?"

He hesitated—it was such an edifice to shake. "Well, we don't know. There's very little *to* know. He covered His tracks as no other human being has ever done."

She was still in her public costume and hadn't taken off the gloves she made a point of wearing as a part of that uniform; she remembered how the rustling housekeeper in the Border castle, on whom she had begun modelling herself, had worn them. She seemed official and slightly distant. "To cover His tracks. He must have had to exist. Have we got to give *that* up?"

"No, I don't ask you to give it up *yet*. But there's very little to go upon."

"And is that what I'm to tell Them in return for everything?"

Gedge waited—he walked about. The place was doubly still

after the bustle of the day, and the summer evening rested on it as a blessing, making it, in its small state and ancientry, mellow and sweet. It was good to be there and it would be good to stay. At the same time there was something incalculable in the effect on one's nerves of the great gregarious density. This was an attitude that had nothing to do with degrees and shades, the attitude of wanting all or nothing. And you couldn't talk things over with it. You could only do that with friends, and then but in cases where you were sure the friends wouldn't betray you. "Couldn't you adopt," he replied at last, "a slightly more discreet method? What we can say is that things have been *said;* that's all *we* have to do with. 'And is this really'—when they jam their umbrellas into the floor—'the very *spot* where He was born?' 'So it has, from a long time back, been described as being.' Couldn't one meet Them, to be decent a little, in some such way as that?"

She looked at him very hard. "Is that the way *you* meet them?"

"No; I've kept on lying—without scruple, without shame."

"Then why do you haul me up?"

"Because it has seemed to me we might, like true companions, work it out a little together."

This was not strong, he felt, as, pausing with his hands in his pockets, he stood before her; and he knew it as weaker still after she had looked at him a minute. "Morris Gedge, I propose to be *your* true companion, and I've come here to stay. That's all I've got to say." It was not, however, for "You had better try yourself and see," she presently added. "Give the place, give the story away, by so much as a look, and—well, I'd allow you about nine days. Then you'd see."

He feigned, to gain time, an innocence. "They'd take it so ill?" And then as she said nothing: "They'd turn and rend me? They'd tear me to pieces?"

But she wouldn't make a joke of it. "They wouldn't *have* it, simply."

"No—They wouldn't. That's what I say. They won't."

"You had better," she went on, "begin with Grant-Jackson. But even that isn't necessary. It would get to him, it would get to the Body, like wildfire."

"I see," said poor Gedge. And indeed for the moment he did see, while his companion followed up what she believed her advantage.

"Do you consider it's *all* a fraud?"

"Well, I grant you there was somebody. But the details are naught. The links are missing. The evidence—in particular about that room upstairs, in itself our Casa Santa—is *nil*. It was so awfully long ago." Which he knew again sounded weak.

"Of course it was awfully long ago—that's just the beauty and the interest. Tell Them, *tell* Them," she continued, "that the evidence is *nil,* and I'll tell Them something else." She spoke it with such meaning that his face seemed to show a question, to which she was on the spot of replying "I'll tell Them you're a—" She stopped, however, changing it. "I'll tell Them exactly the opposite. And I'll find out what you say—it won't take long —to do it. If we tell different stories *that* possibly may save us."

"I see what you mean. It would perhaps, as an oddity, have a success of curiosity. It might become a draw. Still, They but want broad masses." And he looked at her sadly. "You're no more than one of Them."

"If it's being no more than one of Them to love it," she answered, "then I certainly am. And I'm not ashamed of my company."

"To love *what*?" said Morris Gedge.

"To love to think He was born there."

"You think too much. It's bad for you." He turned away with his chronic moan. But it was without losing what she called after him.

"I decline to let the place down." And what was there indeed to say? They *were* there to keep it up.

V

He kept it up through the summer, but with the queerest consciousness, at times, of the want of proportion between his secret rage and the spirit of those from whom the friction came. He said to himself—so sore his sensibility had grown—that They were gregariously ferocious at the very time he was seeing Them as individually mild. He said to himself that They were mild only because *he* was—he flattered himself that he was divinely so, considering what he might be; and that he should, as his wife had warned him, soon enough have news of it were he to deflect by a hair's breadth from the line traced for him. *That* was the collective fatuity—that it was capable of turning on the instant both to a general and to a particular resentment. Since the least breath of discrimination would get him the sack without mercy, it was absurd, he reflected, to speak of his discomfort as light. He was gagged, he was goaded, as in omnivorous companies he doubtless sometimes showed by a strange silent glare. They'd get him the sack for that as well, if he didn't look out; therefore wasn't it in effect ferocity when you mightn't even hold your tongue? They wouldn't let you off with silence—They insisted on your committing yourself. It was the pound of flesh—They *would* have it; so under his coat he bled. But a wondrous peace, by exception, dropped on him one afternoon at the end of August. The pressure had, as usual, been high, but it had diminished with the fall of day, and the place was empty before the hour of closing. Then it was that, within a few minutes of this hour, there presented themselves a pair of pilgrims to whom in the ordinary course he would have remarked that they were, to his regret, too late. He was to wonder afterwards why the course had at sight of the visitors —a gentleman and a lady, appealing and fairly young—shown for him as other than ordinary; the consequence sprang doubtless from something rather fine and unnameable, something for example in the tone of the young man or in the light of his eye, after hearing the statement on the subject of the hour. "Yes, we know it's late; but it's just, I'm afraid, *because* of that. We've had rather a notion of escaping the crowd—as I suppose you mostly have one now; and it was really on the chance of finding you alone—!"

These things the young man said before being quite admitted, and they were words any one might have spoken who hadn't taken the trouble to be punctual or who desired, a little ingratiatingly, to force the door. Gedge even guessed at the sense that might lurk in them, the hint of a special tip if the point were stretched. There were no tips, he had often thanked his stars, at the Birthplace; there was the charged fee and nothing more; everything else was out of order, to the relief of a palm not formed by nature as a scoop. Yet in spite of everything, in spite especially of the almost audible chink of the gentleman's sovereigns, which might in another case exactly have put him out, he presently found himself, in the Birthroom, access to which he had gracefully enough granted, almost treating the visit as personal and private. The reason—well, the reason would have been, if anywhere, in something naturally persuasive on the part of the couple; unless it had been rather again, in the way the young man, once he was in the place, met the caretaker's expression of face, held it a moment and seemed to wish to sound it. That they were Americans was promptly clear, and Gedge could very nearly have told what kind; he had arrived at the point of distinguishing kinds, though the difficulty might have been with him now that the case before him was rare. He saw it suddenly in the light of the golden midland evening which reached them through low old windows, saw it with a rush of feeling, unexpected and smothered, that made him a moment wish to keep it before him as a case of inordinate happiness. It made him feel old shabby poor, but he watched it no less intensely for its doing so. They were children of fortune, of the greatest, as it might seem to Morris

Gedge, and they were of course lately married; the husband, smooth-faced and soft, but resolute and fine, several years older than the wife, and the wife vaguely, delicately, irregularly, but mercilessly pretty. Somehow the world was theirs; they gave the person who took the sixpences at the Birthplace such a sense of the high luxury of freedom as he had never had. The thing was that the world was theirs not simply because they had money—he had seen rich people enough—but because they could in a supreme degree think and feel and say what they liked. They had a nature and a culture, a tradition, a facility of some sort—and all producing in them an effect of positive beauty—that gave a light to their liberty and an ease to their tone. These things moreover suffered nothing from the fact that they happened to be in mourning; this was probably worn for some lately-deceased opulent father—if not some delicate mother who would be sure to have been a part of the source of the beauty; and it affected Gedge, in the gathered twilight and at his odd crisis, as the very uniform of their distinction.

He couldn't quite have said afterwards by what steps the point had been reached, but it had become at the end of five minutes a part of their presence in the Birthroom, a part of the young man's look, a part of the charm of the moment, and a part above all of a strange sense within him of "Now or never!" that Gedge had suddenly, thrillingly, let himself go. He hadn't been definitely conscious of drifting to it; he had been, for that, too conscious merely of thinking how different, in all their range, were such a united couple from another united couple known to him. They were everything he and his wife weren't; this was more than anything else the first lesson of their talk. Thousands of couples of whom the same was true certainly had passed before him, but none of whom it was true with just that engaging intensity. And just *because* of their transcendent freedom; that was what, at the end of five minutes, he saw it all come back to. The husband, who had been there at some earlier time, had his impression, which he wished now to make his wife share. But he already, Gedge could see, hadn't concealed it from her. A pleasant irony in fine our friend seemed to taste in the air—he who hadn't yet felt free to taste his own.

"I think you weren't here four years ago"—that was what the young man had almost begun by remarking. Gedge liked his remembering it, liked his frankly speaking to him; all the more that he had offered, as it were, no opening. He had let them look about below and then had taken them up, but without words, without the usual showman's song, of which he would have been afraid. The visitors didn't ask for it; the young man had taken the matter out of his hands by himself dropping for the benefit of the young woman a few detached remarks. What Gedge oddly felt was that these remarks were not inconsiderate of him; he had heard others, both of the priggish order and the crude, that might have been called so. And as the young man hadn't been aided to this cognition of him as new, it already began to make for them a certain common ground. The ground became immense when the visitor presently added with a smile: "There was a good lady, I recollect, who had a great deal to say."

It was the gentleman's smile that had done it; the irony *was* there. "Ah there has been a great deal said." And Gedge's look at his interlocutor doubtless showed his sense of being sounded. It was extraordinary of course that a perfect stranger should have guessed the travail of his spirit, should have caught the gleam of his inner commentary. That probably leaked in spite of him out of his poor old eyes. "Much of it, in such places as this," he heard himself adding, "is of course said very irresponsibly." *Such places as this!*—he winced at the words as soon as he had uttered them.

There was no wincing, however, on the part of his pleasant companions. "Exactly so; the whole thing becomes a sort of stiff smug convention—like a dressed-up sacred doll in a Spanish church—which you're a monster if you touch."

"A monster," Gedge assented, meeting his eyes.

The young man smiled, but he thought looking at him a little harder. "A blasphemer."

"A blasphemer."

It seemed to do his visitor good—he certainly *was* looking at him harder. Detached as he was he was interested—he was at least amused. "Then you don't claim or at any rate don't insist—? I mean you personally."

He had an identity for him, Gedge felt, that he couldn't have had for a Briton, and the impulse was quick in our friend to testify to this perception. "I don't insist to *you.*"

The young man laughed. "It really—I assure you if I may—wouldn't do any good. I'm too awfully interested."

"Do you mean," his wife lightly enquired, "in—a—pulling it down? That's rather in what you've said to me."

"Has he said to you," Gedge intervened, though quaking a little, "that he would like to pull it down?"

She met, in her free sweetness, this appeal with such a charm! "Oh perhaps not quite the *house*—!"

"Good. You see we live on it—I mean *we* people."

The husband had laughed, but had now so completely ceased to look about him that there seemed nothing left for him but to talk avowedly with the caretaker. "I'm interested," he explained, "in what I think *the* interesting thing—or at all events the eternally tormenting one. The fact of the abysmally little that, in proportion, we know."

"In proportion to what?" his companion asked.

"Well, to what there must have been—to what in fact there *is* —to wonder about. That's the interest; it's immense. He escapes us like a thief at night, carrying off—well, carrying off everything. And people pretend to catch Him like a flown canary, over whom you can close your hand, and put Him back in the cage. He won't *go* back; he won't *come* back. He's not"—the young man laughed—"such a fool! It makes Him the happiest of all great men."

He had begun by speaking to his wife, but had ended, with

his friendly, his easy, his indescribable competence, for Gedge—poor Gedge who quite held his breath and who felt, in the most unexpected way, that he had somehow never been in such good society. The young wife, who for herself meanwhile had continued to look about, sighed out, smiled out—Gedge couldn't have told which—her little answer to these remarks. "It's rather a pity, you know, that He *isn't* here. I mean as Goethe's at Weimar. For Goethe *is* at Weimar."

"Yes, my dear; that's Goethe's bad luck. There he sticks. *This* man isn't anywhere. I defy you to catch Him."

"Why not say, beautifully," the young woman laughed, "that, like the wind, He's everywhere?"

It wasn't of course the tone of discussion, it was the tone of pleasantry, though of better pleasantry, Gedge seemed to feel, and more within his own appreciation, than he had ever listened to; and this was precisely why the young man could go on without the effect of irritation, answering his wife but still with eyes for their companion. "I'll be hanged if He's *here*!"

It was almost as if he were taken—that is, struck and rather held—by their companion's unruffled state, which they hadn't meant to ruffle, but which suddenly presented its interest, perhaps even projected its light. The gentleman didn't know, Gedge was afterwards to say to himself, how that hypocrite was inwardly all of a tremble, how it seemed to him his fate was being literally pulled down on his head. He was trembling for the moment certainly too much to speak; abject he might be, but he didn't want his voice to have the absurdity of a quaver. And the young woman—charming creature!—still had another word. It was for the guardian of the spot, and she made it in her way delightful. They had remained in the Holy of Holies, where she had been looking for a minute, with a ruefulness just marked enough to be pretty, at the queer old floor. "Then if you say it *wasn't* in this room He was born—well, what's the use?"

"What's the use of what?" her husband asked. "The use,

you mean, of our coming here? Why the place is charming in itself. And it's also interesting," he added to Gedge, "to know how you get on."

Gedge looked at him a moment in silence, but answering the young woman first. If poor Isabel, he was thinking, could only have been like that!—not as to youth, beauty, arrangement of hair or picturesque grace of hat—these things he didn't mind; but as to sympathy, facility, light perceptive, and yet not cheap, detachment! "I don't say it wasn't—but I don't say it *was*."

"Ah but doesn't that," she returned, "come very much to the same thing? And don't They want also to see where He had His dinner and where He had His tea?"

"They want everything," said Morris Gedge. "They want to see where He hung up His hat and where He kept His boots and where His mother boiled her pot."

"But if you don't show them—?"

"They show *me*. It's in all their little books."

"You mean," the husband asked, "that you've only to hold your tongue?"

"I try to," said Gedge.

"Well," his visitor smiled, "I see you *can*."

Gedge hesitated. "I can't."

"Oh well," said his friend, "what does it matter?"

"I do speak," he continued. "I can't sometimes not."

"Then how do you get on?"

Gedge looked at him more abjectly, to his own sense, than ever at any one—even at Isabel when she frightened him. "I don't get on. I speak," he said—"since I've spoken to *you*."

"Oh *we* shan't hurt you!" the young man reassuringly laughed.

The twilight meanwhile had sensibly thickened, the end of the visit was indicated. They turned together out of the upper room and came down the narrow stair. The words just exchanged might have been felt as producing an awkwardness which the young woman gracefully felt the impulse to dissipate. "You must rather wonder why we've come." And it was the first note for Gedge of a further awkwardness—as if he had definitely heard it make the husband's hand, in a full pocket, begin to fumble.

It was even a little awkwardly that the husband still held off. "Oh we like it as it is. There's always *something*." With which they had approached the door of egress.

"What is there, please?" asked Morris Gedge, not yet opening the door, since he would fain have kept the pair on, and conscious only for a moment after he had spoken that his question was just having for the young man too dreadfully wrong a sound. This personage wondered yet feared, and had evidently for some minutes been putting himself a question; so that, with his preoccupation, the caretaker's words had represented to him inevitably: "What is there, please, for *me*?" Gedge already knew with it moreover that he wasn't stopping him in time. He had uttered that challenge to show he himself wasn't afraid, and he must have had in consequence, he was subsequently to reflect, a lamentable air of waiting.

The visitor's hand came out. "I hope I may take the liberty—?" What afterwards happened our friend scarcely knew, for it fell into a slight confusion, the confusion of a queer gleam of gold—a sovereign fairly thrust at him; of a quick, almost violent motion on his own part, which, to make the matter worse, might well have sent the money rolling on the floor; and then of marked blushes all round and a sensible embarrassment; producing indeed in turn rather oddly and ever so quickly an increase of communion. It was as if the young man had offered him money to make up to him for having, as it were, led him on, and then, perceiving the mistake, but liking him the better for his refusal, had wanted to obliterate this aggravation of his original wrong. He had done so, presently, while Gedge got the door open, by saying the best thing he could, and by saying it frankly and gaily. "Luckily it doesn't at all affect the *work*!"

The small town-street, quiet and empty in the summer eventide, stretched to right and left, with a gabled and timbered house or two, and fairly seemed to have cleared itself to congruity with the historic void over which our friends, lingering an instant to converse, looked at each other. The young wife, rather, looked about a moment at all there wasn't to be seen, and then, before Gedge had found a reply to her husband's remark, uttered, evidently in the interest of conciliation, a little question of her own that she tried to make earnest. "It's our unfortunate ignorance, you mean, that doesn't?"

"Unfortunate or fortunate. I like it so," said the husband. " 'The play's the thing.' Let the author alone."

Gedge, with his key on his forefinger, leaned against the door-post, took in the stupid little street and was sorry to see them go—they seemed so to abandon him. "That's just what They won't do—nor let *me* do. It's all I want—to let the author alone. Practically"—he felt himself getting the last of his chance —"there *is* no author; that is for us to deal with. There are all the immortal people—*in* the work; but there's nobody else."

"Yes," said the young man—"that's what it comes to. There should really, to clear the matter up, be no such Person."

"As you say," Gedge returned, "it's what it comes to. There *is* no such Person."

The evening air listened, in the warm thick midland stillness, while the wife's little cry rang out. "But *wasn't* there—?"

"There was somebody," said Gedge against the door-post. "But They've killed Him. And, dead as He is, They keep it up, They do it over again, They kill Him every day."

He was aware of saying this so grimly—more than he wished —that his companions exchanged a glance and even perhaps looked as if they felt him extravagant. That was really the way Isabel had warned him all the others would be looking if he should talk to Them as he talked to *her*. He liked, however, for that matter, to hear how he should sound when pronounced incapable through deterioration of the brain. "Then if there's no author, if there's nothing to be said but that there isn't anybody," the young woman smilingly asked, "why in the world should there be a house?"

"There shouldn't," said Morris Gedge.

Decidedly, yes, he affected the young man. "Oh, I don't say, mind you, that you should pull it down!"

"Then where would you *go*?" their companion sweetly enquired.

"That's what my wife asks," Gedge returned.

"Then keep it up, keep it up!" And the husband held out his hand.

"That's what my wife says," Gedge went on as he shook it.

The young woman, charming creature, emulated the other visitor; she offered their remarkable friend her handshake. "Then mind your wife."

The poor man faced her gravely. "I would if she were such a wife as you!"

VI

It had made for him, all the same, an immense difference; it had given him an extraordinary lift, so that a certain sweet aftertaste of his freedom might a couple of months later have been suspected of aiding to produce for him another and really a more considerable adventure. It was an absurd way to reason, but he had been, to his imagination, for twenty minutes in good society—that being the term that best described for him the company of people to whom he hadn't to talk, as he phrased it, rot. It was his title to good society that he had, in his doubtless awkward way, affirmed; and the difficulty was just that, having affirmed it, he couldn't take back the affirmation. Few things had happened to him in life, that is few that were agreeable, but at least *this* had, and he wasn't so constructed that he could go on as if it hadn't. It was going on as if it had, however, that landed him, alas! in the situation unmistakeably marked by a visit from Grant-Jackson late one afternoon toward the end of

October. This had been the hour of the call of the young Americans. Every day that hour had come round something of the deep throb of it, the successful secret, woke up; but the two occasions were, of a truth, related only by being so intensely opposed. The secret had been successful in that he had said nothing of it to Isabel, who, occupied in their own quarter while the incident lasted, had neither heard the visitors arrive nor seen them depart. It was on the other hand scarcely successful in guarding itself from indirect betrayals. There were two persons in the world at least who felt as he did; they were persons also who had treated him, benignly, as feeling after *their* style; who had been ready in fact to overflow in gifts as a sign of it, and though they were now off in space they were still with him sufficiently in spirit to make him play, as it were, with the sense of their sympathy. This in turn made him, as he was perfectly aware, more than a shade or two reckless, so that, in his reaction from that gluttony of the public for false facts which had from the first tormented him, he fell into the habit of sailing, as he would have said, too near the wind, or in other words—all in presence of the people—of washing his hands of the legend. He had crossed the line—he knew it; he had struck wild—They drove him to it; he had substituted, by a succession of uncontrollable profanities, an attitude that couldn't be understood for an attitude that but too evidently *had* been.

This was of course the franker line, only he hadn't taken it, alas! for frankness—hadn't in the least really adopted it at all, but had been simply himself caught up and disposed of by it, hurled by his fate against the bedizened walls of the temple, quite in the way of a priest possessed to excess of the god, or, more vulgarly, that of a blind bull in a china-shop—an animal to which he often compared himself. He had let himself fatally go, in fine, just for irritation, for rage, having, in his predicament, nothing whatever to do with frankness—a luxury reserved for quite other situations. It had always been his view that one lived to learn; he had learned something every hour of his life, though people mostly never knew what, in spite of its having generally been—hadn't it?—at somebody's expense. What he was at present continually learning was the sense of a form of words heretofore so vain—the famous "false position" that had so often helped out a phrase. One used names in that way without knowing what they were worth; then of a sudden, one fine day, their meaning grew bitter in the mouth. This was a truth with the relish of which his fireside hours were occupied, and he was aware of how much it exposed a man to look so perpetually as if something had disagreed with him. The look to be worn at the Birthplace was properly the beatific, and when once it had fairly been missed by those who took it for granted, who indeed paid sixpence for it—like the table-wine in provincial France it was *compris*—one would be sure to have news of the remark.

News accordingly was what Gedge had been expecting—and what he knew, above all, had been expected by his wife, who had a way of sitting at present as with an ear for a certain knock. She didn't watch him, didn't follow him about the house, at the public hours, to spy upon his treachery; and that could touch him even though her averted eyes went through him more than her fixed. Her mistrust was so perfectly expressed by her manner of showing she trusted that he never felt so nervous, never tried so to keep straight, as when she most let him alone. When the crowd thickened and they had of necessity to receive together he tried himself to get off by allowing her as much as possible the word. When people appealed to him he turned to her—and with more of ceremony than their relation warranted: he couldn't help *this* either, if it seemed ironic—as to the person most concerned or most competent. He flattered himself at these moments that no one would have guessed her being his wife; especially as, to do her justice, she met his manner with a wonderful grim bravado—grim, so to say, for himself, grim by its outrageous cheerfulness for the simple-minded. The lore she *did* produce for them, the associations of the sacred spot she developed, multiplied, embroidered; the things in short she said and the stupendous way she said them! She wasn't a bit ashamed, since why need virtue be ever ashamed? It *was* virtue, for it put bread into his mouth—he meanwhile on his side taking it out of hers. He had seen Grant-Jackson on the October day in the Birthplace itself—the right setting of course for such an interview; and what had occurred was that, precisely, when the scene had ended and he had come back to their own sitting-room, the question she put to him for information was: "Have you settled it that I'm to starve?"

She had for a long time said nothing to him so straight—which was but a proof of her real anxiety; the straightness of Grant-Jackson's visit, following on the very slight sinuosity of a note shortly before received from him, made tension show for what it was. By this time, really, however, his decision had been taken; the minutes elapsing between his reappearance at the domestic fireside and his having, from the other threshold, seen Grant-Jackson's broad well-fitted back, the back of a banker and a patriot, move away, had, though few, presented themselves to him as supremely critical. They formed, as it were, the hinge of his door, that door actually ajar so as to show him a possible fate beyond it, but which, with his hand, in a spasm, thus tightening on the knob, he might either open wide or close partly or altogether. He stood at autumn dusk in the little museum that constituted the vestibule of the temple, and there, as with a concentrated push at the crank of a windlass, he brought himself round. The portraits on the walls seemed vaguely to watch for it; it was in their august presence—kept dimly august for the moment by Grant-Jackson's impressive check of his application of a match to the vulgar gas—that the great man had uttered, as if it said all, his "You know, my dear fellow, really—!" He had managed it with the special tact of a fat man, always, when there *was* any, very fine; he had got the most out of the time, the place, the setting, all the little massed admonitions and symbols; confronted there with his victim on the spot that he took occasion to name afresh as, to *his* piety and patriotism, the most sacred on earth, he had given it to be understood that in the first place he was lost in amazement and that in the second he expected a single warning now to suffice. Not to insist too much moreover on the question of gratitude, he would let his remonstrance rest, if need be, solely on the question of taste. *As* a matter of taste alone—! But he was surely not to be obliged to follow that up. Poor Gedge indeed would have been sorry to oblige him, for he saw it was exactly to the atrocious taste of unthankfulness the allusion was made. When he said he wouldn't dwell on what the fortunate occupant of the post owed him for the stout battle originally fought on his behalf, he simply meant he *would*. That was his tact—which, with everything else that has been mentioned, in the scene, to help, really had the ground to itself. The day *had* been when Gedge couldn't have thanked him enough—though he had thanked him, he considered, almost fulsomely—and nothing, nothing that he could coherently or reputably name, had happened since then. From the moment he was pulled up, in short, he had no case, and if he exhibited, instead of one, only hot tears in his eyes, the mystic gloom of the temple either prevented his friend from seeing them or rendered it possible that they stood for remorse. He had dried them, with the pads formed by the base of his bony thumbs, before he went in to Isabel. This was the more fortunate as, in spite of her enquiry, prompt and pointed, he but moved about the room looking at her hard. Then he stood before the fire a little with his hands behind him and his coat-tails divided, quite as the person in permanent possession. It was an indication his wife appeared to take in; but she put nevertheless presently another question. "You object to telling me what he said?"

"He said 'You know, my dear fellow, really—!' "

"And is that all?"

"Practically. Except that I'm a thankless beast."

"Well!" she responded, not with dissent.

"You mean that I *am*?"

"Are those the words he used?" she asked with a scruple.

Gedge continued to think. "The words he used were that I give away the Show and that, from several sources, it has come round to Them."

"As of course a baby would have known!" And then as her husband said nothing: "Were *those* the words he used?"

"Absolutely. He couldn't have used better ones."

"Did he call it," Mrs. Gedge enquired, "the 'Show'?"

"Of course he did. The Biggest on Earth."

She winced, looking at him hard—she wondered, but only for a moment. "Well, it *is*."

"Then it's something," Gedge went on, "to have given *that* away. But," he added, "I've taken it back."

"You mean you've been convinced?"

"I mean I've been scared."

"At last, at last!" she gratefully breathed.

"Oh it was easily done. It was only two words. But here I am."

Her face was now less hard for him. "And what two words?"

"'You know, Mr. Gedge, that it simply won't do.' That was all. But it was the way such a man says them."

"I'm glad then," Mrs. Gedge frankly averred, "that he *is* such a man. How did you ever think it *could* do?"

"Well, it was my critical sense. I didn't ever know I had one—till They came and (by putting me here) waked it up in me. Then I had somehow, don't you see? to live with it; and I seemed to feel that, with one thing and another, giving it time and in the long run, it might, it *ought* to, come out on top of the heap. Now that's where, he says, it simply won't 'do.' So I must put it—I *have* put it—at the bottom."

"A very good place then for a critical sense!" And Isabel, more placidly now, folded her work. "*If*, that is, you can only keep it there. If it doesn't struggle up again."

"It can't struggle." He was still before the fire, looking round at the warm low room, peaceful in the lamplight, with the hum of the kettle for the ear, with the curtain drawn over the leaded casement, a short moreen curtain artfully chosen by Isabel for the effect of the olden time, its virtue of letting the light within show ruddy to the street. "It's dead," he went on; "I killed it just now."

He really spoke so that she wondered. "Just now?"

"There in the other place—I strangled it, poor thing, in the dark. If you'll go out and see, there must be blood. Which, indeed," he added, "on an altar of sacrifice, is all right. But the place is for ever spattered."

"I don't want to go out and see." She locked her hands over the needlework folded on her knee, and he knew, with her eyes on him, that a look he had seen before was in her face. "You're off your head, you know, my dear, in a way." Then, however, more cheeringly: "It's a good job it hasn't been too late."

"Too late to get it under?"

"Too late for Them to give you the second chance that I thank God you accept."

"Yes, if it *had* been—!" And he looked away as through the ruddy curtain and into the chill street. Then he faced her again. "I've scarcely got over my fright yet. I mean," he went on, "for you."

"And I mean for *you*. Suppose what you had come to announce to me now were that we had *got* the sack. How should I enjoy, do you think, seeing you turned out? Yes, out *there*!" she added as his eyes again moved from their little warm circle to the night of early winter on the other side of the pane, to the rare quick footsteps, to the closed doors, to the curtains drawn like their own, behind which the small flat town, intrinsically dull, was sitting down to supper.

He stiffened himself as he warmed his back; he held up his head, shaking himself a little as if to shake the stoop out of his shoulders, but he had to allow she was right. "What would have become of us?"

"What indeed? We should have begged our bread—or I should be taking in washing."

He was silent a little. "I'm too old. I should have begun sooner."

"Oh God forbid!" she cried.

"The pinch," he pursued, "is that I can do nothing else."

"Nothing whatever!" she agreed with elation.

"Whereas here—if I cultivate it—I perhaps *can* still lie. But I must cultivate it."

"Oh you old dear!" And she got up to kiss him.

"I'll do my best," he said.

VII

"Do you remember us?" the gentleman asked and smiled—with the lady beside him smiling too; speaking so much less as an earnest pilgrim or as a tiresome tourist than as an old acquaintance. It was history repeating itself as Gedge had somehow never expected, with almost everything the same except that the evening was now a mild April-end, except that the visitors had put off mourning and showed all their bravery—besides showing, as he doubtless did himself, though so differently, for a little older; except, above all, that—oh seeing them again suddenly affected him not a bit as the thing he'd have supposed it. "We're in England again and we were near; I've a brother at Oxford with whom we've been spending a day, so that we thought we'd come over." This the young man pleasantly said while our friend took in the queer fact that he must himself seem to them rather coldly to gape. They had come in the same way at the quiet close; another August had passed, and this was the second spring; the Birthplace, given the hour, was about to suspend operations till the morrow; the last lingerer had gone and the fancy of the visitors was once more for a look round by themselves. This represented surely no greater presumption than the terms on which they had last parted with him seemed to warrant; so that if he did inconsequently stare it was just in fact because he was so supremely far from having forgotten them. But the sight of the pair luckily had a double effect, and the first precipitated the second—the second being really his sudden vision that everything perhaps depended for him on his recognising no complication. He must go straight on, since it was what had for more than a year now so handsomely answered; he must brazen it out consistently, since that only was what his dignity was at last reduced to. He mustn't be afraid in one way any more than he had been in another; besides which it came over him to the point of his flushing for it that their visit, in its essence, must have been for himself. It was good society again, and *they* were the same. It wasn't for him therefore to behave as if he couldn't meet them.

These deep vibrations, on Gedge's part, were as quick as they were deep; they came in fact all at once, so that his response, his declaration that it was all right—"Oh *rather;* the hour doesn't matter for *you*!"—had hung fire but an instant; and when they were well across the threshold and the door closed behind them, housed in the twilight of the temple, where, as before, the votive offerings glimmered on the walls, he drew the long breath of one who might by a self-betrayal have done something too dreadful. For what had brought them back was indubitably not the glamour of the shrine itself—since he had had a glimpse of their analysis of that quantity; but their critical (not to say their sentimental) interest in the queer case of the priest. Their call was the tribute of curiosity, of sympathy, of a compassion really, as such things went, exquisite—a tribute *to* that queerness which entitled them to the frankest welcome. They had wanted, for the generous wonder of it, to judge how he was getting on, how such a man in such a place *could;* and they had doubtless more than half-expected to see the door opened by somebody who had succeeded him. Well, somebody *had*—only with a strange equivocation; as they would have, poor things, to make out themselves, an embarrassment for which he pitied them. Nothing could have been more odd, but verily it was this troubled vision of their possible bewilderment, and this compunctious view of such a return for their amenity, that practically determined in him his tone. The lapse of the months had but made their name familiar to him; they had on the other occasion inscribed it, among the thousand names, in the current public register, and he had since then, for reasons of his own, reasons of feeling, again and again turned back to it. It was nothing in itself; it told him nothing—"Mr. and Mrs. B. D. Hayes, New York"—one of those American labels that were just like every other American label and that were precisely the most remarkable thing about people reduced to achieving an identity in such other ways. They could be Mr. and Mrs. B. D. Hayes and yet could be, with all presumptions missing—well, what these callers were. It had quickly enough indeed cleared the situation a little further that his friends had absolutely, the other time, as it came back to him, warned him of his original danger, their anxiety about which had been the last note sounded among them. What he was afraid of, with this reminiscence, was that, finding him still safe, they would, the next thing, definitely congratulate him and perhaps even, no less candidly, ask him how he had managed. It was with the sense of nipping some such enquiry in the bud that, losing no time and holding himself with a firm grip, he began on the spot, downstairs, to make plain to them how he had managed. He routed the possibility of the question in short by the assurance of his answer. "Yes, yes, I'm still here; I suppose it *is* in a manner to one's profit that one does, such as it is, one's best." He did his best on the present occasion, did it with the gravest face he had ever worn and a soft serenity that was like a large damp sponge passed over their previous meeting—over everything in it, that is, but the fact of its pleasantness.

"We stand here, you see, in the old living-room, happily still to be reconstructed in the mind's eye, in spite of the havoc of time, which we have fortunately of late years been able to arrest. It was of course rude and humble, but it must have been snug and quaint, and we have at least the pleasure of knowing that the tradition in respect to the features that do remain is delightfully uninterrupted. Across that threshold He habitually passed; through those low windows, in childhood, He peered out into the world that He was to make so much happier by the gift to it of His genius; over the boards of this floor—that is over *some* of them, for we mustn't be carried away!—his little feet often pattered; and the beams of this ceiling (we must really in some places take care of *our* heads!) he endeavoured, in boyish strife, to jump up and touch. It's not often that in the early home of genius and renown the whole tenor of existence is laid so bare, not often that we are able to retrace, from point to point and from step to step, its connexion with objects, with influences—to build it round again with the little solid facts out of which it sprang. This therefore, I need scarcely remind you, is what makes the small space between these walls—so modest to measurement, so insignificant of aspect—unique on all the earth. *There's nothing like it,*" Morris Gedge went on, insisting as solemnly and softly, for his bewildered hearers, as over a pulpit-edge; "there's nothing at all like it anywhere in the world. There's nothing, only reflect, for the combination of greatness and, as we venture to say, of intimacy. You may find elsewhere perhaps absolutely fewer changes, but where shall you find a *Presence* equally diffused, uncontested and undisturbed? Where in particular shall you find, on the part of the abiding spirit, an equally towering eminence? You may find elsewhere eminence of a considerable order, but where shall you find *with* it, don't you see, changes after all so few and the contemporary element caught so, as it were, in the very fact?" His visitors, at first confounded but gradually spellbound, were still gaping with the universal gape—wondering, he judged, into what strange pleasantry he had been suddenly moved to explode, and yet beginning to see in him an intention beyond a joke, so that they started, at this point, they almost jumped, when, by as rapid a transition, he made, toward the old fireplace, a dash that seemed to illustrate precisely the act of eager catching. "It is in this old chimney-corner, the quaint inglenook of our ancestors—just there in the far angle, where His little stool was placed, and where, I dare say, if we could look close enough, we should find the hearthstone scraped with His little feet—that we see the inconceivable child gazing into the blaze of the old oaken logs and making out there pictures and stories, see Him conning, with curly bent head, His well-worn hornbook, or poring over some scrap of an ancient ballad, some page of some such rudely-bound volume of chronicles as lay, we may be sure, in His father's window-seat."

It was, he even himself felt at this moment, wonderfully done; no auditors, for all his thousands, had ever yet so inspired him. The odd slightly alarmed shyness in the two faces, as if in a drawing-room, in their "good society" exactly, some act incongruous, something grazing the indecent, had abruptly been perpetrated, the painful reality of which stayed itself before coming home—the visible effect on his friends in fine wound him up as to the sense that *they* were worth the trick. It came of itself now—he had got it so by heart; but perhaps really it had never come so well, with the staleness so disguised, the interest so renewed and the clerical unction demanded by the priestly character so successfully distilled. Mr. Hayes of New York had more than once looked at his wife, and Mrs. Hayes of New York had more than once looked at her husband—only, up to now, with a stolen glance, with eyes it hadn't been easy to detach from the remarkable countenance by the aid of which their entertainer held them. At present, however, after an exchange less furtive, they ventured on a sign that they hadn't been appealed to in vain. "Charming, charming, Mr. Gedge!" Mr. Hayes broke out. "We feel that we've caught you in the mood."

His wife hastened to assent—it eased the tension. "It *would* be quite the way; except," she smiled, "that you'd be too dangerous. You've really a genius!"

Gedge looked at her hard, but yielding no inch, even though she touched him there at a point of consciousness that quivered. This was the prodigy for him, and had been, the year through —that he did it all, he found, easily, did it better than he had done anything else in life; with so high and broad an effect, in truth, an inspiration so rich and free, that his poor wife now, literally, had been moved more than once to fresh fear. She had had her bad moments, he knew, after taking the measure of his new direction—moments of readjusted suspicion in which she wondered if he hadn't simply adopted another, a different perversity. There would be more than one fashion of giving away the Show, and wasn't *this* perhaps a question of giving it away by excess? He could dish them by too much romance as well as by too little; she hadn't hitherto fairly grasped that there might *be* too much. It was a way like another, at any rate, of reducing the place to the absurd; which reduction, if he didn't look out, would reduce *them* again to the prospect of the streets, and this time surely without appeal. It all depended indeed—he knew she knew that—on how much Grant-Jackson and the others, how much the Body, in a word, would take. He knew she knew what he himself held it would take—that he considered no limit could be imputed to the quantity. They simply wanted it piled up, and so did every one else; wherefore if no one reported him as before why were They to be uneasy? It was in consequence of idiots tempted to reason that he had been dealt with before; but as there was now no form of idiocy that he didn't systematically flatter, goading it on really to its *own* private doom, who was ever to pull the string of the guillotine? The axe was in the air—yes; but in a world gorged to satiety there were no revolutions. And it had been vain for Isabel to ask if the other thunder-growl also hadn't come out of the blue. There was actually proof positive that the winds were now at rest. How could they be more so?—he appealed to the receipts. These were golden days—the Show had never so flourished. So he had argued, so he was arguing still—and, it had to be owned, with every appearance in his favour. Yet if he inwardly winced at the tribute to his plausibility rendered by his flushed friends, this was because he felt in it the real ground of his optimism. The charming woman before him acknowledged his "genius" as he himself had had to do. He had been surprised at his facility until he had grown used to it. Whether or no he had, as a fresh menace to his future, found a new perversity, he had found a vocation much older, evidently, than he had at first been prepared to recognise. He had done himself injustice. He liked to be brave because it came so easy; he could measure it off by the yard. It was in the Birth-room, above all, that he continued to do this, having ushered up his companions without, as he was still more elated to feel, the turn of a hair. She might take it as she liked, but he had had the lucidity—all, that is, for his own safety—to meet without the grace of an answer the homage of her beautiful smile. She took it apparently, and her husband took it, but as a part of his odd humour, and they followed him aloft with faces now a little more responsive to the manner in which on *that* spot he would naturally come out. He came out, according to the word of his assured private receipt, "strong." He missed a little, in truth, the usual round-eyed question from them—the inveterate artless cue with which, from moment to moment, clustered troops had for a year obliged him. Mr. and Mrs. Hayes were from New York, but it was a little like singing, as he had heard one of his Americans once say about something, to a Boston audience. He did none the less what he could, and it was ever his practice to stop still at a certain spot in the room and, after having secured attention by look and gesture, suddenly shoot off: "Here!"

They always understood, the good people—he could fairly love them now for it; they always said breathlessly and unanimously "There?" and stared down at the designated point quite as if some trace of the grand event were still to be made out. This movement produced he again looked round. "Consider it well: *the* spot of earth—!" "Oh but it isn't *earth*!" the boldest spirit—there was always a boldest—would generally pipe out. Then the guardian of the Birthplace would be truly superior—as if the unfortunate had figured the Immortal coming up, like a potato, through the soil. "I'm not suggesting that He was born on the bare ground. He was born *here*!"—with an uncompromising dig of his heel. "There ought to be a brass, with an inscription, let in." "Into the floor?"—it always came. "Birth and burial: seedtime, summer, autumn!"—that always, with its special right cadence, thanks to his unfailing spring, came too. "Why not as well as into the pavement of the church?—you've *seen* our grand old church?" The former of which questions nobody ever answered—abounding, on the other hand, to make up, in relation to the latter. Mr. and Mrs. Hayes even were at first left dumb by it—not indeed, to do them justice, having uttered the word that called for it. They had uttered no word while he kept the game up, and (though that made it a little more difficult) he could yet stand triumphant before them after he had finished with his flourish. Only then it was that Mr. Hayes of New York broke silence.

"Well, if we wanted to see I think I may say we're quite satisfied. As my wife says, it *would* seem your line." He spoke now, visibly, with more ease, as if a light had come: though he made no joke of it, for a reason that presently appeared. They were coming down the little stair, and it was on the descent that his companion added her word.

"Do you know what we half *did* think—?" And then to her husband: "Is it dreadful to tell him?" They were in the room below, and the young woman, also relieved, expressed the feeling with gaiety. She smiled as before at Morris Gedge, treating him as a person with whom relations were possible, yet remaining just uncertain enough to invoke Mr. Hayes's opinion. "We *have* awfully wanted—from what we had heard." But she met her husband's graver face; he was not quite out of the wood. At this she was slightly flurried—but she cut it short.

"You must know—don't you?—that, with the crowds who listen to you, we'd have heard."

He looked from one to the other, and once more again, with force, something came over him. They had kept him in mind, they were neither ashamed nor afraid to show it, and it was positively an interest on the part of this charming creature and this keen cautious gentleman, an interest resisting oblivion and surviving separation, that had governed their return. Their other visit had been the brightest thing that had ever happened to him, but this was the gravest; so that at the end of a minute something broke in him and his mask dropped of itself. He chucked, as he would have said, consistency; which, in its extinction, left the tears in his eyes. His smile was therefore queer. "Heard how I'm going it?"

The young man, though still looking at him hard, felt sure, with this, of his own ground. "Of course you're tremendously talked about. You've gone round the world."

"You've heard of me in America?"

"Why almost of nothing else!"

"That was what made us feel—!" Mrs. Hayes contributed.

"That you must see for yourselves?" Again he compared, poor Gedge, their faces. "Do you mean I excite—a—scandal?"

"Dear no! Admiration. You renew so," the young man observed, "the interest."

"Ah there it is!" said Gedge with eyes of adventure that seemed to rest beyond the Atlantic.

"They listen, month after month, when they're out here, as you must have seen; then they go home and talk. But they sing your praise."

Our friend could scarce take it in. "Over *there*!"

"Over there. I think you must be even in the papers."

"Without abuse?"

"Oh we don't abuse every one."

Mrs. Hayes, in her beauty, it was clear, stretched the point. "They rave about you."

"Then they *don't* know?"

"Nobody knows," the young man declared; "it wasn't any one's knowledge, at any rate, that made us uneasy."

"It was your own? I mean your own sense?"

"Well, call it that. We remembered, and we wondered what had happened. So," Mr. Hayes now frankly laughed, "we came to see."

Gedge stared through his film of tears. "Came from America to see *me*?"

"Oh a part of the way. But we wouldn't, in England, have missed you."

"And now we *haven't*!" the young woman soothingly added.

Gedge still could only gape at the candour of the tribute. But he tried to meet them—it was what was least poor for him—in their own key. "Well, how do you like it?"

Mrs. Hayes, he thought—if their answer were important—laughed a little nervously. "Oh you see."

Once more he looked from one to the other. "It's too beastly easy, you know."

Her husband raised his eyebrows. "You conceal your art. The emotion—yes; that must be easy; the general tone must flow. But about your facts—you've so many: how do you get *them* through?"

Gedge wondered. "You think I get too many—?"

At this they were amused together. "That's just what we came to see!"

"Well, you know, I've felt my way; I've gone step by step; you wouldn't believe how I've tried it on. *This*—where you see me—is where I've come out." After which, as they said nothing: "You hadn't thought I *could* come out?"

Again they just waited, but the husband spoke: "Are you so awfully sure you *are* out?"

Gedge drew himself up in the manner of his moments of emotion, almost conscious even that, with his sloping shoulders, his long lean neck and his nose so prominent in proportion to other matters, he resembled the more a giraffe. It was now at last he really caught on. "I *may* be in danger again—and the danger is what has moved you? Oh!" the poor man fairly moaned. His appreciation of it quite weakened him, yet he pulled himself together. "You've your view of my danger?"

It was wondrous how, with that note definitely sounded, the air was cleared. Lucid Mr. Hayes, at the end of a minute, had put the thing in a nutshell. "I don't know what you'll think of us—for being so beastly curious."

"I think," poor Gedge grimaced, "you're only too beastly kind."

"It's all your own fault," his friend returned, "for presenting us (who are not idiots, say) with so striking a picture of a crisis. At our other visit, you remember," he smiled, "you created an anxiety for the opposite reason. Therefore if *this* should again be a crisis for you, you'd really give us the case with an ideal completeness."

"You make me wish," said Morris Gedge, "that it might be one."

"Well, don't try—for our amusement—to bring one on. I don't see, you know, how you can have much margin. Take care—take care."

Gedge did it pensive justice. "Yes, that was what you said a year ago. You did me the honour to be uneasy—as my wife was."

Which determined on the young woman's part an immediate question. "May I ask then if Mrs. Gedge is now at rest?"

"No—since you do ask. *She* fears at least that I go too far; she doesn't believe in my margin. You see we *had* our scare after your visit. They came down."

His friends were all interest. "Ah! They came down?"

"Heavy. They brought *me* down. That's *why*—"

"Why you *are* down?" Mrs. Hayes sweetly demanded.

"Ah but my dear man," her husband interposed, "you're not

down; you're *up*! You're only up a different tree, but you're up at the tip-top."

"You mean I take it too high?"

"That's exactly the question," the young man answered; "and the possibility, as matching your first danger, is just what we felt we couldn't, if you didn't mind, miss the measure of."

Gedge gazed at him. "I feel that I know what you at bottom *hoped*."

"We at bottom 'hope,' surely, that you're all right?"

"In spite of the fool it makes of every one?"

Mr. Hayes of New York smiled. "Say *because* of that. We only ask to believe every one *is* a fool!"

"Only you haven't been, without reassurance, able to imagine fools of the size that my case demands?" And Gedge had a pause while, as if on the chance of some proof, his companion waited. "Well, I won't pretend to you that your anxiety hasn't made me, doesn't threaten to make me, a bit nervous; though I don't quite understand it if, as you say, people but rave about me."

"Oh *that* report was from the other side; people in our country so very easily rave. You've seen small children laugh to shrieks when tickled in a new place. So there are amiable millions with us who are but small shrieking children. They perpetually present new places for the tickler. What we've seen in further lights," Mr. Hayes good-humouredly pursued, "is your people *here*—the Committee, the Board, or whatever the powers to whom you're responsible."

"Call them my friend Grant-Jackson then—my original backer, though I admit for that reason perhaps my most formidable critic. It's with him practically I deal; or rather it's by him I'm dealt with—*was* dealt with before. I stand or fall by him. But he has given me my head."

"Mayn't he then want you," Mrs. Hayes enquired, "just to show as flagrantly running away."

"Of course—I see what you mean. I'm riding, blindly, for a

fall, and They're watching (to be tender of me!) for the smash that may come of itself. It's Machiavellic—but everything's possible. And what did you just now mean," Gedge asked—"especially if you've only heard of my prosperity—by your 'further lights'?"

His friends for an instant looked embarrassed, but Mr. Hayes came to the point. "We've heard of your prosperity, but we've also, remember, within a few minutes, heard *you.*"

"I was determined you *should,*" said Gedge. "I'm good then—but I overdo?" His strained grin was still sceptical.

Thus challenged, at any rate, his visitor pronounced. "Well, if you don't; if at the end of six months more it's clear that you haven't overdone; then, *then*—"

"Then what?"

"Then it's great."

"But it *is* great—greater than anything of the sort ever was. I overdo, thank goodness, yes; or I would if it were a thing you *could.*"

"Oh well, if there's *proof* that you can't—!" With which and an expressive gesture Mr. Hayes threw up his fears.

His wife, however, for a moment seemed unable to let them go. "Don't They want then *any* truth?—none even for the mere look of it?"

"The look of it," said Morris Gedge, "is what I give!"

It made them, the others, exchange a look of their own. Then she smiled. "Oh, well, if they think so—!"

"You at least don't? You're like my wife—which indeed, I remember," Gedge added, "is a similarity I expressed a year ago the wish for! At any rate I frighten *her.*"

The young husband, with an "Ah wives are terrible!" smoothed it over, and their visit would have failed of further excuse had not at this instant a movement at the other end of the room suddenly engaged them. The evening had so nearly closed in, though Gedge, in the course of their talk, had lighted the lamp nearest them, that they had not distinguished, in connexion with the opening of the door of communication to the warden's lodge, the appearance of another person, an eager woman who in her impatience had barely paused before advancing. Mrs. Gedge—her identity took but a few seconds to become vivid—was upon them, and she had not been too late for Mr. Hayes's last remark. Gedge saw at once that she had come with news; no need even, for that certitude, of her quick retort to the words in the air—"You may say as well, sir, that they're often, poor wives, terrified!" She knew nothing of the friends whom, at so unnatural an hour, he was showing about; but there was no livelier sign for him that this didn't matter than the possibility with which she intensely charged her "Grant-Jackson, to see you at once!"—letting it, so to speak, fly in his face.

"He has been with you?"

"Only a minute—he's there. But it's you he wants to see."

He looked at the others. "And what does he want, dear?"

"God knows! There it is. It's his horrid hour—it *was* that other time."

She had nervously turned to the others, overflowing to them, in her dismay, for all their strangeness—quite, as he said to himself, like a woman of the people. She was the bareheaded goodwife talking in the street about the row in the house, and it was in this character that he instantly introduced her: "My dear doubting wife, who will do her best to entertain you while I wait upon our friend." And he explained to her as he could his now protesting companions—"Mr. and Mrs. Hayes of New York, who have been here before." He knew, without knowing why, that her announcement chilled him; he failed at least to see why it should chill him so much. His good friends had themselves been visibly affected by it, and heaven knew that the depths of brooding fancy in him were easily stirred by contact. If they had wanted a crisis they accordingly had found one, albeit they had already asked leave to retire before it. This he wouldn't have. "Ah no, you must really see!"

"But we shan't be able to bear it, you know," said the young woman, "if it *is* to turn you out."

Her crudity attested her sincerity, and it was the latter, doubtless, that instantly held Mrs. Gedge. "It *is* to turn us out."

"Has he told you that, madam?" Mr. Hayes enquired of her—it being wondrous how the breath of doom had drawn them together.

"No, not told me; but there's something in him there—I mean in his awful manner—that matches too well with other things. We've seen," said the poor pale lady, "other things enough."

The young woman almost clutched her. "Is his manner very awful?"

"It's simply the manner," Gedge interposed, "of a very great man."

"Well, very great men," said his wife, "are very awful things."

"It's exactly," he laughed, "what we're finding out! But I mustn't keep him waiting. Our friends here," he went on, "are directly interested. You mustn't, mind you let them go until we know."

Mr. Hayes, however, held him; he found himself stayed. "We're so directly interested that I want you to understand this. If anything happens—"

"Yes?" said Gedge, all gentle as he faltered.

"Well, *we* must set you up."

Mrs. Hayes quickly abounded. "Oh *do* come to us!"

Again he could but take them in. They were really wonderful folk. And with it all but Mr. and Mrs. Hayes! It affected even Isabel through her alarm; though the balm, in a manner, seemed to foretell the wound. He had reached the threshold of his own quarters; he stood there as at the door of the chamber of judgement. But he laughed; at least he could be gallant in going up for sentence. "Very good then—I'll come to you!"

This was very well, but it didn't prevent his heart, a minute later, at the end of the passage, from thumping with beats he could count. He had paused again before going in; on the other side of this second door his poor future was to be let loose at him. It was broken, at best, and spiritless, but wasn't Grant-Jackson there like a beast-tamer in a cage, all tights and spangles and circus attitudes, to give it a cut with the smart official whip and make it spring at him? It was during this moment that he fully measured the effect for his nerves of the impression made on his so oddly earnest friends—whose earnestness he verily, in the spasm of this last effort, came within an ace of resenting. They had upset him by contact; he was afraid literally of meeting his doom on his knees; it wouldn't have taken much more, he absolutely felt, to make him approach with his forehead in the dust the great man whose wrath was to be averted. Mr. and Mrs. Hayes of New York had brought tears to his eyes, but was it to be reserved for Grant-Jackson to make him cry like a baby? He wished, yes, while he palpitated, that Mr. and Mrs. Hayes of New York hadn't had such an eccentricity of interest, for it seemed somehow to come from *them* that he was going so fast to pieces. Before he turned the knob of the door, however, he had another queer instant; making out that it had been, strictly, his case that was interesting, his funny power, however accidental, to show as in a picture the attitude of others—not his poor pale personality. It was this latter quantity, none the less, that was marching to execution. It is to our friend's credit that he *believed,* as he prepared to turn the knob, that he was going to be hanged; and it's certainly not less to his credit that his wife, on the chance, had his supreme thought. Here it was that—possibly with his last articulate breath—he thanked his stars, such as they were, for Mr. and Mrs. Hayes of New York. At least they would take care of her.

They were doing that certainly with some success when he returned to them ten minutes later. She sat between them in the beautified Birthplace, and he couldn't have been sure afterwards that each wasn't holding her hand. The three together had at any rate the effect of recalling to him—it was too whimsical—some picture, a sentimental print, seen and admired in his youth, a "Waiting for the Verdict," a "Counting the Hours," or something of that sort; humble respectability in suspense about humble innocence. He didn't know how he himself looked, and he didn't care; the great thing was that he wasn't crying—though he might have been; the glitter in his eyes was assuredly dry, though that there *was* a glitter, or something slightly to bewilder, the faces of the others as they rose to meet him sufficiently proved. His wife's eyes pierced his own, but it was Mrs. Hayes of New York who spoke. "*Was* it then for that—?"

He only looked at them at first—he felt he might now enjoy it. "Yes, it was for 'that.' I mean it was about the way I've been going on. He came to speak of it."

"And he's gone?" Mr. Hayes permitted himself to enquire.

"He's gone."

"It's over?" Isabel hoarsely asked.

"It's over."

"Then we go?"

This it was that he enjoyed. "No, my dear; we stay."

There was fairly a triple gasp; relief took time to operate. "Then why did he come?"

"In the fulness of his kind heart and of *Their* discussed and decreed satisfaction. To express Their sense—!"

Mr. Hayes broke into a laugh, but his wife wanted to know. "Of the grand work you're doing?"

"Of the way I polish it off. They're most handsome about it. The receipts, it appears, speak—"

He was nursing his effect; Isabel intently watched him and the others hung on his lips. "Yes, speak—?"

"Well, volumes. They tell the truth."

At this Mr. Hayes laughed again. "Oh *they* at least do?"

Near him thus once more Gedge knew their intelligence as one—which was so good a consciousness to get back that his tension now relaxed as by the snap of a spring and he felt his old face at ease. "So you can't say," he continued, "that we don't want it."

"I bow to it," the young man smiled. "It's what I said then. It's *great*."

"It's great," said Morris Gedge. "It couldn't be greater."

His wife still watched him; her irony hung behind. "Then we're just as we were?"

"No, not as we were."

She jumped at it. "Better?"

"Better. They give us a rise."

"Of income?"

"Of our sweet little stipend—by a vote of the Committee. That's what, as Chairman, he came to announce."

The very echoes of the Birthplace were themselves, for the instant, hushed; the warden's three companions showed in the conscious air a struggle for their own breath. But Isabel, almost with a shriek, was the first to recover hers. "They double us?"

"Well—call it that. 'In recognition.' There you are." Isabel uttered another sound—but this time inarticulate; partly because Mrs. Hayes of New York had already jumped at her to kiss her. Mr. Hayes meanwhile, as with too much to say, but put out his hand, which our friend took in silence. So Gedge had the last word. "And there *you* are!"

A NOTE ON

THE BIRTHPLACE

(1903)

MANY of James's stories measure the tension between two kinds of people—the specifically Jamesian characters, or perceivers, and "the fools," or non-perceivers. The work of the world, or what is loosely known as "living," is largely performed by the non-perceivers. The comprehension of this work, of this "living," is the act of a minority of perceivers. The rounded, wry humor of "The Birthplace" turns on an act of perception. The perceiver is Morris Gedge, later re-enforced by the American couple. The non-perceivers are his wife, plus all the other characters in the story. What is being perceived and non-perceived in "The Birthplace" is something quite large and permanently interesting: the nature of greatness, and also the manner in which greatness is honored by human beings who retain the old-fashioned virtue of intellectual scrupulousness, or dishonored by the more numerous ones who merely pay lip-service to that virtue.

"The Birthplace," like "Brooksmith," is the story of a work of art, for I do not know how otherwise to describe the carefully constructed deception which Morris Gedge, toward the close of the tale, practices on the non-perceivers. This deception (reaching the apex of its humor in the great parody-lecture) saves his job, his sanity, his self-respect, and, in a strange way, saves Shakespeare, saves the values of the imagination. Gedge's act of insight, humble as it is, and limited, nevertheless links him to all the great sensitives who have ever lived. "The Birthplace" is written on the level of comedy but, like most of James's comic tales, it leaves in the mind of the reader the sense of something large and serious. Which is to say that it is like all true comedy, deeply moral.

THE BEAST IN THE JUNGLE

I

WHAT determined the speech that startled him in the course of their encounter scarcely matters, being probably but some words spoken by himself quite without intention—spoken as they lingered and slowly moved together after their renewal of acquaintance. He had been conveyed by friends an hour or two before to the house at which she was staying; the party of visitors at the other house, of whom he was one, and thanks to whom it was his theory, as always, that he was lost in the crowd, had been invited over to luncheon. There had been after luncheon much dispersal, all in the interest of the original motive, a view of Weatherend itself and the fine things, intrinsic features, pictures, heirlooms, treasures of all the arts, that made the place almost famous; and the great rooms were so numerous that guests could wander at their will, hang back from the principal group and in cases where they took such matters with the last seriousness give themselves up to mysterious appreciations and measurements. There were persons to be observed, singly or in couples, bending toward objects in out-of-the-way corners with their hands on their knees and their heads nodding quite as with the emphasis of an excited sense of smell. When they were two they either mingled their sounds of ecstasy or melted into silences of even deeper import, so that there were aspects of the occasion that gave it for Marcher much the air of the "look round," previous to a sale highly advertised, that excites or quenches, as may be, the dream of acquisition. The dream of acquisition at Weatherend would have had to be wild indeed, and John Marcher found himself, among such suggestions, disconcerted almost equally by the presence of those who knew too much and by that of those who knew nothing. The great rooms caused so much poetry and history to press upon him that he needed some straying apart to feel in a proper relation with them, though this impulse was not, as happened, like the gloating of some of his companions, to be compared to the movements of a dog sniffing a cupboard. It had an issue promptly enough in a direction that was not to have been calculated.

It led, briefly, in the course of the October afternoon, to his closer meeting with May Bartram, whose face, a reminder, yet not quite a remembrance, as they sat much separated at a very long table, had begun merely by troubling him rather pleasantly. It affected him as the sequel of something of which he had lost the beginning. He knew it, and for the time quite welcomed it, as a continuation, but didn't know what it continued, which was an interest or an amusement the greater as he was also somehow aware—yet without a direct sign from her—that the young woman herself hadn't lost the thread. She hadn't lost it, but she wouldn't give it back to him, he saw, without some putting forth of his hand for it; and he not only saw that, but saw several things more, things odd enough in the light of the fact at the moment some accident of grouping brought them face to face he was still merely fumbling with the idea that any contact between them in the past would have had no importance. If it had had no importance he scarcely knew why his actual impression of her should so seem to have so much; the answer to which, however, was that in such a life as they all appeared to be leading for the moment one could but take things as they came. He was satisfied, without in the least being able to say why, that this young lady might roughly have ranked in the house as a poor relation; satisfied also that she was not there on a brief visit, but was more or less a part of the establishment—almost a working, a remunerated part. Didn't she enjoy at periods a protection that she paid for by helping, among other services, to show the place and explain it, deal with the tiresome people, answer questions about the dates of the building, the styles of the furniture, the authorship of the pictures, the favourite haunts of the ghost? It wasn't that she looked as if you could have given her shillings—it was impossible to look less so. Yet when she finally drifted toward him, distinctly handsome, though ever so much older—older than when he had seen her before—it might have been as an effect of her guessing that he had, within the couple of hours, devoted more imagination to her than to all the others put together, and had thereby penetrated to a kind of truth that the others were too stupid for. She *was* there on harder terms than any one; she was there as a consequence of things suffered, one way and another, in the interval of years; and she remembered him very much as she was remembered—only a good deal better.

By the time they at last thus came to speech they were alone in one of the rooms—remarkable for a fine portrait over the chimney-place—out of which their friends had passed, and the charm of it was that even before they had spoken they had practically arranged with each other to stay behind for talk. The charm, happily, was in other things too—partly in there being scarce a spot at Weatherend without something to stay behind for. It was in the way the autumn day looked into the high windows as it waned; the way the red light, breaking at the close from under a low sombre sky, reached out in a long shaft and played over old wainscots, old tapestry, old gold, old colour. It was most of all perhaps in the way she came to him as if, since she had been turned on to deal with the simpler sort, he might, should he choose to keep the whole thing down, just take her mild attention for a part of her general business. As soon as he heard her voice, however, the gap was filled up and the missing link supplied; the slight irony he divined in her attitude lost its advantage. He almost jumped at it to get there before her. "I met you years and years ago in Rome. I remember all about it." She confessed to disappointment—she had been so sure he didn't; and to prove how well he did he began to pour forth the particular recollections that popped up as he called for them. Her face and her voice, all at his service now, worked the miracle —the impression operating like the torch of a lamplighter who touches into flame, one by one, a long row of gas-jets. Marcher flattered himself the illumination was brilliant, yet he was really still more pleased on her showing him, with amusement, that in his haste to make everything right he had got most things rather wrong. It hadn't been at Rome—it had been at Naples; and it hadn't been eight years before—it had been more nearly ten. She hadn't been, either, with her uncle and aunt, but with her mother and her brother; in addition to which it was not with the Pembles *he* had been, but with the Boyers, coming down in their company from Rome—a point on which she insisted, a little to his confusion, and as to which she had her evidence in hand. The Boyers she had known, but didn't know the Pembles, though she had heard of them, and it was the people he was with who had made them acquainted. The incident of the thunderstorm that had raged round them with such violence as to drive them for refuge into an excavation—this incident had not occurred at the Palace of the Cæsars, but at Pompeii, on an occasion when they had been present there at an important find.

He accepted her amendments, he enjoyed her corrections, though the moral of them was, she pointed out, that he *really* didn't remember the least thing about her; and he only felt it as a drawback that when all was made strictly historic there didn't appear much of anything left. They lingered together still, she neglecting her office—for from the moment he was so clever she had no proper right to him—and both neglecting the house, just waiting as to see if a memory or two more wouldn't again breathe on them. It hadn't taken them many minutes, after all, to put down on the table, like the cards of a pack, those that constituted their respective hands; only what came out was that the pack was unfortunately not perfect—that the past, invoked, invited, encouraged, could give them, naturally, no more than it had. It had made them anciently meet—her at twenty, him at twenty-five; but nothing was so strange, they seemed to say to each other, as that, while so occupied, it hadn't done a little more for them. They looked at each other as with the feeling of an occasion missed; the present would have been so much better if the other, in the far distance, in the foreign land, hadn't been so stupidly meagre. There weren't apparently, all counted, more than a dozen little old things that had succeeded in coming to pass between them; trivialities of youth, simplicities of freshness, stupidities of ignorance, small possible germs, but too deeply buried—too deeply (didn't it seem?) to sprout after so many years. Marcher could only feel he ought to have rendered her some service—saved her from a capsized boat in the Bay or at least recovered her dressing-bag, filched from her cab in the streets of Naples by a lazzarone with a stiletto. Or it would have been nice if he could have been taken with fever all alone at his hotel, and she could have come to look after him, to write to his people, to drive him out in convalescence. *Then* they would be in possession of the something or other that their actual show seemed to lack. It yet somehow presented itself, this show, as too good to be spoiled; so that they were reduced for a few minutes more to wondering a little helplessly why—since they seemed to know a certain number of the same people—their reunion had been so long averted. They didn't use that name for it, but their delay from minute to minute to join the others was a kind of confession that they didn't quite want it to be a failure. Their attempted supposition of reasons for their not having met but showed how little they knew of each other. There came in fact a moment when Marcher felt a positive pang. It was vain to pretend she was an old friend, for all the communities were wanting, in spite of which it was as an old friend that he saw she would have suited him. He had new ones enough—was surrounded with them for instance on the stage of the other house; as a new one he probably wouldn't have so much as noticed her. He would have liked to invent something, get her to make-believe with him that some passage of a romantic or critical kind *had* originally occurred. He was really almost reaching out in imagination—as against time—for something that would do, and saying to himself that if it didn't come this sketch of a fresh start would show for quite awkwardly bungled. They would separate, and now for no second or no third chance. They would have tried and not succeeded. Then it was, just at the turn, as he afterwards made it out to himself, that, everything else failing, she herself decided to take up the case and, as it were, save the situation. He felt as soon as she spoke that she had been consciously keeping back what she said and hoping to get on without it; a scruple in her that immensely touched him when, by the end of three or four minutes more, he was able to measure it. What she brought out, at any rate, quite cleared the air and supplied the link—the link it was so odd he should frivolously have managed to lose.

"You know you told me something I've never forgotten and that again and again has made me think of you since; it was that tremendously hot day when we went to Sorrento, across the bay, for the breeze. What I allude to was what you said to me, on the way back, as we sat under the awning of the boat enjoying the cool. Have you forgotten?"

He had forgotten and was even more surprised than ashamed. But the great thing was that he saw in this no vulgar reminder of any "sweet" speech. The vanity of women had long memories, but she was making no claim on him of a compliment or a mistake. With another woman, a totally different one, he might have feared the recall possibly even of some imbecile "offer." So, in having to say that he had indeed forgotten, he was conscious rather of a loss than of a gain; he already saw an interest in the matter of her mention. "I try to think—but I give it up. Yet I remember the Sorrento day."

"I'm not very sure you do," May Bartram after a moment said; "and I'm not very sure I ought to want you to. It's dreadful to bring a person back at any time to what he was ten years before. If you've lived away from it," she smiled, "so much the better."

"Ah if *you* haven't why should I?" he asked.

"Lived away, you mean, from what I myself was?"

"From what *I* was. I was of course an ass," Marcher went on; "but I would rather know from you just the sort of ass I was than—from the moment you have something in your mind—not know anything."

Still, however, she hesitated. "But if you've completely ceased to be that sort—?"

"Why I can then all the more bear to know. Besides, perhaps I haven't."

"Perhaps. Yet if you haven't," she added, "I should suppose you'd remember. Not indeed that *I* in the least connect with my impression the invidious name you use. If I had only thought you foolish," she explained, "the thing I speak of wouldn't so have remained with me. It was about yourself." She waited as if it might come to him; but as, only meeting her eyes in wonder, he gave no sign, she burnt her ships. "Has it ever happened?"

Then it was that, while he continued to stare, a light broke for him and the blood slowly came to his face, which began to burn with recognition. "Do you mean I told you—?" But he faltered, lest what came to him shouldn't be right, lest he should only give himself away.

"It was something about yourself that it was natural one shouldn't forget—that is if one remembered you at all. That's why I ask you," she smiled, "if the thing you then spoke of has ever come to pass?"

Oh then he saw, but he was lost in wonder and found himself embarrassed. This, he also saw, made her sorry for him, as if her illusion had been a mistake. It took him but a moment, however, to feel it hadn't been, much as it had been a surprise. After the first little shock of it her knowledge on the contrary began, even if rather strangely, to taste sweet to him. She was the only other person in the world then who would have it, and she had had it all these years, while the fact of his having so breathed his secret had unaccountably faded from him. No wonder they couldn't have met as if nothing had happened.

"I judge," he finally said, "that I know what you mean. Only I had strangely enough lost any sense of having taken you so far into my confidence."

"Is it because you've taken so many others as well?"

"I've taken nobody. Not a creature since then."

"So that I'm the only person who knows?"

"The only person in the world."

"Well," she quickly replied, "I myself have never spoken. I've never, never repeated of you what you told me." She looked at him so that he perfectly believed her. Their eyes met over it in such a way that he was without a doubt. "And I never will."

She spoke with an earnestness that, as if almost excessive, put him at ease about her possible derision. Somehow the whole question was a new luxury to him—that is from the moment she was in possession. If she didn't take the sarcastic view she clearly took the sympathetic, and that was what he had had, in all the long time, from no one whomsoever. What he felt was that he couldn't at present have begun to tell her, and yet could profit perhaps exquisitely by the accident of having done so of old. "Please don't then. We're just right as it is."

"Oh I am," she laughed, "if you are!" To which she added: "Then you do still feel in the same way?"

It was impossible he shouldn't take to himself that she was really interested, though it all kept coming as perfect surprise. He had thought of himself so long as abominably alone, and lo he wasn't alone a bit. He hadn't been, it appeared, for an hour—since those moments on the Sorrento boat. It was *she* who had been, he seemed to see as he looked at her—she who had been made so by the graceless fact of his lapse of fidelity. To tell her what he had told her—what had it been but to ask something of her? something that she had given, in her charity, without his having, by a remembrance, by a return of the spirit, failing another encounter, so much as thanked her. What he had asked of her had been simply at first not to laugh at him. She had beautifully not done so for ten years, and she was not doing so now. So he had endless gratitude to make up. Only for that he must see just how he had figured to her. "What, exactly, was the account I gave—?"

"Of the way you did feel? Well, it was very simple. You said you had had from your earliest time, as the deepest thing within you, the sense of being kept for something rare and strange, possibly prodigious and terrible, that was sooner or later to happen to you, that you had in your bones the foreboding and the conviction of, and that would perhaps overwhelm you."

"Do you call that very simple?" John Marcher asked.

She thought a moment. "It was perhaps because I seemed, as you spoke, to understand it."

"You do understand it?" he eagerly asked.

Again she kept her kind eyes on him. "You still have the belief?"

"Oh!" he exclaimed helplessly. There was too much to say.

"Whatever it's to be," she clearly made out, "it hasn't yet come."

He shook his head in complete surrender now. "It hasn't yet come. Only, you know, it isn't anything I'm to *do,* to achieve in the world, to be distinguished or admired for. I'm not such an ass as *that.* It would be much better, no doubt, if I were."

"It's to be something you're merely to suffer?"

"Well, say to wait for—to have to meet, to face, to see suddenly break out in my life; possibly destroying all further consciousness, possibly annihilating me; possibly, on the other hand, only altering everything, striking at the root of all my world and leaving me to the consequences, however they shape themselves."

She took this in, but the light in her eyes continued for him not to be that of mockery. "Isn't what you describe perhaps but the expectation—or at any rate the sense of danger, familiar to so many people—of falling in love?"

John Marcher wondered. "Did you ask me that before?"

"No—I wasn't so free-and-easy then. But it's what strikes me now."

"Of course," he said after a moment, "it strikes you. Of course it strikes *me*. Of course what's in store for me may be no more than that. The only thing is," he went on, "that I think if it had been that I should by this time know."

"Do you mean because you've *been* in love?" And then as he but looked at her in silence: "You've been in love, and it hasn't meant such a cataclysm, hasn't proved the great affair?"

"Here I am, you see. It hasn't been overwhelming."

"Then it hasn't been love," said May Bartram.

"Well, I at least thought it was. I took it for that—I've taken it till now. It was agreeable, it was delightful, it was miserable," he explained. "But it wasn't strange. It wasn't what *my* affair's to be."

"You want something all to yourself—something that nobody else knows or *has* known?"

"It isn't a question of what I 'want'—God knows I don't want anything. It's only a question of the apprehension that haunts me—that I live with day by day."

He said this so lucidly and consistently that he could see it further impose itself. If she hadn't been interested before she'd have been interested now. "Is it a sense of coming violence?"

Evidently now too again he liked to talk of it. "I don't think of it as—when it does come—necessarily violent. I only think of it as natural and as of course above all unmistakeable. I think of it simply as *the* thing. *The* thing will of itself appear natural."

"Then how will it appear strange?"

Marcher bethought himself. "It won't—to *me*."

"To whom then?"

"Well," he replied, smiling at last, "say to you."

"Oh then I'm to be present?"

"Why you *are* present—since you know."

"I see." She turned it over. "But I mean at the catastrophe."

At this, for a minute, their lightness gave way to their gravity;

it was as if the long look they exchanged held them together. "It will only depend on yourself—if you'll watch with me."

"Are you afraid?" she asked.

"Don't leave me *now,*" he went on.

"Are you afraid?" she repeated.

"Do you think me simply out of my mind?" he pursued instead of answering. "Do I merely strike you as a harmless lunatic?"

"No," said May Bartram. "I understand you. I believe you."

"You mean you feel how my obsession—poor old thing!—may correspond to some possible reality?"

"To some possible reality."

"Then you *will* watch with me?"

She hesitated, then for the third time put her question. "Are you afraid?"

"Did I tell you I was—at Naples?"

"No, you said nothing about it."

"Then I don't know. And I should *like* to know," said John Marcher. "You'll tell me yourself whether you think so. If you'll watch with me you'll see."

"Very good then." They had been moving by this time across the room, and at the door, before passing out, they paused as for the full wind-up of their understanding. "I'll watch with you," said May Bartram.

II

The fact that she "knew"—knew and yet neither chaffed him nor betrayed him—had in a short time begun to constitute between them a goodly bond, which became more marked when, within the year that followed their afternoon at Weatherend, the opportunities for meeting multiplied. The event that thus promoted these occasions was the death of the ancient lady her great-aunt, under whose wing, since losing her mother, she had to such an extent found shelter, and who, though but the widowed mother of the new successor to the property, had succeeded—thanks to a high tone and a high temper—in not forfeiting the supreme position at the great house. The deposition of this personage arrrived but with her death, which, followed by many changes, made in particular a difference for the young woman in whom Marcher's expert attention had recognised from the first a dependent with a pride that might ache though it didn't bristle. Nothing for a long time had made him easier than the thought that the aching must have been much soothed by Miss Bartram's now finding herself able to set up a small home in London. She had acquired property, to an amount that made that luxury just possible, under her aunt's extremely complicated will, and when the whole matter began to be straightened out, which indeed took time, she let him know that the happy issue was at last in view. He had seen her again before that day, both because she had more than once accompanied the ancient lady to town and because he had paid another visit to the friends who so conveniently made of Weatherend one of the charms of their own hospitality. These friends had taken him back there; he had achieved there again with Miss Bartram some quiet detachment; and he had in London succeeded in persuading her to more than one brief absence from her aunt. They went together, on these latter occasions, to the National Gallery and the South Kensington Museum, where, among vivid reminders, they talked of Italy at large—not now attempting to recover, as at first, the taste of their youth and their ignorance. That recovery, the first day at Weatherend, had served its purpose well, had given them quite enough; so that they were, to Marcher's sense, no longer hovering about the headwaters of their stream, but had felt their boat pushed sharply off and down the current.

They were literally afloat together; for our gentleman this was marked, quite as marked as that the fortunate cause of it was just the buried treasure of her knowledge. He had with his own hands dug up this little hoard, brought to light—that is to within reach of the dim day constituted by their discretions and privacies—the object of value the hiding-place of which he had, after putting it into the ground himself, so strangely, so long forgotten. The rare luck of his having again just stumbled on the spot made him indifferent to any other question; he would doubtless have devoted more time to the odd accident of his lapse of memory if he hadn't been moved to devote so much to the sweetness, the comfort, as he felt, for the future, that this accident itself had helped to keep fresh. It had never entered into his plan that any one should "know," and mainly for the reason that it wasn't in him to tell any one. That would have been impossible, for nothing but the amusement of a cold world would have waited on it. Since, however, a mysterious fate had opened his mouth betimes, in spite of him, he would count that a compensation and profit by it to the utmost. That the right person *should* know tempered the asperity of his secret more even than his shyness had permitted him to imagine; and May Bartram was clearly right, because—well, because there she was. Her knowledge simply settled it; he would have been sure enough by this time had she been wrong. There was that in his situation, no doubt, that disposed him too much to see her as a mere confidant, taking all her light for him from the fact—the fact only—of her interest in his predicament; from her mercy, sympathy, seriousness, her consent not to regard him as the funniest of the funny. Aware, in fine, that her price for him was just in her giving him this constant sense of his being admirably spared, he was careful to remember that she had also a life of her own, with things that might happen to *her,* things that in friendship one should likewise take account of. Something fairly remarkable came to pass with him, for that matter, in this connexion—something represented by a certain passage of his consciousness, in the suddenest way, from one extreme to the other.

He had thought himself, so long as nobody knew, the most disinterested person in the world, carrying his concentrated burden, his perpetual suspense, ever so quietly, holding his tongue about it, giving others no glimpse of it nor of its effect upon his life, asking of them no allowance and only making on his side all those that were asked. He hadn't disturbed people with the queerness of their having to know a haunted man, though he had had moments of rather special temptation on hearing them say they were forsooth "unsettled." If they were as unsettled as he was—he who had never been settled for an hour in his life—they would know what it meant. Yet it wasn't, all the same, for him to make them, and he listened to them civilly enough. This was why he had such good—though possibly such rather colourless—manners; this was why, above all, he could regard himself, in a greedy world, as decently—as in fact perhaps even a little sublimely—unselfish. Our point is accordingly that he valued this character quite sufficiently to measure his present danger of letting it lapse, against which he promised himself to be much on his guard. He was quite ready, none the less, to be selfish just a little, since surely no more charming occasion for it had come to him. "Just a little," in a word, was just as much as Miss Bartram, taking one day with another, would let him. He never would be in the least coercive, and would keep well before him the lines on which consideration for her—the very highest—ought to proceed. He would thoroughly establish the heads under which her affairs, her requirements, her peculiarities—he went so far as to give them the latitude of that name—would come into their intercourse. All this naturally was a sign of how much he took the intercourse itself for granted. There was nothing more to be done about *that*. It simply existed; had sprung into being with her first penetrating question to him in the autumn light there at Weatherend. The real form it should have taken on the basis that stood out large was the form of their marrying. But the devil in this was that the very basis itself put marrying out of the question. His conviction, his apprehension, his obsession, in short, wasn't a privilege he could invite a woman to share; and that consequence of it was precisely what was the matter with him. Something or other lay in wait for him, amid the twists and the turns of the months and the years, like a crouching beast in the jungle. It signified little whether the crouching beast were destined to slay him or to be slain. The definite point was the inevitable spring of the creature; and the definite lesson from that was that a man of feeling didn't cause himself to be accompanied by a lady on a tiger-hunt. Such was the image under which he had ended by figuring his life.

They had at first, none the less, in the scattered hours spent together, made no allusion to that view of it; which was a sign he was handsomely alert to give that he didn't expect, that he in fact didn't care, always to be talking about it. Such a feature in one's outlook was really like a hump on one's back. The difference it made every minute of the day existed quite independently of discussion. One discussed of course *like* a hunchback, for there was always, if nothing else, the hunchback face. That remained, and she was watching him; but people watched best, as a general thing, in silence, so that such would be predominantly the manner of their vigil. Yet he didn't want, at the same time, to be tense and solemn; tense and solemn was what he imagined he too much showed for with other people. The thing to be, with the one person who knew, was easy and natural—to make the reference rather than be seeming to avoid it, to avoid it rather than be seeming to make it, and to keep it, in any case, familiar, facetious even, rather than pedantic and portentous. Some such consideration as the latter was doubtless in his mind for instance when he wrote pleasantly to Miss Bartram that perhaps the great thing he had so long felt as in the lap of the gods was no more than this circumstance, which touched him so nearly, of her acquiring a house in London. It was the first allusion they had yet again made, needing any other hitherto so little; but when she replied, after having given him the news, that she was by no means satisfied with such a trifle as the climax to so special a suspense, she almost set him wondering if she hadn't even a larger conception of singularity for him than he had for himself. He was at all events destined to become aware little by little, as time went by, that she was all the while looking at his life, judging it, measuring it, in the light of the thing she knew, which grew to be at last, with the consecration of the years, never mentioned between them save as "the real truth" about him. That had always been his own form of reference to it, but she adopted the form so quietly that, looking back at the end of a period, he knew there was no moment at which it was traceable that she had, as he might say, got inside his idea, or exchanged the attitude of beautifully indulging for that of still more beautifully believing him.

It was always open to him to accuse her of seeing him but as the most harmless of maniacs, and this, in the long run—since it covered so much ground—was his easiest description of their friendship. He had a screw loose for her, but she liked him in spite of it and was practically, against the rest of the world, his kind wise keeper, unremunerated but fairly amused and, in the absence of other near ties, not disreputably occupied. The rest of the world of course thought him queer, but she, she only, knew how, and above all why, queer; which was precisely what enabled her to dispose the concealing veil in the right folds. She took his gaiety from him—since it had to pass with them for gaiety—as she took everything else; but she certainly so far justified by her unerring touch his finer sense of the degree to which he had ended by convincing her. *She* at least never spoke of the secret of his life except as "the real truth about you," and she had in fact a wonderful way of making it seem, as such, the secret of her own life too. That was in fine how he so constantly felt her as allowing for him; he couldn't on the whole call it anything else. He allowed himself, but she, exactly, allowed still more; partly because, better placed for a sight of the matter, she traced his unhappy perversion through reaches of its course into which he could scarce follow it. He knew how he felt, but, besides knowing that, she knew how he *looked* as well; he knew each of the things of importance he was insidiously kept from doing, but she could add up the amount they made, understand how much, with a lighter weight on his spirit, he might have done, and thereby established how, clever as he was, he fell short. Above all she was in the secret of the difference between the forms he went through—those of his little office under Government, those of caring for his modest patrimony, for his library, for his garden in the country, for the people in London whose invitations he accepted and repaid—and the detachment that reigned beneath them and that made of all behaviour, all that could in the least be called behaviour, a long act of dissimulation. What it had come to was that he wore a mask painted with the social simper, out of the eye-holes of which there looked eyes of an expression not in the least matching the other features. This the stupid world, even after years, had never more than half-discovered. It was only May Bartram who had, and she achieved, by an art indescribable, the feat of at once—or perhaps it was only alternately—meeting the eyes from in front and mingling her own vision, as from over his shoulder, with their peep through the apertures.

So while they grew older together she did watch with him, and so she let this association give shape and colour to her own existence. Beneath *her* forms as well detachment had learned to sit, and behaviour had become for her, in the social sense, a false account of herself. There was but one account of her that would have been true all the while and that she could give straight to nobody, least of all to John Marcher. Her whole attitude was a virtual statement, but the perception of that only seemed called to take its place for him as one of the many things necessarily crowded out of his consciousness. If she had moreover, like himself, to make sacrifices to their real truth, it was to be granted that her compensation might have affected her as more prompt and more natural. They had long periods, in this London time, during which, when they were together, a stranger might have listened to them without in the least pricking up his ears; on the other hand the real truth was equally liable at any moment to rise to the surface, and the auditor would then have wondered indeed what they were talking about. They had from an early hour made up their mind that society was, luckily, unintelligent, and the margin allowed them by this had fairly become one of their commonplaces. Yet there were still moments when the situation turned almost fresh—usually under the effect of some expression drawn from herself. Her expressions doubtless repeated themselves, but her intervals were generous. "What saves us, you know, is that we answer so completely to so usual an appearance: that of the man and woman whose friendship has become such a daily habit—or almost—as to be at last indispensable." That for instance was a remark she had frequently enough had occasion to make, though she had given it at different times different developments. What we are especially concerned with is the turn it happened to take from her one afternoon when he had come to see her in honour of her birthday. This anniversary had fallen on a Sunday, at a season of thick fog and general outward gloom; but he had brought her his customary offering, having known her now long enough to have established a hundred small traditions. It was one of his proofs to himself, the present he made her on her birthday, that he hadn't sunk into real selfishness. It was mostly nothing more than a small trinket, but it was always fine of its kind, and he was regularly careful to pay for it more than he thought he could afford. "Our habit saves you at least, don't you see? because it makes you, after all, for the vulgar, indistinguishable from other men. What's the most inveterate mark of men in general? Why the capacity to spend endless time with dull women—to spend it I won't say without being bored, but without minding that they are, without being driven off at a tangent by it; which comes to the same thing. I'm your dull woman, a part of the daily bread for which you pray at church. That covers your tracks more than anything."

"And what covers yours?" asked Marcher, whom his dull woman could mostly to this extent amuse. "I see of course what you mean by your saving me, in this way and that, so far as other people are concerned—I've seen it all along. Only what is it that saves *you*? I often think, you know, of that."

She looked as if she sometimes thought of that too, but rather in a different way. "Where other people, you mean, are concerned?"

"Well, you're really so in with me, you know—as a sort of result of my being so in with yourself. I mean of my having such an immense regard for you, being so tremendously mindful of all you've done for me. I sometimes ask myself if it's quite fair. Fair I mean to have so involved and—since one may say it—interested you. I almost feel as if you hadn't really had time to do anything else."

"Anything else but be interested?" she asked. "Ah what else does one ever want to be? If I've been 'watching' with you, as we long ago agreed I was to do, watching's always in itself an absorption."

"Oh certainly," John Marcher said, "if you hadn't had your curiosity—! Only doesn't it sometimes come to you as time goes on that your curiosity isn't being particularly repaid?"

May Bartram had a pause. "Do you ask that, by any chance, because you feel at all that yours isn't? I mean because you have to wait so long."

Oh he understood what she meant! "For the thing to happen that never does happen? For the beast to jump out? No, I'm just where I was about it. It isn't a matter as to which I can *choose*, I can decide for a change. It isn't one as to which there *can* be a change. It's in the lap of the gods. One's in the hands of one's law—there one is. As to the form the law will take, the way it will operate, that's its own affair."

"Yes," Miss Bartram replied; "of course one's fate's coming, of course it *has* come in its own form and its own way, all the while. Only, you know, the form and the way in your case were to have been—well, something so exceptional and, as one may say, so particularly *your* own."

Something in this made him look at her with suspicion. "You say 'were to *have* been,' as if in your heart you had begun to doubt."

"Oh!" she vaguely protested.

"As if you believed," he went on, "that nothing will now take place."

She shook her head slowly but rather inscrutably. "You're far from my thought."

He continued to look at her. "What then is the matter with you?"

"Well," she said after another wait, "the matter with me is simply that I'm more sure than ever my curiosity, as you call it, will be but too well repaid."

They were frankly grave now; he had got up from his seat, had turned once more about the little drawing-room to which, year after year, he brought his inevitable topic; in which he had, as he might have said, tasted their intimate community with every sauce, where every object was as familiar to him as the things of his own house and the very carpets were worn with his fitful walk very much as the desks in old counting-houses are worn by the elbows of generations of clerks. The generations of his nervous moods had been at work there, and the place was the written history of his whole middle life. Under the impression of what his friend had just said he knew himself, for some reason, more aware of these things; which made him, after a moment, stop again before her. "Is it possibly that you've grown afraid?"

"Afraid?" He thought, as she repeated the word, that his question had made her, a little, change colour; so that, lest he should have touched on a truth, he explained very kindly: "You remember that that was what you asked *me* long ago—that first day at Weatherend."

"Oh yes, and you told me you didn't know—that I was to see for myself. We've said little about it since, even in so long a time."

"Precisely," Marcher interposed—"quite as if it were too delicate a matter for us to make free with. Quite as if we might find, on pressure, that I *am* afraid. For then," he said, "we shouldn't, should we? quite know what to do."

She had for the time no answer to this question. "There have been days when I thought you were. Only, of course," she added, "there have been days when we have thought almost anything."

"Everything. Oh!" Marcher softly groaned as with a gasp, half-spent, at the face, more uncovered just then than it had been for a long while, of the imagination always with them. It had always had its incalculable moments of glaring out, quite as with the very eyes of the very Beast, and, used as he was to them, they could still draw from him the tribute of a sigh that rose from the depths of his being. All they had thought, first and last, rolled over him; the past seemed to have been reduced to mere barren speculation. This in fact was what the place had just struck him as so full of—the simplification of everything but the state of suspense. That remained only by seeming to hang in the void surrounding it. Even his original fear, if fear it had been, had lost itself in the desert. "I judge, however," he continued, "that you see I'm not afraid now."

"What I see, as I make it out, is that you've achieved something almost unprecedented in the way of getting used to danger. Living with it so long and so closely you've lost your sense of it; you know it's there, but you're indifferent, and you cease even, as of old, to have to whistle in the dark. Considering what the danger is," May Bartram wound up, "I'm bound to say I don't think your attitude could well be surpassed."

John Marcher faintly smiled. "It's heroic?"

"Certainly—call it that."

It was what he would have liked indeed to call it. "I *am* then a man of courage?"

"That's what you were to show me."

He still, however, wondered. "But doesn't the man of

courage know what he's afraid of—or *not* afraid of? I don't know *that,* you see. I don't focus it. I can't name it. I only know I'm exposed."

"Yes, but exposed—how shall I say?—so directly. So intimately. That's surely enough."

"Enough to make you feel then—as what we may call the end and the upshot of our watch—that I'm not afraid?"

"You're not afraid. But it isn't," she said, "the end of our watch. That is it isn't the end of yours. You've everything still to see."

"Then why haven't *you*?" he asked. He had had, all along, today, the sense of her keeping something back, and he still had it. As this was his first impression of that it quite made a date. The case was the more marked as she didn't at first answer; which in turn made him go on. "You know something I don't." Then his voice, for that of a man of courage, trembled a little. "You know what's to happen." Her silence, with the face she showed, was almost a confession—it made him sure. "You know, and you're afraid to tell me. It's so bad that you're afraid I'll find out."

All this might be true, for she did look as if, unexpectedly to her, he had crossed some mystic line that she had secretly drawn round her. Yet she might, after all, not have worried; and the real climax was that he himself, at all events, needn't. "You'll never find out."

III

It was all to have made, none the less, as I have said, a date; which came out in the fact that again and again, even after long intervals, other things that passed between them wore in relation to this hour but the character of recalls and results. Its immediate effect had been indeed rather to lighten insistence—almost to provoke a reaction; as if their topic had dropped by its own weight and as if moreover, for that matter, Marcher had been visited by one of his occasional warnings against egotism. He had kept up, he felt, and very decently on the whole, his consciousness of the importance of not being selfish, and it was true that he had never sinned in that direction without promptly enough trying to press the scales the other way. He often repaired his fault, the season permitting, by inviting his friend to accompany him to the opera; and it not infrequently thus happened that, to show he didn't wish her to have but one sort of food for her mind, he was the cause of her appearing there with him a dozen nights in the month. It even happened that, seeing her home at such times, he occasionally went in with her to finish, as he called it, the evening, and, the better to make his point, sat down to the frugal but always careful little supper that awaited his pleasure. His point was made, he thought, by his not eternally insisting with her on himself; made for instance, at such hours, when it befell that, her piano at hand and each of them familiar with it, they went over passages of the opera together. It chanced to be on one of these occasions, however, that he reminded her of her not having answered a certain question he had put to her during the talk that had taken place between them on her last birthday. "What is it that saves *you*?"—saved her, he meant, from that appearance of variation from the usual human type. If he had practically escaped remark, as she pretended, by doing, in the most important particular, what most men do—find the answer to life in patching up an alliance of a sort with a woman no better than himself—how had she escaped it, and how could the alliance, such as it was, since they must suppose it had been more or less noticed, have failed to make her rather positively talked about?

"I never said," May Bartram replied, "that it hadn't made me a good deal talked about."

"Ah well then you're not 'saved.'"

"It hasn't been a question for me. If you've had your woman I've had," she said, "my man."

"And you mean that makes you all right?"

Oh it was always as if there were so much to say! "I don't know why it shouldn't make me—humanly, which is what we're speaking of—as right as it makes you."

"I see," Marcher returned. "'Humanly,' no doubt, as showing that you're living for something. Not, that is, just for me and my secret."

May Bartram smiled. "I don't pretend it exactly shows that I'm not living for you. It's my intimacy with you that's in question."

He laughed as he saw what she meant. "Yes, but since, as you say, I'm only, so far as people make out, ordinary, you're —aren't you?—no more than ordinary either. You help me to pass for a man like another. So if I *am,* as I understand you, you're not compromised. Is that it?"

She had another of her waits, but she spoke clearly enough. "That's it. It's all that concerns me—to help you to pass for a man like another."

He was careful to acknowledge the remark handsomely. "How kind, how beautiful, you are to me! How shall I ever repay you?"

She had her last grave pause, as if there might be a choice of ways. But she chose. "By going on as you are."

It was into this going on as he was that they relapsed, and really for so long a time that the day inevitably came for a further sounding of their depths. These depths, constantly bridged over by a structure firm enough in spite of its lightness and of its occasional oscillation in the somewhat vertiginous air, invited on occasion, in the interest of their nerves, a dropping of the plummet and a measurement of the abyss. A difference had been made moreover, once for all, by the fact that she had all the while not appeared to feel the need of rebutting his charge of an idea within her that she didn't dare to express—a charge uttered just before one of the fullest of their later discussions ended. It had come up for him then that she "knew" something and that what she knew was bad—too bad to tell him. When he had spoken of it as visibly so bad that she was afraid he might find it out, her reply had left the matter too equivocal to be let alone and yet, for Marcher's special sensibility, almost too formidable again to touch. He circled about it at a distance that alternately narrowed and widened and that still wasn't much affected by the consciousness in him that there was nothing she could "know," after all, any better than he did. She had no source of knowledge he hadn't equally—except of course that she might have finer nerves. That was what women had where they were interested; they made out things, where people were concerned, that the people often couldn't have made out for themselves. Their nerves, their sensibility, their imagination, were conductors and revealers, and the beauty of May Bartram was in particular that she had given herself so to his case. He felt in these days what, oddly enough, he had never felt before, the growth of a dread of losing her by some catastrophe—some catastrophe that yet wouldn't at all be *the* catastrophe: partly because she had almost of a sudden begun to strike him as more useful to him than ever yet, and partly by reason of an appearance of uncertainty in her health, coincident and equally new. It was characteristic of the inner detachment he had hitherto so successfully cultivated and to which our whole account of him is a reference, it was characteristic that his complications, such as they were, had never yet seemed so as at this crisis to thicken about him, even to the point of making him ask himself if he were, by any chance, of a truth, within sight or sound, within touch or reach, within the immediate jurisdiction, of the thing that waited.

When the day came, as come it had to, that his friend confessed to him her fear of a deep disorder in her blood, he felt somehow the shadow of a change and the chill of a shock. He immediately began to imagine aggravations and disasters, and above all to think of her peril as the direct menace for himself of personal privation. This indeed gave him one of those partial recoveries of equanimity that were agreeable to him—it showed him that what was still first in his mind was the loss she herself might suffer. "What if she should have to die before knowing, before seeing—?" It would have been brutal, in the early stages of her trouble, to put that question to her; but it had immediately sounded for him to his own concern, and the possibility was what most made him sorry for her. If she did "know," moreover, in the sense of her having had some—what should he think?—mystical irresistible light, this would make the matter not better, but worse, inasmuch as her original adoption of his own curiosity had quite become the basis of her life. She had been living to see what would *be* to be seen, and it would quite lacerate her to have to give up before the accomplishment of the vision. These reflexions, as I say, quickened his generosity; yet, make them as he might, he saw himself, with the lapse of the period, more and more disconcerted. It lapsed for him with a strange steady sweep, and the oddest oddity was that it gave him, independently of the threat of much inconvenience, almost the only positive surprise his career, if career it could be called, had yet offered him. She kept the house as she had never done; he had to go to her to see her—she could meet him nowhere now, though there was scarce a corner of their loved old London in which she hadn't in the past, at one time or another, done so; and he found her always seated by her fire in the deep old-fashioned chair she was less and less able to leave. He had been struck one day, after an absence exceeding his usual measure, with her suddenly looking much older to him than he had ever thought of her being; then he recognised that the suddenness was all on his side—he had just simply and suddenly noticed. She looked older because inevitably, after so many years, she *was* old, or almost; which was of course true in still greater measure of her companion. If she was old, or almost, John Marcher assuredly was, and yet it was her showing of the lesson, not his own, that brought the truth home to him. His surprises began here; when once they had begun they multiplied; they came rather with a rush: it was as if, in the oddest way in the world, they had all been kept back, sown in a thick cluster, for the late afternoon of life, the time at which for people in general the unexpected has died out.

One of them was that he should have caught himself—for he *had* so done—*really* wondering if the great accident would take form now as nothing more than his being condemned to see this charming woman, this admirable friend, pass away from him. He had never so unreservedly qualified her as while confronted in thought with such a possibility; in spite of which there was small doubt for him that as an answer to his long riddle the mere effacement of even so fine a feature of his situation would be an abject anti-climax. It would represent, as connected with his past attitude, a drop of dignity under the shadow of which his existence could only become the most grotesque of failures. He had been far from holding it a failure—long as he had waited for the appearance that was to make it a success. He had waited for quite another thing, not for such a thing as that. The breath of his good faith came short, however, as he recognised how long he had waited, or how long at least his companion had. That she, at all events, might be recorded as having waited in vain—this affected him sharply, and all the more because of his at first having done little more than amuse himself with the idea. It grew more grave as the gravity of her condition grew, and the state of mind it produced in him, which he himself ended by watching as if it had been some definite disfigurement of his outer person, may pass for another of his surprises. This conjoined itself still with another, the really stupefying consciousness of a question that he would have allowed to shape itself had he dared. What did everything mean—what, that is, did *she* mean, she and her vain waiting and her probable death and the soundless admonition of it all—unless that, at this time of day, it was simply, it was overwhelmingly too late? He had never at any stage of his queer consciousness admitted the whisper of such a correction; he had never till within these last few months been so false to his conviction as not to hold that what was to come to him had time, whether *he* struck himself as having it or not. That at last, at last, he certainly hadn't it, to speak of, or had it but in the scantiest measure—such, soon enough, as things went with him, became the inference with which his old obsession had to reckon: and this it was not helped to do by the more and more confirmed appearance that the great vagueness casting the long shadow in which he had lived had, to attest itself, almost no margin left. Since it was in Time that he was to have met his fate, so it was in Time that his fate was to have acted; and as he waked up to the sense of no longer being young, which was exactly the sense of being stale, just as that, in turn, was the sense of being weak, he waked up to another matter beside. It all hung together; they were subject, he and the great vagueness, to an equal and indivisible law. When the possibilities themselves had accordingly turned stale, when the secret of the gods had grown faint, had perhaps even quite evaporated, that, and that only, was failure. It wouldn't have been failure to be bankrupt, dishonoured, pilloried, hanged; it was failure not to be anything. And so, in the dark valley into which his path had taken its unlooked-for twist, he wondered not a little as he groped. He didn't care what awful crash might overtake him, with what ignominy or what monstrosity he might yet be associated—since he wasn't after all too utterly old to suffer—if it would only be decently proportionate to the posture he had kept, all his life, in the threatened presence of it. He had but one desire left—that he shouldn't have been "sold."

IV

THEN it was that, one afternoon, while the spring of the year was young and new she met all in her own way his frankest betrayal of these alarms. He had gone in late to see her, but evening hadn't settled and she was presented to him in that long fresh light of waning April days which affects us often with a sadness sharper than the greyest hours of autumn. The week had been warm, the spring was supposed to have begun early, and May Bartram sat, for the first time in the year, without a fire; a fact that, to Marcher's sense, gave the scene of which she formed part a smooth and ultimate look, an air of knowing, in its immaculate order and cold meaningless cheer, that it would never see a fire again. Her own aspect—he could scarce have said why—intensified this note. Almost as white as wax, with the marks and signs in her face as numerous and as fine as if they had been etched by a needle, with soft white draperies relieved by a faded green scarf on the delicate tone of which the years had further refined, she was the picture of a serene and exquisite but impenetrable sphinx, whose head, or indeed all whose person, might have been powdered with silver. She was a sphinx, yet with her white petals and green fronds she might have been a lily too—only an artificial lily, wonderfully imitated and constantly kept, without dust or stain, though not exempt from a slight droop and a complexity of faint creases, under some clear glass bell. The perfection of household care, of high polish and finish, always reigned in her rooms, but they now looked most as if everything had been wound up, tucked in, put away, so that she might sit with folded hands and with nothing more to do. She was "out of it," to Marcher's vision; her work was over; she communicated with him as across some gulf or from some island of rest that she had already reached, and it made him feel strangely abandoned. Was it—or rather wasn't it—that if for so long she had been watching with him the answer to their question must have swum into her ken and taken on its name, so that her occupation was verily gone? He had as much as charged her with this in saying to her, many months before, that she even then knew something she was keeping from him. It was a point he had never since ventured to press, vaguely fearing as he did that it might become a difference, perhaps a disagreement, between them. He had in this later time turned nervous, which was what he in all the other years had never been; and the oddity was that his nervousness should have waited till he had begun to doubt, should have held off so long as he was sure. There was something, it seemed to him, that the wrong word would bring down on his head, something that would so at least ease off his tension. But he wanted not to speak the wrong word; that would make everything ugly. He wanted the knowledge he lacked to drop on him, if drop it could, by its own august weight. If she was to forsake him it was surely for her to take leave. This was why he didn't directly ask her again what she knew; but it was also why, approaching the matter from another side, he said to her in the course of his visit: "What do you regard as the very worst that at this time of day *can* happen to me?"

He had asked her that in the past often enough; they had, with the odd irregular rhythm of their intensities and avoidances, exchanged ideas about it and then had seen the ideas washed away by cool intervals, washed like figures traced in sea-sand. It had ever been the mark of their talk that the oldest allusions in it required but a little dismissal and reaction to come out again, sounding for the hour as new. She could thus at present meet his enquiry quite freshly and patiently. "Oh yes, I've repeatedly thought, only it always seemed to me of old that I couldn't quite make up my mind. I thought of dreadful things, between which it was difficult to choose; and so must you have done."

"Rather! I feel now as if I had scarce done anything else. I appear to myself to have spent my life in thinking of nothing *but* dreadful things. A great many of them I've at different times named to you, but there were others I couldn't name."

"They were too, too dreadful?"

"Too, too dreadful—some of them."

She looked at him a minute, and there came to him as he met it an inconsequent sense that her eyes, when one got their full clearness, were still as beautiful as they had been in youth, only beautiful with a strange cold light—a light that somehow was a part of the effect, if it wasn't rather a part of the cause, of the pale hard sweetness of the season and the hour. "And yet," she said at last, "there are horrors we've mentioned."

It deepened the strangeness to see her, as such a figure in such a picture, talk of "horrors," but she was to do in a few minutes something stranger yet—though even of this he was to take the full measure but afterwards—and the note of it already trembled. It was, for the matter of that, one of the signs that her eyes were having again the high flicker of their prime. He had to admit, however, what she said. "Oh yes, there were times when we did go far." He caught himself in the act of speaking as if it all were over. Well, he wished it were; and the consummation depended for him clearly more and more on his friend.

But she had now a soft smile. "Oh far—!"

It was oddly ironic. "Do you mean you're prepared to go further?"

She was frail and ancient and charming as she continued to look at him, yet it was rather as if she had lost the thread. "Do you consider that we went far?"

"Why I thought it the point you were just making—that we *had* looked most things in the face."

"Including each other?" She still smiled. "But you're quite right. We've had together great imaginations, often great fears; but some of them have been unspoken."

"Then the worst—we haven't faced that. I *could* face it, I believe, if I knew what you think it. I feel," he explained, "as if I had lost my power to conceive such things." And he wondered if he looked as blank as he sounded. "It's spent."

"Then why do you assume," she asked, "that mine isn't?"

"Because you've given me signs to the contrary. It isn't a question for you of conceiving, imagining, comparing. It isn't a question now of choosing." At last he came out with it. "You know something I don't. You've shown me that before."

These last words had affected her, he made out in a moment, exceedingly, and she spoke with firmness. "I've shown you, my dear, nothing."

He shook his head. "You can't hide it."

"Oh, oh!" May Bartram sounded over what she couldn't hide. It was almost a smothered groan.

"You admitted it months ago, when I spoke of it to you as of something you were afraid I should find out. Your answer was that I couldn't, that I wouldn't, and I don't pretend I have. But you had something therefore in mind, and I now see how it must have been, how it still is, the possibility that, of all possibilities, has settled itself for you as the worst. This," he went on, "is why I appeal to you. I'm only afraid of ignorance today—I'm not afraid of knowledge." And then as for a while she said nothing: "What makes me sure is that I see in your face and feel here, in this air and amid these appearances, that you're out of it. You've done. You've had your experience. You leave me to my fate."

Well, she listened, motionless and white in her chair, as on a decision to be made, so that her manner was fairly an avowal, though still, with a small fine inner stiffness, an imperfect surrender. "It *would* be the worst," she finally let herself say. "I mean the thing I've never said."

It hushed him a moment. "More monstrous than all the monstrosities we've named?"

"More monstrous. Isn't that what you sufficiently express," she asked, "in calling it the worst?"

Marcher thought. "Assuredly—if you mean, as I do, something that includes all the loss and all the shame that are thinkable."

"It would if it *should* happen," said May Bartram. "What we're speaking of, remember, is only my idea."

"It's your belief," Marcher returned. "That's enough for me. I feel your beliefs are right. Therefore if, having this one, you give me no more light on it, you abandon me."

"No, no!" she repeated. "I'm with you—don't you see?—still." And as to make it more vivid to him she rose from her chair—a movement she seldom risked in these days—and showed herself, all draped and all soft, in her fairness and slimness. "I haven't forsaken you."

It was really, in its effort against weakness, a generous assurance, and had the success of the impulse not, happily, been great, it would have touched him to pain more than to pleasure. But the cold charm in her eyes had spread, as she hovered before him, to all the rest of her person, so that it was for the minute almost a recovery of youth. He couldn't pity her for that; he could only take her as she showed—as capable even yet of helping him. It was as if, at the same time, her light might at any instant go out; wherefore he must make the most of it. There passed before him with intensity the three or four things he wanted most to know; but the question that came of itself to his lips really covered the others. "Then tell me if I shall consciously suffer."

She promptly shook her head. "Never!"

It confirmed the authority he imputed to her, and it produced on him an extraordinary effect. "Well, what's better than that? Do you call that the worst?"

"You think nothing is better?" she asked.

She seemed to mean something so special that he again sharply wondered, though still with the dawn of a prospect of relief. "Why not, if one doesn't *know*?" After which, as their eyes, over his question, met in a silence, the dawn deepened and something to his purpose came prodigiously out of her very face. His own, as he took it in, suddenly flushed to the forehead, and he gasped with the force of a perception to which, on the instant, everything fitted. The sound of his gasp filled the air; then he became articulate. "I see—if I don't suffer!"

In her own look, however, was doubt. "You see what?"

"Why what you mean—what you've always meant."

She again shook her head. "What I mean isn't what I've always meant. It's different."

"It's something new?"

She hung back from it a little. "Something new. It's not what you think. I see what you think."

His divination drew breath then; only her correction might be wrong. "It isn't that I *am* a blockhead?" he asked between faintness and grimness. "It isn't that it's all a mistake?"

"A mistake?" she pityingly echoed. *That* possibility, for her, he saw, would be monstrous; and if she guaranteed him the immunity from pain it would accordingly not be what she had in mind. "Oh no," she declared; "it's nothing of that sort. You've been right."

Yet he couldn't help asking himself if she weren't, thus pressed, speaking but to save him. It seemed to him he should be most in a hole if his history should prove all a platitude. "Are you telling me the truth, so that I shan't have been a bigger idiot than I can bear to know? I *haven't* lived with a vain imagination, in the most besotted illusion? I haven't waited but to see the door shut in my face?"

She shook her head again. "However the case stands *that* isn't the truth. Whatever the reality, it *is* a reality. The door isn't shut. The door's open," said May Bartram.

"Then something's to come?"

She waited once again, always with her cold sweet eyes on him. "It's never too late." She had, with her gliding step, diminished the distance between them, and she stood nearer to him, close to him, a minute, as if still charged with the unspoken. Her movement might have been for some finer emphasis of what she was at once hesitating and deciding to say. He had been standing by the chimney-piece, fireless and sparely adorned, a small perfect old French clock and two morsels of rosy Dresden constituting all its furniture; and her hand grasped the shelf while she kept him waiting, grasped it a little as for support and encouragement. She only kept him waiting, however; that is he only waited. It had become suddenly, from her movement and attitude, beautiful and vivid to him that she had something more to give him; her wasted face delicately shone with it—it glittered almost as with the white lustre of silver in her expression. She was right, incontestably, for what he saw in her face was the truth, and strangely, without consequence, while their talk of it as dreadful was still in the air, she appeared to present it as inordinately soft. This, prompting bewilderment, made him but gape the more gratefully for her revelation, so that they continued for some minutes silent, her face shining at him, her contact imponderably pressing, and his stare all kind but all expectant. The end, none the less, was that what he had expected failed to come to him. Something else took place instead, which seemed to consist at first in the mere closing of her eyes. She gave way at the same instant to a slow fine shudder, and though he remained staring—though he stared in fact but the harder—turned off and regained her chair. It was the end of what she had been intending, but it left him thinking only of that.

"Well, you don't say—?"

She had touched in her passage a bell near the chimney and had sunk back strangely pale. "I'm afraid I'm too ill."

"Too ill to tell me?" It sprang up sharp to him, and almost to his lips, the fear she might die without giving him light. He checked himself in time from so expressing his question, but she answered as if she had heard the words.

"Don't you know—now?"

"'Now'—?" She had spoken as if some difference had been made within the moment. But her maid, quickly obedient to her bell, was already with them. "I know nothing." And he was afterwards to say to himself that he must have spoken with odious impatience, such an impatience as to show that, supremely disconcerted, he washed his hands of the whole question.

"Oh!" said May Bartram.

"Are you in pain?" he asked as the woman went to her.

"No," said May Bartram.

Her maid, who had put an arm round her as if to take her to her room, fixed on him eyes that appealingly contradicted her; in spite of which, however, he showed once more his mystification. "What then has happened?"

She was once more, with her companion's help, on her feet, and, feeling withdrawal imposed on him, he had blankly found his hat and gloves and had reached the door. Yet he waited for her answer. "What *was* to," she said.

V

HE came back the next day, but she was then unable to see him, and as it was literally the first time this had occurred in the long stretch of their acquaintance he turned away, defeated and sore, almost angry—or feeling at least that such a break in their custom was really the beginning of the end—and wandered alone with his thoughts, especially with the one he was least able to keep down. She was dying and he would lose her; she was dying and his life would end. He stopped in the Park, into which he had passed, and stared before him at his recurrent doubt. Away from her the doubt pressed again; in her presence he had believed her, but as he felt his forlornness he threw himself into the explanation that, nearest at hand, had most of a miserable warmth for him and least of a cold torment. She had deceived him to save him—to put him off with something in which he should be able to rest. What could the thing that was to happen to him be, after all, but just this thing that had begun to happen? Her dying, her death, his consequent solitude—*that* was what he had figured as the Beast in the Jungle, that was what had been in the lap of the gods. He had had her word for it as he left her—what else on earth could she have meant? It wasn't a thing of a monstrous order; not a fate rare and distinguished; not a stroke of fortune that overwhelmed and immortalised; it had only the stamp of the common doom. But poor Marcher at this hour judged the common doom sufficient. It would serve his turn, and even as the consummation of infinite waiting he would bend his pride to accept it. He sat down on a bench in the twilight. He hadn't been a fool. Something had *been,* as she had said, to come. Before he rose indeed it had quite struck him that the final fact really matched with the long avenue through which he had had to reach it. As sharing his suspense and as giving herself all, giving her life, to bring it to an end, she had come with him every step of the way. He had lived by her aid, and to leave her behind would be cruelly, damnably to miss her. What could be more overwhelming than that?

Well, he was to know within the week, for though she kept him a while at bay, left him restless and wretched during a series of days on each of which he asked about her only again to have to turn away, she ended his trial by receiving him where she had always received him. Yet she had been brought out at some hazard into the presence of so many of the things that were, consciously, vainly, half their past, and there was scant service left in the gentleness of her mere desire, all too visible, to check his obsession and wind up his long trouble. That was clearly what she wanted, the one thing more for her own peace while she could still put out her hand. He was so affected by her state that, once seated by her chair, he was moved to let everything go; it was she herself therefore who brought him back, took up again, before she dismissed him, her last word of the other time. She showed how she wished to leave their business in order. "I'm not sure you understood. You've nothing to wait for more. It *has* come."

Oh how he looked at her! "Really?"

"Really."

"The thing that, as you said, *was* to?"

"The thing that we began in our youth to watch for."

Face to face with her once more he believed her; it was a claim to which he had so abjectly little to oppose. "You mean that it has come as a positive definite occurrence, with a name and a date?"

"Positive. Definite. I don't know about the 'name,' but oh with a date!"

He found himself again too helplessly at sea. "But come in the night—come and passed me by?"

May Bartram had her strange faint smile. "Oh no, it hasn't passed you by!"

"But if I haven't been aware of it and it hasn't touched me—?"

"Ah your not being aware of it"—and she seemed to hesitate an instant to deal with this—"your not being aware of it is the strangeness *in* the strangeness. It's the wonder *of* the wonder." She spoke as with the softness almost of a sick child, yet now at last, at the end of all, with the perfect straightness of a sibyl. She visibly knew that she knew, and the effect on him was of something co-ordinate, in its high character, with the law that had ruled him. It was the true voice of the law; so on her lips would the law itself have sounded. "It *has* touched you," she went on. "It has done its office. It has made you all its own."

"So utterly without my knowing it?"

"So utterly without your knowing it." His hand, as he leaned to her, was on the arm of her chair, and, dimly smiling always now, she placed her own on it. "It's enough if *I* know it."

"Oh!" he confusedly breathed, as she herself of late so often had done.

"What I long ago said is true. You'll never know now, and I think you ought to be content. You've *had* it," said May Bartram.

"But had what?"

"Why what was to have marked you out. The proof of your law. It has acted. I'm too glad," she then bravely added, "to have been able to see what it's *not*."

He continued to attach his eyes to her, and with the sense that it was all beyond him, and that *she* was too, he would still have sharply challenged her hadn't he so felt it an abuse of her weakness to do more than take devoutly what she gave him, take it hushed as to a revelation. If he did speak, it was out of the foreknowledge of his loneliness to come. "If you're glad of what it's 'not' it might then have been worse?"

She turned her eyes away, she looked straight before her; with which after a moment: "Well, you know our fears."

He wondered. "It's something then we never feared?"

On this slowly she turned to him. "Did we ever dream, with all our dreams, that we should sit and talk of it thus?"

He tried for a little to make out that they had; but it was as if their dreams, numberless enough, were in solution in some thick cold mist through which thought lost itself. "It might have been that we couldn't talk?"

"Well"—she did her best for him—"not from this side. This, you see," she said, "is the *other* side."

"I think," poor Marcher returned, "that all sides are the same to me." Then, however, as she gently shook her head in correction: "We mightn't, as it were, have got across—?"

"To where we are—no. We're *here*"—she made her weak emphasis.

"And much good does it do us!" was her friend's frank comment.

"It does us the good it can. It does us the good that *it* isn't here. It's past. It's behind," said May Bartram. "Before—" but her voice dropped.

He had got up, not to tire her, but it was hard to combat his yearning. She after all told him nothing but that his light had failed—which he knew well enough without her. "Before—?" he blankly echoed.

"Before, you see, it was always to *come*. That kept it present."

"Oh I don't care what comes now! Besides," Marcher added, "it seems to me I liked it better present, as you say, than I can like it absent with *your* absence."

"Oh mine!"—and her pale hands made light of it.

"With the absence of everything." He had a dreadful sense of standing there before her for—so far as anything but this proved, this bottomless drop was concerned—the last time of their life.

It rested on him with a weight he felt he could scarce bear, and this weight it apparently was that still pressed out what remained in him of speakable protest. "I believe you; but I can't begin to pretend I understand. *Nothing,* for me, is past; nothing *will* pass till I pass myself, which I pray my stars may be as soon as possible. Say, however," he added, "that I've eaten my cake, as you contend, to the last crumb—how can the thing I've never felt at all be the thing I was marked out to feel?"

She met him perhaps less directly, but she met him unperturbed. "You take your 'feelings' for granted. You were to suffer your fate. That was not necessarily to know it."

"How in the world—when what is such knowledge but suffering?"

She looked up at him a while in silence. "No—you don't understand."

"I suffer," said John Marcher.

"Don't, don't!"

"How can I help at least *that*?"

"Don't!" May Bartram repeated.

She spoke it in a tone so special, in spite of her weakness, that he stared an instant—stared as if some light, hitherto hidden, had shimmered across his vision. Darkness again closed over it, but the gleam had already become for him an idea. "Because I haven't the right—?"

"Don't *know*—when you needn't," she mercifully urged. "You needn't—for we shouldn't."

"Shouldn't?" If he could but know what she meant!

"No—it's too much."

"Too much?" he still asked but, with a mystification that was the next moment of a sudden to give way. Her words, if they meant something, affected him in this light—the light also of her wasted face—as meaning *all,* and the sense of what knowledge had been for herself came over him with a rush which broke through into a question. "Is it of that then you're dying?"

She but watched him, gravely at first, as to see, with this, where he was, and she might have seen something or feared something that moved her sympathy. "I would live for you still—if I could." Her eyes closed for a little, as if, withdrawn into herself, she were for a last time trying. "But I can't!" she said as she raised them again to take leave of him.

She couldn't indeed, as but too promptly and sharply appeared, and he had no vision of her after this that was anything but darkness and doom. They had parted for ever in that strange talk; access to her chamber of pain, rigidly guarded, was almost wholly forbidden him; he was feeling now moreover, in the face of doctors, nurses, the two or three relatives attracted doubtless by the presumption of what she had to "leave," how few were the rights, as they were called in such cases, that he had to put forward, and how odd it might even seem that their intimacy shouldn't have given him more of them. The stupidest fourth cousin had more, even though she had been nothing in such a person's life. She had been a feature of features in *his,* for what else was it to have been so indispensable? Strange beyond saying were the ways of existence, baffling for him the anomaly of his lack, as he felt it to be, of producible claim. A woman might have been, as it were, everything to him, and it might yet present him in no connexion that any one seemed held to recognise. If this was the case in these closing weeks it was the case more sharply on the occasion of the last offices rendered, in the great grey London cemetery, to what had been mortal, to what had been precious, in his friend. The concourse at her grave was not numerous, but he saw himself treated as scarce more nearly concerned with it than if there had been a thousand others. He was in short from this moment face to face with the fact that he was to profit extraordinarily little by the interest May Bartram had taken in him. He couldn't quite have said what he expected, but he hadn't surely expected this approach to a double privation. Not only had her interest failed him, but he seemed to feel himself unattended—and for a reason he couldn't seize—by the distinction, the dignity, the propriety, if nothing else, of the man markedly bereaved. It was as if in the view of society he had not *been* markedly bereaved, as if there still failed some sign or proof if it, and as if none the less his character could never be affirmed nor the deficiency ever made up. There were moments as the weeks went by when he would have liked, by some almost aggressive act, to take his stand on the intimacy of his loss, in order that it *might* be questioned and his retort, to the relief of his spirit, so recorded; but the moments of an irritation more helpless followed fast on these, the moments during which, turning things over with a good conscience but with a bare horizon, he found himself wondering if he oughtn't to have begun, so to speak, further back.

He found himself wondering indeed at many things, and this last speculation had others to keep it company. What could he have done, after all, in her lifetime, without giving them both, as it were, away? He couldn't have made known she was watching him, for that would have published the superstition of the Beast. This was what closed his mouth now—now that the Jungle had been threshed to vacancy and that the Beast had stolen away. It sounded too foolish and too flat; the difference for him in this particular, the extinction in his life of the element of suspense, was such as in fact to surprise him. He could scarce have said what the effect resembled; the abrupt cessation, the positive prohibition, of music perhaps, more than anything else, in some place all adjusted and all accustomed to sonority and to attention. If he could at any rate have conceived lifting the veil from his image at some moment of the past (what had he done, after all, if not lift it to *her*?) so to do this today, to talk to people at large of the Jungle cleared and confide to them that he now felt it as safe, would have been not only to see them listen as to a goodwife's tale, but really to hear himself tell one. What it presently came to in truth was that poor Marcher waded through his beaten grass, where no life stirred, where no breath sounded, where no evil eye seemed to gleam from a possible lair, very much as if vaguely looking for the Beast, and still more as if acutely missing it. He walked about in an existence that had grown strangely more spacious, and, stopping fitfully in places where the undergrowth of life struck him as closer, asked himself yearningly, wondered secretly and sorely, if it would have lurked here or there. It would have at all events *sprung;* what was at least complete was his belief in the truth itself of the assurance given him. The change from his old sense to his new was absolute and final: what was to happen *had* so absolutely and finally happened that he was as little able to know a fear for his future as to know a hope; so absent in short was any question of anything still to come. He was to live entirely with the other question, that of his unidentified past, that of his having to see his fortune impenetrably muffled and masked.

The torment of this vision became then his occupation; he couldn't perhaps have consented to live but for the possibility of guessing. She had told him, his friend, not to guess; she had forbidden him, so far as he might, to know, and she had even in a sort denied the power in him to learn: which were so many things, precisely, to deprive him of rest. It wasn't that he wanted, he argued for fairness, that anything past and done should repeat itself; it was only that he shouldn't, as an anticlimax, have been taken sleeping so sound as not to be able to win back by an effort of thought the lost stuff of consciousness. He declared to himself at moments that he would either win it back or have done with consciousness for ever; he made this idea his one motive in fine, made it so much his passion that none other, to compare with it, seemed ever to have touched him. The lost stuff of consciousness became thus for him as a strayed or stolen child to an unappeasable father; he hunted it up and down very much as if he were knocking at doors and enquiring of the police. This was the spirit in which, inevitably, he set himself to travel; he started on a journey that was to be as long as he could make it; it danced before him that, as the other side of the globe couldn't possibly have less to say to him, it might, by a possibility of suggestion, have more. Before he quitted London, however, he made a pilgrimage to May Bartram's grave, took his way to it through the endless avenues of the grim suburban metropolis, sought it out in the wilderness of tombs, and, though he had come but for the renewal of the act of farewell, found himself, when he had at last stood by it, beguiled into long intensities. He stood for an hour, powerless to turn away and yet powerless to penetrate the darkness of death; fixing with his eyes her inscribed name and date, beating his forehead against the fact of the secret they kept, drawing his breath, while he waited, as if some sense would in pity of him rise from the stones. He kneeled on the stones, however, in vain; they kept what they concealed; and if the face of the tomb did become a face for him it was because her two names became a pair of eyes that didn't know him. He gave them a last long look, but no palest light broke.

VI

He stayed away, after this, for a year; he visited the depths of Asia, spending himself on scenes of romantic interest, of superlative sanctity; but what was present to him everywhere was that for a man who had known what *he* had known the world was vulgar and vain. The state of mind in which he had lived for so many years shone out to him, in reflexion, as a light that coloured and refined, a light beside which the glow of the East was garish and cheap and thin. The terrible truth was that he had lost—with everything else—a distinction as well; the things he saw couldn't help being common when he had become common to look at them. He was simply now one of them himself—he was in the dust, without a peg for the sense of difference; and there were hours when, before the temples of gods and the sepulchres of kings, his spirit turned for nobleness of association to the barely discriminated slab in the London suburb. That had become for him, and more intensely with time and distance, his one witness of a past glory. It was all that was left to him for proof or pride, yet the past glories of Pharaohs were nothing to him as he thought of it. Small wonder then that he came back to it on the morrow of his return. He was drawn there this time as irresistibly as the other, yet with a confidence, almost, that was doubtless the effect of the many months that had elapsed. He had lived, in spite of himself, into his change of feeling, and in wandering over the earth had wandered, as might be said, from the circumference to the centre of his desert. He had settled to his safety and accepted perforce his extinction; figuring to himself, with some colour, in the likeness of certain little old men he remembered to have seen, of whom, all meagre and wizened as they might look, it was related that they had in their time fought twenty duels or been loved by ten princesses. They indeed had been wondrous for others while he was but wondrous for himself; which, however, was exactly the cause of his haste to renew the wonder by getting back, as he might put it, into his own presence. That had quickened his steps and checked his delay. If his visit was prompt it was because he had been separated so long from the part of himself that alone he now valued.

It's accordingly not false to say that he reached his goal with a certain elation and stood there again with a certain assurance. The creature beneath the sod *knew* of his rare experience, so that, strangely now, the place had lost for him its mere blankness of expression. It met him in mildness—not, as before, in mockery; it wore for him the air of conscious greeting that we find, after absence, in things that have closely belonged to us and which seem to confess of themselves to the connexion. The plot of ground, the graven tablet, the tended flowers affected him so as belonging to him that he resembled for the hour a contented landlord reviewing a piece of property. Whatever had happened—well, had happened. He had not come back this time with the vanity of that question, his former worrying "what, *what*?" now practically so spent. Yet he would none the less never again so cut himself off from the spot; he would come back to it every month, for if he did nothing else by its aid he at least held up his head. It thus grew for him, in the oddest way, a positive resource; he carried out his idea of periodical returns, which took their place at last among the most inveterate of his habits. What it all amounted to, oddly enough, was that in his finally so simplified world this garden of death gave him the few square feet of earth on which he could still most live. It was as if, being nothing anywhere else for any one, nothing even for himself, he were just everything here, and if not for a crowd of witnesses or indeed for any witness but John Marcher, then by clear right of the register that he could scan like an open page. The open page was the tomb of his friend, and *there* were the facts of the past, there the truth of his life, there the backward reaches in which he could lose himself. He did this from time to time with such effect that he seemed to wander through the old years with his hand in the arm of a companion who was, in the most extraordinary manner, his other, his younger self; and to wander, which was more extraordinary yet, round and round a third presence—not wandering she, but stationary, still, whose eyes, turning with his revolution, never ceased to follow him, and whose seat was his point, so to speak, of orientation. Thus in short he settled to live—feeding all on the sense that he once *had* lived, and dependent on it not alone for a support but for an identity.

It sufficed him in its way for months and the year elapsed; it would doubtless even have carried him further but for an accident, superficially slight, which moved him, quite in another direction, with a force beyond any of his impressions of Egypt or of India. It was a thing of the merest chance—the turn, as he afterwards felt, of a hair, though he was indeed to live to believe that if light hadn't come to him in this particular fashion it would still have come in another. He was to live to believe this, I say, though he was not to live, I may not less definitely mention, to do much else. We allow him at any rate the benefit of the conviction, struggling up for him at the end, that, whatever might have happened or not happened, he would have come round of himself to the light. The incident of an autumn day had put the match to the train laid from of old by his misery. With the light before him he knew that even of late his ache had only been smothered. It was strangely drugged, but it throbbed; at the touch it began to bleed. And the touch, in the event, was the face of a fellow mortal. This face, one grey afternoon when the leaves were thick in the alleys, looked into Marcher's own, at the cemetery, with an expression like the cut of a blade. He felt it, that is, so deep down that he winced at the steady thrust. The person who so mutely assaulted him was a figure he had noticed, on reaching his own goal, absorbed by a grave a short distance away, a grave apparently fresh, so that the emotion of the visitor would probably match it for frankness. This face alone forbade further attention, though during the time he stayed he remained vaguely conscious of his neighbour, a middle-aged man apparently, in mourning, whose bowed back, among the clustered monuments and mortuary yews, was constantly presented. Marcher's theory that these were elements in contact with which he himself revived, had suffered, on this occasion, it may be granted, a marked, an excessive check. The autumn day was dire for him as none had recently been, and he rested with a heaviness he had not yet known on the low stone table that bore May Bartram's name. He rested without power to move, as if some spring in him, some spell vouchsafed, had suddenly been broken for ever. If he could have done that moment as he wanted he would simply have stretched himself on the slab that was ready to take him, treating it as a place prepared to receive his last sleep. What in all the wide world had he now to keep awake for? He stared before him with the question, and it was then that, as one of the cemetery walks passed near him, he caught the shock of the face.

His neighbour at the other grave had withdrawn, as he himself, with force enough in him, would have done by now, and was advancing along the path on his way to one of the gates. This brought him close, and his pace was slow, so that—and all the more as there was a kind of hunger in his look—the two men were for a minute directly confronted. Marcher knew him at once for one of the deeply stricken—a perception so sharp that nothing else in the picture comparatively lived, neither his dress, his age, nor his presumable character and class; nothing lived but the deep ravage of the features he showed. He *showed* them—that was the point; he was moved, as he passed, by some impulse that was either a signal for sympathy or, more possibly, a challenge to an opposed sorrow. He might already have been aware of our friend, might at some previous hour have noticed in him the smooth habit of the scene, with which the state of his own senses so scantly consorted, and might thereby have been stirred as by an overt discord. What Marcher was at all events conscious of was in the first place that the image of scarred passion presented to him was conscious too—of something that profaned the air; and in the second that, roused, startled, shocked, he was yet the next moment looking after it, as it went, with envy. The most extraordinary thing that had happened to him—though he had given that name to other matters as well—took place, after his immediate vague stare, as a consequence of this impression. The stranger passed, but the raw glare of his grief remained, making our friend wonder in pity what wrong, what wound it expressed, what injury not to be healed. What had the man *had,* to make him by the loss of it so bleed and yet live?

Something—and this reached him with a pang—that *he,* John Marcher, hadn't; the proof of which was precisely John Marcher's arid end. No passion had ever touched him, for this was what passion meant; he had survived and maundered and pined, but where had been *his* deep ravage? The extraordinary thing we speak of was the sudden rush of the result of this question. The sight that had just met his eyes named to him, as in letters of quick flame, something he had utterly, insanely missed, and what he had missed made these things a train of fire, made them mark themselves in an anguish of inward throbs. He had seen *outside* of his life, not learned it within, the way a woman was mourned when she had been loved for herself: such was the force of his conviction of the meaning of the stranger's face, which still flared for him as a smoky torch. It hadn't come to him, the knowledge, on the wings of experience; it had brushed him, jostled him, upset him, with the disrespect of chance, the insolence of accident. Now that the illumination had begun, however, it blazed to the zenith, and what he presently stood there gazing at was the sounded void of his life. He gazed, he drew breath, in pain; he turned in his dismay, and, turning, he had before him in sharper incision than ever the open page of his story. The name on the table smote him as the passage of his neighbour had done, and what it said to him, full in the face, was that *she* was what he had missed. This was the awful thought, the answer to all the past, the vision at the dread clearness of which he grew as cold as the stone beneath him. Everything fell together, confessed, explained, overwhelmed; leaving him most of all stupefied at the blindness he had cherished. The fate he had been marked for he had met with a vengeance—he had emptied the cup to the lees; he had been the man of his time, *the* man, to whom nothing on earth was to have happened. That was the rare stroke—that was his visitation. So he saw it, as we say, in pale horror, while the pieces fitted and fitted. So *she* had seen it while he didn't, and so she served at this hour to drive the truth home. It was the truth, vivid and monstrous, that all the while he had waited the wait was itself his portion. This the companion of his vigil had at a given moment made out, and she had then offered him the chance to baffle his doom. One's doom, however, was never baffled, and on the day she told him his own had come down she had seen him but stupidly stare at the escape she offered him.

The escape would have been to love her; then, *then* he would have lived. *She* had lived—who could say now with what passion?—since she had loved him for himself; whereas he had never thought of her (ah how it hugely glared at him!) but in the chill of his egotism and the light of her use. Her spoken words came back to him—the chain stretched and stretched. The Beast had lurked indeed, and the Beast, at its hour, had sprung it; it had sprung in that twilight of the cold April when, pale, ill, wasted, but all beautiful, and perhaps even then recoverable, she had risen from her chair to stand before him and let him imaginably guess. It had sprung as he didn't guess; it had sprung as she hopelessly turned from him, and the mark, by the time he left her, had fallen where it *was* to fall. He had justified his fear and achieved his fate; he had failed, with the last exactitude, of all he was to fail of; and a moan now rose to his lips as he remembered she had prayed he mightn't know. This horror of waking—*this* was knowledge, knowledge under the breath of which the very tears in his eyes seemed to freeze. Through them, none the less, he tried to fix it and hold it; he kept it there before him so that he might feel the pain. That at least, belated and bitter, had something of the taste of life. But the bitterness suddenly sickened him, and it was as if, horribly, he saw, in the truth, in the cruelty of his image, what had been appointed and done. He saw the Jungle of his life and saw the lurking Beast; then, while he looked, perceived it, as by a stir of the air, rise, huge and hideous, for the leap that was to settle him. His eyes darkened—it was close; and, instinctively turning, in his hallucination, to avoid it, he flung himself, face down, on the tomb.

A NOTE ON

THE BEAST IN THE JUNGLE

(1903)

For me this is the best of James's shorter fictions, combining the utmost concentration of effect with the utmost inclusiveness of meaning. I know of few tales in any literature that I would rank above it. Its significance is timeless and absolute, being dependent on no wind of doctrine, no fashion of style. A myth rather than a story, it gathers up in its sinuosities a part of the prime and universal experience of mankind. From it even the palest stain of the trivial is absent.

The concept of the Faustian man is one we accept as deeply symbolic of our whole culture. Faust, we say, is ourselves, is Western man, the striver, the man to whom things happen, the man who makes things happen, the hero of experience. He comes before us in a hundred guises, as Hamlet, as Ahab, as Don Quixote, as Leonardo da Vinci, as Huckleberry Finn.

Since the Renaissance the Western imagination has been so dominated by the idea of the Faustian man and has figured him forth in such powerful and magnificent embodiments that we have forgotten that where there is Faust there must also be un-Faust. We have forgotten that the Fausts are the exceptions, that they represent the aspirations, the hungers of men rather than reflect men's actual experience. The plain, bare, terrible fact of the matter is that most of us live pitifully un-Faustian lives and die pitifully un-Faustian deaths. The Preacher who said that all was vanity knew this; and many others after him. But, for the most part, poets and novelists have shrunk from presenting the un-Faustian life in imaginative terms. Their very business, they would say, is to show man amid experience. How, then, shall they show him as eternally waiting for the experience that somehow eludes him? The artistic problem seems to admit of no solution.

"The Beast in the Jungle" solves it relentlessly. Its subject is not the life we have had but the life we have missed. Whatever in us is non-sentient, non-perceptive, whatever in us makes us feel, as death approaches, that something has been slipping continually through our hands—this comes to expression in "The Beast in the Jungle." Who among us does not feel from time to time that somewhere ahead there is a magical, or it may be a dread, corner round which Life stands, her attitude full of promise? The saints, the artists, the thinkers, the lovers—these perhaps die in the certainty that they have lived. And (among the commonalty) the egotists, the success-men, the bank-balance men, the power-men—these too die in the same certainty, in their cases born of stupidity. But most of the rest of us die in a kind of bewilderment, holding in our failing hands the thread that should have led us—but did not—into the land of dense, exhaustive experience. This is the feeling, so intensely human, so nearly universal, and so seemingly defiant of dramatic exploitation, that lies at the base of "The Beast in the Jungle."

Marcher stands for un-Faust, for man the coward, not the hero, of experience. "He had been the man of his time, *the* man, to whom nothing on earth was to have happened." He is the tragic, the terrible intensification of all those Jamesian heroes who miss out because they lack the ability to make the decisive gesture of gathering life into their hands. And, before setting him down as an exaggerated, an unnatural figure, let us ask ourselves in all honesty whether there is more of Faust in us—or more of Marcher. "Has it ever happened?" is the key question May Bartram addresses to Marcher when we first encounter them. It is life's key question too, the key question we are afraid to put to ourselves. Many things happen to us, pleasant, unpleasant—but *it,* the thing "rare and strange, possibly prodigious and terrible"—this rarely happens. Most of us are only dimly aware that it never happens; but it is Marcher's horrifying fate to know it intensely. "It wouldn't have been failure," thinks Marcher, "to be bankrupt, dishonoured, pilloried, hanged; it was failure not to be anything."

James's blinding insight into characters who are *manqués* comes in part from the strange pattern of his own life, one lived largely—and with compensatory intensity—in the mind. He must have felt (see the note on "The Jolly Corner") that the circumstances of his parentage, the early accident that partially incapacitated him, the removal to England—all had combined with many other factors to narrow for him the possibilities of direct and passionate experience. That he sensed in himself the troubling pressure of his unlived life we can divine from the frequency with which he exhibits characters who cry out for the experience which their temperaments deny them. Lambert Strether, in *The Ambassadors,* will be remembered as the perfect example of James's projection of his own inner conflict, his sense of the discrepancy between the plenitude of his imagination and the over-refinement of his experience.

But it is "The Beast in the Jungle" that develops this theme with the most concentrated power and greatest generality. Its meaning, as Philip Rahv has so well said, is "so all-inclusive as to refer to every conceivable failure of human energy." It is not that we are all Marchers, but that Marcher is in all of us. He is in the medieval monk suffering from *acedia;* he is in the imperfectly sexed; he is in the ivory-tower dweller; he is in the scholar who establishes no connection with the pulsing outer world. Marcher looks out of the blank face of the subway straphanger and out of the equally blank faces of the middle-aged clubmen of the whisky ads. He is the epitome of the unlived life. He is in you and he is in me.

But he differs from most of us in the intensity of his consciousness. He is saved from blankness by the presence of May Bartram, personifying the life he might have had, holding always before him the possibility of real experience. It is May who, by merely existing, by talking, by an occasional question, and by her piercing insights into the horror of Marcher's predicament, keeps him perceptive. Without her he might have become one of James's non-sentient fools. But she cannot really save him, for his nature is his doom. "Of course one's fate is coming," says May at one point, "of course it *has* come, in its own form and its own way, all the while." One way of describing Marcher's fate is to say that he cannot love. He cannot love even after he realizes what the Beast is. When he perceives that nothing can happen to him, he throws himself on May's tomb, but it is in insane despair, not in passion, that he does so. The moment he understands his life (and that moment is the only real event in it) his life collapses about him. The sense of the collapse is conveyed in the relentless, terrifying last paragraph, an ending matchless in its condensation and finality of effect.

Marcher's special failure (and this is what helps to give "The Beast in the Jungle" its almost Shakespearian universality) is part of mankind's general failure. It is the failure to communicate. The tragedy of men and women is not that we die, but that we die before we have had a chance to communicate to others our pitifully small understanding of ourselves. Literature is but a magnificent protest against this inability, as are indeed all the arts. War, injustice, intolerance form the other side of the picture: they are the monstrous proofs of man's inability to talk to man.

The curious relationship between May and Marcher unforgettably dramatizes this universal inability. For many years these two sensitive, articulate persons sit and talk to each other (only James could conceive of holding one's interest with so fantastic a situation) and yet do not really communicate. May cannot tell Marcher what she feels about him. He cannot tell her exactly what he feels about himself. Painfully they try to build bridges between them; but to no avail. In the end May, the more perceptive of the two, gives up. All she can do for

Marcher is, as she says, "to help you to pass for a man like another." That, of course, is what most women are forced to do for their men—to cover up their weaknesses and inarticulacies and content themselves merely with helping them "to pass for a man like another."

It is customary to praise James for his subtle understanding of the smallest tricks and turns of the mind. This very praise carries with it the implication that he is deficient in large and powerful ideas. But in "The Beast in the Jungle" a large idea is developed with exhaustive subtlety. Masterful technique and overwhelming content have become one, the union producing, as it always does, the highest art.

THE JOLLY CORNER

I

"EVERY one asks me what I 'think' of everything," said Spencer Brydon; "and I make answer as I can—begging or dodging the question, putting them off with any nonsense. It wouldn't matter to any of them really," he went on, "for, even were it possible to meet in that stand-and-deliver way so silly a demand on so big a subject, my 'thoughts' would still be almost altogether about something that concerns only myself." He was talking to Miss Staverton, with whom for a couple of months now he had availed himself of every possible occasion to talk; this disposition and this resource, this comfort and support, as the situation in fact presented itself, having promptly enough taken the first place in the considerable array of rather unattenuated surprises attending his so strangely belated return to America. Everything was somehow a surprise; and that might be natural when one had so long and so consistently neglected everything, taken pains to give surprises so much margin for play. He had given them more than thirty years—thirty-three, to be exact; and they now seemed to him to have organised their performance quite on the scale of that licence. He had been twenty-three on leaving New York—he was fifty-six today: unless indeed he were to reckon as he had sometimes, since his repatriation, found himself feeling; in which case he would have lived longer than is often allotted to man. It would have taken a century, he repeatedly said to himself, and said also to Alice Staverton, it would have taken a longer absence and a more averted mind than those even of which he had been guilty, to pile up the differences, the newnesses, the queernesses, above all the bignesses, for the better or the worse, that at present assaulted his vision wherever he looked.

The great fact all the while however had been the incalculability; since he *had* supposed himself, from decade to decade, to be allowing, and in the most liberal and intelligent manner, for brilliancy of change. He actually saw that he had allowed for nothing; he missed what he would have been sure of finding, he found what he would never have imagined. Proportions and values were upside-down; the ugly things he had expected, the ugly things of his far-away youth, when he had too promptly waked up to a sense of the ugly—these uncanny phenomena placed him rather, as it happened, under the charm; whereas the "swagger" things, the modern, the monstrous, the famous things, those he had more particularly, like thousands of ingenuous enquirers every year, come over to see, were exactly his sources of dismay. They were as so many set traps for displeasure, above all for reaction, of which his restless tread was constantly pressing the spring. It was interesting, doubtless, the whole show, but it would have been too disconcerting hadn't a certain finer truth saved the situation. He had distinctly not, in this steadier light, come over *all* for the monstrosities; he had come, not only in the last analysis but quite on the face of the act, under an impulse with which they had nothing to do. He had come—putting the thing pompously—to look at his "property," which he had thus for a third of a century not been within four thousand miles of; or, expressing it less sordidly, he had yielded to the humour of seeing again his house on the jolly corner, as he usually, and quite fondly, described it—the one in which he had first seen the light, in which various members of his family had lived and had died, in which the holidays of his overschooled boyhood had been passed and the few social flowers of his chilled adolescence gathered, and which, alienated then for so long a period, had, through the successive deaths of his two brothers and the termination of old arrangements, come wholly into his hands. He was the owner of another, not quite so "good"—the jolly corner having been, from far back, superlatively extended and consecrated; and the value of the pair represented his main capital, with an income consisting, in these later years, of their respective rents which (thanks precisely to their original excellent type) had never been depressingly low. He could live in "Europe," as he had been in the habit of living, on the product of these flourishing New York leases, and all the better since, that of the second structure, the mere number in its long row, having within a twelvemonth fallen in, renovation at a high advance had proved beautifully possible.

These were items of property indeed, but he had found himself since his arrival distinguishing more than ever between them. The house within the street, two bristling blocks westward, was already in course of reconstruction as a tall mass of flats; he had acceded, some time before, to overtures for this conversion—in which, now that it was going forward, it had been not the least of his astonishments to find himself able, on the spot, and though without a previous ounce of such experience, to participate with a certain intelligence, almost with a certain authority. He had lived his life with his back so turned to such concerns and his face addressed to those of so different an order that he scarce knew what to make of this lively stir, in a compartment of his mind never yet penetrated, of a capacity for business and a sense for construction. These virtues, so common all round him now, had been dormant in his own organism—where it might be said of them perhaps that they had slept the sleep of the just. At present, in the splendid autumn weather—the autumn at least was a pure boon in the terrible place—he loafed about his "work" undeterred, secretly agitated; not in the least "minding" that the whole proposition, as they said, was vulgar and sordid, and ready to climb ladders, to walk the plank, to handle materials and look wise about them, to ask questions, in fine, and challenge explanations and really "go into" figures.

It amused, it verily quite charmed him; and, by the same stroke, it amused, and even more, Alice Staverton, though perhaps charming her perceptibly less. She wasn't however going to be better off for it, as *he* was—and so astonishingly much: nothing was now likely, he knew, ever to make her better off than she found herself, in the afternoon of life, as the delicately frugal possessor and tenant of the small house in Irving Place to which she had subtly managed to cling through her almost unbroken New York career. If he knew the way to it now better than to any other address among the dreadful multiplied numberings which seemed to him to reduce the whole place to some vast ledger-page, overgrown, fantastic, of ruled and criss-crossed lines and figures—if he had formed, for his consolation, that habit, it was really not a little because of the charm of his having encountered and recognised, in the vast wilderness of the wholesale, breaking through the mere gross generalisation of wealth and force and success, a small still scene where items and shades, all delicate things, kept the sharpness of the notes of a high voice perfectly trained, and where economy hung about like the scent of a garden. His old friend lived with one maid and herself, dusted her relics and trimmed her lamps and polished her silver; she stood off, in the awful modern crush, when she could, but she sallied forth and did battle when the challenge was really to "spirit," the spirit she after all confessed to, proudly and a little shyly, as to that of the better time, that of *their* common, their quite far-away and antediluvian social period and order. She made use of the street-cars when need be, the terrible things that people scrambled for as the panic-stricken at sea scramble for the boats; she affronted, inscrutably, under stress, all the public concussions and ordeals; and yet, with that slim mystifying grace of her appearance, which defied you to say if she were a fair young woman who looked older through trouble, or a fine smooth older one who looked young through successful indifference; with her precious reference, above all, to memories and histories into which he could enter, she was as exquisite for him as some pale pressed flower (a rarity to begin with), and, failing other sweetnesses, she was a sufficient reward of his effort. They had communities of knowledge, "their" knowledge (this discriminating possessive was always on her lips) of presences of the other age, presences all overlaid, in his case, by the experience of a man and the freedom of a wanderer, overlaid by pleasure, by infidelity, by passages of life that were strange and dim to her, just by "Europe" in short, but still unobscured, still exposed and cherished, under that pious visitation of the spirit from which she had never been diverted.

She had come with him one day to see how his "apartment-house" was rising; he had helped her over gaps and explained to her plans, and while they were there had happened to have, before her, a brief but lively discussion with the man in charge, the representative of the building-firm that had undertaken his work. He had found himself quite "standing-up" to this personage over a failure on the latter's part to observe some detail of one of their noted conditions, and had so lucidly argued his case that, besides ever so prettily flushing, at the time, for sympathy in his triumph, she had afterwards said to him (though to a slightly greater effect of irony) that he had clearly for too many years neglected a real gift. If he had but stayed at home he would have anticipated the inventor of the sky-scraper. If he had but stayed at home he would have discovered his genius in time really to start some new variety of awful architectural hare and run it till it burrowed in a gold-mine. He was to remember these words, while the weeks elapsed, for the small silver ring they had sounded over the queerest and deepest of his own lately most disguised and most muffled vibrations.

It had begun to be present to him after the first fortnight, it had broken out with the oddest abruptness, this particular wanton wonderment: it met him there—and this was the image under which he himself judged the matter, or at least, not a little, thrilled and flushed with it—very much as he might have been met by some strange figure, some unexpected occupant, at a turn of one of the dim passages of an empty house. The quaint analogy quite hauntingly remained with him, when he didn't indeed rather improve it by a still intenser form: that of his opening a door behind which he would have made sure of finding nothing, a door into a room shuttered and void, and yet so coming, with a great suppressed start, on some quite erect confronting presence, something planted in the middle of the place and facing him through the dusk. After that visit to the house in construction he walked with his companion to see the other and always so much the better one, which in the eastward direction formed one of the corners, the "jolly" one precisely, of the street now so generally dishonoured and disfigured in its westward reaches, and of the comparatively conservative Avenue. The Avenue still had pretensions, as Miss Staverton said, to decency; the old people had mostly gone, the old names were unknown, and here and there an old association seemed to stray, all vaguely, like some very aged person, out too late, whom you might meet and feel the impulse to watch or follow, in kindness, for safe restoration to shelter.

They went in together, our friends; he admitted himself with his key, as he kept no one there, he explained, preferring, for his reasons, to leave the place empty, under a simple arrangement with a good woman living in the neighbourhood and who came for a daily hour to open windows and dust and sweep. Spencer Brydon had his reasons and was growingly aware of them; they seemed to him better each time he was there, though he didn't name them all to his companion, any more than he told her as yet how often, how quite absurdly often, he himself came. He only let her see for the present, while they walked through the great blank rooms, that absolute vacancy reigned and that, from top to bottom, there was nothing but Mrs. Muldoon's broomstick, in a corner, to tempt the burglar. Mrs. Muldoon was then on the premises, and she loquaciously attended the visitors, preceding them from room to room and pushing back shutters and throwing up sashes—all to show them, as she remarked, how little there was to see. There was little indeed to see in the great gaunt shell where the main dispositions and the general apportionment of space, the style of an age of ampler allowances, had nevertheless for its master their honest pleading message, affecting him as some good old servant's, some lifelong retainer's appeal for a character, or even for a retiring-pension; yet it was also a remark of Mrs. Muldoon's that, glad as she was to oblige him by her noonday round, there was a request she greatly hoped he would never make of her. If he should wish her for any reason to come in after dark she would just tell him, if he "plased," that he must ask it of somebody else.

The fact that there was nothing to see didn't militate for the worthy woman against what one *might* see, and she put it frankly to Miss Staverton that no lady could be expected to like, could she? "scraping up to thim top storeys in the ayvil hours." The gas and the electric light were off the house, and she fairly evoked a gruesome vision of her march through the great grey rooms—so many of them as there were too!—with her glimmering taper. Miss Staverton met her honest glare with a smile and the profession that she herself certainly would recoil from such an adventure. Spencer Brydon meanwhile held his peace—for the moment; the question of the "evil" hours in his old home had already become too grave for him. He had begun some time since to "crape," and he knew just why a packet of candles addressed to that pursuit had been stowed by his own hand, three weeks before, at the back of a drawer of the fine old sideboard that occupied, as a "fixture," the deep recess in the dining-room. Just now he laughed at his companions—quickly however changing the subject; for the reason that, in the first place, his laugh struck him even at that moment as starting the odd echo, the conscious human resonance (he scarce knew how to qualify it) that sounds made while he was there alone sent back to his ear or his fancy; and that, in the second, he imagined Alice Staverton for the instant on the point of asking him, with a divination, if he ever so prowled. There were divinations he was unprepared for, and he had at all events averted enquiry by the time Mrs. Muldoon had left them, passing on to other parts.

There was happily enough to say, on so consecrated a spot, that could be said freely and fairly; so that a whole train of declarations was precipitated by his friend's having herself broken out, after a yearning look round: "But I hope you don't mean they want you to pull *this* to pieces!" His answer came, promptly, with his re-awakened wrath: it was of course exactly what they wanted, and what they were "at" him for, daily, with the iteration of people who couldn't for their life understand a man's liability to decent feelings. He had found the place, just as it stood and beyond what he could express, an interest and a joy. There were values other than the beastly rent-values, and in short, in short—! But it was thus Miss Staverton took him up. "In short you're to make so good a thing of your sky-scraper that, living in luxury on *those* ill-gotten gains, you can afford for a while to be sentimental here!" Her smile had for him, with the words, the particular mild irony with which he found half her talk suffused; an irony without bitterness and that came, exactly, from her having so much imagination—not, like the cheap sarcasms with which one heard most people, about the world of "society," bid for the reputation of cleverness, from nobody's really having any. It was agreeable to him at this very moment to be sure that when he had answered, after a brief demur, "Well yes: so, precisely, you may put it!" her imagination would still do him justice. He explained that even if never a dollar were to come to him from the other house he would nevertheless cherish this one; and he dwelt, further, while they lingered and wandered, on the fact of the stupefaction he was already exciting, the positive mystification he felt himself create.

He spoke of the value of all he read into it, into the mere sight of the walls, mere shapes of the rooms, mere sound of the floors, mere feel, in his hand, of the old silver-plated knobs of the several mahogany doors, which suggested the pressure of the palms of the dead; the seventy years of the past in fine that these things represented, the annals of nearly three generations, counting his grandfather's, the one that had ended there, and the impalpable ashes of his long-extinct youth, afloat in the very air like microscopic motes. She listened to everything; she was a woman who answered intimately but who utterly didn't chatter. She scattered abroad therefore no cloud of words; she could assent, she could agree, above all she could encourage, without doing that. Only at the last she went a little further than he had done himself. "And then how do you know? You may still, after all, want to live here." It rather indeed pulled him up, for it wasn't what he had been thinking, at least in her sense of the words. "You mean I may decide to stay on for the sake of it?"

"Well, *with* such a home—!" But, quite beautifully, she had too much tact to dot so monstrous an *i,* and it was precisely an illustration of the way she didn't rattle. How could any one—of any wit—insist on any one else's "wanting" to live in New York?

"Oh," he said, "I *might* have lived here (since I had my opportunity early in life); I might have put in here all these years. Then everything would have been different enough—and, I dare say, 'funny' enough. But that's another matter. And then the beauty of it—I mean of my perversity, of my refusal to agree to a 'deal'—is just in the total absence of a reason. Don't you see that if I had a reason about the matter at all it would *have* to be the other way, and would then be inevitably a reason of dollars? There are no reasons here *but* of dollars. Let us therefore have none whatever—not the ghost of one."

They were back in the hall then for departure, but from where they stood the vista was large, through an open door, into the great square main saloon, with its almost antique felicity of brave spaces between windows. Her eyes came back from that reach and met his own a moment. "Are you very sure the 'ghost' of one doesn't, much rather, serve—?"

He had a positive sense of turning pale. But it was as near as they were then to come. For he made answer, he believed, between a glare and a grin: "Oh ghosts—of course the place must swarm with them! I should be ashamed of it if it didn't. Poor Mrs. Muldoon's right, and it's why I haven't asked her to do more than look in."

Miss Staverton's gaze again lost itself, and things she didn't utter, it was clear, came and went in her mind. She might even for the minute, off there in the fine room, have imagined some element dimly gathering. Simplified like the death-mask of a handsome face, it perhaps produced for her just then an effect akin to the stir of an expression in the "set" commemorative plaster. Yet whatever her impression may have been she produced instead a vague platitude. "Well, if it were only furnished and lived in—!"

She appeared to imply that in case of its being still furnished he might have been a little less opposed to the idea of a return. But she passed straight into the vestibule, as if to leave her words behind her, and the next moment he had opened the house-door and was standing with her on the steps. He closed the door and, while he re-pocketed his key, looking up and down, they took in the comparatively harsh actuality of the Avenue, which reminded him of the assault of the outer light of the Desert on the traveller emerging from an Egyptian tomb. But he risked before they stepped into the street his gathered answer to her speech. "For me it *is* lived in. For me it *is* furnished." At which it was easy for her to sigh "Ah yes—!" all vaguely and discreetly; since his parents and his favourite sister, to say nothing of other kin, in numbers, had run their course and met their end there. That represented, within the walls, ineffaceable life.

It was a few days after this that, during an hour passed with her again, he had expressed his impatience of the too flattering curiosity—among the people he met—about his appreciation of New York. He had arrived at none at all that was socially producible, and as for that matter of his "thinking" (thinking the better or the worse of anything there) he was wholly taken up with one subject of thought. It was mere vain egoism, and it was moreover, if she liked, a morbid obsession. He found all things come back to the question of what he personally might have been, how he might have led his life and "turned out," if he had not so, at the outset, given it up. And confessing for the first time to the intensity within him of this absurd speculation—which but proved also, no doubt, the habit of too selfishly thinking—he affirmed the impotence there of any other source of interest, any other native appeal. "What would it have made of me, what would it have made of me? I keep for ever wondering, all idiotically; as if I could possibly know! I see what it has made of dozens of others, those I meet, and it positively aches within me, to the point of exasperation, that it would have made something of me as well. Only I can't make out *what,* and the worry of it, the small rage of curiosity never to be satisfied, brings back what I remember to have felt, once or twice, after judging best, for reasons, to burn some important letter unopened. I've been sorry, I've hated it—I've never known what was in the letter. You may of course say it's a trifle—!"

"I don't say it's a trifle," Miss Staverton gravely interrupted.

She was seated by her fire, and before her, on his feet and restless, he turned to and fro between this intensity of his idea and a fitful and unseeing inspection, through his single eye-glass, of the dear little old objects on her chimney-piece. Her interruption made him for an instant look at her harder. "I shouldn't care if you did!" he laughed, however; "and it's only a figure, at any rate, for the way I now feel. *Not* to have followed my perverse young course—and almost in the teeth of my father's curse, as I may say; not to have kept it up, so, 'over there,' from that day to this, without a doubt or a pang; not, above all, to have liked it, to have loved it, so much, loved it, no doubt, with such an abysmal conceit of my own preference: some variation from *that,* I say, must have produced some different effect for my life and for my 'form.' I should have stuck here—if it had been possible; and I was too young, at twenty-three, to judge, *pour deux sous,* whether it *were* possible. If I had waited I might have seen it was, and then I might have been, by staying here, something nearer to one of these types who have been hammered so hard and made so keen by their conditions. It isn't that I admire them so much—the question of any charm in them, or of any charm, beyond that of the rank money-passion, exerted by their conditions *for* them, has nothing to do with the matter: it's only a question of what fantastic, yet perfectly possible, development of my own nature I mayn't have missed. It comes over me that I had then a strange *alter ego* deep down somewhere within me, as the full-blown flower is in the small tight bud, and that I just took the course, I just transferred him to the climate, that blighted him for once and for ever."

"And you wonder about the flower," Miss Staverton said. "So do I, if you want to know; and so I've been wondering these several weeks. I believe in the flower," she continued, "I feel it would have been quite splendid, quite huge and monstrous."

"Monstrous above all!" her visitor echoed; "and I imagine, by the same stroke, quite hideous and offensive."

"You don't believe that," she returned; "if you did you wouldn't wonder. You'd know, and that would be enough for you. What you feel—and what I feel *for* you—is that you'd have had power."

"You'd have liked me that way?" he asked.

She barely hung fire. "How should I not have liked you?"

"I see. You'd have liked me, have preferred me, a billionaire!"

"How should I not have liked you?" she simply again asked.

He stood before her still—her question kept him motionless. He took it in, so much there was of it; and indeed his not otherwise meeting it testified to that. "I know at least what I am," he simply went on; "the other side of the medal's clear enough.

I've not been edifying—I believe I'm thought in a hundred quarters to have been barely decent. I've followed strange paths and worshipped strange gods; it must have come to you again and again—in fact you've admitted to me as much—that I was leading, at any time these thirty years, a selfish frivolous scandalous life. And you see what it has made of me."

She just waited, smiling at him. "You see what it has made of *me*."

"Oh you're a person whom nothing can have altered. You were born to be what you are, anywhere, anyway: you've the perfection nothing else could have blighted. And don't you see how, without my exile, I shouldn't have been waiting till now—?" But he pulled up for the strange pang.

"The great thing to see," she presently said, "seems to me to be that it has spoiled nothing. It hasn't spoiled your being here at last. It hasn't spoiled this. It hasn't spoiled your speaking—" She also however faltered.

He wondered at everything her controlled emotion might mean. "Do you believe then—too dreadfully!—that I *am* as good as I might ever have been?"

"Oh no! Far from it!" With which she got up from her chair and was nearer to him. "But I don't care," she smiled.

"You mean I'm good enough?"

She considered a little. "Will you believe it if I say so? I mean will you let that settle your question for you?" And then as if making out in his face that he drew back from this, that he had some idea which, however absurd, he couldn't yet bargain away: "Oh you don't care either—but very differently: you don't care for anything but yourself."

Spencer Brydon recognised it—it was in fact what he had absolutely professed. Yet he importantly qualified. "*He* isn't myself. He's the just so totally other person. But I do want to see him," he added. "And I can. And I shall."

Their eyes met for a minute while he guessed from something in hers that she divined his strange sense. But neither of them otherwise expressed it, and her apparent understanding, with no protesting shock, no easy derision, touched him more deeply than anything yet, constituting for his stifled perversity, on the spot, an element that was like breathable air. What she said however was unexpected. "Well, *I've* seen him."

"You—?"

"I've seen him in a dream."

"Oh a 'dream'—!" It let him down.

"But twice over," she continued. "I saw him as I see you now."

"You've dreamed the same dream—?"

"Twice over," she repeated. "The very same."

This did somehow a little speak to him, as it also gratified him. "You dream about me at that rate?"

"Ah about *him*!" she smiled.

His eyes again sounded her. "Then you know all about him." And as she said nothing more: "What's the wretch like?"

She hesitated, and it was as if he were pressing her so hard that, resisting for reasons of her own, she had to turn away. "I'll tell you some other time!"

II

It was after this that there was most of a virtue for him, most of a cultivated charm, most of a preposterous secret thrill, in the particular form of surrender to his obsession and of address to what he more and more believed to be his privilege. It was what in these weeks he was living for—since he really felt life to begin but after Mrs. Muldoon had retired from the scene and, visiting the ample house from attic to cellar, making sure he was alone, he knew himself in safe possession and, as he tacitly expressed it, let himself go. He sometimes came twice in the twenty-four hours; the moments he liked best were those of gathering dusk, of the short autumn twilight; this was the time of which, again and again, he found himself hoping most. Then he could, as seemed to him, most intimately wander and wait, linger and listen, feel his fine attention, never in his life before so fine, on the pulse of the great vague place: he preferred the lampless hour and only wished he might have prolonged each day the deep crepuscular spell. Later—rarely much before midnight, but then for a considerable vigil—he watched with his glimmering light; moving slowly, holding it high, playing it far, rejoicing above all, as much as he might, in open vistas, reaches of communication between rooms and by passages; the long straight chance or show, as he would have called it, for the revelation he pretended to invite. It was a practice he found he could perfectly "work" without exciting remark; no one was in the least the wiser for it; even Alice Staverton, who was moreover a well of discretion, didn't quite fully imagine.

He let himself in and let himself out with the assurance of calm proprietorship; and accident so far favoured him that, if a fat Avenue "officer" had happened on occasion to see him entering at eleven-thirty, he had never yet, to the best of his belief, been noticed as emerging at two. He walked there on the crisp November nights, arrived regularly at the evening's end; it was as easy to do this after dining out as to take his way to a club or to his hotel. When he left his club, if he hadn't been dining out, it was ostensibly to go to his hotel; and when he left his hotel, if he had spent a part of the evening there, it was ostensibly to go to his club. Everything was easy in fine; everything conspired and promoted: there was truly even in the strain of his experience something that glossed over, something that salved and simplified, all the rest of consciousness. He circulated, talked, renewed, loosely and pleasantly, old relations—met indeed, so far as he could, new expectations and seemed to make out on the whole that in spite of the career, of such different contacts, which he had spoken of to Miss Staverton as ministering so little, for those who might have watched it, to edification, he was positively rather liked than not. He was a dim secondary social success—and all with people who had truly not an idea of him. It was all mere surface sound, this murmur of their welcome, this popping of their corks—just as his gestures of response were the extravagant shadows, emphatic in proportion as they meant little, of some game of *ombres chinoises*. He projected himself all day, in thought, straight over the bristling line of hard unconscious heads and into the other, the real, the waiting life; the life that, as soon as he had heard behind him the click of his great house-door, began for him, on the jolly corner, as beguilingly as the slow opening bars of some rich music follows the tap of the conductor's wand.

He always caught the first effect of the steel point of his stick on the old marble of the hall pavement, large black-and-white squares that he remembered as the admiration of his childhood and that had then made in him, as he now saw, for the growth of an early conception of style. This effect was the dim reverberating tinkle as of some far-off bell hung who should say where?—in the depths of the house, of the past, of that mystical other world that might have flourished for him had he not, for weal or woe, abandoned it. On this impression he did ever the same thing; he put his stick noiselessly away in a corner—feeling the place once more in the likeness of some great glass bowl, all precious concave crystal, set delicately humming by the play of a moist finger round its edge. The concave crystal held, as it were, this mystical other world, and the indescribably fine murmur of its rim was the sigh there, the scarce audible pathetic wail to his strained ear, of all the old baffled forsworn possibilities. What he did therefore by this appeal of his hushed presence was to wake them into such measure of ghostly life as they might still enjoy. They were shy, all but unappeasably shy, but they weren't really sinister; at least they weren't as he had hitherto felt them—before they had taken the Form he so yearned to make them take, the Form he at moments saw himself in the light of fairly hunting on tiptoe, the points of his evening-shoes, from room to room and from storey to storey.

That was the essence of his vision—which was all rank folly, if one would, while he was out of the house and otherwise occupied, but which took on the last verisimilitude as soon as he was placed and posted. He knew what he meant and what he wanted; it was as clear as the figure on a cheque presented in demand for cash. His *alter ego* "walked"—that was the note of his image of him, while his image of his motive for his own odd pastime was the desire to waylay him and meet him. He roamed, slowly, warily, but all restlessly, he himself did—Mrs. Muldoon had been right, absolutely, with her figure of their "craping"; and the presence he watched for would roam restlessly too. But it would be as cautious and as shifty; the conviction of its probable, in fact its already quite sensible, quite audible evasion of pursuit grew for him from night to night, laying on him finally a rigour to which nothing in his life had been comparable. It had been the theory of many superficially-judging persons, he knew, that he was wasting that life in a surrender to sensations, but he had tasted of no pleasure so fine as his actual tension, had been introduced to no sport that demanded at once the patience and the nerve of this stalking of a creature more subtle, yet at bay perhaps more formidable, than any beast of the forest. The terms, the comparisons, the very practices of the chase positively came again into play; there were even moments when passages of his occasional experience as a sportsman, stirred memories, from his younger time, of moor and mountain and desert, revived for him—and to the increase of his keenness—by the tremendous force of analogy. He found himself at moments—once he had placed his single light on some mantel-shelf or in some recess—stepping back into shelter or shade, effacing himself behind a door or in an embrasure, as he had sought of old the vantage of rock and tree; he found himself holding his breath and living in the joy of the instant, the supreme suspense created by big game alone.

He wasn't afraid (though putting himself the question as

he believed gentlemen on Bengal tiger-shoots or in close quarters with the great bear of the Rockies had been known to confess to having put it); and this indeed—since here at least he might be frank!—because of the impression, so intimate and so strange, that he himself produced as yet a dread, produced certainly a strain, beyond the liveliest he was likely to feel. They fell for him into categories, they fairly became familiar, the signs, for his own perception, of the alarm his presence and his vigilance created; though leaving him always to remark, portentously, on his probably having formed a relation, his probably enjoying a consciousness, unique in the experience of man. People enough, first and last, had been in terror of apparitions, but who had ever before so turned the tables and become himself, in the apparitional world, an incalculable terror? He might have found this sublime had he quite dared to think of it; but he didn't too much insist, truly, on that side of his privilege. With habit and repetition he gained to an extraordinary degree the power to penetrate the dusk of distances and the darkness of corners, to resolve back into their innocence the treacheries of uncertain light, the evil-looking forms taken in the gloom by mere shadows, by accidents of the air, by shifting effects of perspective; putting down his dim luminary he could still wander on without it, pass into other rooms and, only knowing it was there behind him in case of need, see his way about, visually project for his purpose a comparative clearness. It made him feel, this acquired faculty, like some monstrous stealthy cat; he wondered if he would have glared at these moments with large shining yellow eyes, and what it mightn't verily be, for the poor hard-pressed *alter ego,* to be confronted with such a type.

He liked however the open shutters; he opened everywhere those Mrs. Muldoon had closed, closing them as carefully afterwards, so that she shouldn't notice: he liked—oh this he did like, and above all in the upper rooms!—the sense of the hard silver of the autumn stars through the window-panes, and scarcely less the flare of the street-lamps below, the white electric lustre which it would have taken curtains to keep out. This was human actual social; this was of the world he had lived in, and he was more at his ease certainly for the countenance, coldly general and impersonal, that all the while and in spite of his detachment it seemed to give him. He had support of course mostly in the rooms at the wide front and the prolonged side; it failed him considerably in the central shades and the parts at the back. But if he sometimes, on his rounds, was glad of his optical reach, so none the less often the rear of the house affected him as the very jungle of his prey. The place was there more subdivided; a large "extension" in particular, where small rooms for servants had been multiplied, abounded in nooks and corners, in closets and passages, in the ramifications especially of an ample back staircase over which he leaned, many a time, to look far down—not deterred from his gravity even while aware that he might, for a spectator, have figured some solemn simpleton playing at hide-and-seek. Outside in fact he might himself make that ironic *rapprochement;* but within the walls, and in spite of the clear windows, his consistency was proof against the cynical light of New York.

It had belonged to that idea of the exasperated consciousness of his victim to become a real test for him; since he had quite put it to himself from the first that, oh distinctly! he could "cultivate" his whole perception. He had felt it as above all open to cultivation—which indeed was but another name for his manner of spending his time. He was bringing it on, bringing it to perfection, by practice; in consequence of which it had grown so fine that he was now aware of impressions, attestations of his general postulate, that couldn't have broken upon him at once. This was the case more specifically with a phenomenon at last quite frequent for him in the upper rooms, the recognition—absolutely unmistakeable, and by a turn dating from a particular hour, his resumption of his campaign after a diplomatic drop, a calculated absence of three nights—

of his being definitely followed, tracked at a distance carefully taken and to the express end that he should the less confidently, less arrogantly, appear to himself merely to pursue. It worried, it finally quite broke him up, for it proved, of all the conceivable impressions, the one least suited to his book. He was kept in sight while remaining himself—as regards the essence of his position—sightless, and his only recourse then was in abrupt turns, rapid recoveries of ground. He wheeled about, retracing his steps, as if he might so catch in his face at least the stirred air of some other quick revolution. It was indeed true that his fully dislocalised thought of these manœuvres recalled to him Pantaloon, at the Christmas farce, buffeted and tricked from behind by ubiquitous Harlequin; but it left intact the influence of the conditions themselves each time he was re-exposed to them, so that in fact this association, had he suffered it to become constant, would on a certain side have but ministered to his intenser gravity. He had made, as I have said, to create on the premises the baseless sense of a reprieve, his three absences; and the result of the third was to confirm the after-effect of the second.

On his return, that night—the night succeeding his last intermission—he stood in the hall and looked up the staircase with a certainty more intimate than any he had yet known. "He's *there,* at the top, and waiting—not, as in general, falling back for disappearance. He's holding his ground, and it's the first time—which is a proof, isn't it? that something has happened for him." So Brydon argued with his hand on the banister and his foot on the lowest stair; in which position he felt as never before the air chilled by his logic. He himself turned cold in it, for he seemed of a sudden to know what now was involved. "Harder pressed?—yes, he takes it in, with its thus making clear to him that I've come, as they say, 'to stay.' He finally doesn't like and can't bear it, in the sense, I mean, that his wrath, his menaced interest, now balances with his dread. I've hunted him till he has 'turned': that, up there, is what has happened—he's the fanged or the antlered animal brought at last to bay." There came to him, as I say—but determined by an influence beyond my notation!—the acuteness of this certainty; under which however the next moment he had broken into a sweat that he would as little have consented to attribute to fear as he would have dared immediately to act upon it for enterprise. It marked none the less a prodigious thrill, a thrill that represented sudden dismay, no doubt, but also represented, and with the selfsame throb, the strangest, the most joyous, possibly the next minute almost the proudest, duplication of consciousness.

"He has been dodging, retreating, hiding, but now, worked up to anger, he'll fight!"—this intense impression made a single mouthful, as it were, of terror and applause. But what was wondrous was that the applause, for the felt fact, was so eager, since, if it was his other self he was running to earth, this ineffable identity was thus in the last resort not unworthy of him. It bristled there—somewhere near at hand, however unseen still—as the hunted thing, even as the trodden worm of the adage *must* at last bristle; and Brydon at this instant tasted probably of a sensation more complex than had ever before found itself consistent with sanity. It was as if it would have shamed him that a character so associated with his own should triumphantly succeed in just skulking, should to the end not risk the open, so that the drop of this danger was, on the spot, a great lift of the whole situation. Yet with another rare shift of the same subtlety he was already trying to measure by how much more he himself might now be in peril of fear; so rejoicing that he could, in another form, actively inspire that fear, and simultaneously quaking for the form in which he might passively know it.

The apprehension of knowing it must after a little have grown in him, and the strangest moment of his adventure perhaps, the most memorable or really most interesting, afterwards, of his crisis, was the lapse of certain instants of concentrated conscious *combat,* the sense of a need to hold on to something, even after the manner of a man slipping and slipping on some awful incline; the vivid impulse, above all, to move, to act, to charge, somehow and upon something—to show himself, in a word, that he wasn't afraid. The state of "holding-on" was thus the state to which he was momentarily reduced; if there had been anything, in the great vacancy, to seize, he would presently have been aware of having clutched it as he might under a shock at home have clutched the nearest chair-back. He had been surprised at any rate—of this he *was* aware—into something unprecedented since his original appropriation of the place; he had closed his eyes, held them tight, for a long minute, as with that instinct of dismay and that terror of vision. When he opened them the room, the other contiguous rooms, extraordinarily, seemed lighter—so light, almost, that at first he took the change for day. He stood firm, however that might be, just where he had paused; his resistance had helped him—it was as if there were something he had tided over. He knew after a little what this was—it had been in the imminent danger of flight. He had stiffened his will against going; without this he would have made for the stairs, and it seemed to him that, still with his eyes closed, he would have descended them, would have known how, straight and swiftly, to the bottom.

Well, as he had held out, here he was—still at the top, among the more intricate upper rooms and with the gauntlet of the others, of all the rest of the house, still to run when it should be his time to go. He would go at his time—only at his time: didn't he go every night very much at the same hour? He took out his watch—there was light for that: it was scarcely a quarter past one, and he had never withdrawn so soon. He reached his lodgings for the most part at two—with his walk of a quarter of an hour. He would wait for the last quarter—he wouldn't stir till then; and he kept his watch there with his eyes on it, reflecting while he held it that this deliberate wait, a wait with an effort, which he recognised, would serve perfectly for the attestation he desired to make. It would prove his courage—unless indeed the latter might most be proved by his budging at last from his place. What he mainly felt now was that, since he hadn't originally scuttled, he had his dignities—which had never in his life seemed so many—all to preserve and to carry aloft. This was before him in truth as a physical image, an image almost worthy of an age of greater romance. That remark indeed glimmered for him only to glow the next instant with a finer light; since what age of romance, after all, could have matched either the state of his mind or, "objectively," as they said, the wonder of his situation? The only difference would have been that, brandishing his dignities over his head as in a parchment scroll, he might then—that is in the heroic time—have proceeded downstairs with a drawn sword in his other grasp.

At present, really, the light he had set down on the mantel of the next room would have to figure his sword; which utensil, in the course of a minute, he had taken the requisite number of steps to possess himself of. The door between the rooms was open, and from the second another door opened to a third. These rooms, as he remembered, gave all three upon a common corridor as well, but there was a fourth, beyond them, without issue save through the preceding. To have moved, to have heard his step again, was appreciably a help; though even in recognising this he lingered once more a little by the chimney-piece on which his light had rested. When he next moved, just hesitating where to turn, he found himself considering a circumstance that, after his first and comparatively vague apprehension of it, produced in him the start that often attends some pang of recollection, the violent shock of having ceased happily to forget. He had come into sight of the door in which the brief chain of communication ended and which he now surveyed from the nearer threshold, the one not directly facing it. Placed at some distance to the left of this point, it would have admitted him to the last room of the four, the room without other approach or egress, had it not, to his intimate conviction, been closed *since* his former visitation, the matter probably of a quarter of an hour before. He stared with all his eyes at the wonder of the fact, arrested again where he stood and again holding his breath while he sounded its sense. Surely it had been *subsequently* closed—that is it had been on his previous passage indubitably open!

He took it full in the face that something had happened between—that he couldn't not have noticed before (by which he meant on his original tour of all the rooms that evening) that such a barrier had exceptionally presented itself. He had indeed since that moment undergone an agitation so extraordinary that it might have muddled for him any earlier view; and he tried to convince himself that he might perhaps then have gone into the room and, inadvertently, automatically, on coming out, have drawn the door after him. The difficulty was that this exactly was what he never did; it was against his whole policy, as he might have said, the essence of which was to keep vistas clear. He had them from the first, as he was well aware, quite on the brain: the strange apparition, at the far end of one of them, of his baffled "prey" (which had become by so sharp an irony so little the term now to apply!) was the form of success his imagination had most cherished, projecting into it always a refinement of beauty. He had known fifty times the start of perception that had afterwards dropped; had fifty times gasped to himself "There!" under some fond brief hallucination. The house, as the case stood, admirably lent itself; he might wonder at the taste, the native architecture of the particular time, which could rejoice so in the multiplication of doors—the opposite extreme to the modern, the actual almost complete proscription of them; but it had fairly contributed to provoke this obsession of the presence encountered telescopically, as he might say, focussed and studied in diminishing perspective and as by a rest for the elbow.

It was with these considerations that his present attention was charged—they perfectly availed to make what he saw portentous. He *couldn't,* by any lapse, have blocked that aperture; and if he hadn't, if it was unthinkable, why what else was clear but that there had been another agent? Another agent?—he had been catching, as he felt, a moment back, the very breath of him; but when had he been so close as in this simple, this logical, this completely personal act? It was so logical, that is, that one might have *taken* it for personal; yet for what did Brydon take it, he asked himself, while, softly panting, he felt his eyes almost leave their sockets. Ah this time at last they *were,* the two, the opposed projections of him, in presence; and this time, as much as one would, the question of danger loomed. With it rose, as not before, the question of courage—for what he knew the blank face of the door to say to him was "Show us how much you have!" It stared, it glared back at him with that challenge; it put to him the two alternatives: should he just push it open or not? Oh to have this consciousness was to *think*—and to think, Brydon knew, as he stood there, was, with the lapsing moments, not to have acted! Not to have acted—that was the misery and the pang—was even still not to act; was in fact *all* to feel the thing in another, in a new and terrible way. How long did he pause and how long did he debate? There was presently nothing to measure it; for his vibration had already changed—as just by the effect of its intensity. Shut up there, at bay, defiant, and with the prodigy of the thing palpably proveably *done,* thus giving notice like some stark signboard—under that accession of accent the situation itself had turned; and Brydon at last remarkably made up his mind on what it had turned to.

It had turned altogether to a different admonition; to a supreme hint, for him, of the value of Discretion! This slowly dawned, no doubt—for it could take its time; so perfectly, on his threshold, had he been stayed, so little as yet had he either advanced or retreated. It was the strangest of all things that now when, by his taking ten steps and applying his hand to a latch, or even his shoulder and his knee, if necessary, to a panel, all the hunger of his prime need might have been met, his high curiosity crowned, his unrest assuaged—it was amazing, but it was also exquisite and rare, that insistence should have, at a touch, quite dropped from him. Discretion—he jumped at that; and yet not, verily, at such a pitch, because it saved his nerves or his skin, but because, much more valuably, it saved the situation. When I say he "jumped" at it I feel the consonance of this term with the fact that—at the end indeed of I know not how long—he did move again, he crossed straight to the door. He wouldn't touch it—it seemed now that he might *if* he would: he would only just wait there a little, to show, to prove, that he wouldn't. He had thus another station, close to the thin partition by which revelation was denied him; but with his eyes bent and his hands held off in a mere intensity of stillness. He listened as if there had been something to hear, but this attitude, while it lasted, was his own communication. "If you won't then—good: I spare you and I give up. You affect me as by the appeal positively for pity: you convince me that for reasons rigid and sublime—what do I know?—we both of us should have suffered. I respect them then, and, though moved and privileged as, I believe, it has never been given to man, I retire, I renounce—never, on my honour, to try again. So rest for ever—and let *me*!"

That, for Brydon was the deep sense of this last demonstration—solemn, measured, directed, as he felt it to be. He brought it to a close, he turned away; and now verily he knew how deeply he had been stirred. He retraced his steps, taking up his candle, burnt, he observed, well-nigh to the socket, and marking again, lighten it as he would, the distinctness of his footfall; after which, in a moment, he knew himself at the other side of the house. He did here what he had not yet done at these hours—he opened half a casement, one of those in the front, and let in the air of the night; a thing he would have taken at any time previous for a sharp rupture of his spell. His spell was broken now, and it didn't matter—broken by his concession and his surrender, which made it idle henceforth that he should ever come back. The empty street—its other life so marked even by the great lamplit vacancy—was within call, within touch; he stayed there as to be in it again, high above it though he was still perched; he watched as for some comforting common fact, some vulgar human note, the passage of a scavenger or a thief, some night-bird however base. He would have blessed that sign of life; he would have welcomed positively the slow approach of his friend the policeman, whom he had hitherto only sought to avoid, and was not sure that if the patrol had come into sight he mightn't have felt the impulse to get into relation with it, to hail it, on some pretext, from his fourth floor.

The pretext that wouldn't have been too silly or too compromising, the explanation that would have saved his dignity and kept his name, in such a case, out of the papers, was not definite to him: he was so occupied with the thought of recording his Discretion—as an effect of the vow he had just uttered to his intimate adversary—that the importance of this loomed large and something had overtaken all ironically his sense of proportion. If there had been a ladder applied to the front of the house, even one of the vertiginous perpendiculars employed by painters and roofers and sometimes left standing overnight, he would have managed somehow, astride of the window-sill, to compass by outstretched leg and arm that mode of descent. If there had been some such uncanny thing as he had found in his room at hotels, a workable fire-escape in the form of notched cable or a canvas shoot, he would have availed himself of it as a proof—well, of his present delicacy. He nursed that sentiment, as the question stood, a little in vain, and even—at the end of he scarce knew, once more, how long—found it, as by the action on his mind of the failure of response of the outer world, sinking back to vague anguish. It seemed to him he had waited an age for some stir of the great grim hush; the life of the town was itself under a spell—so unnaturally, up and down the whole prospect of known and rather ugly objects, the blankness and the silence lasted. Had they ever, he asked himself, the hard-faced houses, which had begun to look livid in the dim dawn, had they ever spoken so little to any need of his spirit? Great builded voids, great crowded stillnesses put on, often, in the heart of cities, for the small hours, a sort of sinister mask, and it was of this large collective negation that Brydon presently became conscious—all the more that the break of day was, almost incredibly, now at hand, proving to him what a night he had made of it.

He looked again at his watch, saw what had become of his time-values (he had taken hours for minutes—not, as in other tense situations, minutes for hours) and the strange air of the streets was but the weak, the sullen flush of a dawn in which everything was still locked up. His choked appeal from his own open window had been the sole note of life, and he could but break off at last as for a worse despair. Yet while so deeply demoralised he was capable again of an impulse denoting—at least by his present measure—extraordinary resolution; of retracing his steps to the spot where he had turned cold with the extinction of his last pulse of doubt as to there being in the place another presence than his own. This required an effort strong enough to sicken him; but he had his reason, which overmastered for the moment everything else. There was the whole of the rest of the house to traverse, and how should he screw himself to that if the door he had seen closed were at present open? He could hold to the idea that the closing had practically been for him an act of mercy, a chance offered him to descend, depart, get off the ground and never again profane it. This conception held together, it worked; but what it meant for him depended now clearly on the amount of forbearance his recent action, or rather his recent inaction, had engendered. The image of the "presence," whatever it was, waiting there for him to go

—this image had not yet been so concrete for his nerves as when he stopped short of the point at which certainty would have come to him. For, with all his resolution, or more exactly with all his dread, he did stop short—he hung back from really seeing. The risk was too great and his fear too definite: it took at this moment an awful specific form.

He knew—yes, as he had never known anything—that, *should* he see the door open, it would all too abjectly be the end of him. It would mean that the agent of his shame—for his shame was the deep abjection—was once more at large and in general possession; and what glared him thus in the face was the act that this would determine for him. It would send him straight about to the window he had left open, and by that window, be long ladder and dangling rope as absent as they would, he saw himself uncontrollably insanely fatally take his way to the street. The hideous chance of this he at least could avert; but he could only avert it by recoiling in time from assurance. He had the whole house to deal with, this fact was still there; only he now knew that uncertainty alone could start him. He stole back from where he had checked himself—merely to do so was suddenly like safety—and, making blindly for the greater staircase, left gaping rooms and sounding passages behind. Here was the top of the stairs, with a fine large dim descent and three spacious landings to mark off. His instinct was all for mildness, but his feet were harsh on the floors, and, strangely, when he had in a couple of minutes become aware of this, it counted somehow for help. He couldn't have spoken, the tone of his voice would have scared him, and the common conceit or resource of "whistling in the dark" (whether literally or figuratively) have appeared basely vulgar; yet he liked none the less to hear himself go, and when he had reached his first landing—taking it all with no rush, but quite steadily—that stage of success drew from him a gasp of relief.

The house, withal, seemed immense, the scale of space again inordinate; the open rooms, to no one of which his eyes deflected, gloomed in their shuttered state like mouths of caverns; only the high skylight that formed the crown of the deep well created for him a medium in which he could advance, but which might have been, for queerness of colour, some watery under-world. He tried to think of something noble, as that his property was really grand, a splendid possession; but this nobleness took the form too of the clear delight with which he was finally to sacrifice it. They might come in now, the builders, the destroyers—they might come as soon as they would. At the end of two flights he had dropped to another zone, and from the middle of the third, with only one more left, he recognised the influence of the lower windows, of half-drawn blinds, of the occasional gleam of street-lamps, of the glazed spaces of the vestibule. This was the bottom of the sea, which showed an illumination of its own and which he even saw paved—when at a given moment he drew up to sink a long look over the banisters—with the marble squares of his childhood. By that time indubitably he felt, as he might have said in a commoner cause, better; it had allowed him to stop and draw breath, and the ease increased with the sight of the old black-and-white slabs. But what he most felt was that now surely, with the element of impunity pulling him as by hard firm hands, the case was settled for what he might have seen above had he dared that last look. The closed door, blessedly remote now, was still closed—and he had only in short to reach that of the house.

He came down further, he crossed the passage forming the access to the last flight; and if here again he stopped an instant it was almost for the sharpness of the thrill of assured escape. It made him shut his eyes—which opened again to the straight slope of the remainder of the stairs. Here was impunity still, but impunity almost excessive; inasmuch as the side-lights and the high fan-tracery of the entrance were glimmering straight into the hall; an appearance produced, he the next instant saw, by the fact that the vestibule gaped wide, that the hinged halves of the inner door had been thrown far back. Out of that again the *question* sprang at him, making his eyes, as he felt, half-start from his head, as they had done, at the top of the house, before the sign of the other door. If he had left that one open, hadn't he left this one closed, and wasn't he now in *most* immediate presence of some inconceivable occult activity? It was as sharp, the question, as a knife in his side, but the answer hung fire still and seemed to lose itself in the vague darkness to which the thin admitted dawn, glimmering archwise over the whole outer door, made a semicircular margin, a cold silvery nimbus that seemed to play a little as he looked—to shift and expand and contract.

It was as if there had been something within it, protected by indistinctness and corresponding in extent with the opaque surface behind, the painted panels of the last barrier to his escape, of which the key was in his pocket. The indistinctness mocked him even while he stared, affected him as somehow shrouding or challenging certitude, so that after faltering an instant on his step he let himself go with the sense that here *was* at last something to meet, to touch, to take, to know—something all unnatural and dreadful, but to advance upon which was the condition for him either of liberation or of supreme defeat. The penumbra, dense and dark, was the virtual screen of a figure which stood in it as still as some image erect in a niche or as some black-vizored sentinel guarding a treasure. Brydon was to know afterwards, was to recall and make out, the particular thing he had believed during the rest of his descent. He saw, in its great grey glimmering margin, the central vagueness diminish, and he felt it to be taking the very form toward which, for so many days, the passion of his cusiosity had yearned. It gloomed, it loomed, it was something, it was somebody, the prodigy of a personal presence.

Rigid and conscious, spectral yet human, a man of his own substance and stature waited there to measure himself with his power to dismay. This only could it be—this only till he recognised, with his advance, that what made the face dim was the pair of raised hands that covered it and in which, so far from being offered in defiance, it was buried as for dark deprecation. So Brydon, before him, took him in; with every fact of him now, in the higher light, hard and acute—his planted stillness, his vivid truth, his grizzled bent head and white masking hands, his queer actuality of evening-dress, of dangling double eye-glass, of gleaming silk lappet and white linen, of pearl button and gold watch-guard and polished shoe. No portrait by a great modern master could have presented him with more intensity, thrust him out of his frame with more art, as if there had been "treatment," of the consummate sort, in his every shade and salience. The revulsion, for our friend, had become, before he knew it, immense—this drop, in the act of apprehension, to the sense of his adversary's inscrutable manœuvre. That meaning at least, while he gaped, it offered him; for he could but gape at his other self in this other anguish, gape as a proof that *he,* standing there for the achieved, the enjoyed, the triumphant life, couldn't be faced in his triumph. Wasn't the proof in the splendid covering hands, strong and completely spread?—so spread and so intentional that, in spite of a special verity that surpassed every other, the fact that one of these hands had lost two fingers, which were reduced to stumps, as if accidentally shot away, the face was effectually guarded and saved.

"Saved," though, *would* it be?—Brydon breathed his wonder till the very impunity of his attitude and the very insistence of his eyes produced, as he felt, a sudden stir which showed the next instant as a deeper portent, while the head raised itself, the betrayal of a braver purpose. The hands, as he looked, began to move, to open; then, as if deciding in a flash, dropped from the face and left it uncovered and presented. Horror, with the sight, had leaped into Brydon's throat, gasping there in a sound he couldn't utter; for the bared identity was too hideous as *his,* and his glare was the passion of his protest. The face, *that* face, Spencer Brydon's?—he searched it still, but looking away from it in dismay and denial, falling straight from his height of sublimity. It was unknown, inconceivable, awful, disconnected from any possibility—! He had been "sold," he inwardly moaned, stalking such game as this: the presence before him was a presence, the horror within him a horror, but the waste of his nights had been only grotesque and the success of his adventure an irony. Such an identity fitted his at *no* point, made its alternative monstrous. A thousand times yes, as it came upon him nearer now—the face was the face of a stranger. It came upon him nearer now, quite as one of those expanding fantastic images projected by the magic lantern of childhood; for the stranger, whoever he might be, evil, odious, blatant, vulgar, had advanced as for aggression, and he knew himself give ground. Then harder pressed still, sick with the force of his shock, and falling back as under the hot breath and the roused passion of a life larger than his own, a rage of personality before which his own collapsed, he felt the whole vision turn to darkness and his very feet give way. His head went round; he was going; he had gone.

III

WHAT had next brought him back, clearly—though after how long?—was Mrs. Muldoon's voice, coming to him from quite near, from so near that he seemed presently to see her as kneeling on the ground before him while he lay looking up at her; himself not wholly on the ground, but half-raised and upheld —conscious, yes, of tenderness of support and, more particularly, of a head pillowed in extraordinary softness and faintly refreshing fragrance. He considered, he wondered, his wit but half at his service; then another face intervened, bending more directly over him, and he finally knew that Alice Staverton had made her lap an ample and perfect cushion to him, and that she had to this end seated herself on the lowest degree of the staircase, the rest of his long person remaining stretched on his old black-and-white slabs. They were cold, these marble squares of his youth; but *he* somehow was not, in this rich return of consciousness—the most wonderful hour, little by little, that he had ever known, leaving him, as it did, so gratefully, so abysmally passive, and yet as with a treasure of intelligence waiting all round him for quiet appropriation; dissolved, he might call it, in the air of the place and producing the golden glow of a late autumn afternoon. He had come back, yes—come back from further away than any man but himself had ever travelled; but it was strange how with this sense what he had come back *to* seemed really the great thing, and as if his prodigious journey had been all for the sake of it. Slowly but surely his consciousness grew, his vision of his state thus completing itself: he had been miraculously *carried* back—lifted and carefully borne as from where he had been picked up, the uttermost end of an interminable grey passage. Even with this he was suffered to rest, and what had now brought him to knowledge was the break in the long mild motion.

It had brought him to knowledge, to knowledge—yes, this was the beauty of his state; which came to resemble more and more that of a man who has gone to sleep on some news of a great inheritance, and then, after dreaming it away, after profaning it with matters strange to it, has waked up again to serenity of certitude and has only to lie and watch it grow. This was the drift of his patience—that he had only to let it shine on him. He must moreover, with intermissions, still have been lifted and borne; since why and how else should he have known himself, later on, with the afternoon glow intenser, no longer at the foot of his stairs—situated as these now seemed at that dark other end of his tunnel—but on a deep window-bench of his high saloon, over which had been spread, couch-fashion, a mantle of soft stuff lined with grey fur that was familiar to his eyes and that one of his hands kept fondly feeling as for its pledge of truth. Mrs. Muldoon's face had gone, but the other, the second he had recognised, hung over him in a way that showed how he was still propped and pillowed. He took it all in, and the more he took it the more it seemed to suffice: he was as much at peace as if he had had food and drink. It was the two women who had found him, on Mrs. Muldoon's having plied, at her usual hour, her latch-key—and on her having above all arrived while Miss Staverton still lingered near the house. She had been turning away, all anxiety, from worrying the vain bell-handle—her calculation having been of the hour of the good woman's visit; but the latter, blessedly, had come up while she was still there, and they had entered together. He had then lain, beyond the vestibule, very much as he was lying now—quite, that is, as he appeared to have fallen, but all so wondrously without bruise or gash; only in a depth of stupor. What he most took in, however, at present, with the steadier clearance, was that Alice Staverton had for a long unspeakable moment not doubted he was dead.

"It must have been that I *was*." He made it out as she held him. "Yes—I can only have died. You brought me literally to life. Only," he wondered, his eyes rising to her, "only, in the name of all the benedictions, how?"

It took her but an instant to bend her face and kiss him, and something in the manner of it, and in the way her hands clasped and locked his head while he felt the cool charity and virtue of her lips, something in all this beatitude somehow answered everything. "And now I keep you," she said.

"Oh keep me, keep me!" he pleaded while her face still hung over him: in response to which it dropped again and stayed close, clingingly close. It was the seal of their situation—of which he tasted the impress for a long blissful moment in silence. But he came back. "Yet how did you know—?"

"I was uneasy. You were to have come, you remember—and you had sent no word."

"Yes, I remember—I was to have gone to you at one today." It caught on to their "old" life and relation—which were so near and so far. "I was still out there in my strange darkness—where was it, what was it? I must have stayed there so long." He could but wonder at the depth and the duration of his swoon.

"Since last night?" she asked with a shade of fear for her possible indiscretion.

"Since this morning—it must have been: the cold dim dawn of today. Where have I been," he vaguely wailed, "where have I been?" He felt her hold him close, and it was as if this helped him now to make in all security his mild moan. "What a long dark day!"

All in her tenderness she had waited a moment. "In the cold dim dawn?" she quavered.

But he had already gone on piecing together the parts of the whole prodigy. "As I didn't turn up you came straight—?"

She barely cast about. "I went first to your hotel—where they told me of your absence. You had dined out last evening and hadn't been back since. But they appeared to know you had been at your club."

"So you had the idea of *this*—?"

"Of what?" she asked in a moment.

"Well—of what has happened."

"I believed at least you'd have been here. I've known, all along," she said, "that you've been coming."

" 'Known' it—?"

"Well, I've believed it. I said nothing to you after that talk we had a month ago—but I felt sure. I knew you *would,*" she declared.

"That I'd persist, you mean?"

"That you'd see him."

"Ah but I didn't!" cried Brydon with his long wail. "There's somebody—an awful beast; whom I brought, too horribly, to bay. But it's not me."

At this she bent over him again, and her eyes were in his eyes. "No—it's not you." And it was as if, while her face hovered, he might have made out in it, hadn't it been so near, some particular meaning blurred by a smile. "No, thank heaven," she repeated—"it's not you! Of course it wasn't to have been."

"Ah but it *was,*" he gently insisted. And he stared before

him now as he had been staring for so many weeks. "I was to have known myself."

"You couldn't!" she returned consolingly. And then reverting, and as if to account further for what she had herself done, "But it wasn't only *that,* that you hadn't been at home," she went on. "I waited till the hour at which we had found Mrs. Muldoon that day of my going with you; and she arrived, as I've told you, while, failing to bring any one to the door, I lingered in my despair on the steps. After a little, if she hadn't come, by such a mercy, I should have found means to hunt her up. But it wasn't," said Alice Staverton, as if once more with her fine intention—"it wasn't only that."

His eyes, as he lay, turned back to her. "What more then?"

She met it, the wonder she had stirred. "In the cold dim dawn, you say? Well, in the cold dim dawn of this morning I too saw you."

"Saw *me*—?"

"Saw *him,*" said Alice Staverton. "It must have been at the same moment."

He lay an instant taking it in—as if he wished to be quite reasonable. "At the same moment?"

"Yes—in my dream again, the same one I've named to you. He came back to me. Then I knew it for a sign. He had come to you."

At this Brydon raised himself; he had to see her better. She helped him when she understood his movement, and he sat up, steadying himself beside her there on the window-bench and with his right hand grasping her left. "*He* didn't come to me."

"You came to yourself," she beautifully smiled.

"Ah I've come to myself now—thanks to you, dearest. But this brute, with his awful face—this brute's a black stranger. He's none of *me,* even as I *might* have been," Brydon sturdily declared.

But she kept the clearness that was like the breath of infallibility. "Isn't the whole point that you'd have been different?"

He almost scowled for it. "As different as *that*—?"

Her look again was more beautiful to him than the things of this world. "Haven't you exactly wanted to know *how* different? So this morning," she said, "you appeared to me."

"Like *him*?"

"A black stranger!"

"Then how did you know it was I?"

"Because, as I told you weeks ago, my mind, my imagination, had worked so over what you might, what you mightn't have been—to show you, you see, how I've thought of you. In the midst of that you came to me—that my wonder might be answered. So I knew," she went on; "and believed that, since the question held you too so fast, as you told me that day, you too would see for yourself. And when this morning I again saw I knew it would be because you had—and also then, from the first moment, because you somehow wanted me. *He* seemed to tell me of that. So why," she strangely smiled, "shouldn't I like him?"

It brought Spencer Brydon to his feet. "You 'like' that horror—?"

"I *could* have liked him. And to me," she said, "he was no horror. I had accepted him."

"'Accepted'—?" Brydon oddly sounded.

"Before, for the interest of his difference—yes. And as *I* didn't disown him, as *I* knew him—which you at last, confronted with him in his difference, so cruelly didn't, my dear—well, he must have been, you see, less dreadful to me. And it may have pleased him that I pitied him."

She was beside him on her feet, but still holding his hand—still with her arm supporting him. But though it all brought for him thus a dim light, "You 'pitied' him?" he grudgingly, resentfully asked.

"He has been unhappy; he has been ravaged," she said.

"And haven't I been unhappy? Am not I—you've only to look at me!—ravaged?"

"Ah I don't say I like him *better,*" she granted after a thought. "But he's grim, he's worn—and things have happened to him. He doesn't make shift, for sight, with your charming monocle."

"No"—it struck Brydon: "I couldn't have sported mine 'down-town.' They'd have guyed me there."

"His great convex pince-nez—I saw it, I recognised the kind —is for his poor ruined sight. And his poor right hand—!"

"Ah!" Brydon winced—whether for his proved identity or for his lost fingers. Then, "He has a million a year," he lucidly added. "But he hasn't you."

"And he isn't—no, he isn't—*you*!" she murmured as he drew her to his breast.

A NOTE ON

THE JOLLY CORNER

(1909)

This is one of the last stories Henry James wrote, and surely one of the most difficult. Composed in his famous final manner, it serves as a fair example of the complexity of his mind, a complexity that forced him (as with Joyce and other innovators) virtually to invent a style. In these brief notes we have said little about James's style. It is supposed to be the stumbling block that has always hindered him from attracting readers. I do not believe there is much truth to this idea. The difficulty in reading James lies less in him than in education whose effect, if not indeed its aim, is to produce readers in whom the faculty of attention has atrophied. If James is read with sufficient slowness and care, and if he is re-read often enough, he will always at last reveal himself. He is bound to, for his mind was never unclear. He knew what he was up to. It is only that the instruments he chose for the purpose of projecting his own clarity are unconventional and complicated.

Of all James's shorter tales "The Jolly Corner" and "The Beast in the Jungle" seem the ones most profoundly connected, despite their seeming objectivity, with the roots of James's own experience. Of "The Jolly Corner" this is especially true.*

Just at the time of the outbreak of the Civil War, the young Henry sustained an injury ("an obscure hurt," he calls it) which prevented him from following two of his brothers into the Union army. It is highly significant that this accident paralleled one which his father had experienced during his own boyhood, involving the loss to the elder James of one of his legs. In both cases the injury came about in consequence of efforts to extinguish a fire. We do not know precisely how Henry was hurt but from what he tells us it is clear that the disablement wa permanent. It is probable, though not provable, that his handicap prevented him from experiencing normal sex relations. A any rate the trauma was central in his life.

It appears to have developed in him a certain sense of impotence, already implanted as a consequence of the inferiority he felt to his brilliant father and even more brilliant brother William. The wound prevented him from joining in the masculine activity of making war; he may have believed that he was an unconscious malingerer. It symbolized a certain death in him, the death of passion. The withdrawal to Europe, the most important outward event of his long life, was another symbol of his death, of the retreat from the American experience that, in a sense, had been too much for him. During the rest of his life he repressed in himself the memory of this defeat. Like all repressions, this one was imperfect and rose to the surface, partly in action, partly in imagination. The action

*Much of what follows is merely a re-statement of part of the thesis advanced in Dr. Saul Rosenzweig's remarkable monograph, "The Ghost of Henry James: A Study in Thematic Apperception" (Character and Personality, Vol. XII, No. 2, December, 1943).

consisted of three visits to America, the last one (1904-1905) interpretable as a compulsive return to the scene from which many years before he had made a defensive escape. As Dr. Rosenzweig so persuasively puts it, the visit "was largely actuated by an impulse to repair, if possible, the injury and to complete the unfinished experience of his youth. He was, as it were, haunted by the ghost of his own past and of this he wished to disabuse his mind before actual death overtook him."

These ghosts he attempted to lay not only by returning in body to the scene of their engendering, but by projecting them in a series of spectral stories, all composed during the latter third of his life. "The creatures of James's imagination [I again quote Dr. Rosenzweig] represent not the shadows of life once lived, but the immortal impulses of the unlived life." It is obvious that James's ghosts anticipate and dramatize many of the findings of psychoanalysis.

"The Jolly Corner," then, which deals with the return home of a Jamesian expatriate, is just such a working-out of the impulses of James's own unlived life. The ghost of Spencer Brydon is the life Brydon (James) might have lived, not necessarily a beautiful life, but a life the quality of whose experience was totally different from that undergone by the expatriate Spencer Brydon. The missing fingers must represent "the obscure hurt," the symbolic meaning of which James had repressed, and which now forced itself to the surface. The self Brydon-James had rejected, the American self if you will, the active, dominating, Faustian self, comes to light at the end of a long life in the form of the specter in the house on the Jolly Corner. The whole story, then, may be taken as a kind of auto-psychoanalysis, and the very fact that it is so unconscious is what makes it possible for James to treat his material artistically and with seeming detachment.

There is an even more general interpretation possible, which readers of Matthiessen's *Henry James: The Major Phase* may find congenial. The ghost of Spencer Brydon, with its "million a year," its deformity, its ravaged and unhappy face, may represent the America James retreated from, the America Dreiser and his followers attempted to describe. James knew the meaning of this post-Civil War America (see his *The American Scene*) but he could never bring himself to come to close grips with it. Perhaps he has done so obliquely in this fascinating and multi-leveled ghost story.